THE BEST OF
ROSEMARY
SUTCLIFF

THE BEST OF
ROSEMARY SUTCLIFF

WARRIOR SCARLET
THE MARK OF THE HORSE LORD
KNIGHT'S FEE

ILLUSTRATED BY
CHARLES KEEPING

CHANCELLOR
PRESS

Warrior Scarlet first published in Great Britain by
Oxford University Press in 1958
© Oxford University Press 1958

The Mark of the Horse Lord first published in
Great Britain by Oxford University Press in 1965
and in the United States by Dell/Delacorte.
© Rosemary Sutcliff 1965

Knight's Fee first published in Great Britain by
Oxford University Press in 1960
© Oxford University Press 1960

This one-volume edition first published in
Great Britain by
Chancellor Press
59 Grosvenor Street
London W1

All Rights Reserved

ISBN 1 85152 048 1

Printed in Czechoslovakia

50638

CONTENTS

WARRIOR SCARLET

Historical Note

'THE Bronze Age.' The words have the ring of strong magic about them, conjuring up harp music and the clash of weapons, the thunder of ponies' hooves and chariot wheels along the green ridgeways of the Downs, the rattle of the loom-weights where the women are weaving by the house-place door, the wind-torn, smoky flames of a chieftain's funeral pyre. It is a description that could stand, without much alteration, for Homeric Greece; and that, I think, is the secret of the magic. The time of which Homer sang was the Heroic Age of Greece, and the Bronze Age is ours. Far rougher and more primitive than the Greek, of course, but a Heroic Age, all the same, though the heroes are forgotten.

But this story is not about Kings or heroes or battles (not even a Heroic Age could be all heroes and fighting) and there are no chariots in it, because when I came to write it down, I found that although the Golden People had ponies, it was the next wave of invaders who brought chariot warfare into Britain. It is the story of a boy called Drem, who lived with his Tribe on what is now the South Downs, nine hundred years before the birth of Christ. His land and his people were not cut off from the rest of the world; the Baltic amber and blue Egyptian beads that the archaeologists find today in Bronze Age grave mounds show that clearly enough. But probably he never heard much of what went on in the world beyond his own hunting runs; a world in which Troy had fallen three hundred years ago, and Egypt was already past its greatest days, and a hollow among the hills by the ford of a rather muddy river had still more than a hundred years to wait before wild Latin herdsmen pitched their tents there and founded Rome.

CONTENTS

I

Scarlet on the Loom

THE old shepherd sitting with his face turned seaward and his broad-bladed spear across his knees, seemed as much a part of the downs as did the wind-stunted whitethorn trees along the bank behind him: a little man, dark and knotted and tough as a furze root, with fine wrinkles round his eyes, under their jut of badger-grey brows, that told of a life-time of looking into the distance in sun and wind and rain. He was naked save for a sheepskin belted around his waist, and on the bare brown skin of his sides and shoulders showed the puckered silvery lines of more than one wolf-scar. Two great herd dogs lay beside him; one old and wise and grey-muzzled like himself, one young and gangling; and a boy of about nine summers old squatted at his feet, playing with the ears of the young one.

The boy also was half naked, but his kilt was of rough woollen stuff dyed with the red-brown crotal dye, and in all other ways he was as different from the old man as though they came from different worlds; the skin of his broad, hot-

I

tempered face—of his whole body—freckle-dusted and fair, his hair the colour of polished copper, and his eyes grey with golden flecks in them; eyes that would seem when he was excited or angry to be all gold.

The boy stopped playing with the dog's ears, and laid his arm across his updrawn knees and his chin on his arm, gazing southward where the chalk fell in long, slow turf slopes and ridges, between willow and hazel choked combes, into the forest and the Marsh Country far below, and the Marshes spread away and away to the shining bar of the Great Water on the edge of the world. Below him the turf of the steep combe-side was laced with criss-cross sheep-tracks, and the faint formless cropping sounds of the flock at the bottom came up to him along the ground. Far off and lower down on the other side of the combe, he could see the tiny figures of Flann and his dogs, on watch also over the sheep. Flann whistled to one of the dogs, and the sound came clear across the combe, a tiny, shining arrow-point of sound in the great quietness. A little warm wind came up from the south, trailing the cloud shadows after it across the Marshes and up the slow-gathering slopes of the Chalk, thyme-scented and sea-scented and swaying the heads of the blue scabious flowers all one way. The shadow of a hawk swept across the turf below him, and the sun was hot on his head: the day was good.

Drem—the boy's name was Drem—heaved a small sigh of contentment. He liked it up here on the High Chalk with Doli and the others of the shepherd kind. Several times this summer and last, since his legs grew long enough for the journey, he had come up, and spent a night, or two nights, with the sheep. It was good. This time, he had been with Doli two nights already, sleeping in the shepherd's bothie by the dew-pond, and now he supposed it was time to be going home, because he had never been more than two nights away from home before; his mother was one to worry, and when she worried her hand was hard.

'It is good, up here,' he said by and by.

'Aye, it is good up here—when the sun shines and the wind

blows soft without snow in it, and a man need not be away after a straying ewe, knee-deep in snow, and the wolves crying,' Doli said.

Drem screwed his head over his shoulder to grin at the old man. 'You need some of your own sheep medicine. Tell me more about the wolves. Tell me how you came by that long scar on your ribs.'

The old man shook his head, his gaze on the flock in the combe bottom. 'I have told you that story, aye, and more than once.'

'Tell it again.'

'Nay, it is hot, and I am in no mood to tell over again stories that I have told before.' Doli brought his gaze up out of the combe, and let it rest on the boy's face. Nothing else about him moved. He never moved without need. 'I have told you all that there is to tell about wolves and fights with wolves, and it is not good to talk of such things even in the summer. I have told you all the stories and the dreams that are of my people, save for those which may not be told. I have told you about Corn King, and Earth Mother; and I have told you how Tah-Nu, the Father of my people, in a land where the sun casts no shadows, dreamed a dream of the north, and how he hollowed out the trunk of a great tree and put into it his woman and his child and his hunting dog and a basket of barley seed, and paddled after the dream across the Great Water, and how he came to this land after many days, and sprang ashore and found that he had grown a shadow. Surely I am a great teller of stories, but even I must have rest. Maybe when you come again I shall have found in my head another story.'

Drem wriggled round, sticking a leg out sideways on the slope, to come face to face with the old man. He said, partly in the tone of a question, partly as one repeating a thing said before, 'And there was no one in the land before Tah-Nu, and no one after him except his children and his children's children, and his children's children's children, until we came?'

'Nay. Tah-Nu was the first, but there were others after him,

3

before you came,' Doli said. 'There came giants as red-gold as you are, with great spears of bronze against which our flint spears were but brown-tufted rushes. So they set us to tend their herds, and sometimes they took our women to tend their fires and bear their sons; and in a while and a while and a while we became, in some sort, one people. *Then* you came, as it might be yesterday, and treated the children of the giants as they had treated us. Now we are all the Half People, Tah-Nu's children and the children of the giants alike, and we come at your call. But we who have yet the old blood strong in us, we the Little Dark People, we have the long memories, and we remember while we tend your sheep that once, when the long grave-mounds yonder against the sky were new, Tah-Nu's children were the lords of the land.'

Drem nodded. 'Does it ache in your belly, when you re-member that?' If you asked a thing like that of most of Doli's kind, they would only look at you sideways beneath their brows, and make you an answer that slid out from under your question like an eel from under a stone. But Doli was different.

The old shepherd shrugged, his gaze level enough on Drem's face; yet his answer slid a little, all the same. 'The wind from the east is a cold wind, and blood runs from a spear-thrust, and if a man be too long without food he will die. And all these things are bad; yet he would be a fool who spent his life grieving for such things.'

Drem waited, looking into Doli's face; but nothing more came, and the old man's face was shut as he gazed out over his sheep once more. It seemed that the time had come to be on his way again.

He gave a parting pull to the young dog's ears, drew his legs under him, and stood up. 'Now I go, if you will tell me no more stories.'

Doli looked up at him, mocking a little under his brows. 'It is a long trail back to the village, and a sad thing it would be if the evening stew was all of it eaten before you came.'

'As to that, my mother will keep something for me in the pot,'

4

Drem said, with the assurance of the Lordly Ones of the world, for whom something is always kept in the pot. 'Nevertheless, I go now. Maybe I will come again before barley harvest. But if I do not, then surely I will come up and help with the droving when the time comes to bring the flock down at Samhain.'

'Come when you will. You have a way with the sheep; and it is in my heart that you would make none so ill a shepherd.'

Drem cocked up his head and laughed, rocking on his heels. 'Nay, I leave that to Tah-Nu's children. I shall be a warrior, after the way of my kind. Yet when I am a man I shall come up with my kind also, when the time comes to keep the Wolf Guard in the winter nights.'

'I will tell it to the Wolf-people, that they may grow afraid,' Doli said.

Drem flushed, still laughing. 'You laugh at me, and that is not good! But I will come back before barley harvest.'

He swung on a hard brown heel, and set off at a trot, following the curved bank of the great enclosure where the sheep were driven for shelter at night; and a short way beyond, on the crest of the hill, passed the turf-built bothie by the dew-pond, where Hunno, the brother of Flann, was swabbing a raw place on a sheep's back with elder-water to keep off the flies. He did not stop to talk to Hunno, who was a surly little man with small round eyes like jet beads, but went on at a steady wolf-trot, heading for home.

Presently he struck the green Ridgeway that ran from the world's edge to the world's edge along the High Chalk, and followed it for a while, until another track came up from the seaward Marshes and crossed it; and then he turned inland. The sun was westering as he came dipping down into the steep combe that sheltered the home steading; and all the great, rounded, whale-backed masses of the downs were pooled and feathered with coolness, the shadows of a stunted whitethorn tree reaching across half a hillside, every rise and hollow of the land that did not show at all when the sun was high casting its own long, liquid shadow across the gold. The family cattle-

ground in the head of the combe was already in shade, but farther down, where the combe broadened, the turf roofs of the steading—drying up now in the summer heat—glowed tawny as a hound's coat in the sunlight, and the smoke from the house-place fire was blue as the fluttering haze of flower-heads in the flax plot as he trotted by.

He entered the steading garth by way of a weak place he knew of in the thorn hedge, instead of going round to the gateway that faced towards the corn-land down the combe, and made his way between the byre and the shelter where the two-ox plough was kept. Drustic must be out hunting, since there was no sign of him about the farm-land, and would scarcely be home by dusk; but his mother and the Grandfather would be there, and Blai. As he reached the back wall of the house-place and saw the familiar strip of warm darkness where the roof turf had been rolled back to let in more air and light, the idea suddenly woke in him that it would be fun to get in that way and drop on them like an earwig out of the thatch when they did not know that he was anywhere near.

The roof of the house-place came down to within elbow height of the ground all round, and the pitch was not very steep, but the sun-dried turf was slippery, and so it was not as easy to climb up as it looked. He managed it, however, working his way up with infinite care until he could reach the edge of the opening, and after that it was easy. He drew himself up a little farther, then shifted his grip and slipped through between the rafters that showed in the gap, found a one-hand hold inside, and next instant, all without a sound—for few people could move more silently than Drem when he chose—was lying full length along the edge of the loft floor.

The half-loft in the crown of the roof was full of warm, crowding shadows through which the bar of fading sunlight from the gap in the roof fell like a golden sword. There was a warm smell of must and dust, and the sharper, aromatic tang of the dried herbs hanging in bundles from the rafters, and the animal smell of the skin rugs laid aside there until the winter. Spare farm tools were stacked deep under the eaves, and the raw, grey-brown bundles of wool from the last clip, and the wicker kists in which the household kept their clothes and gear. Harness hung among the herbs, and a smoked bear ham; and there, too, were the two-handled crocks full of honey that kept the household in sweetness from one bee harvest to the next.

At the open side, almost in the smoke of the hearth fire that wreathed past on its way to the smoke hole, hung two shields: Drustic's shield that had been their father's, and the great bulls-hide buckler with the bronze bosses that was the Grandfather's and would be Drem's one day.

But at the moment Drem had no interest to spare for the loft. Lying flat on his stomach and shielded from sight by the great roof-tree and the Grand-father's buckler, he was peering down over the edge into the main body of the house-place below. It was fun to see without being seen. Out of the fireglow and the fading sword of dusty gold, the great living-hut ran away on every side into brown shadows with a bloom of wood smoke on them, but where the light fell strongest near the doorway, his

7

mother was working at her loom; a big upright loom, the warp threads held taut by a row of triangular clay weights at the bottom. He could hear the small rhythmical sounds as she passed the weaving-rod to and fro and combed up the woof between each row.

The warm, fatty smell of the evening stew came up to him from the bronze pot over the fire, and brought the warm water to his mouth, for he had not eaten since the morning bowl of stirabout with the shepherd kind. The Grandfather was sitting beside the fire as usual, on the folded skin of the bear that he had killed when the world was young; a man like a huge old brooding grey eagle that had once been golden.

On the other side of the hearth, the Women's side, Blai squatted on her heels, turning barley cakes with small, flinching hands in the hot ash. She was exactly beneath Drem, so that he thought how easy it would be to spit on her, like spitting on the back of a hare as it sunned itself on a far-down ledge of the old flint quarry north of the summer sheep-run. Blai was not his sister; her coming belonged to the time that he could only just remember, when a bronze-smith had come by from the Isles of the West, and his woman with him—a wild, dark creature with hair and eyes like the night. She had been sick already, and in the night she had died and left a new babe bleating in the fern against the wall. The bronze-smith had not seemed much interested, and two days later he had gone off along the track that led inland, leaving the babe behind him. 'What should I want with the creature?' he had said. 'Maybe I will come back one day.' But he never had come back. And now Blai was rising seven years old, black as her mother had been, in a house where everyone else was red-gold like flame, and some-how never quite belonging to them. Blai believed that one day the bronze-smith would come back: 'One day, one day my

8

father will come for me!' seemed to be her talisman against all ills, the faith that she clung to as something of her own. But of course he never would come back; everybody knew that except Blai. Blai was stupid.

Drem decided not to spit on her after all, because that would betray his presence in the loft, and turned his attention back to his mother. The cloth on the loom had grown a little since he saw it last, though not much, because there was so much else to do; a piece of fine chequered wool, blue and violet and flaming red. There was red wool on his mother's weaving-rod now, the true burning Warrior Scarlet that was the very colour of courage itself. No woman might wear that colour, nor might the Half People who came and went at the Tribe's call. It was for the Men's side. One day, when he had passed through the Boy's House, and slain his wolf single-handed, and become a man and a warrior of the Tribe, with his Grandfather's shield to carry, his mother would weave scarlet on the loom for him.

The Grandfather raised his great grey-gold head from watching bygone battles in the fire, and turned his gaze on the woman at the loom. 'It grows slowly, that piece of cloth,' he said, in a voice that came mumbling and rattling up from the depth of his great frame. 'When it is finished, let you use it to re-line my good beaver-skin cloak. The old lining is worn to shreds.'

Drem's mother looked over her shoulder, showing a tired face in which the beautiful bones stood out so sharply that it looked as though you could cut your hand on it. 'I had thought to use this piece for Drustic; he also needs a new cloak, for his old one does not keep out the wind and the rain.'

'Drustic is young, and the wind blows less cold for him. He can wait. Let you set up the loom for him next time.'

'Next time and next time and next time,' Drem's mother said quietly. 'Sometimes I wish that I had been born to the Men's side; sometimes I grow weary of the spinning and the weaving and the grinding corn.'

The Grandfather spat into the fire. 'By right there should be three son's wives to weave and grind for me!'

9

'Then there should be three sons for them to weave for also,' Drem's mother said with a spurt of tired and angry laughter, thrusting back a bright wisp of hair that had strayed as her hair was always straying from the blue linen net in which it was gathered, and looked round again. 'Or would you have them all widows?'

Drem knew his mother in this mood; it came when she was very tired; and he began to feel that it would not be a good idea to play his earwig-out-of-the-thatch trick, after all.

The Grandfather drew his brows together, and glared. 'Aiee! A hard thing it is that I grow old, and of all my three sons there is not one left, and that the wife of my youngest son should taunt me with it! A hard thing it is that I should have but one grandson to carry my spear after me; I who have been among the greatest warriors of the Tribe.'

('The Old One grows forgetful,' Drem thought. 'He has lived so long with old battles that his mind grows dim; and he has forgotten Drustic.')

His mother turned again from her weaving, with a fierceness that struck him even at that moment as odd. 'Two grandsons there are at the hearth fire! Have you forgotten?'

It was then that the Grandfather said the thing that altered the whole world for Drem, so that it could never return to being quite the same as before.

'Nay then, I have not forgotten. I grow old but I can still count the tally of my ten fingers. Two grandsons there are at the hearth fire; but a grandson at the hearth fire is not a grandson among the spear-warriors of the Tribe. Is it likely, think you, that the young one will ever win his way into the Men's side, with a spear-arm that he cannot use?'

There was a sudden silence. Drem's mother had turned back to her loom, but she was not weaving. The Grandfather sat and glowered. And in the warm shadows of the loft above them, the small boy lay on his stomach, staring down at them with dilated eyes, and feeling all at once cold and sick. Only Blai went on turning barley cakes among the hot ashes, her small wan face telling as little as usual of what she thought or felt.

Then Drem's mother said, 'Talore the Hunter is one of the great ones of the Men's side to this day.'

'Talore the Hunter was a man and a warrior before ever he lost a hand to the cattle raiders,' the Grandfather said, deep and grumbling, and he eyed her with a kind of disgusted triumph. 'Na na, it is in my mind that the boy must go to the Half People when the time comes. He is often enough away with Doli and the sheep as it is; maybe he will make a shepherd.' He spat again. 'Lord of the Sun! That I should have a grandson herding sheep! I, who have been such a warrior as men speak of round the fire for a hundred winters!'

'If the child fails, then he must go to the Half People,' Drem's mother said, and her voice sounded tight in her throat. 'But it may be that he will not fail. He is your own grandson, and not lightly turned from the things he sets his mind to.'

'So. But it is not his mind alone that must be set.' The Grandfather flared his nostrils in a derisive snort. 'Say then that he comes through his years in the Boy's House and slays his wolf at the end of them, and the time comes for him to receive his weapons; there must be two warriors, let you remember, and one of them not kin to him, to bring each New Spear before the Clan. And who shall I find, think you—or Drustic if I have gone beyond the Sunset—to stand for a one-armed champion?'

'It is six summers before that question need be answered—and must I then answer it this evening?' Drem's mother cried. 'If he fails, then let him go to the Half People as I say, and let you be thankful that there is Drustic to carry your spear after you!' She gave a swift exclamation and turned from the loom towards the open pottery lamp that hung from the roof-tree just below Drem's hiding-place. 'The light fades, and if I am to finish this stripe before Drustic is home to be fed, I must have the lamp.'

Quick as a lizard, Drem darted back into the shadows.

'Surely there is a rat in the roof. I heard it scamper.' He heard her voice, dry and hard, behind him as he slid out through the opening in the roof. He dropped silently to the ground, driven by an odd panic fear of anyone knowing that he had overheard what passed in the house-place, because somehow—he could not have said why—that would make it quite unbearable.

The little stilt-legged hut where the seed corn was stored seemed to offer refuge and he dived under it and crouched there, breathing hard as though he had been running.

The sun was gone, but a golden after-glow was spread behind the Chalk, and there was still light to see by. And crouching there among the timbers that upheld the floor, he looked at his right arm, as though he had never seen it before: his spear arm that he could not use, the Grandfather had said. It was thinner than his left, and somehow brittle looking, as though it might snap like a dry stick. He felt it exploringly with his left hand. It was queer, like something that did not quite belong to him. He had always known, of course—when he thought about it at all—that he could not use that arm, but it hadn't seemed important. He held things in his teeth and he held things between his knees, and he managed well enough without it. Certainly he had never for a moment thought of it coming between him and his Warrior Scarlet.

But he thought now, crouching under the floor of the corn store and staring straight before him with eyes that did not see the golden after-glow fading behind the Chalk. Never to take his proud place among the Men's side with the others of his kind; to lose the world he knew, and go out into the world of the Half People, the Dark People, the Flint People, whose homes, half underground, were the little green hummocks in the hidden combes of the Chalk; who came and went at the Tribesmen's call, though they never owned the Tribesmen as their masters; to be cut off, all his life, from his own kind . . . He was only nine years old, he could not yet understand all that it would mean; but he understood enough—more than enough. He crouched there for a long time, whispering over and over to himself, 'I *will* be a warrior of the Tribe. Let you say what you like, Old Man! I will show you—I will *show* you'—lashing up anger within himself, for a shield against fear.

When he went back to the house-place it was almost dark. Drustic had returned from the hunting trail, and the newly paunched carcass of a roe hind was hanging from the birch tree beside the door, out of reach of the dogs who were fighting over the offal, the white of her under-belly faintly luminous in the dusk, where the blood had not fouled it. He went in through the fore porch, where the ponies were stabled in winter. The apron of skins over the inner doorway was drawn back, and the tawny glow of the lamp and the low fire came to meet him on the threshold as he checked, blinking. The evening meal was over, and the Grandfather, it seemed, had returned to his watching of old battles in the fire. Drustic, with a half-made bow-stave across his knee and a glue-pot beside him, was busy on the great hunting bow that he was building for himself, while on the Women's side of the hearth their mother sat spinning. She looked up as Drem appeared. 'Cubbling! Here is a time to be coming home! When it drew to sunset I said, "He will not come now until tomorrow." '

'I would have been home by sunset, but—I stopped on the way. There were things to look at and I stopped on the way,' Drem said. But he could not meet his mother's eyes. Keeping his head down, he went to squat beside Drustic, holding out his hand. 'I will hold it steady while you put on the binding.'

But Drustic hated anyone else to meddle in a thing that he was making. He looked up slowly—all his movements were slow and deliberate—and said quite kindly, 'Na, I can manage well enough. Let you learn to shaft a spear; that is the thing for you to do.'

Drem snatched his hand back as though it had been stung. You needed two hands for a bow, but you could learn to use a spear with one. That was another thing that he had not really thought about.

13

And at the same moment, his mother called to him. 'See, there is some stew left. Let you come round here and take your bowl. You are not a man already, that you should eat on the Men's side of the hearth.'

Drem came at her call, and took the black pottery bowl of stewed mutton that she held out to him, and squatted down in the fern. As he did so, he caught sight of Blai squatting far back in the shadows, picking the furze prickles and bits of dirt from a lapful of raw wool, and watching him as she worked. And he realized that Blai also had heard what the Grandfather had said. So he turned his shoulder on her, hunching it in a way that was meant to show her that she mattered so little that he had not noticed that she was there at all.

And somehow in doing that—he overset the bowl.

It was such a small thing, a thing that might have happened to anyone. But to Drem, coming so close on the heels of what had gone before, it was overwhelming. The words that the Grandfather had said, Drustic's refusal to let him help with the bow—they were things that came from outside; and a thing that came from outside could be in some sort shut out; it could be defied and snarled against. But this was different; this came from inside himself; there was no defence against it, and it let in all the rest.

Dismay and something that was almost terror swept over him as the warm stew splashed across his knee and into the fern. The Grandfather grunted; a grunt that said as plainly as words could do, 'See now, did I not say so?' And his mother caught up the bowl, crying in exasperation and something under the exasperation that was as though he had hurt her, 'Oh, you clumsy one! You grow more clumsy every day! Can you never look what you are about?'

Black misery rushed up into Drem's breast, so that it was as though his heart were bursting because there was more misery in it than it could hold. He raised a white, desperate face to his mother's, and shook his head. Then he scrambled to his feet and bolted for the doorway.

'Where are you going?—Come back, cub!' his mother called after him; and he called back mumbling that he was not hungry, that he would come again in a while, and stumbled out through the fore porch into the summer night.

The gateway of the steading was closed, as always after dark, by an uprooted thorn bush, and he went out through the weak place that had let him in earlier that evening before the blow fell that changed the world, and making his way round the steading hedge, started down the chalk-cut driftway between the lower corn-plots and the half-wild fruit trees that were his mother's care.

He had no clear idea what he was doing or where he was going, or why. Blindly, instinctively, he turned to the wilderness, like any small desperately hurt animal seeking solitude from its own kind and the dark and a hole to crawl into.

II

Talore the Hunter

LOWER down, the combe ran out into a broadening valley that swung northward, opening into a vast half moon of rolling chalk hills above the forest and the marshlands far below. Drem followed the valley down, because down was easier than up, but he did not think of which way he was going; he simply went. Down and down, by swirling slopes and plunging headlands of turf, by bare chalk and tangled furze and through the whitethorn bushes of the lower slopes, until at last the great trees of the Wild came climbing up to meet him.

The Great Wild, mist haunted, spirit haunted, rolling away into the unknown; the wilderness of forest and marsh that was the place of wolf and bear and wild pig, the place of the Fear that walked among the trees, so men said, after dark; where only the hunters went at night, taking their lives in their spear hands and trusting their souls to the charms and talismans of amber and bear's teeth and dried garlic flowers that they wore about them.

At first it was quite easy travelling, for anyone used, as Drem was, to wandering about in the dark. The hazel and elder and wayfaring trees of the forest verge grew well apart, and there was little undergrowth; but as time went by, the trees crowded closer and closer; oak and ash, alder in the damper places, holly everywhere, great thickets of it, mingled with black masses of yew, matted together with a dense undergrowth of thorn and brambles. And wherever the trees fell back a little, the bracken grew head high to the small boy who thrust his way on, deeper and deeper into the fastness, driven by the misery and the furious bewilderment within him like a small wild thing driven by the hounds.

Utterly lost in his own desolation, Drem never noticed how the forest darkened and crowded in on him, until suddenly a piece of rotten tree-trunk gave under his foot, and he all but went through into an ants' nest; and that woke him up, so that as he gathered himself together again, he was suddenly aware of his surroundings. He had never been into the forest at night before; never so far as this, even in day-time, and he did not know where he was. And, swift-footed fear overcoming his longing for refuge, he had enough sense left to tell him that it was not good to be so far into the forest alone at night, and that he must get back to the woodshore. He knew the direction to take without even having to think; the north side of any tree, especially any oak tree, smelled quite different from the south, and he had only to head south to strike the Chalk again at last.

So he turned his face southward, and set off. But he was desperately tired, and he dreaded going home, because going home would mean facing the thing that he had run away from; and his dread somehow made it harder to find the way.

The trees that should have begun to thin out crowded thicker and thicker about him as he went, and there was no way through the tangled thickets of bramble and holly, so that he must cast about for the narrow game-tracks worn by the feet of the deer, that never led in the right direction. It seemed that he would never win free of the choking tangle, and he was too tired, too wretched to care very much. Only—only it seemed that a change was coming over the forest.

Or maybe it was that he was awake and aware of the forest now as he had not been before; awake to the darkness and the crowding trees that were suddenly—not quite what trees should be, not quite what they were in the day-time; to the furry hush that was full of voices, the whispering, rustling, stealthy voices

of the forest, that were not the voices of the day-time, either. There were little nameless rustlings through the undergrowth, the soft swish of wings through the branches overhead; in the distance a small animal screamed, and Drem knew that somewhere a fox had made its kill. Surely the whole forest was disturbed tonight. But those were not the sounds that raised the hair on the back of his neck. Once he thought he heard the breathing of a big animal close at hand, and as he checked, his own breath caught in his throat; something brushed through the undergrowth towards him, and there was a sudden silver pattering like rain among the leaves—but it was not raining. He pushed on again, more quickly now, carelessly, stumbling often among the underbrush; and when he stopped once more, to listen and make sure of his direction, suddenly the breathing was there again; a faint, slow panting, just behind him. He whirled about, his hand on the knife in his belt, but there was nothing there. Nothing but the furry darkness. And far off through the trees, he thought that something laughed. His heart was racing now, sickeningly, right up in his throat; he struggled on again, blindly. Mustn't stop any more; it was when you stopped that you heard things. But even as he blundered on, above the brushing and crackling that he made, above the drubbing of his heart, he heard that soft, stealthy panting, as though the Thing prowled at his heels. But it was not only at his heels now, it was all around him, in front as well as behind, and the forest itself, the whole forest was like some great hunting cat crouched to spring. 'Don't run!' said the hunter that was born and bred in him and that knew the ways of the wild through a hundred generations. *'Don't run!'* But terror had him in its power, and he was running, with no more sense of direction than a mouse with a stoat behind it.

Brambles tore his skin, fallen branches tripped him, low-hanging boughs slashed across his face as he crashed through the undergrowth that seemed to lay hold of him with wicked, clawing hands. This was what the hunters spoke of under their breaths around the fire. This was the Fear that walked the forest, the Terror of the Soul. He had never felt it before, but the hunter within him knew it; the Fear that prowled soft-footed beyond the cave mouth and the firelight.

Panting, sweating, sobbing, he crashed through a screen of alder scrub on the edge of a little clearing, and next instant had pitched forward and was rolling over down a slope rustling with last year's leaves. He reached the bottom with what breath he had had left all knocked out of him, and found himself almost under a great hollow bole of roots and uptorn earth where a huge oak tree had come down in some past winter gale. It seemed to offer shelter, the shelter that even a very small cave gives from the Fear that prowls outside; and with a shuddering gasp, Drem crawled in as far as he could over the deep, rustling softness of drifted oak leaves, and crouched down, pressed against the roughness of the torn roots.

For a long while he crouched there with drubbing heart, still shivering and sweating, while the Fear snuffled about the opening of his refuge. But little by little the Fear faded and went farther away. Strength and steadfastness seemed to come out to him from the torn roots of the great tree that had been a forest king in its day; his heart quietened and his breath came slower. And gradually his terror and his misery alike grew dim. He did not know that he was falling asleep like a small, exhausted animal . . .

He woke with a crash, and the taste of terror in his throat. There was hot breath panting in his face, and something was snuffing at his shoulder.

For a moment he lay quite still, everything in him seeming to curl in on itself and turn to ice, knowing that the thing could only be a wolf, and that if he made the slightest movement it would be at his throat before ever he could whip the knife from his belt. Then a voice said softly, 'Sa, what have we here, then? Off, Swift-foot! Back now, Fand!' And his eyes flew open to see a man—or something in the shape of a man—bending over him, head and shoulders blotted dark against the white light of moon-rise; and the thing that had been snuffing at his shoulder drew back with a whine.

There was a swift exclamation, and a hand flashed down on him as he flattened back against the earthy root-tangle behind him; and like a wild thing cornered, with nothing in him but a blind instinct to fight for life, he snapped at it, his teeth meeting in a finger. He was shaken off, and in the same instant, as it seemed, the hand was on his shoulder, and he was jerked bodily out from under the tree roots and set on his feet, still kicking and struggling and trying to bite, in the full moonlight. The hand held him at arm's length in a grip that he could not break though he twisted and squirmed like an otter cub; but the man's voice when he spoke again was not harsh, despite his bitten finger. There was even something of laughter in it.

'Softly, softly now! There is no need for such a snarling and snapping!' Then, as Drem, reassured by something in the voice, ceased his struggling: 'Why, it is old Cathlan's grandson!'

Drem stood quite still now, and looked at the man, while

three great hounds sat down around them with lolling tongues and eyes shining in the moonlight. The man was slight and dark—dark for one of the Golden People—and had faintly the smell of fox about him; and even in his stillness, as he stood holding Drem at arm's length, was the swift, leashed power of a wild thing. He was naked save for a fox's pelt twisted about his loins; and the moon caught the blade of the long hunting-knife thrust into his girdle, and the coils of a great snake of beaten copper that coiled again and again about his left forearm, the head lying level with his elbow, the tail curled downward into a hook that served him instead of a left hand.

'So it is you who walks the forest tonight, making all the Wild uneasy,' said Talore the Hunter.

Drem nodded.

'A small cub, surely a very small cub, to be sleeping out in the forest.'

Drem said fiercely, 'I have seen nine summers, and I sleep in the forest because I choose.'

'Surely that is as good a reason as any other,' said the man, with the laughter deepening in his tone. 'But now, I think, the time comes to be going home.'

There was a silence among the crowding trees. Then Drem said, 'Let me be. I will go back in a while and a while.'

'Na, not in a while and a while,' Talore said, and he looked down at Drem in the moonlight, with eyes that missed nothing of the small, desperate figure before him. 'This part of the forest is no place for small cubs, alone. Therefore we go together, you and I; and we go now.'

He released Drem's shoulder, and stooping with the lithe and lazy swiftness that was in all his movements, caught up from among the brown leaves and white-flowering dead-nettle at his feet his hunting-spear, and a newly flayed badger pelt, which he flung across his shoulder. 'Come,' he said, and with an almost soundless whistle to his hounds, turned to the steep slope behind him.

And rebellious and resentful, bewildered by the swiftness

with which the unknown terror whose hand he bit had become
Talore the Hunter, and by the man's mastery over him, which
was different from anything he had experienced before, Drem
came. The Fear was gone from the forest, and the chill freshness of the dawn was in his face as, with the three hounds, he
followed at the shadow-silent heels of the hunter, threading the
mazy deer-paths that seemed to have turned themselves about
to lead in the right direction after all. He felt spent and empty
as though he had cried until he had no more tears to cry with;
and nothing of last night seemed quite real; it was all dark and
confused and had the sick taste of nightmare that remains in the
back of one's mind after one wakes. He wished he could talk
about it to Talore. Talore with his copper snake would understand as no one else in Drem's world could. It would be good to
tell Talore. But he knew that if the hunter was to stop in his
tracks, and turn, and say 'Cub, what Thing was it that you ran
from, into the forest?' the words would never come. So there
was no good thinking about it.

The light was growing all around them, wherever the trees
fell back a little; moonlight and dawn-light watered together;
and as they came down to a narrow brook a willow wren was
singing among the alders. They followed upstream a little way,
and suddenly Drem knew where he was. He knew this brook,
he knew the ancient willow bending far out over the water,
where the brook broke up into a chain of pools. Just up yonder
through the trees was the track, the ancient track under the
scarp of the downs that echoed the Ridgeway along the High
Chalk far above. Even as he realized it, they came out on the
edge of a clearing, and Talore checked among a tangle of elder
bushes with a swift gesture that halted boy and hounds alike.

Ahead of them in the clearing the light was so strong that
already the foxgloves were touched with colour; and the low
ground-mist of the summer morning lay like gossamer in the
hollows among the fern. And peering, breath in check,
through the low-hanging elder branches, Drem saw that on the
far side of the clearing a herd of roe deer were grazing, their

fawns all together at a little distance. One big hind was grazing a little apart from the rest, between them and the elder scrub; and Drem judged that she was well within spear throw, knowing that in the hands of a skilled hunter a light throw-spear could kill at forty or fifty paces. One of the hounds was standing against his leg, and he felt the tremors running through the brute's body, though no whimper of excitement broke from him, or from the other two. They had come on the herd upwind, and so there was nothing to carry the smell of danger to the deer, and they grazed on undisturbed. Every moment Drem expected to see Talore throw and make his kill; but the moments passed, and when he stole a sideways glance at Talore, the hunter was watching the herd through the white curds of the elder blossom, with a keen, quiet pleasure narrowing his dark eyes, and the throw-spear still at rest in his hand.

A few moments later, he gave a soft whistle. A curious, low note at sound of which the nearest hind raised her head and looked towards the elder tangle, then began, obviously not in the least startled, to drift back to the main herd. One or two others looked up and began to drift also, a hind barked to her fawn, and in a few moments the last of the deer had melted into the trees and the morning mist.

Drem looked again at Talore, puzzled, and spoke for the first time since they had set out on the home trail. 'You could have killed her—the one this side of the herd.'

'So. Very easily.' Talore had been on the point of moving again, but he checked, looking down at the boy.

'Then—why not?'

'I have killed once already tonight and have no need to kill again,' Talore said. 'There is meat enough in my house-place, and a deer-skin fetches but a small price from the traders.' And then, seeing Drem still puzzled, 'Never kill what you cannot use. If you kill for skins, kill for all the skins you need; if for food, fill your belly and the bellies of hound and woman and child at your hearth and set store by, that they may be full another time. But to kill for the sake of killing is the way of the weasel and the fox, and the hunter who kills so angers the Forest Gods. Let you remember that when you are a man and hunt with the Men's side!'

Drem had not meant to say it, a moment before he would not have thought that he could say it, but the words seemed to burst out past the silence in his throat in a small, hoarse rush that had nothing to do with his will. 'Most like, when I am a man, I shall not hunt with the Men's side.'

There was a pause, and a little wind riffled through the elder branches, fetching down a shower of petals. Then Talore said, 'Who with, then?'

'The Half People.'

'And who says so?'

'The Old One, Cathlan my Grandfather.'

Talore stood leaning on his spear and frowned down at Drem with a suddenly quickened interest. 'Let you tell me why.'

Drem scowled at him, the old misery aching in his throat, and did not answer; and after a moment Talore flicked the tail of his copper snake at the arm which the boy carried trailing like a bird with a broken wing. 'Because of that?'

Drem nodded.

'So. Men call me Talore One-Hand as often as Talore the Hunter, yet no man has ever questioned my right to the scarlet.'

'Sabra my mother said that—something of that. But you were a warrior and a—a great one of the Clan before ever you lost a hand to the cattle raiders.'

Talore smiled, his swift, dark smile that raised his lip over the strong dog teeth at the corners of his mouth. 'The Grandfather again.'

And again Drem nodded, and again Talore leaned on his spear and looked down at him. 'Listen, cub,' he said at last. 'If the thing is worth a fight, fight for it and do not hear the Grandfather too clearly. There are ways—ways round, and ways through, and ways over. If you have not two hands for a

bow, then learn to use a throw-spear with such skill that your enemies, and your brothers, forget that it is not from choice.'

Drem looked at him in wonder. How could Talore—even Talore—know about Drustic's bow? And then he realized that Talore did not know about *that* bow, but that for him also there had been a bow that he could not draw, and a spear that must take its place. There were things to think about, here. But first there was something more; a question to be asked. Drem looked at the ground while he asked it, because he could not bear to look into Talore's face. 'If I did—all those things, and learned to kill a buck at—at sixty paces with a spear; and slew my wolf at the Wolf Slaying—a—a greater, fiercer wolf than most, would there—might it be that someone among the warriors would stand for me with the Grandfather, when the time comes for me to go before the Tribe, after all?'

The silence that followed seemed to him so long that he began to give up his new hope. Then Talore said, 'When the time comes that your mother weaves scarlet on the loom for you, let you remember this dawn in the forest, and bid the Grandfather send word to me.'

Just for a moment, he could not believe it. Then he looked up, slowly, his eyes suddenly all golden. '*You?*'

'Who else has so good a right, small brother?' Talore said.

They looked at each other for a moment, steadily; a look that was the sealing of a bond. Then Talore straightened, shifting his hold on his spear. 'Come now, it is near daylight, and they will be half mad for you at the home steading. You will know your way, now?'

Drem nodded.

'So. Then our ways part here. Good hunting, cub.'

And in a little, while the hunter melted in among the trees, going on up the streamside towards the village, Drem struck up through the fringes of the forest on to the swelling flanks of the Chalk.

It was almost broad daylight, the moon pale as a bubble in the shining sky; and the red plough oxen were stirring and

stamping in their stalls, when Drem came up the chalk-cut driftway to the gate of the home steading. The thorn tree was drawn aside and the gateway open, and he walked through and across the garth to the house-place, suddenly so weary that he could hardly drag one leg after the other. He heard Drustic's voice as he came to the door, 'Na, he is not with Doli. The Gods alone know where he is or what has come to him!' and saw his brother standing over the Grandfather, who sat hunched in his cloak beside the fire that looked as though it had been kept up all night. He caught the Grandfather's rumbling answer. 'The child is bad; always I have said that the child is bad. He has no respect for *me* his Grandfather! If the Sun Lord so wills it, he will come back when he is hungry enough.'

And then they saw him, both it seemed in the same moment, and also in the same moment old Kea, the mother of all Drustic's hounds, got up with waving tail, yawning her pleasure, and came to greet him. But Drustic reached him first, in a couple of strides, and caught him by the scruff of the neck and jerked him forward into the fireglow beside the hearth, demanding, 'Son of blackness, where have you been?'

Drem stood and rubbed his neck and glared. 'It was a very bright night. I went to catch a fish, but they were all shy.'

The Grandfather snorted, a snort that might mean unbelief or only derision; and Drustic said, 'And so, because you chance to feel like catching a fish, our mother must seek you all night through the woodshore, and I must trail up along the High Chalk lest you had gone back to Doli and the sheep!' As he spoke he took down a whip of tanned ox hide that he used for the hounds, and stood drawing the dark leash again and again through his hands. 'You know what happens to a puppy of the dog pack when he runs off in such a way?'

Drem faced him squarely. He had known that this must happen, and he was ready for it. 'You thrash him.'

Drustic glanced for an instant, questioningly, at the Grandfather, the lord of the house; but the Grandfather spat into the fire, hunching his blanket farther round his shoulders. 'Na na, I

am too old to be troubled with the training of puppies. The thing is for you to do—and see that you do not hold your hand.'

'I shall not hold my hand,' Drustic said roughly. He was clearly very angry, his young, ruddy face dark with his anger. He reached out and fetched Drem a buffet on the side of the head that sent him sprawling across the wood pile by the fire. Drem crouched there, his head ringing from the blow; and waited with shut teeth. He knew that by the end he would be yelping like a puppy, but he would not yelp before he must. He sensed that his brother's arm had swung up, and waited for the sting of the descending lash across his shoulders.

But it never came. Instead, something small and fierce out of the shadows flung itself on Drustic and bit him, as last night Drem had bitten Talore the Hunter.

Drustic yelped with surprise and pain, and shook his attacker off and cuffed her aside, then raised his whip again. But as he did so, Drem heard his mother's voice from the doorway, crying with a rush of thankfulness, 'Ah! You have found him!' And then, 'No, Drustic. No!'

Everything was very confused and confusing, but it seemed to Drem that he might be going to escape a beating after all. He got up from where he had been crouching, as his mother came swiftly in, her heavy hair falling loose and her kirtle torn and mired. 'Cubbling, where have you been? You were with Doli then?'

Drustic was standing, solid and still angry and beginning to be bewildered, sucking his bitten thumb, while Blai crouched snarling silently, and holding her head, among the hounds where his cuff had sent her. He spat blood into the fire. 'Nay, you were wrong, my mother; he has but now come in, so bold as the King himself in his high Dun, to tell me he went to catch a fish.' Then, rounding once more on Drem, 'Get down again. I have not finished with you yet.'

'No, Drustic,' their mother said again. 'You shall not beat him—not this time.'

The Grandfather raised his great grey-gold head and looked

27

at them with eyes that went golden when he was angry or glad, just as Drem's did, but it was anger now. 'Woman, this is for the Men's side. Leave it for the Men's side's handling, and tend to your distaff!'

Drem's mother paid no heed to the old man. '*Not this time!*' she said again.

'But why not?' Drustic demanded, his brows puckered with bewilderment. 'Am I not to train the cub at all? *Why not?*'

'Because I say not, I who gave both of you life!' their mother said; and she caught the whip from Drustic and flung it into the far shadows. Then she turned to Drem, with her hands held out, and the crooning softness in her voice that came there all too seldom. 'Baba, cubbling, why did you run off like that? I would have given you more stew—the bowl was not broken——'

Her eyes were searching his face. He thought she guessed that it had not been a rat in the roof; guessed why he had gone; and that was why she would not let Drustic beat him. But she could not be sure, and while she was not sure she could not speak of it to him. He did not want her to speak of it to him. So he stepped back, and stood with his feet apart and his head up, while Drustic shrugged and went to pick up his whip and hang it in its accustomed place. 'I did not want any more stew. I wished to catch a fish. I went down to the river, into the forest to catch one; but the fish were all shy.'

'But what did you do by yourself, all alone the long night in the forest? You are torn to pieces, and your kilt in shreds. Aiee, baba, you look as though you were new come from battle —and you must be so hungry.'

'I am hungry,' Drem agreed, 'and the brambles are sharp in the forest. I crawled into a hole under an oak tree and slept.' He had not forgotten the Great Fear, but he shut his mind to it. 'And later I met Talore the Hunter in the forest, and we walked together, and talked, in the way of men!'

His mother was already taking a barley bannock out of the bannock basket that hung from the edge of the loft. 'Eat now, and you shall have better in a little.' Then, as she gave the

28

bannock into his hand, 'Talore the Hunter? And what could there be for you and Talore the Hunter to talk of?'

That was one of the things about Drem's mother; often she wanted to know too much. He stuck his chest out, swaggering a little, with his mouth already full of bannock. 'Did I not say that it was man's talk?' Then he looked over his shoulder at his angry brother. 'I am tired of trapping fish. Let you give me one of your old throw-spears—the one with the three nicks in the blade that you never use now.'

III

First Kill

BARLEY harvest came, but Drem did not go up to Doli and the sheep again. Wheat harvest followed, and they threshed, and then winnowed the grain with an old grey goose wing, and saved the best for seed, and parched the rest to prevent it sprouting, before it went into the skin-lined store pits in the chalk. Samhain came, the feast of in-gathering when the year turns to the dark; the flocks were driven down from the high pastures for branding, and there was all the excitement of the great cattle round-up and the red business of the winter slaughtering. And Drem did not go up, as he had promised, to help with the droving. That way was closed to him; he could not go to Doli and the shepherd kind again . . .

Winter came, and the wolves howled closer and closer in the darkness, while Tribesmen and Half People alike kept the Wolf Guard over the lambing pens. Spring came, and Drustic ploughed the family corn plots with the two red plough oxen, followed by a wheeling, crying cloud of gulls, the shadows of wings mingling with the shadows of the drifting clouds along the shoulder of the downs. Seed-time came, and with all the other children of the Outland farms and the village away down the valley, Drem was busy all day long at the bird scaring. And so almost a year went by.

On an evening about the time of sheep shearing, Drem went down the valley towards the village and the house-place of Talore the Hunter, with a message from his mother for Wenna

30

about a sitting of mallard eggs. He had been to Talore's house-place more than once since that summer dawn in the forest. Talore had three sons, all grown men, even the youngest of them who had gained his scarlet last Beltane, but they were kind to Drem in an off-hand way, tossing him a word in passing as though tossing a scrap of meat to a well-intentioned puppy. Fat Wenna, the wife of the eldest son, who looked after the household, was kind to him too, when she was not too taken up with the stew or the wet girl-child squalling in the rushes. And there was always the hope that Talore would be there.

He was hoping that now, as he came dropping down from the Chalk at a steady wolf trot, with his throw-spear over his shoulder. It was a wild day, the wind driving a racing tumble of cloud low across the downs, and the stray gleams of sunshine scudding before the rain; and the long tongue of the woods that thrust up from the valley was roaring like a forge fire as he came down through the head of it with the rain in his face. Rain trailed across the crest of the Hill of Gathering, above the village, blurring the outline of the round grave-mound of the long forgotten warrior who slept there with his copper sword beside him; and the cluster of turf-roofed huts and house-places about the Chieftain's steading seemed to huddle under the bluff hill shoulder with the head-down dejection of ponies sheltering under a bank. But ever after in Drem's memory that was to be a shining day—one of the cluster of shining days that a man may hold in the hollow of one hand when he is old and looks back.

The steading of Talore the Hunter had fewer out-sheds than most, for though he and his sons farmed a little, their wealth was not in herds or corn-land but in dressed skins, and their own skill and cunning on the hunting trail, with spear and bow and dead-fall trap. Æsk, the eldest son, was squatting by the doorway now, cleaning a raw beaver skin with a bronze scraper, while a couple of great hounds beside him snapped up the scrapings; and when Drem had stopped to give him the day's

greeting, he said with a jerk of his head behind him, 'Something fine to see in there.'

'Is it the puppies—Fand's puppies?' Instantly Drem was alight with eagerness.

'Maybe. Go in and look.'

More than two moons ago, when winter was quickening into spring, Talore had taken Fand, the wisest and most beautiful of his hounds, and rubbed her brindled hide with certain herbs to take away the Man smell, and tied her to an alder tree by the forest pool where the wolves came to drink. The hunters and shepherds did that sometimes, for a hound bitch mated with a wolf had fine cubs, and brought strong new blood into the dog pack. And in the morning there had been the pad marks of a he-wolf all about her, and the wolf smell on her hide, and they had known that presently there would be strong puppies born to Fand the Beautiful.

Drem swooped through the low doorway into a warm, smoky gloom laced with firelight, pitched his throw-spear in the direction of the place where it was the custom to stack weapons on entering a house, and not even noticing Wenna setting curd cakes to dry by the fire, made for the place against the wall, fenced off with hurdles and piled with russet fern, from which came small unmistakable squeaks and rustlings. Talore had shifted back one of the hurdles, and was squatting on one knee in the opening, giving little bits of meat to Fand, who half lay, half sat, her eyes luminous in the gloom, surrounded by small things that Drem could not really see in the crowding shadows, save as a wriggling and a squirming among the dried bracken fronds.

Talore turned on his knee and looked up at the boy with a swift, dark flash of shared pleasure that made nothing of the difference in years and status between them. 'I heard your voice. See now, the cubs are come.'

Drem, who had checked his headlong arrival, squatted down beside the hunter, his own eyes very bright under his wild, rain-wet flame of hair.

Fand dropped her muzzle and sniffed at one of the tiny rat-like creatures against her flank, with a kind of proud bewilderment. She had had many litters in her time, but just at first she always seemed a little puzzled by the puppies.

'Ah, my beautiful, that was bravely done!' Talore said, with a leaping gentleness in his voice, as he gave her the last piece of meat, and turned his hand to caress the warm hollow under her chin.

There were five of the whelps, Drem could see now; blind, helpless, squirming, yet already thrusting among each other for first place against their mother's flank and the chief share of the warm milk that meant life.

Talore slipped his hand under one of the puppies, and scooped it up. Fand licked his wrist as he did so, but when Drem tried to pick up one of the tiny creatures she rumbled warningly in her throat, the rumble rising to a sing-song snarl; and he drew his hand back empty, saying, 'But you know me, I am Drem. Do you think that I would harm your cubs?'

Talore smiled, and the dog teeth showed white at the corners of his mouth. 'In a little, ah, before their eyes open, she will let you take them even from under her. Now her temper is shaken and unsure; it is no more than that.' He returned the puppy, and took up another, whose coat was brindled black and amber. 'Aye, they are fine cubs. But this one, it is in my heart, will be the finest of the litter.' And while Fand watched with only a faint warning growl, he set the puppy on Drem's knee.

With strange things happening inside him, Drem slipped his hand under its small chest and sat it up, its fore paws dangling over his wrist. It was as rat-like as its brothers, its still damp hide soft as a mouse's skin, its stomach pinkish and almost naked, palpitating with very new life against his palm. And on its breast and throat there shone already a blaze like a small silver flame. The creature whimpered, its soft muzzle thrusting and fumbling against Drem's hand, seeking for the warm milk that it had lost. And Drem, looking down at it, saw it with the

eyes of love, so that his whole heart went out to it, his whole
soul caught up in longing. It was not just because it was a
puppy, he had held many puppies before now, in his world that
lived by its hounds and herd dogs; and of them all, it was to
this one that his heart cried out, 'Brother, we are for each other,
you and I!' This one, with the white flame on its breast.

Ah, but what was the use? If it had been a weakling, the
outcast of the litter, maybe Talore would have given it to him
instead of drowning it; but it would be the finest of them all,
Talore had said so, and he could see the truth of that for himself. And there were always hunters throughout the Clan who
would pay any price that Talore liked to ask for one of Fand's
puppies, for Fand's puppies always had her wisdom and her
beauty.

Now the puppy was nuzzling harder and more urgently
under his hand. Talore said, 'He is hungry. It is time that he
goes back to his mother,' and picked him up and set him again
among his brothers, laughing as he thrust his way back to his
mother's flank.

'Come,' said Talore, rising. 'Better that we leave her to
herself now.'

So Drem got up, with one last, longing look at the tiny rat-
like thing squirming among its litter brothers, and presently,
quite forgetting to give Wenna the message about the sitting of
mallard eggs, went his way, out into the gusty greyness of the
evening, leaving his small fierce heart behind him.

In the days that followed, he seized on every excuse to go
down to the village, until at last the time was almost come for
the cubs to leave their mother. By that time Fand was growing
tired of her family and had returned to her usual place at
Talore's heels; and the low hurdles of their pen were the only
thing that kept them from exploring all over the house-place at
all times of the day and night and probably ending by being
trodden on by Wenna or killed in a fit of exasperation by one
of the other hunting dogs.

On a summer evening, a grey evening as the other had been,

but full of the soft, regretful stillness of mizzle rain instead of the wet turmoil of wind, Drem, who for several days had not been able to escape from the work on the farm, met Talore on his way home from visiting his traps, and came trotting back among the hounds at his heels. And now, the hurdle shifted back, he was squatting on his heels in the fern, with the cubs all about him. The rain dripped from the eaves, and the flames fluttered under the pot in which Wenna was seething deer meat in milk; the wet girl-child chirrupped and bubbled to herself on a deer-skin beside the hearth, and the puppies squealed and whickered together. Fand pushed past Drem and snuffed among her cubs, thrusting them  this way and that with her broad muzzle; but she no longer lay down among them, for her time for feeding them was gone, and she was tired of being nipped and crawled over.

They were twice the size that they had been when first he saw them; they had become woolly and venturesome and had long since ceased to look like rats. He looked up at Talore, who had come across the hut to join him, after hanging up his kill. 'Does Fand not feed them any more?'

'Nay, the time for that is over; they eat meal stirabout and meat now.'

Something seemed to twist in Drem's stomach, and he put out his hand to the cub with the white throat, and bowled it on to its back, feeling the nip of its little sharp teeth in his thumb. 'Ah—ee! Fierce wolf-dog! You would bite, would you?' He rolled it from side to side while it squirmed with delight; and still playing with the puppy, so that he need not look up, he asked in a carefully levelled voice, 'Then—their new masters will be taking them soon?'

'Any day now,' said Talore.

Drem swallowed. 'You will—have chosen who they go to?'

35

'Surely. The little red one I keep myself, and the mealy grey. This one, Belu from above the ford will trade me a length of cloth for—poor Wenna cannot clothe four men with her weaving—and this one goes to Gwythno of the Singing Spear.'

That left only the cub with the silver blaze, now muzzling into the hollow of Drem's neck, for without quite knowing that he did so, he had caught it up and was holding it against his breast.

'And that one——' said Talore, and let the end of the sentence fall, watching the small, braced, tell-tale figure crouched among the fern, with the puppy held fiercely, protectively, against his breast.

Drem looked up, and met Talore's dark, narrowed gaze upon him, and waited, with a sudden intensity of waiting that hurt him somewhere beneath his breast-bone. He heard the drip of the summer rain from the eaves, and Wenna crooning to the girl-child as she turned barley cakes among the hot ash. The puppy whimpered protestingly at being held so close, its little body warmly alive against his, its breath like the breath of all puppies, smelling of garlic. Soon its warmth and liveness would be under someone else's hand, it would learn to come to someone else's call, and hunt with a master who was not Drem. . . And still the rain fell, drip-drip-drip from the eaves, very loud.

'Do you want him so badly, then?' Talore said.

Drem lifted bright, grave eyes to his face and nodded. He could not speak.

'Then it is in my mind that I will sell him to you,' Talore said, 'at a price.'

It seemed to Drem that the rain was louder than ever. '*Drip-drip-drip*' marking off the silence with little dark arrow-heads of sound. Price? What price could he give for the cub? He was not Belu to have fine cloth to trade. His eyes searched Talore's face, looking for the meaning behind it.

'What is the price?' he asked at last, and his voice sounded husky in his own ears.

Talore smiled. 'I grow weary of mutton and of deer meat.

36

The price is a bird for the pot—but it must be brought down with the throw-spear.'

Drem frowned at him a moment in bewilderment, knowing that Talore could bring down wild fowl for himself at any time he chose, and had besides, three sons to hunt for him. And then he understood. It was proof of his own skill with the throw-spear that was really the price of the cub.

Well, it was a year since he had first set himself to master the throw-spear; he had some skill, he knew. Suddenly he grinned, flinging up his head like a pony, in a way that always showed when he was ready for battle; and the dripping of the rain under the eaves went back to its proper place. 'I will pay the price,' he said, 'I will pay it tomorrow, Talore.'

Drem did not say anything in the home house-place about what he was going to do; he could not speak of it to anyone until it was done. He slept fitfully that night, waking often, until the first faint paling of the sky where the roof turf was rolled back warned him that it was time to be on his way. Then he pushed back the deer-skin covering and got silently to his feet, feeling to make sure that his knife was safely in his belt. There were a few bad moments while he felt for his own spear among the others in the rack, and got it out, but he managed it without the blade clattering against its neighbours, and with a sigh of relief turned to the entrance. Old Kea raised her head beside the fire to watch him, but made no outcry, for the hounds were well used to night-time comings and goings; and since it was summer time there was no stirring and stamping of ponies in the fore porch to betray his passing that way.

Yesterday's rain had gone over, and there was a new-washed cleanness in the air, a smell of wet, refreshed earth. The curlews were already calling over the High Chalk, but at this time of year they called almost all through the short nights; and there would be plenty of time to reach his chosen hunting ground before dawn.

He had left the last of the corn plots behind him, and was

turning down to the little brook that had its spring in a deep hollow under the grazing ground, when his ear picked up the pad of running feet behind him—very small, swift feet on the downland turf—and he had scarcely time to swing round before a flying shadow came down the slope and Blai was beside him, panting with the speed she had made.

Drem was angry. 'What do you come after me for?' he demanded. 'Go home, Blai.'

'I saw you go,' Blai said in the little clear voice that had somehow the note of a bird call in it and never seemed to belong to the same person as her narrow, shut-up face, 'and I thought maybe—if it was a hunting, you would need food for the day.'

Food; yes, he had not thought about food. Well, it was for the Women's side to think of such things. 'What have you got?' he demanded.

'Only a barley cake. That was all I could steal without waking them. But it is a big one.'

'It will serve,' said Drem handsomely, and tucking his throw-spear under his arm, took the hard, crusty bannock that she thrust into his hand. 'Go home now, Blai, and do not you be telling anyone that I have gone hunting.'

'I will not, then.' Blai hesitated on one foot, half going, half staying. 'Drem—let you take me too!'

Drem said with harsh reason, 'You! What use would you be?'

'I would do anything—I would be your hound——'

But Drem was already turning away. 'Na, I do not need a hound today. And'—suddenly he could not hold it back—'soon I may have a hound of my own to hunt with me!'

Behind him as he went, he heard her cry out in a little defiant voice, 'One day—one day my father will come back for me——' But she was crying it out to herself, not really to Drem.

Drem crossed the brook—it was so narrow still that it did not even need a stepping stone—and went on to his day's hunting, leaving her standing there.

A faint bar of amber light was broadening in the east as he came down through the oak and hazel and whitethorn scrub of the lower slopes, eating the bannock as he went so as to have it out of the way, and headed for the marshes. A great, slow, full-bodied river, winding south from the forest uplands far inland, found a pass in the hills just there, and went winding and looping out to join the Great Water. Many streams rising in the lower flanks of the Chalk ran down into it, and in several places across it beavers had built their dams—generation after generation of beavers that had been there, Drem supposed, as long as the river had been there, and would stay while the river stayed. And the choked river had flowed out over its banks, spreading far and wide; and so came the Marsh. Sometimes after the winter rains the water spread far up into the forest, making a lake that was a day's trail, two days' trail, from end to end, and all the pass through the Chalk was a winding arm of water out of which the alders and sallows raised their arms to the sky. But in the summer it was mostly land of a sort, sour and sodden and very green: reed beds and alder brakes, and dense covers of thorn and sallow, and thickly matted fleeces of yellow iris, all laced with winding, silver riverways and spreading, shallow lakes alive with the wild fowl that came inland at the breeding season and did not go back to the coast until autumn came again.

No one lived in the Marshes that lay inland of the Chalk, for at night mists rose from them and evil spirits prowled abroad in the mists to give men the sickness that filled their bones with shivering fire; and even at high noon in summer time there was always a dank smell of things wet and rotting, for the cleansing wash of the tides that came up and went down again twice in every day over the sea marshes could not reach so far through the Chalk. But the hunters went there after the wild fowl and the beaver.

So Drem headed for the Marsh now, and in a clump of sallows on the edge of one of the many spreading sheets of water, settled himself to wait.

He was shivering with mingled cold and excitement and a

breathless sense of the importance of that day's hunting. Away eastward the bar of amber light was brightening to gold, and the gold was catching echoes from the water that lay everywhere, and all around him was a stirring as the Marsh woke into life. Light and colour were coming back into the world; and suddenly something dark, almost like a rat, darted from among the pale roots of the rushes close to Drem, hesitated, half doubled back, and then scuttled across to the next clump. When the water-rail moved, other things would soon be stirring. Very soon now, Drem thought, any moment now, and drew his knee farther under him. His hand cramped on the spear shaft, and he opened it, feeling it wet and sticky with the long tightness of his grip; and went over feverishly in his mind everything he had ever been told, everything he had ever found out for himself about the throw-spear; and licked his lower lip, and waited again.

He was so twanging taut that when, without an instant's warning, a mallard drake beat up from the rushes not three spears' lengths away to his right, he was thrown completely off his balance. Next instant he had recovered himself, and sent the light throw-spear, thrumming as it flew, after the quarry. It missed so narrowly that it carried away the tip of a wing feather, and for one instant he thought he had made his hit, before the spear plunged back into the rushes and the mallard darted off, raising its wild alarm call to the morning skies. And suddenly with a great bursting upward, the Marsh was alive with startled and indignant wings.

In a while, the morning fell quiet again, and he could hear teal and widgeon, curlew and sandpiper crying and calling in the distance; but all around him the Marsh was silent; empty under a shining and empty sky.

Drem hit the stem of the nearest sallow with a passionate fist; but that only hurt his knuckles and did nothing to mend what had happened. He was almost crying with fury as he slid out of his cover and searched among the reeds for his throw-spear. It took him a few moments to find it, because he was

40

blind with rage and disappointment; but he found it at last, and
settled again to wait. But the wild fowl did not return though
he heard them calling in the distance; and at last, with the sun
well up and the level light streaming across the Marshes, he
knew that it would be no use waiting any longer.

He left his hiding place, slipping along in the lea of the sallow
bushes. Maybe he would be able to flush something and knock
it down before it got out of range. But though he hunted far
and wide as the shadows shortened, he never got within spear-
throw of a bird; and something was growing in him that was
frightened and a little desperate. There would be other days;
Talore would not sell the cub away from him at once, because
he failed on the first day of all. But last night he had said, 'I will
pay the price tomorrow.' And somehow for him there was only
this one day; that was the bargain. Somehow, in his mind, the
thing was mixed up with his Warrior Scarlet; he must earn the
price of the cub today, he must keep his bargain perfectly and
completely, and give proof of his skill with a throw-spear *today*,
if his mother was ever to weave scarlet on the loom for him.

It must have been noon or later, when, as he came crouching
down the fringe of a long straggle of alder trees, he heard the
rhythmical creaking sound, half eery, half musical, of a swan in
flight, and turning, saw the great bird flying low towards him

across the level of jewel-green turf between two spreading sheets of water. The sun was on its feathers, and its shadow flew beneath it like a dark echo along the ground; a bird of snow and a bird of shadow ... Drem saw the proud spread of shining wings, beating with slow, almost lazy power and beauty, as it flew with outstretched neck; he heard louder and louder the half musical throb of the wing beats; and the great swan swole on his sight. It seemed rushing towards him, blotting out the world with the white spread of its wings. He was caught up in a piercing vision of white, fierce beauty that was like thunder and lightning and an east wind, like a sunburst. He was scarcely aware of rising to his feet as the great bird swept towards him, climbing into the sunlight, scarcely aware of his spear-arm swinging up and back in its own perfect curve of movement ...

The spear went thrumming on its way. It took the swan in the breast, and the great bird pitched in the air, half turning over its own length, and dropped.

Drem started from cover of the alder trees and ran towards it. The swan was still alive, and threshing where it had fallen, with a dreadful, broken struggling. Drem ran in among the flailing wings that could have broken his leg even now, if a blow had landed square, and finished the work with the knife from his belt. The struggling ceased with a last quiver.

The swan—a big cob—lay dead, its neck outstretched as in flight; and Drem pulled out the spear which was still embedded in it. There was blood on the white feathers. Blood on snow, Drem thought, standing over it; blood on his own hand, too; and the living, flashing beauty was gone. Desolation as piercing as the moment of vision had been stabbed through him. How could a little spear that he had thrown almost without knowing it, blot out in an instant all the power and the swiftness and the shining?

But the desolation passed as the vision had done, and he was left with the fierce hot pride of his first real kill. He stabbed his knife into the turf to clean it, and thrust it back into his belt; then stood to think what he must do next.

IV

The Price of Whitethroat

THE first thing he realized was that he could not possibly get his kill back to Talore alone. He had seen himself proudly walking into the steading with a teal or a widgeon hanging from his hand; how much more proudly with a swan on his shoulder, the huge white wings drooping all about him! But those wings must be as far from tip to tip as the height of a man. And when he tried, he found that he could not even get the swan on to his shoulder without help, let alone carry it all the way back. The only thing to do was to hide it, and go and tell Talore.

He got hold of the bird, and began to drag it back towards the alder trees. It took him some time to do, because instinctively he was trying not to spoil it. It was his kill, and still beautiful, though with a moveless beauty now; and he wanted it to keep the beauty until Talore saw it. Little by little, the great wings fanned out on the grass, he got it back: in at last among the tangle of alders and the thick-growing rushes and wild iris.

43

Dragging it deep into the tangle, he folded the great wings close so that it might take up as little space as possible, and dragged up handfuls of brown, flowering rushes and cool, sword-shaped iris leaves and spread them over it in a thick layer until there was no gleam of white to betray it to the magpies and the ravens. Then he got up, picked up his spear and cleaned it as he had cleaned his dagger, by stabbing it into the turf, and taking a last careful look round him to be sure of knowing the place again, set off for the village and the steading of Talore the Hunter.

He had wandered long distances to and fro in search of his kill, but turned back often on his trail, so that he was not so far out into the Marsh as he had expected. But even so, the way up through the midge-infested hazel woods and along the flank of the Chalk was a long, hard one, and his bare, briar-scratched legs were beginning to be very weary when he came within sight—and smell—of the village.

It was the time of the wild garlic harvest, when the women and girls went down the stream sides and through the cool, dark places of the forest fringe, searching for the rank-smelling star-white flowers, and gathering the plants into big rush baskets; and for days the village and every outlying steading reeked of the white flowers spread out on the south sides of the low turf roofs to dry. Yesterday it had been no good trying to dry the flowers, but today the sun shone hot, and the swallows were flying high for fine weather, darting and swerving against the blue of the sky, and every roof had its patch of wilting white stars; the pungent waft of them came to meet Drem as he climbed up between the village corn plots towards the steading of Talore the Hunter.

Talore was not there, nor any of his sons. Only fat, good-natured Wenna sat on her heels in the house-place doorway, grinding corn for the next day in the big stone quern; and she cried out at sight of him, '*Now* what thing have you been doing? Tch tch, you're hurt—there is blood on your forehead——'

Drem had not known that; it must have come off his hand

when he pushed back his hair. 'Na, I am not hurt,' he said. 'I have been hunting, and I have killed. Now I would speak with Talore.'

'He is away down the valley about a heifer calf,' said Talore's son's wife, smiling at him across the quern, now that she knew he was not hurt. 'Do you want to go in and look at the cubs? Gwythno came for his today, and Belu also, but there are still three cubs left.'

Drem shook his head. That was a thing that he was saving.

'Are you hungry, then?' Wenna asked.

Drem thought about this a little. In the intensity of his thinking about other things, he had forgotten about being hungry, but now he realized that having eaten nothing but Blai's bannock all day, he was as empty as a last year's snail shell. 'I am hungry,' he agreed.

'Bide you——' Wenna rose, and disappeared into the house-place, leaving him alone with the girl-child, who lay in a soft deerskin, sucking the bead of red coral that hung round her neck, and gazed at him out of solemn, sloe-black eyes. Drem stared back at the girl-child, then poked it gingerly in the middle with one toe, to see what would happen, prepared to retreat and swear he hadn't been near it if it screamed. But it kicked inside the deerskin, and made pleased noises. So he poked it once more, then abandoned it rather hurriedly as Wenna came back.

'Here—take this, then,' she said, and gave him a wheaten cake smeared with dark honey, and squatted down again to her grinding.

Drem sat down with his back against the rowan-wood door-post in the sunshine, and ate his wheaten cake, licking the golden dribble of sweetness round the edges, and watched Wenna scoop the grain from her basket into the hole in the upper stone of the quern, and the coarse creamy meal that came out between the two stones as she rubbed, on to the spread skin under the quern. Every now and then she stopped rubbing, and scooped up the meal into a crock beside her.

Drem did not offer to help; it was woman's work, and he was of the Men's side, a hunter, and had made his first big kill.

The shadows were lengthening though it would not be evening for a long while yet, and Wenna had finished her grinding, and gone in again, carrying the baby with her on her hip, and Drem was alone before the house-place door, when at last Talore came home, driving a small, dispirited brown heifer calf on the end of a rope.

Drem scrambled up and went to meet him as he came up between the store shed and the woodstack, with the calf lurching from side to side on the end of the rope, and the three hounds loping at his heels.

'Well?' Talore said questioningly when he saw him, leaning back to check a sudden rush by the calf.

'I have come for the cub,' Drem said. 'I can pay the price.'

Talore's dark brows went up. 'Where is it then? In the pot already?'

'I could not bring it with me. It is too big.'

'Have you killed a wild ox with your throw-spear?' Talore's voice deepened, as it always did with laughter; and the dog teeth showed at the corners of his mouth. 'It was a bird I said, remember.'

'It is a swan!' Drem's pride came rushing up into his throat. 'A cob swan—big, big as a cloud!'

'So? That is a kill indeed!'

They were all heading for the byre by now, and the calf had set up a dismal bawling. Drem nodded urgently. 'Down in the Marsh, it is. I could not carry it, so I hid it and came back. I thought maybe—we could go for it—now.' His voice trailed away a little, as it dawned on him that perhaps that was rather a lot to ask at the day's end.

Talore glanced down at him, at the same time putting out a leg to fend the calf from a determined sideways rush in the wrong direction. He was tired, and wanted nothing but to sit down and stretch out his legs and polish his spears while he

46

waited for Wenna to make ready the evening meal. But looking at Drem's proudly eager face with the doubt already beginning to shadow it, he said, 'Let you help me to stall the calf, and then we will go down together and fetch this kill.'

They stalled the calf in the warm-shadowed byre, and left it to Wenna's tending; and, in a little, were heading down again toward the Marsh, Talore loping ahead with the long, light stride of the hunter, the hounds and Drem close at his heels.

The blue summer dusk had deepened into the dark, and the white owl who lived in the shed of the Chieftain's great herd bull was hawking to and fro like a silver shadow across the corn land, when they came up again towards the huddle of the village under the Hill of Gathering. Talore walked ahead as before, and Drem and the hounds padded at his heels; but now the hunter carried Drem's swan on his shoulder, the great wings drooping wide behind him—pale, paler than the soft wings of the hunting owl in the darkness, or the white, wilting stars of the garlic spread on the hut roofs to dry.

The skin apron over the house-place doorway was drawn back, and a stain of light came to meet them, thick and golden like honey trickling from a tipped jar. Inside, the sons had returned from their hunting and were gathered about the hearth where the fire sank low, for the evening meal was long past, burnishing their weapons, while Wenna stitched at a piece of yellow cloth by the light of a mutton-fat lamp hanging from the roof tree.

There was another man sitting by the fire, his back to the doorway, a big, broad-shouldered man who turned as they crossed the threshold, revealing the heavy, reddish face of Morvidd, the Chieftain's brother. And behind him in the shadows squatted a boy of about Drem's age, nursing his father's spear—a boy with a quarrelsome and unhappy face; but Drem, who had run with him in the same pack all his life, did not of course see that. He only knew that Luga the son of Morvidd was apt to be at the root of any trouble that broke out among their own kind.

'So. You are here at last,' the man said, rather loudly, while the two boys cocked their heads at each other.

Talore checked just within the doorway and returned the greeting more courteously. 'And you, Morvidd the Chieftain's brother, you also are here, and welcome. I had not thought you would be back from your trading until the moon was on the wane.'

'I am but this evening returned to my house-place; and one told me that Fand has whelped and the whelps are ready to leave their dam. Therefore I am come to make my choice of one of them.'

Talore stood smiling a little, the great swan on his shoulder, its wings falling wide behind him. 'Others have made their choice already. There is none of the cubs left without a master.'

Æsk, the eldest son, looked up from the spear he was burnishing, and said swiftly, 'I told him that, my father, but he would wait for you none the less.'

Morvidd's face had turned a deeper red as it always did when he was crossed, so that his eyes looked like little bright splinters of glass in the redness of it; and he began to bluster. 'Did I not say to you, last Fall-of-the-leaf, that I would give you a fine copper cooking pot that had never known the fire, for the best cub in Fand's next litter?'

It seemed to Drem that everything stopped, between breath and breath, and there was a sudden cold emptiness inside him. He saw the grin of triumph on the face of the boy Luga. Then Talore said, 'Did I not say to you last Fall-of-the-leaf that I do not promise unborn cubs to any man?' And everything went on again, and the grin faded on Luga's face.

Morvidd forced a laugh, and an air of joviality; clearly he wanted one of the cubs very badly. 'Nay then, we will leave that part of it. I come now, and there are three cubs yet in the litter. I've a mind to the one with the white blaze on its breast—the best cub of the three, without doubt; and I'll give you the cook pot for him—a good big cook pot—and a length

48

of fine bleached linen cloth thrown in. What do you say to that?'

'I say that above all the litter, that one is already sold,' Talore said.

'Who to, then? Who to?'

'To the boy here.'

Morvidd stared for a moment, then flung up his head with a roar of laughter. 'And since when does Talore sell his hound cubs to children for a handful of wild raspberries? Ah, but of course if that is the way of the thing it is easily undone. I see the thing is more than half a jest!'

Talore slipped the swan from his shoulder and flung it down beside the hearth. 'Nay, it is not a jest, the bargain was fairly made and the boy has paid the price—the agreed price—and the thing is finished.'

The great swan lay there, spread-winged in the firelight and the lamplight; one of the hounds sniffed at it and was cuffed aside by the second son. Morvidd finished his laugh rather abruptly, and stared down at the swan and then at Drem and then back at Talore, angry again, and the more angry because he was puzzled. 'This—*this*?' He reached out a foot and prodded the great bird contemptuously in a way that made the rage rise in Drem's throat—his swan, his beautiful kill, the price of the hound of his heart, to be treated so! 'Surely it is not a hand but a head that you lack, Talore! What sort of price, beside a fine copper cook pot, is a dead swan for a hound puppy? Tell me that!'

Drem clenched his sound hand into a fist; and then above him, Talore said with that leaping gentleness of his, '*This* swan is a better price than if it were as many copper cook pots as there are fingers on my one hand.'

The two men stood facing each other beside the fire, the one big and red-gold and blustering, swaying a little on his heels, the other slight and dark, and still as a forest pool; while the rest of the big firelit hut looked on, the boy Luga watching his father out of the shadows, expectantly.

Then Morvidd said, 'And that is your last word as to the thing?'

'That is my last word.'

'Then you're mad!' Morvidd let out a kind of baffled roar. 'You're a fool, Talore One-hand! To shake your head at a fine copper——'

Talore cut across his blustering, with the same gentleness. 'That you have said before. Nay then, Morvidd the Chieftain's brother, there is a thing that you forget, in all this. It is I who choose what master Fand's cubs shall go to, and what master Fand's cubs shall not go to; I, and no other. And I choose only masters who to my mind are worthy of them.'

For a moment Drem thought that Morvidd was going to burst like an old skin bottle filled too full, then he seemed to collapse as though the bottle had been partly emptied. He blinked, and swallowed loudly, then gathered himself together and strode to the doorway. On the threshold he turned, some of his bluster coming back to him, and shouted: 'Then here is *my* last word. There are better cubs easily come by for a smaller price; and do not you be trying to sell a cub to *me* when Fand litters again and maybe no man needs another hound!'

50

'I will not, assuredly, I will not,' Talore said, looking after the big angry man as he flung away into the night; and the familiar note of laughter was deepening in his voice.

The boy Luga made after his father, turning also on the threshold with a long, lowering look that took in everybody in the house-place but rested longest upon Drem, before he too was gone.

'He was very angry,' Drem said, when the sound of footsteps had died away.

'He will forget,' Talore said. 'He blusters—like a west wind he blusters; but a west wind blows itself out in a while.'

But Drem had a feeling that however quickly Morvidd's fury blustered itself out, it would be a long time before Luga forgave having seen his father worsted and made to seem foolish.

Ah, but what did that matter? The thing was over; and Drem drew a long breath, and turned his gaze again to the swan lying spread-winged in the firelight. They were all look-ing at the swan now, while Wenna set aside her stitching, and rose to set out the deer meat which she had been keeping hot for the lord of the house in a pot among the embers. 'Gwythno was here at noon, and Belu from the ford a while before. I gave

51

them the puppies as you bade me . . . I would have liked a copper cook pot, but I suppose we can do without.'

'Nay then,' said Talore, laughing. 'We are none so poor that we must trade a puppy for a cook pot. If your heart is set on such a thing, then go and speak with Kian the Smith, and tell him he shall have two dressed wolfskins from me, for making it.'

Talore's sons were all round Drem now, laughing. 'That was a great hunting,' they said. 'Little brother, that was a fine kill—see, it is all but as big as himself!' And the eldest son caught him a friendly buffet between the shoulders that landed like the blow of a bear's paw and all but sent him sprawling into the fire.

Triumph rushed up into Drem's throat, all the fiercer and more sweet for what had gone before. Just for one dreadful moment following on Morvidd's words, he had seen his swan, his beautiful kill, as so small a price for the cub that it was not really a price at all. Just a big dead bird, beginning to be tattered and unlovely. But then Talore had said that it was worth as many copper cooking pots as there were fingers on his one hand, and the white rumpled feathers on which the bright blood had turned brown were shining with pride and beauty again.

'It is a fair price,' said Talore, seeing where he looked. 'Let you take the cub now.'

Drem nodded, for the moment beyond speech, and crossed to the hurdled-off place where Fand stood with her muzzle down and her tail slowly swinging, among the yippings and whimperings that came from the piled fern.

His heart was beating right up in his throat with the joy of the moment as he pulled the low hurdle aside and reached down among the small, sleepy forms in the bracken, and grasped the one with the silver blaze by the scruff of the neck and lifted him out from between his brothers. Fand made no protest, and indeed seemed scarcely interested. He held the puppy up, swinging a little from its loose scruff; he laughed as it tried from

arm's length away to lick his nose, and knew that the perfect moment, the best moment of all had come.

'I have bought my hound!' he said to the world at large. 'I have paid the price for him, and he is mine! I shall call him Whitethroat!'

'So, that is a good name,' Talore said. 'And now it is time to be going home.'

Drem looked up from the puppy. 'I shall need to leave my spear here until tomorrow,' he said, 'so that I can carry the cub.'

'Assuredly,' Talore nodded. 'His legs are but two moons old, and the way will be over long for them; yet first make him follow you a little. It is so that he will understand that he is your hound to follow at your heel.'

Drem looked at the hunter doubtfully a moment, then squatted down and set the puppy on its legs. 'Will he come, do you think?'

'Call him, and see.'

Drem got up and took a step backward. 'Hi! Whitethroat, come!' The puppy continued to sit on its haunches. It was too small as yet to prick its ears, but it fluttered them, gazing up at Drem with the air of one trying to understand what he would have it do. Drem drew another step towards the doorway. 'Come! We go home now, brother.' The puppy whimpered and made a small thrusting motion towards him. Aware that everyone in the house-place was watching them, Drem took yet another backward step. He was almost at the threshold now. 'Whitethroat—here!' His throat ached with urgency, and the words came hoarse. He whistled a two-note call that he had never thought of before, but that seemed to come to him now as the proper call between him and Whitethroat. The small, brindled, half-wolf cub got up, sneezed, shook itself and waddled towards him, its stomach brushing the ferny ground. Once it hesitated, and looked back at Fand its mother with an air of uncertainty, and then padded forward again. And Drem knew that he had been wrong in thinking that the moment

when he picked it out from the litter was the best moment of all.

He was across the threshold now, looking back over his shoulder as he went; and the cub gave a bounce and quickened to a rolling trot. They went down between the outsheds together, the hunter leading, the hound at his heels, as it should be; as it would be in all their lives together. But at the edge of Talore's steading, Drem stopped in answer to a protesting whimper, and scooped up the puppy and settled it against his shoulder, in the crook of his sound arm.

So Drem walked home up the sweeping flanks of the Chalk, through the still summer darkness, with his hunting dog asleep, warm and live and unexpectedly heavy, in the crook of his arm; and a kind of chant of triumph singing itself over and over again within him. 'I have bought my hound! I bought him with a great white swan—a swan like a sun-burst, that I slew with my throw-spear! I have bought my hound, and he is mine! He was sired by a wolf, out where the wolves pass at the Spring Running; and he will be the swiftest and the bravest hound that ever ran with the Clan, and he is mine! Mine is the cub to me because I paid the price for him—I, Drem the Hunter; I bought him with my kill!'

It had been a long day and a hard one, and it had given him his hound and his first big kill, and the proof of his own skill with a throw-spear that brought him just so much nearer to his Warrior Scarlet. It had been a good day.

But he had been right in thinking that it would be a long time—a very long time—before Luga the son of Morvidd forgave, or forgot.

V

The Dagger and the Fire

AT most places the brook ran deep sunk between steep
alder-fringed banks; but at the loop just below the
ancient trackway, the current had formed a low spit
which was a favourite bathing place with the boys of the Clan.
It was a good place, in the blue and green noon-tides of summer
when the high sun splashed through the alder leaves and fell in
freckles of gold on the dark water, and the shadows might be
lit at any moment by the irridescent flash of a dragon fly.
Summer was over now, and the water turning cold, so that you
splashed in and out again, shouting, and tumbled over each
other in sham fight on the bank to get warm, while you dried
off and got your kirtle on again; but it was still a good place, on
a fine autumn evening, with the westering sunlight slanting in
spears of tawny brightness through the alders and the nut leaves,
and the shadows blue as woodsmoke.

There were some boys down there now; Luga the son of
Morvidd, and fat, good-natured Maelgan, and little dark Erp of
the Half People, who could swim like an otter under water, and
two or three more, with the usual pack of dogs. Drem sat a
little farther up the bank than the rest, re-tying the ankle
thongs of his rawhide shoes, a thing which always took him
rather longer than it took the others, because of having to do it
one handed. And beside him, nose on paws, and superb bush-
tail curving away into the tangle of the past summer's willow-
herb, lay the great, brindled, black and amber hound whom

more than a year ago he had picked, small and woolly and half a leep, from among his litter brothers in Talore's house-place, and whistled to follow him.

Drem made the thong fast, and half drew his legs under him, beginning to think about going home to supper. He wondered what there would be; stew of some sort, he hoped, for as usual he was hungry. And if Blai, who had gone down the brookside with a withy basket, came back in time, maybe his mother would have made some of the sweet, dark, pippy mess that she brewed with blackberries and honey to spread on barley cakes; but more likely that would be tomorrow.

For the moment they had fallen quiet, and in the quiet, a flash of living blue lit across Drem's eyes, as a kingfisher swooped down to a low-hanging branch of the great willow, upstream.

Luga picked up a flint from the grass beside him—there were always a few along the spit, rolled down from the made-place where the cattle came to drink—and flung it. It missed its mark and skittered over the top of the branch into the water beyond with a sound like a fish leaping, and the kingfisher darted off with a gutteral anger-call.

Drem hooted derisively, and Luga scowled. 'I was not trying to hit it.'

'Yes you were,' Drem said.

'I was not, then.'

'You can never see anything alive and—and *liking* being alive without wanting to throw something at it and make it be dead,' Drem said, and added, more for the sake of arguing than anything else, 'Talore says that killing for the sake of killing, in the way of the fox and the weasel, makes the Forest Gods angry.'

'Talore! Talore!' said Luga, skimmering another flint into the water, and trying to mimic Drem's way of speaking. 'Of course we all know you are Talore's pet. Didn't he give you Whitethroat just for a dead swan that you like enough found dead of old age on the Marshes and stole from the magpies,

when *my* father would have given him a fine copper cooking pot?'

Drem rose in his place and was just about to fall on him and avenge the insult to himself and his swan alike, when White-throat sprang to his feet and stood alert, his head up to reveal the silver blaze that had given him his name, his amber eyes wary, muzzle testing the wind; and almost in the same instant, Erp, who had been lying on his stomach investigating a water rat's hole under the bank, rolled over and sat up, cocking his narrow, dark head towards the track: the ancient green track along which, as often as along the Ridgeway, the world went by; bands of skin-clad hunters from distant hunting runs; herdsmen in the droving season; warriors with stripes of woad and ochre on their foreheads, following their princes to war; traders from across the Great Water with salt and scented yellow amber and fine bronze in their ponies' bales.

Somewhere, a long way off as yet, someone or something was coming along the track between the hazels and the whitethorn trees, and instantly the quarrel was forgotten, and boys and hounds in a knot went scrambling up the bank to where they could get a view of the track through the scrub.

'Maybe it is a war-band!' said Luga, hopefully. It was exciting when a war-band came by; and there was no need to be afraid, for if their business was with the village under the Hill of Gathering, as it had been in the time when Talore lost his hand and Drem's father went beyond the sunset, then they would not be on the track at all.

'More likely it is a hunting party, now in the Fall-of-the-leaf,' Maelgan said.

Little Erp lay with his ear pressed against the ground. 'Ponies,' he said, 'The earth speaks of ponies—I think two ponies—and one man. No more.'

'Then it must be a trader of some kind.'

They waited, peering between the hazel branches, and listening. They could all hear it now, very faintly, the light beat of hooves on the summer-hard ground, and then the pad

of human feet; nearer, and nearer. There was a flicker of saffron yellow through the alder leaves; and a few moments later a man came into view: a tall, dark man in a tattered cloak whose greens and purples had dimmed with weather and mud to the colour of storm clouds, leading two dejected ponies one behind the other, the foremost bowlegged under the weight of two great bales wrapped in yellow cloth, the hindmost loaded with the tools of a bronze-smith's trade.

A trader or travelling craftsman was always of interest, for his stories of the outside world as well as for the wonders that might be hidden in his bales. And as this one drew level, walking with the long, slow stride of a man who walks from the sky's edge to the sky's edge and knows that there is no hurry, the knot of boys swarmed from cover with the hounds at their heels, and flung themselves upon him, demanding, 'Where are you from?—Where are you away to?—Do you sleep in our village tonight?—What have you in those bales?'

The tall man looked down at them, laughing, as they padded alongside him. 'Sa hah! Here is a fine welcome, then! I am from the last village behind me, and it may be that I spend the night in your Chieftain's steading, or it may be that I shall sleep as sound under a hawthorn bush with a fire to keep the Wild away. I am for the West towards the Sunset; and as to what there is in my bales, let you see when I open them before the Chieftain's door.'

And they went on together, only Erp was not with them, for he was of the Little Dark People whose instinct was to run and hide instead of coming out to ask questions; but the others knew that he was watching them from under the whitethorn bushes.

Maelgan ran ahead to give warning of the bronze-smith's coming, and when they reached the outskirts of the village, one

58

of the Men's side came down to meet them, with reversed spear for a sign of peace, saying, 'Greeting, stranger. We have our bronze-smith already among the huts of the Half People; but Dumnorix the Chieftain sends you greeting, and bids you come and open your bales before his threshold, according to the custom.'

'Sa, I will come as the Chieftain bids me, and open my bales before his door according to the custom,' the stranger said. 'It is in my mind that the Chieftain will not regret it. All the world knows that the finest bronze-smiths are from the Green Isle in the West; and in all the Green Island there is no smith with cunning to match mine whether in the forging of weapons for a hero, or the working of ornaments for a queen's white neck.'

When they reached the clear space before the Chieftain's house-place, the only things alive in it were an old hound sleeping outstretched on the dung heap, and Midir the Priest sitting in the last echo of the sunset, against the wind-break beside the house-place doorway, with his soft bull's-hide robe huddled about his shoulders against the chill of the autumn evening, and his chin sunk on his breast as though he also slept. But it was commonly believed that Midir never slept, only went away small inside himself and talked with the Gods in the silence he found there. He did not look up or make any sign as they drew near. But almost in the moment of checking the ponies, two older boys—next year's warriors—came across from the Boys' House to take charge of the poor tired beasts as they were unloaded; and several of the Men's side who were home early began to trickle up, gathering for a sight of the things in the yellow bales, so that the small boys who were only there on sufferance anyway, were thrust farther on to the fringe of things.

Then the dyed deer skins over the house-place doorway were flung back and Dumnorix, the lord of three hundred spears, came out; a big man with a mane of red-gold hair tumbling about his bull neck and on to his shoulder, and the bright hairs of his beard spreading over his breast almost to the bronze

buckle of his belt. He was followed by his hounds and a square-built boy a few months older than Drem, with bandy legs and a pair of round, very blue eyes; his son Vortrix, who had not been one of the bathing band, because he had trodden in Midir's shadow that morning, and so had been taboo until sunset.

'Greeting and welcome to you, stranger Bronze-smith,' said Dumnorix, 'for your own sake, and for what is in your bales. It will be a while before the evening stew comes from the fire; therefore if you are not over-weary, let you open your bales now, for I am eager to see if you have fine weapons to trade.'

The stranger touched palm to forehead, then stood up straight before the Chieftain with a pride to match his own, like a prince on a journey, rather than a wandering bronze-smith in a tattered cloak. 'Greeting, Lord of three hundred spears. Did ever a bronze-smith come out of the Green Isle yet, that had not fine weapons to show? And am I not the most skilled in the craft that ever the Green Isle bred? I am on my way home towards the Sunset, and much that I had is sold, yet there are still a few treasures worth the seeing in these bales of mine.' His long, strong fingers were busy on the bale-cords even as he spoke. 'And what better way to pass the time while we wait for the food bowls to be filled?'

The Chieftain had seated himself on his stool of carved and painted wood before his door, and the others of the Men's side were squatting on to their heels, huddling their cloaks about them. Drem, squirming his way through from the outcast fringe to get a better view, came up under the arm of Talore the Hunter, and Talore made room for him, so that in the end he had as good a view as Vortrix the Chieftain's son himself.

And so, while the flame of the sunset blazed and sank behind the Hill of Gathering, as though the sacred fires burned there as they did at Beltane, and the faint smell of frost and dead leaves stole up from the forest to mingle with the sharp, blue reek of wood smoke and horse droppings, the bronze-smith brought forth his treasures, laying them first before the Chieftain, then passing them among the eager knot of tribesmen:

beautifully shaped axe-heads, spear blades all of bronze, neck rings and arm rings of shining bronze and silver and copper, ornaments for a pony's harness, and a sword with studs of red coral in the unguarded hilt. There was little bargaining as yet; men looked at the things they wanted, making no comment; and in a little they would go home and think about it, and see what they had to give in exchange, and come back in the morning maybe with a length of cloth or a couple of fine beaver skins or a lathe-turned beechen bowl.

All the while Midir the Priest sat hunched in his bull's-hide robe, seemingly oblivious of all that went on around him. When you saw him so, Drem thought, it was hard to believe that he was that Other One, the One red with bull's blood at the sacred slaying when the Need Fires burned on the Hill of Gathering; whose voice was like a storm wind when he spoke from the Sun Lord to the people on Midsummer mornings. He was just a tired old man making little breath-puffings in his beard, Drem thought, and then hurriedly made the sign to avert evil, because it was dangerous to think such things.

'And is this, then, the last of the things that you have to show?' Dumnorix asked at last, handing back a pony's breast ornament that had the curve of a breaking wave.

There was a little silence, and then the smith said, 'Na, there is one thing more, though not of my forging—and maybe a strange thing for a bronze-smith to be carrying in his bales.'

He took up something wrapped by itself in a piece of woollen cloth, and unwrapped it and set it in the Chieftain's broad hands.

Dumnorix the Chieftain looked up swiftly. 'The light fades, and I must see this thing. Bring a torch.'

Vortrix slid from his place at his father's feet, and disappeared into the house-place, returning in a few moments with a smoking torch that he must have taken down from its sconce against the roof tree, for there was a faint sound of protest from within, as of a woman left to weave by firelight. With the coming of the torch, the misty twilight seemed to deepen behind the shoulders

61

of the tribesmen, though it had still been almost daylight the
moment before. As the whole circle gathered closer, Drem saw
that there was something strange, something very strange indeed, about the dagger in the Chieftain's hands. It was the
wrong colour: not the familiar sun-colour of bronze, but a
kind of dim moon-colour, fish-scale colour, as the Chieftain
tipped it towards the torch, and the light ran like water along
the blade.

'Sa, what is this thing—this grey metal?' said Dumnorix,
testing the blade gingerly with a finger.

'It is called iron,' said the stranger.

A murmur ran round the circle. They had heard of iron. It
was strong magic.

'So this is iron. I have heard of it, but never held it in my
hand until today,' Dumnorix said.

'Nor I, until three moons since, and I paid a heavy price for
it to the yellow-haired giant out of the land of Mist-forests
across the Great Water, for this one piece to carry away with
me.'

'How is it greater than bronze?' someone asked, out of the
torch-lit circle.

'How? It is much harder, it remains keen when bronze
grows blunted, therefore it calls less often for the sharpening
stone and does not dull in the midst of battle. It is to bronze
what bronze is to copper, what copper is to flint. See now, and
I will show you.' The stranger held out his hand. 'Let Dumnorix the Chieftain give me back my dagger, and draw his
own as for battle—so.'

Dumnorix laughed, and flashed the slim bronze dagger from
his belt. The stranger's blow was as swift and fierce as the
strike of a viper. Bronze and iron rang together, and the smith,
with a thin, triumphant smile on his dark face, and no glance at
the dagger in his hand, held it out to Dumnorix again, saying,
'Take it, and look now at both blades.'

Frowningly, the Chieftain did so. Then he gave a low
exclamation, half of wonder, half of disgust.

'You see?' said the smith.

'I see. Aye, I see well enough.' Dumnorix frowned at the blade a moment longer, then to his tribesmen, 'Look you, and see also.'

The two daggers were passing from hand to hand, heads bent over them, men turning to look at each other, and the murmur running from one to another, 'Ha! This is a strange thing! A strange thing indeed!'

Talore leaned forward and took first one and then the other into his hand; and Drem, peering over his arm, saw that there was a great notch in the edge of the bronze blade; but the moon-coloured blade was unmarked. Lying across Talore's thigh, it had a look of power, a lean, dark look of menace; this strange new beast that had bitten a piece out of the Chieftain's dagger. Greatly daring, he reached out and touched it; and felt that it was strong magic under his hand.

'This is a thing and a most wonderful thing, my brothers,' Talore said. 'Surely in the time to come, men armed with weapons such as this will be the masters of men whose weapons are of bronze.'

Suddenly Midir the Priest stirred in his bull's-hide robe, and leaned forward, his eyes—narrow dark eyes with a gleam of gold behind them, like dark sunlight—turned upon the strange grey dagger. Talore laid it before him with a deep courtesy; and the old man put out a thin, blue-veined hand and touched it as it lay, but did not take it up. He shook his head. 'I like not this strange new magic. The God forfend that this cold grey metal should ever master bronze. Aye, aye, I see the notch. I hear what ye all hear and see what ye all see. Yet we are the Sun People, and it is in my heart that bronze is of the Sun, and this cold iron only of the earth. As the little Dark People are the people of the blue flint, so we are the people of the shining bronze; our day is the day of bronze as theirs was the day of flint; and in a world where iron rules, we shall rule no longer. Aiee, Aiee! It will be a cold grey world, and the kings and the heroes will be dead.'

63

'But if we can come by such weapons as that——' began the Chieftain, pointing.

The stranger bronze-smith shook his head, answering them both. 'The man who carries an iron dagger will be the lord of the man who carries a bronze one; but it is in my mind that there will never be many such men, nor many such weapons.'

'Why so, then?' Dumnorix demanded.

'For this reason: that it is only in the Mist-forests across the Great Water that they have the secret of the fire—ah, many times hotter than the fire we raise to work our bronze—that will melt the grey metal and make it workable. It is only the giants of the Mist-forests who have the magic of the fire and the magic of the grey metal.'

'Yet to be one of the few would be a fine thing,' Dumnorix said. 'A fine thing indeed,' and he looked up suddenly. 'I will give you the price of three bronze daggers for the grey blade.'

The smith shook his head, and took up the dagger again. 'Can strong magic be bought for the price of three bronze daggers? The thing is not for sale.'

'Yet you spoke of a heavy price that you gave for it, to the man of the Mist-forests.'

'Aye—of a sort.'

'What was it, then?'

'A woman,' said the bronze-smith. 'And I was not yet tired of her.' He saw the idea in the Chieftain's face, and laughed. 'Na, na, I want none of your little dark slave women. If the dagger was worth more to me than one woman, why should I now trade it for another?'

Midir spoke again. 'Why indeed? Let you take your dagger on towards the Sunset, friend; it is in my mind that we do better without its cold grey magic.'

The bronze-smith checked in the act of reaching for the piece of yellow cloth in which the thing had been wrapped, and cast one of his dark, mocking glances at the old Priest. 'None so cold and none so grey is the magic of this dagger of mine, Holy One. .See, I will show you——' Still holding the dagger, he slipped

a hand into his mantle, and brought out from somewhere about himself the flint of his strike-a-light, and struck it upon the blade. They all saw the sparks fly out, golden and fiercely bright from the moon-grey blade, and again a murmur, a marvelling ran through the circle.

'See you? It is not the warm bronze of the sun, but there is fire at the heart of it, none the less, this cold grey metal. Did I not say that it was strong magic? Who shall say what strange thing it can do?' The bronze-smith glanced about him, triumphantly, at the eager, torch-lit faces; and as he did so, it seemed that his eyes were caught and held—held so that he could not look away.

A sudden stillness took him; and his hand slackened on the dagger so that it dropped from his fingers, and stood quivering in the turf before him. 'Surely the cold iron is indeed a strong magic,' he said, as though he found it difficult to speak. 'But even I did not know that it could raise ghosts.'

Drem craned round with all the rest in the direction of the bronze-smith's startled gaze and saw that a knot of girls, returned from the bramble picking, had come to hover on the outskirts of the little crowd, eager as the others to see what treasures the stranger bronze-smith had spread before the Chieftain's door. And among them was Blai; Blai, not hanging back as she generally did when she was with the other girls, but pressing boldly to the fore, her dark gaze fixed on his face, as his was fixed on hers.

It was the time of evening, between the lights, not full dusk yet no longer daylight, when all things seem a little insubstantial; and standing there almost beyond the reach of the torchlight, Blai with her wan, narrow face and huge, dark eyes did indeed look like something not of the day-time world—as though if the wind blew she might waver in it like weed in flowing water.

But almost in the same instant before the dagger had ceased to quiver where it fell, the bronze-smith seemed to have recovered himself, and crooked a finger to her as a man might

crook a finger to a hound. 'You—if you are there in truth—
come you here to me.'

And amid a sudden hush, Blai came and stood before
him. She carried a rush basket half full of blackberries on
her hip, and there were stains of blackberry juice about her
mouth that somehow made her look more transparent than
ever.

'What do they call you?' said the bronze-smith.

'I am called Blai.' The stillness that had been in him seemed
to have crossed into her; only suddenly she smiled.

'From whose house-place?'

'From the house-place of Cathlan the Old, away yonder
where the cattle way comes up through the Chalk from the
Marshes and the Great Water.'

'So, the track inland. I remember the track,' the stranger
said, half under his breath.

Midir, who, it seemed, had not gone so far away inside
himself as usual, leaned forward, his gaze narrowed on the

66

stranger's face. 'Maybe you also remember the house-place? And the woman who died there? Were you tired of her, too?'

And suddenly Drem understood. They all understood, the big golden Chieftain and the hunters gathered in the torch-light, and the children who had crowded up to see what came out of the yellow pack bales; and Blai.

But as Drem cast a startled look at Blai, he saw that somehow she had known, even before the stranger called her out to him. This was the thing that she had clung to all her years, all those many times when she had cried out defiantly in the face of all ills. 'One day—my father will come back for me!' Now it had happened, and something about it was wrong—horribly wrong.

The bronze-smith glanced aside at the Priest, a mocking and a challenging look. 'Aye, I remember the house-place,' he said. 'But I did not know that it was so near.' He knelt upon one knee, and reaching out, set a long forefinger under Blai's chin, and tipped her face to the torchlight. But there was no gentleness in the finger, and none in his face as he stared long and hard into hers; so that slowly the smile grew uncertain, became a pathetic little grimace, and died. 'Now by the Song of the Silver Branch, here's a strange thing to come about!' he said at last. 'Aye, you're like the woman your mother; the same whey face and goggle eyes; but at least there was fire in her—like the secret fire within the heart of this grey dagger of mine; and a man might warm his hands at it—aye, and burn his fingers too! But you—faugh! You're like a damp cobweb.'

Abruptly he dropped his hand. 'So, it is enough. Away with you and carry your blackberries home.'

67

Blai did not move. She stood as though she had struck root, still carefully holding the basket of blackberries, staring into his face as though she were trying to understand. There was a crimson mark on her jaw bone, where his finger had been.

'Well, what do you wait for?' the stranger said; and then, as he stared, his mouth curled into a slow, cruel smile. 'Ah, so, that is the way of it? You thought that I had come for you? You small fool, I had forgotten your existence until this twilight! And if I had indeed come so, what should I want with such a whey-faced thing as you are?' And he flung up his head in laughter; dark, flashing, wicked laughter.

Blai drew back very slowly, like one walking in her sleep, her eyes still fixed on his face; and there were shadows under them the colour of the blackberry stains about her mouth. As she did so, he leaned forward, laughing still, and caught up a bronze ring-brooch from the shining tumble on the yellow bale-cloth, and tossed it towards her like one tossing a bone to a dog. 'Never let it be said that I failed to furnish a dowry for my own daughter, though I'm thinking it would take a bigger dowry than that—I'm thinking it would take a whole herd of milch mares, to tempt any man to take such a grey thing to his hearth. There—take it, you poor, pale moth.'

Drem hoped that she would leave it lying there, but still with that wide, horrified sleep-walker's gaze on the bronze-smith's face, she crouched down and felt for it, and took it up, very slowly. Then she turned and ran.

Some of the other children shouted after her, hooting and jeering; Luga called out, trying to mimic her high silvery voice: 'One day—one day my father will come! Yah!—and fetch me away on a horse with a golden bridle!'

Talore suddenly withdrew his hand from Drem's shoulder. It was a gesture like slipping a hound from leash. But Drem did not need it. He had no particular fondness for Blai; but she was of his hearth fire, and that was enough. He sprang up, Whitethroat at his heels, and began to push his way out through the circle, glaring about him at his own kind, especially

68

at Luga, whose ankle he managed to kick in passing, and went with his freckled nose in the air after the small, desolate figure disappearing into the dusk.

She was right down by the brook before he caught up with her, Whitethroat bounding ahead to nuzzle his head against her—oddly enough she was the one person in Whitethroat's world, apart from Drem himself, to whom the great hound ever paid any attention. But Blai took no notice of White-throat, not this evening. She was standing on the steep bank where it almost overhung the water above the sloping cattle-place, holding the ring-brooch in her hands. And the basket lay overturned beside her, with the little, dark bramble-fruit scattered in the grass. She turned as Drem came up, and stood there like a little wild thing cornered, with the drop to the stream behind her. 'Have you come to laugh at me too? The others all laughed at me.'

'Na,' Drem said. 'I came because they laughed.'

'Did you, Drem?' Blai said, in a small aching voice. 'Did you truly?'

He scowled fiercely, swinging on his heels. 'You are of my hearth fire.' Then in a rough attempt at comfort. 'You should be glad that he will not take you away with him. We are much better to be with than he is!'

Blai looked at him in silence, her narrow white face set in the twilight; and he had a feeling that she was older than he was, much, much older, which was foolishness because he had seen eleven summers and she only nine.

'You have spilled all your blackberries,' he said, because he didn't like the silence. 'What will you do with the brooch that he threw at you?'

Something happened in Blai, like the moment when the bronze-smith had struck at the strange grey dagger blade with his flint, and fire sprang out under the blow, so that watching her with his mouth open, Drem thought that the bronze-smith had been wrong about Blai, after all. 'This!' she cried, and spat on the bronze circle in her hand, with the savagery of a cat

69

spitting; then whirled about to the stream and flung it from her into the deep water under the bank.

It struck the surface with a plop like a trout leaping, like the stone that Luga had thrown at the kingfisher, and peering down, Drem saw the ring-ripples spreading out and out in the shadowy water, with a faint gleam of light in the curve of each ripple, as though a trout had leapt there; no more. And then the last ripple touched the bank and was gone.

Blai said, 'That was not my father. Something happened to *my* father so that he could not come back. And now he will not ever come. He will not—ever—come.'

VI

The Boys' House

NEXT day Drem heard that the bronze-smith had moved on, taking with him the strange grey dagger with the fire at its heart, despite all the Chieftain's efforts to make him part with it; and Dumnorix the lord of three hundred spears had gone to look for a bear to kill, to ease his temper.

Blai never spoke of what had happened, and when the other children taunted her with it she cried out on them as though amazed that they could be so foolish. 'That was not my father! Something happened to *my* father so that he could not come back!' Nothing would shake her in that. It was almost as though she believed it herself. Drem's mother was gentler to her than usual in those days, but being gentle with Blai, it seemed, was no good; she merely shrank away, like a wild thing backing from a kind hand, looking sideways and showing its teeth.

So that winter came and wore away, and the year came up again out of the dark. The whitethorn of the steading hedge was curdled with blossom, and there were young calves to bring in and stall in the hurdled-off part of the house-place; that year's new warriors were made, in the night and the day before Beltane, and the Beltane fires blazed on the Hill of Gathering, before the grave mound of the forgotten champion who slept there; and it was time for Drem to go to the Boys' House.

The Boys' House stood in the garth of the Chieftain's steading, among the other turf-thatched bothies that made up the
Hall of Dumnorix. From their twelfth spring until the spring
that they were fifteen years old, the boys of the Clan were
brought up there, as it were at the Chieftain's hearth. They
learned the use of broad spear and throw-spear, sword and
buckler and the long war-bow of the tribes. They learned to
handle hound and pony; they hunted with the young hunters
of the Clan, learning to follow a three-day-old spoor as though
it were a blazed trail. They fought and wrestled together and
grew strong; and together they learned to go cold and hungry,
and to bear pain without flinching. And so, under the eyes
of the Chieftain and of old Kylan who ruled the Boys' House
with his oxhide whip, the warriors of the Clan were made.

When the morning came for Drem to be setting out, Drustic
gave him much useful advice, remembered from his own years
in the Boys' House, and a particularly well-balanced throw-
spear of his own, which Drem thought a great deal more of
than he did of the advice. And his mother gave him a cloak of
thick brown wool with a stripe of kingfisher blue along the
edge, a fine cloak, though it was too long for him, as yet. When
he had eaten his morning barley cake and mare's milk curds—
always it must be mare's milk curds flavoured with wild garlic,
on the day one went to the Boys' House—he went and knelt before Cathlan the Old as he sat on his folded bearskin beside
the fire, and set his hand on the old man's thigh in leave-taking.

'I go now, my Grandfather.'

'Sa, you go now, son of my youngest son, little red fighting
cock,' Cathlan said, leaning forward to peer down at him with
those fierce, gold-irised eyes, 'and truly I think that you will
be a seasoned fighter before you come again with your Wolf
Slaying behind you—if ever you do—Aiee, if ever you do. But
I will tell you this: it is good, for you, that your years in the
Boys' House will be the years of Vortrix the Chieftain's son, also.
For ever after, the men who trained together as boys, and slew
their wolves and passed into the Men's side together are a

brotherhood; and the Chieftain does not forget the men who did these things with him. I know, ah, I know, I who slew my wolf in the same year with Belutugradus, the great grandsire of this one.'

Drem bent his forehead on to his hand as it rested on the old man's thigh; then rose and took leave of his mother, driving his head for a moment into the hollow between her neck and shoulder that was warm and white and soft even though her voice was often harsh with scolding. Then he caught up his new spear and flung his cloak across his shoulder, and went out into the morning, whistling Whitethroat to heel. He forgot to take his leave of Blai at all.

The parting from his family sat lightly on him, for he was used to being away from home, and had come and gone as the mood took him, since the days when he had gone up to Doli and the shepherds on the High Chalk. But at the foot of the driftway, between the waking green of the young barley, and the sleeping fallow, he halted, knowing that the time had come for a harder leave-taking. He had known that it would be no good tying Whitethroat up to keep him from following, when he went down to the Boys' House, and so for a long time past he had been training the great hound to go home alone when he bade him. And now it was the time for putting the training to the test.

Suddenly the three years that had seemed a proud thing earlier that morning, looked very long and grey; and there was an ache in his throat as he dropped his spear and called White-throat from snuffing among the coarse grass and the pimpernels and yellow vetch at the side of the rough chalk, and squatted down to talk to him, holding his muzzle and rubbing behind his ears in the warm hollows where he loved to be rubbed. 'I must go down to the Boys' House, brother, and I cannot take you with me. Soon I will come again, soon and often, and we will hunt together. But now you must run with Drustic's hounds, and do as Drustic bids you.'

And Whitethroat talked back in the singing growl he always

73

made when Drem rubbed behind his ears, holding his head low and flattened, and turning it for Drem to come at yet more delicious places.

Drem stopped rubbing at last, and pressed his face down for a moment on to the top of the dog's rough head; then he sprang up. 'Go home! It is time to be going home, brother!'

Whitethroat pressed his head against Drem's knee, his tail swinging.

'Go home! Home now!' Drem ordered, pointing. And the great hound looked from his face to the pointing finger and back again, whimpering; understanding what Drem wanted of him, understanding also that this time was not like the other times that he had been ordered home.

Drem caught him by the studded collar and dragged him round to face up the driftway. 'Home! Off now! Go home, can't you!' His voice was rough and angry with the unshed tears in his throat; and he thumped Whitethroat hard on the rump with his clenched fist.

Whitethroat went then, with a piteous puppy-whimpering, his head down and his proud bushy tail that came from his wolf father tucked between his legs. And Drem caught up his throw-spear and ran, with his shoulders hunched and the ball of tears swelling in his throat.

When he reached the garth of the Chieftain's steading, he found a little knot of boys already gathered before the empty doorway of the Boys' House. Vortrix the Chieftain's son, and a boy with a round head and a mouth like a frog whose name was Gault, and Luga kicking moodily at tussocks of coarse grass that grew against the wall. Otherwise there was no sign of life in the steading, save for the old hound sleeping on the dung heap as he had been on the day last autumn when the bronze-smith came, and a half tame mallard drake with his dun wives behind him, waddling about the brushwood pile. Drem walked across to the three boys. They opened their ranks for him, and the four of them stood and looked at each other and

74

away again, half grinning, but somehow a little uneasy. None of them spoke.

Drem leaned against the wall of the Boys' House. The flints in the wall were tawny and white and grey-blue. He had never really noticed flints before. One of them was striped grey and white and looked like a badger's mask peering out of the wall. He watched the mallard drake, seeing the glint of metallic green on his wings as he turned in a gleam of sunlight. It was a pale, dry, windy day, with a constant changing of light as cloud and clear chased across the sky; and little whirls of chalky dust hurried about the steading garth, that stung when they got in one's eyes. He wished someone would come. Old Kylan or some of the older boys—because until they did he was stuck and could not go forward into the start of the three years' training time that must be got through before he was a warrior and could be with Whitethroat again. They must all be away to the hunting or the weapon practice; and he could hear the emptiness of the Boys' House behind him.

In a while, Urian the son of Cuthlyn came stalking across the steading garth with his thumbs in his belt, and brought their numbers up to five; and then fat Maelgan appeared, with little black-eyed Tuan in his shadow; and the gathering of that year's New Spears was complete.

There before the door of the Boys' House they stood and looked at each other, still in silence. Drem saw them all with a new clearness, an awareness of them as though he had never seen them before; and it was the same with all of them. They had run and tumbled and fought together all their lives, like puppies of the same pack; but now, suddenly, they were aware of each other, and a little shy of each other, caught up in a relationship that was new to them.

A sudden spatter of rain came down the wind, freckling the ground with dark, and streaking the flints of the Boys' House wall; and a woman slave passed across the garth from the byre, carrying a high-shouldered milk pail, and turned to stare at them before she disappeared. They ignored her with an

75

elaborate air of unconcern, trying to look as though they were not at all at a loss and were standing round the Boys' House door because they chose to.

But when she was gone, Vortrix hunched his shoulders and said, 'It grows wet, here in the garth. Let us go inside.'

'Will they not be angry?' Tuan said doubtfully. Tuan was always inclined to be cautious.

'I don't see why. No one seems to be coming to tell us what we are to do.'

Luga stopped kicking at the tussocks of grass. 'So long as you remember if Kylan comes with his whip, that it was your idea!'

It seemed a bold thing to do, to go in without leave; into the Boys' House where none of them had ever been before; and their breaths caught a little at their own hardihood, as, one after another, following Vortrix, they ducked under the door curtain and prowled in out of the wind and the bright rain, and looked about them. After the sharp spring wind and the changing light out of doors, the air in the great round hut was still and heavy, and the light was dim and brown, thickened by the inevitable bloom of wood smoke over the shadows. There were sleeping stalls round the walls, spread with sheepskin over the piled fern, but they would be for the great ones, the lordly ones who had reached their second and even their third year; the likes of Drem would sleep like hounds around the central hearth. There was a half-made hunting bow before one of the stalls, and a cloak with a green patch at the shoulder in another; a clutter of cook pots beside the hearth and weapons stacked against the roof tree; and several pelts in various stages of curing hung from the rafters.

The twelve-year-olds felt their own boldness in their chests. Here they were, for the moment, in possession of the Boys' House, and they grinned at each other, strutting a little. The fire on the hearth had sunk low, to a red glow and a few charred logs in the midst of the white ash. 'They have let the fire sink,' Drem said. 'They should be grateful to us for coming in and mending it for them before it goes out!' And greatly

daring, he kicked the logs into a blaze, and threw on a couple of birch logs with the bark still on them from the pile beside the hearth. Vortrix had led them in here, he, Drem, would be the one to wake the fire. The logs were dry and the bark like tinder; a little tongue of saffron flame licked up, and the silver bark blackened and curled back, edged with red jewels. There was a sudden flare, a flickering amber light that warmed the shadows; and they looked at each other with kindling excitement born of their own boldness and the likelihood that the older boys would make them pay for it later.

The sudden flare of the flame-light caught the bronze face of a great war shield that lay tilted against the roof tree as though some champion had just cast it down there, and woke sparks of shifting fire among the raised bosses with which it was covered. It caught at their attention, and they gathered round, looking down at it. Each of them knew a shield, maybe more than one, in their own homes; nevertheless, this one caught and held their interest. They squatted about it and heaved it up to examine it in the firelight. Truly it was a mighty shield, a hero's shield, formed of layer upon layer of bull's-hide, the whole face sheathed in shining bronze, and the bronze worked in circle within circle of raised bosses, the outermost circle lying just within the hammered strength of the shield rim, the innermost close against the thrusting swell of the central boss. And looking at it as the firelight played and ran on every curve, Drem thought it was like the spreading ripples made by a leaping fish, or when you dropped a pebble—or a brooch—into the water.

'It is a fine shield,' Maelgan said.

'Ugh! It is heavy!'

Urian thrust his arm through the straps, and staggered upright, panting a little under the weight, his fierce brown face flashing into laughter. He pulled a spear from among those against the roof tree, and stood straddling his legs and thrusting out his chest though the weight of the great shield dragged his shoulder down. 'See! I am a man! I am a warrior already!

Why should I spend three years running with little boys like you?'

They pushed him over—it was quite easy for he was off balance already with the weight of the great shield—and rubbed his nose in the fern; and Vortrix heaved the shield on to his own shoulder, and stood proud and bright-eyed in the firelight, braced under its weight. 'I am a warrior too! I am the Chieftain, the lord of all your spears!'

'Stop crowing, and let me try it,' Luga said.

One after another they all tried their strength with the great shield. Maelgan, who was the biggest of them all, with the slow strength of an ox, even managed to walk a few steps carrying it. Tuan, who was the smallest, only just managed to lift it clear of the ground. One after another, breathless and intent, until there was only Drem left to try.

'Drem! Hai! Drem, wake up!'

Drem woke up. He had hung back to the last, which was not his way: and suddenly his heart was pounding as he stepped to the great war shield. He thrust his sound arm through the straps, and setting his teeth, lurched up again. The weight bore down on his shoulder, as he stood to face the others. The war spear that each of them had taken in turn lay in the brown bracken at his foot; he felt it there. And it had already dawned on him that he could not take it up.

It dawned on the others at the same moment. They were all round him, watching him with sudden speculation. Then Luga pointed down at the spear and his face was alight with malice. 'Aren't you going to take up your spear? A warrior must needs carry a spear as well as a shield; do you forget that?'

Drem faced him, faced them all. 'Na,' he said. 'I do not forget that. But it is in my mind that a warrior might do well enough carrying only his spear and not a shield at all! I took up the shield to try its weight as you have all done. No more.'

'Ya-ee! Hark to Drem One-arm!' Luga cried. 'Drem One-arm cannot carry his spear and his shield together; he would

make only half a warrior—and what use is half a warrior to the Men's side?'

Drem was sharply aware of the silence all about him, and in the silence the spattering rain on the thatch and the distant scolding of a woman. He did not move, he was too proud to move before them, even though his arm and shoulder were beginning to tremble under the weight of bronze and bull's-hide; but if he had been a hound, the hair would have risen on his neck. The others were still staring at him, not hostile as yet —though that was coming—but somehow no longer strange with each other, bonded together under Luga's leadership; and *he* was the only stranger. He understood about Luga; Luga had never forgiven him for the matter of Whitethroat and the swan; that was simple. The rest was less simple; but something far down in Drem that had nothing to do with thinking, understood that too. All their lives they had run together in one pack; a mingled pack of children and hounds from the Clan and Half People alike; but now it was different, now Erp and his dark brothers must follow their own ways, and the Clan and the Half People were no longer one. This was the Boys' House; this was the beginning of the Men's side, the Spear Brotherhood, the beginning of the question whether Drem's place was inside with the Spear Brotherhood or outside with the Half People.

'Let you go and learn to weave with the women,' Luga said, bright-eyed and taunting, and there was a splurge of laughter.

'But you'd need two arms for that, too,' Gault squealed in sudden excitement; and—he was a great one for playing the fool—he began to jig up and down, making the gestures of a woman working at an upright loom. They were crowding in on Drem, beginning to jostle him. It was more than half in jest at first, but the jest was an ugly one, and wearing thin over what lay underneath. 'Ye-ee! Drem One-arm—Drem One-arm!'

It must be Luga or himself, Drem thought, and the only thing he could do was to fight, and if need be go down fighting.

He did not stand the faintest chance, of course, but that made no difference. He let go the great shield. It fell with a ringing clash and crash against the edge of the hearth stone, momentarily scattering the little fierce knot, and in the same instant, with the life still tingling back into his arm, he hit Luga fair between the eyes, with all the strength that was in his body behind the blow. And he cried out on a shrill note of challenge, 'One arm is enough to hit with!'

Luga staggered backward, shaking his head, as though for the moment he was not at all sure what had hit him. Then he recovered himself and came in again with flailing fists.

Drem hit him again in the instant before the other boy's fist crashed into his own cheekbone, filling one eye with a red burst of stars. Having only one serviceable arm, he could do nothing to guard against the blows that came pounding in on him. He tucked his head down to save his face as much as possible, and somehow got his back against the great roof tree. The whole lot of them were on him at once, giving tongue like hound puppies at the kill. He saw their faces pressing in on him, their open mouths and bright eyes; and their shrill clamour rose and rose in his ears. He knew that he was fighting for his place in

the Clan, fighting for his whole life—
all that made life worth having; and
he hit out wildly, desperately, yelling
his defiance. He never knew what it
was he yelled, only that it was defiance.
He kicked somebody's legs from under
them so that they came down across
the great shield with a hollow clangour;
but while the thrumming of it still hung
upon the air, a buffet landed on the
side of his
head that sent
him stagger-
ing sideways, and instantly they were
on him, dragging him down though
he struggled and tore and bit like a
cornered wild cat.

And then, when he was all but
done, somebody dived low through
the flailing mass of arms and legs, and
whirled about at his side, flinging
Maelgan off him with one shoulder,
and driving his fist into Urian's howling face. And as Drem grasped the
moment's respite to drag himself free
and stagger upright again, shaking
his head to clear it, he realized vaguely
that he was no longer alone.

'Sa sa sa! Come on then! Come on
all of you and see what you'll get!' he
heard his new comrade yelling. He
had his back against the roof tree again
now, and the other boy's shoulder
was against his, guarding where he
could not guard for himself, and a
sudden warm sense of increase was in

him. The smell of blood came into the back of his nose, far up between his eyes; the Warrior Smell. And suddenly, from feeling like a cornered animal, the joy of battle leapt in him like a flame.

He cared nothing now for the blows he got, only for the blows he gave. It was a great fight, though a short one; a stand against hopeless odds such as no warrior of the Tribe need have been ashamed of. But it was a last stand, and the odds were hopeless; five against two, and Drem had only one arm to fight with.

In their shrill and bloodthirsty absorption in the matter in hand, none of them saw the sudden dark swoop of figures into the doorway as several of the older boys came ducking in; nor the squat, hairy figure of Kylan of the Boys' House straddling there with his whip in his hand, looking on. They were not aware of anything but themselves and their own affairs; until someone behind Kylan spoke a deep-voiced word, and suddenly Kylan was among them, wading into their midst with his lash busy in his hand, as a man wades into a fight among his own hound puppies. 'Break off! Back, I say! Back—get back!' And the long supple lash of oxhide curled and cracked again and again as he laid about him. Drem felt it sear like a hornet sting across his neck and shoulders. The shrill yammer died down, and slowly, sullenly, the fight fell apart and the fighters stood rather sheepishly looking at each other, and at Kylan, and at the Chieftain himself, standing in the doorway with his great golden head bent under the lintel and the last of the shower shining behind him.

Dumnorix the Chieftain looked them over with interest, his frowning grey eyes moving from one to another in little darts and flickers that missed nothing. His gaze rested a long moment on Drem and the boy beside him; and he said to Kylan, with the merest flicker of a smile under his long moustaches, 'You spoke too soon when you swore but now that the bad days were here, and there were no more champions coming up to take their stand in the Spear Brotherhood.'

'So it seems,' Kylan said, breathing loudly through his

hairy nostrils as he stood now drawing the supple lash again and again through his broad hairy hands. 'If the snapping and snarling of puppies gives any proof in the matter.'

Drem, his breast still heaving, the blood trickling from a cut under one eye, stared rather muzzily at Luga's face. Luga was working at a loose tooth, and his nose was bleeding and seemed to have spread over his face like a bannock. Yes, he'd set his mark on Luga. He'd set his mark on a good many of his own kind—he and the other at his shoulder. For the first time it occurred to him to wonder who it was; and he turned his head carefully, as though it were loose on his neck, to see.

He saw that it was Vortrix, the Chieftain's son. Vortrix turned his head at the same moment, licking a cut lip; and they looked at each other gravely, almost warily, and then, as though making up their minds, broke into slow and rather wavering grins.

The voice of Dumnorix the Chieftain called them back to the matter in hand. 'And what thing brought it about, this mighty battle?'

No one answered; they looked straight before them and scuffled among the strewed fern, while the older boys looked on as the lords of the world look on at the antics of a litter of puppies. 'Well?' said Dumnorix. 'Are you all dumb? You yelped loud enough but now!' and the frown gathered on his face like the shadow of thunder clouds gathering on the face of the High Chalk. Dumnorix the Chieftain was not a good man to defy.

For one agonized moment more, the silence held, not even Vortrix found his voice; and then Drem cocked up his head and grinned into the Chieftain's frowning face. 'We were practising to be warriors. O Dumnorix, Lord of three hundred spears, is it not for that, that we live three years as the Chieftain's hounds, at the Chieftain's hearth?'

For a moment after he had said it, he was so frightened that his mouth dried up and he could not have spoken again if he had wanted to. And then the storm broke—into a gale of

laughter, as Dumnorix the Chieftain flung up his head among the rafters, and roared. His great laughter filled the Boys' House, so that a log fell on the hearth, and the sparks whirled upward, and even Kylan chuckled grumblingly in his deep chest, and the older boys nudged one another, grinning. But to the twelve-year-olds it was no laughing matter.

'Sa sa sa! We have champions indeed!' Dumnorix said, still laughing. 'The good days are not gone yet, Kylan old wolf; and we shall not be without cunning champions in the Men's side, when our time comes to sit by the fire and dream of old battles!' And then, already turning to the low doorway, he added to the knot of silent twelve-year-olds, 'It is in my mind that there has been enough *practice* for one day. Maybe now the time comes to be washing off the blood.'

When he was gone, they looked at each other uncertainly, while the older boys turned away to their own affairs as though they no longer existed. They wondered a little, now that it was over, what it had all been about. Only Luga, still working at the loose tooth, looked as though he remembered. Then Maelgan grinned suddenly, blinking pale eyelashes, and began the drift towards the doorway and the spring below the village.

Drem and Vortrix were the last to go, and as the drift became a scramble, Vortrix flung an arm of friendliness round Drem's neck. He had cut his knuckles on Urian's front teeth and a crimson trickle from the cut under Drem's eye splashed on to his hand where it was still bleeding. They both saw it, and looked at each other. Vortrix laughed, and then grew sober, for it was no laughing matter after all. 'See, we have mingled our blood. Now we are brothers, you and I.'

VII

The King-Making

O N an evening well into the Fall-of-the-Leaf, Drem came
down the long flank of the Chalk towards the village.
His hunting spear was over his shoulder, and he had
just left Whitethroat at the foot of the home driftway. Two and
a half years had gone by since the first time that he had left his
hound there, to go down to the Boys' House—two and a half
years in which Drem had become the finest spearman among
his fellows and a rider who could control his little fiery mount
with the grip of his knees alone when he needed a hand free
for his weapons—and by now it was a thing that they were both
used to. It had become a definite pattern. Always, when Drem
was free to hunt with him, Whitethroat would seem to know,
and would refuse to go with Drustic about the farm or on the
hunting trail, though at other times he went willingly enough;
and when Drem and Vortrix came up through the alder brake
beside the stream, he would be waiting at the foot of the driftway, smelling the wind for their coming, quivering with hope.
Then he would leap up, baying, and come with great leaps and
bounds down over the springy turf to fling himself upon his
lord, and they would roll over together, laughing—the hound
as well as the boy—Drem with his arm round Whitethroat's
neck, and Whitethroat growling and roaring in mock ferocity
while all the while his bushy tail lashed to and fro behind. And
then they would go off, the boys with their spears on their
shoulders, the hounds—Vortrix also had his hound—padding

85

at their heels. And when the hunting was over, Drem would bring Whitethroat up the combe again to the foot of the drift-way, or sometimes even to the gateway of the steading where he might speak with his mother or Blai, though he might not cross the threshold while he was of the Boys' House. But if he went up to the steading, Whitethroat always came down again to the foot of the driftway with him. There, by the lowest of the little ragged corn plots, was their place for parting.

Drem and Vortrix had hunted together since that first day in the Boys' House, the day that they had become blood brothers whether they would or no; but Vortrix was never present at these partings. Drem was one to keep his loves in separate stalls; and Vortrix, though not in general over-quick to sense such things, was wise in the ways of his blood brother, and always went back to the Boys' House alone, while Drem ran his great, white-breasted hound back to the foot of the driftway.

The autumn dusk was coming up blue as wood smoke across the rolling dimness of the Wild, quenching the russet flame of the forest far below, as Drem came down through the higher field plots of the village. There was a black and white flicker of plovers' wings over the fallow, and the starlings swept home-ward overhead; and already firelight was beginning to strengthen in house-place doorways. It all looked very quiet, a faint mist stealing among the huts, made up of wood smoke and the first promise of frost and the warm breath of the cattle byres. But as he drew nearer, as he came in among the crowding bothies, Drem found that it was not so quiet as it had seemed. There was a strange activity in the village that evening; a coming and going of figures dim-seen in the dusk, a fitful mur-mur of voices, a general air of making ready for something. And in the Boys' House, too, when he reached it, was the same air of preparation. Vortrix, who had arrived some while before him, was squatting by the fire on which the evening stew bubbled in its great, slung cauldron, his light hunting bow lay beside him; and he was skinning the hare that he had shot that day, with an air of one attending to first things first. But the

other boys of his year and Drem's, sprawling or standing around him, were talking eagerly as they burnished cloak pin and dagger blade, and furbished their trailing pony harness as though for battle, while Kylan sat on his skin-spread stool with his spear across his knees and watched them with a bright and vigilant eye.

'What is it, then?' Drem said. 'Is there a raid?'

Two or three voices answered him, taking up from one another. 'The King is gone beyond the Sunset!'

Drem whistled. 'How do you know?'

'The runners were here when I got back,' Vortrix said, intent on his hare.

'What killed him, then? He was not old?'

Urian tested the blade of his dagger. 'They say it was a boar. He went hunting yesterday—but it was the boar who killed, and not the King.'

Excitement shivered through the little group. There was no sorrow in them; they had never seen the King in his high Dun, they knew from their fathers that he was a hard man and a shining warrior, and that was all. And now he was dead, gone back beyond the Sunset because of a long-tusked, red-eyed boar, turning at bay.

'Now there will be a great Death Feast, and a King-Making for a new King to lead the Tribe,' said Tuan.

'A three day feast, with wrestling and foot races, and all the Men's side gathered in the Royal Dun——'

'My father says that when the last King was made,' Maelgan put in, blinking pale eyelashes in the firelight, 'there was so much cattle roasted that the smell of roasting fat reached from the Wild to the Great Water.'

There was a shout of laughter. 'That is the thing that you would care about, Fat One! . . . When Maelgan was small, they drove him down with the swine in the autumn to fatten on acorns!—Let you be careful, Maelgan, that they do not mistake you for one of the fattened porkers for the cooking pits!'

Drem's eye ran over the preparations that were going on,

while Maelgan, who was used to being a butt, grinned peaceably. The swift excitement that was rising in the others took hold of him. 'Is it that we also go to this feast?'

'Surely.' Old Kylan grunted, speaking for the first time. 'Are ye not of the Chieftain's household, hounds of the Chieftain's pack? Let you stop asking questions now and get to making ready for the morning. It grows late, and you are away behind the others, and I'll not have it said that any of Dumnorix's hounds looked like a mangy flint-knapper's cur when he followed his lord to the Death Feast and the King-Making!'

Luga, who was burnishing a bronze bridle bit, looked up with a sneer. 'You forget, Old Father, that Drem has always to take that most precious hound of his home, before he can come back to us in the Boys' House. Sometimes it is in my mind, Drem One-arm, that I wonder you can bear to come back at all, leaving him behind you.'

'Is it?' Drem said, stacking his spear in the rack beside the hearth. 'Maybe if you had more thought for your own hound, Luga, he would answer to you better on the hunting trail.'

It was queer how long Luga could carry a grudge and still find pleasure in it, he thought, as he clattered up the ladder to the loft in the crown of the roof, and began to delve among the gear of the rest of the Boys' House for the things that were his own. But there were other things to think about than Luga and his dark, rankling humours. He got out his brown cloak with the kingfisher stripe, which was now as much too short for him as it had been too long when his mother cut it from the loom, and his good saffron kirtle, and his belt with the bronze studs, and brought them down again. And when the evening meal was over he sat with the rest, round the fire, burnishing his dagger and the bronze belt studs, and combing and combing his hair to make it shine, as the Men's side combed their hair. For they were almost men now, he and Vortrix and the rest. The twelve-year-olds, thrust away from the fire to shiver in the door draughts, watched them enviously. *They* had no need to comb their hair, they would not be going to the Death Feast

and the King-Making. That was for the third year of the Chieftain's hounds, who sat lordlywise around the fire, and talked as men, with their spears beside them.

Next morning at first light, when the village was already seething like a pan of warming yeast with last-moment preparations, the men from the outlying steadings of the Clan began to arrive, riding their small, shaggy ponies whose harness was rich with bronze and narwhal ivory, and leading others to serve as pack beasts. Cattle were being driven in from the grazing grounds, for the Royal Dun could not feed the whole Tribe, and so every Clan would drive its own meat with it, on the hoof. Supplies were being brought out and laid before the riders, or bound on to the backs of the pack animals: barley loaves and white cakes of ewes'-milk and mares'-milk curds, and meal in sewn skins. And everywhere children and dogs were under foot; children squealing, dogs barking, ponies trampling.

Drem had bitted and bridled his own mount—the Boys' House did not have ponies of their own, but rode the fiery little brutes out of the Chieftain's stable—and was standing with Vortrix near the Chieftain's door, when a cold muzzle was thrust into his hand, and he looked down to see Whitethroat beside him with waving tail. 'Greetings, brother!' he said, pulling the great hound's ears. Then to Vortrix, 'It must be that Drustic is here.' And at that moment Drustic rode into the crowded open space below the Chieftain's steading, his own hounds loping among the ponies' hooves; and a little behind him, leaving him to force their way through the throng, rode the Grandfather!

Drem had known of course that Drustic would come, but he had not thought of the Grandfather coming with him. He let out a soundless whistle. '*And* the Old One! It must be years since he had his legs astride a pony, and he's too old by far and far for such a journey!'

Vortrix laughed. 'He looks very well pleased with himself, the old Golden Eagle!'

89

'Always he is pleased with himself,' Drem said. 'It is the rest of the world that he is not pleased with!' and leading his own mount with him, he plunged into the throng, weaving his way through to join his kinsmen.

Drustic grinned at his young brother as he came up, but he had a somewhat harrassed look; and the Grandfather, seated on his bearskin that had been flung over the pony's back for a riding rug, splendid in his beaver-skin cloak with the scarlet lining, with his best bronze bracelets on his arms and his heron-tufted war-spear in his hand, was alight with triumph. Clearly, Drem thought, there had been a battle.

The Grandfather, it seemed, was still in something of a fighting mood, for he ignored Drem's salutation, and said in his deep crackling voice, 'So! You also think I am too old!'

'Did I say so, my Grandfather?' Drem said.

'It looks at me out of your eyes. It looks at me out of every-one's eyes. Aiee! I grow old indeed, and *because* I grow old, it is bad for me not to do as I wish! Now, I wish to see once more the full gathering of the Tribe. I wish to wear my bronze bracelets and talk with the men who stood up with me in arms when the world was young—with such as are left of them. Is it so great a thing to ask?'

'It is in my mind that you are not one for asking, my Grand-father,' Drem said, grinning, and put up his hand to caress his pony which was growing restive in the crowd. 'And surely you are wearing your bronze bracelets, and surely you are going to the gathering to talk with whoever you wish to talk with.'

'You—you were always an impudent whelp!' the Grand-father began, shooting out his lips and his ragged brows; and then unwillingly he chuckled. 'But it is true as you say. It is Sabra your mother's fault: I have argued so long with that woman that now I cannot stop. Also with so much arguing, my throat is dry. Go you and bring me some barley beer instead of standing there grinning like a frog on a hot stone!'

By the time Drem had found some barley beer and brought a cup of it to the old man, and reclaimed his own mount which

he had left for the moment in charge of one of the second year boys, Dumnorix the Chieftain had come out from his house-place, burning on the grey autumn morning in his scarlet cloak and the gold-work on his arms and about his bull neck, and mounted the raven black stallion that Vortrix was holding for him before the door. The elders and the great ones of the Clan were all assembled by now; and most of them already mounted. Drem saw Talore sitting a young red mare close behind the Chieftain; Talore seeming as always very slight and dark among the tawny warriors of his kind. He saw Morvidd with a necklace of blue beads showing under his wolfskin cloak, as small and hard and bright as his hot-tempered blue eyes, and old Kylan from the Boys' House, and the rest. Now suddenly Midir was in their midst, all men urging their ponies back from him lest any should step in his shadow; Midir with the amber Sun Cross on his breast and his grey hair straggling out from under the folded eagle wings of his head-dress. The holy man settled himself on a litter of skins slung from birch poles, and was lifted on the shoulders of six runners. The great bull's horns brayed and bellowed to the mist-pearled morning sky, and the foremost riders following the Chieftain kicked their ponies from a stand into a canter. One after another they swung in a jostling stream, away between the crowding huts of the village, then up towards the Ridgeway that followed the crest of the Chalk from Sunrise to Sunset. And behind them rode Drem and the other boys, with their dogs running among them, driving the lowing, wild-eyed cattle.

All that day they followed the ancient green ridgeway along the High Chalk, with their faces towards Sunset, the Wild falling away below them on the Sword side; and on the Shield side, wherever the long upland ridges fell back, the far off shining line of the Great Water—only for Drem it was the other way round, because he used sword and spear left handed, and carried his shield, when he must carry one for appearance, on a harness over his right shoulder; and so when anyone said 'Shield side' or 'Sword side' he had to turn the things round in his mind.

Other ways branched from the way that they were following; some grassy, some white, making a spider-web of communication along the tawny ridges of the high downs. They passed grazing sheep, who ran into startled huddles as they went by, stamping and staring at the scarlet and the bronze and the dull thunder of hooves and the streaming ponies' manes; so that the little dark shepherds sent their curses after the Golden People, who crashed by, lordlywise, startling the sheep. They passed the round grave mounds of the forgotten heroes that were strung out along the ridges, helping to mark the way. That night they camped beside one of the ancient, fortified dew-ponds; and about noon of the next day they came in sight of the Royal Dun, high on its vast wave-lift of the Chalk.

By that time they had become one of several such bands, following their Chiefs and great men, all drawing in by the white trails of the Chalk towards the huge fortress of turf banks that lay like a girdle, like a triple crown, like a coiled snake, about the highest crest of the downs.

The autumn day was a gleaming one, the hawthorn bushes glowing copper red with berries in the sunlight, against the staring white of the chalk-cut ramparts, and the turf below the Dun fiercely green where the autumn rain had brought it up from the tawny dryness of late summer: a day of sharp edges and colours clear and hard as the enamels on a shield boss. But away towards the Great Water, a long low bank of cloud was creeping inland, and already the distant Marshes were growing blurred as though a grey finger had been smudged across their blue and green and violet.

'Mist,' Drem said to Vortrix riding at his shoulder. 'We shall have cheerless camping tonight, up on these high downs,' and then, as the Dun drew nearer, forgot about it in the noise and excitement of their arrival.

Up the white chalk of the ancient track and over the turf on either side, the riders let their ponies out, and they leapt forward with tossing manes, shaking their heads and spilling foam on their breasts; and Midir's litter bearers, changed many times

since the journey started, quickened from their long, swift lope into a run that must have all but shaken the holy man's head from his shoulders. So they swept forward towards the massive triple gateway, where the silent warriors of the Royal Clan lined the chalk-cut ramparts, their bucklers darkly glinting against the dappled autumn sky. Now they were threading the zigzag causeway that spanned the outer ditch; now the timber facings of the gateway towered on either hand; and the riders poured through. Last of all, Drem and his fellows dug their heels into their ponies' flanks and swept yelling after them, driving the wild-eyed, sickle-horned bullocks through the narrow-necked entrance.

Within the Royal Dun was an open space where the whole Tribe could gather in time of trouble, with the cattle driven into the berms between the vast concentric rings of defensive banks; and in the highest part of the stronghold the round turf roofs of the Royal Village clustered about the high hall of the King. But Drem, casting eager glances about him as he dropped from the back of his shaggy little mount, saw that from all the huddled roofs no smoke rose into the air. No hearth fires burned in the Royal Dun, nor would any, until the new King was made. And from the King's high hall he heard the keening of the women: 'Ochone! Ochone!'

When the cattle had been handed over to the men who waited to pen them, he made his way with Maelgan and the rest, down through the swarming encampment where already the horsehide tents were being set up, to picket the ponies in the inner berm. There were many ponies there already, and they were restless, stamping and fretting, made uneasy by the strangers all around them, or by the feeling that lay like a shadow, like the thick heaviness and sense of waiting before thunder, over the Royal Dun. They had almost finished picketing and feeding the ponies, when Vortrix, who had been kept back to attend on his father, came down to join them, leading the Chieftain's black stallion. They gathered round him as he set about the task that they had just finished, and looked on.

But it seemed that the general uneasiness was in Vortrix's usually easy temper, for he turned on the perfectly unoffending Maelgan, saying, 'Must you stand there looking like a pig? Give me the other picket rope.'

Maelgan took up the coiled hide rope and tossed it to him. 'I do not know about a pig,' he said peaceably. 'I wish I was a pony. Nobody expects the ponies to fast until the new King is made!'

'Try pawing the ground and whinneying,' Gault said, 'and maybe someone will give you an armful of bracken fodder.' And he pulled his hair into a forelock between his eyes, and began to prance, playing the fool as he used to do when they were twelve-year-olds; and the others laughed as they had done when they were twelve-year-olds, and Urian thumped him on the head, and suddenly they were in the midst of a rough and tumble—anything to ease the tension, the sense of waiting that was like something twisted too tight in their stomachs.

A young mare, pied like a wagtail, who was being led by at that moment, chose to play startled at their laughter, and flung up her head with a snort, dancing a little. She would have been quiet again the next instant, but the boy in charge of her struck at her head with the bunched reins in his hand, cursing; and that did the mischief. Squealing between fear and temper the mare went up in a rearing half turn, and began to swing on her hind legs, with the boy hanging on to her headgear. She crashed into the Chieftain's black stallion, who squealed in his turn and flung round, dragging on the picket rope, and bit at her crest. In an instant all was confusion.

Vortrix, struggling to quieten his father's angry pony, shouted furiously over his shoulder. 'Oh, fool! Who let you loose with anything on four hooves?'

There was a cry of, 'Look out, she's broken free!' and Drem saw the mare upreared almost above him, and leaping clear of the lashing hooves, sprang for her headgear.

'Well enough—I have her!'

A few trampling and sweating moments followed, and the

mare was down on all four legs again, trembling, but quite docile. The two boys faced each other, both breathing quickly, while the mare swung her head to nuzzle exploringly at Drem's breast. 'Hasn't anyone every told you not to jab at the head of a frightened horse like that?' Drem said.

The other boy thrust out his jaw. 'What frightened her, then? *You* all yaffling like a treeful of green woodpeckers under her nose!'

'She was well enough until you hit her with the bridle.'

The other boy flushed crimson. 'I do not need that the like of you should tell me how to handle a pony!' He caught back the bridle into his own hand, taking care, however, not to startle the mare again.

'It is in my mind that you sorely need *someone* to tell you how to handle a pony!' Drem said, laughing, and turned away to his Spear Brothers.

Behind him the laugh was caught up by the little crowd that had gathered, and another boy's voice said, 'You got the worst of that, Cuneda, *and* you deserved it! Na, na, come away. There will be trouble if you start a fight here at the King's Death Feast.'

And the thing was over; over as swiftly as it had blown up; and Drem thought no more about it as they helped Vortrix to feed and rub down the Chieftain's still angry stallion; and presently made their way back all together to the encampment below the Royal Dun.

In the crowd and the enclosed space between the high turf banks, they had not seen how the mist—that far-off mist that had been a cloud bank along the Great Water—came creeping up across the marshes, rising higher and higher like the ghost of a long dead sea. But suddenly as they came out into the open space in the midst of the camp it was all about them, wreathing up from the trampled ground in a faint, wet smoke that seemed to gather most thickly about the King's hall in the highest part of the Dun. And with the mist, it seemed to Drem that there came upon the Royal Dun a deeper sense of waiting—waiting . . .

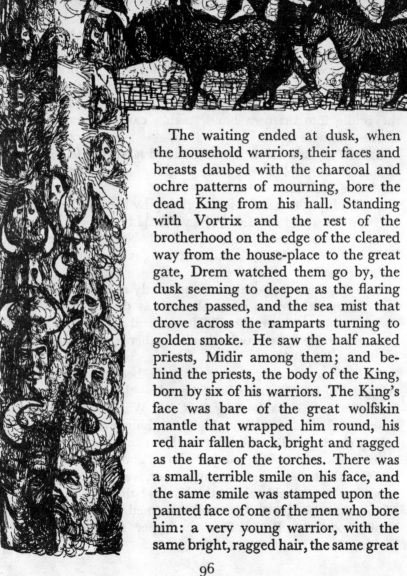

The waiting ended at dusk, when
the household warriors, their faces and
breasts daubed with the charcoal and
ochre patterns of mourning, bore the
dead King from his hall. Standing
with Vortrix and the rest of the
brotherhood on the edge of the cleared
way from the house-place to the great
gate, Drem watched them go by, the
dusk seeming to deepen as the flaring
torches passed, and the sea mist that
drove across the ramparts turning to
golden smoke. He saw the half naked
priests, Midir among them; and behind the priests, the body of the King,
born by six of his warriors. The King's
face was bare of the great wolfskin
mantle that wrapped him round, his
red hair fallen back, bright and ragged
as the flare of the torches. There was
a small, terrible smile on his face, and
the same smile was stamped upon the
painted face of one of the men who bore
him: a very young warrior, with the
same bright, ragged hair, the same great

96

beak of a nose, so that Drem knew, though no one had told him, that he was looking at father and son, the old King and the new King, yesterday's and tomorrow's.

The crowd swayed and stirred, catching up the wailing from the women, and behind the King's body came the warriors of the Royal Clan, with his favourite ponies and hounds, who would go with him beyond the Sunset, and others driving a bull and a ram and a black, bristling boar for the sacrifice.

The Tribe turned in behind them, Men's side and New Spears alike, all with their weapons. And so, in a long comet tail of torches, they bore the dead King from his Dun and away over the downs in the mist, while the wailing of the Women's side fell away behind them.

It was quite dark when they reached the Holy Place, and the mist was thickening. Drem, far down the long tail of torches, sensed rather than saw

97

the huge, bush-grown mass of the ancient grave-mound on their right, as they carried the dead King Sunwise about it, in a circling snake of torch light, a Sun-snake coiled about the darkness. When they had made the circle, they laid their burden on the tall pyre that had been built on the level hill-top turf. Then the bull and the ram and the boar were sacrificed by the High Priest with his black flint knife, and flayed, and the skins and fat wrapped about the King's body. Hounds and ponies were slain, though the ponies were mares and therefore almost beyond price, and their carcasses ranged upon the pyre with the flayed carcasses of the beasts of sacrifice. Great two-handled jars of honey and tallow were stacked among the logs and brushwood, and all was ready.

The High Priest with the gilded horns of the Sun upon his head, stood out with arms upraised, chanting the Invocation. 'Spear in the Noonday, Lord of Light, Lord of Life, Lord of the Cleansing Fire, take back by fire the warrior whose warring is finished, the hunter whose hunting is done . . .'

And while he yet chanted, the King's son stepped out from among his kind, and took a torch from one of the priests, and turning to the pyre, plunged it again and again into the brush-wood. Then, with the flames already licking up, he flung the torch into the very heart of the great mass, and setting a foot on one of the projecting logs, mounted lightly to the muffled shape on the crest. For a long moment he crouched there, his arms across his father's body, bending his head on to the dead man's breast so that in that last moment of farewell their bright hair flowed together as one. Then he sprang down again, with the blood of the flayed skins on him, and the sparks hanging on the hem of his kirtle.

At dawn they quenched the sinking flames with barley beer, and when the dark fire scar was cool enough, they gathered the half-burned bones of the King and wrapped them in a cloth of scarlet linen, and put them in a great jar. In the growing light Drem saw that a little chamber had been cut in the flank of the grave mound, and in it the priest kind set the jar, making a

singing magic as they did so. They ranged about it all that was left of the ponies and hunting dogs, the weapons and the ornaments of a warrior, and roasted meat and jars of mead and grain for the King's journey. Then the warriors closed in, and laid back the chalk and the cut turfs over all. And only the black fire scar remained to tell that the King had gone beyond the Sunset.

And now another waiting was upon the assembled host; and all faces, eager, strained with anticipation in the thin dawn light, were turned up towards the crest of the sacred mound. The mist had thinned a little, growing ragged, and out of the trailing scarves of vapour loomed the low-growing darkness of thorn and yew and juniper that clothed the wide shoulder of the downs and the swelling green breast of the ancient grave-mound. Mist was in the hair of the warriors, a grey-silver bloom of mist clinging to the rough wool of their cloaks and the coats of the hounds who padded among them. And somewhere a bird rose crying, unseen in the drifting greyness of the morning.

Then that waiting, too, was over, with a hollow booming of bulls' horns; and there on the crest of the sacred mound, where no man had seen them come, stood the High Priest, and with him the young warrior with the old King's face. A gasp, a great shout rose from the crowd. 'The King! The High Chieftain comes again!' And it seemed to Drem, staring up through the drifting mist wreaths, that the two poised high on the crest of the sacred mound were taller than any mortal man; giants and heroes, not men. The High Priest raised his arms, and his voice came down to the waiting host, thin and piercing as the bird's cry in the grey morning. 'The King is gone into the West. The King comes again. The Sun sets and the Sun rises. See and acknowledge the King, O ye warriors of the Tribe.'

And Drem saw, as he had not seen before, that between his upraised hands, between the golden sweep of the Sun horns on his head, was a twisted circle of red gold that caught a gleam of flame even in that milk-pale morning. In a silence so complete

99

that suddenly it was as though one could hear the mist wreathes trailing through the dark juniper branches, he brought his hands down, slowly, slowly, and pressed the shining circlet low on the young King's brows.

Roar on roar of acclamation burst from the assembled warriors; a beating rush of sound, rising to the crescendo of the Royal Salute, as every man brought his spear butt crashing down across his shield. When it was stilled, the High Priest had gone, melted into the mist, no man seeing him go as none had seen him come; and the young King stood alone above them, alone with the mist and the twisted thorn trees, in the sudden isolation of his kingship. The mourning paint had been wiped from his face. He turned slowly, his hands held out, showing himself to his Tribe as the custom demanded; and when the circle was complete, cried out in a hard, clear voice, 'I am the King!'

'You are the King!' came back the shouted answer.

'I am the King! Ye who are my warriors, let you now swear faith with me!'

And the answer came back in a deep chant; in the ancient three-fold oath of the Golden People. 'You are the King. If we break faith with you, may the green earth gape and swallow us. May the grey sea burst loose and overwhelm us; may the sky of stars fall and crush us out of life for ever!'

And so the ceremony was over, and the King was made. And the new King, with his priest kind going before, led his warriors back to the Royal Dun.

VIII

The Hound Fight

THERE was a smell of roasting in the Royal Dun; the cooking smoke hung low in the mist, and there was firelight again in house-place doorways and the openings of the horse-hide tents; and in a while, when the ponies had been tended, the feasting began. It was such feasting as Drem had never dreamed of; whole baked carcasses of cattle and sheep and pig lifted smoking from the pits of hot stones, black puddings made of blood and fat roasted in the paunches of sheep, great baskets of wheaten cakes and mares'-milk curds, and jars of mead and barley beer that the slaves and the women carried round. All day it went on, while from time to time the young warriors and the champions would leave feasting around the fires, and betake themselves to wrestling and all kinds of trials of strength or skill, and then return to their feasting again. And all the while the new King sat on his stool of painted wood spread with sheepskin beside the High Fire, the Royal Fire, and with him the Clan Chieftains and the great men of the Tribe, each attended by his New Spears, who served him as cup bearers and ceremonial guard, according to the custom.

Drem, squatting with the rest of Dumnorix's New Spears, a little behind their Chieftain, and gloriously full of black pudding, could see the Grandfather and Talore the Hunter both here at the High Fire, and felt the pride rise in his chest that it should be so. He tore a last mouthful from the piece of rib he had been gnawing, and gave the bone to Whitethroat

against his knee; and turned with a sigh of contentment to listen to the blind harper who sat at the King's feet, striking music like a shower of shining sparks from the slim, five-stringed harp of black bog oak in his hands. Once or twice since he could remember, such a harper had come to the home village, and played beside Dumnorix's fire, and each time he had been blind. Sometimes the power of song came to a man who was blind in the first place—as though the Sun Lord had reached out to touch him with a bright finger, that he might have another kind of seeing, another kind of light in place of the light he lacked. But if the song came to a sighted man, then as soon as it became clear that he was touched by the Sun Lord's finger, often while he was still only a child, he was blinded by the priests, that his other kind of seeing might grow the stronger. It was the custom. Drem shut his eyes, hearing the winged notes fly upwards in the darkness, above the deep surf of voices round the fire. And when he opened his eyes again, the firelight seemed brighter than it had done before, and the flower petal shape of Whitethroat's pricked ears gave him an almost painful stab of pleasure.

Vortrix, squatting at his shoulder, said, 'I suppose it is fair enough. Anyone can be a warrior and see the sky and the way the shadows run, but only one in a host can make the Harp Magic.' It sometimes happened like that between him and Vortrix; they did not talk to each other much, but often they knew what the other one was thinking.

Dusk was again creeping over the crowded Dun by now, and much mead and barley beer had been drunk since the feasting started; eyes were growing brighter and tongues looser, and there were wild bursts of laughter and swift flaring quarrels as men grew fierce and merry in their cups. The main business of eating was over, and there was a breaking up and shifting all round the great fires; but the drinking would go on for a long while yet. The young King, lounging sideways on his painted stool with the head of a favourite wolfhound on his knee, held up his great cup of wrought red gold, and looked about him at

his Chieftains and warriors in the firelight. 'My Chieftains, my brothers, I drink to you. The Sun and the Moon on your path.' And flinging back his head he drained off the thick yellow mead.

And from all round the fire the answer came back as the Chiefs and Warriors raised their cups and horns in reply. 'The Sun and the Moon be on the King's path also.'

Dumnorix drank with the rest, and turned, laughing his deep, slow laughter, to drink again with the man whom the general shifting had brought to sit beside him; a fat man whose paunch bulged over his gold studded belt, and whose eyes bulged also, on either side of a mottled nose. Drem rose swiftly, taking up one of the tall mead jars that stood ready, and stepped forward to pour again for his Chieftain; and it was so that he saw the thing . . . As the fat man flung up his arm and leaned back to drain the horn he held, his fine plaid cloak fell back, and Drem and his Chieftain saw, both in the same instant, the dagger that he wore thrust into his belt; a little grey dagger that caught the firelight fish-scale colour instead of golden.

Dumnorix stopped laughing and set down his mead cup, and leaned forward. 'Brother Bragon, show me the dagger that you wear in your belt.'

Bragon hiccupped, clearly gratified, pulled the dagger from his belt and held it out. 'Sa. I show it to you. It is in my mind that you will not have seen a dagger the like of that before? There are few such daggers, and they are strong magic. Have a care, therefore, how you handle it.'

Dumnorix's hand tightened on the haft. 'I have seen the like of this dagger before; aye, more than that, for I have seen and handled this very dagger before. But the bronze-smith in whose pack it was would not sell it, not for the price of three bronze daggers nor yet for a fair woman slave. How then comes it about that you wear the thing in your belt, brother Bragon?'

'Did you think, then, that yours was the only fire at which a bronze-smith might open his bales?' said Bragon, with blurred

triumph, holding up his mead horn to be filled by one of his New Spears.

'Said I not that he would not sell the thing?' Dumnorix leaned closer still, his frowning gaze fixed on the mottled face of the other Chieftain. 'I asked you how it came to be in your belt; now let you answer me my question!'

'Sa. I will answer you your question. It comes to be in my belt because maybe I have sharper wits than you, my brother Dumnorix!' Bragon laughed jibingly, showing wolf-yellow teeth. 'What a man will not sell, he may be got to throw the knuckle bones for, if he be first made drunk enough. They are great gamblers, the men of the Green Isle; and I—I have a way with the knuckle bones. If my brother Dumnorix also wished for the little grey dagger, my brother Dumnorix should have shown more wit in the matter!'

So the bronze-smith had lost his grey dagger with the fire at its heart, Drem thought. He would tell Blai that, when he got home. He would say, 'That bronze-smith who came once—*you* know—has been cheated of his grey dagger with the fire at its heart.' And Blai would be glad; it was pleasant to make Blai glad, now and then when it wasn't any trouble.

The frown had deepened between Dumnorix's eyes until the thick golden brows met in a single bar, and he drew his legs under him and rose as though to find another place to sit, where the air was fresher. 'It may be that I lack the wit of my brother Bragon—Bragon the Fox! But I do not make drunk the stranger at my hearth, to cheat him of what he will not sell!'

Bragon leapt up after him, with unlikely swiftness in so fat a man, thrusting his face into that of his fellow Chieftain. 'When any man crows to me in righteousness of what he does or does not do, that is the time that I look to my goods and gear!' he shouted, his voice thick with passion and much mead. 'Give me back now my grey dagger, lest maybe you confuse it with your own!'

There was a moment's deadly silence. Then Dumnorix, whitening to the lips, cast the dagger down at the other's feet. 'Take it, then. Mine is no more than bronze, but it will serve

its purpose well enough!' And as he spoke, deliberately, he drew his own dagger from his belt.

It had all flared up as swiftly as the sudden spurt of flame when a log falls on the hearth. A few moments ago they had been laughing together, and now . . .

One of Bragon's New Spears slipped in low, and caught up the grey dagger and gave it to his lord almost before it had ceased to quiver. A kind of rustling and murmuring hush had fallen on the circle of watchers, and in the silence, there was an ominous forward thrust of men out of the farther dusk, as Clansmen from the lower fires, drawn by the raised voices of their Chieftains, came up to their support. Daggers were out in a score of places, and any moment now there was going to be trouble; bad and tragic trouble.

Then the young King flung aside his half empty drinking cup, spattering those nearest to him with the sticky golden mead, and crashed up from his painted stool. 'Na na, my brothers!' He stood over the scene, dominating it, young as he was. 'Will you fight like dogs at my father's Death Feast and my own King-Making? Here is no time nor place for such brawling; put up your daggers—put them up, I say!'

The two chieftains never turned their gaze from each other's faces. 'He has put an insult on me,' Dumnorix said, 'and I demand fighting to wipe it out.'

'If ye must have fighting, then let it be the fighting of dogs indeed,' the King said, and glanced about him, laughing, at the many hounds among their masters' legs. 'Surely there are dogs enough about my Dun tonight. Let you take each a dog— nay, three dogs will make a better showing. Bragon, let you take three hounds from among your own pack, and Dumnorix, let you take three hounds also, and let them fight to the death, here in the circle beside the fire. So, we may have good sport with our mead, and the insult will be wiped clean.'

There was a little silence after he had spoken. Then Bragon slid the grey dagger back into his belt. 'It is as the King says.'

'It is as the King says,' Dumnorix growled, echoing the action.

All around them there was a sheathing of daggers, a sudden slackening of the tension that had sprung up so swiftly; and the danger was past. A splurge of voices rose, eager, fiercely laughing. 'So, it is good—a dog fight. Come, Cerdic, there is going to be a dog fight.'

Bragon called to one of his warriors. 'Ho, Llew! That dog of yours is a fighter; bring him here.' And a man came shouldering through the throng, holding by the collar a big, heavily built dog whose ragged ears and scarred muzzle told their own tale.

For answer, Dumnorix whistled. 'Whee-ee!' and a young prancing hound of his own sprang up at his side. Again Bragon called out a hound; and Dumnorix glanced over his shoulder. 'Fynn, have you the red devil with you?'

'He is here,' said an old warrior, and thrust forward into the open space a reddish hound whose ears and muzzle were scarred like those of the first.

The King looked them over. 'Sa, two pairs we have, and I the King, will make choice for the third.' Under the twisted golden circlet, his gaze went carelessly to and fro among the nearest of the hounds, and singled out from among those of Bragon's Clan a huge brindled brute with a mane on him like a full bred wolf. 'That one I choose. And for the other——'

At that unlucky moment, Whitethroat, standing beside Drem, flung up his head to nuzzle the boy's arm, in one of the sudden little bursts of affection that he was given to; and the firelight caught the silver blaze that had given him his name. 'Sa! That one!' the King said, pointing. 'That one with the white throat.'

For one shocked instant of time, Drem did not believe it. It couldn't be Whitethroat he meant—not Whitethroat. But there was no mistaking the direction of the King's gaze and his pointing finger. Drem looked down at the great hound standing against his knee. Whitethroat's tail was swinging, and he gazed up at Drem trustingly, with amber eyes a little puzzled as

though he caught the smell of something around him that he did not understand.

Drem looked at the other dog, the cunning, scarred veteran of many fights, his head lowered, the hackles already rising on his neck as though he understood perfectly what was expected of him; and in his eyes the red glint, the unmistakable red glint of the killer. Whitethroat could fight when need arose, though he was no fighter by nature, but Drem knew with a sickening certainty that if they were matched together, Whitethroat would be killed because he himself was not a killer.

They were looking to him to thrust the dog forward. The pause could only have lasted a couple of heart beats, but it seemed to Drem to have dragged on for a hundred. And then, setting down the mead jar that he still carried, he walked forward, with Whitethroat as usual pacing beside him, and turned, head thrown up, to face the King, to face Dumnorix his Chieftain and the big-bellied Bragon. He heard his own voice, level and challenging, though his heart had lurched into the base of his throat. 'We also, the New Spears, are called the Hounds of Dumnorix, and should we then have no part in this setting-on of hounds? Let one come out to me from among the New Spears who are the Hounds of Bragon, that we may fight it out here, beside the fire, for the third pair!'

There was a startled grunting, a startled rustle of voices round the fire. It was an unheard of thing that a boy who had not yet come to his Wolf Slaying should raise his voice in challenge before the Great Ones of the Tribe, before the King himself. But his challenge suited the wild humour of the assembled Tribesmen none the less; and the King smote his knees with an open hand, laughing. 'Well spoken, Hound of Dumnorix! And what say the Hounds of Bragon to that?'

Bragon stuck his thumbs in his belt under his broad paunch, and whistled. And one by one his New Spears slipped through the throng of Chieftains, and came to him. Eight of them, Drem saw: and one was the boy Cuneda, of yesterday's scene in the pony lines.

'Well,' said Bragon. 'Which of you takes up the challenge?'

There was a long pause, a harsh, dragging pause. And Drem, looking bright-eyed and defiant from one to another of the eight faces that looked back at him without any sign, understood it all too well. Understood that none of Bragon's Hounds was eager to face the possible shame of being defeated by a one-armed champion, nor yet of defeating him, for that, in its way, could carry almost as little honour. His mouth was dry, and he ran the tip of his tongue over his lips, smiling at them, a smile that was as much an insult as he could make it. If they refused him fight . . .

He was aware of the Grandfather, of Talore, of Drustic who had come thrusting up with the Clansmen from the lower fires; the whole Tribe, it seemed, looking on. Dumnorix had not whistled up his Hounds; but suddenly they were there, all the same, slipping through the crowds as Bragon's had done; and Drem felt their coming as they gathered in a knot behind him, Vortrix's shoulder against his; the bond of the Boys' House, the Brotherhood, close drawn between them. Save perhaps for Luga, he thought, they would stand by him whatever happened. If Bragon's Hounds refused him fight, they would stand by him still, in the face of the world, and make a mock of Bragon's Hounds who feared to fight a one-armed champion; but when they were by themselves they would look at his right arm again, as they had looked at it on their first day in the Boys' House, and he would have lost the strong place that he had won for himself among them. Drem knew his world; and it was a harsh one in which the pack turned on the weakest hound, in which little mercy was asked or given.

Bragon straddled his legs and wagged his thumbs under his belt, grinning. 'A pity it is that none of my young Hounds runs on three paws. It is in my mind that after all——'

The sickness rose in the pit of Drem's stomach. And then close beside him, Luga turned his head a little, and looked the boy Cuneda up and down with a faint sneer. 'And yet even a hound on three paws has his uses,' he said, and then, as though

on quite a different subject, 'Is it that you need anybody to help you hold a pony?'

Drem flashed a startled look at him. He had thought—if he had given a thought to the thing at all—that Luga might be glad to see him humiliated before the Tribe; glad even, to see Whitethroat killed. Was it that he would be even more glad to see Drem killed? Even as the thought came to him, he knew that it was not that; but there was no time to seek the answer now.

To the Chieftains and elders about the fire, the taunt had no meaning, but Bragon's Hounds knew what it meant, and so did the Hounds of Dumnorix, and each knew that the other knew. There could be no escaping it. The boy Cuneda shrugged with an attempt at carelessness, though the angry colour flushed up to his forehead as it had done yesterday; and caught the dagger from his belt. 'I'll take you, then, with an arm bound behind my back if need be.'

'Na,' Drem said, smiling, though he felt the sweat prickle on his upper lip. 'That would be to tip the chances all one way. I have learned to fight one-handed.'

Men were crowding in on them more and more thickly from the other fires; the hounds, scenting what was in the wind, were straining at their broad studded collars, snarling and with raised hair. The King stood looking down his great beak of a nose, fondling the pricked ears of his wolfhound. 'So, it will be a dog-fight indeed . . . Wait though, should the third of our pairs go up against each other as it were naked, while the rest have their wolf collars to their throats? No shields, I think, in this dog fight—no, no shields. Irdun, bring out the hunting straps.'

And so the strips of thick yet supple pony-hide that men wore on the wolf or boar trail were brought out from the King's Hall; and Drem pulled off his saffron kirtle, and stood as though in a dream while Vortrix, thrusting the others aside, bound the straps about his belly and loins and left forearm; Vortrix, very bright and truculent of eye, and with an odd grimness about his

mouth. And all the while, Whitethroat thrust and fawned against him, whining.

'Here, let you give me your dagger, and take mine,' Vortrix said when he had finished. 'It is better than yours.'

It was not, it was almost identical; but Drem knew that if this had been Vortrix's fight, he would have done the same thing because to lend Vortrix his own dagger would have been the only thing he could do for him in help and friendship. 'So, I take your dagger,' he said. 'Hold Whitethroat for me.'

The crowd was falling back, clearing a space beside the fire. The King had seated himself again on his painted and skin-spread stool with his blind harper at his feet. The four hounds dragged against their collars with renewed urgency, their snarling rising to a sing-song note of hate and menace; most of the others had been thrust out of the circle, lest they seek to join in. 'Good hunting, my brother in blood,' Vortrix said, and Drem heard him through the advice that the rest of his kind were showering upon him and which he did not hear at all. Then he stepped out into the clear space.

Across the crowding circle he saw the Grandfather sitting with his beaver-skin cloak huddled to his ears, gazing into the middle distance, for it was not the custom for any of the Men's side to show a public interest in a young kinsman who had not yet slain his wolf. Drustic, close beside him, was clearly deep in trouble; poor Drustic, who took life heavily and was always troubled about something, and was now in all likelihood wondering what he was going to tell their mother afterwards. Talore was looking straight at him despite the custom; Talore, slight and darkly fierce in the firelight that glowed in the brilliant folds of his scarlet cloak and struck shifting sparks of light from the coils of the great copper snake about his maimed forearm; and between the man and the boy, across the cleared space, unseen by the rest of the Tribe, there passed the old salute.

Then he was walking forward with stiff legs, houndwise, to meet his enemy.

They came together in the midst of the circle, and checked. The mist seemed to have thickened again, a golden smoke in the firelight, dimming a little the farther shapes of the crowd. He was aware of the moment's hush, everything save for the sing-song snarling of the hounds caught into stillness; of the eyes of the Men's side upon him. He was not aware, for his pride did not run on that particular trail, that standing there poised in the firelight and the golden mist, on the edge of intense and deadly action, he was beautiful to see. A tall, red-haired boy, with the lean, strong grace of the King's wolfhound; all the more beautiful, in a queer, crooked way, because he carried his right arm trailing, like a bird with a broken wing.

Then the hounds, slipped from leash, sprang snarling past him, for each other's throats, and the frozen instant was over.

Drem and his enemy did not spring as the hounds had done; they were circling warily, crouching a little. Drem was watching the other boy's eyes. 'Watch his eyes.' How often old Kylan of the Boys' House had said that: 'Watch his eyes, and let his dagger hand look after itself.' Cuneda was the first to spring, but Drem had seen the flicker in his eyes in the instant before, and slipped sideways, feeling the wind of the dagger past his shoulder. Then he sprang in himself, to be met by a lightning guard-stroke. Dagger and dagger rang together, and he felt the jar of the impact all up his arm. On either side, all around him, the snarling tumult of the dog fight rose, and the voice of the crowd surged to and fro; but Drem heeded neither the one nor the other. His world had narrowed to a circle of sea-smelling, fire-gilded mist, and he was alone in it with his enemy. Once before, he had fought in deadly earnest—on that first day in the Boys' House; but this was a very different thing, no wild, squealing hurly-burly of random blows, no warrior's smell of blood at the back of his nose. This was something almost of ritual, a duel rather than a battle, and the more deadly for that. Yet it was linked, as the other had been, with his Warrior Scarlet.

Cuneda sprang in again, and again there was that ring of

bronze on bronze; and Drem, breaking free his dagger, leapt
in under the other boy's guard and drew blood from his upper
arm before he could spring back out of range. One of the dogs
had begun to howl, and there was a hideous worrying noise.
For a few moments the boys circled at a distance, then sprang in
again in a swift, fierce flurry of thrust and counter-thrust.

Drem felt a hot flick of pain in his side, as though old Kylan's
bull's-hide whip had flicked him there. He laughed, and drove in
for closer fighting, momentarily pressing the other back. He saw
Cuneda's face, the lips drawn back and nostrils flaring. Cuneda
was losing his temper, as yesterday he had lost it with the pony
mare; all the better, for with temper gone, judgement went too.

For a few moments the thing had the swiftness of a battle between wild cats rather than a dog fight, before both sprang back out of touch, and the wary circling began once more.

The end came suddenly; and by chance rather than his enemy's skill, very nearly in disaster for Drem. He saw again the warning flicker, just in time, and again side-sprang clear of the other boy's stroke, but even as he did so, he heard a shout behind him, and something crashed snarling into the back of his legs, and he went down sprawling over two hounds locked together, the one with jaws fast in the other's throat.

Cuneda was on him in the same instant. He saw the flash of the descending blade, and twisted wildly, flinging up his arm. There could be no parrying the blow. He took it on his dagger arm instead of in the breast, and the keen blade, landing square, sheared through the pony-hide straps and laid his dagger arm open from wrist to elbow, and in the same instant he stabbed upward and felt the blow go home in the other boy's shoulder.

The King, on his painted stool, bent his head to listen to something that it seemed his blind harper had to say; then nodding briefly, rose to his feet, and stood hands on hips, surveying the scene.

Drem knew nothing of that. But as Cuneda grunted and lurched sideways, and he got to his feet panting, he heard the King's voice raised above the splurge of other voices. 'Finish! It is enough! The fight was good and it is over!' And just at first he did not understand. But he saw a flicker of a new kind in Cuneda's eyes, as the other boy scrambled up, clutching his shoulder; a flicker of relief.

For a moment Drem and his enemy, no more his enemy now, stood and looked at each other, while the uproar of the Men's side rose about them. Of the two victorious hounds, one was being dragged off by his master, and the other, bleeding from a score of wounds, stood licking his muzzle over the body of his foe. The fourth dog writhed horribly on the stained ground with his throat torn open. One of the warriors bent and put the poor brute out of its agony with a thrust of his dagger.

Drem turned and walked back to meet his own kind, stiff-legged still, swaggering his shoulders as he went. But the blood from his gashed forearm was trickling over his hand, and it was hard to hold the dagger. Whitethroat, tearing free of the hands on his collar, had come leaping to meet him, with bushy tail flying. They were all about him now; Vortrix had an arm across his shoulders. 'My heart is glad!' Vortrix said. 'It was a good hunting.' And then old hairy Kylan of the Boys' House was there, and one of the priest kind with linen strips and evil-smelling, black salve.

Meanwhile the King stood with his Chiefs about him, swinging a little on his wide-planted heels, the golden mead cup again in his hand. 'Nay,' he said, in answer to the grumbling protest of an old Chieftain, that the fight should have been allowed to find its own end. 'We have had our sport: why should the Tribe lose a warrior, maybe two?'

'Aye, but see,' said another Chieftain. 'The matter of the dagger is not yet wiped clean, for look you, a dog of Bragon's clan and a dog of Dumnorix's have won their fight, and you called off the boys with their fighting not yet finished. Therefore the thing stands equal and unfinished still.'

'You speak truth, Findabair,' said the King, and there was a small and rather grim smile in the shadow of his young golden beard. 'The matter of the dagger is not yet finished. Therefore we will make an end of it now . . . It is in my mind that surely it is not fitting that a strong magic such as this grey dagger seems to be, should lie in the hands of a Clan Chieftain—even so great a Clan Chieftain as you, Bragon my brother—while the King carries only a bronze dagger such as all men have in their belts. Therefore doubtless it has been in the mind of Bragon the Chieftain to give the grey dagger into the hands of the King.'

Bragon swallowed thickly, and turned as red as a withy when the sap rises. 'The King—surely the King jests.'

'Na, the King left jesting behind him on his father's death-pyre,' said the big golden man, smiling still, and he held out his hand.

Bragon, now almost purple, took the little grey dagger from his belt, and pressed it to his forehead, then gave it into the outstretched hand.

The King took his own dagger rich with inlaid silver and red amber from his belt, saying. 'So. Now let you take this in exchange, that the gift of a knife may not break the friendship between the King and his Chieftain.' And so the thing was robbed of its sting.

Dumnorix flung up his big russet head and laughed, and the laughter was caught up by the Chieftains and the warriors around him, until even the red face of Bragon cracked into an unwilling grin. The King's dagger was a fine one, after all. And on the outskirts of the throng, Cathlan the Old gave a deep appreciative chuckle, and said to Talore who stood beside him: 'Sa, sa, the young bull has an old head on his shoulders. Behold, he has turned aside the trouble that there might have been between the Clans; and he has the grey dagger for himself.'

Talore showed the dog teeth at the corners of his mouth, in that swift, dark smile of his. 'Surely the young bull is a wise one —or has a wise counsellor in that blind harper of his. It is in my mind that it was wisdom to call off the fight when he did, that Bragon's boy should not be put to shame by a one-armed fighter—a thing which also might have bred trouble between the Clans at a later time.'

The Grandfather peered up at him under his thick, grey-gold brows. 'You think it would have ended so?'

'After that shoulder blow, I—think that it would have ended so,' said Talore the Hunter. 'He is a born fighter, that hound cub of yours.'

Drem heard the laughter of the Men's side, though he did not know what it was about. The small gash in his side had been salved, and his forearm tightly bound with linen strips to stop the bleeding and bring the edges of the wound together; and his own kind were thronging about him; and he was very thirsty. 'I am thirsty,' he said. And it was Luga who brought him a pot of barley beer, and held it for him to drink, because

his arm was so stiff in the tight binding that he could scarcely bend it. And looking at Luga's dark face over the tilting rim of the pot, he thought suddenly: 'I know you; you're a trouble-maker, always one to pick a quarrel and bear a grudge; but you're one of the Brotherhood still, and let any threat come against the Brotherhood from the outside, and you'll stand with the rest of us until the threat is beaten back.' Nothing was changed between himself and Luga, they would be hackles-up with each other tomorrow as they had been yesterday. But today they grinned at each other across the beer pot as Luga set it down empty.

The firelight was in Drem's eyes, and the taste of triumph in his mouth was hot and sweet as wild honey. He had made a good fight with his enemy, Whitethroat was safe, and he had held and strengthened his place among his spear brothers; now, surely, nothing but his Wolf Slaying was between him and his Warrior Scarlet.

And his Wolf Slaying would be before the spring came again.

IX

The Black Pebble

DREM walked proudly among his fellows of the Boys'
House in the moons that followed, while the long gash
on his forearm healed and faded to a pinkish line that
would be silvery by and by, and autumn gave place to winter,
and the mid-winter fires blazed on the crest of the Hill of
Gathering. And when the year turned towards spring and the
wolves left the winter pack to mate, it was time for the Wolf
Slaying to begin.

For two winters, Drem had watched the boys in their third
year go out to the Wolf Slaying; and now the time had come
for him and Vortrix and the rest of them. The time that, he
realized now, had lain like a kind of darkening gulf across his
path ever since he entered the Boys' House, making everything
on the far side of it seem fiercely bright and at the same time
remote. That was the same for all of them, he knew; they did
not speak of it, but it was in their eyes as gaze caught gaze,
every time they drew the sacred lots.

Since the choice of the Tribe's warriors must lie with the
Sun Lord, the boys drew pebbles out of a narrow-mouthed
jar—one black pebble and the rest white—to determine each
time who should have the next hunting. And after each Wolf
Slaying, one pebble was cast away, so that there were always
so many pebbles in the pot as there were boys with their Wolf
Slaying yet before them; one black pebble, and the rest white.

And in the dawn after each lot drawing, the hunting would

117

begin. There were no hounds with the Wolf Slayers, but the whole of the little brotherhood would set out together as a hunting band; and together they would track down the beast and bring it to bay. Only the actual kill must be left to the one of them who had drawn the black pebble. For at the last, the thing must be fought out in single combat between the hunter and his wolf, matched together by the Sun Lord, so that from that time forward there was room for only one of them in the world of the living.

The time of Wolf Slaying went by slowly, and the white pebbles dwindled in the narrow-mouthed jar; and one white pebble was smeared with red ochre before it was cast away. That was for Gault who had missed his spear thrust and would never play the fool again. They made his death fire as it had been made for the old King; but this was a small fire, for a boy who had never come to the Warrior Scarlet.

Vortrix drew the black pebble and killed his wolf; Luga also, and Tuan and fat Maelgan, while still Drem drew only white pebbles, and waited for his turn to come. Spring came early that year, and the curlews were calling over the upland country and the first blackthorn foaming on the forest fringe, when Urian and he drew the last two pebbles from the jar. Once again, Drem drew the white pebble. And after Urian had slain his wolf, the weather turned wild and wet, so that for many days on end the white rain drove lashing before the spring gales across the roof of the Boys' House, and there was little to do but crouch over the smoking fire and go out to try one's weapons and come in half drowned and deaf with the wind, to crouch over the fire again; waiting, waiting, no hope of a wolf in this weather, while the days went by. Drem scarcely ate in those days of waiting; he grew gaunt as a famine wolf himself, and tense as an over-strung bow, so that even Vortrix scarcely dared to speak to him.

Then one evening the wind died, and the sun set wetly yellow over behind the Hill of Gathering, and the rain drifted away, leaving the world sodden and gale-weary. 'Give it two

days,' old Kylan said. 'Two days, and the game trails will be alive and fit for following again.'

Drem looked up from beside the fire, where he sat burnishing his wolf spear. 'Give it two days, and the storms may return on their track. Already there are too few days left of Wolf Slaying. Give the word, old Lord of the Boys' House, and I go tomorrow.'

Kylan considered, his eyes that were yellow like a wolf's frowning into the eyes of the boy before him; and at last nodded his ragged head. 'So be it then; it is your trail, your wolf trail. Let you follow it.' And he gave the black pebble into Drem's hand.

And so in the dark before the next day's dawn, the hunting band rose and began to make ready. Standing naked by the fire, with the others about him, and the whole of the Boys' House awake and eager in the shadows as always when there was a Wolf Slaying in the wind, Drem tied back his hair with a thong, that it might not get in his way; and stood for Vortrix to bind the supple, sweat-darkened straps of pony hide about his belly and between his legs and round his left forearm, just as he had done beside the Royal Fire when the King called for a hound fight.

'Too tight?' Vortrix asked.

Drem twisted and crouched. 'Na, not too tight—tight enough, though.' And their eyes met in the light of the roof-tree torch, one pair very blue, the other suddenly golden, remembering that other time. The others stood looking on; one less of them than there should have been, and Drem, glancing round at them, saw in his own mind the missing one among them; a smallish ghost in the firelight with a mouth like a frog, and felt the skin prickle a little at the back of his neck. Beside Gault's death fire he had felt that quiver for the first time. Each of the New Spears were well aware, when they went out to the Wolf Slaying, that they might not come back, but he had realized then, as he had not quite realized before, that for him, because of his arm, the chances of not coming back

were greater than for the others. Maybe tomorrow they would build the death-fire for him . . . But he would not think of that. He would think of coming back to the village at Sunset with the blood of his wolf on his breast and forehead, and the newly flayed skin on his shoulder.

He reached out and took his broad wolf spear from the rack beside the roof tree, and turned to the door, while behind him the others caught up the spears and the light wicker hunting shields that they carried for self defence, and Vortrix took down the flaring torch from its sconce. Kylan was waiting for him in the doorway, old fierce Kylan with his bull's-hide whip laid aside, oddly gentle as he always was at this moment, and set his hand on Drem's shoulder, saying, 'Show the wolf kind that I have taught you well. Good hunting, my son.'

The sky had begun to lighten, a luminous water-green above the dark peaks of the turf roofs, as Drem with his hunting band behind him crossed the steading garth towards the doorway of the Chieftain's house-place; and his own shadow ran dark and spider-tall before him, in the light of the torch that Vortrix carried. Midir came to meet them on the threshold, with the golden eagle cap upon his head, and the amber Sun Cross on his breast catching the warmth of the torchlight.

'Who do you bring here to the sacred threshold of the Chieftain's house?' said Midir as they halted before him; and to the ritual question, Vortrix, the torch bearer, gave the ritual answer. 'A New Spear to be marked for his Wolf Slaying, Holy One.'

'Let him kneel down,' said Midir.

And while Drem knelt before him on sacred ground—every threshold was sacred, the Chieftain's above all others—the old priest made the three slim lines of the Wolf Pattern with charcoal and red ochre on his forehead. Lastly, with a hand so thin, despite its strength, that the torchlight seemed to shine through it, he took the amber Sun Cross on its thong, and touched Drem with it on the forehead above the Wolf marks, and again on the breast.

'Go forth and slay the wolf that waits your coming, my son. The Light of the Sun be with you through this day.'

And Drem rose, marked for his Wolf Slaying, set apart from the world of other men, and turned away to his hunting.

'What is the plan?' Vortrix asked softly, when they had left the still sleeping village behind.

'It is in my mind that the Under-Hill track is a good place to pick up a trail,' Drem said, moving a little ahead of the rest; and as they went down through the village barley plots he lifted his head and sniffed the morning, his nose almost as sensitive as a hound's, so that for him, running water and bare chalk and the north side of trees all had their clear, distinctive smells. The morning smelled chill and fresh, the wind still blowing in long, soft gusts that died away into stillness between; but his questing nose could discover no scent of wolf in it as yet. He felt the Wolf mark on his forehead as though the charcoal and red clay pressed against his skin. The light was broadening in the sky when they came down to the track under the steep northern scarp of the Chalk. The ancient trackway was sticky and slippery after so much rain, set with great pools that reflected back the pale shining colours of the sunrise beyond the interlacing hazel and sallow twigs. And for the trained eyes of the boys who came down to it spear in hand through the scrub, it bore a complete record of all the coming and going that there had been on it since the rain stopped yesterday evening.

Drem, his eyes moving unhurriedly here and there, as he checked beside the way and then began to follow it, was reading the signs with the ease of long use. Here a hedgehog had crossed the track from left to right, there a herd of deer had followed it for a little way, then turned off into the scrub towards the river: four head of deer, with three yearling fawns among them. A little farther on, a fox had crossed the track, going down to drink at sunset, and his spoor was crossed by that of a hunter coming that way a little after, carrying his kill on his left shoulder. Drem saw where he had halted to change it to the

other shoulder, and left the tale in a single blood spot on the sodden ground, and in the changed balance of his footprints when he went on again. And then, just beyond that place, clear in a patch of fine gravel, were three padmarks that might have been the prints of a huge dog.

Vortrix saw them in the same instant as Drem, and said softly, 'Here's your wolf, brother.'

Drem nodded, slipping to one knee and bending low over the prints for a closer view, for the light was still poor, though growing stronger every moment. The tracks were new; the wolf could not have passed much before first light, and the depth and spacing of the pad marks showed that he was travelling easily, almost lazily. Probably he had killed somewhere up on the hill, and was now on his way back to his lair.

The others were standing round him, careful of their feet and where their shadows fell, in the way of the trained hunter. 'Well, do you take it?' Luga asked impatiently. 'Or is it that you need that dog of yours to tell you what to do?'

'I take it,' Drem said quietly, 'when I am ready.' And he went on studying the tracks, learning all that he could about his wolf. It was a big dog wolf, and from the angle at which the prints crossed the open ground, he judged that it was heading for the shallows of the stream below, as though to cross over into the dense forest that choked up the valleys on the farther side. He rose from his knee at last, his hand tightening on the white ash shaft of his spear, his heart giving the little lurch of excitement with which he always began a hunting; and with his hunting band at his back, melted into the budding hazel scrub beside the way, leaving the wet track empty in the day-spring until a magpie flew down on to it to drink at one of the puddles.

They forded the stream, picking up the pad marks again in the soft earth on the far side, and pressed on. All that morning while the sun rose high into a sky of drifting cloud and storm-washed blue, and the broken tumble of light and shadow sailed lazily across the High Chalk, Drem and his companions followed the trail of the big dog wolf through the deep mazes of

the forest; very occasionally by a pad mark, more often by a single brindled hair on a low-hanging thorn branch, by a few side-brushed blades of grass, by the distant alarm call of a jay; by all the thousand and one signs, not there for any save the trained hunter, that told of a wolf passing that way. The hazel scrub and wild fruit trees and the red, sap-bloomed alders of the forest fringe had given way by little and little to the small, dense damp-oaks of the Wild, and as they pushed farther and farther into the dark heart of the forest, dense tangles of yew and holly crowded ever more thickly about them. It was not a tall forest, but a dark one; grey-misted, brown-shadowed, green-gloomed, and the hunting band, moving with the light swiftness of quest-ing hounds, moved in a twilit world, where the sunlight splash-ing in through the tangle of bursting oak twigs overhead or between the black rook-wing branches where a yew had fallen, seemed to burn with a brilliance that was sharp-edged as a sword cut and gave off none of its light into the misty glooms of the surrounding forest. When summer came and the trees were in full leaf there would be no sunlight at all, even to stripe and dapple the darkness. A cold and heavy smell hung between the trees, and there were few birds here. Only suddenly, not far off, a jay screamed its warning.

Drem checked an instant, the little cold thrill closing round his heart; then he began to run, circling wide so as to come up-wind on the place where the jay had sounded its alarm call. And the rest of the band were hard behind him; a swift and silent running of shadows among the trees.

Stronger light glimmered through the twisted and crowding trunks ahead, and somewhere to the right the jay called again; and slipping low under the drooping branches of a great forest yew, he found himself crouching on the edge of a clearing. In the midst of the open space, a dense mass of thorn and elder and wayfaring trees thrusting up into the light and air, almost hid from sight a kind of low, overhanging cliff of earth and rock, caused maybe by some landslide in the rains of a long past winter, that closed the far side of the clearing. But Drem knew

as surely as though he could see the cave mouth with his own eyes, that somewhere in there, under the dark overhang and the crowding bushes, was the lair of the wolf that they had trailed so far.

He made a small, swift sign to the others behind him; and knew, though no breath of movement told him so, that they had slipped away, right and left, to draw their ring about the place. Drem crouched motionless in the brown gloom under the yew branches, his hand clenched on the spear shaft until the knuckles shone white. His nostrils widened, and little tremors ran through his body, houndwise, as the smell of wolf came to him down the wind.

The faintest movement, the swaying of a branch in one place, the stirring of a tall bramble spray in another, signalled to him that the others were in place all round the clearing. This was the moment, then! He stood up. The others were up almost in the same movement; he could see them all round the circle, closing in towards where, somewhere in the dense scrub before them, the wolf must be aware of their coming and watching them come. The time for silence was past now, and they began to shout, their voices chiming together and rising into the tree tops. 'Ty-yi-*yah*-eee!' And with the rising voices, Drem's heart seemed to rise too, beating upwards with a wild exultancy: 'Ty-yi-ee! Yah-ee-ty-yi-yi!' as they came closing in through the long grass and the brambles.

And then suddenly the wolf was there. With a crashing of twigs and small branches it sprang into the open, then, seeing the hunters all about it, checked almost in mid spring, swinging its head from side to side, with laid-back ears and wrinkled muzzle: a great, brindled dog wolf, menace in every raised hackle. Then, as though it knew with which of the hunters it had to deal, as though it expected him, it looked full at Drem. For a long moment it stood there, tensed to spring, savage amber eyes on his as though it knew and greeted him. The rest of the band had checked at a small distance, spears ready; but Drem was no longer aware of them; only of the wolf, his wolf.

The thing was between him and his wolf, life for life, and the Warrior Scarlet.

It seemed to him that the open jaws with their lolling tongue were grinning at him as he leapt forward and ran in low, his spear drawn back to strike. And at the same instant the wolf sprang.

Quite what happened he never knew; it was all so quick, so hideously quick. His foot came down on something agonizingly sharp that stabbed through the soft raw-hide of his shoe and deep into his flesh—a torn furze root perhaps—throwing him for one instant off his balance. It was only for the merest splinter of time, but twisting to regain his balance, somehow he missed his thrust; and the wolf was on him. He had one piercing flash of realization; a vision of a snarling head that seemed to fill his world—yellow fangs and a wet black throat;

and then sky and bushes spun over each other. He was half under the brute, he felt a searing, tearing pain in his right shoulder, he smelled death. The wolf's hot breath was on his face as he struggled wildly to shorten his spear for a dagger-stab, his chin jammed down in a despairing attempt to guard his throat; while at the same moment something in him—another Drem who was standing apart from all this—was knowing with a quiet and perfect clearness like a sky at summer evening: 'This is the end, then. It is Gault's fire for me . . .'

He heard shouting, and at the edge of his awareness caught the downward strike of another spear blade. There seemed to be another struggle rolling over him, and confusedly he knew that the wolf had turned from his throat. He heard its snarl rise to a sudden yelping howl; he was aware of a great weight gone from him, a crashing away through the bushes, a burst of more distant shouting; a moment of oddly terrible quiet. And in the quiet, scarcely knowing what he did, he dragged himself to his knees, shuddering and gasping for breath, his spear still in his hand. And Vortrix's arm came down to him, helping him to his feet.

Blood from the long fang-slash in his shoulder spattered down, bright on to Vortrix's hand, just as it had done on the day so long, long ago, when they had become blood brothers. They looked at each other across the silence, and then, ashamed to look at each other because of what had come between them, looked away. The other boys were gathering about them, breathing fast. Someone said, 'The brute is clear away—na, the lair is empty. We shall not see that one again.' And someone said: 'It was no ordinary wolf. Surely it was a ghost wolf, or it could never have escaped after that thrust of yours, Vortrix.'

Drem leaned weakly on his spear and looked at Vortrix again. 'You should have left the thing between my wolf and me,' he said, but his mouth was so dry that the words came out only as a choking whisper.

Vortrix was deadly white, grey-white to the very lips, and

his eyes looked blind. He shook his head, but said no word. There was nothing to be said, Drem knew, nothing to be done. Even if he could stop the bleeding in his shoulder and track down the wounded wolf again and slay it—before sunset, it must be before sunset—it would do no good, for Vortrix would have had a hand in the killing; and the killing must be between wolf and New Spear alone. That was the custom.

Everything seemed unreal and far off. Somebody brought him a handful of moss to press against his shoulder, and he took it, slipping his arm through the thong of his spear, and gathered himself slowly upright. He looked about him at his fellows; and the familiar faces looked back, silently, not quite meeting his eyes. He saw that as though by common consent, they had parted their circle about him, and understood that the gap was for him to walk out through; out and away. His brothers of the Boys' House were offering him the only mercy that they had it in their power to give; that he might go now, to live, or more likely die, as the forest chose, instead of coming back to face the shame. He was free to turn to the forest as he had turned to it that night six summers ago, when it had all begun. It would be the easiest way. But that night six summers ago had been the last time that Drem had turned tail. He had fought so long and so hard that now he couldn't stop fighting; he couldn't take the easy way, though he longed for it.

'The forest is all around you,' Luga said.

Drem shook his head. 'Na,' he said. 'Na.' And could say no more because of the dryness in his mouth. He gathered himself together, and slipped the spear thong up to his shoulder; then, still pressing the reddened moss against his hurt, turned back in the direction that they had come. The others fell a little behind, but Vortrix walked with him.

X

'Brother, My Brother!'

A T dusk that evening, having faced Kylan, having faced
the Boys' House, Drem went home.

They were all at the evening stew, round the hearth in
the familiar house-place; and they looked up and saw him leaning in the doorway, on the dim edge of the firelight, with the
remains of the Wolf Pattern still on his forehead, and the dried
and clotted wound in his shoulder. And for one moment it
was in the hearts of all of them that he was a ghost. He saw it
there; he saw the fear in his mother's eyes. Well, in a way he
was a ghost—dead to the Tribe. A boy who failed in his Wolf
Slaying and did not die was dead to the Tribe. It was the
custom.

Then Whitethroat, who had sprung up with the other hounds
at his coming, gave a piercing whine and came running to him,
crouching low, in very different manner from his usual joyous
greeting, and the still moment, the icy moment, was past. His
mother had risen swiftly to her feet. 'What is it? Ah, you are
hurt—your shoulder——'

Drem looked about him. He saw that the loom by the door
was empty, and a piece of cloth lay folded at its foot as though
it had been newly cut from it; fine chequered cloth of Warrior
Scarlet woven with the dark green of juniper leaves. And his
heart twisted with a physical pain under his ribs. He said
hoarsely, 'If that was meant for me, my mother, let you take it
for a new cloak for Drustic. I have failed in my Wolf Slaying.'

128

He thought that he should never forget his mother's cry. It was not loud; quite a little cry, but it seemed to be torn from her raw and bleeding, and it hurt him as he had not known that it was possible to be hurt.

Cathlan, the Grandfather, on his folded bearskin beside the fire, leaned forward to peer at him through the wreathing smoke fronds, his golden eyes almost hidden under the down-twitched grey-gold brows. Then he tossed the bone he had been gnawing over his shoulder to a waiting hound, and spat harshly and disgustedly into the flames. 'What did I say, son's wife? What did I say, six summers ago?'

Drustic was staring at him, too, his pleasant square face bogged deep in trouble. He opened his mouth and then shut it again, as though he wanted to say something but couldn't think what.

Drem came in to the fireside—the first time in three years that he had crossed the threshold of his home; the last time, maybe, in all his life—and squatted down, with Whitethroat crouched against his knee. 'Is there no food for me?' he demanded, harshly defiant. 'I have not eaten for a night and a day.'

His mother was pressing her hands across her forehead. 'Food? Yes—yes, there is food. But first—at least let me bind your wound.'

'It will do well enough as it is,' Drem said. 'I want food before I must be away, no more.'

Blai, unnoticed in the shadows until that moment, had risen to her feet. 'I will see to it,' she said; and brought him a bowl of stew and a barley cake, and gave them to him without another word.

He took them from her and ate furiously. He had not eaten for a day and a night, as he said; one did not eat before hunting, and besides, he had been too afraid. But there was nothing to be afraid of any more, because the worst thing that could possibly happen to him had happened. So he ate fiercely and swiftly, tearing the meat from the bones with his teeth, and

tossing the bones to Whitethroat against his knees. It was his mother and brother and the silent Blai, watching him, who did not eat. The Grandfather ate, but then nothing in the world would come between him and his food.

When at last Drem could eat no more, he rubbed his hand in the brown, piled fern to cleanse it, and looked round him; a long, long look; at the faces of his kin, at the familiar, firelit, shadowy house-place. He saw the firelight falling saffron coloured across the hearth stone, the long, jagged knot high up on the roof tree where a branch had been when it was a growing oak tree in the forest, the dappled cream and tawny deerskin hanging before his mother's sleeping stall, and the bronze and bull's-hide shield hanging from the edge of the loft, that would never now be his to carry. All the long-familiar things that he had not seen for three years, and after tonight, would never see again.

Then he got to his feet, saying to Whitethroat, 'Come, brother, it is time that we were away.'

His mother, who had remained standing all the while, braced against the roof tree, as though she were bound there, came and set her hands almost timidly on his shoulders. 'Where are you away to? Cubbling, what will you do?'

'I will go to the Half People, as you said six summers ago—you and the Grandfather both—that I must go if I failed,' Drem said. 'I will go to Doli and the sheep.'

'So you heard,' his mother said; and he saw her eyes straining in her beautiful, dagger-thin face, and the desire to hurt as he had been hurt rose within him. He had not forgiven her for that small, agonized cry.

'You always wondered, didn't you? Aye, I heard, every word. I was in the loft; I had come in by the roof strip meaning to drop on you like an earwig out of the thatch—a child I was; but I was never so much a child again, after that day . . . That was why I ran to the forest; only Talore One-hand found me and bade me come back and fight for the thing if I would have it. And I have fought, the Sun Lord knows that I have fought,

these six years gone by. But the Grandfather was right after all.' His voice, which had become a man's voice in the past year, cracked, and steadied again. 'Let you be glad of Drustic, as you bade the Grandfather to be glad of Drustic. You'll not be without a son to stand with the Men's side, when I am herding sheep.'

She cried out again at that, and her second cry seemed to undo what the first had done. He wanted to put his arm round her and drive his head into the warm, soft hollow of her neck as he had used to do when he was small, but he did not dare, lest he should weep like a woman. It was better to go on being angry. Anger was a kind of shield. His mother had dropped her hands from his shoulders. 'Drustic is a good son, but it is better to have two sons—better two sons than one . . . And this time there will be no coming back.'

'Na, this time there will be no coming back.'

He turned, with Whitethroat at his heel, blundering past Blai, whose pinched, white face swam for an instant into his sight as though it floated in dark water, and went out into the spring dusk. The ponies in the fore porch advanced soft muzzles to him, but he blundered past them also. Behind him he heard a movement as though his mother made to rush after him; and Drustic's voice saying urgently 'Na na, my mother, there is no good that you can do!'

And he plunged on into the dusk with the sound of sudden wild weeping in his ears.

He was going out, stripped and alone, from his whole world, leaving behind him his people, the comradeship of his own kind, even his own gods. Many of the Half People bowed themselves to the Sun Lord, but he was going not only to the Half People but to Doli; to the little Dark People, the children of Tah-Nu; and he knew that little by little he would lose his own faith that was sharp and fierce and bright as a spear blade; turn from the Sun Father and the open sky, to the older faith of Doli and his kind, to the warm suffocating darkness and the Earth Mother who gave all things birth.

He turned his steps towards the sheltered fold of the downs high above the village, where the turf-walled lambing pens stood for use each winter. In a little now, after the Beltane fires were burned out, the shepherd kind would take the ewes and their lambs up to the High Chalk again, to the summer sheep runs, but now sheep and shepherds would still be there, and Doli with them.

It was long after dark when he came up the combe and saw the gleam of firelight from the doorhole of the low turf bothie beside the pens, and heard the faint rustle of the penned flock and the bleating of a lamb that had woken to find itself apart from its mother; and a great baying of herd dogs broke out, making him stoop quickly and catch Whitethroat by his bronze-bossed collar. Then a voice sounded, silencing the dogs, and a little bent figure came ducking out through the firelit doorway, and turned to peer down the combe.

'Who comes?'

'It is I, Drem,' Drem called back.

Doli, for it was Doli, spoke to the dogs again, and they lay down on either side of him. He stood without any movement, leaning on his broad-bladed spear, and waited for Drem to come up to him.

'It is past barley harvest,' he said, when the boy stood before him; and that was all.

'It is past six barley harvests,' Drem said, 'but I am come at last. You said once that I should make none so ill a shepherd. Do you think so still?'

'How shall I say, I who have not spoken with you these six barley harvests past?' And then as a silver wing of moonlight slipped over the shoulder of the combe and spread towards them, the old man looked up at him, slantwise under the grey tangle of his brows. A long considered look. Then he shook his head. 'I am none so sure. I think that you are more ungentle than you were, six barley harvests ago. Yet it may be that you are gentler with the four-footed kind than with men and women. Why do you ask?'

There was a little silence, filled by the delicate riffling of the wind through the short grass, and the stirring of the sheep in the fold behind them. A curlew cried from the head of the combe, and one of the herd dogs, still lying obediently at Doli's side, gave a warning growl as Whitethroat's exploring muzzle came too near. Then Drem said, 'I have had too much fighting of late, to care much for the gentle things. But I have lost my fight. I have failed in my Wolf Slaying.'

Doli showed neither surprise nor sorrow—but then Doli very seldom showed anything. 'Sa, that is a bad thing,' he said. 'And so now you come to me and the sheep.'

'So now I come to you and the sheep,' Drem said dully.

'Then let you come in to the fire, and I will salve that shoulder,' Doli said. No surprise, no questions asked. And deep in his raw and angry heart, so deep that he did not realize it, Drem was grateful, as he ducked under the low lintel and followed Doli into the shepherd's bothie. Someone sat beside the fire, a dark boy of his own age, and he saw that it was Erp who had run with the rest of them in the days before the Boys' House. Their eyes met, black eyes and golden, and then both looked away again.

Doli brought rank-smelling yellow ointment in a pot, and smeared Drem's shoulder as though he had been a wolf-bitten ewe, saying, 'This is good against a wolf gash, whether in man or sheep.'

Drem bore with the salving, then sat down with Whitethroat against his knee, beside the fire, not avoiding Erp's dark, curious gaze any more, not seeking it out, too tired to care either way. He felt oddly adrift, like something with its roots hacked from under it, spent and empty. Even his rage had gone from him, and there seemed nothing to take its place, nothing; just emptiness where yesterday his life had been: and he was so tired.

Bv and by he lay down beside the fire, with his head on Whitethroat's flank, and fell asleep like a tired child, the traces of the Wolf Pattern still on his forehead. So deeply

asleep that he did not wake even when Flann and his brother came back from the village.

It was the eleventh morning after that, and his shoulder, thanks to Doli's salve, was three parts healed, when he looked up from helping the old shepherd to spread the same stinking yellow stuff on a ewe's back where she had been pecked by ravens—and saw Vortrix standing by the opening of the fold.

He was not surprised, he had known that Vortrix would come, before his initiation cut them off from each other for all time. And this was the last day of all.

No word passed between them, only one long look, and when the ewe had been released, bleating after her lamb, he said to old Doli, 'I will come back in a while,' and whistling White-throat to heel, walked out of the fold to where Vortrix waited for him.

Still without a word, they turned together, and walked up the combe, with their hounds loping behind them.

'Why did you not come before?' Drem asked at last, staring straight before him as they walked. He had not meant to ask it; but he asked, none the less.

'I have been nine days and nine nights enclosed. Taboo in my father's house,' Vortrix said. 'Midir sealed the door with clay, and sealed it again every time he came—he and the warriors with him—and I might not break the seal.'

Drem had not thought of that; that Vortrix had broken custom by coming between him and his wolf, and would have to pay for it in ritual purification. 'Was it bad?' he said.

'It was—not good,' Vortrix said, quite quietly, but it sounded as though he had spoken through shut teeth. Drem looked at him sideways. Vortrix's square, cleft jaw was set, and there were great stains like bruises under his eyes. What had they done to him, those nine days and nights, in the hut with the clay seal on the door? Drem realized that he would never know; that he must not even ask.

All that day they hunted together as of old. They killed

at last among the wooded combes of the High Chalk, and evening found them making their way home with the carcass of a young roe hind slung from Vortrix's spear between them. The hounds padded at their heels; the shadows of boys and hounds and kill long-drawn on the downland turf. All as usual, everything as usual, save that it was for the last time.

They came over a last lift of the Chalk, and on the edge of a little solitary wood of wind-stunted oak and thorn trees that crested the ridge, halted to rest. But they had carried home heavier kills before now, and never thought of resting. And there among the budding oak trees, with the body of the hind at their feet, they turned to look at each other. All day they had contrived somehow to hide from themselves the fact that this was their last hunting together, but now they could not hide it any longer. It was in the sea-song of the wind in the budding oak branches, and the distant crying of the gulls, in the cool scent of the moss that grew thick under the trees, and in the bleak and hopeless desolation of their own hearts.

'We have had good hunting,' Vortrix said.

Drem nodded. They had had good hunting; not only today, but all the days of their hunting together. He would hunt again, and so would Vortrix, but never again together. That was over. The fore-shadow of tomorrow's parting hung over them; a parting as sure and more final than it would have been if one of them was to die in the morning, and one to go on living. It was not that they would not see each other again, but that they would see each other only across the gulf that divided the Men's side, the free Tribesmen of the warrior cast, from the Half People without the Tribe. There was nothing they could do. They were in the grip of the custom of the Tribe; and the custom was stronger than they were, stronger than all the men of the Tribe together.

Drem stared down at the roe hind at his feet. There was a scarlet stain on the white of her belly, like the scarlet stain on the white breast feathers of the swan. Warrior Scarlet . . .

He cried out hoarsely, as though under sudden sharp pain. 'Why did you come between my wolf and me?'

'I had no time to think—even now I cannot think. I—it is none so easy a thing to stand leaning on one's spear to see a brother die.'

'And so tomorrow I must stand to see you and all our company go away from me—and turn back alone, after you are gone.'

'My brother—oh, my brother—we have hunted the same trails and eaten from the same bowl and slept in the same bed when the hunting was over. How shall I go on or you turn back alone?'

'I do not know,' Drem said. 'It must be—it must be; but how, I do not know.'

They reached out their hands to each other, Vortrix's two hands, Drem's one, gropingly as though both of them were blind. Their arms were round each other in a close, hard embrace. They had always been equally matched, a team that had neither leader nor follower; but now in their parting it was Drem who was the stronger of the two, and Vortrix who cried like a woman, with his head bent into the hollow of Drem's shoulder, while beyond the wind-stirred branches of oak and

137

thorn the low sun set fire to the clouds, and the west was suddenly kindled to furnace gold.

Higher and higher burned the fires of the sunset, deepening from gold to copper, to fierce and glowing red. The branches of the oak trees were black against it, and the wings of the gulls were black as they swept by; and the crimson light splashing far in through the little wood flushed the vivid moss under the trees, and stained the breast of the roe hind so that it was as though the blood spread until the whole of the white fur was stained pink.

When the fires began to fade, dying out into pale rose-flecks overhead, so that all the sky was freckled like the skin of a trout, and the shadows thickened among trees, they stooped again to their kill. The village, though out of sight below them, was not far off, and, 'I will come no farther with you,' Drem said. 'It is in my mind that you can carry her alone from here.'

'Aye, I can carry her. I will take your half of the kill to your mother.'

He helped Vortrix to get the carcass of the deer across his shoulders, fore feet in one hand and hind feet in the other, and to settle his spear. Then without another word between them, he turned and went blundering down through the little wood. He could not bear any more. He did not even remember to whistle Whitethroat after him, did not remember the great hound at all, until a brindled black and amber shadow brushed past his knee and circled before him with bushy tail flying. He had forgotten Whitethroat; he would not be quite alone.

It was dusk when he got back to Doli and the shepherd kind; and he settled down to his evening stew keeping well away from the fire, that the light of the flames might not show them his face.

Drem tried to keep away from the village the next day, but nevertheless, when sunset drew near and it was time for the

start of the ceremonies, he came up the stream, through the alder brake, and stood among the alder trees in their haze of young leaf, looking across the irregular barley plots to the familiar huddle of turf roofs. He heard the soft, formless murmuration of the gathering crowd that rose to a long-drawn cry as the boys appeared from the Boys' House doorway; and he bent his head on to his fist on the spear shaft, seeing against the darkness of his closed eyes the scene that he had watched so often before. He saw them coming down through the now silent crowd, walking one behind another, very proud and erect, and looking straight before them. Another cry—almost a wail— told him that the first boy had stepped out into the open space about the Council Fire where Dumnorix stood with the greatest of his warriors about him. That would be Tuan, the youngest of them; always it was the youngest first, the eldest last—the eldest who this year would be Vortrix. Against the darkness he saw two warriors step out from the Men's side, to either side of him. But it was no longer Tuan between them, and the warriors that he saw in his mind were not Tuan's father and his friend but a huge and stooping old grey-gold man with a beak like an eagle's, and a slight, dark one with a great copper snake twisted about a left forearm that lacked a hand. They were bringing him to Midir beside the Council Fire; Midir bending a little to receive them, his thin hair straggling from beneath the golden eagle cap of the priest kind. He seemed to hear the ritual questions and answers. 'Who is this that you bring before me?'

'It is a boy, that he may die in his boyhood and return a warrior to his Tribe.'

'And who speaks for the boy?'

'I, Cathlan the Old, Cathlan the Mighty, I his Grandfather, speak for the boy——'

Drem, leaning on his spear among the alder bushes, drew a hoarse breath that was like a sob. Why had he come? But he knew that his coming had made no difference; if he had stayed with Doli and the sheep as he had tried to do, the thing

that was happening beside the Council Fire would have reached him just as surely.

Across the little barley plots and the young flax, he heard the women taking up one from another the death chant for the sons who were going out to their ritual dying, and knew that it was over; it never took long, that first ceremony. Now they would be coming down after Midir, through the crowd that swayed back to let them through, the boys who had been his companions of the Boys' House, who would have been his fellows of the Spear-ring—Vortrix . . . He raised his head, and saw them, no longer against the darkness of his inner eyes, a slim line of young proud figures, with the winged figure of Midir at their head, and the fires of a stormy sunset that he had not seen come, blazing behind them; and as they walked, their shadows reached out towards him across the springing barley as though in farewell. Now, for a night and a day, until the fires of tomorrow's sunset flared beyond the Hill of Gathering, they would be as dead to the Tribe; and then they would come back, as warriors from victory, with the tattooed patterns of their new manhood raw on their breasts, and there would be a great rejoicing, a triumphal blowing of war horns before presently the Beltane fires were lit.

But Drem knew that he would not see that triumphal home-coming. He had come because he must, to see his brothers of the Boys' House away; the return of the young warriors was no more to do with him.

They had turned right hand, now, and were walking straight up the slopes of the Hill of Gathering, while behind them the women lamented still. 'Ochone! Ochone!' And the death chant fell heavy on Drem's ears and on his heart. The boys dwindled smaller and smaller on his straining sight, winding up the long slope towards the sleeping-place of the unknown champion on the crest, and as they dipped over the sky-line towards the Place of New Spears beyond, it seemed as though they walked straight into the blazing brightness of

the sunset. And the brightness opened for them, and they were gone.

Drem turned away alone, blind with more than the sun in his eyes, and plunged back through the alder scrub. And still behind him rose the wailing of the Women's side. 'Ochone! Ochone!'

XI

The News-Bringers

THE next night Drem stood alone by the empty lambing pens, when the flocks and herds had all been driven down to the village, and watched the Beltane fires blazing red on the crest of the Hill of Gathering; and knew that the young warriors had returned out of the sunset. Behind him in the shepherd's bothie the hearth was black and cold, just as his own heart felt black and cold within him, and with the same empty desolation. But the hearth only waited, like every hearth throughout the Clan and the Half People, to spring to life again at the touch of the sacred fire . . .

Then far down the combe a red bud of flame pricked out in the darkness, and Erp came running with a torch, as all up and down the Clan territory the youngest man of every household would be running. And the black hearth in the shepherd's bothie woke and kindled and uncurled petals of living flame. But the coldness and darkness within Drem was as cold and as dark as ever.

Next day, when the Beltane fires were burned out, the sheep were taken up to the high summer pastures, and Drem, whose life was now the life of the shepherd kind, went with them. And little by little, as the days went by, the slow, solitary rhythm of the new life closed round him. Every night at twilight they folded the sheep in the great, turf-banked enclosures. (Even in summer the sheep only had to be left unfolded for a few nights for the wolves to come up from the forest and hunt the grazing

142

lands. They were no fools, the wolf kind.) Every morning, when the light returned to the world, they were let loose again. And morning and evening they must be taken to the dew-pond a bow shot from the enclosures, to drink. All day long as they grazed, they must be watched and guarded, moved from place to place so that there was always fresh grass, kept from the parts of the Chalk where harmful herbs grew, and from danger spots such as the old flint quarries; rounded up when they became too scattered; tended when they were sick or hurt. At night when the sheep were safely folded, there was the low turf bothie by the dew-pond, and stew—mutton stew for the most part, from the carcass that hung in the hearth smoke out of reach of the dogs—cooked by one of the Little Dark Women who came and went and seldom seemed to belong to any of the shepherds in particular. There were sheep salves to be mixed and shepherd's gear to be mended; while sometimes old Doli would blossom into a story, and sometimes young Erp would play a little wandering, tuneless air on the elder pipe that by day he played to his sheep. But for the most part they sat in silence. They were a silent people, the shepherd kind.

When Drem had been more than a moon with Doli and his people, it was time for sheep shearing.

Three times a year the Tribe and the Half People without the Tribe came together at a common need. One was at the great cattle round-up at the Fall-of-the-Leaf, one was at lambing time, when every able-bodied man, Dark or Golden, must take his turn in the Wolf Guard; and one was at sheep shearing. But it was chiefly the women of the Tribe who came to mingle with the Half People at the sheep shearing.

It was early summer as yet, but already the rolling chalk hills quivered in the heat. Swifts darted high in the blue air, or skimmed low above their own shadows along the flanks of the turf, and the whole wide sky shimmered with lark song. Drem, bringing down a small flock from the high Chalk to the shearing pens above the village, heard the larks and smelled the dry thyme bruised under his feet and the little sharp hooves of the

sheep, and felt the sun hot between his shoulders. But the old
fierce joy that he had once taken in such things was lost to him.
He kept his ears on the bleating of the ewes and their half
grown lambs, his eyes on their bobbing rumps, and on the grey
herd dog circling on the flanks of the flock. Cu, the older of
Doli's two dogs, who had been the young one, six summers
ago, would not work with anyone but his master, but Asal,
the young one now, would work with Drem well enough, and
there was no trouble between him and Whitethroat so long as
Drem remembered never to fondle Asal when the great hound
was by. Whitethroat padded at his lord's heels now, with a
long fluted strap of pink tongue dripping from his mouth. He
would never make a herd dog, he had been a hunting dog too
long, but he understood that the sheep were not for hunting but
for protecting, and already he had proved that he could earn
his keep as a guardian of the flock.

It was the first time that Drem had been within sight of the
village since the day when he had watched the opening ceremonies of the New Spears from afar; and as he dropped lower,
and the distant blueness of the Wild was lost to sight behind
the rolling bluffs of the Chalk, he looked for the familiar roof-
huddle under the Hill of Gathering, and the full and noisy
scene on the level turf above the corn plots, where the shearing
pens had been set up and the shearers were already at work;
half longing for the sight of familiar things, familiar faces, half
flinching from it.

Drem could not work among the shearers. There were few
things that he could not do one-handed, but to deal with a
struggling and indignant sheep and work the heavy bronze
shears, one must have two hands. So through the rest of that
crowded and sweating day, when the droving was over, he
worked at the pens, and ran the sheep down, bleating and protesting, to the shearers, from whose hands they were turned
loose at last, pale and shorn, to trot quietly off in search of their
bleating lambs. It was hot work. His hair stuck to his forehead
and his kilt to his thighs, and his hand was greasy with the yolk

of the fleeces that seemed to have got inside his nostrils so that he could not smell anything else.

When a girl, passing with a tall jar full of buttermilk for the shearers on her hip, paused beside him, he turned to her eagerly —and it was Blai.

For almost the first time in his life he was glad to see her. She would be able to tell him of his house, of the old life that he had left behind him. For the moment, in his swift surge of longing, he forgot even his thirst and the buttermilk, and letting go the sheep he had just taken from the pen, stretched out his yolky hand and caught her wrist as though he was afraid she might be away before he could get out the things he wanted to say, the questions he wanted to ask. 'Blai! Blai!' He was almost stammering. 'It is good to see you!'

She looked up quickly, and for a brief moment it was as though a light sprang up in her face. 'Is it, Drem?'

'Of course.' He was impatient at her stupidity. 'You can tell me how it is with my kin at home! How is it with my mother, Blai?'

The light died again, and Blai said after a moment, 'Yes— I can tell you of your home. It is well with your mother, Drem.'

'She is—not here?'

'Na. She is not here.'

They looked at each other a moment, then Blai raised the wide-necked jar, holding it for him because he had not the two hands to take it. 'Now drink. You must be thirsty.'

Drem drank. The buttermilk was cool and thin and smooth, and he drank his fill. When he had done so, he stood back, wiping his hand across his mouth; and then wished that he had not because of the yolk on it.

In swift little scattered sentences, Blai was telling him the news of his home; of the Grandfather's cough and Drustic's hunting, of the birth of hound puppies, of how the half wild fruit trees did, of his mother, and the red mare who was ready for breaking.

When it was all told, she was silent a short while, staring down into the jar. Then she said a little breathlessly, 'I could come and bring you news of your home again—sometimes—if you would like.'

'I shall be up on the High Chalk again tomorrow. That's a long way,' Drem said quickly; and then, without meaning to say it, heard his own voice adding, 'It is lonely, up on the High Chalk, Blai.'

Blai was still staring into the jar. 'I could come—sometimes,' she said. 'I would not mind the long way, and—then maybe it would be—less lonely.'

Drem looked at her with a little frown between his eyes. He was puzzled. 'Why would you do that—come all that way, for me, Blai?'

Blai raised her head, and a slow painful wave of colour flowed up over her narrow face. 'You came after me once—years ago—when *that man* came, and all the other children laughed. You came after me because I was of your hearth, you said; and so now—surely if I am of your hearth, then you must be of mine.'

There was a little silence—silence to Drem and Blai, though filled with all the crowding sounds of sheep shearing going on around them. Drem was still puzzled, not so much by Blai now, as by something in himself that was strange to him. Just for a moment he seemed to be looking at Blai for the first time, and for the first time really seeing that she was there. He saw that there was a knot of white elder flowers caught into the dark coils of her hair. The other girls often wore a flower caught in the neck pin of a kirtle or braided into their hair, but he had never seen Blai, who was not like the other girls, with a flower about her, before. Or maybe it was that he had never noticed before. Somewhere deep inside him, a small faint fellowship curled open, delicately like a bud curling back its petals. And yet with the fellowship, with his sudden awareness of her, he was shy of her for the first time in his life.

'Blai——' he began uncertainly. 'Blai——'

A triumphant bleat awoke him to the fact that the ewe he had been taking down to the shearers had of course wandered off. Fool that he had been to forget about the ewe! It was at a little distance by now, already mingling with the shorn sheep that had been turned loose. One of the Half People shouted to him, pointing. As though he could not see! He began to run, and the ewe, seeing him coming, broke away and began to run too, bleating as though he were the butcher, her matted fleece flouncing up and down above her thin legs. He caught her in a few moments, but before he could get a firm grip on her fleece she whirled about, bawling, and dived between his legs, tripping him up. Somebody at the pens laughed, and as he picked himself up and went after her again, he felt that he was a fool—one armed, humiliated. He shut his teeth, and getting her again, twisted his hand in the fleece at her neck, and swung her round with a savage thrust of his knee in her flank, all but bringing her down. She cried out in earnest that time, in pain and terror; and in the same moment Erp passed him, carrying the pot of wood ash that was for dabbing on any cut made by the shearers. 'It is a poor shepherd that loses his temper with the sheep,' Erp said, not quite looking at him, as usual. 'Also it is foolishness, for she will remember and be the more trouble another time.'

From one of the older men, Drem might have taken it, but from Erp, who was no older than himself, who was not even shearing, but only ash-boy to the shearers . . . 'Maybe I should find it easier if I were like you, you little black bush-creeper, born for nothing better than to tend the sheep!' he began furiously; and then he caught sight of old Doli, standing leaning on his spear beside the opening of the lower pen; and what he saw in the old man's weather-wrinkled face made him swallow the rest. With shut teeth, and the blood burning up to his forehead, he ran the ewe down to the shearers, and then returned for the next. Doli was still leaning on his spear beside the lower pen. 'You should not lose your temper with Erp, either, as though he were another sheep that would not go your way,' Doli said. 'That also is foolishness.'

Drem stood before him, his breast heaving a little. 'I forgot that the Little Dark People are my equals now. It is a thing still strange to me. Maybe I shall learn in time!' he said. It was the most insulting thing that he could think of to say.

But Doli, it seemed, was not insulted. That was one of the maddening things about the Dark People; they were often in some way beyond the reach of an insult. 'Nay, there is no question of equals,' Doli said. 'Since you have come to us, by our standard you must be judged. Hunno and Flann and I are older than you, and wiser; and even Erp knows more about the sheep. Therefore you are the least among us . . . Go now, and bring down another sheep lest there be a shearer waiting.'

Drem brought down the sheep, and another, and another. He worked on, furious and heart sick; and when, a little later, he straightened to wipe the sweat out of his eyes and thrust back the heavy red hair that was stuck to his forehead, and found Blai with her jar beside him again, he turned on her so roughly

that she shrank back as though he had struck her. 'No need that you follow me about with the buttermilk, for I am not thirsty. No need that you follow me up to the summer pasture. I shall do well enough—better maybe—without news of my home, for I have no home now. I am no more of your hearth!'

Blai was white enough now, a grey, thin white like the buttermilk in her jar; she stood looking at him for a moment, in the way that he had seen her stand looking at someone once before, but he didn't remember who it had been, or when, and he didn't care. He noticed with a kind of savage satisfaction that the elder flowers in her hair were limp and tarnished already.

He turned away with hunched shoulders, and went after another sheep, leaving her standing there.

Summer wore on. Below, along the skirts of the downs, the wild garlic flowers were gathered and spread to dry on the roofs of the village, and the flax harvest was got in, and the barley stood tall and golden, rustling when the wind blew over, in the village corn lands and the little lost plots among the downland folds that belonged to Tah-nu's children who had known the secret of the barley before ever the Golden People came. But up on the High Chalk there was little sign of how the seasons passed. The turf grew dry and tawny, and the noontide shadows of shepherd and flock grew shorter, and then began to lengthen again, and that was all, save that the elder trees that grew in the corners of the sheep enclosures for a medicine, shed their creamy blossom and began to darken with blue-black berries that the birds loved.

Drem was no happier than he had been, but he began to grow used to what had happened, as one may grow used to the ache of an old wound until it is possible almost to forget about it and to think of other things, though the ache is still there, just the same, and the weariness of the ache.

Harvest came, and among the clustered turf hummocks in the high combe that was the nearest thing Tah-Nu's children had to a village, the Little Dark People made strong magic of

their own that had nothing to do with the harvest of the Golden People on the lower slopes. Magic that was made with the open palm on stretched sheep-skin drums, while one of the young men danced the dance of the Corn King until he fell twitching to the ground. 'Once we killed the Corn King every year, that the next year's harvest might be good, but now there are not enough young men among the Dark People, and we kill him only once in every seven harvests,' old Doli said to Drem, when the ceremony was over. 'And the harvests are not what they used to be. Na na.'

On an evening a little after harvest, Drem took part of the flock to the dew-pond, to drink before they were folded; a task that sometimes fell to him and the young dog Asal, now that they had begun to learn the ways of the sheep and how to handle them. He had half the flock with him; if you took the whole flock together half of them would never get near the water. Whitethroat was loping at his heels as usual, Asal circling on the flanks of the sheep. As they came over the last rise, and saw the water before them, they surged forward in a bobbing flood, suddenly purposeful. He heard the quick putter of their little sharp hooves on the turf. The pond had sunk very low in the long, hot summer, a shining round boss of water in a great shallow buckler of puddled clay that was almost⁻ white at its upper edge, deepening to the pinkish brown under a mushroom as it neared the water. Sometimes it was blue and staring, that water, sometimes changeable with cloud shadows, or sullen grey when the mist came up. Now it lay pearl and palely golden, quiet in the sunset, and a magpie rose from the water's edge, chattering, as the flock swept down towards it. There were always birds at the dew-pond; they dropped feathers round the margin of the water, wagtail and hawk and magpie; warm, russet curlew feather curved like a flower petal, speckled starling feather; once, far out on the water, the white pinion feather of a swan.

The sheep were spreading out all round the margin of the pool, working down over the hard clay to the water. Drem

stood leaning on his spear and watching them, the two dogs at his side. The dogs were thirsty, panting and with dripping tongues, but they knew—even Whitethroat knew by now—that they must wait their turn until the sheep had drunk. The sheep drank thirstily, the water riffling round their muzzles, every ripple with a flake of the sunset caught in its spreading curve. It was a very peaceful thing to watch.

In a while the sheep had drunk their fill, and began to lose interest in the water and turn away. Asal and Whitethroat were looking up into Drem's face, their tongues hanging from their jaws, their tails giving little beseeching flicks and flutters. 'Go then,' he said, and they bounded away into the longed-for water, crouching belly deep in the coolness as they lapped.

He had just whistled the dogs out, shaking the shining drops from their rough coats in showers, and set Asal to rounding up the flock—not that much rounding up was needful now, for the sheep, their thirst gone, were beginning to drift of their own accord in the direction of the night enclosures—when little dark Erp came over the brow of the Chalk carrying a meal-skin on his shoulder, and headed down for the bothie beside the pond.

Drem lingered a little behind his sheep, half waiting for the other boy to draw near. Erp had been down to the village that day, for fresh barley meal; and it was seldom that he came up from the abodes of men without news of some kind; he was all eyes and ears, was little dark Erp. And so now Drem, sick for the news of his own kind that he was too proud to ask for, lingered behind his flock, making belief to do something to the belt that held his sheepskin close about his narrow waist, while the other boy flung down the meal sack before the bothie door.

'Surely you have been a long time down in the village,' he said, his eye half on the flock, as Erp came up to him a little sideways as a dog comes.

'The meal sack was heavy,' Erp said, and wriggled his shoulder. 'And it is a long way from the village, and the meal sack grew heavier all the way.'

There was a little silence. Drem longed to say, 'Well, then, and how was it with the village? How is it with my house? What word runs through the Clan?' but pride stuck in his throat; and Erp glanced sideways into his face, torn as he always was between his wish to please the boy who seemed to him so tall and golden and splendidly heedless of where his feet fell, and his wish to be revenged on him for being what he was. At last he said, 'There is a new man-child in the house of Talore.'

'So?' Drem said.

'And a new red bull calf in the Chieftain's byres, and Urian has slain a bear, but they do say that it was little more than a cub. And Caradig and Morvidd have returned to their quarrel—the old quarrel about the line where their corn plots come together.' He looked at Drem again, sideways under his brows, bright-eyed and curious. 'And Drustic the brother of Drem has asked Belu from above the ford for the third daughter at his hearth.'

Drem looked round quickly. He remembered that third daughter: Cordaella he thought her name was. A plump, pink girl who smelt like new bread. So she would be coming to spin beside the fire in his old home. Suddenly, and rather oddly, since he had never troubled about it himself, he hoped that she would be kind to Blai.

'And Drustic is not the only one,' Erp said. 'They do say that Vortrix also has a girl under his cloak.'

Drem did not answer for a short space. Then he said: 'What girl is that?'

'Rhun, the daughter of Gwythno of the Singing Spear. I have seen her myself, grinding corn before her father's door, and she grows very fair.' Erp grinned. 'See now, do I not bring you back news—much news, from the Golden People?'

'Much news,' Drem said. 'Much news, little Eyes-and-Ears. But now it is time that I go after my sheep, lest they begin to scatter.'

It seemed to him that the sunset was fading very quickly to-night. The gold of it was quite gone, as he turned from the dew-pond; and there was a new and sharper ache in the old wound. He had a harsh desire to make the sheep suffer for it, to set Asal snapping at their heels, and hustle them along, and see their silly fleeces flouncing above their thin legs as they ran; but he had learned that lesson—among other lessons that summer on the High Chalk. He walked slowly, using his spear as a staff, the dogs on either side of him, the flock drifting ahead, a grey cloud of sheep along the tawny downland turf. One of the ewes swung out sideways from the rest, and he whistled to Asal, pointing with his spear, and the dog streaked off to gather her in. 'Easy!' Drem called after him; Asal, being young and over-eager, was sometimes inclined to chevy his charges exactly as he, Drem, was longing to see them chevied. Despite the warning, he was doing that now, snapping over close at the heels of the straying ewe. Drem whistled again, shrill and compelling, and the dog checked and looked back. 'Softly,' Drem called. 'Softly, brother.' And the dog returned to his task more gently, heading the ewe in again to the main flock.

'Sa, that was well done,' said Doli's voice, and he found the old man beside him, leaning on his spear, and looking, as always, as much part of the downs as did the elder trees in the corner of the sheepfold; as though he had not moved in a hundred years.

'I begin to learn,' Drem said. 'It is well that I begin to learn.' There was a hard and heavy note in his voice, and the old shepherd gave him a swift, searching look under his grey brows.

'Erp is a great one for hearing news.'

They were walking together now, behind the flock; and Drem looked quickly at the old man, realizing that he must have met with Erp as the dark boy came up with the meal sack, and also heard the news of the Golden People. 'Little Eyes-and-Ears could always hear the thoughts of a man's heart a day's trail away, by putting his ear to the ground.'

They were drawing near to the entrance of the great turf-walled fold, where Flann and his brother waited with their notched tally sticks to count in the sheep as they did every night; and Drem fell back a little, for Doli to take over the task of getting the flock through the narrow opening; but Doli shook his head. 'Na na, if the old dog does all the work, how shall the puppy ever learn? Let you take them through.'

So Drem went on; he and Whitethroat and the young dog Asal, while old shepherd and old dog watched behind them. He was lost in a great loneliness; he thought he had not really known what loneliness was, until now. He tried to be glad about Vortrix—glad that now Vortrix would be comforted and would forget his blood brother. But it was lonely—so lonely, for the one forgotten; and the downs looked very wide and dark and desolate in the fading light. And surely the wind had grown cold.

But he got the sheep safely through the gap between Flann and his brother with their tally sticks; and later that evening, when they were safely folded, and Drem and the old man were alone for a moment in the bothie, Doli said, seemingly to the red heart of the fire: 'It is a good shepherd that can think of his sheep when his heart is full of other things. It is in my mind that maybe Drem will make none so ill a shepherd, after all.'

XII

The Wolf Guard

AUTUMN came, and the rams were turned loose to run with the ewes, while far below in the rolling distance of the Wild, the weary green of late summer caught fire and flamed tawny and amber, bronze and gold, the wild apple trees of the woodshore were bowed with little russet crabs, and the brambles dark with fruit among their gold and crimson leaves, and the village swine were driven down into the valleys to fatten on acorns. And then it was Samhain, and with the last leaves falling in the forest, they brought the sheep down to the winter pastures, where there would be more hope for them in snow or hard frost. There was all the tumult of the great cattle round-up and the winter slaughtering. And when the slaughtering was over, only the best and strongest of the rams and the ewes were left, for there would not be enough food for the hoggets or the weaker ones through the winter.

So winter came, and in the long dark nights the shepherds huddled close about the fire in the turf bothie, with their sheepskin or wolfskin cloaks drawn close about them, listening, as somehow one never seemed to listen in the summer, to the great loneliness of the Chalk beyond the firelight. It was an open winter at first, a winter of gales and rain, but not cold, and there was little danger to the folded sheep from their ancient enemy; and the midwinter fires of the Golden People had burned out, and it was within a moon of the start of lambing time when the first hard frosts came.

A few nights later, they were huddled round the fire in the smoke-filled bothie, over the evening meal of barley stirabout and broiled deer meat—Drem and Whitethroat had been hunting. They were all there save Flann, who had a woman among the little green hovels of the Half People, and so was often missing when winter brought flocks and shepherds alike down to the lower pastures. Drem, who had finished eating, was polishing a new spear shaft with a piece of sandstone. The white ashen shaft came up silvery pale and smooth in the fire-light; the rubbing stone, crumbling a little under his fingers, shed an occasional trickle of yellow sand, like pollen, like dust of gold, into the lap of his sheepskin mantle. From time to time he glanced across through the smoke at Erp and the girl who had cooked the evening meal. More than once, that particular girl had come up, in the past moon, and Erp had bought her a neck-lace of jet and blue glass beads, paying an otter skin for it to the trader. She showed her teeth like a young vixen when he sat too near her; but she was wearing the necklace. Drem could see it in the opening of her sheepskin. Pretty it was, with little blue sparks where the firelight caught the glass beads.

Drem shifted his hold on the spear shaft under his arm to come at another length of it; and drew closer to the fire, though his shins were scorching under the cross-bound deerskin leggings. That was always the way in frost or wind, one's front scorched and one's shoulders froze. He hunched deeper into his cloak, and said, because he was tired of the silence: 'See, the fire burns red all through. There is a frost tonight.'

Hunno looked up from the piece of rib that he was chewing. 'I should know that without a fire to tell me,' he growled, 'by the gash that I carry here in my shin where the she-wolf caught me seven winters ago. Always it aches in a frost.'

And in that moment, as though the mention of wolf had been a spell, first one and then another of the dogs pricked its ears and growled softly. Old Doli raised his head to listen. 'So. It comes,' he said. 'Always it comes; later in some winters than others, but always it comes.'

Drem listened, aware of Whitethroat suddenly tense and quivering beside him. They all listened, dogs and men alike, hearing afar off in the starry darkness the long-drawn, desolate, cry of the wolves on the hunting trail.

'So, the time comes to be keeping the Wolf Guard,' Hunno said.

It was the thing that Drem had been dreading; knowing that it must come, yet unable to bring himself to face it. The Wolf Guard would bring his brother Drustic, and the young warriors who had been boys with him in the Boys' House—and Vortrix. At shearing time he had not had to face that fear, for the Men's side did not concern themselves greatly with the sheep shearing, considering it work only for the women and the Half People; but the Wolf Guard was another matter, that was man's work, and all must take their turn when the wolves hunted among the sheep runs and the lambing time drew near.

The rubbing stone slipped in Drem's fingers, a jagged angle of it making a long score in the silvery smoothness of his new spear shaft, and he cursed with the small, bitter, adder's-tongue curses of the Dark People.

So the men of the Tribe stood the Wolf Guard with the men of the Half People, through the long bitter nights that followed. Men who had been great warriors and hunters before Drem was born, men who had been boys with him only a year ago.

He did not mind the older men so bitterly—even Talore, who never tried to speak with him, but set a hand on his shoulder once in passing, as he bent over a sick ewe. But his own fellows he minded with a minding that cringed in his belly. They talked easily enough with Doli and the Half People, squatting round the fire that had been built at the mouth of each fold, easily and with no sense of barriers between; there had been no barrier between Drem and the Half People before the Grandfather raised it, six summers ago. But they did not know how to speak to Drem, nor he to them; their eyes slid away from meeting; and in the end they pretended, both he and they, not

to see each other. Even when Drustic came, they pretended not to see each other. It was better that way.

As yet, Vortrix had not come at all.

At least, when lambing began, Drem had plenty of work to fill in days and nights, and that helped. Never a night went by for the next two moons or more, that several lambs were not born in it; and all the while the ewes must be watched and tended, the lambing pens constantly crossed and re-crossed to keep a look-out for trouble. When there was a moon it was easier, with the silver light to see by; in the darkness there was only the ewe's bleating, and your own hands—hand—to tell you when she was in trouble; and then she must be got down to the fire, where there was light to work by, for you could not carry a torch among them without frightening the whole flock. And trouble came more and more often as the time went by, and the winter shortage began to tell on the ewes. There were foolish ones too, who would drop their lambs in the trampled fern and wander away; that also was a thing that must be watched for, for a lamb left long to lie on the frozen ground was a lamb dead. Then there were lambs who lived though the ewe died, and must be reared beside the bothie fire, cared for as a woman cares for a babe, until maybe they could be given to a ewe who had lost her lamb. Yes, there was work enough for Drem as for all the shepherd kind, now that the lambing time was here.

On a night midway through the lambing season, Drem squatted with Hunno beside the fold fire, working over a straining ewe, while the men of the Wolf Guard leaned on their spears and looked on. It was a bitter night, with a shrill north-east wind blowing, and snow whirling down the gusts; snow that became visible like a cloud of eddying and swirling feathers as it entered the firelight. They had got the ewe close in against the turf wall for whatever shelter there was, but even there the snow reached her, pale-freckling her fleece that the wind parted in zigzag lines. But Drem doubted whether she felt it. He doubted whether she felt anything clearly, any more. She

was beautiful, too. Sheep had ceased to be just sheep to Drem by that time, and he had begun to see them as the shepherd kind saw them, as he saw men and women; this one beautiful and that one sour-faced, this one cross grained and that one placid. Beautiful and proud she was, but old Doli had said for some time that it would go hard with her when the lamb came.

And now the lamb was here; a fine little black-faced ram lamb limp and sprawling on the handful of brown bracken fronds that they had hastily spread to keep it from lying on the snow; and they left it to itself for the moment while they turned themselves to do what they could for the ewe. Small, surly Hunno rose and turned to the fire for the barley gruel that was warming beside it. But the ewe was already stretching herself out.

Drem leaned over her. 'Quickly, Hunno!'

And then Hunno was kneeling beside him again, with the bowl in his hands, and the growling gentleness in his voice that was only there when he spoke to a sick sheep, and never for his own kind. 'So now, the work is over. Now gruel, my girl.'

The ewe seemed to know that they were trying to help her, and raised her head a little. But a shudder ran through her under Drem's hand, and her head fell back on to the snow. And they were left, Drem and Hunno, as they had been left before, with a lamb flickering into life, and a dead ewe between them.

It had happened before, and each time Drem had hated it, but tonight, perhaps because he had actually felt the shudder that was the life going out of her under his hand, perhaps because she had been proud and beautiful like the great swan that had been his first kill, he hated it more than ever; and the old wailing bewilderment rose in him, crying out to know where the life had gone to . . . but it was no time to be asking such questions, with the movements of the lamb already growing fainter.

'Sa, the thing is over,' Hunno said, setting down the gruel with a slow, expressive shrug. 'Let you take the lamb down to

the bothie before it goes the same way. I must see how it is
with the speckled one with the torn ear.'

So, carrying the lamb like a mere rag of wet wool trailing
from his hand, Drem made his way across to the bothie that
looked more than ever like a little knoll of the hillside, with the
snow to muffle its outlines. The bothie was empty but the
fire burned low and red, and a crock of ewe milk stood ready as
always in the lambing season. Drem set the lamb down on the
spread fern beside the hearth, and left it to be licked and
nuzzled by Whitethroat, who, though no sheep dog, seemed to
have the love of all small and young things that some very big
dogs possess, and an instinctive feeling for what to do with a
new-born lamb, while he set some of the milk to warm in a
bronze pipkin, and with fingers numb with cold brought out
from the dark recesses of the bothie the feeding bottle of
stitched sheepskin, and a short length of elder twig with the
pith scraped out. When the milk was warm, he poured it into
the bottle, wrapped the elder twig in a scrap of rag so that it
would be soft and the lamb might be persuaded to suck on it,
and pushed it into the neck of the bottle; then, taking the lamb
from Whitethroat, he settled down beside the fire, with the

little creature against his knee, to the business of getting it to suck.

Patience never came easily to Drem, but he had more patience with animals than he had with people; and besides, he was learning. He was learning many things, those days and nights. Again and again he dipped his fingers into the drops of warm milk left at the bottom of the pipkin, and painted the lamb's mouth with them; again and again the little thing wavered its head away, or merely lay there making no response whatever. But it was stronger; he was sure that it was stronger. That was Whitethroat's licking and the warmth of the fire. Little sprawling tremors began to run through it; and then quite suddenly the battle was won, and it began to suck. 'Sa, that is the way of it, small one,' Drem said, and dipped his fingers again in the warm drops and gave them once more to the little sucking mouth, and then hastily took up the feeding bottle; and the lamb butted at it as though it was its mother's flank.

It was half standing against Drem's knee, its tail awag behind it as it sucked, while Whitethroat looked on with prick-eared interest, when old Doli came ducking down the entrance step, with the snow thick in his sheepskin mantle. Drem looked up with a kind of wry triumph. 'If we are no good for anything else, Whitethroat and I, at the least we do well enough in the place of a dead ewe.'

The old man crouched down beside the fire, taking in the little scene with those shrewd, weatherwise eyes of his. 'There are worse things for a man or a hound to do well at,' he said.

The next night it happened the other way round; a lamb dropped in the snow that no skill even of old Doli could stir to life, and a ewe was left bleating pitifully without understanding. Drem went across to the shepherd's bothie with the dead lamb hanging from his hand as yesterday the living one had done. And there, leaning against the squat roof tree, with a barley bannock in one hand, the firelight flickering upwards warmly

saffron over his square, bandy-legged figure and steady face, was Vortrix.

Drem checked an instant, crouching in the low doorway, and as he did so, Vortrix's head went up; and for a long moment their eyes met through the drifting, firelit smoke, while Erp and Hunno looked on.

It seemed to Drem that there was a pain, a physical, dragging pain, under his breast bone. Then, deliberately, as Vortrix made the beginning of a movement towards him, he turned away, as he had done from the others of his kind. Only this was not just another of his kind, this was Vortrix, with warrior patterns blue upon his breast; and the sudden wild weeping rose against the base of his throat as he bent to the next thing he had to do.

Laying the dead lamb down beside the fire, and thrusting away Whitethroat's exploring nose with a, 'Na na, brother, not this time,' he drew the knife from his belt.

'The ewe?' Hunno grunted.

'It is well enough with the ewe,' Drem said, and his voice sounded hoarse and heavy in his own ears, as he set about the task of skinning the dead lamb.

'You will give her the other one in its place, then?' Hunno jerked his head towards where last night's motherless lamb slept curled into a little grey hummock against the wall.

Drem nodded and went on with his task. Hunter though he was, he had never found an easy way to skin an animal one handed. It would have been much simpler to pass the task over, lordlywise, to Erp. The other boy would have done it for him, he knew, though he was in the middle of his evening bannock. But if he did that, he would have no excuse to keep his head bent over his hand; he would have to look up. He did look up once, and saw Vortrix watching him, the bannock still untouched in his hand. Then he bent his head again over his flaying-knife.

When the skin was off he did turn to Erp. 'Bring the small one and help me get him into it.'

So Erp brought the live lamb, bleating in scared protest, and between them they worked his back legs into the pelt of the dead one; then his forelegs, finally drawing up the head over his own like a little hood. Hunno laughed, and little dark Erp laughed; there was always something funny in the sight of a lamb wearing another lamb's skin over its own; and the little creature's shrill, indignant clamour made them laugh the more. Only Drem, tying the skin lightly at neck and belly to keep it in place, did not laugh; nor did Vortrix, looking down on them from his stance against the roof tree.

When the thing was done, Hunno tossed a bannock towards him, saying, 'Best eat before you take it out.'

Drem shook his head, and left the bannock. 'Later, maybe.' He got up without looking again at Vortrix, and carrying the living lamb in the pelt of the dead one, shouldered out blindly into the grey, snow-lit darkness.

He went down, Whitethroat as always at his heels, through the big lambing enclosures, parting the ewes and turning them aside with his knee where they were most densely packed, until he found the ewe he sought. The ewe was restless, calling for her lamb. He set his small burden down beside her, and stood to see that all was well. The little creature staggered to its feet, bleating, and made instinctively for the warm woolly flank that meant milk. The ewe swung her head and sniffed at it, suspiciously; but the smell was the smell of her own lamb; all was well. Seemingly quite satisfied, she stood, passive and peaceful, while the fosterling, accepted as her own, butted at her flank to make the warm milk flow faster. Both of them were perfectly content.

If only there was as simple a cure for all ills, Drem thought dully, and turned away, holding himself bent a little as though to ease the ache of a physical wound.

Another figure, short and bandy-legged and dearly familiar even in the darkness, had come down towards him through the sheep, and Vortrix's voice said, 'They are happy now.'

'They are happy now,' Drem echoed. He drew a quick breath. 'Why have you come down after me?'

'You left your bannock lying,' Vortrix said. 'Therefore I have brought it down to you. Why did you turn from me as from a stranger, up yonder in the bothie?'

'Maybe because I was a fool,' said Drem wearily. 'I am tired of things that hurt in my belly.' And he took the bannock that the other held out to him in the darkness, and began to eat; but the bannock seemed to be made of dust instead of barley meal, and his stomach revolted at it though he was wolf hungry.

'I also. I am tired of things that hurt in my belly,' Vortrix said.

Wading through the grey, huddled shapes of the flock, they had come out to the opening of the great fold, and stood together, looking away down the curve of the snowbound valley. It was a very still night, still with the brittle, waiting stillness of hard frost. The seven stars of the Great Hunter seemed to hang out of the sky, pulsing with cold fires; the Great Hunter, swaggering as he always swaggered, above the pale shoulder of the snow-covered downs. Far off in the distance a wolf howled, and the sheep stirred uneasily, and were quiet again, their breath and the warmth of their bodies making a faint smoke in the starlight. With their backs to the fire beside the fold opening, Drem and Vortrix might have been the only living men in a frozen and forgotten world.

They were standing very close, and Vortrix brought up his

arm and laid it across his blood brother's shoulders. Drem felt the warm weight of it through the thick rough sheepskin of his mantle, and let it lie there. But the gulf was between them, nevertheless, and neither of them could cross it to the other's side.

'How is it with you, my brother?' Vortrix asked, very quietly, in a while.

'It is well enough with me,' Drem said. 'I have let go my own kind, and I hunt with the Dark People in all things now.'

'Is it truly so?—in all things?'

There was a long silence, and again, far off among the woods that lay dark and soft like furs flung across the whitened hills, the wolf cried, and again the sheep stirred in the fold, snorting and stamping. Then Drem said, 'Na, we cannot think with one mind, the Dark People and I. We speak the same words but they do not mean the same things. We laugh together, but I do not know the things that stir behind their eyes. Maybe one day I shall learn . . .' He turned to Vortrix. 'And with you? How is it with you?'

'I am—lonely without my brother.'

'One was telling me that there is a girl—the daughter of Gwythno of the Singing Spear. One was telling me that she grows very fair.'

The silence fell between them again. Only a short silence this time, and then Vortrix said, 'If there were a girl under your cloak, though her hair were as bright as the sun and her arms as white as mare's milk, would she fill my place?'

There was no more to be said; and in a little they went out from the lambing pen, drawing the gate hurdle to again behind them, and turned towards the watch fire, round which several of the Tribesmen stood or squatted, leaning on their spears. Vortrix's spear picked up the firelight in a slim leaf of flame against the bluish darkness of the snow and the stars; but Drem saw only the dark side of the blade, a leaf of darkness against the firelight, for he had dropped behind a little, walking not as brother with brother, but as one of the Half People behind one of the lordly Golden Ones.

XIII

The Grey Leader

THE winter had been late in starting, but before it ended,
it was one of those winters which men speak of years
afterwards, round the fire when the earth is frost-bound
and snow comes drifting down the wind. And when the first
signs of spring should have been waking in the forest and the
curlews coming up from the seaward marshes, the earth was
still deep in snow and held by frost as keen and deadly as the
blade of the strange grey dagger that the King wore now in his
girdle. On fine days the snow melted a very little in the sunshine; in the shade where it was blue as the hyacinths in the
woods at Beltane (but surely that was in another world) it
froze without ceasing, day after day; and it seemed that as the
days grew longer the cold increased. The sheep had to be
kept folded all day as well as at night, and with no grazing the
fodder ran short. Drem and his fellows cut branches all along
the woodshore and stripped the lower-slope birch trees of their
bark, pressing farther and farther afield as time went by. But
there was little good in such fodder, and the sheep grew thinner
and thinner, the weaker of them scarcely able to stand on their
legs, and many of the late lambs were born dead. They killed
the more weakly sheep and lambs, so that the strong ones
might have their share of the poor fodder; and there was so
little flesh on the poor, starved carcasses that even when they
could get them down to the village they added nothing to the
meat supply for Clan or Half People.

The wolves, driven by famine beyond their normal fear of the guard fires, were growing ever more bold, howling closer and closer in the darkness about the folds. Farther along the run of the Chalk, the sheep folds themselves were attacked; and everywhere a sheep that strayed was a sheep lost, and no man cared to step beyond the firelight and the sound of his brother's voice after dark.

On a day about the end of the lambing, Drem came up from the woods, carrying on his shoulder a bundle of hardly-gathered fodder branches; and flinging it down beside the gate-gap of the fold, looked about him hastily as he always did, for Doli. The old man, spent with over-much labour and hardship that was sharper even than the shepherd kind were used to, had been ill on his feet for days, after becoming chilled to the bone over a lambing ewe, and Drem had been constantly anxious about him; but to all suggestions that he should go down to the village, or even remain beside the fire in the shepherds' bothie, he had only replied impatiently, 'Na na, there is too much that I have to do.' And now, not seeing him, Drem's anxiety flared up. 'Where is Doli?' he demanded of Hunno, who was spreading fodder.

'One of the ewes has broken out.' Hunno jerked his head towards the High Chalk that closed the head of the valley. 'A strong one such as we can ill afford to lose, and she near her time with the lamb. Doli is gone after her up towards the summer folds. He said it was in his mind that she was gone that way.'

Drem hitched his sheepskin higher on his shoulder, frowning. 'Is Flann with him, or Erp?'

Hunno shook his ragged head. 'Na. As for Flann, his woman has come to her time also, and all men know the fool that he is about her. One brought him word to come, and he went. Therefore, with Drem away down the woods, and the Golden Folk not yet come up for tonight's Wolf Guard, there were but the three of us here when we found the ewe gone.'

'And of the three of you, it must be Doli that went after her?

Why not you or Erp? You are younger than he is, also he is sick.' He swung round on Erp who had come ducking out from the bothie. 'Why did you let him go alone?'

Behind him Hunno growled something only half spoken about an old man being of less worth to the village than a young one, and Erp gave him a swift upward look under his dark brows. 'Not to us the blame. Doli said to us that being old and wise he knew more of the ways of the sheep kind than we could do. Therefore he bade us to stay and guard the fold, and left us Asal and took Cu with him and went. There will be no harm come to him; not to Doli in his own sheep runs . . . There is lamb stew in the hut if you are hungry.'

If he was hungry. As if any of them were ever not hungry these days. Drem hesitated, looking about him. It was drawing towards dusk already; low sky and snow-covered hills alike yellowish grey in the fading light. In the fold, the ewes and lambs—such as were left of them—huddled close, standing or lying in the puddled snow and the litter that was frozen hard where they had wetted it. Icicles hung from the long wool under their bellies, that rang together when they moved so that the fold was full of a faint chiming as well as the pitiful bleating of the ewes as the weight of ice tore at their skins. A bitter wind was gusting over the shoulder of the downs from the north-east, making jagged, bluish partings in the wool of the sheep and the rough hair of the herd dogs; and Drem, sniffing at it, could catch the faint but unmistakable smell of more snow on the way. He shrugged, and turned into the shepherds' bothie, where the dung smoke stung his eyes, and the warmth of the fire seemed to mix with the icy eddies of wind as oil and water mix together but without ever mingling. One of the Little Dark Women was within, huddling over the rough hearth. She looked up as he ducked through the door hole with Hunno behind him, and pointed to the pot that she had just taken off the fire. And Drem took himself a bannock from the basket in the corner, and settled down to stay his chilled and empty belly with the lamb stew.

He began hungrily enough; one mouthful, two mouthfuls, scooping up the lumps of meat with bits broken from his bannock. He ate the third mouthful, more slowly; the fourth he swallowed at a gulp, and drawing his legs under him as he did so, got up, pushing the remains of his bannock into the breast of his rough woollen kirtle, and reached for one of the spears that lay against the turf wall.

Hunno looked up, his mouth full of lamb stew. 'Where away?'

'Up towards the summer folds.'

'There is more snow coming.'

Drem was already half turned to the door. He checked, looking down at the little surly man beside the fire. 'I too can smell other things than garlic with my nose. There is more snow coming, and that is the more reason why I should go after Doli.'

'It is in my mind that you are a fool if you do,' Hunno said simply. And as though to give point to the words, at that moment there came to the ears of both of them, far off and faintly down the wind, the long-drawn and infinitely mournful cry of a wolf. They were silent, looking at each other, while the cry was taken up by another wolf, and then, still farther off, by a third. '*They* are early on the trail tonight,' Hunno said.

Drem's grip tightened on his spear shaft. 'The men from the village will be here soon. Meanwhile keep a good fire up by the fold,' and heedless of Hunno's growling retort that he had been keeping the Wolf Guard when he, Drem, was not yet thought of, he turned again to the door hole, whistling Whitethroat to heel with lips so chapped by the cold that he could scarcely form the sound, and plunged out into the bitter dusk, past the guard fire where the boy Erp stood leaning on his spear, with the herd dogs beside him, and away into the great, white loneliness.

All around the fold the snow was cut up, trampled to a frozen brown mud by the feet of men and dogs and sheep, but within a spear throw the tracks thinned out, and in a little there was

only Doli's track and the strayed ewe's, and that of the dog Cu, faintly visible in the whiteness, reeling out before him into the gathering of the winter dusk.

Drem huddled his sheepskin mantle more closely about him, and trudged on, head into the wind that came swooping down the combe. Something like a tiny frozen feather eddied past his face to alight on the thick fold of sheepskin in which his chin was sunk, and clung there. Another settled with an icy touch on his right eyebrow; another on his lip, and suddenly there was snow flurrying all about him.

It was snowing hard when he came up out of the combe-head on to the open Chalk, and already Doli's track was becoming blurred by the fresh fall. There was still some light left to see by, for there was a moon behind the cloud roof, and the snow threw a faint upward light of its own. But the wind was rising steadily, blowing up from the dark immensity of the Wild far below, with the sea-surge roaring of wind through bare branches and the desolate, long-drawn hushing of wind across open snow. And the snow was worsening with every bow-shot that he pressed on. It was whirling down the gusts now in a fine, choking powder to mingle with the dry snow already fallen that the wind drove sideways across the ridges in a mealy spray. It was growing hard to find the trail, harder all the while. Growing harder, too, to know exactly where he was, in the whirling icy cloud that blotted out the familiar shapes and smells and underfoot feel of the downs.

Drem, already weary from a hard day's work, pressed on in a desperate attempt at speed, stumbling in the deep snow, crouching double at times to search out the faint hollows in the smooth whiteness that were all that was left now of old Doli's track, then struggling on again. Whitethroat, long since trained not to spoil a trail by running on it, floundered at his heel, belly deep in the snow. On the north side of the slope, Drem lost the track in the drifting of the new fall. He struggled down to the bottom of the little dip, casting desperately to and fro, houndwise, and on the farther side, where the snow lay

thinner, picked up the faint trace again, and with a gasp of
relief, pressed forward once more. But on the farther crest,
where the whole flank of the hill turned over into a long, level
slope towards the north, the tracks faded out into the drifts, and
for all his searching, and the great hound's sniffing to and fro, he
could not find any trace of it again.

As he stood at fault, rather desperately, it seemed to him that
the snow was passing. A faint cobwebby gleam of moonlight
slid through the clouds; but only to show him the whiteness
ahead as pure and unmarked as though no living thing had
passed that way since the first man was a thought in the darkness of the Earth Mother. Then the gleam was gone again, as
swiftly as it had come, and the snow came whirling back as
though in triumph. With very little hope of any answer, Drem
propped his spear in the crook of his arm, and cupping his
frozen hand about his mouth, shouted at full pitch of his lungs.
'Coo-oo! Coo-aoh-ee-*yah*!' The seeking cry of the hunters and
herdsmen of the High Chalk wailed out into the storm. Boy
and dog listened, head up into the wind, but there was nothing
to hear save the desolate hushing of the wind and the whisper of
the snow. They pushed on a short way farther, as nearly as
Drem could judge it in the direction of the summer folds, but
his sense of direction was confused by the whirling whiteness,
and he had no clear idea of his own whereabouts, let alone that
of the folds.

In a while he halted, and called again, 'Coo-oo! Coo-aoh-
ee-yah!' and this time, to their straining ears, there came a
reply—a long-drawn howl from far ahead of them, at sound of
which Drem's mouth dried and his hand tightened on the ashen
shaft of his spear. But the howl ended in a burst of barking.
'That's Cu!' Drem said aloud, his numbed lips scarcely moving;
and his heart leapt between relief and an added fear. He called
again, and tried to run, stumbling, floundering in the deep
snow. Ahead of him he heard the dog howling, and he called
again, gasping, 'I come! Doli, I come!' and plunged on.

A few moments later a wolf-like shadow seemed to scramble

from the whirling paleness almost at his feet, and old Cu was weaving round his legs, panting and whining. And Drem realized that he had all but gone straight over the edge of the old open flint quarry in the steep hillside. A torn-away place at the edge told its own story, and below him as he peered down, the chalk dropped away so sharply as to be clear of snow save where the whiteness clung about the roots of the bushes that grew here and there on the sheer surface of the drop. The darkness of more bushes gathered thick at the foot; and among them, something moved and bleated; and he thought that there was something else down there, darker than the bushes, that lay unmoving.

The old dog had launched himself from the crest again, and gone slithering and scrambling down at a rush, to the dark thing that did not move. Drem never paused to remember that there was a perfectly easy way down the hillside and into the old working at its lower end. He took the steep chalk slope much as Cu had done, in a landslide of snow and falling chalk and grass tufts. Whitethroat went past him as a rushing shadow, and somehow, with most of the breath driven from his body, he was at the bottom. The sheep was on her legs, so she was not likely to have come to much harm, although she bleated distressfully at his coming, and made no attempt to move. Drem was kneeling over the still figure of old Doli, lying face downwards with the snow already building up against his weather side. In frantic haste he turned the little shepherd over with hand and knee, and felt for his heart. His own was drubbing so that for a moment he could not be sure; then he felt the faint beat of life under his fingers, and a sob of relief burst from him. 'Doli! Doli!' But Doli never moved. His exploring fingers found a hard lump on the old man's temple and the stickiness of blood among his hair. The ewe must have scrambled and slithered down much as he and the dogs had done, but Doli, following on her track before it was swallowed up, ill and blind weary, and away north of where he thought he was, even as Drem had been, and maybe giddy with the whirl-

ing snow, must have pitched clean over as from a cliff, striking his head somewhere on the way down.

Drem thought desperately, crouching over the old shepherd. What was the thing to do now? At fifteen he had not yet come near to his full strength, and he knew that, one-armed as he was, he could not get Doli across his shoulders and carry him back unaided. Even if he had had the strength of an ox, to carry Doli he would have had to leave his spear behind, and that would most likely mean death for both of them, with the wolf-kind abroad and the smell of Doli's blood to draw them. Here at the foot of the old flint quarry the bushes gave some shelter from the wind and snow, and in case the wolf kind came he would at least have his spear-arm free and the solid chalk behind him. He was fumbling with the bronze pin of his sheepskin cloak even as he thought. He tore it off and spread it over Doli, feeling the wind strike like a knife through his own body without it. Then he turned to Whitethroat and pointed. 'Back—go back, brother. Fetch the others.'

Whitethroat looked along the line of his pointing finger and then up into his face, whimpering. Drem got up and caught his collar, and urged him out to the open mouth of the quarry, where the chalk cliff sank into the hillside; then pointed again. 'Back! Go back to the fold! Fetch Hunno!' He had no means of sending any message, but there was no need: anyone seeing Whitethroat apart from his master would know that it meant trouble—bad trouble, and there would be plenty of men at the fold, for the men of the village would have come up long since to keep the Wolf Guard. Maybe even Vortrix; Vortrix had come up more than once in the past moon. He held the hound's big rough head for a moment with his hand under the raised muzzle. 'Go back, brother. *Bring Hunno!*' Then he pointed again, and gave the hound a light, open-palmed blow on the rump.

Whitethroat looked up into his face again, whimpered, and, turning, ploughed away into the darkness and the flurrying snow.

Drem waited until he was lost to sight, then turned and went back to Doli. Cu, crouching over his master, greeted him with an agonized whine, and he spoke gently to the old hound, and began to drag the shepherd farther back against the chalk cliff, where there was more shelter. It was not easy, with only one hand for the task, but he managed it little by little. When he got Doli where he wanted him, in a little bay of the chalk where a dense clump of spindle bushes broke the wind, he spread his cloak again over the old man, and saw with relief how Cu crawled close and lay down almost on top of his master. That should give him a little warmth.

He turned to the ewe, running his hand over her as best he could in the dark. Her lamb was on the way, but it would not come just yet. Like enough the wolves would be here first, he thought grimly. Her also he urged in close against the foot of the chalk, into the same sheltered spot where he had dragged Doli. Then he found Doli's spear and laid it beside his own, where it was easily come by; and fell to collecting loose turfs and lumps of chalk and frozen snow—anything to throw when the time came. And when that was done, there was nothing more that he could do. If only he could have made a fire! That would have helped to keep away the wolf kind, at any rate for a while. He had his fire stones, but there was nothing in the frozen bushes that would make a blaze, nothing at all. All that he could do now was to wait.

How far would Whitethroat have got on his way back to the fold by now? He had no idea, no means of knowing how time was going by, as he crouched, spear ready to hand, over the old shepherd, trying to add the shelter of his own body to that of the spindle bushes. Maybe Whitethroat would never get back to the fold at all; maybe he would meet the wolves, his father's kind, instead. Peering out through the bushes, with every strained sense on the alert for danger, it seemed to him once again that the snow was slackening. A little later he was sure of it. That was one thing to the good. It was scarcely snowing at all now; there might be something left of their track for the

others to follow—if Whitethroat ever got through. It was growing lighter, too, the low sky breaking up into hurrying masses through which every now and then a greasy blur of tarnished silver showed where the moon rode high. Behind him the ewe was becoming restless. The lamb would be here soon.

Ah, but it seemed that he had been right in his thinking. The wolf kind would be here first!

From somewhere ahead of him in the grey murk, it rose; long-drawn, savage, and unutterably sad, the cry of a wolf on the hunting trail. Another cry echoed it, nearer than the first— and then there was only the wind in the silence. Drem felt as though all the blood in his body had jumped back to his heart, and an icy stillness took him. The ewe stirred behind him, snorting and stamping her foot; he prayed that she might not bleat in terror—not that it would make much difference if she did, for the wolves were down wind of them, and the gusts would carry their scent, if indeed the brutes were not running on it already. Something brushed against his knee, and Cu was crouching beside him; he could feel the tremors running through the old dog's body: tremors of fear and fury and hate. He laid his hand for an instant on the dog's neck, and felt the harsh hairs rising against his palm.

Nothing more happened for so long that he felt he could not bear the waiting for a heart-beat longer; he must yell, beat his spear against the chalk, anything to break the thin-drawn agony of waiting. But still he crouched silent, his heart beating with a slow, heavy drub that seemed to wait to listen between each beat, and the old hound crouching against his knee. The ewe was snorting again, in pain and terror. She had gone off her feet, and Drem thought she needed help, but he could not help her; not now. The moon swam out suddenly, free of the scudding, curdled cloud into a lake of clear sky—and in the sliding silver light, something moved on the smooth whiteness of the snow before the quarry mouth. Something dark, and running low, like a great hound. But it was no hound; and behind it came two more.

Now that the moment had come it was almost a relief; and as the wolves swerved in their tracks and headed in towards him, Drem began to yell; yell and throw the lumps of chalk that he had gathered. That might frighten them back for a while, but not for long. If only he had some means of making a fire—fire to singe their hides! The great grey leader flinched from the lump of chalk that caught him on the shoulder, and gave back a little. But they were famine-driven; even in that fitful light Drem could see how their bones stared through their hides; and seeing that there was none against them but one lone shepherd and a dog, they would not be long held from their attack by yelling and lumps of chalk.

They slunk to and fro, dodging the clods he flung at them, and he saw their shining eyes in the moonlight, their lolling tongues and the thick, raised hair of their manes. There was a kind of hideous mirth about them, as though they knew that there could be but one end to the thing, and could afford to laugh.

Already the great grey leader was slinking forward again, his belly almost on the snowy ground, his jaws widening in that obscene grin . . . Drem had no idea how long he had held them off with his lumps of chalk. He had nothing to throw now, except Doli's spear. He caught that up and flung it; but the broad fighting spear was not meant for throwing, and in the

uncertain light it did no more than graze
the leader's shoulder as it flew. He had
nothing left to throw at all now; and the
wolves knew it. This was the kill. Drem
had caught up his own spear and half risen
to his feet, crouching there, his eyes wide
and fixed on the oncoming grey leader.
His mouth was very dry. The old hound
crouched snarling at his side, and behind
him he was aware, though he did not know
how, that the ewe had struggled to her feet
again, bleating in wild pain and terror.

Nearer and nearer, circling warily,
came the grey leader, squirming and
slinking low-bellied over the snow. In the
last moment it seemed to Drem that he had
known this wolf before; and the wolf had
known him. The wicked grin, the welcome
in the savage yellow eyes belonged to a
before-time as well as to now. But then it
had been the wolf who waited for the meeting. Now it was Drem.

Then the great beast gathered himself on

his haunches, and sprang. Drem leapt to meet him, while Cu flung himself with a snarl at the throat of the second wolf, the she-wolf. Even as they came together, there was a distant shout—a burst of shouting—but Drem did not hear it. In all his world there was only himself and his wolf, and old Doli; and the ewe struggling to bring her lamb to birth behind him.

And then not even Doli and the ewe, only himself and his wolf. He had side-slipped as the wolf sprang forward, and his spear took the great brute behind the shoulder and was all but wrenched from his grasp as it turned, yowling, almost in mid leap. Fiery pain slashed at his right shoulder just as it had done before; but he scarcely felt it as he drove his shortened spear home again. He was dragged to his knees, the wolf almost on top of him, tearing at his shoulder, striving to come at his throat. He drove his chin down on to his breast, and stabbed his spear dagger-wise again and again into its body as they rolled together in the snow. The third wolf was on him now; there was a terrible stricken howling—he did not know whether it was himself or his wolf that howled—a worrying and a snarling and a yelling. There was the taste of blood in his mouth, and a darkness flaring into ragged lights before his eyes . . .

And then the yelling was a different yelling, neither his own nor his wolf's; and the lights were the saffron mares'-tails of torches carried by running men—and it was all over. In some unbelievable way it was all over. He was crouching with hanging head in the churned and trampled snow, staring down at the red that blotched and spattered the whiteness. Scarlet on white; Warrior Scarlet; and for a moment he thought hazily that it was the scarlet on the white breast of the swan that had been his first kill. Then his brain cleared somewhat, and he saw that it was blood on snow—hot blood on cold snow, steaming a little in the flaring light of the torches. Old Cu and the she-wolf lay sprawled together, both with their last fight fought, and at a little distance; the third, a young one, snapped and snarled in its death agony, with somebody else's spear

through it. But the torch light fell fullest and fiercest on the body of the great grey leader lying outstretched almost against Drem's knee.

There were men all around him; Whitethroat nuzzling into his face, trying to lick all at the same time the torn and streaming wounds in his right arm and breast and shoulder. Someone was supporting him, and he knew that it was Vortrix; and Vortrix's voice was in his ears, lit with a ringing triumph. 'He has killed his wolf! See, Luga, Urian, a fine Wolf Slaying there has been here! He has killed his wolf!'

'And I think that his wolf has killed him,' Urian said.

But Drem only heard them vaguely and a long way off. 'Look to Doli,' he mumbled. 'The ewe too—she——'

'It is well with the ewe.' That time it was Hunno's voice. 'She needs no looking to.' And suddenly he was aware of the thin crying of a new born lamb; and a moment of swift exultancy leapt in him, not because he had slain the great grey leader, but of all unlikely reasons, because a lamb had come unscathed into the world.

It was the last thing he knew with any clearness for a long time.

XIV

Warrior Scarlet

AFTER that there was a time that Drem remembered only as a darkness and confusion, with two fires burning in it, one in his head and one in his shoulder. Sometimes the confusion thinned a little, and there were faces in it; his mother's face, and Blai's, and Midir the Priest's with its eyes like dark sunlight; and sometimes the face of Vortrix. But he knew that it could not really be so, because all those faces were of the Tribe, and something had come between him and the Tribe, between him and Vortrix—a kind of black gulf. He couldn't remember what it was, and always when he tried to, the confusion came back and all the faces were lost to him again.

And then, like someone waking from a sleep that has been uneasy and full of crowding dreams, he opened his eyes and knew by the angle of the sword of sunlight striking through the smoke hole in the crown of the roof, that it was evening; knew also that he was lying on piled fern, under deerskin rugs in his own sleeping stall, where he had lain before he went down to the Boys' House a whole lifetime ago—or maybe only yesterday. He felt quiet and clean, and he was sharply and shiningly aware of the delicate, fork-tongued flicker of the fire on the hearth, and the golden dust dancing in the beam of sunlight, and the little rhythmic sounds that meant somebody weaving—his mother, or Blai. The hairs of the dappled deer-skin were tickling his neck, and he made to thrust it down, finding to his surprise that he had barely the strength

to fumble his hand clear of
the folds. There was a swift
movement beside him, and Blai
leaned forward and did the thing for him. She bent closer
a moment to look into his face, and then cried out something
—he did not know what, but the sound of it was glad;
and the sounds of weaving stopped and next instant his
mother was kneeling at his side, feeling his forehead, looking
into his face with eyes that looked as though they were aching
in her head, her bright, heavy hair bursting as always out of its
net. 'Small cub! Heart-of-my-heart——' She gave a little laugh
that broke in the middle, and put down her cheek against his.
'You have come back. Soon, quite soon, you will be well again.'

He tried to come up towards her, and press his face in the soft
hollow of her neck as he had used to do when he was small. But
at the first movement, pain tore at his shoulder, where the fire
had been, and he realized that shoulder and breast were
tightly bound. That must be where the wolf had mauled him.
There had been a wolf—or was that only another dream?

Blai had risen, and brought a bowl from the fire, with warm, strong broth in it, and his mother fed him, calling him all the while by the small soft names that the Women's side kept for the smallest of their children. And by and by, when he was already beginning to grow sleepy, she rose and went back to her weaving.

Drem lay still blinking at the disc of singing gold that was the sunset beyond the smoke hole. Then Whitethroat crawled up from where he had been lying at his feet, to thrust his muzzle under the palm of his lord's hand. Drem fondled the great rough head, drawing the twitching ears through his fingers with a small, sharp-edged pleasure in their warm, silken texture. Odd how soft the ears of even the harshest coated dogs were. 'Greetings, brother,' he said. He could hear the sounds of his mother weaving, and somebody scouring the cook-pots—that must be Blai—and the buzzing, sing-song snore of the Grandfather who must have fallen asleep over the fire after his supper, as he so often used to do. There were other sounds behind these, too, little formless, green, trickling sounds; a dripping under the eaves. An indefinable sense of relief and quickening reached him even under his piled deerskins and told him that at last the thaw had come.

The faint, familiar rattle of the loom weights teased at his ears. He wondered what his mother was weaving, and manage to turn his head to see. The big standing loom by the door had been set up afresh quite lately; there was a new piece of cloth just begun on it—scarlet cloth.

Was it for the Grandfather? Or for Drustic? he wondered. Drustic must have had the piece that she had woven for him, Drem, a year ago. Vaguely he seemed to remember something heard in one of his dreams: the Grandfather saying with the familiar, wide-nostrilled snort, 'Let you wait to see that the boy will live, before you set the loom up and maybe have your trouble for nothing!' But that did not seem to fit in anywhere; and he was too tired to think it out, too tired and spent even to care that the scarlet could never be for him. He had spent

so much caring over that, that his caring seemed to have grown numb.

All that he cared for now, was to sleep.

He slept that night, a long, dark sleep without dreams, and woke at dawn to hear the thaw still dripping under the eaves, and feel the life running back into his own torn and battered body, and with the life, old unhappiness, old complications that he did not want to look at as yet; the beginning of a half formed idea that there was something odd about his being in the home house-place at all.

But in a little, he slept again, while the rest of the household woke around him; and when he roused the second time, they had already scattered to the work of the day, Drustic to see to the beasts, his mother to the store shed, even the Grandfather gathering his huge frame together and hobbling out to see how much snow had gone from the world since yesterday. He was alone save for Whitethroat, and for Blai grinding the day's corn beside the doorway, until suddenly a pony whinnied in the entrance porch and somebody came ducking in over the threshold.

Drem turned his head towards the doorway, thinking to see his mother or Drustic; and saw instead Vortrix with something that looked like a brindled wolfskin under his arm.

He gave a little croaking cry, and fumbled his hand clear of the coverings, and next instant Vortrix had come striding across the house-place and flung down the bundle and was squatting beside him with Drem's hand in both of his. 'My brother—oh my brother, they told me that you were come back into your body.'

Drem looked at him, frowning a little. 'I thought—I dreamed—that you were here before.'

'One may dream many things, with a wolf-mauled shoulder such as that,' was all Vortrix said; but looking into his square steady face with the very blue eyes, Drem knew that it had not been a dream.

'That was a great fight—a great Wolf Slaying!' Vortrix said;

and his eyes were shining. 'I shall not forget how we came down the slope at Whitethroat's tail—running we were, running until our hearts were like to burst—and saw you down there, with a whole pack it seemed upon you, and the snow trampled and scarlet as though two wolf-packs had fought there. Aiee! They speak your name round the fires in the village, these nights!'

Things came rushing back to Drem as he listened; things that had been hovering on the fringe of his memory since last evening, but they brought with them no triumph in his Wolf Slaying. He was too weak for triumph. 'Doli!' he said. 'What of Doli?'

'Doli went to his own place, back to the Earth Mother, five days since,' Vortrix said. 'The little man was worn through, and there was the breathing-fever on him.'

There was a small harsh pause; and then Vortrix laid Drem's gaunt hand back on his breast with a kind of clumsy gentleness, and took up the brindled wolfskin. 'See, I have brought you your wolfskin. I have scraped it and begun the curing, lest it should be beyond curing before you could come to it. But now it can wait until you are strong again to finish the task.'

Drem looked from him to the wolfskin and back again; and his heart began to beat heavily, unevenly, though he did not as yet understand—did not dare to understand. Vortrix was brushing aside the harsh, brindled hair at the shoulder of the pelt, high up near the base of the neck, showing him a scar that there was on it, a place where the hair had not grown again over an old wound, saying something about his own wolf. 'It is your own wolf!' Vortrix was saying. 'Your own wolf! Here is the mark from the first time!'

Drem stared at the puckered, hairless line on the pelt, and his hand on the soft deerskin coverings clenched into a fist. 'I did not so much as scratch the hide of my wolf.'

'Na,' Vortrix said, 'but I did. A brindled dog wolf, and I wounded it here, high on the shoulder; here where I found the scar when I came to flay this one, nine days since!'

They looked at each other with the great wolfskin lying half across Drem's body between them. And Drem's hand crept

down to rest on the harsh hairiness of it. 'It was between him and me in the first place. My heart is glad that I have slain my wolf, even though—it is too late.'

Vortrix said, 'It is not too late. Do you not see that there is scarlet on the loom for you already?'

Drem stared at him, his breath caught in his throat. Vortrix could not really have said that; it must be that he was still dreaming . . . But Vortrix was saying it again, bending close over him, suddenly ablaze with his own eagerness. 'I thought they would have told you! Wake up, Drem, you have slain your wolf, and your place waits for you among the New Spears!'

Drem shook his head, denying it because he did not dare to believe it. 'Many times the Half People kill their wolves as I killed that one. There can be but one Wolf Slaying, and—I failed in mine.' His voice dried up into a cracked whisper. 'It is not true; it could not be true.'

Neither of them was aware that Blai had left her grinding and stolen out like a grey shadow, leaving them alone. They had not noticed that she was there. And the only sound in the world was the drip of the thaw under the eaves.

'I am your blood brother, not your sorest enemy,' Vortrix said at last. 'Why should I tell you this thing if it were not true? Listen, Drem. Three days since, it was spoken of round the Council Fire. It is true, I swear to you by—my own spear hand that it is true.'

And Drem knew that it was so. He reached out and caught the other's wrist, straining up from the piled fern, heedless of the pain that clawed at his breast and shoulder. 'How then——? I—I do not understand. Tell me what passed at the Council Fire—all that passed——'

Vortrix pressed him back again. 'Let you lie still; if you burst the wounds, I shall be blamed . . . See then; when I had flayed the wolf and found the scar on it, then I went to Dumnorix my father, and showed him the scar as I have showed it to you.' Vortrix grinned. 'It is useful, now and then, to be the Chieftain's son. And my father laughed that great laugh in his

chest, and said, "Sa. The cub was always a fighter, from his first day in the Boys' House, as I remember; and the Men's side may have need of its fighting men one day." And so when the Spring Council gathered three nights since, he took and showed the pelt to the Men's side of the Clan, beside the Council Fire, and said, "See, the Shining One has sent to Drem One-arm his Wolf Slaying again, and this time he has not failed!" Then there was much talk, and some among the elders said—even as you—that there can be but one Wolf Slaying. And at last the thing went to Midir where he sat gone-away-inside-himself beside the fire. So Midir came back and looked out of his eyes again, and said, "I have seen the wounds in the boy's shoulder; they cover the scar of that first Wolf Slaying, so that the scar of that first Wolf Slaying is no more. The thing was not finished, and now it is finished; therefore let one among you be found to stand for the boy, beside Cathlan his Grandfather, on the Day of the New Spears, for the Sun Lord and the Lords of the Tribe and the Hunting Trail have shown that they would have it so." And truly I think that there would have been more than one come forward to stand with Cathlan; but before any other man could move, Talore sprang up—you know how swift he is, like a wild cat when it springs—and stood there before the Clan, smiling so that his lip curled up over those great strong dog-teeth; and he cried out: "Seven summers ago, I found the boy curled under the roots of an oak tree, like a wolf cub himself, far into the Wild, where he had run from his own kind, fearing to fail in this very thing; a small, hairless cub and very much afraid, but fierce even then, and bit my finger to the bone before I had him out of his lair. Because he was small and valiant, and one-handed even as I am myself, my heart turned to him; and I promised him that night that when he had slain his wolf and the time came for him to stand before the Clan on the Day of New Spears, I would stand for him beside Cathlan his Grandfather. Therefore the thing was settled seven summers ago." (You never told me that, Drem.) And then all the elders—all the Men's side looked at each other and

nodded their heads, and said, "Aiee! It is well!" And Maelgan and I and the rest of us drummed our spears on our shields and made a great noise—and so the thing was done.'

Drem lay with his eyes fixed on the other's face, trying to lay hold of what had happened and draw it in and make it part of himself. He began to laugh at Vortrix's attempt to mimic Talore's swift dark vehemence; and then, because he was to be let in to his own world after all, returned to the company of his own kind after all, and because he was very weak, found the laughter breaking in his throat, and hid his face in his sound arm and cried.

The days went by, and Drem grew steadily stronger. Every third day Midir came and pointed the Fingers of Power at the wounds in his breast and arm and shoulder, driving new life into them; and his mother and Blai dressed them with salves made of yarrow and comfrey and the little pink centaury that grew on the High Chalk, reciting the proper charms over them as they did so, so that they healed cleanly, leaving only the puckered, thunder-purple scars behind. There was a third woman in the house-place, these days, for Drustic had brought home the plump, pink Cordaella to be his wife; but she took no part in tending Drem. It was not that she was unwilling, but the only time she tried to bring him his food bowl, Blai took it from her, showing her teeth like a young vixen; so that Drem, watching in bewilderment, thought that he had been wrong in hoping that Cordaella would be kind to Blai, he should rather have hoped that Blai would be kind to Cordaella.

As soon as he was strong enough, he crawled out to sit in the sunshine before the house-place doorway, and work at his wolf-skin pegged out on the ground there, curing it with herbs crushed in salt, and working in grey-goose grease until it was as supple as the finest deerskin. He wanted to be quiet, in those spring days, while suddenly there were washed-faced primroses in the hollow banks of the driftway, and the alders by the brook were dropping their little dark catkins into the water; he wanted a kind of threshold time between one thing and the next.

There was something else, besides his wolfskin, that he must have ready before the time came for him to stand with the New Spears before the Clan. And one evening when the supper stew was finished, he took down from its place among the smoky rafters, the heavy bronze and bull's-hide shield that had been the Grandfather's and would be his after all when the Feast of Beltane was over; and squatting beside the low fire with the rest, fell to fixing the shoulder harness of pony-hide straps, such as he had carried his buckler on in the Boys' House.

The Grandfather, looking up for a while from his bygone battles in the fire, eyed him as he worked, with a grudging interest that increased until he was leaning far forward to see more clearly how the straps went. 'Sa, this is a cunning thing,' he said at last. 'I see—ah, I see. Not even Talore carries his shield that way.'

'No need,' Drem said round the strap he held in his teeth. 'Talore has his shield arm almost to the wrist.'

The old man glanced up at him under the shaggy, grey-gold jut of brow. 'Why did you never tell me of that promise between Talore and you, seven summers ago?'

Drem did not answer at once. There were hard and hurting things that he could have said to the Grandfather about that. Once he would have said them, but not now. He spat out the strap and turned the buckler round to come at it from the other side. 'It is good to have a secret, when one is small. With a secret in one's chest, one feels larger.'

Drustic, mending a piece of plough harness, looked up with his slow grin. 'There was never anything needed to make you feel large, little brother.'

'Surely the cub who comes behind so fine a brother as mine— with so long a whip—has need of *anything* that makes him feel larger,' Drem said with an answering grin. 'Let you throw me over that piece of thong.'

And then it was the day before Beltane. Time for Drem to go down to the Boys' House. He did not eat when the rest of

the household ate that morning; for a New Spear must go fasting to his initiation. He washed all over in the brook, a ritual washing, and came up naked and shining and scarred, to stand beside the hearth stone, while his mother and Blai belted on his new kilt of scarlet cloth—Warrior Scarlet; he felt it lapping about him like a flame—and settled the finely dressed wolfskin over his shoulder, belting that also about his narrow waist with a strap of leather dyed violet blue and bright with studs of bronze, and combed his hair and bound it back with thongs; so that when all was done he stood up like a warrior for battle, but with no war paint on his face, and no weapon in his hand. He looked up and saw the Grandfather's shield hanging in its usual place. Tonight they would take it down and lay it beside the hearth with his new war spear that he had not yet seen; tonight when he was—where? No one who had been that way before him, not Drustic, not even Vortrix, could tell him. They were bound by the oath of silence, as tomorrow, he also would be bound.

Blai was doing something to the fold of his wolfskin; he looked down at her, but saw only the top of her bent head, before she turned away without looking up. She never looked at him now. She had stopped looking at him when he began to get better. She did anything he wanted, willingly, but she didn't look at him any more, and he felt vaguely hurt.

But now it was time for him to go. He knelt and set his hand on the Grandfather's thigh as custom demanded; and as custom demanded, the old man put his huge, blue-veined one over it and said: 'Go forth a boy and come home a warrior.' Then his mother kissed him on the forehead with the same words, and took him to the threshold and sent him out with a light blow between the shoulders. Whitethroat followed him as usual; and at the foot of the driftway he parted from the great hound as he had done so many times before, and went on to the Boys' House alone.

There was a little wind running through the grass, and the hawthorn bushes of the lower slopes were in flower, the scent of

them coming and going like breath, and a small brown bird flashed through the alder brake ahead of him. It seemed to Drem suddenly that the world was very kind. He had known its beauty often; a fierce and shining beauty like that of his great white swan, but he had not had time for the kindness. After this, maybe he would not have time for it again, but he thought that he would not quite forget . . .

He had been wondering what it would be like in the Boys' House, with the New Spears who were not of his year at all, but the year behind him. But he found that his name had become great in the Boys' House, greater even than after he fought Bragon's Hound at the King-making; and his companions were more interested in the purple scars on his shoulder than in the fact that he belonged to last year. But they had none of them much time or thought to spend on anything save what lay before them.

There were long rituals of strengthening and purification to be gone through under the eye of old Kylan; and Kylan himself painted the white clay patterns of initiation on their foreheads. And when all was done and made ready, they sat in silence about the low fire in the Boys' House, from which the younger boys had been sent away, listening to the sounds of life going on in the village around them; and even Vran, the stupidest of them, was afraid.

At last the sounds of life began to fall away, and in the quiet a distant voice or the barking of a dog sounded unnaturally loud. They heard feet and then more feet going down towards the centre of the village. And then Kylan rose and ranged them before him and looked them over with those wolf-yellow eyes of his, and said: 'So, it is time. Remember the things that I have taught you, children.' And to Drem he said: 'You also, who have already had a year to forget them.'

And they ducked out through the low doorway, and stood blinking in the sudden blast of sunlight after the gloom of the Boys' House.

The familiar ritual that came then seemed not quite real to

Drem, like an echo of something real that had come before. He saw the faces of the Clan as the line of New Spears went winding down towards the space beside the Council Fire. He saw the Chieftain's face and the Priest's face with the sun behind its eyes; he heard the ritual questions and the ritual answers.

'Who is this that ye bring before me?'

'It is a boy that he may die in his boyhood and return a Warrior to his Tribe . . .'

But he had lived through it all so vividly, a year ago, that now it seemed to have little meaning, less reality than the pressure of his own spear shaft against his forehead as he crouched in the alder brake . . .

And now, one behind another, looking neither to right nor left, they were following Midir out from the village and away up the long slope into the eye of the setting sun, while behind them the women raised the death chant, 'Ochone! Ochone!'

The fires of the sunset still flamed behind the Chalk as they came up over the broad shoulder of the Hill of Gathering, passing close by the grave mound of the champion who slept on its crest, and dipped down again on the far side towards the hollow place among the hills where the warriors of the Tribe were made. And the hollow was brimming with shadows, so that as they looked down the ancient turf circle with its nine thorn trees seemed drowned in them as though it lay under water. They dropped down out of the sunset into the shadows that rose about them and closed over their heads.

The place seemed empty of all life; lost in its own solitude. But as they drew near a horn brayed somewhere ahead of them from within the thorn trees, and out of the shadows there sprang up smoky golden light; and out of the brightness figures came filing to meet them. Naked and golden in the light of the torches, hooded with the heads of animals; the animals that the Tribesmen hunted—the wolf, the wild, black boar, the red fox and the brindled badger. They closed round the boys in

silence, and turned back with them
towards the half moon of piled brushwood that had been set
up screening the entrance to the sacred circle.

Here there was a kind of low bier of turfs spread with a huge
red oxhide, and still without a word, they took the youngest of
the New Spears and laid him upon it as for sacrifice. One with
the head of a badger took up something that lay beside the
bier, and for an instant Drem's breath caught in his throat.
Then he saw that it was only a wooden haft set with slim bright
pins of bronze, and realized that this must be the time and place
to receive the warrior tattooing of the Men's side.

It was a long time before it came, last of all, to Drem's turn;
and when he flung back the wolfskin from his shoulder and
gave himself proudly into the hands of the tattooers, it had
grown quite dark, and looking up past the tawny flare of the
torches and the snarling masks of those who bent over him, he
saw the stars very far off and uncaring, and already, behind the
Hill of Gathering, the silvery snail-shine spreading before the
rising moon. The man with the badger's mask took up his tools
for the seventh time, and began to paint the zigzag and flowing
lines on the skin of his breast and shoulders with a wisp of
sheep's wool dipped in his woad pot, and then to prick along
them with the sharp bronze pins, grinding in more woad as he
went. It felt like being stung by a crawling trail of insects, and
where the lines crossed the newly healed scars the insects
became hornets, and it was all he could do, lying there with
shut teeth, not to flinch under the small, merciless, stinging
points. And all the while he was knowing that this was the easy
part; that the real thing, the dark and terrible and shining
thing was yet to come.

Save for that first blaring of a war horn as they drew near the Holy Place, complete silence had held the scene; not even a night bird's call or the whisper of a little wind over the turf to break the stillness; but now Drem became aware of a sound— no, a sensation rather than a sound, a rhythmic pulsing that might almost have been his own heart. But even as he listened, it grew and strengthened, changing—changing—from a pulse beat to a fierce, confusing rhythm that made Drem think of that harvest magic of the Dark People, beaten out with an open hand on the sheepskin drums. It never grew loud, that drumming, but moment by moment it became more intense, more potent, until it seemed to Drem to be inside himself, in his head, in his heart, so that he could no longer think clearly, like a man who was drunk with much mead.

He was vaguely aware of getting up from the bier and standing with the other New Spears, the proud new patterns smarting like fire on his breast—on all their breasts, for while the drumming lasted they all seemed to be part of each other, so that each felt the sting of the others' wounds and the sharp, confused fear in the others' hearts—and then, suddenly, as though it had been cut by the swift downward flash of a sword-blade, the drumming stopped, and there was silence again; silence that was more potent, more clearly and irresistibly a call than any blare of war horns could have been.

The New Spears looked at each other, their blood jumping oddly within them. And while the silence yet seemed to tingle, two of the beast-headed figures took the youngest of the New Spears and led him to the shielded entrance of the sacred circle, and in a while came back alone.

Then the drumming started again.

Again and again came the tingling silence, and each time another of the New Spears went away into the sacred circle, and none of them ever came back.

And then the drumming ceased for the last time of all, and the call was for Drem. He stepped forward, with a sense of moving in a dream, the two beast-headed figures on either side

of him, out from the shelter of the brushwood curve, and turned to the entrance of the sacred circle. There was light, a smoky dazzle of torchlight among the thorn trees; he glimpsed figures like the figures of a dream—beast-headed as the others had been, striped badger mask and upreared antlers and snarling grey wolf muzzle—and the torchlight under the thorn trees making the white blossom shine against the moony darkness, and the sparks flying upwards. But his whole awareness was caught and held by the tall figure of Midir the Priest, naked as the rest, and crested with the folded wings of the golden eagle, standing in the midst of the circle, in the very heart of the brightness. He was no longer aware of the men on either side of him, not aware of walking forward, until suddenly he was close before Midir; not aware of anything but Midir's eyes.

But Midir's eyes, that were like dark sunlight, were no longer eyes at all. They had contracted to two pin points of intense yellowish light, and the light ate into his very soul . . . Yet even as he gazed and gazed, his whole spirit caught up and held powerless, they were eyes again; yet such eyes as he had never seen before. Eyes that burned with a fire beyond fire, a blasting and shrivelling glory; and he was aware of a face growing up around them, and a figure, but not Midir's. He had forgotten Midir. This was One who leaned on a spear as vast as the shaft of light when the sun strikes through storm clouds. And the face——? Afterward Drem only remembered that looking into it was like trying to look into the sun at noonday. He was aware of a shining and unbearable glory, a power that seemed to beat about him in fiery waves; and he knew in a moment of terror and ecstasy that he was looking into the face of the Sun Lord himself, which no man might see and live. The voice of a thousand war horns rang in his ears, and he was flying forward, plunging, swooping like a hawk, like a shooting star, into the heart of the singing brightness, the heart of all things.

XV

The Flower of the Sun

THE warmth of the sun was on his body, and above him great grey and white clouds were drifting across a sky that had in it already a hint of evening. There was a lazy, blustering wind blowing—a south wind, it must be, for there was the salt of the sea in it: the honey of hawthorn flowers in it too, and garlic, which was odd and did not seem to fit with the rest. He felt as though he had been on a very long journey; so weary that he wanted to do nothing ever again but go on lying on his back and staring up past the lazy clouds into the blue heights of heaven. But he had a feeling that somebody had called him by name, and he stirred himself to look about him.

He was lying at the heart of the ancient circle, and the other New Spears with him; lying with their feet to the centre and their heads towards the ring of thorn trees, like the rays of a seven pointed star. And instantly he remembered the splendour and the terror that had been. The warrior patterns on his breast and shoulders were sore and stiff, and as he moved, a knot of dried garlic flowers fell from his breast, where they must have been set to keep his body safe while he was away from it.

The others were stirring now, sitting up one by one and looking about them. Nothing remained of last night's mystery; no beast- and bird-headed figures among the thorn trees; no smoky blaze of torches; nothing left of the supremely beautiful and terrible moment when each had looked into the face of the

Shining One—only Midir the Priest, sitting peacefully under one of the thorn trees and gone away small inside himself, with his bull's-hide robe about him and his thin, grey hair wisping out in the wind from under the eagle head-dress, and the amber sun cross on his breast catching and losing the light with his old, quiet breathing, and a few fallen hawthorn petals lying in his lap, as though he had sat there unmoving all night.

Then as they stirred and rubbed their eyes and looked about them with an air of having lost something, the old Priest stirred also, looking out of his eyes again, and brought out from under his cloak a bowl of black lathe-turned shale. 'Sa, it is over,' he said, and smiled a little, the bowl between his hands. 'Come now to me, ye who return again out of the West, new and weak as thy mothers brought thee into the world afore-time. Come now and drink, and grow strong again.'

One after another, still a little dazed, they got themselves to their feet and went to him, and took the bowl he held up, passing it among themselves from one to another. There was milk in the bowl, and other things in the milk. What they were Drem never knew, things that tasted bitter, with an under-taste that clung evilly to the back of one's throat after the milk was swallowed—but new strength ran through him as he drank, and some of the weariness fell away.

'Now ye are warriors and men of the Clan, and of the Tribe,' Midir said when they had all drunk. 'Now ye have seen those things which are forbidden to all save the Priest kind and the warrior at his initiation, and which none may speak of afterwards. Therefore now ye shall swear the silence, by the ancient threefold oath of the Golden People, that no boy not yet come to his manhood shall ever learn from you the things that lie before him.'

And so, each in turn, kneeling before the old priest, they swore, just as the warriors had sworn fealty to the new King. 'If I break faith, may the green earth gape and swallow me, may the grey seas burst out and overwhelm me, may the sky of stars fall and crush me out of life for ever.'

It was near to sunset again when they came down the last sloping shoulder of the Chalk towards the village, following Midir, one behind another; and their long shadows ran away before them, pointing the way home.

The village was swarming with life, the poor thin sheep and cattle left from the famine winter all driven in close to wait for the Beltane fires. As the New Spears drew nearer, suddenly the voice of a war horn rang to and fro between the hills, and a throng of young warriors burst out from among the huts and came, tossing up their weapons as they ran, to close around the New Spears and swing back with them, shouting and chanting, towards the village.

How often Drem had seen this triumphal return of the New Spears that was the start of the Beltane Festival. How often he had looked forward to the fierce and shining day when he would be one of those for whom the Clan roared in their rejoicing. Then had come last year; last year that was not good to think about; and now, after all, against all seeming possibility the fierce and shining day had come, and he was returning out of the Sunset like a warrior from victory. And he cried out inside himself, 'It is real, it is true! I am a warrior like my brothers,' and could not quite believe it.

Afterwards, that sunset time, the final ceremonies of his initiation remained with Drem only as a blur, shining but without form; but out of it stood up small, clear-edged memories. He remembered the heat of the Council Fire on his cheek as he stood beside it to receive his weapons. He remembered the Grandfather towering over him as he towered over most people when he cared to stand erect, setting the great new war spear in his hand with a grumbling, 'There, take it. Did I not always say that the boy would make a warrior?' and a golden glare under his eyebrows for anyone who dared to contradict him. He remembered Talore's swift, dark smile lifting his lip over the strong dog-teeth as he raised the ancient bronze and bull's-hide shield. 'Small fierce cub, was it well that I found you under the oak tree, seven summers ago?' And the proud smart of the

shoulder harness as the heavy shield dragged its straps down on the lately healed wolf scars and the sore new lines of tattooing. He remembered the flash of his spear blade as he tossed it up in salute to the setting sun, and brought it crashing across his shield. He remembered Whitethroat's growling song of gladness at finding him again, and the taste of the piece of rib that he and Vortrix shared between them, sitting shoulder to shoulder, when the ceremonies were over, and the cooking pits had been opened, and the feasting began.

But Drem was to remember the day of his Warrior Scarlet for another thing; a thing that he did not as yet dream of, as the dusk deepened into the dark, and the Council Fire sank to red embers.

Save for the Council Fire, all the fires in the village had been quenched before the feasting started, and when that too had sunk, and the last red embers been scattered and stamped out under the heels of the young warriors, the village was a village without fire, dark save for the glow of a great, broom-yellow moon just shaking clear of the Chalk.

With the dying of the last fire, the Feast of New Spears was over, and the Feast of Beltane was begun; and it was time to raise the New Fire, the Living Fire. A strangeness came over the village, as it came every year between the fires; and it was in silence and a breath-caught expectancy and something very like fear that presently they laid aside their weapons and Clan and Half People together wound their way out of the village and up the Hill of Gathering, driving with them a young red bull garlanded for sacrifice with vervain and green broom and whitethorn blossom.

They thronged the crest of the hill, a crowd of shadows touched by the silver of the moon, no sound among them save the wind hushing through the furze and whitethorn bushes; and in their midst the twin stacks of the Beltane fires, dark on one side, brushed on the other with that same silver of the moon, waiting as the whole night waited, for the Wonder.

Now the red bull who must die for the rest of the herd had

played his part, and certain of the warriors were laying aside their cloaks and stepping forward to the trailing raw-hide ropes of the fire drill that stood reared beside the stacks.

On and on, as the moon rose higher into the glimmering, wind-streaked sky, they worked the fire drill, one team of nine taking over as another tired, while Midir, with the blood of the red bull on his breast and forehead, stood by to add his magic to their labour. Team followed team, while the whole awareness of the watching crowd, blent into one spearhead of intense concentration, was fixed upon the dark point where the sharpened spindle whirled in its socket, every soul waiting, waiting for the Wonder, half fearful, as they were half fearful every year, that this year the Wonder would not come.

Always the New Spears and the youngest warriors tried to hang back till towards the end, each eager to be in the team that actually woke the spark; and several teams had followed each other, when Drem, standing by among his own year, felt Vortrix's hand on his shoulder. 'See, they are beginning to tire,' Vortrix said, 'and it is in my mind that the fire is not far off. Our turn now, my brother. Urian—Maelgan——'

They stepped forward, the rest of last year's warriors with them, and three of the New Spears, to make up the team; each taking up his stand beside one of the toiling men. The hide ropes changed hands, the old team fell back, and Drem and Vortrix, facing each other through the dark framework, with the rest ranged behind them, took up the swift, rhythmic pull and release, pull and release, the long step forward and the long swing back, that set the fire drill spinning. The hide rope thrummed under Drem's hand, the whirring squeal of the drill was in his ears, and the sense of being one with his own kind again, joined with his Spear Brothers in this, that was the very life and death of the Clan, rose hot in his breast until he felt it pressing out against the smarting patterns of his new manhood. He had tried so hard, down there through the ceremonies by the Council Fire, to believe in what was happening, and somehow never quite succeeded. And now suddenly it was

all real and came piercing home to him, and he could have wept, as he had wept when Vortrix first told him that he was to be let into his own world after all.

In the same instant he caught the smell of charring, and from the sharp nose of the spindle a thread of smoke wisped up into the moonlight.

His eyes flew to meet those of his blood brother, as Vortrix also looked up; and in the hushed moment the excitement and the triumph and the swift, awed delight leapt between them like a shout. They were together in this thing, and the Wonder was coming, and it was good—everything was good. Instinctively they quickened the rhythm of the pull, and the squeal of the drill grew higher and more urgent.

The thread of smoke had become a whisping frond, a feather; suddenly a spark flew out to fall upon the dry moss with which the socket was packed, cling there an instant like a red jewel, and go out. Another followed, and another; and a soft, long-drawn gasp of relief and exultation burst from the watching throng as a little clear tongue of flame sprang up, yellow as a broom flower in the moony darkness.

Old Midir stirred as one rousing quietly from a thousand-year sleep, and brought from within his bull's-hide robe a torch of plaited straw, and bent to dip it into the flame. Then, drawing himself erect, he began to whirl it in the air until it burst into swooping circles of fire, as though a bird of flame flew about and about his head. And his deep throbbing cry rang out over the Hill of Gathering. 'Fire is come again! Behold, O ye people, O all ye people, there is fire again in the world of man!'

This year also, the Wonder had come! Roar on roar of fierce rejoicing beat up from the crowd, and as the old priest went from one stack to the other, kindling them from the torch in his hand, they broke into the chant of the Reborn Fire. 'We were in darkness and fire came again to us, the Red Fire, the Red Flower, the Flower of the Sun . . .' The little fork-tongued flames ran crackling through the brushwood and laid hold of the bigger branches, flaring up to light the eager,

crowding faces of Golden and Dark People, and the Half People between, to flicker in men's eyes and jink on copper arm-ring and bronze, leaf-bladed spear, and kindle the eyes of the hounds to green lamps against the moon-watered dark.

Higher and higher leapt the flames, sending their fierce and fitful glare far out over the Hill of Gathering, warming the threshold of the great, quiet mound where the nameless champion slept with his copper sword beside him. And with the flames, the crowd's excitement mounted too. The young warriors sprang forward and began to whirl and stamp in the fierce glare between the fires, to the rhythm that the girls clapped for them, until with a lowing and a trampling out of the darkness, the first of the driven herds came pelting up. And then a yet wilder turmoil broke out, a chaos of gaunt, up-tossed heads, horns flashing in the firelight, an uproar of shouting and bellowing, barking and bleating, as the terrified sheep and cattle were driven through between the fires by their yelling and laughing herdsmen, that they might be protected and made fruitful for the year to come. Lastly the half wild pony herds were driven through, the mares with their foals running at heel, in a flood of streaming manes and trampling hooves; and the tumult was ripped across by their terrified neighing.

The uproar was sinking a little, by and by, when Drem, re-turning from helping to gather in some of the ponies, caught sight of little dark Erp on the edge of the fire glow, with the dog Asal beside him. 'Erp!' he called. 'Erp!' and turned in his tracks, threading his way towards him through the shifting throng of men and beasts.

The boy stood to wait his coming, but did not look round. And when they stood side by side, he asked: 'Well then, what is it that you want with me?'

Drem looked at him, half puzzled, half already beginning to understand, while Asal and Whitethroat sniffed muzzles in the way of old friends. 'You have the dog, then,' he said at last. It was not what he had meant to say.

'Aye, I have the dog.'

Drem waited a moment, then, as it seemed the other had nothing more to say: 'Let you tell me of Doli.'

'Doli is gone back to the Dark. There is no more to tell.'

Another pause, full of the shouts of men and the lowing of scattered cattle—a fine job it would be to get them rounded up again. Drem looked down, a frown between his coppery brows, at the boy beside him. But Erp's face was shut fast in the firelight, his own gaze caught between the pricked ears of his dog.

'At least let you tell me where they have laid him,' Drem said.

The little dark shepherd looked up then, looked him full in the face for almost the first time in their lives, then let his gaze slide downwards. 'What is it to the Golden People where Tah-Nu's children lay their dead?' He whistled Asal to heel, and turned away about the business of the sheep.

Drem made a swift movement as though to catch him, then checked. What was the use? He shrugged and swung on his heel—to find himself face to face with Luga standing close by and looking on. 'Even the great Drem One-arm cannot hunt in two worlds at once,' Luga said.

'If Luga viper-tongue does not have a care, he will not hunt long in any world!' Drem retorted furiously, and thrust past him with his nose in the air, and went shouldering back to the fire.

The flames were sinking, and the warriors and their women who wished for sons in the coming year had for the most part already leapt hand in hand through the fire; and now some of

202

the young warriors who had no wives as yet had begun to take
the girls of their choice out of the Women's side—girls with
star-wort and the magic vervain in their hair—to leap with
them for the same purpose. Just as Drem reached the forefront
of the crowd again, Vortrix had pulled out from among her
own kind a tall, laughing girl with bright hair round her head.
They cleared the fire easily, the girl shrilling like a curlew, and
scattered a few hot embers on the edge as they landed. And
Drem, watching, thought that little Eyes-and-Ears had spoken
the truth; she was indeed fair, the girl that Vortrix had under
his cloak.

And now, before the fire sank too low, it was time to be taking
home the New Fire to rekindle the dark hearths for another
year; and in ones and twos the youngest grown men in every
household began to come forward to take their fire; those whose
homes were in the village merely dipping a branch into the
flames and running with it streaming out in rags of smoking
brightness behind, while those whose homes were the outland
farms and the herdsmen's and shepherds' bothies among the
Chalk took carefully chosen embers and stowed them in fire-
pots. It dawned on Drem, watching, that it was no longer for
Drustic to carry home the New Fire, but for himself.

He went in search of the Grandfather to tell him.

He found the Grandfather sitting defiantly on a pile of cut
turfs, with a horn of heather beer on his knee, with Drem's
mother and Cordaella hovering over him, and Drustic standing
by at a safe distance. 'You should come home now,' Drem's

203

mother was saying. 'It grows late, and so much heather beer is not good for your belly. You will be ill, and then I must tend you.'

The Grandfather was scowling at all of them under his thick, grey-gold brows. 'I am old, and it is not good for my belly that I do not have what I wish! What I wish is to be left in peace to enjoy myself, on this, the night that the youngest son of my youngest son becomes a man. The Fire will burn for a long while yet. Woman, I shall remain here so long as I choose, and *when* I choose, then Drustic shall bring me home. Let Drem go now and carry home the New Fire, that the hearth may be bright when I choose to come!'

And so in a little, Drem was loping back along the moonlit flanks of the Chalk, with the red seeds of the New Fire glowing in the fire-pot his mother had given him, under his wolfskin.

The steading lay quiet in the moonlight as he came up the driftway between the little irregular barley plots, pausing once to blow gently on the glowing embers in his fire-pot. As he came through the gate gap in the steading hedge, he saw Blai in the house-place doorway, sitting sideways against the rowan wood doorpost, with her head drooping as though she were very tired. He had forgotten that she must be at home; he had not missed the sight of her among the other girls about the Beltane fires. The wind fell away between one long, soft gust and another, and in the moment's stillness the shadows and the moonlight were sharply pied as a magpie's feathers; the shadows of the birch tree lay all across the threshold, across Blai's skirt and her hands that lay palm upward, empty, in her lap.

Whitethroat padded ahead, across the moon-washed garth, and thrust his muzzle against her neck, and she started and looked up, then rose to her feet. She had taken off the woollen net that usually bound her hair, and it hung about her neck and shoulders like black smoke. There were no flowers in it, no star-wort nor magic vervain. 'Drem,' she said, a little questioningly.

'I have brought the New Fire,' Drem said.

'Where are the others?'

'The Grandfather would not come away yet. They will be here in a while; but I have come now, to bring the New Fire.'

Not really aware that he did so, he held out the fire-pot towards her in a gesture of sharing. They stood with it between them, their heads bent to peer into it, like a pair of children holding a miracle cupped between their hands. The red seeds of the fire glowed in the darkness of the pot; Drem blew on them gently and the seeds brightened, casting a faint glow around them.

'Come, let us wake the fire on the hearth,' said Blai.

It was very dark in the house-place, with the moonlight shut out, a waiting darkness. They had to grope their way to the hearth. Kneeling beside it, Drem blew on the spark until it grew strong, and Blai dipped in a dry twig, and as they watched, suddenly there was a slender bud of flame at the tip of the twig. Then she kindled a piece of dry birch bark on the hearth, and then another and another, and dropped in the twig as the flame reached her fingers.

Drem blew on the little tender new flames, on the birch bark whose crumbling edges were suddenly strung with red jewels; then sat back on his heels, as the fire quickened and spread, watching the pale, eager tongues and petals of flame spring up out of the dark.

'It is like a flower,' Blai said very softly, feeding it with bigger and bigger bits of wood. 'A flower of the Sun.'

And they looked at each other, in the first firelight, both aware of having been joined in something potent and lovely.

'Blai,' Drem said after a while. 'Blai, why were you here?'

'I—saw you come back with the New Spears.' Blai set a piece of wild pear branch with infinite care in the midst of the fire. 'And then I came away. I had things to do.'

'What things could you do, without fire to see by?'

'The moon is very bright,' Blai said.

There was a small silence. The new flames fluttered on the

hearth, and a long sigh of wind came over the shoulder of the Chalk and brushed across the thatch, and Whitethroat, who had settled himself beside the hearth, stretched out and began to lick his paws. At last Drem said: 'You were not doing anything when I came.' And then, as she still remained silent— 'Blai, why *did* you come away?'

She looked up then, but the stillness in her never stirred. 'What place have I yonder with the Women's side? I have no place among the maidens of the Tribe. I am not one with them, I am not one with the Half People either. It is better that I come away . . .'

It was as though her words called to something in Drem; something that called back in recognition and greeting. Suddenly he was aware of her as he had been only once before, but more strongly and clearly now, out of a new compassion, a new power of seeing that had grown in him through his outcast year: Blai, who was not quite a handmaid nor yet quite a daughter in his home, who had no dowry of cattle nor any beauty to take its place and make her desirable in the eyes of some young warrior. For a moment it was only compassion, and then quite suddenly and simply he understood that he and Blai belonged together, like to like; that no other girl could ever come as near to him as Blai could do, because she knew the things that he knew.

'They were still leaping through the flames when I came away,' he said; and then, as she did not answer, 'Vortrix leapt through with Rhun the daughter of Gwythno of the Singing Spear, when the flames still burned high, and neither of them was scorched. That means many sons for them by and by.'

Blai was watching him, but still she did not answer.

He drew his legs under him and made to rise. 'This fire is well enough now; if we bank it up, no harm will come to it. Blai, it may be that there will still be some fire left up yonder, if we go back now—if we run very quickly.'

Blai sat and looked at him, her face whiter and narrower than

ever, in the black smoke of her hair. 'You are kind,' she said wonderingly. 'You did not use to be kind.'

He had sprung up, and taken a long pace towards the doorway, followed as ever by Whitethroat; but he turned, and stood looking at her across the hearth that was alive with fire again. He was understanding more things now. He was understanding why Blai had not looked at him these past moons; that it was not that she hadn't looked at him since he began to get well, but that she hadn't looked at him except when he was sick since last sheep shearing. He remembered with sharp-edged clearness that small bitter scene at sheep shearing, and the white blind look on her face; the look that he had seen there once before—when the bronze-smith came with his magic dagger.

He thought he had left it too late. And as always with him, he met fear with anger. 'I am not kind!' He flung the word away as though it were a wasp that had settled on him, and swung round to the doorway; then checked again to look back at her. 'Well, are you coming, or is it that I must go back alone? There are other girls on the Hill of Gathering tonight.'

There was a sudden white flash of anger in Blai, answering his own as the fire in the grey dagger answered to the flint. 'Then let you take one of them to leap through the fire with you, my young Golden Lord!'

But Drem's anger had escaped him. He shook his head. 'I do not wish for any of them, Blai.'

She looked at him in silence, a long, clear look; and for a moment he was still afraid that he was too late. Then she smiled, and still without a word, began to tend the fire, so that it could be safely left. When that was done, she sprang up and came to Drem where he waited in the doorway; and he caught her hand in his sound one, and they ducked out into the moonlight and the blustering spring wind, and ran laughing, with Whitethroat at their heels, back towards the Beltane fires.

Postscript

A while after finishing *Warrior Scarlet*, I began to read up for another book, *Knight's Fee*, about two other boys living in Drem's countryside two thousand years later. And in a small, battered, locally printed book about Downland shepherds, I came on the description of a flint implement that had been found by one of them in Victorian times. A kind of double axe-head with no hole for a haft to go through and no place to bind one on. This kind of implement or weapon was made for holding in the hand, and quite a lot of them have been turned up on the Downs from time to time. But there was something a little unusual about this one. It was shaped and hollowed for use by a left-handed man.

R.S. August 1978

THE MARK OF THE HORSE LORD

CONTENTS

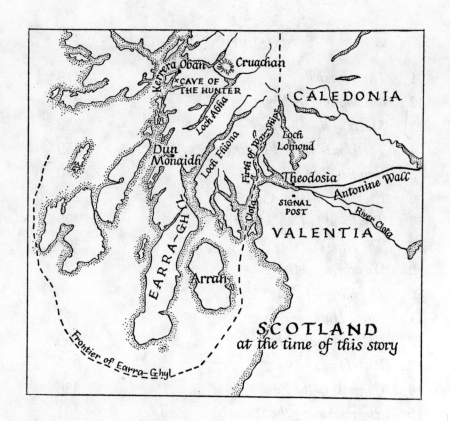

Kerrera Oban Cruachan
CAVE OF
THE HUNTER
CALEDONIA
Loch Abha
Dun
Monaidh
Loch Fhiona
Loch
Lomond
Firth of War-Ships
Theodosia
Antonine Wall
Clota
SIGNAL
POST
River Clota
EARRA-GHYL
VALENTIA
Arran
SCOTLAND
at the time of this story
Frontier of Earra-Ghyl

Historical Note

EVERYONE knows that at one time Scotland was inhabited by Picts and Scots, but most people are a little hazy as to the difference between them. Broadly (very broadly) speaking, they started out the same; both part of the great Western drift of peoples who rose somewhere in the great emptiness of Asia and spread across Europe in succeeding waves through the last two thousand years or so before Christ. The Picts were a confederacy of tribes whose 'Master Tribe', the Caledones, settled in the land that later became Scotland. The Scots were the tribes who went on farther to make their homes in Ireland and, long after, returned—some of them—to settle in the Western Islands and coastal districts of Scotland. At the time of this story, the Caledones had begun to be great among the tribes, but the Pictish confederacy did not yet exist; while 'Scot' or rather 'Scotti' was the Roman name for a people who called themselves Gael, or Dalriad. So in *The Mark of the Horse Lord* I have written of Caledones and Dalriads, and not of Picts and Scots, but it comes to much the same thing in the end.

In the years since they parted company, the Gael had become a Sun People, worshipping a male God, while the Caledones had held to the earlier worship of the Great Mother, and like most people with a woman-worship, they traced their family and inherited even the kingship through the mother's side. (Even in medieval Scotland it was quite common for a king's eldest son to find his claim to his father's throne after him indignantly denied by his sisters' husbands, who claimed that they were the true heirs by right of being married to the Royal Women.)

The traditional founder of the Dalriads is the Irish Prince Cairbre Riada, who, driven out from his own land of Munster by famine, led his kinsmen and followers first north into Ulster and then overseas to the Western Islands and Highlands, in the year A.D. 258, which is quite a bit later than the date of this

217

story. But there are traces and traditions of Irish settlement on the West Coast in A.D. 177, in 200 B.C., and even 300 B.C.; so that the answer would seem to be that no one knows quite when they came, but that they probably arrived in waves over several hundred years, and the most famous Irish leader would come in time, in the usual way of folklore, to have the credit for all the rest.

You will not find the Cave of the Hunter anywhere; but on the coast, close by Oban, there are caves that show clear traces of Stone Age occupation, and the coastline has changed so much through the ages, that the cave with the Horned One daubed on its back wall might have been among them once, and been claimed by the sea.

Nor, at present, will you find the ruins of a Roman Naval Station at Dumbarton Rock; though a strong tradition says that there was once one there, and that it was called Theodosia.

But if you go looking for it a few miles south of the head of Loch Awe, not far from the modern Crinan Canal, you will find Dunadd, which was once Dun Monaidh, with the traces of its five courts cropping through the turf, and in the highest court but one, the great Rock of the Footprint, where Phaedrus and Gladiator (whom you will not find anywhere outside this book) was crowned Horse Lord and King of the Dalriads.

I

The Threshold

IN the long cavern of the changing-room, the light of the fat-oil lamps cast jumping shadows on the walls; skeleton shadows of the spear-stacked arms-racks, giant shadows of the men who crowded the benches or moved about still busy with their weapons and gear; here and there the stallion shadow of a plume-crested helmet. The stink of the wild beasts' dens close by seeped in to mingle with the sharper smell of men waiting for the trumpets and sweating a little as they waited. Hard to believe that overhead where the crowds had been gathering since cock-crow, the June sun was shining and a fresh wind blowing in from the moors to set the brightly-coloured pennants flying.

219

But the man in the farthest corner, who sat hunched forward, arms crossed on knees, seemed lost to all that went on around him, deep sunk in his own thoughts. One or two of his fellows glanced at him in passing, but left him alone. They were used to Red Phaedrus's moods before a fight; he would come out of it, and laugh and turn tiger when the trumpets sounded.

Phaedrus was indeed very far away, back beyond the four years that he had been a sword-fighter here in the Gladiators' School at Corstopitum, and two years before that; back in the small, pleasant house in Londinium on the night his father died ... Ulixes the Arcadian, importer of fine Greek wines. He had never owned Phaedrus for his son, only for a slave, the son of Essylt who kept his house for him. But he had been fond of them both, when he could spare a thought from his business; he had seen that the boy got some schooling; he had been going to free them, one day. But in the end he had died too suddenly, slumped over his office table with a half-drafted letter to his agent in Corinth under his hand, and the autumn wind whirling the leaves of the poplar-tree against the window.

Everything had been sold up, the household slaves included. Everything but Phaedrus's mother. 'I am too old to go to a new master,' she had said on the last day before the sale, and she had sent him on an errand into the town. And when he came back from the errand, he had found her in the arbour at the foot of the narrow garden, where the master had liked to have his breakfast on fine summer mornings. She had used the slim, native hunting-dagger that had served Ulixes as a papyrus knife; but there was not much blood because she had stabbed herself under the breast, not cut her wrists as a Roman woman would have done. Phaedrus, not yet come to his fourteenth birthday, had changed from a boy into a man that day.

He had been sold off next morning, along with the part-Lybian chariot-horses, for he had the makings of a charioteer—and after changing hands a couple of times, and learning something of sword-play from his last master who wanted someone to practise on, had been sold into the arena to help pay a gambling debt. ('It's you or the team, and it won't be easy to

get another pair of matched bays,' his master had pointed out.)

At first he had been wild with loathing of his new life, but in four years it had become part of him, so that whether he hated or loved it no longer mattered. It ran in his veins like the fiery barley-spirit that the tribesmen brewed: the roar of the crowd that set one's pulses jumping, the warmth of sunlight and the sweetness of cheap wine and the fierce pleasure in one's own strength and skill, all heightened by the knowledge that tomorrow, next week, in an hour's time, it might all end on the squared point of a comrade's sword.

Four years. Not many lasted so long at the deadly trade. If he could last another year or so, they might give him his wooden foil with the silver guard, and he would be free. But his mind never got beyond the first triumphant moment of gaining his freedom, any more than it got beyond the sting of the death-blow, because he had been born a slave and knew no more of what it would be like to be free than he knew of what it would be like to die.

'Wooden foil?' Somebody's voice exploded beside him. 'You've been dreaming lad!' And the words, striking in so exactly upon his own thoughts, splintered them apart and brought him back to the present moment and the scene around him.

'I have not, then,' said Lucius the Bull, leaning back and stretching until the muscles cracked behind his thick shoulders. 'Someone is to get their wooden foil, earned or no. Trouble and expense no object in *these* games, so long as the Province remembers them afterwards and says, "Good old Sylvanus! *Jolly* old Governor Sylvanus! Gave us the best games we ever had." I heard the Captain talking to Ulpius about it—neither of them best pleased by the sound of it; Ulpius was cursing by all the Gods he knows.'

'Well, you couldn't expect any arena master to be *pleased*,' someone said. 'Maybe he reckons he's going to lose enough of his little game-cocks without losing that one more.' And there was a burst of reckless laughter from those near enough to overhear and join in.

Phaedrus stopped and rubbed his palm on the sanded floor, an old trick when one's sword-hand grew sticky. In the moment of silence that followed the laughter he heard the rising murmur of the crowd, and from the beast-dens a wolf howled, savage and mournful as a lost soul; *they* knew that it was almost time. Without meaning to he glanced across the crowded place to where Vortimax stood under a flaring lamp, preening the crest plumes of his helmet before he put it on. The big-boned Gaul turned his head in the same instant, and their eyes met. Then both looked away. . . .

In the ordinary way, the master of a frontier circus could not afford to use up his gladiators too fast, but Sylvanus Varus, the new Governor, who was giving these games to celebrate his appointment, had paid for four pairs of sword-and-buckler men to fight to the death. Four pairs—including Phaedrus and Vortimax. Phaedrus still could not quite believe it. They had come up the School together from the first days in the training yard. They knew each other's sword-play as well as they knew their own; they had shared the same food-bowl and washed each other's hurts in the same water; and in all the School, the big fair-haired Gaul was the only man Phaedrus had ever counted as a friend.

A forceful step sounded in the corridor, and Automedon, the Captain of the gladiators, appeared in the dark entry. He stood an instant looking down at them, and the livid scar of his own gladiator days burned in a crimson brand across his cheek, as it always did in the moments before the trumpets sounded.

'Time to helm-up, lads.'

Phaedrus got to his feet with the rest, catching up his plumed helmet from the bench beside him, and stepped forward from his dark corner. The light from the nearest lamp showed him naked like the other sword-fighters, save for the belted leather loin-guard and the sleeve of supple bronze hoop-mail on his sword-arm; a young man with hair the colour of hot copper, lithe and hollow-flanked as a yearling wolf, the tanned pallor of his face slashed across by red brows and a reckless, faintly smiling mouth.

He put on the heavy helmet and buckled the chin-strap. Now he was seeing the world through the long eye-slits in the moulded mask, and thought, testing the buckle, 'My last sight of the world will be like this, looking out at it sharp-edged and bright from the darkness inside my helmet.' And then he pushed the thought away. It wasn't lucky to have that kind of thought, going into the arena. That was the way one's nerve began to go.

Automedon stood in the entrance, watching from the vantage point of the two steps that led up to it, while they took down spears and heavy, bronze-rimmed oblong shields from the arms-racks and straightened themselves into roughly ordered ranks; then looked them over with a nod. 'Good enough. Now you know the order of events for the day: The wild beast show first, the boxers and then the General Fight; the Net-and-Trident men, and to wind up with'—his glance went to Phaedrus and Vortimax and the rest of the rear rank, and his voice was grimly sardonic—'you lucky lads in the place of honour ... For the rest of you—I don't want any more careless casualties like we had last month! Casualties of that kind don't mean courage—nought but slovenly sword-play, and the circus doesn't pay for your keep and training for you to get yourselves hacked to bits before it has had its money's worth out of you! Any man who comes out of the arena today with a hole in his hide deep enough to keep him out of the Consualia Games will have to account for it to *me*, and if I am not satisfied with the accounting'—he smiled at them with narrowed gaze and lip lifted over the strong, yellow dog teeth—'both he and the man who gave it to him will wish they had never been born! Understood?'

They grinned back, one or two tossing up their weapons in mock salute. 'Understood, Automedon! Understood, noble Captain!'

'That's well.' His face lost something of its grimness in a gleam of humour. 'This new Governor is fresh out from Rome, and maybe he doesn't expect much from a frontier circus, so show him that even if he has seen bigger fights in the Colosseum, man for man the Corstopitum lads can give Rome a bloody nose any day of the week!'

They shouted for him then in good earnest, tossing up swords and javelins as though to Caesar himself, and while their shouts still rang hollow under the roof-beams, Phaedrus heard the silver crowing of the trumpets, and the grinding clang as the arena doors were flung wide.

Automedon turned on his heel with a rapped-out command, and the arena guard stood back on each side of the broad stone stairway that led up to the open air. Two by two, the gladiators stepped off and swung forward.

Phaedrus shortened his stride at the foot of the stairway, clipped steps, head up, sword drawn, and shield at the ready. The lamplit gloom fell away behind, and the light of day came down to them with the swelling voice of the crowd. They were out from the echoing shadows of the arched stairway into the sudden space and wind and sunshine of the arena, the yielding sand underfoot, the greeting of the multitude bursting upon them in a solid wave of sound, hoarse under the clash of the cymbals and the high strident crowing of the trumpets. They swung left to circle the arena, falling into the long swaggering pace of the parade march, past the Altar of Vengeance at which they had sacrificed at first light, as always before the games; past the mouth of the beast-dens, past the dark alleyway giving on to the rooms where the Syrian doctor and his slaves were waiting to deal with such of the wounded as seemed worth trying to save, past the shovels and sand-boxes and the Mercuries with their little, flapping gilded wings and long hooks. Phaedrus looked up, seeing the tiered benches of the amphitheatre packed to their topmost skyline: Roman and Briton, townsfolk and tribesmen, easy figures in purple-bordered tunics in the Magistrates' Gallery, and everywhere—for Corstopitum was a depot town for the frontier—the russet-red cloth and glinting bronze of the Legions. Faces stared down at them, hands clutched the barriers in the excitement of what was to come. The usual flowers and sweetmeats began to shower down upon favourite gladiators. Phaedrus caught a white briar-rose in the hollow of his shield, and flashed his trained play-actor's gesture of thanks up at the fat woman in many jewels who had thrown it.

224

Full circle round the wide rim of the arena, they were close beneath the Governor's box now. Automedon snapped out a command, and they clashed to a halt, and wheeled to face the big, bull-necked man who leaned there with the glowing wine-red folds in his cloak flung back from the embossed and gilded breastplate beneath: Caesar's new representative, the giver of the games. Their weapons flashed up in the windy sunlight, and they raised the full-throated shout as though Caesar himself had leaned there.

'Hail Caesar! Those about to die salute you!'

Then they were breaking away to take station round the barricades. Phaedrus swung his shield into its resting position behind his shoulder, and straddling his legs, stood with hands on hips, deliberately wearing his courage at a rakish angle. That was what the crowd liked to see; the crowd that had come to watch him or Vortimax die.

The attendant Mercuries were hauling back the bars that closed the dark mouth of the dens, and the proud ten-point stag came flying in, half mad already with fear of the wolf-smell in his nostrils; and a few moments later the wolves were loosed after him. Six wolves in a dark, low-running pack. He killed two with his terrible antlers and left them ripped and broken on the bloody sand, before the rest pulled him down to a red rending death amid a great yelling from the onlookers. The bodies were dragged away; a third wolf who lay snapping and snarling with a broken back was finished off by one of the Mercuries. The remaining three were decoyed back to their cages for use another day, and fresh sand was spread over the stains in the arena. After that came the boxing-match, and the big sham fight which pleased the crowd better, especially when blood began to flow—for despite Automedon's orders, there was seldom a sword-fight that did not end in a few deaths and maimings. Now it was the turn of the Net-and-Trident men, and all across the arena they and the swordsmen matched against them were zigzagging like mayflies in a wicked dance of death.

Suddenly Phaedrus realized that the open expanse before him was empty of tense and running figures, the Mercuries with their

hooks were dragging another dead man away, and for the last time the filthy sand was being raked over and the worst of the stains covered.

And he thought in a perfectly detached way, 'Our turn now.'

The trumpets were crowing again, and as one man, the chosen eight strode out from their station close under the Governor's box to the centre of the arena, where Automedon now stood waiting for them.

They were being placed in pairs, ten paces apart and with no advantage of light or wind to either. It was all happening very quickly now; from the Governor's box came the white flutter of a falling scarf, and the trumpets were sounding the 'set on'.

Phaedrus took the customary two steps forward and one to the left, which was like the opening move in a game of draughts, and brought sword and shield to the ready. With that movement he ceased to be aware of the other pairs, ceased even to be aware of the suddenly hushed onlookers. Life sharpened its focus, narrowed to a circle of trampled sand, and the light-fleck of Vortimax's eyes behind the slits of his visor. ('Watch the eyes,' Automedon had said on the very first day in the training-school. 'Always be aware of the sword-hand, but watch the eyes.') They were circling warily, crouching behind their bucklers, ready to spring. Phaedrus's head felt cold and clear and his body very light, as it always did the moment the fight began, whether in earnest or in practice. Practice. He had fought out so many practice bouts with Vortimax. The surface of his mind knew that this was different, that this was kill or be killed, but something in him refused to believe it. This *could* be no more than a trial of skill between himself and Vortimax; and afterwards they would slam the swords back into the arms-racks, and laugh and go off to the wine-booth together. ... He made a sudden feint, and the Gaul came in with a crouching leap. Their blades rang together in thrust and counter thrust, a fierce flurry that struck out sparks from the grey iron into the windy sunlight. The sand rose in little clouds and eddies round their feet; they were circling and weaving as they fought, each trying to get the sun behind him and the dazzle of it in the other's eyes. Phaedrus felt the hornet-

sting of the other's blade nick his ribs, and sprang back out of touch. Vortimax was pressing after him, and giving back another step before the darting blade, he knew that the Gaul's purpose was to drive him against the barricade, where he would have no space to manoeuvre. He could sense the wooden barrier behind him, some way off still, but waiting—waiting—and side-sprang clear, at the same time playing a thrust over the shield that narrowly missed the other's shoulder. 'A feint at the head, a cut at the leg, and come in over the shield with a lunge.' Automedon's voice sounded in his inner ear as he had heard it so often at practice. The crowd were crying 'Habet!' as a fighter went down; and almost at once the shout was repeated, one wave crashing on the tail of another, and the Mercuries were dragging two bodies away. Only two pairs left now. Phaedrus knew it, on the outer edge of his consciousness, but it had no meaning for him; it was beyond the narrow circle of trampled sand and the sparks of living danger behind the eye-slits of Vortimax's visor. They had returned for a while to more cautious play, and the blades rang together lightly, almost exploringly; but they had no need to explore, they knew each other's play too well. It was that, partly, that made the whole fight seem faintly unreal, a fight in a dream. And the sense of unreality took the edge from Phaedrus's sword-play; he knew it, and tried to break through, and could not.

Ah! Vortimax's guard was a shade more open that time! Phaedrus's blade leapt, and it was the other's turn to spring back out of touch, with a red gash opening like a mouth in the brown skin over the collar-bone. He had the Gaul now, and began to press him back—back—Vortimax's turn to feel the waiting barrier. But still the odd sense of fighting in a dream was upon Phaedrus, and the inability to bring his sword-play out of the practice yard and set it to the real work of killing. . . .

He saw the flicker behind Vortimax's eye-slits in the split instant before the deadly low stroke came. He sprang sideways, pivoting on the ball of his foot, and felt a white-hot sting like that of a whip lash across the side of his left knee. The stroke which, had it landed square, would have cut the tendon and left him

ham-strung and helpless on the sand. It was a brilliant, wicked stroke, an almost outlawed stroke for it crippled instead of killing, and could bring your enemy down broken and at your mercy; but if it failed, if left your own guard wide open. Like the sudden opening of a cavern in his head, reality burst upon Phaedrus, and in that ice-bright splinter of time he understood at last that this was a fight to the death; that he was fighting, not his comrade Vortimax, whom he had fought scores and hundreds of times before, but death—red rending death such as the stag's had been, and the hooks of the Mercuries in the dark alleyway. And the man before him was the enemy, and he sprang to finish him. But in the same instant the Gaul, almost knee-down in the sand, twisted aside and up in an almost miraculous recovery, and again sprang back out of touch.

Phaedrus set his teeth and went after him, warned by the warm flow down his leg that he had not much time. He did not hear the crowd cry 'Habet!' for the third time, nor the mounting roar as all along the benches they shouted for himself or Vortimax. He had another enemy to fight now: the rising weakness of blood-loss creeping through him. Soon he felt his sword-play growing less sure. No onlookers could guess it as yet, but he knew, and so did Vortimax. Once, the Gaul's blade was within a nail's breath of his throat before he turned it aside. His heart was lurching in the sick hollow of his body, his teeth were clenched and his breath whistled through flared nostrils. The crowd had fallen suddenly oddly silent, but he heard their silence no more than he had heard their yelling. He was fighting on the defensive now, he had begun to give ground—a little—a little—and then a little more—and he knew with sick despair that he was very nearly done. Suddenly his blade wavered glaringly out of line, and Vortimax sprang in under his guard. How he avoided that thrust he never knew, but as he leapt sideways without thought—like a wounded wolf, Vortimax's foot slipped on Phaedrus's own blood in the sand, and in the instant that he was off balance with lowered shield, Phaedrus gathered the last of his strength and struck home.

Vortimax gave a small surprised grunt, and pitched forward,

twisting as he fell, so that he landed face upward, still part covered by his buckler.

Phaedrus stumbled to one knee over him, and caught himself back from crashing headlong. He heard the voice of the crowd now, but distantly, as one heard it from the underground changing-rooms, and stood with raised sword, drawing his breath in great sobbing gasps, while he waited to hear the 'Habet' and see the thumbs turned down. But the signal did not come; instead, a long roar of applause, and then he understood. Vortimax's chin-strap had snapped in his fall, and the plumed bronze helmet had fallen off, leaving his face bare. He was quite dead.

Phaedrus thought without emotion, looking down at him, 'That was almost me.'

He just remembered to turn and salute the Governor's box, which swam in his sight as the arena floor was swimming under his feet, then Automedon was beside him, growling in his ear, 'Hold on! Hold up, lad! If you go down now I swear I'll get the Mercuries with the hot irons to you!' And the Captain's hand was clenched on his arm, turning him back towards the arched entrance of the changing-rooms. The Mercuries were already dragging Vortimax's body away. 'Come on now, a drink is what you need!' And he thought with a sick shock of laughter, 'I'm being decoyed away, just like the wolves from their kill—decoyed away for another day.' He managed something of his usual swagger as he passed out of the westering sunlight, leaving a heavy blood-trail behind him, into the gloom of the stairhead and the smoky glimmer of the lamps still burning below. His foot missed the top step, and he stumbled forward, and somebody caught him from a headlong fall, saying cheerfully, 'Drunk again? This is no time to go breaking your neck!'

He was sitting on a bench, with head hanging, while the long, crowded changing-room swirled around him. They had taken off his helmet, and the Syrian doctor was lashing his knee in linen strips, so tightly that he could not bend it. There was a sudden splurge of voices with his own name and the words 'wooden foil' tangled somewhere in the midst of them. They

were thumping him on the shoulders to rouse him, pouring the promised drink down his throat. The barley-spirit ran like fire through his veins, and the world steadied somewhat.

'Now—up with you!' Automedon said. 'Up!'

And he was being thrust back towards the entrance stairway and the evening sunlight wavering beyond the great double doors; and all at once the truth dawned on him!

Somehow—the barley-spirit helped—he pulled himself together and put on the best swagger he could with a rigid knee, and managed the few paces to the Governor's box with a kind of stiff-legged, fighting-cock strut. Sylvanus's coarse, clever face seemed to float in clouds of bright nothingness and the rest of the world was the merest blur so that he never saw the sandy, withered-looking man with silver and coral drops in his ears, who leaned forward abruptly from a near-by bench to stare at him out of suddenly widened eyes.

He saw nothing but the Governor's big fleshy nose and small shrewd eyes, and the foil with its blade of smooth ash-wood as white almost as the silver guard. He took it from the Governor's hands into his own, feeling how light it was after the heavy gladius that he was used to, how lacking in the familiar balance when he brought it to the salute.

The crowd were shouting for him: 'Phaedrus! Red Phaedrus!' The fat woman who had tossed him the briar-rose threw an enamelled bracelet at his feet, and two or three others followed her example. But Phaedrus was scarcely aware of the gifts. He knew only that he was a free man; that he had come to one of the two thresholds that had waited for him, and for all the triumph and the shouting, he must step over it alone, into the unknown world that lay beyond.

2

Corstopitum by Night

HE stood outside the gateway of the Gladiators' School, under
the sculptured helmet and weapons of the pediment, and pulled
his cloak round him against the chill mizzle rain that was
blowing in from the moors. It was a new cloak, very fine, of
saffron-coloured wool with a border of black and crimson and
blue, and had been given him by a certain admiring merchant
who had seen him kill Vortimax and win his wooden foil. A tall
man, dried and withered and toughened like a bit of old
weather-worn horsehide, but with heavy drops of silver and
coral swinging in his ears. He had brought his gift in person, on
the morning after the games, and stared into Phaedrus's face as
he gave it, so intently that the gladiator laughed and said,
'You'll know me another time, even if I should not be wearing
this sunburst of a cloak!'

231

And the man had lowered the fine-wrinkled lids over his eyes, but gone on staring, under them, and said, 'Aye, I'd know you another time,' with something in his tone behind the words that had made Phaedrus suddenly wary. But he had kept the cloak; it was a rich cloak and he had not lived four years in the Gladiators' School without learning never to turn down a gift.

He looked up the street towards the transit camp, and down the street towards the baths and lower town, wondering which way to go, now that all ways were open to him, and feeling suddenly a stranger in the town that he knew as well as he did the cracks in the wall plaster beside his sleeping-bench. Well, no good standing here all day, he must find another sleeping-bench. He hitched up the long bundle containing his few possessions, including the wooden foil, and set off down the street, limping because the half-healed gash on his knee (they had kept him until it was half healed; a clear fortnight) was still stiff.

He found lodgings at the third attempt, a filthy room in a house down by the river, kept by an ex-army mule-driver with one eye, and leaving his bundle there, went out again to the baths. He had the full treatment, with a breath-taking cold plunge after the scalding steam of the Hot-room, and then lay like a lord while a slave rubbed him with scented oil and scraped him down with a bronze strigil; finally, he had the tawny fuzz of his young beard shaved. It cost a good deal, but there was the fat woman's bracelet and a few other bits and pieces in the small leather bag which hung round his neck, and in the circus one got out of the way of saving for tomorrow in case there was no tomorrow to save for. Also it helped to pass the time.

But the Depot trumpet was only just sounding for the noon watch-setting when he came out again into the colonnade. Two or three men strolling there looked at him and said something to each other, recognizing him. The rain had stopped and a pale gleam of sunlight was shining on wet tiles and cobbles and drawing faint wisps of steam from sodden thatch. He went down the colonnade steps, the red hair still clinging damply to his forehead, and the beautiful cloak, flung back now from his shoulders, giving him a kind of tall, disreputable splendour like a

corn-marigold, and strolled off along the street as though he were going somewhere, because he knew that they were still watching him.

For the next few hours he wandered about Corstopitum. He bought a brown barley loaf and strong ewe-milk cheese at a stall, and ate them on the river steps in another scurry of rain, and then wandered on again. He was free! A free man for the first time in his life! His official manumission, signed by the circus master and a magistrate, in the small bag round his neck, his name struck off the muster roll of the Gladiators' School with the words 'Honourably discharged' instead of the more usual 'Dead' against it. No man was his master, there was nowhere that he must report back to after his day's leave. Yet more than once that day he found himself back at the double doors with the sculptured weapons over them, or wandering in the direction of the turf-banked amphitheatre beyond the South Gate.

The last time it happened, he pulled up cursing, and looking about him, saw that it was dusk and a little way down the street someone had hung out the first lantern of the evening. The first day was drawing to a close, and suddenly he thought, 'This is only one day, only the first day, and there'll be another tomorrow, and another and another. . . .' And panic such as he had never known in the arena, where one only had to be afraid of physical things, whimpered up in him so that for a moment he leaned against a wall, feeling cold in the pit of his stomach. Then he laughed jeeringly and pushing off from the wall, turned back the way he had come, towards the narrower streets where the less respectable wine-shops were to be found. 'Fool! You want a drink, that's what's the matter with you—a lot of drinks. You can get as full as a wineskin tonight, and sleep it off like an Emperor! Won't have to be out on the practice ground with a head like Hephaestus's forge and seeing two of everything, at first light tomorrow.'

The first wine-shop he came to, he passed by. It was a favourite haunt of the gladiators on town leave, and he didn't want to run into old comrades. It was odd how he shrank from that idea now—a kind of embarrassment, a feeling that they

233

would not know quite how to meet each other's eyes, There was only one of them he would not have minded meeting again, and he had killed him the week before last.

Jostling and jostled by the people who still came and went along the streets, he pushed on until the 'Rose of Paestum' cast its yellow stain of lamplight and its splurge of voices across his way. He went in, swinging his cloak behind him with the play-actor's swagger of his old trade, and thrusting across the crowded room to the trestle table as the·far side, demanded a cup of wine. He grinned at the girl with greasy ringlets hanging round her neck, who served him, and flung down the price of the wine lordly-wise on the table, with a small bronze coin extra.

She half moved to pick it up, then pushed it back. 'This is over.'

'Best keep it for yourself then.'

'Best keep it for *yourself*,' she said. 'I reckon you've earned it hard enough, lad.'

'*Sa, sa*, have it your own way. This instead——' Phaedrus leaned across the table, flung an arm round her shoulders, and kissed her loudly. She smelled of warm unwashed girl under the cheap scent, and kissing her comforted a little the coldness of the void that had opened before him in the street.

He picked up his cup and the extra coin—she was his own kind, part of his own world, and to leave the coin after all would have been a sort of betrayal—and lounging over to a bench against the wall, sat down.

He gulped down most of the wine at a draught, though it hadn't much flavour somehow, and sat for a long time with the almost empty cup in his hand, staring unseeingly over the heads of the crowd towards the opposite wall and the faded fresco of a dancing-girl with a rose in her hand which gave the wine-shop its name.

What was he going to do with the days ahead? It had been stupid, that moment of panic in the twilit street, the appalling vision of emptiness that was simply today repeated over and over again for all eternity; stupid for the beautifully simple reason that to go on living you had to eat, and go on eating you

had to work—the fat woman's bracelet wouldn't last for ever. What about the Eagles? Oh, not the regular Legion, the Auxiliaries of the Frontier Service? It might be worth trying, but he didn't see old, one-armed Marius who commanded up at the Depot taking on an ex-gladiator. Well then, if he could get a job as a charioteer? Any kind of job to do with horses? But men who owned horses didn't want free grooms and drivers when they could get a slave for twelve aurei. No, sword-play was the only trade for him; he could probably get himself taken on by a fencing-master somewhere in one of the Southern cities, and end up teaching the more showy and safest fencing-strokes to young sprigs of the town. The prospect sickened him.

There was a movement in the crowd, and a shadow fell across his hand holding the winecup, and he looked up quickly to see that a young man had risen from a near-by table and checked beside him. Phaedrus knew him by sight, Quintus Tetricus, the Army Contractor's son, and recognized one or two others among the faces at the table, all turned his way.

'See who sits drinking here alone!' Quintus said, clearly speaking for the rest. 'Ah now, that's no way for a man to be celebrating his wooden foil!'

'I fought for it alone, and I may as well drink the Victory Cup alone—the wine tastes just as sweet,' Phaedrus said harshly, 'and snore alone under the table afterwards.'

'Come and drink with us, and we'll all snore under the table afterwards,' Quintus said, and the men about the table laughed.

'I do well enough where I am.' In the mood they were in, if a showman's sad bear had shambled in through the door they would have called it to drink with them, and Phaedrus was in no mood to dance to their whim.

'Even with an empty cup? *Na, na*, my Red Phaedrus! Come and drink off another with us; we've got a flask of red Falernian—Eagles' blood!'

Other voices were added to his; the rest were shifting closer on the benches, making room for one more.

And suddenly, because nothing mattered much anyway, it was too much trouble to go on refusing. He shrugged, and got

235

up, and not quite sure how it happened found himself sitting with Quintus and his friends, the cup brimming with unwatered Falernian in his hand. Flushed faces grinned at him round the wine-dabbled table. A complete stranger with hair bleached lint-white as some of the young braves among the tribesmen wore it—it was the fashion just then to be very British—leaned forward and clapped him on the shoulder, shouting, 'Here he is then; let's drink to him! *Aiee*, my lucky lad, that was a pretty fight!'

Cups were raised on all sides: 'Red Phaedrus! Joy and long life to you!'

Phaedrus laughed, and drank the toast with them, gulping the cup dry. It would be good to get drunk. 'A pretty fight. You saw it?'

'Wouldn't have missed it for all the gold in Eburacum's mint!'

'I thought the Gaul had you with that low stroke,' another said.

'I thought so, too.' Phaedrus drained his cup and threw the lees over his shoulder, where they lay dark as the grains of old blood on the dirty floor. 'What's a friend after all? I'll drink again if anyone asks me.'

Presently, he had no idea how many winecups later, he realized that the place was emptying, and the serving-girl and a couple of slaves were gathering up empty cups and mopping spilled wine, while at the far side of the room, benches were being stacked one a'top the other. 'Shutting up, by the look of things.' A plump, dark youth who had been quieter than the rest of them all evening looked about him somewhat owlishly. 'S'tonishing how quick an evening runs its course in—good comp'ny.'

'Ah now, who says it's run its course? I'm shtill—*still* thirsty.' Quintus flung himself back against the wall behind him, and beckoned imperiously to the girl. '*Hai!* Pretty! More wine.'

The girl looked up from her task. 'We're shutting up now.'

'Not while I'm here, we're not.'

She glanced towards the wine-shop owner, who came wad-dling across the room towards them, his paunch thrust out

beneath a dirty tunic stained with old wine splashes. 'We don't keep open all night in the "Rose of Paestum". This is a decent house, sirs, and we need our sleep the same as other folks.'

Quintus lurched to his feet, flushing crimson, his hand fumbling for his knife, but Phaedrus, with a few grains of sense still in him, put a hand on his shoulder and slammed him down again. 'Softly! The "Rose of Paestum" isn't the only wine-shop in Corstopitum.'

And a big red-faced young man with a loose mouth grinned in agreement. 'Tired of that girl on the wall, she's coming off in flakes, anyhow. Le's go 'nd find some real dancing-girls.'

Somehow matters were sorted out, and the remains of the score paid, with a good deal of bickering, and they were spilling out into the street,. hotly arguing as to where they should go next. They had been no more than loudly cheerful and from time to time a little quarrelsome in the hot room, but the fresh air went to their heads and legs like another kind of wine. 'I'm drunk,' Phaedrus thought. 'I haven't been as drunk as this since Saturnalia!'

Well, he had meant to get as drunk as an Emperor tonight, and the feeling was good. He was not lonely or cold any more, and tomorrow could look after itself; he felt eighteen hands high and curiously remote from his own feet. He could fight a legion single-handed, and whistle the seven stars of Orion out of the sky. It was not such a grey world after all.

They had forgotten about the quest for dancing-girls, and for a while they wavered their way about the streets, singing, with their arms round each other's necks. Respectable people scurried into doorways at their approach, which seemed to all of them a jest for the Gods, so that they howled with laughter and began to kick at doors in passing and yell insults at any protesting face that appeared at an upper window. They had no clear idea of where they were heading, but presently they found themselves in the centre of the town, with the square mass of the Forum buildings and the Basilica rising before them cliff-wise out of the late lantern-light into the darkness. Among the small lean-to shops, closely shuttered now, that lined the outer

colonnade, the gleam of a lantern here and there where a late wine-booth was still open, and the sight of the little groups gathered about them made Phaedrus and his boon companions thirsty again.

'C'mon,' Quintus said. 'Let's have another drink.'

'Had enough,' The dark, plump boy still had more sense left in him than any of the others. 'Maybe we'd best be jogging home.'

'Roma Dea! The night's still in swaddling-bands, there's two full watches of it left yet.' And another of the band lifted up his voice in mournful song:

> '*Oh do not drink so deep, my son,*
> *My dear and only child!*
> *And do not lie down in the street*
> *And look so strange and wild.*'

The others joined in the chorus:

> '*Yellow wine of Chios*
> *And dark wine of Gaul,*
> *But the blood-red Falernian,*
> *The ruby-red Falernian,*
> *The fire-red Falernian,*
> *Is the Emperor of them all.*'

Then in a blurred gabble, '*I've-a-fine-and-noble-reason-for-lying-here-a-season-but-what-it-is-I-cannot-quite-recall.*'

And baying each other on to further efforts, they headed for the nearest of the still open wine-booths, close beside the main gate, with its triumphal inscription and attendant stone lions.

The booth, which was no more than a trestle table under the roof of the colonnade, with a couple of coarse wine and water jars behind it, a few horn cups and a red pottery lamp in the midst of all, was kept by an ex-Legionary who had had trouble with drunks before. He eyed them with grim disfavour as they drew near, and began ostentatiously to stack the horn mugs together.

'And what might you be wanting?'

Quintus propped himself agains the trestle table. 'What's one generally come to a wine-booth for, eh?—Tell me that. Wha's one gener-ally——'

'Well, you've come too late,' said the booth's owner. 'Can't you see I'm shutting for the night?'

Quintus shook his head, while the rest crowded closer, and said with elaborate care, 'That was what they said at the "Rose of Paestum". The very words they—and it wasn't *true*! They jus' di'n'—*didn't* like our faces. You don' like our faces either, do you?'

'I've seen ones I've liked better.'

'Our money's good 'nough, though.' Quintus flung down a scatter of coins and thrust a suddenly darkening face into that of the ex-Legionary. 'An' tha's all that matters t'you, isn't it? Now we'll have some wine. Me an' my frien's, we'll *all* have some wine.'

'Not here, you won't.' The man pushed the money back at him. 'Now pick up this lot, and get off to bed, the pack of you.'

The rest of the party had begun crowding closer, and there was an ugly murmur. Phaedrus, with his beautiful prancing mood suddenly checked, aware once more, through the bright haze of the Falernian, of the grey, flat future that he had thought successfully drowned, had a strong desire to fight somebody. It did not much matter whom. He elbowed his way to the forefront of the group beside Quintus. 'And supposing there's no wish in us for bed? Suppose we feel like a cup of wine all round, and nothing else in the world?'

The mood of the whole band was turning ugly; he felt the ugliness growing and gathering strength behind him, and saw the recognition of it in the ex-Legionary's suddenly alerted gaze. Legionary of the Eagles that he, Phaedrus, was not good enough to join! For the moment it seemed to him that he had actually gone up to the Depot, and been turned away.

'Then you'll have to try another booth, gladiator. *I'm shutting up for the night!*' The man raised his voice abruptly to a parade-ground bellow, as he clattered horn cups into a basket that a boy

behind him had dragged out from under the trestles. Out of the tail of his eye, Phaedrus was aware of several other men moving up; the wine-booth owners were mostly old Legionaries, and held together when there was trouble.

'Right! Then we'll help you!' Quintus shouted, and kicked over the biggest wine-jar; and in the same instant, even as the booth keeper lunged into battle like a bull with a gad-fly on his tail, Phaedrus seized one end of the trestle board and heaved it up, sending everything on it to the pavement with a deeply satisfying crash. On the instant a free fight was milling round the wreckage, and the raw-red Sabine wine running like blood between the cobbles. The lamp had gone over with the rest, and little rivulets of burning oil mingled with the wine. Then someone shouted, 'Look out! It's the Watch!' And the thing that had begun as little more than a savage jest tipped over into nightmare.

Somebody—in the confusion Phaedrus did not know who it was—drew a knife. He caught the flash of it in the flickering light of the burning oil about their feet; somebody shouted, 'Don't be a fool! For Gods' sake——' and a Legionary of the Watch went down with a sharp bitten-off cry.

One of the little runnels of fire caught the dry timber of a shop-front near by; a wavering tongue of flame licked up as though tasting it and then the fire was roaring up the shutter, and in the red flare of it, Phaedrus saw the crested helmet and mailed shoulders of the officer of the Watch-patrol lowered to charge, and more men thrusting grimly behind him. The little band of revellers was scattering, melting away at panic speed. Phaedrus sprang back into the shadows and turned to run. But some time in the fighting he had caught a kick on the half-healed wound, and now suddenly his knee gave under him.

He heard a shout and the pounding of feet and even as he struggled up from his headlong fall, two of the Watch had flung themselves upon him. 'Here's one of them, anyhow!' a voice shouted, and merciless hands dragged him to his feet and back into the light of the blazing shop-front, where others of the patrol were already getting to work with water from the Forum

fountain. He caught a brief glimpse of the officer's crest, tall and arched like a stallion's against the sinking fire; and a coldly disgusted voice from under it said, '*One* of them! And they have half-gralloched Gerontius.'

All sounds of the chase were pounding away into the distance. Phaedrus twisted in his captors' hands and began to fight. Four years of the Gladiators' School where private quarrels were settled without weapons and far from the eye of authority, had taught him other ways of battle than those of the sword and he used them all, every clean and dirty trick of them. But the part-reopened wound hampered him, and when he tried to knee one of his captors in the groin it again played him false.

'Ah! You would, would you, you stinking pole-cat!' someone snarled, and he was wrenched sideways, and something that felt like a thunderbolt took him under the left ear. Jagged flame shot from the point of impact through the top of his head, and he plunged down into a buzzing blackness between spinning sun-wheels of coloured light.

3

Midir of the Dalriads

PHAEDRUS sat on a pile of filthy bedstraw in the corner of the cell, scratching at the blood-stained rag that was tied round his knee, and watching the last daylight fade out beyond the high, narrow window-hole.

It had been noon when they hauled him out of the main prison hall and flung him in there. At the time he had been too sick to care, almost too sick to notice. There was something odd about that sickness; it had leapt upon him as soon as the morning bannock and water was down his throat, so suddenly and horribly that he had wondered if he were poisoned—until he stopped being able to wonder at all. His head still ached, but dully, a leaden soreness instead of the pounding of a few hours ago; and his belly crawled clammily within him; but he no

longer sweated and shivered. And he had begun to wonder with a growing urgency why he had been shifted into this small cell shut away from the rest of the prisoners. Because of that sudden sickness? Had they feared that it might be something that would breed and spread and break loose of the prison into Corstopitum. Or had the wounded Legionary died? He had not been dead when Phaedrus was thrust into the city goal six days ago, that much they told him, but he could have died since. Was this solitary cell perhaps the place where prisoners on a death charge were held for trial? It was one thing to make a good end with one's sword in hand and the packed theatre benches baying, quite another to die like this. ... Not a pleasant thought, and it brought with it an unpleasant sense of the damp stone walls closing in.

He pushed the walls back with care, and steadied his breath. The fact that he had not struck the blow would stand him in no kind of stead; he realized that. In the eyes of Roman justice, they had all struck, had all, equally, drawn the knife. And the others had all got clear. Well, he would do for a scapegoat—exgladiator, paid off with the wooden foil, gets drunk to celebrate and knifes one of the Watch in a street brawl; it made a nice neat story for the records, all the ends properly tied in, no need to look any further.

There was a heavy step outside, and the gaoler appeared beyond the iron grid of the cage-like door, stopped to thrust the evening food bowl under the lowest bar, and tramped on without a word; a few moments later Phaedrus heard the sudden uproar from the main hall that always greeted the food. He looked at the bowl which the man had left on the floor, but the look of the black rye-bread and watery bean-stew made his stomach heave, and he left it where it was and went on sitting. It was dusk in the cell now, though there was still light in the sky outside the small, high window; and beyond the cage-work door there began to be a faint tawny glow, an echo of the torch that burned all night at the head of the steps.

Presently the gaoler returned, but instead of merely reaching in for the bowl and passing on, halted and produced from his

243

belt something that jangled. His hands were out of sight beyond the edge of the door, but Phaedrus heard the metallic kiss and click of the lock; the long bar which held the door was freed and dragged back, and the door itself swung open.

'Out with you,' the man said, standing back.

Phaedrus's muscles had already tensed to the chance of freedom, with the quick reaction of the arena-trained, but he made no movement. No point in trying to rush the door when it was already open—and the Gods knew what lay beyond. ...

'Out, I said! Come on now, outside.'

Phaedrus stood up in no hurry. 'Am I to go before the Magistrate? Well, it's about time—six cursed days he's kept me waiting.'

'At this hour of night? Besides, he's not back yet. Do you think he's going to shorten his hunting trip for the likes of you?'

'Hardly,' Phaedrus said, and then, 'Is the man dead?'

'Him as you knifed? Not that I've heard of.'

That was something, anyway, but still Phaedrus stood wary, back against the wall, misliking the man's furtive manner. 'Then where are you taking me? *Why* am I to leave my cell at this hour?

The gaoler shrugged broad shoulders. 'How should I know? My orders don't go beyond the guardroom steps. Are you coming or do I have to call my mate?'

'I am coming,' Phaedrus said, and pushed off from the wall. As he ducked through the cell doorway, the man side-stepped, quick as a cat for all his size, and he felt the prick of a knife-point under his ribs. 'Quietly now.'

Phaedrus checked an instant at the touch of the cold iron. He had half hoped for the moment that someone was working his rescue; but the knife would seem to put an end to that idea. It had been a stupid one, anyway; the School stood by its own, bound by odd pack loyalties however much it fought among itself, but once you were out, living or dead, you were *out*, and the pack hunted without you.

'Down here—out of the light.'

Well, whatever was happening, whatever all this meant, he

hadn't much to lose. Phaedrus was used to taking chances. Now, quite deliberately, he let go, and abandoned himself to events like a swimmer pushing off into the current; and as the prick of the knife came again, warningly, under the ribs, he gave a low breath of a laugh and moved off down the stone-flagged corridor away from the torchlight. The main hall was behind them, with its wild-beast stink; once more they crossed a patch of torchlight, shining across a narrow courtyard from the open guardroom door, then they turned another corner, mounted some steps, and cool air stirred in their faces, clearing Phaedrus's head somewhat from the fumes of the strange sickness.

Another figure, tall, but shapeless in the dusk, moved from beside an open postern doorway; there was a quick, muttered exchange between him and the gaoler: 'All well?' and 'All well.' And then to Phaedrus, 'Put on this cloak—so, the hood forward over your face. It is a fine night for a walk, my friend.'

Then he was out in a back alleyway, walking as though all this was a perfectly usual thing to happen, beside the muffled figure of his new guide.

'Walk as though we were bound for the nearest wine-shop—nowhere more important,' said a dry voice under the other's hood; a voice that seemed faintly familiar, speaking in the British tongue.

Phaedrus glanced aside at him. 'And since that seems un-likely, where *are* we bound for, on this fine night's walk?'

'Not into any trap, if that is what you are thinking.'

'I can be sure of that?' Phaedrus said on a faint note of mockery.

'*Na*, you cannot be sure until the thing is proved. You have only my word for it, but there are places where the word of Sinnoch the Merchant is counted binding.'

Phaedrus wondered whether this was one of them, then shrugged beneath the greasy-smelling folds of the cloak, and, his weakness beginning to wear off, fell easily into step beside the other man.

Among the drifting evening crowds, they went by narrow ways and back streets, emerged at last into the Street of the

Trumpeter, and turned down it. It was almost dark now, with a faint mist creeping in from the moors to make a yellow smear about the lanterns that hung here and there at street corners or over shop doorways. A stain of light fell across the roadway from an open door, and with it the blur of voices and throaty blackbird notes of a pipe, and Phaedrus realized, with a nightmare sense of having travelled in a circle, that the doorway and the voices and the lamplight were those of the 'Rose of Paestum.'

But the man beside him touched his arm, and instead of passing in beneath the hanging ivy-bush, they turned off short into the mouth of a small, dark passageway beside the wineshop; and the circle was broken.

A few paces into the darkness, Phaedrus sensed rather than saw the door that barred their way. It opened to the merchant's hand as though it had been left on the latch for them, but once inside the man said, 'Wait!' And standing in the dark, Phaedrus heard the sounds of key in lock, and then the light grating of a bar being slipped into place. If this were a trap after all, he had walked into it, and the trap was sprung. It was odd, still to hear the voices and the blackbird piping, and know that on the far side of the lath-and-plaster wall was the lamplight and the cheerful evening gathering of the wine-shop, while he was here in the dark with whatever was coming towards him out of the Unknown.

Sinnoch the Merchant led the way to another door, which also opened to his touch, and this time did not pause to secure it behind them. They were in a narrow, walled space, half courtyard, half garden, where a lantern hanging from a rickety vine-trellis lit up the nearest of a few dejected rose-bushes growing in old wine-jars. There was a stable close by, to judge from the smell of hay and horse dung, and at the far side of the place a thin line of light showed through the clink of a door in what looked like a barn or a range of store-rooms.

The man crossed to it, breaking into a soft, haunting whistle, as though to give warning of his coming to someone inside, and lifting the wooden door-pin, went in. Phaedrus followed close behind.

The light of a fine red earthernware lamp hanging by a chain from the rafters showed him a store-room of sorts, with dim-seen bales and boxes stacked along the walls together with coiled hide-ropes, a couple of riding-pads and all manner of horse gear; showed him also a couple of benches strewn with rugs and pillows of striped native cloth, and a table with a bronze wine-jug and cups on it. Clearly this was a private room of the 'Rose of Paestum', such as a merchant who did not wish for the company of the big posting inn by the South Gate might take for himself and his wares.

But though his first glance took all these things, his whole attention went in the next instant to the man seated at the table, and remained there. A man in his full prime, certainly well under forty, and of giant strength, to judge by the almost grotesque thickness of neck and shoulder and the hand clenched, as though it did not know how to hold anything lightly, about the bronze winecup he had just set down. His mouth was dry and ragged at the edge, as though he had a habit of chewing his

247

lower lip; black brows almost met across the bridge of his nose, and on cheek and forehead showed the fine spiral lines of tattooing that had earned the far Northerners the name of the Painted People.

Whatever Sinnoch might be, *this* was certainly no merchant, Phaedrus thought.

He heard the door-pin falling, and Sinnoch passed him, pushing back the hood of his cloak and letting it drop from his shoulders, and the lamplight jinked on a silver and coral ear-ring. It was the man who had given him the saffron cloak.

More and more, there were things here that he did not understand.

'I have brought him,' Sinnoch said.

The man at the table answered him with a nod, and spoke directly to Phaedrus in an outlandish form of the Celtic tongue: 'Take off that cloak.'

Still deliberately going with the current, Phaedrus flung back the hood without a word and let the heavy folds drop to the floor, and stood confronting the stranger, his head up and on his lips the faintly insolent smile that his comrades of the arena knew.

There was a long moment of complete silence, in which Phaedrus could hear the distant hubbub from the wine shop, mingled with the drubbing of his own heart. Then the stranger said, 'It is in my mind that you will have spent an evil day.'

Phaedrus took one long pace to the table, and stood looking down into the eyes that were tawny as a wolf's. 'That was your doing?'

'It was needful to make sure you would be lodged alone. It was needful also that there should be something—some mark of sickness on you to be remembered afterwards.'

'Afterwards?'

'After they find the body.'

Phaedrus felt a small icy shock in the root of his belly, and his hand flew to the place where his dagger should have been, then dropped away. It was in that instant that he became aware, for the first time, of a curtained inner doorway half lost in the farther shadows.

'Ach no, not *your* body,' Sinnoch, who had sat himself down on the bench a little to one side, said in his dry, amused voice. 'There are always bodies to be had in every city—a beggar in a back street—anybody not too closely seen, will serve the purpose—and once it has been tipped into a hole in the prison yard. . . .'

Phaedrus said slowly, 'And all that is arranged?'

'All that is arranged. It might have been a harder matter if he they call the Chief Magistrate had not been off on the hunting trail; but it is wonderful what a few little lumps of yellow gold will do among them; most wonderful. Merchant that I am, I know the buying-power of gold. . . . They will put him in his hole quickly, lest the thing spread in the summer heat, and when the hunter returns from his hunting, there will be nothing left to see of Phaedrus the Gladiator, but a little turned earth in the prison yard.' The dry tone deepened into melancholy. 'It is very sad. He was young and strong and good to look upon; but he took a sudden sickness in the gaol, and was gone like a lamp pinched out between thumb and finger.' Sinnoch made the gesture sharply and precisely, then dusted his leathery finger-tips together as though to rid them of the smitch of the charred wick.

Phaedrus caught the gesture out of the tail of his eye; he had never taken his gaze from the man at the table, while he listened to Sinnoch the Merchant.

'You must have wanted me sorely, to go to so much trouble,' he said, and his mouth felt dry.

'We—had a certain need of you.'

'What need?'

All this while, the other man had sat unmoving, the bronze winecup gripped in his hand. Now he pushed it away, so sharply that a few drops of wine leapt over the rim and splashed like blood upon the table-top, and lunging to his feet, came tramping round the table to where Phaedrus stood. Seated, he had seemed a big man, but the gladiator found with a sense of shock that he was looking steeply down at him, for his body was set on strong bow legs so short that he was almost a dwarf.

249

'Turn to the light.'

Phaedrus obeyed. He could scarcely see the other's face now, only the darkly blotted shape of him with the lamplight on the top of his head and shoulders: but he was aware of the bright tawny stare that raked him from head to foot; and aware also, though he could not have said how, when the purpose of the stare changed, and it was no longer his outer seeming but his mettle that was being judged.

Until now, he had gone unresisting where the current carried him, but something in that ruthless probing scrutiny raised his hackles, and he locked his gaze with the other man's and strove to beat it down as though it were an opponent's weapon.

It was the merchant, lounging among the striped rugs on the bench, who broke the silence at last. 'I was right, Gault the strong?'

The other nodded, turning back to the table. 'You were right, Sinnoch my brother. He may serve the need.'

Phaedrus shot out a long arm to the shoulder of Gault the Strong, and swung him round again. 'And now that seemingly you are satisfied, in Typhon's name you shall tell *me* this need, and we will see if *I* am satisfied also!'

Suddenly the dark man smiled, and with a lightning movement, chopped Phaedrus's gripping hand away, so that he felt for an instant as though his wrist was broken. 'When you lay hands on me, do it in fellowship and not in anger! Now pull that stool to the table and sit down, for you have a long listening before you.'

Phaedrus stood for a moment, his fists clenched, then shrugged, and pulled up the stool. When they were facing each other across the table, Gault said, 'Can you be understanding all that I say, or shall Sinnoch here turn the words from my tongue to yours?'

Indeed, the tongue he spoke was full of odd inflexions and cadences that would have made it almost a foreign tongue to most of Phaedrus's kind. But his mother had been part of the spoils of some far Northern battle before ever she came to a Roman slave-market, and had spoken in much the same way

when they were alone together. 'I understand well enough,' he said.

'*Sa*. First then, drink, my friend.' Gault the Strong splashed more wine into his own cup and pushed it across the table.

Phaedrus left it standing there. 'I've an empty belly and I'd as soon listen to what you tell me with a clear head.'

'Maybe there is wisdom in that. Later then, we will eat and drink together.' Gault had dipped a finger in the spilled wine, and as though not conscious of what he was doing, he had begun to draw patterns on the table-top as he talked. It was a trick that Phaedrus was to come to know well as time went by.

'In my grandfather's time, we, the Dalriads, the People of the Gael, came from Erin over the Western Sea and conquered the land and the people of the hills and sea-lochs below Cruachan; the people who were called the Epidii in those days; and we made our hunting-runs where theirs had been, so that all that land became Earra-Ghyl, the Coast of the Gael.' He looked up, his finger pausing an instant in its making of curved and crosswise lines. 'Since long and long before that, we have been a Horse People, a people of Lugh the Sun Lord, holding to kings who passed the kingship down from father to son. But the Epidii, though they, too, were a Horse People, were even as the Caledones are still, a people of Cailleach, the Great Mother, and to them the queen was all, and the king for little save to give the queen children. Therefore our king mastered and mated with their queen, as the Sun Lord masters and mates with the Mother who is both Earth and Moon; and we and the Epidii became in some sort, one.'

'This one may learn from any harper who sings of the old days and the death of kings. Why will you be telling it to me now?'

'For a good reason, that you shall know in time. ... Seven winters ago, Levin of the Long Sword died when the boar of his hunting turned at bay; and the kingdom should have gone to Midir, his young son. Maybe that would have been the way of it, if the boy's mother had been yet living; but she was dead, and Liadhan the King's half-sister was the Royal Woman of the tribe—a woman like a she-wolf in a famine winter. The earth-

ling blood was in her, and the Old Ways, for her mother was a princess among the Caledones. She chose out one of the Royal Body-guard to be her mate—her first marriage-lord was lately dead—and seized the rule. So for seven years we have followed the Old Ways again.'

'Just like that. Did you not fight?'

'Some of us fought.' Gault fingered a long white scar that writhed up his forearm, and left it streaked with the crimson of the spilled wine that stained his fingers. 'Most of us died. She had the Northern clans, where the old blood runs strong, behind her; she had the support of the priest-kind, who hoped for greater power under the Mother than they had known in the Sun Lord's day; she had made sure of young Midir. The thing was done between a winter's dusk and a winter's dawning and we of the Southern clans were weak with fighting, for we had joined shields with the Caledones in the past summer, to break the Red Crest's Northern Wall. We had no rightful king to raise for a battle-cry against her. The longer-sighted among those that were left of us urged peace; and in the end we made what peace we could—such peace as may be made with the wolf-kind—and waited for a later time.'

He paused, and dipped his finger yet again in the spilled wine, and added a carefully judged flourish to his pattern. A small muscle twitched in his cheek. 'At Midwinter, it will be the seven years that we have waited.'

'Seven years?' Phaedrus said, puzzled.

And from the rug-piled bench, Sinnoch the Merchant put in dryly, 'You have been too long among the Roman kind, for all the colour of your hair. You forget the ways of your own people.'

'Every seventh year the king dies,' Gault said, as though there had been no interruption. 'Liadhan has chosen already the man who is to fight the Death Fight with Logiore and take his place, until in another seven winters it is time for his own death, and another king.'

For instance, Phaedrus's arena training almost made him say, 'What if it is the Old King who wins the Death Fight?' He had lived all his life among the Roman kind, but something in him

was beginning, all the same, to remember the ways of his own people, a memory of the nerve-ends rather than the mind. And he knew that the Old King would not win the Death Fight. Maybe there was a drug used; maybe it was simply that he knew winning that fight was not in the pattern of his fate.

He began to catch the first and most distant flicker of an idea as to where all this might be leading. 'And the Old King does not care for the end made ready for him?'

Sudden and unexpected laughter twitched at the corners of Gault's bitten lips. 'Ach no. The Old King has the old blood in him. For him it is the pattern of things. It is the Young King who baulks. At Beltane, the Queen sent her token to young Conory of the Kindred. The gift proved unwelcome.'

'And so?'

The dark man leaned forward, one elbow smearing out his pattern to a red blur on the table-top; and all at once his eyes were burning like those of a man with fever. 'And so the time has come that the Dalriads set aside Liadhan the Queen, having borne her rule long enough. Already the horns are blowing in the hills, and the black goat dies. Even among the Northern clans many have come over to us in their hearts, weary of this dark Women's-rule that calls for the death of men. We of the Kindred, the Royal Clan, are of one mind in this matter; Conory stands with us, and certain of the Companions, the Bodyguard will follow him. There is yet one more than we need—Midir!'

Phaedrus stared at him under frowning brows. 'And since Midir is dead?'

Gault made a quick gesture of one hand, as though to say, 'Let that pass for a moment,' and went on, 'We need our rightful King to raise and follow against the Woman, as we needed him seven winters ago. He would have been worth two—three thousand fighting men to us then, boy that he was. As a man, he would be worth more.' The tawny eyes were fixed upon Phaedrus face. 'A man much about your age; much such a one to look at, too.'

'I am not certain what you mean.' Phaedrus heard his own

253

voice after a sharp pause, without even being aware that he had spoken. 'But it is in my mind that you would have me play this lost prince for you.'

'We need Midir.'

Phaedrus flung back his head and laughed. 'Fiends and Furies! You're more of a fool than you look, if you think I could be doing *that*.'

The tawny eyes never swerved. 'You can if you will.'

'If I will? I have the choice then?'

'It is a thing that can only be done of the free choice.'

'Are you asking me to believe that if I refuse, you will let me go free, loaded with all this that you have told me? Tell that to the green plover.'

'*Na* we will not be troubling the green plover. Refuse, and bide captive in our hands until all is over, then go free and shout your story where you will. I will swear that, if you like, on all our hopes of victory.'

Phaedrus said, 'But if he is dead, she will know—all the tribe will know it for a trick.' It seemed to him as he spoke, that the rug that hung across that inner doorway stirred, but when his gaze whipped in that direction, the heavy folds were hanging straight and still. It must have been only a trick of the lamplight.

'The tale runs that the boy was drowned bathing in the loch, and his body never washed ashore. Only the Queen, and those who did her will, can know it for a trick, and for good reasons they will not be seeking to prove it.'

'A pity, for her, that she did not have the body washed ashore, for all men to see.'

'That would have been beyond even her powers,' Gault said. 'He was not dead.'

The words seemed to hang echoing among the bales and boxes, until Phaedrus said at last, 'Not dead?'

'Even Liadhan would not quite dare the slaying of the King. She—made sure of him.'

'Then what if he comes back to claim his own?'

'He will not come back to claim his own.'

'How can you know? If he is lost——'

'He is not lost.' Gault's finger had returned to its half-unconscious pattern tracing in the spilled wine. 'He works for a leather merchant in Eburacum. We sought him from the first, and found him three years and more ago.'

Phaedrus was beginning to feel that he was caught up in some fantastic dream. 'Then if you have your own prince to your hand, why me? *Why me?* There is something here that smells strange to me, and I do not think that I like the smell!'

'There is a price offered.'

'This time, I am not for sale.'

'For gold, maybe no. There are other kinds of price.'

'A kingdom? How much of a king should I be when all is done?

'As much of a king as you would be showing yourself strong for. That I promise you, I who am not without power in the tribe. .... The price I had in mind was no more than the balance of a sword in your hand, a few risks to be run, maybe a lost flavour to be caught back into life.'

'You choose the price you offer well,' Phaedrus said after a moment.

'And your answer?'

'Give me a sword, and I'll use it well for you. I'll not meddle with a kingship that isn't mine; ill luck comes that kind of way.'

Silence lay flat and heavy in the room, a silence that seemed as tangible as the air one breathed. And in the silence, Sinnoch the Merchant looked on as though at some scene that interested him but was no concern of his; and the two pairs of eyes, slate-grey and tawny, held each other across the table.

Then Gault turned on the bench, and shouted into the gloom behind him: 'Midir!'

And even as Phaedrus's gaze whipped towards the inner doorway, the hanging rug was dragged aside, and a man stood on the threshold. A young man in the rough tunic of a craftsman, who checked on the farthermost edge of the lamp-light, his head alertly raised like a hound's when it scents the wind. Phaedrus caught the glint of red hair, and something in

255

the shadowed face and the line of throat and shoulders and long flank that made the hair lift a little on the back of his neck. He might have been looking at his own fetch.

'Did someone call my name?' The voice was different at all events, lighter and harder, glinting with a bright febrile fierceness that flashed into Phaedrus's mind the image of a panther he had once seen in the Londinium Circus.

'I called,' Gault said. 'I have failed, Midir. Now let you try if you can do better.'

The young man walked forward, Phaedrus with a quick suspicion of the truth, thought that he followed the sound of the other man's voice, and as he came full into the lamplight, saw that there were only scarred hollows under the straightened brows where his eyes should have been. Saw also the great puckered scar on his forehead where something, some pattern that had been tattooed there, had been dagger-gashed across and across in a sickening savagery of destruction, a long time ago.

He had enough of his mother in him to know that among the tribes no maimed or blind or crooked man could hold the kingship, lest his rule bring disaster on the people. So that was how the Royal Woman had made sure of Midir, the rightful King, whom she had not quite dared to kill! His gorge rose in his throat.

'Will you speak, Phaedrus the Gladiator, that I may hear where you stand.'

'I stand here, a spear's length from you, Midir of the Dalriads.'

'You give me a name that I have not borne these seven years. I am Midir the leather-worker.' The other had turned full face to him at the first sound of his voice, and came towards him unerringly, seeming to know the position of table and benches by the sound of his own footsteps, or by that mysterious 'shadow' that blind men speak of. 'And so you are like-looking to me. Like enough to take my place?'

'It is in my mind at least that any man who has seen neither of us in seven years might well take one for the other.'

256

'That should make you proud. It is not every slave gladiator who could pass for a prince of the Dalriads.'

Phaedrus felt the angry blood rushing to the roots of his hair, but before he could retort, the other added with a crack of laughter, 'Or, of course, every prince of the Dalriads who could pass for a leather-worker.'

'I do not see why not, if he had the training of his craft,' Phaedrus said in a tone of cool effrontery; but his sudden anger had begun to flicker out.

'I wonder. Is it the same with the prince's craft, should you be thinking?' The laughter still lingered in Midir's voice.

'*Na*. The prince's craft is another matter. No man needs to be born a leather-worker and the son of a leather-worker, but can you think of any training that would change a slave gladiator, in truth and not mere seeming, into a prince of the Dalriads?'

'The seeming might be enough—if he were not afraid.'

'Afraid?'

'A man who set out to play such a part would have good cause to be afraid. . . . But if you are like enough to pass for me, and not easily made afraid, then maybe the God has sent you to us.'

Phaedrus asked with a detached interest—he could still think himself detached, because he still believed that he was going to refuse—'And you? Could you stand aside while another man took your place?'

Midir's head was up, the lines of laughter in his face suddenly thin and hard as sword-cuts. 'Listen, my friend, Gault has used me as a weapon against you tonight—Ach, yes, he has, you know it as surely as I do—and if old Fox Sinnoch had not found you, they would have used me as a weapon against Liadhan, for want of a better. They would have made me their accusation against her before all the tribe. "See, warriors of Earra-Ghyl, lords of the horse-herd, here is Midir who should have been your King, but the She-Wolf clawed out the daylight for him and made him an insult to the Gods! Strike now against the Woman who has done this accursed thing!" It is better than no weapon at all. But to shout: "Brothers! Here is Midir your King! Liadhan would have slain him, but he escaped and now he is come back

to be the Battle Standard of the War Host!"—that is a sharper weapon, and the sharpness of the weapon is all I care for, now.'

His hands had come up while he spoke, feeling for Phaedrus's shoulders, and clamped down on them with a fiercely urgent grip.

And Phaedrus thought again of the chained panther, and was not sure why; only as surely as though he had shared these seven years, he knew that this red-haired other self had never come to any kind of terms with his fate, never for an instant accepted, never for an instant ceased to rage against the darkness, unbroken, unsubmitting, unreconciled. Knew also that he was without pity either for himself or for anything under the sky. For that instant, as though one life flowed through them both through the other's hands on his shoulders and his own that he had brought up to cover them, he knew the Prince Midir as he had never known anyone since the day he was born.

The two onlookers had ceased to matter; the world contracted and sharpened its focus as it had used to do in the arena, until it contained only himself and the man before him.

'You bid me to take your place, Midir?'

Midir was faintly smiling, and he spoke lightly, but the words came widely spaced like small bright drops of blood. 'Take my place, Phaedrus, and with it, take my vengeance and keep it safe—warm with your own warmth, like a little polished throwstone in the hollow of your shield, until time comes to throw. But cry my name when that time comes, so that both the Sun Lord and the Woman may know that it is *my* vengeance, not yours.'

4

The House of the Fighting-cocks

COCK-CROW had just sounded from the fort, and the long, narrow sprawl of native hovels, wine-shops and bath-houses, granaries, married quarters, horse corrals, and temples to a score of alien Gods, that made up the town of Onnum on the Wall, was stirring into wakefulness. Not that any of the Wall towns ever slept, save twitching and with one ear cocked and one eye open.

In the loft of a ramshackle house close to the fortress gate, where Florianus the old Syrian archer bred his fighting-cocks, the birds roused and rattled their feathers, stretched their necks and crowed defiance to the Roman trumpets.

Most mornings, the crowing of the cocks roused Phaedrus and Midir in their quarters beyond the rough partition wall. Then whoever's turn it was to forage would go down the rickety loft

ladder and out to the well at the street corner, draw himself a pail of water for hurried splashing wash, and on the way back, collect the platter of oaten bannock and jug of buttermilk or sour watered-wine which the old crone who owned the house would have left out for them overnight. The one whose turn it was to have his food brought up to him like an Emperor, went without washing that day. They never broke cover together, for though it was still half dark the lantern burned until dawn above the doorway of the 'Bacchus's Head' close by, and they took care not to impress it needlessly on the minds of chance beholders that there were two men lodging in the House of the Fighting-Cocks, two men who looked exactly alike, unless you came near enough to realize that one was blind.

But today they had been astir before the cocks, and were sitting on the edge of the makeshift plank bed, the jug and platter almost finished with, between them. The lamp on its niche high on the wall was getting short of oil; the flame leapt and fluttered, and its unstable light sometimes found and sometimes almost lost the two young men, showing them stripped to their plaid breeks as they had slept, for it was close in the little room, and already the day creeping up behind the narrow window gave promise of heat later.

Perhaps it was because of the thundery heat, Phaedrus told himself, that he was not hungry. But he knew it was not. Fiends and Furies! One would think to be glad enough at the prospect of getting out of this place!

He looked round at Midir, sitting with a half-eaten lump of the mouth-drying oatcake in his hand, and realized with a kind of exasperation that the heat had killed Midir's hunger as well. The flaring lamp made harsh shadows where his eyes should have been, and cast the puckered scar on his forehead into cruel relief. It was almost a month now, since the night just after they came here, when they had lain side by side while Gault with his curious skill for such things, had remade the lost pattern with a cock's hackle dipped in woad, and then copied the main lines of it on to Phaedrus's forehead; those potent, interlocking lines and spirals and double curves of Sun Cross and Stallion Symbol that

260

formed between them a device not unlike a four-petalled flower. And after that, the old woman he had brought with him had taken over, with her tattooing needles and pots of woad and crimson dye. The memory of that small, prickling torment made the nerve-ends crawl between his brows even now, and Phaedrus put up his hand unconsciously and felt the faintly raised lines on the skin. The Royal Flower, the old woman had called it, the Mark of the Horse Lord.

'Does it still feel strange?' Midir said, with that disconcerting awareness he sometimes had of what one was doing.

'Not so strange as it did a month ago.'

'A few months older, and I'd have had more than the Mark of the Horse Lord for the beldam to prick into your hide with her sharp needles.'

Phaedrus thought of Gault who had gone north again now; Gault the Strong, with the warrior pattern tattooed on breast and shoulders, thighs and cheeks and temples.

'All the warrior patterns that they prick on to the boys' skins at the Feast of New Spears,' Midir was saying. 'At the next Feast it would have been my turn to go into the darkness of the Place of Life, and come out from it a man, to take my place among the Men's Side, with the warrior patterns princely thick upon me.'

Beyond the thin partition a cock crowed in fiercely shining challenge, and was answered faintly across the roof-tops from some other cock-loft on the far side of the town.

'Why not Sinnoch?' Phaedrus asked suddenly.

'Sinnoch is only half of the tribe. His father was a Roman merchant—they get everywhere, the merchant-kind—who came to his mother on the night she hung up her girdle for the Goddess. There was a bad harvest that year, so I've heard. The priestess said the Great Mother was angry and must be appeased; and when they drew lots among the maidens, to sleep at the river crossing for the first stranger who passed that way, the lot fell upon her. And so Sinnoch was born and she died bearing him. ... I think he never greatly wanted to be a warrior; I suppose his father's wandering was in him, too, so he trades horses to the Roman kind, with an unmarked skin, and Gault

says there is not a noble of the tribe he could not buy up if he wanted to. It is strange—he did not want to be a warrior, and the Dalriads have always accepted him in other ways; but it hasn't made him love the folk who whisper in the dark to the Great Mother.'

'I think it would not make me, either,' Phaedrus said.

He got up and crossed to the window. The lamp was finally dying in little gasps of flame, and the roofs opposite were already touched with morning, though night still lingered in the narrow chasm of the street below. He stood gazing down into it while he tied his hair back out of the way with a leather thong as he had been used to do before putting on his helmet. He knew that street—what one could see of it from the window—as well as he knew the room behind him, with its gap-toothed floorboards and the scattering of bright feathers that drifted through with the smell of droppings from the cock-loft, and the places where the daub had fallen from the walls and the laths showed through like the bare ribs of something dead.

'Close on time for you to be away,' Midir said behind him.

'*Sa, sa.* No time for a wrestling-bout this morning.'

Every morning, since they had been cooped up here, they had wrestled together, at first simply to keep themselves from going soft, because they had no other way of getting exercise; but later, because they enjoyed pitting strength and skill against each other. Well, all that was done with now. ... 'I must not be keeping my new master waiting,' he added, and thought, 'It seems a lifetime that I have been mewed up in this place, learning my trade, and in a little while, it will still be here, but I shall be gone. I shall be away up the street to join Sinnoch and take the pack-beasts north—to win myself a kingdom that isn't mine, or more likely end as wolf-bait. And Midir?' Somehow the past month had seemed so shut away from the run of life, so turned in on itself that he had never wondered before. He swung round from the window. 'And you? What road for you now, Midir?'

Deep in the shadows the other shrugged. 'The road back to Eburacum and my *old* master and the dressed hides. This was

only to be a free time to visit my Aunt in Segedunum. He's a good old man; he said I had earned a holiday.'

'One advantage of being a free man. A slave never earns a holiday.' (Midir had never been sold as a slave, Phaedrus knew. Who would buy a blind slave unless he could sing? He had simply been turned adrift like an unwanted dog among the beggars of Eburacum, and his one piece of good fortune had been when the harness-maker who was now his master had seen him rough-mending a broken pack-strap for a traveller outside the posting inn, and noticed the skill in his hands.)

'I've an idea he did not mean so long a holiday as this one,' Midir said wryly.

'But he will take you back?'

'Ach, yes. I'm a good craftsman. You don't need to be able to see to work the skins or cut a belly-strap—only to be a king. ... I am wondering if this looks a noble jest to any God that chances to look this way. I wonder if the Gods laugh at the things that happen to men, as we laugh at someone slipping on a kale stalk—or if they simply don't care. ... My father went out to meet his boar. There had been much fighting, and the Red Crests had burned off all the pasture that they could reach, and then a wet autumn and the cattle died. It was famine time, you see. And look what came of it. That will have made Gods laugh, too.'

'Don't be talking like that,' Phaedrus said quickly. He did not understand what Midir was talking about, but he knew that it was dangerous. 'It is only a fool who sets out like a man poking at a stallion with a little stick, to make the Gods angry!'

Midir shrugged. 'Ach, well, it is I that said the thing, not you.' He leaned forward and felt for the jug, and with a quick gesture, flung the lees of the watered wine on the already stained and filthy floor. 'See, I am making an offering—what is it you call it in your Roman tongue? I pour a libation to the Sun Lord, a peace offering.' Then leaning back against the wall, hands behind head, 'Come now, I'll be hearing you your lessons one more time while you make ready for the road.'

Phaedrus had begun to move about their cramped quarters, gathering his few belongings and bundling them into an old cloak. A small part of his mind was wondering what had happened to his wooden foil and the fat woman's bracelet— probably the lodging-house people had taken them and what- ever else was in the bundle, when they heard he was dead. The rest of him was waiting, his mind poised to leap this way or that, for whatever question Midir would toss at him first.

Midir said, 'What happened after Liadhan had you stunned and flung into the river?'

Phaedrus frowned. ('Do not seem too sure,' Sinnoch had said when his training began, 'not so sure as to make men think "this is a lesson learned by heart".') 'How would I be knowing in the

264

dark and I hit on the head with a stone? The last thing I remember is Liadhan's man; the one of them with a stone in his hand. For the rest——' He shrugged. 'I suppose the man did not strike hard enough—maybe he did not mean to. Or else it was that my time had not come. I must have lodged among the rocks under the overhang of the shore, with my face above water. And seemingly they did not wait to be sure the work was finished, for when I woke, there was no one there. I was half drowned and very sick, and there was no strength in me to make the bank again and I—I must have struggled, and rolled clear of the rocks, and run of the river took me and carried me away, and washed me up at last, away down at the Crinan ford, where the chariot road runs south. A trader going that way with horses to sell to the Wall garrisons found me——'

'What was he like?'

'A small man—I do not remember clearly. I was in no state to be taking account of faces; and it was a long time ago.'

'That is fair enough. Go on.'

'He would not believe me when I told him who I was; he was a stranger and did not know the Royal Mark. He took me south with the horses and sold me when he sold them; and the man who bought me sold me again, and—shall I go on?'

'No need. So far the story is a credit to Sinnoch. For the rest— you should know your own story well enough without my hearing it again. *Na*, we'll try something else.' He made no move from his lounging position, but the next question came silken swift as a dagger thrust. 'You see a man with a small sickle-shaped scar slicing through one eyebrow. Who is he?'

'Dergdian, Son of Curoi, one of the Guard in my grandsire's day.'

'Which eyebrow does the scar cut through?'

'The left.'

'How is it that you remember so clearly? It is a longer time since you saw Dergdian than it is since you saw the horse-trader.'

'It was I that gave him the scar, throwing a stone at what I thought was a fox in the bracken; and he gave me the choice of

taking my beating from my father, or from himself and no more said.' Phaedrus sounded rueful, hitching at his shoulders as he spoke, as though indeed remembering the weight of Dergdian's arm. It was like that with him sometimes, now. He turned to the narrow window and stood looking out. 'Conory helped me wash the blood off, and begged some wound-salve from old Grania to ease the smart.'

'Conory?' said Midir's voice behind him.

'Conory was—is my cousin, born in the same summer to Iorwen, my father's younger sister. I know him by his having one eye set higher than the other, and a brown fleck in the apple of it.' There were other things he knew about Conory, a great many other things, including some that Midir had never told him. But he did not recite them now. They had had to be learned, but though the arena years had hardened him to most things, he still disliked trampling more often than need be in another man's private territory. 'It was to Conory that the Queen sent her token at Beltane,' he said, and then, watching a pigeon on the opposite roof, 'It seems the Queen likes her kings young.'

'The Sacred King must be always young, and strong, lest the harvest fail and the mares grow barren. It is maybe a fine thing for the Queen, but the needs of the harvest come first.'

'You've not told me much of Liadhan the Queen. Very little beside all that you have told me of other men and women.'

'What should I tell you of her? She has long fair hair and a long fair face, and all her movements are slow and strong and rich— like corn that is heavy in the ear. They say that Maeve of Connacht was such a one, who fought against us in the High and Far Off days, in the land our people came from. But there's small need to tell you the look of her, you'll not be mistaking her for another woman. I saw her in the Royal Woman's place at the feasts and sacrifices, but her life never touched against mine, until——' He broke off and Phaedrus, looking round, saw his face for the moment no more than a mask—like the calmly moulded features of the helmet mask over the sweating, snarling features of the gladiator beneath. Even his voice seemed masked

with that same artificial calm, when he spoke again. 'The boy Midir hated and feared her always, that is all that the Prince Midir, returned to his rejoicing tribe, need remember of Liadhan. Not even that she had him blinded to make him unfit for the kingship, and stood by to see it done. That story is done with and best forgotten, now that there is a new story to take its place.'

'Nevertheless, the part of me that remains Phaedrus the Gladiator will not quite forget that story until the account is settled with Liadhan.'

'*Na!* Forget it!' Midir dropped the mask, and springing up, came striding across to him. 'You've a wild enough team to drive without *that* mare yoked among them.'

'It was you who bade me to avenge you, that first night behind the "Rose of Paestum".'

'I spoke in a black moment,' Midir said.

And there was a small, sharp silence. Then Phaedrus said, 'You must have hated me.'

'You can scarce expect I would be loving you.'

A cart came rumbling up the street, the wagoner cursing his team; there was the crack of a long raw hide whip, the slow hoofbeats of the file of oxen died into the distance. Then Phaedrus said:

'Give me a right to the kingship, Midir.'

'I have told you——'

'I want more than words.'

Midir stood thoughtful for a moment, then he pulled the dagger from his belt where he wore it night and day ('A man needs to know where to lay hand on his knife in the dark,' he had said once), feeling with a finger along the blade to the tip, and made a small precise movement quicker than the eye could follow. A thread of crimson sprang to life on the fine brown skin inside his wrist, and a few beads of blood welled up. He reversed the knife with a flick, and held it out by the blade. 'Now you.'

Phaedrus took it, and stood for a moment balancing it in his hand. He was not even sure that he liked this uncomfortable man, certainly he felt none of the easy comradeship with him

that he had felt with Vortimax; but none of that mattered. During this long enclosed month they had grown together at the edges in a way that had nothing to do with liking, but belonged somewhere far down at the root of things.

He made his own small quick movement; watched the blood spring out on his own wrist.

Midir flicked up his head at the sound of the movement. 'Done?'

'It is done.'

'Bring yours to mine, then.'

Phaedrus did so, feeling the mouth of the tiny wound on the mouth of the other as they pressed their wrists together. Three drops of mingled blood escaped between them and made three brighter spots among the spilled lees of the wine on the floor where Midir had poured his libation to the Gods.

'So now we are of one life blood, you and I,' Midir said, 'and you have the blood of the Horse Lord mingled with your own, if ever the Gods call you to account for taking the kingship.' There was a note almost of laughter in his voice. Then as he took back the knife and sheathed it and brought up his hands to feel for Phaedrus's shoulders, he spoke in deadly earnest. 'Listen! *You* cannot be taking the kingship from me. Liadhan did that, once and for all. But it is not hers, even by riever's right, for she has turned back to the Old Ways and so there is no Horse Lord to lead the Dalriads and answer for them to Lugh of the Shining Spear. The kingship lies free and waiting. ... Take it if you can—and a good war-trail to you, Phaedrus, my brother-in-blood.'

Phaedrus set his own hands for an instant on the other's, as he had done that first night of all. 'It may be that we shall meet again one day,' he said. 'The Sun and the Moon on your path, Midir.'

He turned and caught up his bundle, and went clattering down the rickety stair and out into the street, all but colliding with a man carrying hot loaves. The man swore at him, and Phaedrus swore back, with flowers and flourishes of insult learned in the arena which left the other open-mouthed and

envious, then turned to look up at a small window high under the gap-toothed slates, from behind which came the sound of whistling, a short five-note phrase jaunty as a water wagtail, that he and Midir had used for a signal at their comings and goings, all this month. He whistled back, and hitching up his bundle, set off for the inn on the outskirts of the town, where Sinnoch and the horses were lodged, falling as he went into the old play-actor's swagger.

He had entered into this business partly for the sake of the thing that Gault had offered as a price, partly because of that sudden feeling of oneness with Midir; and then he had not been sure what strange waters he was getting into, nor where he was heading. But now, striding up the already crowded street where light and colour were seeping back into the world, and the pigeons wheeled above the roof-tops, suddenly he felt light on his feet and lucky. Every gladiator knew that feeling; the day when the God's face was towards you, your lucky day, when it was your adversary's guard and not yours that flew wide. He dodged a cart laden with wineskins, and swaggered on. Once or twice a head turned to watch the tall man with the red hair under a Phrygian cap pulled down to his eyebrows, who wore the rough clothes of a pack-train driver and walked with the braced instep of a dancer or a swordsman.

It was almost full daylight when he came to the stable court of the 'Golden Fleece'.

5

Frontier Post

TOWARDS evening, sixteen days later, with all the broad, slow
heather hills of Valentia between them and the Onnum Gate,
the little pack-train swung northward from the broadening
Cluta which they had been following since dawn, and turned
into the track that rose gently from the river marshes. And it was
then that Phaedrus saw a faint haze of smoke hanging beyond
the ridge, and said to the merchant riding beside him, 'What lies
ahead? It does not look like heath fire, though Typhon knows
the furze is dry enough.'

'It isn't heath fire,' Sinnoch said. 'That is the smoke of the Northern Wall cooking its supper.'

It was late into August by now, and the dust-cloud rose from the track under the ponies' hooves, and settled slowly again after their passing; a grey bloom of dust that powdered beasts and men from head to foot, parched the throat and stung the eyes, and seemed to fur over even the sound of the bell that the train leader wore about his neck to warn off the evil eye. And Phaedrus, constantly on the move to and fro along the plodding line, envied Vron, who had been Sinnoch's fore-rider for a score of years, ambling ahead on his small, ragged pony, his feet almost brushing the ground on either side, his old sheepskin hat hanging loose and easy on the back of his head.

It was a very small pack-train, only four burden-beasts and the three riding ponies; for Sinnoch was a horse-trader before all else. Once a year he made the trip south with a score or more rough-broken three-year-olds, herded by drovers on little shaggy ponies much as sheep-dogs herd their flock. He would give the lads a few days to make Corstopitum a still wilder place than it was the rest of the year, and then send them north again, and himself follow later with no one but Old Vron and maybe one other, his ponies' yellow bale-cloths laden with a few luxuries chosen with care and long experience of knowing his market: a few fine bronze weapons, ornaments of amber and jet, a cup of violet-coloured glass, a length of emerald silk, a couple of jars of Etruscan wine slung one on either side of a pack-saddle.

Phaedrus had asked him one day why he did not keep the drove-boys with him to act as guard for his small, rich cargo, and Sinnoch had said, 'Ah now, that would be to cry aloud to the very hills that the goods in my bales were worth taking; and what could a handful of drove-lads do against a rieving party? *Na, na*, it is better not to be putting ideas into honest folks' heads.'

A short while later they had crested the ridge, and were looking down at the Cluta marshes again, where the river flung one of its great loops northwards. A broad tongue of low, sodden land reaching far back into the hills, flaming with gorse along its

backward fringes, blurred with saltings and mouse-pale dunes towards the coast. And away across the flatness of it, where the land began to rise again, was the square-set mass of a big turf and timber fort with the usual huddle of native bothies in the stockaded cantonment; and on either side, the turf banks and ditches of the Wall itself. The Wall that ended, westward, in some kind of blockhouse or signal-station far out on the marshes, and eastward, climbed away on to higher ground, strung with other forts—Phaedrus could make out two, from the low ridge where they had checked to breathe the ponies—until it lost itself in distance and heat-haze and the great, dust-dark Caledonian Forest that lay like a thundercloud over all the inland country. And beyond the Wall, range behind range, trembling and transparent on the sultry air, the mountains of the North, seeming less substantial than the smoke of the cooking-fires that hung above the fort. ...

Eight years ago, the smoke hanging above the forts of the Northern Wall had been war-smoke, the dark smitch of burning timbers, rolling over dead men in the ditch. That was the last time that Dalriads and Caledones had joined spears; the second time that the Wall of Lollius Urbicus had gone up in flames. But each time it had been patched up and garrisoned again, and now the smoke was the quiet evening smoke of cooking-fires and the place looked secure and set in its ways between the marshes and wooded hills.

'A pleasant change, to see smoke rising from a hearth again,' Phaedrus said, his mind going back over the cold hearths, the remains of deserted villages, the steadings and cattle-folds whose stones were laced together with brambles and bindweed about their doorways, that they had passed more than once on their way north. Oh there had been living settlements, too, but even they had had a chill about them: too many old women with hollow faces, too few men, and too few children.

'*Aiee!* Lollius Urbicus made a fine clean sweep of Valentia while he was about it,' Sinnoch said. He spoke the General's name as though it smelt: a tone which Phaedrus had heard before among the men of the North. 'More than forty summers

272

ago, but the scars still show. *And* still ache when the wind is in the east, as old scars have a way of doing.'

Phaedrus glanced round, with quickly raised brows. 'Meaning another rising, one day?'

But the merchant, sitting loosely on the saddle rug, the great ox-hide whip resting across his pony's withers, had nothing in his eyes but distance and heat-haze. 'Maybe one day when and if the lowland tribes grow strong enough. That won't be in your time or mine; Lollius Urbicus knew what he was doing when he made his demands on the province—draughts for the Auxiliaries has a fine respectable sound to it—and marched all the young men away to serve the Eagles at the other end of the Empire.'

'One might be calling that a kind of murder,' Phaedrus said thoughtfully, 'only the murder of a whole people instead of one man.'

Sinnoch's voice was dryly and bitterly amused. 'Ah, *na*, it is just the Red Crests making the *Pax Romana*.' He whistled to the pack team, cracking the long whip above their backs to set them moving again.

'And then he built his fine new Wall,' Phaedrus pondered, as they plodded on and the choking dust-cloud rose again,' 'to say to all men: "The *Pax Romana* runs to *here*. This far the sun shines, and beyond it is the dark, that had best keep out."'

'Not quite. There were forts along that line a hundred years ago, so I've heard, and there are still outpost forts and the old warship base at Are-Cluta, a full day's trail beyond it. And as for keeping anything in or out. ....'

'What purpose does it serve, then?'

Sinnoch shrugged. 'It serves as a check-line, by which the Red Crests can keep track—after a fashion—of who comes and who goes, and how many, and how often.'

'After a fashion?'

'There are ways through without troubling the Red Crests. There are the coastwise marshes at either end, if one knows the tides and troubles to learn the habits of the patrols. But the game's not worth the lamp-oil unless there is something of especial value to be smuggled through.'

'Such as?'

'Arab mares, for instance. The Romans will wink quite happily at the odd stallion, fairly bought in the horse-market, going through to improve the stock—the more so that they buy our three-year-olds for Cavalry re-mounts. But mares are another matter.'

Phaedrus nodded. A stallion could sire many foals in a year, but a mare bears only one. That was why no War Host ever put its mares in the fighting-line unless it was desperate for horses, why no province would allow good mares out over its borders if they could possibly be stopped. 'Then if it is only to improve the stock, why not leave the mares alone and bring north only the stallions that the Red Crests wink at?'

Sinnoch looked round at him. 'A charioteer, you have been, among other things, but it is in my mind that you know little of horse-breeding. Have you never heard that a horse gets his strength from his sire, but his courage from his dam? And valiant though our little hill-run mares may be, there's nothing like an Arab mare for setting fire in her foals. Besides, it would be a poor cold world in which a man was only doing what the Red Crests allowed.'

Phaedrus said softly, 'Have you taken mares through, yourself?'

'I may have done, from time to time, when I was young and rash. If it served no other purpose, it taught me the hidden ways of my own hills as few save the little Dark People know them. But *this* trip we are not looking for trouble; also I've a mind to visit an old friend who keeps the wine-shop in the Cantonment yonder. So tonight we shall sleep safe and respectable under the fortress walls, and pass through with Rome's blessing in the morning.'

And so late that evening, having unloaded the pack bales and left Sinnoch in the back room of the wine-shop, exchanging the news of the Frontier with his old friend, who proved to be an immensely fat old woman in a dirty pink tunic, Phaedrus and Vron took the ponies down to water them at the stream below

the fort, that, born somewhere among the furze and birch scrub inland, came down in a chain of looped shallows and widening pools on its way to join the Cluta.

A patrol of the Frontier Scouts had just come in and were watering their mounts, and Phaedrus, well aware of the cast-difference between pack-pony and cavalry mount—though, indeed, these particular cavalry mounts were just as rough-coated as his own charges and not much larger—followed Vron down to the pool below that at which the troop ponies were drinking. It was cool under the alders that trailed their branches towards the water, though the midges still danced in the sunlight, and a breath of air stole up from the marshes, salt-laden after the heat of the day. You could see the long, soft breath of it coming, silvering the marsh grasses all one way. Phaedrus and old fore-rider dismounted, knotted up the halters, and let the ponies make their own way down the bank, and the cold peat-brown water rippled round the seven eager muzzles as the weary little beasts dropped their heads to drink.

Vron squatted on to his heels, his back against an alder trunk, tipped his sheepskin hat over his eyes and became instantly and peacefully one with the landscape. But Phaedrus, making sure that the halters were secure so that the ponies could roll without danger of getting entangled, before going back to the corral, kept one eye on the men upstream.

He had seen bands of the Frontier Scouts once or twice since coming north of Hadrian's great wall, but they were a strange breed to him, not like the Legionaries, or the Auxiliaries of the Wall garrisons who came down to Corstopitum on leave. Of course he had heard stories. . . . They were lean, rangy men who he knew could cover the hills on foot almost as quickly as on horseback if need be; many of them British born. A wild lot, the stories said, but said it in a tone of unwilling respect, and watching them as they stood by, relaxed but watchful while the ponies drank, one leaning against a hazel trunk and whistling through his teeth, one frowning over some adjustment to his bow—a light horn bow such as the Cretan Auxiliaries used, good for work on horseback; two more arguing softly and fiercely, an

argument that looked as though it had gone on all day and might well go on all night, but each with an eye on his mount to make sure that he drank what he needed and no more, Phaedrus could believe something of their reputation and understand something of the respect. No Legion would have been seen dead in their company, breeched like barbarians, wolfskin cloaked, some with the wolf's head drawn forward over their own in place of cap or helmet. Something about them seemed familiar, waking an odd pang of longing in Phaedrus that surprised and puzzled him, until he realized that it was the oneness of the pack, the strong bond that he had known in the Gladiator's School.

But the little, red-roan pack-mare was water-greedy, and in seeing that she did not guzzle half the pond and give herself colic, he lost track of the Frontier Scouts until a twig cracked, and he looked round to see that the Captain of the band had come strolling down the stream side with an eye cocked on the ponies.

He nodded towards the mare. 'She looks as though she had a bit of breeding to her.'

'She's not——' Phaedrus began, instantly on the defensive.

And the other laughed. He was a thin, very dark man, maybe in his late twenties, with a hooked nose too big for his narrow face, and a pleasant pair of eyes set deep and level on either side of it. 'Ah no, I'm not accusing her of Arab blood! I was thinking merely that she seemed a bit too good for pack duty. She might make a hunting-pony. I wonder if Sinnoch would sell her.'

Phaedrus, beginning to coax the mare back from the water ('Enough, greedy one! Back, now! Back, I say!'), looked round at the soldier. 'You know my master?'

'I have been in these parts three years now—seen him through three times into Valentia with his re-mounts, and three times back into the hills again with his wine and amber. Everyone on this sector of the Wall knows Sinnoch, and relies on him for news of the outer world. But as to the mare——'

'You had better ask him.'

'Maybe I will.' The man had put up a hand that was thin and

dark like himself, and began fondling the mare's wet muzzle as she turned unwillingly from the water, coaxing her to him. 'There's my girl. See, we are friends already, you and I.' But his gaze was still on Phaedrus's face, considering; and suddenly he said, 'You're a new man of Sinnoch's, aren't you?'

'Yes.'

'And like the mare, you have not the look of the pack-train.'

'I have been other things—more than one—in my time.'

'Among them, perhaps, a gladiator?'

Phaedrus's head jerked up. 'I gained my wooden foil something over two months ago.'

'So—o. This seems an unlikely way of life for a gladiator to turn to.'

'It's meat and drink. My kind still needs to eat, even when the arena gates are closed to us. It is written all over me, then?'

'It is my business to know the looks of fighting-men. You are a fighting-man, but you have the look that does not come from Legionary training.'

Phaedrus grinned. 'Is it only the training then, that makes the war hound or the arena wolf?'

'Generally something more, I grant you. Assuredly the gladiator, once trained to the sand, makes a very bad soldier.'

'I was right then. I did think to go up to the Fort—that was at Corstopitum; but I reckoned it would be a waste of time.'

The other nodded, his hand still on the little mare's neck, while she nuzzled with delicately working lips against his breast. Then he added abruptly, 'The Frontier Wolves, of course, might be another matter. We also make very bad soldiers by Legionary standards.'

Phaedrus was silent a moment in blank surprise. 'You would not be offering me a Scout's dirk for my wooden foil?' he said at last.

'Hardly. But if you were to go to the Commandant at Credigone, I *think* you might not find it a waste of time.'

They stood confronting each other while the slow heartbeats passed; the silence full of the soft stamping and sucking of the horses, and the woodwind call of an oyster-catcher from the

marshes. Phaedrus thought, with detachment, what it would be like to break away from the wild venture he was bound on, and ride behind this man or another to his kind, one of a close-knit company again. It was a thought to play with for an instant, like a little sharp dagger that one throws up and catches by the blade. . . .

Then he shook his head. 'Too late now; I've another trail to ride.'

'No turning aside from it?'

Phaedrus had a sudden vision of the kind of thing that would happen to him if he tried to turn aside from this particular trail now; and knew in the same instant that if there had been no bargain made in the back room of the 'Rose of Paestum', no mark like a blue-and-crimson four-petalled flower tattooed on his forehead under the close Phrygian cap, still he would have done no more than play with the thought for an instant.

'No turning aside. To speak plain, I'd not care to spend the next twenty years patrolling this desolation of Valentia, with a skirmish with cattle-raiders now and then by way of salt in the stirrabout. Not that I'd be lasting twenty years. I'd be cutting my throat by spring.'

'So? Are you so much of a townsman? The hills are lonelier, north of the Wall, than the hills of Valentia.'

'But maybe not so desolate. There are too many dead villages and cold hearths between here and the Southern Wall.'

'That is an old story now, though it was an ugly one in its day,' said the Roman officer. 'Punitive work is always ugly.'

'More than forty years old, they tell me, but the little villages are still dead and the hearths cold, as Lollius Urbicus left them.'

'You're British, aren't you?' the Captain said. 'Well, upward of half my scouts are native to the land.'

'They have chosen their loyalties, and I choose mine,' Phaedrus said, and checked, trying to find words for what he meant. 'My mother was from somewhere in these Northern parts, and knew the inside of a slave-market. My father was—of another conquered people. There are too many conquered people in Rome's world.'

'At least we have brought some kind of order, even some kind of peace, to a world that was ancient chaos before.'

'The *Pax Romana*,' Phaedrus said. 'My fa—my first master had me taught to read and write, though I have lost the trick of it now. He let me read books. There was one, a history that a man called Tacitus wrote of the General Agricola's campaigns, a hundred years ago. He fought a great battle, this Agricola, with a war-leader called Calgacus, far to the north somewhere; and there was a fine fiery speech that Calgacus was supposed to have made to his warriors before the battle joined—no Roman could have heard a word of it and so it must have been Tacitus's speech really—you see that? He made Calgacus say of the Romans, "They make a desolation, and call it peace." So even Roman Tacitus could have his doubts.' He was surprised and infuriated, even while he was speaking, to find how much of his mother's race those dead villages had roused in him. Fool, to be crossing swords with this dark man, just when it was most needful that he should not get into trouble, or draw attention to himself in any way! But still, he did not stop until the thing was said.

Mercifully it seemed that the Roman officer was unusually slow to take offence. There was no gathering frown of affronted dignity on his face, only the look of a man arguing with another who has different beliefs from his own, and who respects those beliefs even while he will not yield to them one hair's breadth.

'I think you must have been almost as unlikely a gladiator as you are a pack-driver. I'm sorry I can't persuade you; I believe you would have made a good Frontier Wolf.'

There was the jink of a hanging-bridle-bit as one of the cavalry ponies tossed up his head, and from the fort, a trumpet call sounded through the evening air; and Phaedrus realized that the shadows were beginning to thicken among the alder roots. 'Aye, well, I'll have a word with Sinnoch about the mare,' the Captain said, and turned on his heel to stroll back upstream to his own men.

Phaedrus stirred Vron out of his sleep with a friendly foot.

'Come on, old one, time to be getting them penned for the night.'

Late that evening, in the lamplit store-shed behind the wine-shop, when the fat woman had gone waddling off to attend to her customers and Vron had betaken himself to a cock-fight, Sinnoch said, 'And what were you and the Captain, Titus Hilarian, talking of so earnestly, down at the horse-pool?'

'*That* will be Vron,' Phaedrus said. 'I doubted he could have gone to sleep so suddenly.'

'Vron always sleeps like a hound—one ear cocked and one eye open.'

'*Sa*—I have noticed. Well then, he can tell you what we talked of.'

A dry smile twitched at the corner of Sinnoch's mouth. 'Alas, you spoke in the Latin tongue. Vron has only three words of Latin, and one of them is "drink". . . . What did the Captain want?'

'He was interested in buying the roan mare.'

Sinnoch nodded. 'I thought he might. He was needing a new hunting-pony when I came by on the road south, so I kept my eye open in the Corstopitum horse-markets.'

'You thought—then why all this pretence of her being a pack-pony?'

'Why bring her all this way like a fine lady eating her head off, when she can earn her keep on the trail? Besides, it was in my mind that he would be well pleased with himself to discover breeding under a pack-saddle, and a man pleased with himself pays the better.'

'You wily old fox,' Phaedrus said in admiration.

Sinnoch made a small depreciatory gesture, as of one modest-ly turning aside a compliment. 'It is merely a matter of knowing one's market. He is a bright enough lad, our Captain—good at his job. He'll be commanding one of the outpost forts in a year or two, if he isn't broken for going too much his own way, or dead in a bog with an arrow of the little Dark People in him; but like most of his kind, his mind works in straight lines. Maybe that is

what has made Rome the ruler of the world, but there's no denying that when it comes to buying or selling a horse, the man who can think in curves has the advantage.' He leaned forward abruptly, his face in shadow, one heavy ear-drop of coral and silver catching the lamplight as it swung. 'What else did he say?'

Phaedrus frowned, and was silent an instant before answering. 'That an ex-gladiator might do well enough among the Frontier Scouts.'

'And you are thinking it, maybe; a sad pity that you never thought of that before you went the first time to the "Rose of Paestum", and ended in the town gaol.'

Phaedrus rubbed his knee, where the scar was pulling as it still did when he was tired. 'We have a saying in the circus, that life's **too** short to waste it in saving for the future or regretting the past. I told the Captain Hilarian I'd be cutting my throat by spring, if I took service in this desolation.'

'You may not last so long in Earra-Ghyl.'

6

Eyes!

NEXT day when the bargaining for the red mare was over and
she had changed owners, they pushed on north-westward into
the tribal lands beyond the shadow of Rome. Gault met them
two nights later, a picked handful of warriors with him. And
after that there were days and nights—so many that Phaedrus
lost count of them—among the coastal marshes and steep
woodland glens and great inland-running arms of the sea, with
always the huge mountain mass that Sinnoch said was
Cruachan the Shield-boss of the World, towering higher and
higher into the northern sky. A constant shifting from place to
place, strange faces seen in the fire-light and gone again next
morning; word spoken softly and passed on, in herdsman's bothy
or at river ford. Little bands of men with spears who appeared as
it were from nowhere in the half-light of dusk or dawn, and were
given their orders and merged into nowhere again.

They came at last to three great cliff caves that must once have had their feet in the western waters, though now there was a strip of rocky shore between them, and made their fire in the heart of the largest of them; and after that for a while there was no more changing camp.

It was well into autumn by now; the great gales came booming in from the sunset, leaping the back of Inshore Island that crouched as though to give what shelter it could to the rocky coast behind it, and the seals had left their basking rocks for deep water. And a certain autumn night came, a soft dark night between storms, bringing with it a moment that seemed to Phaedrus very like the moment before the first trumpets sounded and one heard the clashing open of the arena gates.

The branching gallery in which he stood was no more than a fault in the living rock, so narrow that a man's shoulders might brush against either side, but running up to unknown heights overhead. The rocks were slippery underfoot and somewhere in the depth of them was the sound of running water; and the heavy cold air was full of hollow sighings of the sea. There was a faint blur of light at the far end where the lamp still burned in the small inner cave, and close at hand a fiercer gash of torchlight shining through a chink in the heavy sealskin curtain that covered the mouth of the gallery.

Low voices sounded beyond the curtain, as the three of them checked an instant in the all-enveloping dark between the two gleams, and they, too, had a hollow sound, and set strange whispering echoes running. Then Gault—he knew that it was Gault by the kind of leashed ferocity of the movement—reached out and dragged the heavy skins aside; and torch- and fire-light flooded in to meet them.

Phaedrus, caught full in the smoky light, with all the darkness of the gallery behind him, checked an instant on the lip of the rock-tumble that led down into the huge main cavern. Trained as he was to make an entrance and an impression, he was vividly aware of himself, aware that gladiator and pack-rider had both gone, and that in their place stood a prince of the Dalriads, in breeks of chequered stuff and tunic of fine saffron wool, raw hide

283

brogues on his feet, a bronze-sheathed dagger at his belt, and everywhere about him, on arms and neck and in the fillet of twisted wires that bound back his hair, the glint of yellow river-gold.

The voices in the cave had suddenly stopped. Faces were turned and eyes fixed hungrily upon him. He sprang down over the loose stones into the cave, Gault and Sinnoch following more soberly in his wake.

As always in the first instant of coming into the great cavern, he cast one swift glance towards the innermost wall, where the masses of volcanic rock which elsewhere upheaved themselves in gigantic zigzag layers, rose in sheer slabs as flat and level as though cut by hand, and on the smooth surfaces still showed the dim and fragmentary traces of animals and birds drawn in red and ochre and black: wild ox and bear, boar and wolf, and what looked like a wild duck rising, and in the midst of them, towering into the upper gloom, gaunt and grotesque but mag-nificent, the figure of a man with the head of a twelve-point stag. No one knew how long he had stood there, only that he was very, very old. And Sinnoch, who knew many things beside how to sell horses, had said once that he was the Lord of Herds and the Hunting Trail, and something strange about his dying for the people whenever the Sacrifice was needed.

It was only a flung glance as his feet touched the cave floor, then he turned to the five men who sat or stood beside the driftwood fire on the raised central hearth.

'Well?' Gault said, beside him, and then, 'Look him over, my brothers; will he serve?'

It seemed to Phaedrus that there were nothing but eyes in all that great sea-echoing cavern, and behind the eyes, the judge-ment of five men, focused on him. He felt them burning him up, as he stood confronting them, head raised and mouth curving into a smile that he did not know was faintly insolent.

A big, freckled man with the blurred outlines of an athlete run to flesh was the first to speak. 'It is hard to tell, with a boy of fourteen summers, what like the man will be; but the King his father'—he checked an instant and corrected himself—'this man

is much such a one to look at as the King, Midir's father, was at his age.'

Another nodded in agreement, and the third said, 'It takes more than the shape of a nose to be making one man able to pass for another, but so far as outward seeming goes, aye, he will serve.'

But the fourth member of the group, an oldish man with hot, clever eyes and a sour mouth with no teeth in it, said fretfully, 'I wonder, Gault the Strong, that you are troubling yourself to bring him to the Council fire at all, since it seems that you have decided the thing to suit yourself already. Or do I dream in my old age, and only *think* to see the Mark of the Horse Lord on his forehead?'

'*Na*, you do not dream, Andragius my Chieftain,' Gault said. 'The Mark is there. But maybe your memory plays you tricks, and you forget that because *you among the rest of the Council* chose me, I am the leader in this matter as I have been from the first. There was no time to call a Council; indeed, if Sinnoch had not had calm weather for the boat crossing and found me in my own Dun of the Red Bull, but had come on north to Dun Monaidh seeking me, it is in my mind that there might have been no time to carry the thing through at all. The Mark had to be made at the first possible moment, that there might be time for the look of fresh tattooing to wear off from it, and in such a case it must be for the leader to decide what shall and what shall not be done! Will any of you say that I have gone beyond the powers you gave me?'

There was a moment's silence, broken only by the sea-echoes and the crackle of the driftwood spitting on the fire. Then Andragius shrugged and said unpleasantly, 'If my brothers are satisfied, then I suppose I have little choice but to be satisfied, too.'

Gault dropped the subject as though it was a dead mouse and turned to the fifth member of the Council. 'You have not spoken yet, Tuathal the Wise, Cup-bearer of the Sun: you who should speak first among us.'

The fifth man, who had been sitting on a skin-spread stool, unmoving all this while, his eyes fixed on Phaedrus's face, got to

his feet, slowly uncoiling his full magnificent height, and instantly became the core and centre of the scene. He was, maybe, not much younger than Andragius, but of a very different kind. A man with a great curved nose like the hooked beak of a bird of prey; his robe of finely dressed horse-skins, supple as cloth, fell around him in folds like a king's mantle; his head was shaved save for a single broad strip from forehead to nape, which sprang up and arched back with the proud sweep of a silver stallion's crest. His eyes, too, were like those of a bird of prey—a falcon, not a hawk, the dark, full, glowing eyes that, alone of all eyes of men or beasts, could outstare the sun without being blinded. He said, 'Come here to me, you who are now called Midir.'

Phaedrus went to him, and found himself caught and held by those eyes.

'You understand, to the full, what we demand of you? Not only the Council here, but the people who will be your people?'

'I know and I understand the demands of the Council. Can any man not born to it understand the demands of a people, save by learning them as they come?'

'No,' said Tuathal the Wise. 'No. ... Yet even that is a thing worth understanding, and the rest may come with the need. ...' He seemed to be speaking to himself, rather than to Phaedrus, his gaze going past him to the great daubed figure on the wall behind. Then abruptly the bright, piercing gaze returned to Phaedrus's face. 'You have learned the part that you must play? The ways and customs—and the memories? You know your way through the five courts of Dun Monaidh? When a kinsman speaks to you, you will know what name to call him by?'

'I was a full month with Midir, and I think I did not waste it.'

'No?' Tuathal waited, clearly for some proof.

Phaedrus smiled, knowing that he could give it. 'Shall I call you by all your titles, Tuathal the Wise, High Priest of the Burning One, Mouthpiece of Lugh Shining Spear, Cup-bearer, Foal of the Sun? And—the one more, not for speaking aloud.' He leaned closer, and murmured the fifth name, the Taboo name that could only be spoken between the Horse Lord and the Priests of the Sun.

Something flickered far back in Tuathal's eyes, and the proud arched lids widened a little, but he gave no other sign.

Phaedrus turned to the big, fleshy man who had been the first of the five to speak. 'Oscair Mac Maelchwn, is there still a cub of white-breasted Skolawn's among your hearth hounds?'

Then as Oscair nodded, he turned to the third man, meeting little, bright, lively eyes like a grass-snake's, in a big-boned, ruddy face. 'You will be here in the Chief your father's stead, Cuirithir? He was a sick man, growing old before his time, seven years ago, and yet you do not wear the Chief's arm-ring.'

And then it was old Andragius's turn, and Phaedrus longed to say to him, 'Poor old man! Do you know that they only brought you into the Council because you are too great a Chieftain to be left outside?' Instead he said, 'My Lord Andragius, you were never quite believing that I did not trip your grandson on purpose in the boys' Spear Dance, so that he went heels over head and everybody laughed. But truly, it was no more than clumsiness. I have learned to use my weapons better now.'

And last of all, to a thickset, dark man, younger than the rest, with a gay and ugly face, he said, 'Gallgoid, are you still the Prince of Charioteers in all Earra-Ghyl? You used to take me up into your chariot, and drive like the west wind with me, and I'd not have changed places with all the Gods and heroes rolled into one!'

'There's none risen to supplant me yet,' Gallgoid said, with a flash of white, crooked teeth.

'You have put your month to good use,' the Sun Priest said after a moment, 'but let you tell us one thing more. Why are you doing this?'

Oscair put in gruffly, 'He *is* doing it. Does the reason matter?'

'It is in my mind that there are reasons and reasons—though maybe this one is not far to seek. A kingship must seem good enough reason to such men as I have heard fight to the death to amuse a Red Crest crowd, for the price of their next meal.'

'Both Gault and Sinnoch will bear me out that at first I swore I'd not meddle with a kingship that was not mine.'

'*Sa, sa*—what made you change your mind?'

There was a long silence, and Phaedrus heard by the changed sea-echoes in the cavern that the tide was on the turn. 'Midir, as much as any other thing,' he said at last. Then with a kind of defiance, '*Na*, it is simpler than that. Gault offered me a price— oh, not in gold; the whetted edge to life that I had missed somewhat since I gained my freedom from the Gladiators' School. The price seemed to me a fair one, and so I am your man, in the way of any other Mercenary who strikes a fair bargain for his sword.'

'So, you give us two reasons; and together, I find them good.' Tuathal turned to the others beside the fire. 'For myself, I am with Gault the Strong in this. How say you, my brothers?'

'I also,' Gallgoid said vehemently.

'And I.'

'And I.'

Only Andragius shrugged and held his hands to the fire. He would be able to say that he had warned them all along, he would even be able to claim that he had never agreed but been over-ruled by the rest of the Council, if trouble came later.

Presently they were all sitting about the fire, while the mead horn passed from hand to hand and Phaedrus, as the youngest man there, tended the thick hunks of pig-meat broiling on the red peat heart of the blaze.

They went over plans as they waited for the food to be ready; the plans that were to become action on the night before the Midwinter Fires. But, indeed, all things had been worked out long since ('Already the horns are sounding in the hills, and the black goat dies,' Gault had said, months ago in Corstopitum), and there was only some small point here and there to be altered because now, instead of a blinded prince to avenge, they had a long-lost prince to set back in his father's place.

Even the mark that would tell friend from foe had been decided on, and every man of the Sun Party would wear the temple locks of his hair plaited, the rest hanging loose. Conory, it seemed, was to manage that, setting the fashion and making sure

that it spread naturally as a fashion does, between this and the night of the uprising.

Oscair said suddenly, 'You are sure that Conory can handle it? He is more skilled with the sword than the ways of guile.'

'He'll handle it. He's no fool, and he has only to cut the tip off his nose one day for half the young braves of the tribe, to be lacking theirs the next.'

'I still think,' Gallgoid the Charioteer put in, 'that we should have been telling Conory the truth of this matter.'

'If he suspects——'

'Why should he suspect?' Gault demanded harshly. 'It is seven years since he last saw Midir, and they were both fourteen. And in any case, it is a less risk than telling him would be. He's as unpredictable as a woman and once told, it would be too late to untell the thing again.'

The Sun Priest, who had seemed to be far withdrawn into some inner distance of his own, looked up from the fire. 'Furthermore, in Conory we have our one sure test. They were closer to each other than most brothers, those two; if Conory does not know that this is not Midir, then unless he makes some very great mistake, no one will ever know.'

Many torches burned at the upper end of the cavern, and in the unaccustomed light that leapt from his feet to the proudly antlered head high among the hearth smoke, the painted figure of the Horned God seemed to stand clear of the rock wall behind him. An apron of skins across the seaward entrance had been drawn tight over its pegs against the wild autumn night, and the stormwind coughed and roared against it like the open palm of a giant on the stretched skin of some mighty drum. And between it and the driftwood fire on its raised hearth, the Chiefs and Captains of the tribe were gathered.

Phaedrus, standing alone at the huge rock-daubed feet of the God, saw them only as thickened shadows, lit here and there with the blink of bronze or gold, here and there with the life-spark of an eye. The shadows, that had had deep-murmuring voices before his coming, had fallen silent, even the wind had

ceased for a moment its drumming on the entrance skins; only the sea pitching on the rocky foreshore still boomed and roared, flinging its echoes about the cave.

Then Gault, standing with his knot of household warriors a spear's length to one side, cried out in a voice which leapt back from the rock walls with the rough ring of war horns, 'Here he is, then! Here is the Prince Midir, your true Horse Lord, whom the woman Liadhan would have slain, seven winters ago!'

And among the crowding shadows below the fire there was a stirring and an indrawn breath that was almost a sob.

Then a voice shouted back, 'What proof can you give us that this is indeed Midir, and not some other with the look of him?'

'What is proof to do with myself or with Sinnoch the Merchant? We have found and brought to you the Prince Midir. The proof is for him to give, if it's more than the sight of your own eyes you're needing!'

'Let him give it, then!'

Phaedrus put his hands to the circlet of braided gold wires that pressed low on his temples, and lifted it off and flung it down ringing on the rock floor at his feet, baring his forehead to the torches. 'Here is your proof! Come closer and look!'

A formless smother of voices answered him, lost in the boom of the storm-wind as it swooped back, and the shadows parted and came crowding up past the fire, taking on the substance of living men as the flaring torchlight met them. An oldish man whose hair showed brindled as a badger's pelt, thrust out from the rest; his voice, deep and glad, crashed through the bell-booming of the storm. 'Midir! It *is* Midir, after all these years!'

'Seven years,' Phaedrus said, and reached out to him, the gold and copper arm-rings clashing on his wrists. 'It is good that they are over and I come back again!'

But the doubt lingered in some of them. A tattoo mark could, after all, be copied, and they had learned caution under Liadhan's rule. 'You do not speak like us,' someone called from the heart of the throng.

And Phaedrus dropped his hands and turned on him. 'Set a wolf-cub among the hound-pack, and he'll learn to bark like

a dog. Great Gods, man, I have been seven years in the South!'

Then another spoke up. 'Why did you not come back before?'

'Why does the mare not foal before she is mated, or the bramble ripen before the flower falls? What would have happened if I had come creeping to your hunting fires one night, or worse still, burst in upon you shouting war-cries, before the time was ripe? Before you called me back? I heard no man call till now.'

'We did not know that you yet lived.'

And somewhere out of the knot of warriors a third voice rose, with others in support: 'How does it happen that you did not drown as we were told? Tell us what passed that night and after.'

The drumming of the wind about the cave mouth filled the expectant hush, but Phaedrus had a sense of silence. He had known that this would come, and come again and again; he had his story ready, so familiar that it seemed part of his own memory; but suddenly, every nerve on the stretch, he knew that this first time, he must not tell it; that to tell in answer to a shouted demand would not have been Midir's way.

His head was up and his hand caressing his dagger. He laughed a little, but without mirth. 'Ach now, did they not tell you that tale when they summoned you here? Did the messengers only whisper in your ear, "Midir is back from the slain! Come!" and you came, asking no question?'

'We would hear it from yourself, Midir.'

'Would you so?' Phaedrus looked them up and down, then flashed out at them in a fine blaze of anger. 'Now by Lugh of the Shining Spear! To hear you, a man might think the Prince Midir stood on sufferance, here among his own! Shall I come to you with my hands held out, and bend my neck and stand before you like a beggar before the master of the house, telling my story for a crust of bannock and a corner by the fire? It is not for you to wag your heads and take me in as the master of the house takes in a beggar of his charity; it is I, Midir the Horse Lord, who comes back to take the place among you that is mine; mine to me! I am the spearhead of this rising that shall drive the

She-Wolf from the place that she has snatched, and free the tribe to walk in the daylight again! I am the Lord of the Horse People as my father was before me; if you do not believe me, kill me for an impostor; if you do, then take me for what I am, and be glad of my coming!'

For a moment longer the hush endured, and then the badger-haired man broke it. 'That had the true ring of Midir about it. There was never a shred of respect he had for his elders!'

And someone laughed deep in his throat, and the hush broke into the hubbub of slackened strain.

And in the midst of it all, Phaedrus was handfast with the badger-haired one, and saw in the torchlight the line of an old scar slicing through one bushy eyebrow, and said, suddenly quiet, 'What, Dergdian, no doubts at all?'

'None!' Dergdian said. 'I knew you from the first moment. I am not like some fools who forget a face they have not seen for a week! Ah well, I set my mark on you, as I remember.'

'And I on you! The scar still shows a little—but you made me pay for it! My back still smarts when I remember that day!' He hitched at his shoulders. 'I still say it was a simple mistake; you were red as a fox in those days. Not so red now, Dergdian.'

'*Na, na!* I will not be called a fox! That is for Sinnoch. I am a hound growing grey about the muzzle.' Laughter-lines deepened about Dergdian's eyes. 'But I am your hound as I was your father's.' And still holding Phaedrus's hands, he got stiffly down on to one knee, and pressed his forehead against them, in the way of a tribesman swearing loyalty to his Chief.

One by one the other followed his lead, pressing about Phaedrus to take their allegiance. Their faces were alive with reborn hope. And suddenly Phaedrus wanted to fling the next man off and shout at them: 'Don't! In Typhon's name don't. I'm not Midir—if you want him go and look for a blind leather-worker in Eburacum!'

And then behind the rest, with some kind of great fur collar round his neck, he saw a man holding back, taking his time; watching him out of eyes that seemed, even in the gloom beyond

the torchlight, to be oddly set—
one a little higher than the
other. . . .

Their gaze met, and Phaedrus
saw in that instant that the fur
collar had eyes too. A striped-
grey-and-dark thing with eyes
like green moons. The young
man made a sound to it, and the
thing rippled and arched itself
into swift, sinuous life, became
a wildcat, poised and swaying
for an instant on his shoulder,
and leapt lightly to the floor,
and advanced beside him with
proudly upreared tail, as he
came forward to take his place
among the rest.

For an instant, as they came
face to face, and the wildcat
crouched at his foot, Phaedrus
thought that this could not, after
all, be the cousin born in the
same summer, who had helped
Midir to wash the blood from his
back after that long-ago beating.
Not this wasp-waisted creature
with hair bleached to the silken
paleness of ripe barley, who
wore a wildcat for a collar, and
went prinked out like a dancing-
girl with crystal drops in his ears
and his slender wrists chiming
with bracelets of beads strung on
gold wires! But one of the man's
eyes was certainly set higher
than the other; and on the

293

bright hazel iris was a brown fleck the shape of an arrow-head.

For a long moment they stood confronting each other, and Phaedrus knew that this was indeed the danger moment. He saw a flicker of doubt in the odd-set eyes, quickly veiled, and something tensed in his stomach, waiting for what would happen next, while the men around him looked on.

The young man said, 'Midir.' Just the one word, and his hands came out. Phaedrus, with an unpleasant consciousness of the wildcat crouched with laid-back ears on the floor, followed his lead so instantly that the onlookers could scarcely have said which made the first move. But next instant their arms were round each other in a quick, hard embrace that looked like the reunion of long-parted brothers, but had actually nothing in it but a kind of testing, an enquiry, like the first grip of a wrestling-bout.

The wildcat spat as though in warning, but made no move.

Then both stepped back, and stood looking at each other at arm's length.

'Conory—you have changed!' It was the only thing that Phaedrus could think of to say, and it seemed safe.

'Have I?' Conory said. 'So have you, Midir. So—have—you,' and the doubt was still in his eyes; indeed, it had strengthened, Phaedrus thought, but it would not be there for anyone but himself to see. At any rate—not yet. What game was he playing? Or was he playing any game at all? Had he, Phaedrus, only imagined that flicker of doubt? It was gone now. Unless it was only veiled once more. . . .

With Conory's grip on his shoulders, he discovered that there was more strength in those slender wrists than anyone could have expected. He made another discovery, too. He did not know, looking into those oddly set eyes that were so silkily bright, whether he and Conory were going to be heart-friends or the bitterest of enemies, but he knew that it must be one or the other; something between them was too strong to end in mere indifference.

7

The Road to Dun Monaidh

THE Chiefs and Captains went their ways, even Gault and Sinnoch were gone, and there was still a moon and a half to pass before the time of the Midwinter Fires. But for Phaedrus, in his hide-out on the wild west coast, while the gales beat in from the sea and the days grew shorter and the nights longer and more cold, the time did not hang heavy, for he was kept too hard at his training.

Gallgoid the Charioteer, who had remained behind (officially he was lying sick in his own hall under Red Peak) to captain the little guard of warriors who were left with him, took a large hand in the training. It was the month in the Onnum cock-loft over again, but whereas that had been enclosed, a training of the mind, this was a thing of the open moors, a training in the skills of hand and foot and eye that the Horse Lord must possess. With Gallgoid and sometimes one or another beside, there were long days out in the hills inland, always leaving and returning in the dark, and gradually he learned the things, strange to him, that

Midir must have known since childhood; he learned how to move silently without loss of speed on the hunting trail, how to ride on the fringes of a flying horse-herd and cut out one chosen colt from the rest, how to bring down game in full run with the three cord-linked stone balls of the hunter's bolas, even such small things as how to mount by vaulting on his spear instead of the more familiar steed-leap with one's hands on the horse's withers.

Then, too, the Dalriads were all charioteers. It was four years since Phaedrus had handled a chariot, and the first time that he took out Gallgoid's, he found with disgust that in growing used to the short sword and heavy circus shield his hands had lost much of their old cunning. At least he was thankful that the master who had made him a charioteer before he sold him into the arena had driven a British-built chariot, and not one of the graceful scallop-shells that the Romans called by that name. At least he knew the kind of vehicle he was driving, with its greater weight and different balance, the wider set wheels for stability on a rough hill-side, its open front that gave one a sense of being almost on top of the flying ponies. And little by little, the thing came back to him, in the way of old skills that are seldom quite lost, but only stored deeply away.

By the end of a month he and Gallgoid had grown so used to each other's ways that one day, up in the hills above the Loch of Swans, reining in from a sweeping gallop, Gallgoid said to him, 'You'll do! Didn't I be telling you you'd make a driver one day, when you stood no taller than a wolf-hounds's shoulder——' and he checked, and they looked at each other and laughed, though the laughter was awkward in their throats.

Four days before the Midwinter Fires, they set out from the Cave of the Hunter, Phaedrus in a rough plaid with his hair gathered up into his old leather cap, turning for the last time to salute the great horned figure with something of the same grim flourish with which he had been used to salute the Altar of Vengeance before going into the arena, and headed south for the Royal Dun.

It was already dusk when they mounted the waiting ponies in

the sheltered hollow inland of the sea-ridge, but there was a young moon sailing behind the hurrying storm-clouds when they came riding like a skein of ghosts past the Serpent's Mound at the foot of the Loch of Swans, and by the time the full dark closed down, Phaedrus reckoned that they were the best part of ten Roman miles on their way. They found cold shelter for themselves and the ponies for what was left of the night, among the woods of a steep-sided glen; and pushed on again at first light, across ridges where the thin birch woods grew leaning all one way from the western wind, round the heads of grey sea-lochs, where many islands cut the water with yeasty froth and the swirl of tide races. Towards evening, with the wind dying down, they were following a narrow track that snaked along the seaward slopes of the hills, hazel woods bare and black with winter rising sheer on the left hand—dropping like a stone into the broad firth on their right; and at dusk, came down at last into the fringes of a sodden marsh country of reed beds and sear yellow grass and saltings that, in the failing light, seemed sinking away into the sea while one watched. And there, in what shelter a tangle of furze could give them, they settled down to wait for darkness. In all that way they had seen no one save a few herdsmen in the distance, and once a hunting band of the little Dark People jogging along beside the track. But it was well to run as little risk as possible of being seen on the next stage; better that no stray onlookers should know of any link between the little knot of Sun People coming down from the north, and the larger band heading from the south next day. Besides, they must wait for the tide.

It was a long wait while darkness came; a black darkness, for tonight the moon was almost hidden; and then gradually a strange sound stole into the air, a distant, wet roaring that was yet vibrant as a struck harp or a human voice, and Phaedrus, shifting one chilled and soaking knee from the ground, asked under his breath, 'What is that?'

'That roaring? That is the Old Woman Who Eats Ships. She always calls when the tide is on the turn.'

'And who—what is this Old Woman?'

'The whirlpool—out yonder where the waters dash between two islands. A coracle can pass safely at slack water, but when the tide turns, that is another matter. That is why they say that the Old Woman calls.'

'The sound of death is in her calling,' Phaedrus said.

'She's far out of your sea-road.'

Phaedrus laughed softly. 'An old woman who used to tell fortunes outside the circus gates once told me that I should not die until I held out my own hands to death, so assuredly I am safe tonight, for I've no wish to go answering the call of the Old Woman Who Eats Ships.'

Gallgoid turned his head quickly to look at him in the dark, as though he had said something startling. But he only said, 'I've known a two-man coracle caught in the pull and escape, all the same. The seamen of these coasts are seamen and no mere paddlers about in pond-water.' And then, 'Come, it is time that we were on our way.'

Leaving the ponies and the rest of the band behind them, they went on alone, far out into the maze of sour salting and little winding waterways and banks of blown dune-sand. Stranded on the tide line in the shelter of a sandy spur, a two-man coracle lay tipped sideways like an abandoned cooking-pot, and to Phaedrus's landsman's eyes not much larger, and the black shadow of a man rose from beside it, and stood waiting.

He and Gallgoid exchanged a low mutter of greetings and then as the man picked up his small craft and heaved it into the water, Gallgoid spoke quickly to Phaedrus in parting. 'Now listen, for there is always a chance of betrayal. We have seen no one likely to be a danger to us on the trail south, but that is not to say for sure, that no such one has seen *us*. Gault may not come himself to meet you on the far side. If you do not know the man you find there, say to him that the flower of four petals is opening in the woods. If he replies that there is a promise of an early spring, for the horse-herds are growing restless, you will know that he is to be trusted.'

'And if not?'

'You have your dagger,' Gallgoid said meaningly. 'Struan the

boatman will wait for you a spear's throw off shore, until he knows that all is well.'

'*Sa*. Then if I do not see you again tonight, I will be looking for you tomorrow in Dun Monaidh.'

The boatman was squatting in the stern of the coracle now, and had got out the rowing-pole. 'As I will be looking for you,' Gallgoid said. 'Steady! Don't rock her. It is easy to see that you have long been among inland folk!'

Phaedrus, splashing through the icy shallows, got himself gingerly over the side of the coracle without shipping more water than, say, a hound would have done, and settled into the bottom of the bowl-shaped craft. He had never been in any kind of boat in his life before, and with an eye on the yeasty water beyond the sand bar, blurring into the dark, he wished that he were a better swimmer.

The boatman grunted something, and pushed off with the rowing-pole, and they were heading out across the mouth of the broad sea-loch that ran inland to lose itself somewhere away eastward in the marshes and the peat moss below Dun Monaidh. The sea took the small, crazy shell of stretched skins and wicker work as she cleared the sandspit, and she began to dance. Phaedrus would have felt deadly sick, but that he was too numbed with cold to feel anything; it was bitterly cold, and the spindrift burned like white fire on the skin. But crouching there with his cloak huddled to his ears, feeling the little craft lift like a gull to each wave, and noting the skill with which the boatman handled her, he found after a while that he was beginning to enjoy himself. The man never spoke to his passenger, but had begun to sing to himself softly and deeply, in time to his rowing: to himself, or maybe to the coracle, as men will sing and shout and croon to a horse for encouragement and companionship. The crossing, which would have been only a mile or so direct, was made much longer by the run of the sea, and the unseen moon was down, leaving the world, that had been dark enough before, black as a wolf's belly, when at last the sea gentled and they grounded lightly among more rushes and coarse grass and sand-dunes on the farther shore.

Phaedrus scrambled out, landing knee-deep in the shallows. The lightened coracle bounced high at the bows, and instantly, still crooning to himself, the boatman backed off. A figure uncoiled from among the broom scrub, a darkness on darkness. There was no possibility of seeing whether it was one that he knew or not. Phaedrus spoke softly, with his hand ready on his dagger.

'The flower of four petals is opening in the woods.'

The voice of one of Gault's household warriors said as softly, 'You wouldn't think it now, but there's promise of an early spring. Already the horse-herds are growing restless.'

'*Sa*, I have no need of my dagger. That is good,' Phaedrus said.

'That is most certainly good!' replied the voice with a quiver of laughter. The man's shadow turned seaward again, and gave the whistling call of a Dunlin, three times repeated. 'That will tell Struan that all is well.'

A few moments after, as they turned inland, the man asked, 'Do you remember what he was singing?'

'How should I? I—I have forgotten our songs in the past seven years—we sang other songs after supper in the Gladiators' School.'

The other glanced round at him, surprised, but not suspicious. 'It was the King's Rowing-song that keeps time for the oars when the King goes seafaring. I'd not think it was ever sung in a two-man coracle before, but he must have been glad to be raising it again.'

'What about the Queen's seafaring?'

'It is a song of the Men's Side; even Liadhan would be knowing that.'

Again there was that faint note of surprise; and Phaedrus thought, 'Typhon! I must not be making that kind of mistake too often!'

They walked in silence after that, cross country through birch and heather and bilberry scrub that was ill-going in the dark, and maybe an hour later, hit the old trade road from the south and the mainland crossing. And a short way down it, came upon a small rath or a farmstead within its ring stockade, with a

saffron flicker of fire-light shining from an open doorway, and three or four chariots squatting with yoke-poles cocked up against the house-place wall.

Someone was waiting to draw aside the dead thorn-bush that stopped the gateway; somebody quieted the baying hounds. Coming in out of the cold and dark of the midwinter night, the blast of fire-light and warmth, the smell of warm animal skins and broiling meat, and the crowding of men in the small, rough hall met them like a buffet. There must have been a score of men there beside the lord of the house and his sons. Gault looked up from the pattern he was tracing among the hearth ashes with a bit of charred stick. 'So, you come at last. Now we can shut the night out and fill our bellies.'

One of the sons rose and went to slam the heavy timbered door, and the lord of the house rose without word, and came and dropped to one knee before Phaedrus and took his hands and held them to his forehead as the Chieftains had done in the Cave of the Hunter. His front hair, like that of every man in the houseplace, hung in slim braids on either side of his face.

Next morning they slept late—no knowing when they might sleep again—and spent a good while in burnishing their gear and the bronze horse ornaments and whetting their short dirks to a final keenness. And when, well past noon, they headed north again by the old trade road, Gault had a new charioteer.

It was a fine chariot that Phaedrus found himself driving, not so fine to look at as that of the master who had sold him into the arena, for it lacked all ornament that could add a feather's weight, but so finely balanced that one scarcely realized that it was heavier than Gallgoid's, and like many British chariots, it was nowhere pinned or dowelled but lashed together with thongs of well-stretched leather, so that the whole structure was lithe and whippy, almost vicious underfoot, giving to every rut in the trackway, every hummock and hole and furze root when a stretch of track washed out by the winter rains turned them aside into the heather, like a living thing, a vixenish mare that one loves for her valour.

Phaedrus, shifting his weight on wide-planted feet, to trim the chariot on the slope of a hill shoulder, felt the vibrating of the woven leather floor under him, felt the proud and willing response of the team flowing back to him through the reins that were like some living filament between them, hearing the wheel-brush through the heather, and the axle-whine, and the softened hoof-beats, and the shouts of the other charioteers behind him, began to whistle softly through his teeth.

He heard a brusque laugh beside him, where Gault sat on the sealskin cushion of the Warrior's Seat. 'It begins to be good.'

'It begins to be good,' Phaedrus said, with only half his mind, steadying the team down once more to the track ahead. The countryside that had seemed so empty yesterday, was suddenly alive with riders and chariots; even—well clear of the trails— little bands of the Dark People loping along, with paint on their arms and faces, and their full ritual finery of dyed wildcat skins and necklaces of animals' teeth, and here and there a girl with green woodpecker feathers in her hair. And the track from the south, which had been bad enough before, was rapidly sinking into a quagmire under the passing feet and hooves and chariot wheels, as Earra-Ghyl gathered in to the Royal Dun and the Midwinter Fires and the seven-year King-Slaying and King-Making.

The grey light of the winter's day was fading into slate colour when they came down from the low grazing hills where the horse-herds ran loose even in the coldest weather, into the sodden flatness of Mhoin Mhor, the Great Moss, and westward a faint, chill mist that had been kept at bay by the wind, now that the wind had dropped was creeping in over the marshes from the loch of last night's crossing. Northward, the hills rose again, and everywhere was the gleam of water, sky-reflecting pools like tarnished silver bucklers, winding burnlets that wandered down from the hills to join the broad loop of the river that flowed out through the Mhoin Mhor to the sea. And on the nearside of the river, not much more than a mile away, stood Dun Monaidh, on its fortress hill that rose abrupt and isolated out of the waste wet mosses.

At that distance, and in the fading light, Phaedrus could not make out much more than the crown of ramparts, and a haze of smoke that hung low over the hill-top. But as they drew nearer, the ramparts stood up high, timber-faced, pale with lime-daub against the tawny winter turf; and the faint gleam of torches, strongly yellow as wild wallflowers in the way of torches at first twilight, began to pick out here and there, and the blurred freckling of things no larger than ants along the foot of the slope became chariot ponies grazing, for the most part two by two as they had been loosed from under the yoke, in the narrow infields between fortress hill and the marsh. To judge by the number of teams, especially remembering that the horses of the Chiefs and Captains would be stabled above in the Dun, a huge company must be gathered already, for on the track that Gault and his party followed, and dim-seen on the track from the north, and on foot by the unseen paths of the marsh, men were still drawing in from the farmost ends of the tribal hunting-runs, to Dun Monaidh.

Their own trail ran on into the marsh, paved with logs over a bed of brushwood, winding to follow the firmest ground, to the foot of the fortress hill, giving better travelling than the hill tracks had done—so long as one did not overrun the side.

'Let them feel the goad, you're not driving a pack-train now,' Gault said. But Phaedrus had not waited for the words. If it had not been in his nature in the first place, the circus would have taught him the importance of making a good entrance, and on this entrance, so very much might depend. For afterwards, men would remember, and say to each other, 'That was the first that we saw of Midir at his home-coming.'

He tickled up the flanks of the team with the goad that he had scarcely used before—he had never been one to drive on the goad—shouting to them, 'Ya-a-ya! *Hi*-a-hup! Come up now. Hutt—Hutt—Hutt!' And the ponies, snorting from the sting, sprang forward with stretched neck and laid back ears into a full gallop. The wind of their going ripped by, filling his dark plaid, the chariot leapt like a demon underfoot, its axles screeching,

and the rest of the little band, riders and chariots, came drumming along behind.

There was another chariot on the track ahead of him, and he misliked the sight. It was not for the Prince Midir to enter the Dun Monaidh at the tail of another chariot. He passed it going like an arrow, with an inch to spare between hubs and his off wheel skimming the drop to the marsh; and when he was back in the centre of the track again, Gault, who had not moved or spoken, said simply. 'It is a fine thing to make a hero's entrance, but I'll be reminding you that other lives hang on yours—and even on mine.'

'It was not right that the Prince Midir should come home with his mouth full of another team's mud. There was no risk; you have good horses.'

The black-browed warrior seemed on the point of choking. 'And you know how to handle them. Nevertheless, if you fail as a king, do not you be coming to me, to be my charioteer!'

'If I fail as King, I'll have no need to come to anybody for anything,' Phaedrus said, his eyes unswerving on the track that had begun to rise as they reached the first slopes of the fortress hill. He eased the team from their flying gallop, steadying them as the slope steepened. The track turned sharply back on itself where a small rocky stream came leaping down to join its lowest stretch, and yoke-pole and axles groaned as he gentled the team round it and urged them forward again. Not a good place to attack. Phaedrus thought, no reasonable way up, seemingly, save for this one steep hill-side gully that looked as though it would be as much torrent as track, after heavy rain, and which, moreover, was angled so that in the last stretch, the unguarded right side of any man making for the gate must be open to the spears of the defenders. He could see now why Gault and the rest of the Council had been so decided that the rising must have its begining *within* the ramparts.

The huge timber-framed gateway was close before him. He caught the dark glint of iron and bronze, saw the dappled red and white of the bull's-hide bucklers where the warriors and hunters thronged the turf ramparts to watch the late-comers in.

The rest of the band behind him, the chariot that he had overtaken still caught among them, he drummed across the ditch causeway. The great carved gate timbers lurched past on either side, the iron tyres howled on the broad lintel stones, the sparks flying from under them as from blade on anvil. He swept through into the broad outer court of the Royal Dun, and brought the team to a plunging halt before the tall, grey Pillar Stone of the Horse Lord.

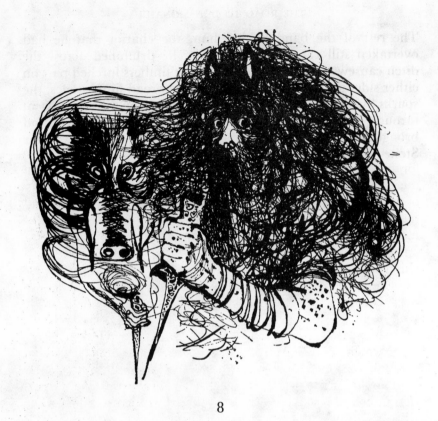

8

The King-Slaying

LATER that evening Phaedrus feasted among the charioteers of
the Chiefs and nobles, in the foreporch of the great, round,
heather-roofed Fire Hall. They were not slaves after the way of
charioteers among the Romans, nor even servants; they were
sons and younger brothers, close friends, lesser kinsmen, but
there was quite simply no room for them in the Hall. There was
little enough room for them here, and they were packed like
spearheads in an armourer's basket, but that was a thing that
had its advantages, for little warmth reached them from the peat
fire that glowed on the central hearth, filling the high crown of

306

the roof with smoke, and small spiteful draughts that cut the ankles like a fleshing-knife hummed under the outer door; but close-packed as they were, their cloaks huddled about them, they had worked up a steaming fug that was the next best thing to the warmth of the fire, and they ate whatever came their way, and filled and refilled the mead-horns from the bronze-bound vat with the boar's-head handles just beyond the inner doorway.

Phaedrus, drinking as little as might be—the smell in the foreporch was enough to make a man drunk without the help of mead, and he would need a clear head later—was sharply aware of the winter darkness beyond the smoky torch-flare; the blurred moon and the mist thickening over the icy marshes. Aware of men crouching in that ghostly mist, among the furze and winter-pale rushes, behind alder stumps and the tangle of hawthorn wind-breaks. Each man with his spear beside him—waiting for the signal. . . . Men within the Dun, too, gathered about the fires over which whole pig and oxen were roasting. Men here in the Hall itself. . . .

He had managed to get a seat on the third rung of the loft stair from which, craning his neck, he could see most of the Hall through the open doorway, which was larger than any outer door could be. He saw the circle of seven great standing timbers that upheld the roof, and between the crowding shoulders of the warriors stray glints and flame-flickers of the fire on its central hearth. The pine-knot torches in their iron sconces on each of the seven roof trees, flooded the heart of the place with a fierce tawny light, though it left the walls in crowding shadow; and letting his gaze wander, as though idly, from face to face, he saw many that he knew; Gault and Sinnoch, Dergdian, Gallgoid the Charioteer. Wherever he looked he saw men with red or dark grey or russet hair, or the bleached locks that many of the young warriors affected, hanging in slender braids against their cheeks. But he saw, too, that they were outnumbered by men whose hair hung loose in the usual way. More than ever he realized that their one real advantage was surprise, and that even with surprise on their side, in the first flare of the attack, the thing would hang by a thread. . . .

Most of the Gate Guards were their own men, but everything would depend on whether, having raised the war-cry, they could keep their feet with only the short dirks they had used for eating (for there was no certainty that they would be able to gain the armoury before the Queen's Party) until the men from the outside dark could swarm in to their support.

A picked handful of the Bodyguard, the Companions, the only men who might carry weapons at such a gathering as this, stood leaning on their spears behind the High Place, and Phaedrus's questing gaze found Conory in their midst. Not that he needed much finding. He must have bleached his hair freshly for the occasion, for it shone almost silver against the brown of his skin, and his odd-set eyes were painted like a woman's. Under the dark folds of the cloak flung back from one shoulder, he wore kilt and shirt of some soft, fine skin, dyed green. There were fragile wirestrung bracelets on his wrists, and strings of crystal and gold and blue faience about his neck; and on his shoulder, arched and swaying to his every movement, the striped hunting-cat, whose collar, like his own belt, was studded with enamel bosses. But it was something more than all this, Phaedrus thought, that singled him out from his fellows. Perhaps it came from the fact that in this hour, whatever was to happen later, he was the Chosen One, the King-Slayer and the Young King. It was a kind of lustre on him, a sheen such as one may see when the light strikes aright on the petals of certain flowers; the purple orchis or speckle-throated arum, the dark wild hyacinth. . . .

Someone jerked an elbow into his ribs, and he found that the mead-horn was being thrust under his nose. 'Wake up, my hero! The man who sleeps when his turn comes round, maybe doesn't get another chance!' It was a youngster with a mouth like a frog, and a thatch of rough, broom-yellow hair, the fronts locks doing their best to burst out of rather unsuccessful plaits.

Phaedrus took the mead-horn, grinning. 'I was not asleep then. I was taking a look at this new Seven-year King.'

And an older man leaned across to him from the other side. 'A good long look, then. Aye well, he's worth looking at, *and* he

knows it,' he snorted, but there was a hint of admiration in the snort. 'Ever since he came to manhood he's been one that women watch—aye, and men too, and there's times I think he makes a sport of seeing just how far he can go. He only has to come out one day with his cloak caught in a particular fold, or a woman's ear-ring in one ear, and next day half the young braves of the tribe are doing the same. If he cut off a finger-tip tonight, the other half would lack a finger-tip tomorrow. Fools!'

Phaedrus drank, and wiped the back of his hand across his mouth. 'Someone else was saying the same thing—almost the same thing—a while since.'

The other held out his hand for the horn, and drank in his turn, still grumbling. 'Now it's this new notion of plaiting their front hair. You can't expect sense from young fools like Brys'— here jabbing a finger towards the yellow-haired boy—'who only Took Valour at the last Feast of New Spears, and scarcely counts for a man yet at all; but when it's the grown men, the seasoned warriors who should be having more sense——'

But Phaedrus seemed to have lost interest in both the new Seven-year King, and his own sour drinking companion, and was craning his neck as he had done more than once that evening, for a better sight of the woman seated on the piled crimson-dyed sheepskins of the High Place. The woman who had stood by to see Midir blinded. Others of the Women's Side were moving to and fro to keep the mead-cups filled, for among the tribes, slaves did not serve in the Hall. But Liadhan sat to be waited on, for no man there, not Conory who would sit beside her in the King's place tomorrow at the Midwinter Feast, certainly not the dark, silent man who sat there now, were her equals; she who was Goddess-on-Earth, the beginning of all things, without whom there could be neither sons to the tribe nor foals to the horse-herd nor barley to the fields.

She sat leaning a little back among the piled skins and pillows, one hand resting idly on the bronze-work branch with its nine silver apples that lay in the lap of her blood-red gown, relaxed as a great cat half asleep in the sun. Her pride, like a cat's, was huge, too complete in itself to need any outward showing. She

must have been beautiful when she was young. The broad heavy bones of her face were beautiful still, framed in the braids of still fair hair that were thick as a warrior's wrist, and her forehead was broad and serene under the tall, silver head-dress she wore. But looking at her, Phaedrus felt a little cold creeping of the skin that was not so much fear as a kind of physical revulsion such as some people feel for spiders—big female spiders who devour their mates.

The dark man beside her sat very upright, his stillness tense as hers was relaxed, his brooding gaze fixed on the torches as though he would drink the light of them into his soul. 'The Old King has the old blood in him,' Gault had said, that night in the back room of the 'Rose of Paestum'. For him it is the pattern. . . .'

Logiore had accepted his destiny and there could be no saving him.

The feasting was long since finished, even the mead-horns had begun to go round more slowly. The buzz of voices and bursts of laughter and the stray struck notes of a harp that had filled Hall and foreporch alike, began to die down. There began to be a quietness and a sense of waiting. Phaedrus, too, was waiting for the thing to begin. He had been told what to expect, but something in him, even so, expected war-horns—a clash of weapons— some kind of outcry to fill the place of the silver braying of circus trumpets. And he was taken by surprise to find that waiting was over and the thing begun almost before he noticed it.

The curtain of heavy stuff over the doorway to the women's quarters was flung back, and a girl came stooping through, and stood erect as the folds swung to again behind her. A tall girl, holding between her hands a wonderful shallow cup of worked amber. Her tunic of dark chequered stuff that seemed almost black in the torchlight, was hung about with thin disks of bronze that kissed and rang lightly together as she moved; heavy gold serpent bracelets were on her arms, and her face, with the peat smoke curling across it, was like a ritual mask. There was a look of Liadhan in that mask, but it was lighter boned than Liadhan

could ever have been, and the thick braids of hair that ended in swinging balls of enamelled bronze, were of a very different colour, almost as fair, but warmer, with the gold softened and somehow greyed—dove-gold, he thought suddenly; dove-gold, and soft and unmanageable, so that it was springing free of its braids much as the broom-yellow hair of the boy Brys was doing; hair that was almost living a life of its own in flat contradiction to the face that was only a mask.

Murna, the Royal Daughter, who, if tonight's rising failed, would be Queen one day in her turn—if they failed. But they would not fail. He thrust the thought aside as unlucky.

The girl moved forward with small, swaying steps. Her shadow, cast by the nearest torch, fell across Logiore as she stooped and gave him the cup. He took it without rising, without looking at it, and sat an instant, holding it in his hands, his eyes still full of the torchlight; then flung back his head and drank, and gave the cup into her hands again.

Phaedrus wondered if the drink were drugged.

For the first time, Liadhan turned to look at the man beside her, and it was clear that she was waiting. The whole crowded Fire Hall was looking to him now. It was he who must make the next move in the ritual pattern, and Phaedrus saw that he knew it, and perhaps had a last moment of dark laughter in making them all wait. Even Liadhan for this one time. But he would make the move, all the same.

Someone unseen had opened the outer door, and the cold mist blew in. And in the foreporch the charioteers were on their feet, crushing back against the dry-stone wall to leave a clear path, forcing Phaedrus farther up the loft stair as they crowded the lower rungs, a few even slipping out through the open door.

Logiore got to his feet, and stood an instant, then came walking stiffly across the paved central dancing-floor, past the fire, and through the foreporch, moving a little like a sleep-walker, and out into the winter night. Two of the Guard had stepped forward to follow him, each lighting a fresh torch from the fire as they passed, and behind them went two more, naked swords in hand. Then Conory, his striped cat clinging lithely to

his shoulder; behind him, the rest of the Guard with drawn swords and torches. Then the Chiefs and nobles, draining out of the Hall like wine out of a cup, and leaving it to the women gathering on to the dancing-floor.

The charioteers and armour-bearers had spilled outside, Phaedrus among them, but in the shadow of the door-post he hung back until the squat, bow-legged figure of Gault the Strong came by, then slipped out to join him.

Gault never turned his head or gave any other sign of being aware of him, only as they came to the gateway of the Citadel he muttered, 'Pull that cap off; no time for fumbling later.'

In a patch of dark between torch and torch, Phaedrus dragged off the close-fitting charioteer's cap and tossed it away, shaking his head as he felt his hair fall loose, and the unaccustomed touch of the two slim braids against his cheeks. Then he pulled the loose hood of his cloak well forward to shadow his face and the device on his forehead.

Sinnoch had come up on the other side, and glancing round as he walked, he saw Gallgoid, black-browed and grimly cheerful, close behind. Other faces that he knew caught the torch-light, and he realized without knowing quite how it had been managed, that he was walking in the midst of a kind of bodyguard of his own.

The mist had thickened since he stabled the horses. It came smoking in over the turf and dry-stone walls of the Dun, smudging the torches into blurred mares' tails of flame. More and more torches as the crowds came thrusting in from feast-fire after feast-fire to join them. Surely, Phaedrus thought, Dun Monaidh could not seem more of a blaze from end to end, if this were tomorrow night; the night of the Midwinter Fires.

So they went down, a growing river of men and torches and wreathing golden fog, from the Citadel, looping through one after another of the five courts of the Royal Dun, until each had been visited, and they came to the lowest and outermost court of all.

In the wide outer court, seven fires—the farther ones already blurred with mist—were blazing in a wide circle about the

mighty upreared shape of the King Stone; and already the crowd was thickening between the fires, a crowd without visible weapons, and—strange among the tribes—without dogs, for the hound-pack, like the slaves, had been shut safely out of the way for the ceremony that was to follow.

Phaedrus and the knot of warriors with him, took up their places not far from where the Companions already stood leaning on their spears, with Conory in their midst. Of Logiore there was now no sign.

And then they heard it, winding down from the Citadel; a wild, wordless chanting of women's voices, and the thin white music of pipes wailing in and out through it. 'I must be careful!' Phaedrus thought suddenly. 'Gods! I must be careful or this music will draw me into it and I shall be lost! I must think of something else—think of the arena sand underfoot and the swing of the parade march! Here we go, past the knackers' sledges and the Altar of Vengeance. If that woman on the third bench eats another honeycake she'll have a seizure. Typhon! This helmet-strap's rubbing. I ought to have had it seen to after the last fight. Ah! Here's the Governor's box; "*Ave Caesar! Morituri te salutant.* ..."' The swaggering stamp and go of the parade march came to his help out of the world of familiar and daylight things, and he thrust it between him and white wailing music that something in him understood rather too well.

It was very close now. Something stirred in the mist at the edge of the fire-light, and Liadhan stepped into the circle of seven fires. The girl Murna, who seemed to be priestess of the rite, followed close behind her, and the women crowded after, bearing among them the crimson-dyed sheepskins of the High Place. They were chanting still, but the piping had separated itself, and while they piled the sheepskins into a throne it ran on in little thrills and ripples round the circle of fires. Phaedrus half saw grotesque shadow-figures that ran and flitted behind the fires and the torchlit crowd, the piping going with them; thin shimmers of sound, flutings and half bird-calls that were as though they talked to each other on the pipes in some tongue older than human speech. Something made Phaedrus look over

313

his shoulder, and he saw one of the shadows standing quite close to him. A man—a thing like a man, stark naked in the bitter cold that made men's breath smoke into the mist, save for the streaks of red ochre that daubed his body, and the bracelets and anklets of shells and feathers and dried seed-pods; a pipe that might have been made from the thigh-bone of some big bird was in his hands and on his shoulders, where his head should have been, was the snarling mask of a wild boar. For an instant the hair rose on the back of Phaedrus's neck, and then the thing crouched, and raised the pipe to some hole hidden in the black shadow under the grinning snout, and he realized that there was a human mouth within the bristly hide. Masked priests, then, but priests of a very different kind from Tuathal the Wise. The man's long fingers moved on the pipe, and the shrill bird-twittering notes scurried up and down, and Phaedrus felt eyes upon him from somewhere within the mask, and turned back to the lighted circle.

Liadhan had taken her seat on the piled sheepskins, between two of the sacred fires, with the women and the Companions of the Guard about her. She sat very upright now, still as the great standing stone that formed the hub of the wheel of light. Her eyes going past it, out past the blurred fires of the farther side, into the darkness beyond. This was her hour, and the small, still smile on her lips was such a smile as no mortal man or women should wear.

The chanting had ceased now, and the fluting pipe calls had grown silent. Only the Royal Daughter sang on, a high white singing that had nothing human in it. She was moving from one to another of the fires, weaving an intricate dance pattern of swaying and shuffling steps, and at each fire she paused to feed the flames with leaves and herbs from a basket she carried on her hip.

A strange smell began to rise in the smoke, bitter and pungent, yet dangerously pleasant, bringing forgotten things hovering in from the edges of the mind ... somewhere in the drifting, milky dark beyond the flame-light, the wolfskin drums began to throb, softly, like a sleeping heart, and something

seemed to stir into wakefulness and run through the concourse, like the chill breath of wind before a thunderstorm.

Standing at Gault's side, his head bent and shoulders hunched into shapelessness under his cloak, Phaedrus stole a quick glance at Conory. His head was up, eyes and nostrils wide in his face, the look of a hound still in leash that scents the boar. One of the Companions had taken both spear and sword from him and he had loosed his cloak and slipped it free from one naked shoulder; but the striped cat still clung to its accustomed perch. He could not be going to carry it into the actual fight with him, but meanwhile, everyone seemed to take as little heed of it being there as though it were a part of Conory, like his sword-hand.

Murna, her circle of fires completed, had come to stand beside the Queen, and while the bronze disks on her skirt still clashed softly as they swung, Liadhan raised the slender branch with its nine silver apples, and shook it once. The thin, sweet ripple of the little bells seemed to make strange echoes in the mist, and the throb of the wolfskin drums changed to a coughing roar that rose and rose—then ceased with a suddenness that left a woollen numbness in the ears.

Liadhan shook the silver branch again, and a long-drawn sigh, almost a moan, rose from the throng, as something moved in the darkness where she looked, and out into the fire-light stepped Logiore, the Old King.

It was an instant before Phaedrus realized that it *was* Logiore, this wild, uncanny figure in the trappings of the Horse Lord. He was stripped to the waist, in warrior style. Heavy bronze arm-rings circled his upper arms, and about his neck hung collar upon collar of jet and amber beads and dark heron-hackles. Clay and ochre patterns had been painted on his skin, overlaying the fine blue lines of tattooing. On his head was a war-cap that seemed to be made from the scalp of a red horse, the proud stallion crest still springing erect between the ears, the long mane tumbling on his shoulders; and out of the death-paint on his face, his eyes blazed on the world like those of a man who has taken nightshade. The naked knife in his hand caught the fire-

315

light and became a tongue of flame, as he came forward with a curious high-stepping walk, to stand before the woman on the throne of piled sheepskins.

Conory flung off his own cloak, and under it, he also was stripped for battle. He drew his own dagger without haste, and took the one long pace forward that brought him to the Queen's side and face to face with his adversary. The drums had begun to throb again, the smell of the strange smoke drifting from the fires seemed at once to heighten and confuse the senses. And still she striped cat clung to its lord's shoulder, its eyes enormous and fur fluffed up along its arched back until it seemed to bloat to twice its normal size. In the last few moments, Conory had been murmuring to it, its furry cheek against his, but now—surely he must have forgotten it was there. Others thought so too. One of the Companions spoke to him, pointing to the creature, holding out his hand to take the leash.

Conory answered with a sound in his throat that was for the cat alone, and the small fiend laid back its tufted ears and with a

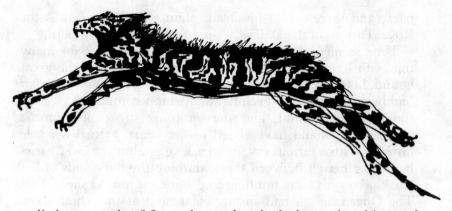

splitting screech of fury, the unsheathed claws ploughing red furrows in Conory's bare shoulder as it launched itself, sprang straight for Logiore's face.

In the same instant, so that both movements were one, Conory flashed round with his dagger upon Liadhan the Queen.

In the same instant also, there happened one of those small unforeseeable mischances that can tear an empire down. It was no more than a hound, tied up in the stable court, that had chewed through its leash and come to find its master. Nobody, certainly not Phaedrus who had his back to it, saw the wolf-shadow in the mist, poised on the crest of the broad dry-stone wall and searching the crowd with anxious tawny eyes. But in the barest splinter of time before the cat leapt screeching at Logiore's face, the hound gave a joyful bark of recognition and sprang out and down. He had leapt for a gap in the crowd, but something—maybe the grotesque figure with the boar's head—made him swerve in mid-air. He was no mere herd-dog but one of the great wolf-hounds of Erin, feather-heeled, and for size and weight almost the equal of a yearling pony colt. His swerve brought him crashing full into Phaedrus, and flung him head-long, full into the light of the nearest torches. The hound landed on top of him, driving most of the wind from his body, and went bounding on across the circle to join its master on the farther side. Best part winded as he was, Phaedrus was up again with a speed learned in the arena, but the hood of his cloak had fallen

back, and there on his forehead, plain for all to see, was the Royal Pattern of the Dalriads, the Mark of the Horse Lord.

Time seemed to go slow, so that there was space for many things to happen between one leap and another of the great hound. Liadhan, perhaps already half alerted by something that had been in the air all evening, had whipped round to face the sudden small tumult, and the lightning stroke of Conory's dagger that should have ended in her heart, gashed her side instead. With a furious cry, he struck again, but the girl Murna had flung herself between them, dashing the dark folds of her cloak across his face, muffling and blinding him as she did so. The Queen herself had sprung clear, and as the whole scene dissolved in howling chaos, Phaedrus saw, in the very act of regaining his feet, her terrible eyes fixed on the mark of his forehead. Then she screamed, and in screaming, raised the agreed war-cry: '*Midir!*'

The women, their knives out, were swirling in upon Conory; and Logiore, his face now a streaming mask of blood, the wild cat still clinging to him, came crashing in with the shrill fury of an angry stallion.

Phaedrus, plunging forward with no thought save to reach Conory before it was too late, heard Gault beside him take up the war-cry, raising the terrible bull-below that was the signal for those waiting in the outer darkness: 'Midir! *Midir!*'

The perfect timing on which so much might depend, had been lost to them, but there was no help for that now. All around the Pillar Stone and among the seven fires, the warriors were reeling to and fro, as the men of the braided forelocks ripped out their dirks and hurled themselves upon the Queen's followers. But for the moment all that was lost on Phaedrus; in the heart of that hideous struggle before the High Place, he was fighting back to back with Conory. Fighting for his life and something more than his life, for no man likes the idea of being torn to pieces, against a screaming throng of women, whose weapons, beside their knives, were the wild beast's weapons of teeth and claws. He did not know what had happened to Liadhan or the girl Murna, nor even what had happened to Logiore; there was nothing in this

world but the screaming furies about him, and the feel of
Conory's back braced against his. A knife gashed his shoulder,
claws were at his throat; if no help came, it could not be long
before he or Conory went down, and once that happened. ...

Suddenly the press was slackening, breaking up, the blood-
screams of the women changing to howls of baffled fury, as a
solid wedge of the Companions, heads down behind cloak-wrapt
forearms, came charging through to their support.

The fighting had spread through into other courts by the
sound of it. Someone shouted, 'They're fighting for the
armoury!' And from somewhere in the heart of the Dun, a
tongue of flame leapt up, blurred and wavering in the mist. Men
were pouring through the great gate that had been opened to
them, swarming in over the ramparts, men who carried each a
spare weapon with him. Phaedrus with one such sword in his
hand, Conory racing beside him with his own again, was
storming forward at the head of a swelling band against the
main mass of the Queen's Party, who, after the first moments of
random fighting, were gathering in closed ranks before the
gateway to the stable court. They, too, had weapons now;
seemingly some of the Queen's people had reached the armoury
first. Away to his right he heard Gault's bull-roar, and yelled the
war-cry in answer: 'Midir! *Midir!*'

Another band of men and women, headed by the wild figure
of Logiore with his horse-mane flying, came charging in across
their path. They also were fully armed, for by now weapons
were springing into every hand; and in the light of scattered fires
and guttering torches, Phaedrus thought he glimpsed in the
midst of the battle-throng around the gateway, the moon-silver
gleam of the Queen's diadem. Others had seen it too, for a new
shout went up: a baying of hounds that sight the kill. Gault
bellowed, 'There she is! The Hag! The She-Wolf!' as they
crashed together with Logiore's band, hell-bent to come at the
gleam of that distant diadem. The patterns of the fighting were
changing and reforming so quickly that everything was shapeless as a dream; and now Logiore's band had been flung back,
and they were at reeling grips with the warriors about the gate,

locked knee against knee, blade against blade, snarling faces and flying hair.

And now the Queen's Party were falling back. Slowly, stubbornly, battling for every inch of the way. Somehow, the outer court was cleared, and then the Horse Court, and they were falling back on the gate-gap of the King's Court, the Citadel itself. There were men on the crest of the rock outcrop that formed part of the King's Court wall, and stones and spears came whistling among the attackers. And still, somewhere ahead in the swirling press, like a flicker of moonlight between racing storm-clouds, the gleam of a silver head-dress came and went.

They were back to the gate again now and every foot of the outcrop wall had become a reeling battle-line. The mist was red about them, for somebody had fired the heather thatch; and in the fiery murk, Phaedrus had come together with Logiore the Old King.

And then a strange thing happened, for the rest of the fight surging all about them seemed to fall away a little on every side, and in the space so cleared, they fought, as Old King and Young King were fated to fight according to the ancient custom; Phaedrus still in the rough dress of a charioteer, his red, mist-wet hair flying about his head, and the man in the trappings of the Horse Lord, with the terrible burning eyes in the terrible painted and blood-streaked face. Even Conory held aloof from that fight, and found plenty of work for his sword elsewhere; and in this isolation they crouched and thrust and parried, with the sparks from the burning Hall falling about them. Logiore was a fine swordsman; Phaedrus the Gladiator, used to the quick judging of an opponent, knew that, but knew also that thanks to Automedan's training, he was a better.

The struggle for the Citadel did not last long, for the Queen's Party were by now heavily outnumbered, and though the numbers were equal enough in the actual gateway, they were too few to hold the inner wall against those who swarmed over. They made their last desperate stand, while before the flame-lit gateway, Old King and Young fought the ancient ritual fight

that was ritual no longer. Both were bleeding from gashes on breast and arms and shoulders; no space to manoeuvre, no sprining back out of touch; they fought where they stood, close-locked as battling stags. Phaedrus could see the mist drops on the horse head-dress, and the sparks of the burning thatch that died among them, the other-world glare in his enemy's eyes. He saw the eyes change, as he had once seen Vortimax's do, and parried the deadly lunge, turning the other's blade at the last instant, and lunged in his turn, in past the open guard. He felt his own blade bite deep, and saw those eyes widen and had time to wonder at the triumph in them, before the Old King staggered back and went down.

Everywhere the line of the defence was going, and the followers of the Horse Lord were crashing in through the gate and over the broad low walls. Hounds were baying and the screams of terrified and angry horses tore the air. But in the Citadel itself there seemed for the moment to be a strange silence. Logiore, with his head-dress torn off and most of the death-paint washed from his face by blood, lay like any other dead man— and there were plenty—crumpled against the right-hand gatestone where he had been trampled and kicked aside in the break-through. But the look of triumph was still in his eyes.

And Phaedrus knew the reason for it now, as he stood leaning on his crimsoned sword, drawing his breath in great whistling gasps; and looked at Murna the Royal Daughter, standing between two of the Companions, on the threshold of the burning Hall. Murna with blood on her ripped and tattered tunic, and a little smile that echoed Logiore's triumph lifting the corners of her lips. And on her head the tall, silver moon head-dress of the Queen.

9

'You are not Midir!'

GAULT said in a rasping voice, 'Where is Liadhan?'

'The Queen, my mother, is in a place where you will not find her—Gault the Traitor!'

Gault shrugged his bull shoulders. 'I have other things to do than be playing hurly with evil names for a ball.' Then to the two Companions, 'Take her away and lodge her safely—remembering that she is the Royal Daughter, and not to be mishandled.'

'Sa, sa, I have to thank you,' the girl said. 'Would you have given my mother the same cause to thank you, if you had taken *her*?'

'*When* we take her, you will have the answer to that question.'

Gault jerked his chin at the Companions, to take her away. She half turned in obedience to their hold on her arms, then checked, and looked back full at Phaedrus for the first time. A long, strange look, completely unreadable, and meeting it, Phaedrus wondered if she knew how her mother had in truth disposed of the real Horse Lord. If she did, she must know, even as Liadhan must have known it when the first shock was over, that whoever else he might be, he was not Midir. And like Liadhan, there would be nothing that she could do about it. He returned the long, cool stare, and in a few moments she turned away between her guards.

The fiery fog seemed to get into Phaedrus's head after that, and everything became like a dream in which there was no ordered sequence of events. He heard Gault shouting orders, and was aware of men tearing off the burning heather thatch and beating out the flames that had spread to the timbers, aware of fighting still going on in odd corners of the Dun, with now and then a cry to tell how some fight had ended. There was a search going on, swift and desperate and very thorough, among the mist-shrouded buildings and the huddled dead. He was bleeding from a score of gashes, none of them serious, and beside him, Conory was cursing softly as he tried to staunch a deeper wound in his upper arm with a strip torn from a dead man's kilt; and somewhere a cat was raising its wild squalling cry. Stupidly he looked about for it, and saw in the dying flame-light, a striped shape with eyes like green moons and blood dripping from a gashed flank, clinging to the edge of the foreporch roof and singing a triumph-song that might have been made by all the fiends in Ahriman's deepest pits of torment. Conory left off cursing long enough to call, 'Shân,' and the thing leapt to his shoulders, trailing the remains of its leash behind it, and settled across his neck, singing still.

A man was panting out some message to Gault, and then there was a time of running, in the midst of which Phaedrus stumbled on the body of an almost naked man with an otter's mask for a face. And then he was in the outer court again, over in the far angle away from the gate, staring at the place where

the overflow from the spring that formed the Dun's water supply disappeared into a narrow gully and dived under a rough-cut lintel stone through the rampart wall. Three men with braided forelocks lay dead there, each tangled as though from a distance, in the thongs of a hunting bolas, and stabbed where they lay. Someone was holding a torch low to the dark mouth of the tunnel, and the light showed a glint of silver apples under the water.

Someone fished out the silver branch.

'So that's the way she went,' Gault said, chewing at a lower lip that was chapped and red-raw.

'She will be heading for Caledonia, and her own kin,' Conory said. He had knotted the rag round his wounded arm, and save for the blood on him he looked as unruffled as the striped cat who had dropped from his shoulder and was now sitting a little way off, unconcernedly licking its flank wound. 'Can we stop up the runs before she gets clear away?'

Gault shook his head. 'I doubt it. The People of the Hills will stand her friends, and no one save the red deer know all *their* runs. None the less, we must try it, for she carries maybe the life or death of the tribe in her keeping.' He swung round on the young warrior with the torch. 'Brys, find me your Lord Gallgoid, with Dergdian if the life is still in him—and that horse-smuggler Sinnoch; there are few men know the border hills as he does.'

Phaedrus had not recognized the boy for his cheerful neighbour of the crowded foreporch; his face was so grey and old, with the laughter all gone from it. 'My Lord Gallgoid is dead.'

'Cuirithir then. Those three—quickly.'

The boy went, running. And presently Dergdian was there, Sinnoch with him and Cuirithir hard on his heels, and Gault was speaking quick and harsh. 'The She-Wolf is away— you'll all be knowing that, and she must be heading for Caledonia by one way or another—there's nowhere else for her, unless she takes to sea. Sinnoch, you know the border hills better than any of us, how many trails into the Cailleach's country at this time of year?'

324

Sinnoch thought a moment. 'As many as there are fingers and thumb on my right hand.'

'One to each of us here, then.'

'There are six of us here,' Dergdian said, hackles up, and with a glance at Phaedrus.

There was an instant's pause, and then Phaedrus said, 'It is a long while since I was in the border hills. I will ride behind one of you.'

'One to each of us here, then,' Gault said, as though there had been no interruption. 'Conory, take what men you can raise quickly—two-score should be enough—and follow the track up Loch Fhiona, the Royal Water, and across the mountains into the Glen of Baal's Beacon. Not beyond; it will not profit the tribe that you run wild into the Cailleach's hunting-runs and never come back! Dergdian, and you, Cuirithir, make for the great Gap of Loch Abha, and divide there; take one of you the Glen of the Alder Woods and the other the Glen of the Black Goddess.'

'She will not be taking *that* way,' Cuirithir said. 'Ach now, it is close on twice as far, and the trail runs a full two days through the very heart of Earra-Ghyl.'

'She will not likely be taking that way,' snapped Gault, 'but if the little Dark People choose to be her guide and cast their mists about her, for the very reason of its unlikeliness she might take it, and we'd be fools to leave it alone. Myself, I will be for Rudha-Nan-Coorach, and the fisherfolk shall lend me their coracles to cross Loch Fhiona. The trail down the Glen of the Horns keeps hard enough at this season, and with fisherfolk all down the far shore to see her across the Firth of War-Boats, I'm thinking that's the trail she might choose. That is four. Where runs the fifth trail, Sinnoch?

'It is in my mind that I miscounted. There are two more trails—two more at the least, between the Royal Water and the Firth of War-Boats. But it is all wild country, and the Caledones hunt over it almost as often as we. It is hard to be sure in one's head, without seeing the state of the trails; there have been heavy rains in the past moon.'

'Go and look, then. Those trails I leave to you. Take the best hunters with you; you'll need them.'

'*Sa*, that means my old Bron for one. Some of the best hunters in Dun Monaidh are hammering from within on the slave-house door at this moment.'

'Men of the little Dark People?' Gault interrupted.

'The little Dark People are the best hunters in the world.' The dry smile was in Sinnoch's voice, though his face was lost now in darkness. 'And as for those in the slave-house, Liadhan's slaves do not learn to love her—even for Earth Mother's sake.'

'So be it then, hunt your little dark hounds.'

'Those and others—a mongrel pack, shall we say—open to any who are not too proud to hunt with it.'

'I will hunt with your mongrel pack,' Phaedrus said, and decided, by the moment of sudden silence about him, that that had been a mistake. But to change now would have been an even worse mistake, and beside—surely even a prince of the Dalriads need not dance always to other men's piping. 'Unless I am too out of skill as a hunter,' he added, pretending to misunderstand the silence.

And Sinnoch said with that dry amusement out of the darkness, 'You are the Prince of the Dalriads. Surely you may hunt with any pack—even the Hounds of Hell—that you will.'

For four days Phaedrus hunted with Sinnoch's mongrel pack, on foot or on one of the small mountain ponies they had rounded up beyond the heather hills and steep forested glens between the two great sea-lochs. But if Liadhan had passed that way, she had been too swift for them, and left no trace behind her. And on the fourth evening, when they forgathered with Conory and his band, far up the Glen of Baal's Beacon, they, too, had had bad hunting.

They were fog-wet and bone-weary and their wounds had had little chance to heal. The dried meat that the tribes carried with them on trial had begun to run short and there had been no time to hunt for themselves, and so they were hungry. They made camp dourly, on the strip of turf and heather between the river and the forest that seemed to reach its hands towards them

in the gathering shadows as though it, too, were hungry; and tended and picketed the rough-coated ponies—they dared not let them graze loose with the trees so near.

And meanwhile Phaedrus and Conory had come together, and as though the thing were arranged between them, gone down river a short way towards the head of the loch. The rest of the camp had seen them go without surprise or remark: they had always been best content with each other's company, as boys.

They did not speak at once of the thing that both knew had brought them out from the camp. Indeed, for a while they did not speak at all, but simply stood looking across the river to where the great hills of Caledonia caught the last red of the winter sun, while the striped cat, who had stalked after them through the heather and bog myrtle, sat down for another lick at the healing wound in her flank.

'So—the She-Wolf is safe away into her kinsman's hunting-runs,' Phaedrus said moodily at last.

'Unless Gault or Dergdian have had better hunting than we.'

'They will not.'

'No, I am not thinking it likely.'

'Was it my doing? Or the dog's? Or the chance fall of the dice?'

• Conory shrugged. 'Can the dice fall chance-wise from the God's hand?'

'I have wondered that, before. It is the way they cast for pairs of fighters in the arena. ... What will happen now?'

'Nothing now, in the black of winter. You know what the tracks are like, and not even Liadhan can move a War Host over these mountains and mosses when the high passes are deep in snow and there's no grass for the chariot ponies. But when the birch buds thicken and the burns come down in spate from the melting snows, then there will be a great hosting among the Caledones.'

Phaedrus looked round quickly. 'It will really come to war?'

'She is the King's kinswoman. And do you think that the Great Mother—the Lady of the Forest, they call her—will not rise up in war-paint to protect her own? Have you forgotten that

the Caledones follow the Old Way, too?' Conory turned his head slowly, and the mocking, veiled gaze was on Phaedrus's face. 'You have forgotten many things in these seven years.'

'There is time to forget many things in seven years.'

For an instant gaze held gaze, carefully blank.

Conory's cloak had fallen back from his shoulder, and glancing down, Phaedrus saw that the rags about his upper arm were dark and juicy. 'That wants rebinding,' he said.

'I'll see to it, by and by.'

'Better now, while there's still enough daylight to see by. I'll do it for you.' Then at something he saw on the other's face, 'It is not the first time that you and I have bathed each other's hurts.'

There was a small, sharp silence, empty save for the rush and suck of water, and the sudden desolate calling of some bird among the winter-black heather. Then Conory said slowly and deliberately, 'Is it not?'

Phaedrus's heart gave a small, sick lurch under his breastbone, but there was no shock of surprise in him. This was the thing between them, the thing that had brought them down here away from the camp. He tried once more, prepared to fight it to a finish, all the same. He forced a laugh. 'There is one time that sticks in my mind above all others. But you did not have the beating, so there's less reason for you to remember helping me wash the blood off my back after Dergdian had thrashed me for half braining him with a throw-stone.'

Conory whirled round on him. 'Who told you that?'

'Who should tell me? It was I that had the beating, and I remember well enough without being told.'

'Oh no, you don't,' Conory said, silken-soft. 'It was Midir who had that beating, and *you are not Midir!*'

'You are out of your wits! It must be that you have the wound fever,' Phaedrus said.

'Both the wound and my wits are quite cool.'

'Very well then, tell me who I am.'

The other's hands shot out and clenched on his shoulders with that unexpected strength that he had felt before in the Cave of the Hunter. Conory's face was thrust into his, the odd-set eyes

narrowed under the traces of paint that still clung to the lids. '*You* shall tell *me* that!'

Phaedrus made no attempt to break the other's hold, though with Conory's arm wound he could have done it without much trouble. For one thing, the cat had stopped licking its flank, and was crouching ready to spring, with laid-back ears, and mask wrinkling in a silent snarl. It made no sound, it did not move, but he knew that at the first movement of his that looked hostile, it would fly at him. The added complication of being attacked by a wildcat, he felt, was more than he could handle just then.

But another kind of recklessness took him like a high wind. He did not know whether or not this was the end of the trail, but he laughed in the other's face. '*Sa, sa!* I will tell you! My father was a Greek wine-merchant, and my mother was his slave who kept his house for him. I was born a slave and bred a slave—you can see now how suitable was my choice of pack to hunt with! I was bought and sold, bought and sold, until I came into the Corstopitum Circus, and was a slave still. Most gladiators are slaves, did you know? *That* is what you cried "Midir!" for, five nights ago!'

'And so Sinnoch saw you in your circus and saw the likeness—and the opportunity. Well may men call him "Sinnoch the Fox!" What price did he pay you?'

Phaedrus asked quietly, 'Was that meant for an insult?'

'If it seems so to you, then yes. But chiefly, I was asking a question.'

'One that I cannot answer. I gained my wooden foil on the day he first saw me— that means freedom with honour, for a gladiator. I was free for a whole day after they had pushed me out, until the howling boredom of it drove me into a street brawl, and my freedom ended in the town gaol. If you would know how much it cost in bribes to get me out, you must ask Sinnoch—or Gault.'

'I am not interested in the cost of unbarring a prison door. What was *your* price? And in what kind? Did they buy you, or force you? Or did you come because anything was better than this howling boredom?'

329

'Something of all three. Also they called in Midir to their aid. He—was a master of persuasion.'

The hands on his shoulders gave a little jerk, and released their hold. Conory let them drop limply to his sides and half turned away. 'Midir ... yes, of course. Nobody but he could have told you about washing off the blood of that beating ... and the other things—all the other things. He was always thorough.' Phaedrus saw him swallow. 'Will you tell me something. If Midir still lives, why did they need another man to take his place?'

'He is blind,' Phaedrus said.

'Blind!' Conory's voice sounded sick in his throat, and he made a strange gesture, pressing the heels of his hands into his own eye-sockets as though for a moment he felt them empty. 'So that was how she made sure of him. ... Where is he?'

'He went back to the man he works for, a harness-maker in a Roman city far south of the Southern Wall.'

'How long have Gault and Sinnoch known all this?'

'Three years, I believe.'

'And who else beside?'

'Tuathal the Wise, Gallgoid—but he's dead.' (It was odd, that it had hardly struck home to him until he said the words.) 'Two or three more.'

'And never told me; even when the She-Wolf sent me her token last Beltane and the time came to begin sharpening our swords. I that was closer to him than most brothers.'

'There was a great while still to wait. They are all grey-muzzles except—Gallgoid, and maybe they feared that you might do something hot-headed.'

'Did they fear the same thing at summer's end, when they told me the same tale as the rest of the tribe, concerning the Prince Midir come back from the dead?' Conory's voice had a bite to it.

'It seemed to them good that you should be the test. If you did not know that I was not Midir, then nobody would know it. But you knew, and so I have failed.'

They had come a long way from the dangerous mood of so short a while before.

330

'No,' Conory said absently, 'I'd not be saying that, for the test was not a fair one.' He looked round at Phaedrus with his gentle, almost sleepy smile. 'This arm of mine begins to ache. Is there light enough, do you think?'

A few moments later, they had scrambled down the bank and were kneeling among the tangled alder roots at the water's edge, and Phaedrus had begun easing off the filthy rags that left dark juicy stains on his fingers as though he had been picking overripe blackberries. Conory squinted down to watch him. 'Ach no, I would not be saying you had failed at all. Unless you make some glaring mistake, you will pass well enough—with everyone else.'

'What mistake did I make with you?' The last clotted fold came away, and Phaedrus stooped to cup the icy water in his palm and bathe the stale blood from the wound before he could see how it did.

'More than one; small things enough. When Gault was ordering away the hunting-bands, it came to you that you did not know these hills, and there was an instant when you did not know what to do. You covered up well, though; to choose Sinnoch's mongrel pack to hunt with was just the kind of thing Midir would have done. He was always one to take a devil's delight in seeing how far he could go in outraging the Grey Muzzles and the customs of the tribe.'

'As you do in seeing how wild a fashion you can make the young braves follow for their own befoolment?'

'It is always amusing to see what can be done in that way,' Conory said, catching his breath a little at Phaedrus's probing fingers on the wound, and glancing up at the striped cat who had remained at the top of the bank and was now crouching there with her face a little above his. She was staring into some inner distance of her own, but when he put up his hand, she rubbed her broad furry head into his palm. 'They will tell you it is not possible to tame a wildcat, and most times it will be true, but not—quite always. I found Shân as a kit, before her eyes were well open. Her mother had been killed by an eagle, *aiee!* a great fight that must have been—and the rest of the litter were dead for lack of her. But there was still a spark of life in this one

and so I took her. She bit my thumb to the bone in the hour that she first had teeth enough to bite with, but now—you see?' He smiled reflectively, and Phaedrus knew that he was taking refuge from the thought of Midir alive and blind, until he had had time to get used to it. 'Only the first time I put a leash on her and brought her into the Fire Hall on my shoulder, every fool in Dun Monaidh thought that Conory was starting a new fashion. . . . The Healer Priests were busy cleansing bites and clawings for the best part of a moon before the thing wore itself out.'

'You had best take *this* to the Healer Priest, when we get back,' Phaedrus said, 'but it will do for now. . . . Well, she proved her ancestry when you flung her in Logiore's face. Did you think to see her again with the life in her striped hide?'

Conory gave a small, one-shouldered shrug. 'It was a risk we all took. She is a fighting animal, as we all are. But it was good to hear that wicked triumph-song of hers, afterwards.'

He returned to the thing they had been speaking of before Shân came into it. 'Only small mistakes. But I would not be needing any mistake at all. Way back in the Cave of the Hunter—what name did you answer to, before you answered to Midir?'

'In the arena, they called me Red Phaedrus.' He was tearing a strip from the end of his cloak. It would make a better bandage than that foul rag, anyway.

'Then, Red Phaedrus, tell me—in the circus, were you wont to draw your weapons from some common store, or did you each have your own?'

'You do not have anything of your own, in the Gladiators' School, save the clothes you stand up in, and the gewgaws that your patrons and admirers give you; but as far as maybe, you stick always to the same sword.'

'*Sa*. Then you will know how it is with weapons; to the eye they may be as like as one grain of sand is like another, but each comes from the armourer a little different in balance, with some nature of its own that no other weapon has, and your hand grows to know it, so that if you take up another in its stead, though there is no difference to the eye, your hand knows.'

332

Phaedrus nodded.

'Midir and I were two halves of the same nut when we were boys. I was not sure at first, that night in the Cave of the Hunter, but when we put our arms round each other and made a show for all those onlookers, *then* I was sure. The balance of the blade was not right.'

'Why did you not speak out, then?'

'It was in my mind to see what would happen—to learn what you were, since you were not Midir. Also it was *not* in my mind to wreck the uprising we had waited and planned for so long, and perhaps be the death of many friends.'

Phaedrus was binding up the wound, and his eyes and Conory's were very close together. 'And now? If you denounce me now, you will split the People of the Horse from top to bottom, and Liadhan will walk back unchecked into the red ruins of her queendom.'

'If we needed the Prince Midir in throwing off the She-Wolf's yoke—we will be needing the Prince Midir still.'

Phaedrus tied off the knot. 'You will stand with me, then?'

'When a man binds up a gash in my hide for me, I must be counting him as a friend. And most times I stand with my friends. Is it so with you?'

'Ach, don't you be putting overmuch trust in my friendship—we learn to take such trifles easily, in the arena,' Phaedrus said, lightly and harshly. 'The only man I ever counted for a friend, I killed in winning my wooden foil.'

They looked at each other an instant, and then Conory said, 'It's a chance I'll take.'

They went back towards the camp, with their arms lightly across each other's shoulders. And this time it was not altogether for show. The striped cat stalked ahead, tail uplifted like a banner.

Gault and his band had just ridden in to the forgathering as they got back to the camp. Well on into the night, Cuirithir and a knot of horsemen came in with word that Dergdian would be in next day. None of them had had any success with their

333

hunting. And later still, when the meagre food had been eaten in dulled silence, and the weary men were already huddling into their cloaks and the heather wind-brakes close about the fires, Gault gathered the leaders about him, and kept them waiting until he was ready to speak, then looked up from drawing in the ash with a bit of stick and said abruptly, 'We have two moons— three if the spring comes later, but assuredly no more, to have our swords whetted before the Caledones take the war-trail. It is time enough, but no more than time enough. Therefore, the sooner we bring the King to the Crowning Stone, the better, for when that is done—' The wolf-yellow gaze whipped round, singling Phaedrus from the rest, so that for the first time Gault's words were directly for him: 'The sooner that is done, and he has taken the Princess Murna for his woman, the sooner we shall be free for the whetting of our swords.'

Phaedrus had sprung up before the last words were spoken. 'The Princess Murna?'

The wolf-stare never wavered. 'Who else?'

'It was not in the bargain!'

'What bargain?' Gault's voice had the ring of iron. 'If Liadhan had not escaped to her left-hand kin, the thing might not have been so direly needful, at least not so urgent. As it is, you must take the Royal Daughter for your woman, even as your great grandsire took the Royal Woman of the Epidii, that the two people might become one, and you must take her as soon as you are crowned King. The little Dark People, the Woman's Side, all those who make their foremost prayers to Earth Mother, will accept you the more readily if you hold by the ancient right, as well as by the right of the Sun People, and you must make your claim strong, before any rise to question it.'

Phaedrus was seeing inside the darkness of his head, the white mask-like face under the silver moon head-dress, with the look in the eyes that he could not read. The face of Liadhan's daughter. 'How if I refuse?' he demanded, his voice thick in his throat.

The dark brows lifted a little. 'You will not refuse. You are the King.'

Phaedrus made one desperate effort to beat down the tawny

334

wolf's gaze that would not leave his face, but he was trapped, and he knew it, and knew also, raging inwardly, that he was hamstrung in this battle of wills by the fact that he had been a slave too long, trained to obey as a thing that had no right to any will of its own, and the training had left scars and weak places in him like an old wound that lets you down when you least expect it.

He turned the thing into an ugly jest. 'So, I will take Liadhan's daughter for my woman. But "like mother like daughter", they say. Will you promise not to let her eat me and choose another king, seven Midwinter Fires from now?'

He dared not meet Conory's eyes, lest he should see scorn in them, or worse still, the look of a man making allowance for a friend.

The King-Making

PHAEDRUS opened his eyes into complete darkness, and lay for a while trying to remember where he was, trying to pierce back through the black sleep that had come down like a curtain between him and some strange, shadowy half-world on the other side of it. Three days, they had said—someone had said—three days and three nights for the Horse Lord before he came back to life. But surely it had been longer than that, whole years longer than that. Or had there perhaps never been a beginning to it, and would there never be an end?

He made a sudden panic movement, and the pain and stiffness of his body seemed to tear apart the feeling of nightmare that had begun to rise in his throat, so that he remembered where he was and what was happening to him. He turned his head cautiously, and saw a little way off, the few red gleeds of a

dying fire. There had been many fires in this place where the little Dark People had laid their dead Chiefs away, when they were the lords of the land; he had seen the dark scars of them on floor and roof, at the beginning, when there were torches to see by. The Place of Life, they called it, this place where now the boys came at their initiation mysteries, and the Horse Lord must lie for his three days and nights among the dead.

He had not been alone in the tomb-chamber. Vaguely he could remember now the Sun Priests coming and going about him; silent figures in horse-hide cloaks and aprons, their heads shaved save for the broad centre crest. The strange-smelling herbs that they had burned in the fire, the ritual patterns of sound and movement that they had woven round him. Dreams there had been, too, that seemed to come from the smoke of the fire, dreams of having four legs and a heart like flame, and running with a four-legged herd of kindred, in a thunder of hooves and a sky-wide flying of manes and tails. Strange wild dreams of freedom such as no mortal man had ever known.

He moved again, carefully, testing out his body, and the stiffened smart of the new tattoo marks on breast and shoulders brought him fully back to himself with a rush, and to wondering why, in the name of all the Gods that ever man had prayed to, he had got into that fight at the wine-booth. Why hadn't he simply hitched up his bundle and turned south, the moment the gates of the Gladiators' School closed behind him? He might have been in Londinium, a free trainer in some other school, perhaps, by now; his own master among his own kind. Even when Gault came, why hadn't he pretended to agree, and waited his chance and run as though all the fiends of Tartarus were after him? He supposed he had grown so used to thinking no more than one day ahead that when Gault and Sinnoch had put the scheme to him, and when he was with Midir, it had only seemed like a wild adventure to set out on, and he had not realized that it was for all the rest of his life.

To the end of his life, he was Midir the Horse Lord, and when he came to the end he would be laid in much such a place as this, with a sword to his hand and a pot of heather-beer to cheer him

on the dark journey, and be remembered by a name that was not his, by a people who were not his, either.

Meanwhile, wasn't it time that somebody came? How much longer? Soon the last gleeds of the fire would dim and go out. ... Suddenly the darkness was bearing down on him with all the weight of piled stone and turf between him and the world of living men, suffocating and engulfing him, crushing him out of existence. There was a drumming sound all about him, quicker and quicker, and a strange, animal panting that seemed to echo back from the unseen walls, and he did not realize that he was hearing his own heartbeats and his own hurrying breaths. He thrust back the soft, skin rug in which he was wrapt, and struggled to an elbow, then into a sitting position, groaning as every stiffened fibre of his body twinged in protest.

There was a stir and a flicker of torchlight far off at the entrance to the tomb-chamber, as though someone on watch there had only been waiting for some sound of movement to tell them he was awake, and figures came ducking in along the low tunnel. After so long in the dark, the sudden light of the torches they carried jabbed at Phaedrus's eyes, half blinding him, so that it was a few moments before he could see that the foremost of the torch-bearers was Conory, for once without his cat, and with two more of the Companions at his back.

'It was a good sleep?' Conory asked the ritual question.

And Phaedrus gathered his wits to make the ritual answer: 'A good sleep. And a good waking.'

The Companions were setting their torches into the makeshift stands of crossed spears that stood ready for them against the walls, and the light, flaring upward, splashed the great in-curving stones with honey colour, till they ran in to meet at the great fire-blackened lintel-stone high overhead. It was like a giant beehive, Phaedrus thought suddenly. It was easy to imagine the wild bees nesting up there, filling the chamber with their deep song—would the rib-cage of a dead Chieftain make a good framework for a honeycomb? ...

'It is time to be making ready,' said Conory's voice in his ear. And he pulled himself together and straightened his mind from

338

its wandering with an effort. There were so many things he wanted to ask. So much could have happened during these three days and nights that he had been shut away from the world of living men. He wanted to know if there had been any word of Liadhan and what had happened to her priests—those that had not died in the fighting—how many of the tribe had died on either side, how the rising had fared in the farther parts of Earra Ghyl. But all that must wait. He had been well drilled by Gault in how he must behave during this time of being made ready. So he drank the dark, bitter-tasting brew in the bronze cup that Conory gave him, and got stiffly and awkwardly to his feet, the floor dipping and side swimming under him, until whatever was in the drink took effect, and the world steadied somewhat; and stood to be decked out for his King-Making, like a sacrificial bull for the slaughter, he thought, and had a moment's insane desire to laugh.

In silence, Conory and the Companions combed his hair and bound it back with thongs as though for battle, and dressed him in breeks and tunic that they had brought with them. They hung round his neck an ancient clashing necklace of river-gold, amber, and cornelian, and a broad collar of heron-hackles; sheathed a leaf-shaped dagger with a gold pommel-mount at his side and sprang on to each arm a pair of coiled bronze arm-rings that he seemed to have seen before. It was a few moments before he remembered when, and where, and that it was not the arm-rings alone; and then, looking down, he saw the dark clotted patch where Logiore's blood had sunk into the heron-hackles.

They gave him a spear with a collar of black horsehair. And lastly, they set on his head the great maned and crested head-dress of the Horse Lord. He felt the scalp-cap gripping, from his brows to the nape of his neck, and the side fringes with their little gold disks that swung against his cheeks and chimed at every movement of his head, felt the heavy balance of the great arched stallion crest and the sweep of the mane between his shoulders, and for the last time before they faded altogether, he remembered those dreams of racing four-legged among the horse-herd.

He crouched his way down the arched tunnel followed by the

339

three Companions, his head ducked low between his shoulders to keep the great crest clear of the roof, and stood erect on the threshold, between the huge stone entrance posts; then stalked forward into the flare of pine-knot torches, where the rest of the Companions waited for him, and beyond the standing-stones of the forecourt, horses were being walked to and fro in the bitter dark. After the still and heavy air of the tomb-chamber, the thin wind of the winter night seemed to whine through his very bones, and the torchlight was flecked with spitting sleet. The warriors raised a great clamour at sight of him, drumming their spears across the rims of their bucklers. Then someone—Phaedrus saw that it was the boy Brys—brought him a red horse with a mealy mane and tail, and he made the steed-leap on his spear, and was away, the others mounting and pounding after him—Conory a bare half length behind, lest at any time he should be uncertain of the way.

Down every narrow side glen as he headed south, from every rath and village among the snow-puddled moors, mounted men came in to join them, many carrying torches, until the whole countryside was speckled with flame; herdsmen on little, sure-footed hill-ponies, ragged-fleeced in their winter coats, men in their best cloaks and carrying their finest weapons; here and there a knot of men on fine horses with the Arab strain in them; once a fat man with a flame-red beard, riding a mare with twin foals at heel. More and more, until Phaedrus found himself riding at the head of a fiery cloud of horsemen, that churned the glen trails to a puddled slush; and his ears were full of the soft, rolling thunder of hooves and the exultant throat-cries of the riders.

It was midnight when they set out on that wild ride, and dawn was not far off when they came in sight of Dun Monaidh across the marshes; dark-humped against the half-thawed, half-frozen snow that pooled and pale-dappled Mhoin Mhor, and crowned with torches. The men set up great shouts at the sight, heels were struck into horses' flanks, and the whole mass drummed forward into a gallop, strung out along the looping causeway track, splashing through the paved ford, and sweeping

left-hand wise to come at the fortress track. A flying skein of horsemen were out from the Dun itself, sweeping down to meet them at the foot of the fortress hill; and all around him was a great shouting above the smother of hooves; saffron and black and crimson cloaks flying in the torch-flare and the spitting sleet, weapons tossed up and caught again.

So with a great riding of horsemen before and behind him, Phaedrus swept on up the steepening track and in for the second time through the gates of Dun Monaidh, and reined in before the tall Pillar Stone.

The Sun Priests were there, and their chanting rose into the pallor of the winter dawn, full-voiced and strong in the invocation to Lugh of the Shining Spear; and there also were the elders of the Kindred, to receive him as he swung down from the red horse. Tuathal the Wise stood foremost among his priests, wrapt in his horse-hide robe, with the amber sun-cross on his breast: he came forward and put a stone-hilted dagger with a strange, leafshaped copper blade into Phaedrus's hand. A knot of young warriors were bringing up the sacred white stallion.

Midir, and later Gault, had warned him that he would have this to do, this making of the Horse Sacrifice before the Pillar Stone of the Royal House. 'I am no priest and no butcher,' he had said angrily. 'I have killed men but not horses; I shall bungle it.' And Gault had said, in the tone of one giving an order he will have obeyed:

'You will not bungle it! A clumsy killing is taken as an ill omen, and there will be no room for ill omens, that day.'

And he did not bungle it, or not much. A clean kill enough, though the white horse reared up, screaming defiance as a stallion screams in battle, when he felt his death upon him, tearing at the ropes and swinging the men who held them from side to side. For one moment he towered over Phaedrus like a great wave before it breaks, ready to come plunging down and engulf him. Then the powerful haunches gave way, and the great horse crashed sideways to the ground, gave one convulsive shudder, and lay still. Tomorrow there would be a new Lord of the Sacred Horse-herd.

341

There was a smell of blood mingling with the smell of burning that still clung about scorched timber and blackened thatch, and a great wailing rose from the watching crowd. The old High Priest dipped a finger in the blood and made a sign with it on Phaedrus's forehead, above the Mark of the Horse Lord. And the wailing of the Women's Side was taken up and engulfed by a triumphant roar from the men, and that in turn was drowned in the deep booming splendour of sound that seemed to loosen the very thoughts in one's head, as two of the priests raised and sounded the huge, curved bronze trumpets of the Sun that had not been heard in Dun Monaidh for seven years.

The torches were quenched and the

342

grey light of dawn all about them, as Phaedrus was led up through the Dun, the Sun Priests going ahead, the Companions and Kindred, and then a great comet-tail of people following on behind, until they came to the court next below the Citadel, where the Rock of the Footprint jutted up from the natural outcrop; the Crowning Stone of the Dalriads.

There were more things to be done, but they were short and soon over; mare's milk to be drunk from a battered black pottery bowl that was never used save at the King-Making; a ritual washing of hands and feet in the bowl-shaped depression at one end of the same great rock slab, where the gathered sky-water was more than half-melted sleet; the priests with short prancing steps making sacred patterns of words and movements that passed him by like a dream. They had brought the freshly flayed hide of the King Horse, and spread it across the end of the stone opposite to the bowl depression, so that it covered the third thing that was cut there: the wild boar beloved of warriors.

Sleet was still spitting down the wind, but the yellow bar of a low dawn edged the eastern sky, and as Phaedrus mounted the Crowning Stone, and with his left foot on the hide of the King Horse, set his right into the deep-cut footprint that had held the right foot of every king of the Dalriads since first they came from Erin across the Western Sea, the first sunlight struck the high snow-filled corries of distant Cruachan.

Gault brought the spear of Lugh, and put it into his hand in place of the other that he had brought with him from the Place of Life. Conory knotted the sheath thongs of the King's sword to his belt. Now they were loosening the bindings of the stallion head-dress, lifting it away. Tuathal the High Priest was standing on the horse-hide beside him, holding up a narrow circlet of fiery pale gold that caught the morning light for an instant in a ripple of white fire, like the leaves of the white aspen when they blow up against the sun. Phaedrus bent his head to receive it, felt it pressed down on to his brows.

The bronze Sun Trumpets were sounding again; the deep earth-shaking note booming out over the marshes and the hills

and the high moors, to be caught up from somewhere on the very edge of hearing, and passed on, carrying the word from end to end of Earra-Ghyl that there was a Horse Lord again in Dun Monaidh.

11

Royal Hunt

THE next time Phaedrus woke, it was to the flicker of fire-light
through eyelids still half gummed together with sleep and the
morning sky milk-silver beyond the smoke-hole in the crown of
the King's Place roof. He lay for a few moments basking in the
sense of well-being that lapped him round; the aching stiffness
and the leaden weight of exhaustion all washed away by the
black warm tide of sleep. Then gradually a weight of some other
kind settled on him in its place as he remembered. Yesterday he
had been crowned Horse Lord, but today was the day of his
marriage to the Royal Woman.

He opened his eyes and came to one elbow with something
between a groan and a curse; and a small rhythmic sound that
had been going on all the while without his noticing it, stopped

abruptly. The young warrior Brys, squatting by the great fire that glowed warmly in the centre of the big square hut, looked up alertly from the great war-spear with the black horsehair collar he had been burnishing across his knee.

Phaedrus scowled, startled for the moment at finding he was not alone. 'What in Typhon's name are you doing here?'

'I was burnishing your gear and weapons while you slept, Lord. Gault bade me come to serve you.'

'Gault!' Something in Phaedrus seemed to snap. 'Gault bids this thing—Gaults bids that thing—Gault will choose me my armour bearer, *and* my wife——' He checked at sight of Brys's face, and quietened his tone somewhat. 'You have served me well; that spear blade looks as though it had this morning come fresh from the armourer's hands. Now go back to your own Lord, and if you should be seeing Gault on the way, tell him I thank him for his care of me, but I will choose my own armour-bearer.'

There was a moment's pause, and then Brys said, 'My own Lord is dead.'

And suddenly Phaedrus was remembering the place where the fortress stream dived through the outer wall, and Brys holding the torch that called that answering gleam from the silver apples under the water. Gault had said, 'Your Lord Gallgoid,' and the boy had said, 'My Lord Gallgoid is dead.' He rubbed the back of one hand across his forehead, trying to clear the confusion that still blurred all the edges of that night. 'Of course. You will be—you will have been Gallgoid's armour-bearer.'

'His armour-bearer and his charioteer.'

'It is in my mind that to suit Gallgoid, a charioteer would need to be good at his trade.'

'I am,' Brys said with conviction.

'*Sa*—and modest as well. And now you would be mine?'

'I am of the Kindred,' the boy said proudly, stating his claim. 'You would not be remembering; I was only in my first year in the Boys' House when you—when the Bad Thing happened. But I am of the Kindred.'

346

'Gallgoid had no one with him all that moon and more that he was with me in the Cave of the Hunter.'

'He left me behind in his Hall, until the time came to join him here in Dun Monaidh. There had to be those that he could trust, while he was supposed to be lying sick in his own place.'

'And you were one that he could trust.'

'Nobody found out that he was not there.'

Phaedrus looked at Brys with fresh eyes, noticing the good straight look of him, and the stubborn mouth. '*Sa, sa*—it may be that I shall need someone to trust, one day. ... I will take Gallgoid's charioteer after him.'

'In spite of Gault the Strong?' Brys said slowly.

'In spite of Gault the Strong.' Suddenly Phaedrus laughed. 'If Gault had sent me Cuchulain himself this morning to be my armour-bearer and drive my team, I would have spat in Cuchulain's eye, if I could not be coming at Gault to spit in his.' Then as the slow smile broadened on Brys's face, 'Now leave that burnishing, and go and find me something to eat, for my belly's cleaving to my back-bone.'

The unpegged curtain of skins across the doorway had scarcely fallen behind Brys when voices sounded outside and the heavy folds were thrust back once more, and Conory, with Shân draped across his shoulders, strolled in. 'A fine and fortunate day to you,' he said pleasantly, and deposited on the low stool by the fire, a gaming board and a carved wooden box. 'Since there's no going out for the bridegroom until they summon him out to his marrying, it was in my mind that a game of Fox and Geese might serve to pass the time.'

Phaedrus flung off the bed-rugs with a sudden violence, and sat up. 'Conory, it's madness! I can't be going through with this marrying!'

Conory had settled on to his heels, and taken up the gaming box to open it. He said very softly, 'Midir, it is in my mind that you have no choice.'

'She will know!'

'Keep your voice down, you've a King's Guard outside. Here—let you put that cloak round you and come to the fire.'

347

'Fiends and Furies!' Phaedrus swore, but he picked up the heavy saffron cloak that lay tumbled on the bed-place, and flung it round him over the light under-tunic which was all he had on, and came to squat beside the fire, facing Conory across the checkered board on which he had begun to set out the pieces of red amber and narwhal ivory. '*She will know!*' he repeated desperately.

'She will not. She was only ten—eleven summers old when it happened. A babe who would scarcely have begun her weapon training.' (To Phaedrus, it still seemed strange that the women of the Northern tribes shared the training of the young warriors, becoming as used to the throw-spear as to the distaff; and unconsciously, he frowned.) 'You have nothing to fear on that count. She will not know the balance of the blade.'

Phaedrus had just drawn breath for one more furious protest, for, indeed, it seemed to him a horrible thing, not only on his own account but on Midir's also, that he should take this She-Wolf's daughter for his woman; but at that moment Brys returned, with a beer-jar in one hand and a bowl piled with cold pig-meat and barley bannock in the other, and the protest must be left unmade. Instead, while they ate together—Brys had brought more than enough for two—he turned to the questions he had longed to ask yesterday. And Conory answered him as best he could, while Shân, springing down from his shoulder, pounced on and played with and tormented a lump of pig-fat that he had tossed for her beside the fire, until she wearied of the game and stalked out, tail erect, in search of better hunting elsewhere.

By the time they had finished eating, it was all told: the number of the dead, and how many women were among them, the success of the rising that had swept like heath fire through Earra-Ghyl, freeing the Dalriads of the dark bondage that had held them for seven years; the flight with Liadhan of the Earth Priests not killed in the fighting.

'Now it will be for the women once again to make the Mysteries of the Mother, as they have always done,' Conory said.

'Those furies!' Phaedrus gave a small shudder, thinking of the women with their knives and their rending claws, and Conory and himself fighting for life in the middle of them.

Conory flicked a faint, warning glance towards Brys, who was standing by to take up the bowl and beer-jar. 'Do you ever remember them like that before, save when a man intruded on the Women's Mysteries? And any man who does that has himself to blame for the thing that happens to him, as any woman would have only herself to blame, who spied on the boys' initiation ceremonies. Ach no, that night was Liadhan's doing, and the dancing in the Fire Hall, and the flute-magic of the priests.'

When Brys had departed with the empty bowl, Phaedrus looking after him, with his mind full of the things that they had been talking of, found that his thoughts had slipped sideways for a moment, and he was discovering that the Princess Murna could not be more than a year older than Brys himself. For that one moment he was thinking of her as a person, wondering how it had been with her in the days since Liadhan had fled, and where she was held captive, and if she also had woken to a weight on her heart this morning—supposing that she had slept at all.

Then Conory said, 'Shall we begin? Amber plays first.'

They played three games, and Conory won them all.

'Since you have my kingdom,' he said, when he had made the winning move for the third time, 'it is only fair that I should have the games.'

There was a laugh from the direction of the doorway and looking up, Phaedrus saw that several of the Companions had entered, and were standing just inside, watching the end of the game.

Yesterday they had been no more than strange faces and chance-heard names, these men who had been boys with Midir. But now, after the wild ride down from the Place of Life, that they had shared, and last night's feasting that they had shared also, names and faces had begun to join together. Lean, freckled Loarne, and Diamid of the sombre eyes and devil's-quirk

349

eyebrows; Comgal and Domingart who were brothers and seldom apart; the little dark one, probably with Earthling blood in him, whom they called Baruch the Grass-Snake. And in a vague, tentative kind of way, they were beginning to take on a friendly look.

'The day be fortunate to you,' Diamid said, 'and may all the ill luck of it have gone into the gaming board.'

'Fox and Geese was never your game, my Lord Midir.' That was Domingart, shaking his head regretfully as he surveyed the board before Conory began to gather up the pieces. 'And still it would seem that it is not.'

'I am seven years out of practice,' Phaedrus returned. The excuse was unanswerable.

Brys had come in behind them, and began taking many-coloured garments from the big carved chest against the far wall, gravely proud to be the King's armour-bearer, so that Phaedrus thought if he had had a tail like a hound's, it would have been lashing slowly from side to side behind him.

Time to be moving, then. He flung off the saffron cloak and got to his feet and stood ready for them.

When he was once again clad in the ritual dress of the Horse Lord, from the brogues on his feet to the great stallion head-dress that had been brought from the hut where the priests kept the sacred objects, he went out with the Companions, to the Horse Court beside the Court of the Footprint, where the horses stood ready for them, and they mounted and rode down into the great Forecourt.

The Forecourt was already alive with men, and growing more so every moment, as others came in from all over Dun Monaidh. There were few women among them, for the Women's Side were for the most part gathering in the same way to the Royal Court. A shout greeted Phaedrus, when he appeared with the Companions riding about him, and they were caught up in the general movement and swept across towards the gate gap which gave on to the Court of the Footprint and from there into the Citadel.

'The King rides hunting!'

Somebody raised the shout and suddenly it was running through the great gathering, taken up from end to end of the Dun.

'The King rides hunting!' And then, 'Who rides with the King?'

Conory and the Companions crashed out the answer: '*We* ride hunting with the King!'

They were close before the inner gateway now, jostling and jostled; the ponies stamped and snorted, puffing clouds of steam from their nostrils; the colours of cloaks and fringed riding rugs and the glint of bronze from brooch or bridle-bit were darkly brilliant in the grey light of the winter's day that was already far past noon. 'What quarry for the King's hunting? What quarry for the King's hunting?'

For a moment there was no answer, and the crowd fell silent, watching the gate. Then from within that last inner circle of rock walling rose the low wailing of the Women's Side, making the ritual lament for a maiden carried off from among them against her will. Phaedrus, on the red horse with the mealy mane, ignored Gault's dark face among the nobels in the forefront of the crowd and glanced aside under his red brows, at Conory; saw that Conory looked amused and politely interested more than anything else, and could have hit him. There was a little stir among the waiting tribesmen, and then the dead thorn-bush that closed the inner gateway was dragged aside. He could glimpse movement within, and the glint of colours, and the Princess Murna came walking slowly through the gate, with the women of the Kindred behind her and on either side. She walked looking neither to right nor left, down through the Court of the Footprint and out into the wide Forecourt. Her head was held very high and the soft, springing hair, loosed from its braids and drawn forward over her shoulders, hung in thick falls of dove-gold down over the breast of her many-coloured gown. The last time Phaedrus saw her she had been wearing the silver Moon Diadem; now she was crowned only with a narrow head-band of crimson stuff, strung about with shining wires and hung with disks of gold and coral; but under it her face was covered by

a mask of red mare's-skin that gave her the look of something not belonging to the world of men, so that looking at her, Phaedrus felt the skin crawl and prickle at the back of his neck.

'What quarry for the King's hunting?' the men shouted again, and the women flung back the answer:

'A Royal quarry! A Royal quarry for the King's hunting!'

Down at the foot of the outer court, where the timbered gates stood open, two men had just flung a fringed riding rug across the back of a young black mare, which looked, as Phaedrus had thought when he first glanced down towards her past the Pillar Stone, to have been ridden already today. He had said as much to Conory, and Conory had smiled that gentle smile and said, 'A sad thing it would be if the quarry should outrun the hunter.'

The Princess was level with him now. She turned her head once in passing, and he caught the flicker of light behind the eye-slits of the mask. Then she passed on, the men parting to let her through, until she reached the gate and the black mare waiting there. She seemed to come to life then, and scooping up a great fold of her skirt, drew it through her belt and made the steed-leap as lightly as any boy.

A strange high cry like a sea-bird's floated back to them as she wheeled the mare towards the gate, and with a sharp jab of the horse-rod, urged it from a stand into a canter.

She was out through the gate, and under the chanting of the Sun Priests invoking Lugh of the Shining Spear, they heard the hoof-beats trippling down to the outer gap, then burst into the drumming rhythm of full gallop. Phaedrus saw in his mind's eye that steep rocky track down to the marshes—and she was riding it as though it were a level practice field. His hand clenched on the horse-rod of green ash, and unconsciously he must have tightened his knees. The red stallion stirred and buckled forward under him, and instantly Conory's finger flicked up, warningly, on his own bridle-rein. 'Not yet.'

There was a general laugh all about him. 'See how eager he is! This will be fine, fierce hunting!'

The drum of hoof-beats was very faint now, almost lost. The chanting of the Sun Priests died on a last long, glowing note, and

again the finger flicked on Conory's bridle-rein. Phaedrus raised the small, bronze-bound hunting-horn that hung from the stallion's pectoral strap, and putting it to his mouth, set the echoes flying; then while the notes still hung on the winter air, heeled the red horse from a stand to a canter in his turn. The Companions were close behind him, Conory as usual just to his right, as he bore down on the great gate. Behind him he heard cries of, 'Good hunting!' Gault's bull-roar topping all the rest. 'Good hunting to you, Midir of the Dalriads!'

They were out through the gates and across the ditch causeway, the track dropping before them towards the moss. For a moment there was no sign of horse or rider. Then Conory pointed. 'There she goes!' And away northward, Phaedrus saw the flying figure, already dimming into the sear grey and tawny of the marshes.

'She's not going to be easy to follow, once the light begins to go.'

They took the plummeting track at breakneck speed, down from the hill of Dun Monaidh, from the in-pastures where that year's colts scattered, kicking up their heels as they drummed past, and out into the great emptiness of Mhoin Mhor.

The Companions were stringing out like a skein of wild geese threading the winter sky. The red horse snorted and stretched out his neck, and the foam flew back from his muzzle to spatter against Phaedrus's breast and thighs, the mealy silver of the mane flowed back across his bridle wrist as the land fled by beneath the pounding hooves. Excitement rose in them all; laughter and hunting cries began to break from the men behind him. He guessed that in the ordinary way of things the girl's flight would have been only a pretence, like the wailing of the Woman's Side. But this was different; if he wished to catch the Princess Murna, then he would have to hunt her in good earnest; and pity twinged in him, not for her, the She-Wolf's daughter, but for the weary mare she rode.

The track was pulling up now, out of the great flats of Mhoin Mhor, and the quarry, striking away from it, was making northeastward for the hills around Loch Abha head. And the wild

353

hunt swept after her, hooves drumming through the blackened heather, skirting little tarns that reflected the sword-grey sky, startling the green plover from the pasture clearings. Far over to the west the clouds were breaking as they came up into the hills, and a bar of sodden daffodil light was broadening beyond the Island, casting an oily gleam over the wicked swirling water of the Old Woman, while away and away northward, the high snows of Cruachan caught the westering beams and shone out sour-white against the storm-clouds dark behind.

But now the chase was turning tail to the sunset, and all at once Conory let out a startled curse, and urging his horse level with Phaedrus's, shouted, 'By the Black Goddess! She's making for the Royal Water and Caledonia!'

And his words were caught up in a startled splurge of voices and echoed to and fro behind him.

'The vixen!' Phaedrus said, and laughed. 'You were saying it would be a sad thing if the quarry were to outrun the hunt. The Sun's warmth for ever on the shoulders of the man who rode that mare today!'

After that it was a hunt in deadly earnest, and shouting to the rest, Phaedrus crouched lower and dug in his heels and settled down to ride as he had never ridden in his life before. The ground began to be cut up, soon they were into a maze of shallow glens, wooded in their hollows, and tangled with stone-brambles and bilberry and sour juniper scrub along the ridges between; and once they thought they had lost her—until Baruch the Grass-Snake pointed across the glen, yelling, 'There she goes!' and on the crest of the far ridge, the flying shape of horse and rider showed for an instant against the sky. They wheeled the horses and plunged downhill after her, fording the little burn between its snow-puddled edges, and stringing out in a bee-line up the opposite hill-side. When they gained the crest, she was nowhere to be seen, but a few moments later, she came into view again, heading up the glen towards the high moors; she had doubled northward, in an effort to throw them off her trail, relying maybe on the fading light to cover her. But there was just too much light left, and in turning north she had missed the ford

a short way downstream, and was left with a tiring horse, and fast water running between her and her way of escape.

Conory was riding almost neck-to-neck with Phaedrus, a little in advance of the rest. He leaned towards him and said quickly, 'It is seven years since you were in these hills. Will you let me give the orders?'

Phaedrus nodded, and Conory fell back a little, shouting over his shoulder to the smother of horsemen that followed after, 'The mare is tiring fast, and if we can hold her in sight a while longer, she's ours! Baruch, Finn, Domingart, you three ride the lightest of us all—back to the ford with you, and come up the far side. If you can reach the glen head before her, you can turn her back, while we keep her from breaking away on this side, and we'll have her before the last light goes!'

The three young men wheeled their horses and plunged away, while the main chase swept on after their desperate, flagging quarry. But in a short while they appeared again, deliberately showing themselves on the skyline, and going like the Blue Riders of the West Wind. Phaedrus saw the black mare flinch sideways, flinging up her head, as though the hand on her bridle had involuntarily jerked at the bit; the rider snatched a glance over her shoulder; he could almost feel her despairing moment of indecision, then she wheeled about and took to the open hill-side, swinging west again.

It was not quite a hunt now, more like rounding up a runaway colt. The Companions were not only behind her but creeping up on either side, heading her back the way she had come. The light was going fast as they dropped down from the hills on to lower ground. What still lingered of it lay over the wide levels of Mhoin Mhor stretching grey and dun and dreary-pale towards the sea; but on the left, behind the down-thrust tongue of the hills, the gathering twilight could not yet quench the one stretch of full colour in all that winter evening, the luminous, wicked green of bog between its islands of half-thawed snow.

The distance between them and the wild rider was lessening steadily, the mare, despite all her valiant efforts, rocking in her

355

gallop and almost done. Then the girl snatched one more glance behind her, as though judging the distance that she still had in hand, and wrenching the mare round in her tracks, sent her plunging down into the hazel woods that sloped southward into those luminous green shadows.

Conory cried, 'Thunder of Tyr! She's heading straight for the bog!'

So she would take even that last hideous way out! Ahead of them as they crashed after her, heads low against the whipping hazel twigs, the bog lay smooth and deadly, and the girl was heading straight towards it, crouched over the mare's straining neck, drumming her heels into the poor labouring flanks. Her voice blew back to them, crying endearments and encouragement. Phaedrus, driving in his own heels, had somehow flung the red stallion out before the rest; he was circling to ride her off as the herd lads rode to turn a break-away. The divots of soft black earth that spun from the mare's hooves flew past him like a flight of swallows; behind him the muffled hoof-drum of his Companions, ahead and to the right, the mare floundering and swaying in her stride; and the livid greenness of the bog rushing nearer—nearer, in the evening light. The cold rooty smell of it was all about them. A few moments more, and they would be into it. . . .

Shouting would be no use. Desperately, Phaedrus flung the horse-rod point-over-butt as though it were a dagger and saw it arch spinning past the mare and plunge into the bog myrtle just ahead of her and to the left. That was one useful trick learned in the Gladiators' School, anyway. Startled, she swerved aside, snorting, and plunged on, but no longer straight towards the fringe of the bog. Now the red horse's muzzle was almost level with the dark streaming tail, as the Princes struggled to head her mount back to the waiting greenness of the bog that was now so hideously close. But the mare was just about done, and Phaedrus clamped in his knees and hurled the stallion forward, and they were neck and neck. And with only a few strides to go and the ground softening at every hoof-fall, he wrenched round and deliberately took the black mare in the shoulder, all but bring-

356

ing her down. She screamed with fear, and lashed out, but the crash had spun her in her tracks, away from the deadly verge. In the same instant Phaedrus felt his own mount side-slither under him, as one great round hoof slipped into the black quaking ooze beneath the green. For one long-drawn sickening moment the red horse lurched on the brink, and it seemed that in the next, they must be over into the bog, but his own speed carried him on, and the next flying stride found solid myrtle tussocks underfoot again.

The girl had turned with a cry of fury and lashed him across the face with her horse-rod, but he had her reins and they were racing along the flank of the bog, perilously locked together, floundering in and out of solid ground and sinking pocket, but drawing steadily away from the livid greenness of the hungry mire. Then with a sound between a laugh and a sob, Phaedrus had an arm round the Princess Murna and dragged her across the red horse's withers. The wild-eyed mare, lightened of her load, sprang away and went streaking back towards the hills, with a couple of the Companions in pursuit. And Phaedrus, still riding full gallop, was clamping the Royal Woman against him with his free arm, while she struggled to break free and fling herself off.

Then quite suddenly the fight seemed to go out of her as they slackened pace from that wild gallop to a canter. Phaedrus freed one hand—he was controlling the panting stallion with his knees now—and caught at the red mare's-skin mask.

Just for an instant, as his hand touched the hairiness of the hide, he wondered if it were the Moon Diadem trick over again, and the face beneath it would not be Murna's. Wondered, with a little shiver of cold between his shoulder-blades, whether it would be a human face at all, or something else, something that was not good to see. ... Then he pulled away the mask, and flung it behind him among the following horsemen. It was Murna's face looking up at him, grey-white and somehow ragged, as though in pulling off the bridal mask he had torn holes in something else, some inner defence that she was naked and terrified without. And for that one instant, despite the dusk,

he could look into her face instead of only at the surface of it. Still feeling rather sick from the nearness of the bog, he laughed in sudden triumph, and bent his head and kissed her.

Surprisingly, she yielded against him and kissed him back. But as she did so, he felt her hand steal out, light as a leaf, but not quite light enough, towards the dagger in his belt.

His own hand flashed down and caught her wrist, twisting the weapon from her grasp before she well had hold of it, and sent it spinning into a furze bush. 'Softly, sweetheart! Maybe we shall do better if we are both unarmed,' he said, gently dangerous. She could have no other weapon about her, or she would not have gone for his dagger.

She gave a sharp cry of baffled fury, and became a thing as rigid and remote as one of the stocks of wood, charmed into human shape, that the People of the Hills left behind in its place when they stole a child of the Sun Folk. And yet the odd thing—Phaedrus knew it beyond all doubt, was that the kiss she had given him had been as real as her hand feeling for his dagger.

It was long past full dark by the time they came back to the Dun, and all down the steep track and massed in the gateways, the warriors were waiting, with pine-knot torches in their hands, so that they rode through a ragged avenue of light. Midir of the Dalriads, with the Royal Woman conquered and captive across his horse; and after them, the Companions, Conory triumphantly bearing aloft the red mare's-skin mask on the point of his spear, as though it were a trophy.

The King was home from his hunting.

Golden Plover's Feather

WHEN it came to getting away by oneself for a while, Phaedrus
decided, the Lord of the Dalriads was in much the same case as a
gladiator with his town leave stopped. All the past two days up
here in the hill horse-runs, watching Sinnoch's leggy two-year-
olds in the first stages of breaking, the Companions had been
with him, friends and bodyguard in one, alert and willing to go
anywhere and do anything as a knot of hounds at heel, and as
difficult to get rid of.

In the end he had simply gone to the garbage pits—at least
they let him go there alone—and from there strolled round by

359

the back ways of Sinnoch's steading to the stable huts, and bidden Brys whom he found there playing knuckle-bones with three other charioteers, to bring out the dun colt for him.

'Do I ride with you?' the boy had asked.

And Phaedrus had said, 'Neither you nor anyone. If Conory or any other of the Companions ask where I am gone or seek to follow me, tell them I've gone to find better company than theirs.'

And he mounted and clattered off by the lower gate where they brought the colts up to the practice yards. They would probably think that he had gone off after some girl glimpsed yesterday in one of the herdsmen's bothies. Well, they'd not be surprised. The Horse Lord's month-old marriage had been only a form, and nobody would be fool enough to think there was anything in it to keep him from going after other girls, or that the Queen would care or even notice if he did.

She had not changed since the night he brought her back to the Dun, with Conory carrying the red mare's-skin mask on the point of his spear. The torn defence, whatever it was, was whole again, and she still seemed like some cold thing magicked into human-seeming that the Dark People might have left behind in the stealing of the real Murna away. Once he had said to her, 'If I strike you with cold iron, will you fly up through the smoke-hole, or turn back into a log of wood?'

And she had said in a tone of complete indifference, 'Try it, and see.'

He had been half minded to do it, too. But in the end—he had not quite dared to, in case what he had said in angry jest, was true. ... And yet there had been the moment when she kissed him back, even while she felt for his dagger. That had not been a clay-cold changeling's kiss. And sometimes he wondered if the real Murna were there inside her all the while, looking out at him as he had so often looked out at the world through the eye-slits of a gladiator's helmet. Well, it was not anything to him, either way; he simply visited the Queen's Place as seldom as might be, and thought about her very little the rest of the time.

And he had better stop thinking about her now, because he

360

had only been this way once before, and if he let his wits go, wandering off down every gust of wind, he would almost certainly miss the half-dead birch-tree where one left the glen track.

But he found it easily enough in the end, and the little white thread of a burn that came chattering down from the high moors.

It was sear, dark country that he climbed through after that, leading the colt now because it was too steep to ride; outcropped with rock and pocketed with wetness. It would be fair in its own wild way, when the new fern came thrusting through the sodden wreck of last year's bracken and the ancient hawthorns were in flower along the burn; but now, in the dark end of winter with spring still a long way off, it was desolate enough. That was why it was left to the little Dark People, Phaedrus supposed, the dispossessed, whose place was always the rock screes and the waste wet mosses that were no use to the later-come lords of the land.

It was all strange country to him, since leaving the track, and he had no idea how far he had to go. ('Away up the burn—that way,' Sinnoch had said yesterday, when they passed the birch-tree on the way to the outland horse-runs, and that was all), and he had begun to think he must have missed the way when suddenly between one step and the next—there it was.

No more than a tumble of stones and turf laced together with brambles, that might have been only a natural hummock of the hill-side, save for a dark opening in its side that was just too large and just too regular to be the mouth of a wild thing's lair. Midway between the hummock and himself, as he checked to look, a great flat stone cropped through the blackened heather. Nothing moved or sounded but the hill wind and the burn water, and a golden eagle swinging in mile-wide circles far overhead.

He had heard before of places such as this, where one left something that needed mending, together with a gift, and came back later to find the gift gone and the broken thing mended; it was one of those things no one talked of very much,

the places where the life of the Sun People touched the life of the Old Ones, the People of the Hills. Like the bowls of milk that the women put out sometimes at night, in exchange for some small job to be done—like the knot of rowan hung over a doorway for protection against the ancient Earth Magic—like the stealing of a Sun Child from time to time. Save for the few who were their slaves and bond-folk, the tribes had little else to do with the Old People, certainly they were used to taking less account of them than they did of their chariot horses and beef cattle, when it came to casting up the chances of war. Yet, assuredly, it was by the aid of the little Dark People that Liadhan had escaped to her Caledonian kin. Gault had said as much, and now, with the war horns sounding over the edge of spring, Phaedrus with the common sense of his Roman upbringing, felt that the time was come when the Dark People must count at least for as much as ponies and beef cattle. Sinnoch had said that this mender of worn and broken things, who had his lair and his leaving-stone up here, was the Old Man, the Chieftain of his village. A king in his way, and it seemed to Phaedrus that a visit to him was probably the best chance he would ever get of making contact with any leader among the Dark People.

The colt had begun to fidget, and Phaedrus quieted him and hitched his bridle over a hawthorn-bush, then walked forward, and pulling a good serviceable strap of tanned leather and three barley-cakes from the breast of his tunic, stooped and set them on the flat stone.

Then he retreated downstream to where he had left the pony, and turned again to face the dark hole in the turf hammock, that might almost have passed for the mouth of an animal's lair, save for the betraying wisp of smoke that rose from the briar-tangle above it.

Slowly and deliberately, knowing that his every movement was being watched, he laid his spear on the ground, the blade pointing away down the glen, and his dirk beside it. He held out his hands, showing them empty, and called, 'Old Man of the green hillocks—let you come out to me.'

Nothing moved but the thin hill wind. Phaedrus waited—

362

waited—then he walked back slowly, part of the way, and checked again, feeling suddenly how little he knew of the Dark People, wondering what he should do about it if the man did not come. 'Chieftain—see, I carry no cold-iron blade; let you be coming out to me.'

And from just within the dark mouth, a voice answered, speaking the tongue of the tribes in the lighter, softer tone of the Old People, 'You have left me a gift, but nothing that needs my skill to make it whole again. Why should I come out to you?'

'Because I have brought you the gift; and the thing that I ask for it is not the mending of a worn brogue or a sprung rivet in my dagger hilt, but that you should come out and speak with me.'

'So—o, that seems fair enough,' the voice said consideringly. But still nothing moved beyond the mouth of the dark hole. And then—Phaedrus realized afterwards that he must have glanced away, but at the time he could have sworn that he never took his eyes from the door-hole under the briar-tangle—suddenly a man was standing on the far side of the stone. A small, slight-boned man in a kilt of otter skins and with grey hair bushing from his narrow skull, and eyes that seemed at first glance like jet beads, until one looked again and saw that they were not black at all, but the dark-furred brown of a bee's back. Phaedrus made the sign of the Horns behind himself, and then had an uncomfortable feeling that the other knew it. But he only said, looking at the forehead mark that was like a four-petalled flower, 'What is it that you would speak with me about, Midir of the Dalriads?'

'I would speak with you because it has been told me that you are a Chieftain among your own people, and because the war horns are sounding across Druim Alban. When the spring comes, the hosts of King Bruide will take the war-trail, and at such a time it is surely good that the Horse Lord should know something of all those within his hunting-runs, not of his own tribe alone.'

The little man gestured to Phaedrus to sit himself on the flat

stone, and then squatted down at his feet. 'You have more than one of our people among the slaves in your Dun. Why not ask *them* what you would know of the Dark People?'

'Because a slave answers as a slave, and it is the answer of a free man that I am wanting.'

The other nodded. 'Ask, then.'

Phaedrus knew that it would be no good trying to come at the thing slantwise, not with this little man who would understand slantwise methods all too well, so he made his question as direct as a dagger thrust. 'When the fighting comes, this fighting that will not be only for cattle or boundaries, but for deciding whether the Dalriads shall be free people any more, and what kings shall rule us, and what Gods we shall follow—have we to fear your little blue-flint daggers in our back while our shields are turned to the Caledones?'

'If you had, should I tell you?'

'No,' said Phaedrus frankly, 'but I have fought for my life to amuse a Roman crowd too often not to be able to judge men's faces. I had hoped that your face might tell me before you were aware of it.'

'And it does not? See now, I will be telling you myself, and I will be telling you the truth. We count for nothing, we, the people of the dark-blue flint, since the Horse People took our hunting-runs; we count for nothing, and we know it. But the tribes come and go like wind-waves through the heather, and we bide in our hills and let them pass. It is no concern of ours when they fight each other. We shall always be here as long as there are wolves on the hill. Kill and be killed as you choose, it is nothing to us.'

'Yet you helped Liadhan to escape into Caledonia.'

'Surely. She was the Mother, the Lady of the Forests. She was ours to us, and we were hers. Yet because she fled from it when her own Call came—*aiee*, though we helped her in her fleeing—I do not think that many of us will stir from our own fireside for her sake again.'

'When her own Call came?' The phrase caught at Phaedrus's attention, and he was puzzled by it.

The other's dark gaze was on his face, and the burn sounded very loud in the silence. High, high overhead, Phaedrus heard the thin, sharp yelp of the golden eagle. Then the little Dark Man said softly, 'The Horse Lord, of all men, should be knowing what that Call means. ...' And then as though changing the subject, he reached out and took up one of the barley-cakes, and broke a long piece of crust from one side. 'Lord, do you see what I am holding?'

'Surely,' Phaedrus said, surprised.

'What is it, then?'

'A crust of barley-cake.'

'Are you sure?'

From being surprised, Phaedrus was puzzled, and somewhere deep within him was a flicker of warning that he did not understand. 'I am quite sure. It is a crust from one of the barley-cakes I brought you.'

'Look at it well,' the man said.

And Phaedrus found himself obeying, his head bent over the crust as though it were something strange and wonderful that he had never seen before.

'Are you still sure?' said the soft, insistent voice.

And suddenly he was not so sure. Not sure at all. The thing in the narrow dark hand was growing blurred, losing its outline, changing into something else. Something—something——

'What is it, then?' said the voice.

'It is—it is *like* a feather.'

He could see it taking shape, the strong slender line of it, as it were, filled in with mist. But the mist was thickening, taking on substance and colour. He could see the almost blackness of the strong pinion barred with gold—in another moment—but something in him had begun to resist.

'What kind of feather would it be?'

'A golden plover's——' he began, and checked. 'No feather at all!' He forced the words out, his eyes fighting for the lost outline of the barley crust. He could see it now very faintly like a shadow—showing through the feather that was growing misty again. For what seemed an eternity of time the two images hung

365

equally balanced, so that he could see them both, one showing through the other. 'It is only a barley crust—*a barley crust!*'

The feather was no more substantial than a wisp of wood-smoke and with a supreme effort of will, he snuffed it out, the dark slender shape and the golden shadow-bars, and there was nothing in the other man's hand but the strip of crust with the grains of parched barley scattered on top.

He looked up with a gasping breath, and drew the back of one hand across his forehead. Despite the little chill wind, it was wet. 'Why did you do that?'

There was sweat on the little Dark Man's forehead too, as he set the barley crust back beside the cake that it had come from. 'That? It was no more than a small piece of Earth Magic, such as may be made between the eyes of one man and the eyes of another. I made it—for the answering of a question that was in my mind.' He looked up from fitting the crust back into place with a craftsman's care, and his eyes rested consideringly on Phaedrus's face. 'It is strange; I could have sworn that there was not one among the Sun People that I could not have made to see that golden plover's feather and forget altogether the barley crust, until I bade them remember it again.'

There was a little pause, and then Phaedrus said, 'I have spent seven years in the Romans' world, which is a different world from ours; maybe that is why you could not work your magic on me perfectly.'

'Maybe,' the other said, but his eyes still brooded on Phaedrus's face.

And meeting the question in them, Phaedrus conjured up the old swaggering arena smile that he had learned as he learned his sword strokes. '*Na* now, do you think that I am not Midir of the Dalriads, not the Horse Lord after all, but another wearing his forehead mark?'

'I do not know,' the man said slowly. 'But when you see that golden plover's feather again, you will be the Horse Lord; and the forehead mark your own.'

'Rede me the riddle, Old Man.'

'Time will do that. But this I will tell you, that you may be

knowing I speak true: within three days one of the Old People will reach out to touch your life again, but it is in my heart that he will be already dead.'

So—Phaedrus had his answer; it was only the horses and the beef cattle that need be reckoned, after all. The People of the Hills were part of a different world, and no more to be counted as strength or weakness than the glen woods or the snows of Cruachan. . . .

Next day he rode back with the Companions to Dun Monaidh, and after that there was little time for remembering the scrap of Earth Magic that was already fading in his mind like a dream, or for thinking of the things that Old Man had foretold. Little time for anything save the matter in hand. And the matter in hand was war! War, when the wild geese flew north in the spring.

In Dun Monaidh, as in every other dun and rath and steading of Earra-Ghyl, the smiths and armourers, the horse-breakers and chariot-builders were at work. All day long from the huddle of blackened bothies in the outer court came the red lick of flame and the roar of the sheepskin bellows, and the ding of hammer on anvil, as here the fresh iron felloes were fitted to chariot wheels, and there the dints were beaten out of the rim of a dappled oxhide shield; and every warrior sharpened and resharpened his weapons on the great Pillar Stone.

And then on the second day after his return, Phaedrus came out of the long chariot shed with a couple of the Companions behind him, and heard somewhere over towards the northern rampart, a sudden worry of sounds that were all human, and yet made him think of the moment at the end of a hunt, when the hounds close in and make their kill.

The small tumult died out almost as he began to run, the other two at his heels, and when he came out between two store-sheds into the clear space just within the dry-stone curve of the rampart, the little group of warriors he found there were quite silent, their dirks still in their hands, looking down at a body that lay crumpled on the ground among them. One of them was

turning it over with his foot as Phaedrus arrived, much as a man might turn over a dead rat, and as it fell all asprawl, he saw that it was the body of one of the Dark People, stabbed in four or five places about the breast and belly.

'What has happened here?' he demanded.

And the man who had turned the body over answered him, 'A rat-hunt, Midir.'

'It seems that you have made your kill. What was he doing in the Royal Dun?'

Another man shrugged. 'Spying. We found him hiding in the wood-store yonder. He must have come over the rampart in the night.'

'Or up by the way that the She-Wolf went.'

A small crowd had begun to gather; someone came cleaving his way through them like a strong swimmer in a rough sea, and Gault stood there, arms folded on barrel chest, looking down with hard, wolf-tawny eyes at the slight dark body in its blood-soaked deerskin. 'A spy, most assuredly.' He bent forward abruptly for a closer look. 'Aye, he's out of the Caledonian hunting-runs, by the patterns of his hide. Doubtless, if you had not found him he would have been out over the rampart again tonight, and away back to King Bruide with word of how many chariots Dun Monaidh can muster.' He straightened and half turned away, as though, for him, the thing was finished. 'Make a fire on the eastern slopes beyond the outerbank—good and high, for the blaze to show far across country—and burn me this rat.'

There was a sharp, half-surprised silence, and then little

Baruch said, 'Why do more than tip him into the bog—or throw him out for the wolf-kind?'

'Fire is the fitting end for rats.'

Phaedrus, his eyes narrowing under the red brows, suddenly took command. 'Why are you so firm set on this burning, Gault the Strong?'

'His litter-brothers will come to know of it. It will maybe serve for a useful warning.'

'They will come to know that he is killed. Will that not serve for warning enough?'

'I am doubting it,' Gault said harshly. 'The Old Ones are so close to Earth Mother, that death is to them no more than a short journey.'

And so, the fire . . . Phaedrus had been long enough out of the four-square Roman world to have some idea of what all this was really about. To the Sun People it made little difference whether earth or fire took their bodies when they were done with them; but with the children of Earth Mother, it was very different. Grain thrown into the fire would never quicken, and for them, burning took not only the body but the life that had belonged with it. Gault, in fact, was proposing to destroy whatever this little dark creature had of a soul, for a warning to his kind. Phaedrus had never cared overmuch for the laws of men, but this was another thing, and the laws of men had nothing to do with it. Until now, feeling his way in a new and unfamiliar world, he had left the real leadership to Gault and the inner Council. But now he knew, suddenly and with absolute certainty, that he had come to the end of that. . . .

'But to my mind, the killing is enough,' he said, 'and Gault, it is *I* that am the King! Whatever he was doing, his death settles the score. *There will be no burning!*'

Gault's wolf-gaze whipped round to meet his, and Phaedrus read in the other's frown that he, too, knew the time had come for a trial of strength between them. 'You are the King, but it seems that you have forgotten much of your own world in the arena. And until you remember, best be leaving such matters as this to those of us who will better understand what we do.'

'I have forgotten much,' Phaedrus agreed, 'but I learned some things too. Even in the arena, we count the fighting ended with the kill, and do not seek to carry it beyond the death-stroke.'

The knot of onlooking warriors was growing moment by moment, but no one attempted to take any hand in this odd quiet battle of wills. It was a thing between Gault and the Lord Midir, with the body of the little dark hunter lying between them.

'You speak like a gladiator—a mere bought butcher,' Gault said at last.

'There might be worse things to be than a gladiator.'

'Such, for instance, as Lord of the Dalriads?' It was easy enough to read the meaning behind that: 'I made you and I can break you. No need to be lord of the Dalriads another hour, if it displeases you.'

Phaedrus's mouth lifted at the corners in the faint, insolent smile that his fellow sword-fighters had come to know. 'Surely it is a fine thing to be Lord of the Dalriads; and Lugh Shining Spear himself forbid I should forget it was you who took me from Corstopitum city gaol and set my foot on the Coronation Stone.' He let Gault see the meaning behind that, too: 'You made me and you can break me, but you will be broken with me, if you do.'

There was a feeling of battle in him, under the quiet surface. He had again the old sense of life narrowing and sharpening its focus until there was nothing in it but himself and Gault, and both of them knowing that the thing they fought for was the leadership of the tribe.

So they confronted each other, eye looking into eye, neither speaking again nor moving, until the silence between them drew out thin and taut, so that Phaedrus felt he could have plucked sparks from it like notes of a harp-string; and he heard his own voice break it, saying very clearly, each word separated from the next, 'There will—be—no—burning.'

Something flickered far back in Gault's eyes, and he shrugged his bull shoulders. The fight was over, and the victory to

Phaedrus. 'You are the King, the thing must be as you choose. But the Gods help you and all of us, if you choose a'wrong.' But there was no enmity in his tone; indeed, his dark frowning gaze held a new respect.

On the surface, it had been such a small battle; it had not even concerned a warrior of the tribe, only one of the little Dark People, who, in the eyes of the Dalriads, were half animal and half uncanny. Yet it was now, and not in the moment of his King-Making, that Red Phaedrus felt the Lordship of the Dalriads come into his hand.

'Take him away and throw him out for the wolves,' he said to the men who had done the killing. The wolves did not matter; it was only the fire that mattered.

It was only then, watching them dragging the little body away, that he remembered Old Man's foretelling, of just three days ago.

That night, when the evening meal was over and the harping silent in the Fire Hall, and Phaedrus went to the King's Place to sleep, he checked on the threshold with a caught breath of surprise. Beside the central hearth, where Brys should have been waiting for him, sat a woman. She had drawn his own stool to the fire, and sat there, with her loosened mantle dark about her. Her face was hidden from him by her hair which she had unbraided and begun to comb, as though to pass the time while she waited, but the falling curtain of it was unmistakable: the soft dove-gold, mouse-gold hair of the Royal Woman.

'Murna! What is it that you do here?'

She flung back the mass of hair and turned her face to him. 'May the Queen not come to the King's quarters when she chooses?'

'Surely. But has the Queen chosen to come so often?' He pulled off his heavy cloak and flung it across the piled skins of the bedplace, and came to stand beside the fire, and look down at her, his shoulder propped against the roof tree.

'I was wishing to have a word with you,' she said, 'and so I sent your armour-bearer out for a while.'

371

'Yes?' Phaedrus's guard was up.

'You gained a victory today.'

'In the matter of the spy? So you have heard about that?'

'There is little that the Women's Side does not hear about,' she said, and the cool, hazel eyes that he suddenly realized were like Conory's, for all that they were set level, rested on him consideringly. Then, as though making up her mind to something, she added, 'But he was not here for spying.'

'No? For what, then?'

'He came to get speech with me.'

'And did he get it?'

'Yes. He brought me word from my mother—and a gift, for you.'

Phaedrus's red brows flashed up. 'For me? I'd not have thought she loved me so greatly.'

'There are gifts and gifts,' Murna said.

'And this one? Are you going to give it to me?'

For answer, she laid down the ivory comb she was still holding, and brought something from the breast of her gown, and held it out to him.

He took the thing and looked at it warily; a leather flask so small that it lay like a chestnut in the palm of his hand, plugged with a bone stopper carved into the likeness of a tiny snarling head—human or animal, there was no telling which. The thing had an almost palpable smell of wickedness, and he took care not to interfere with the waxed thread that kept the stopper in place.

'What is it?'

'Death,' Murna said.

'Poison?' He had been half prepared for that, but something twisted coldly in the pit of his stomach all the same. He stood for a few moments turning it over and over, and looking at it. Odd to see one's own death lying in the palm of one's hand. 'Why have you told me this—shown me this?'

She held out her hand for the thing's return. 'Because I do not think I will be using it, after all.'

'After all?' Phaedrus, surprised and amused to find what a fool he was, gave it back to her.

She sat cradling it in her hands and looking up at him between the falls of mouse-gold hair. 'You have changed, in seven years. The Midir I knew when I was a child would have let Gault have his burning without another thought—unless it seemed to him amusing to pit his strength against Gault's and he chanced to be in need of amusement just then.'

'And how do you know that I did not chance to feel in need of amusement today?'

For the first time there was the shadow of a smile in her face. 'Did you?'

'No.'

'And most assuredly, if it had been like that, the Midir I knew would not have troubled himself to lie to me.'

'I was a boy, seven years ago. Boys do change, growing into men.'

'It is more than that—another kind of change.'

'You have said "the Midir *I* knew" twice, but in truth you were little more than ten when your mother put an end to that Midir. You were never knowing much of him, were you, Murna?'

Her face tightened, and for a moment he wondered if she was going to fly out at him for that word of her mother. But she let it pass. 'I knew maybe better than others guessed at; more than you remember. But you were never one to care much what you broke, or even remember the breaking of it, were you, Midir?'

'Was I not? If I was never one for remembering, what use to ask me?' He dropped the light, hard tone. 'Tell me—if your mother's messenger had escaped, and so the thing between Gault and me today had not happened, would you have used the poison?'

'In the day that I have a use for poison,' Murna said simply, 'I have no need that my mother should send it to me.'

She snapped the thread and pulled out the bone plug; and poured the contents of the tiny flask into the heart of the fire, then dropped the flask itself after it. The fire spat like an angry cat, and a bluish flame leapt up, wavered, and slowly died out.

As it did so, Murna picked up the ivory comb and rose,

373

wrapping the folds of her cloak about her. '*Sa*, there is no more that I came to say. Brys will be within call, I do not doubt, like the good, well-trained hound he is.'

And she was gone.

Phaedrus did not at once call his armour-bearer, but stood staring after her, a frown bitten deep between the brows, trying to make sense of many things that he did not understand, his own feelings among them.

War-Dance

THE snow was shrinking in the lower corries of Cruachan, and
the nights were alive with the green sounds of running water and
the mating calls of curlew flighting in for the high moors, when
the Caledonian Envoy came.

The Lord of the Dalriads received him and his escorting
nobles seated on the High Place of black ram-skins in the Fire
Hall, with a group of the Companions about him; made them
welcome, feasted them as honoured guests, and afterwards bade
his harper play for them. The pretence must be kept up that the
green juniper brand in the Envoy's hand really meant that he
came in peace.

But the knowledge of what was going forward, and the

presence of the Caledonian nobles in their ceremonial cloaks of wildcat skins was like a thin, dry wind blowing round the Hall, and a mood was rising in the young men that needed more than harping. The Companions had begun to make another kind of music of their own, little Baruch beating out the rhythm with an open palm on one of the cooking-pots, others taking it up from him, clapping and stamping it out on the beaten floor where they had kicked the fern aside. And six or seven of the young warriors spilled out on to the paved dancing space and began to crouch and stamp in a hunting-dance, among the very fringes of the fire.

Diamid of the devil's eyebrows was the hunted, the rest were the hunters—men or hounds, it made no difference. The quarry fled from them, and turned back to them, to dance, as it were, with his own death, and fled from them again, drawing them after him; and the hunters followed, miming the chase to that wild, throbbing rhythm of stamping feet, led by the strangely bell-like drumming of Baruch's open palms on the cooking-pot, until the Old Magic filled the Fire Hall and Phaedrus could have sworn that the roof had become the interlaced branches of forest trees, and the shadows of the dancers, spun outward by the fire, were the shadows of a flying stag and a pack of hounds. They danced the Kill, the rhythm rising to fever pitch, closed in about the panting quarry and pulled him down, and ran in with their spears. The drumming ceased, as though cut by the spear-thrusts, and the dancers stood laughing and breathless, the mystery dropping from them like a cloak—so that they were no more than young men, who had been letting off some of the pent-up strain in the air.

But now the mood was on them and soon the dancing began again, the dancers constantly changing, until the whole night seemed to dissolve into stamping and whirling figures, and even the older men were adding their bit to the heady rhythms beaten out for the dancers.

But presently, in a pause for breath, Forgall the Envoy, seated beside Phaedrus, turned to him with an air of scarcely veiled boredom and said, 'Tell me, it is not the custom with the Dalriads, as it is with us, for the women to dance also?'

'It is, when it pleases them,' said Phaedrus.

'It is in my mind that I would gladly see your women dance. It would be interesting to me to see how they compare for skill with the women of my own people. Will you send word to the women's quarters, that maybe it will please them now?'

Phaedrus was suddenly furious at the cool demand so thinly masked as a request. The Women's Side did indeed dance when it pleased them, but for a stranger within the gates to demand it of them was an insult, and he very much doubted if this Caledonian noble with the full mouth and insolent dark eyes was ignorant of the fact. But before he could speak, Murna, who had led the other women all evening in keeping the mead-horns filled, and now sat at his other side, erect and indrawn as usual under the moon head-dress, said in a clear, high voice, 'It is not for my Lord the King to send such a message to the women's quarters. But since our guest would have it so, I will send the word.' She looked across the great, round Hall to where the few women who yet remained—old ones for the most part—had gathered in a little knot before the doorway. Grania, one of the women, came to her call, and was given some murmured instructions, and went out. And the young warriors lounged back to the places and pastimes they had left earlier: to fondle a hound's ears or start a game of knuckle-bones with a comrade. Phaedrus sat coldly raging behind his best arena smile. That this Envoy should have dared. . . . That Murna should have made it impossible for him to thrust the insult back down the man's throat . . . But of course she would have been eager to avoid that, she was Liadhan's daughter, part Caledonian herself; probably the man was her kin.

There was a sound of women's voices and running feet outside and a knot of girls came in through the foreporch, flinging off hastily donned cloaks. Their skirts were already hitched knee-high and each girl carried a dirk in her left hand and another thrust into her belt or girdle. The woman who Murna had sent, had returned with them, and she also carried two dirks; but clearly she was not going to dance, for her gown still fell in straight folds

to her ankles, and in her free hand she held a long elder-pipe.

Murna rose in her place, and called in a clear, hard tone to the girls by the door: 'The guests in our Hall would have us dance for them, my sisters. So—let us dance.'

One of the girls, a dark, fierce creature, laughed, as though sharing a harsh jest that their hearers did not understand as yet. 'We will dance for them, Murna the Queen—as we used to dance when we called ourselves the Wildcats, and went to the practice grounds together.'

As they came forward between the crowding warriors, Murna walked out, kilting her skirts through her bronze-studded belt as she went, to join them on the dancing-floor.

For a long moment the silence in the Hall was so intense that all men could plainly hear the faint chiming of the row upon row of tiny, hanging silver scales that, stiched on to the tall, leather head-dress, made up the Moon Diadem. Murna held out her hands, and the older woman came and put the two dirks into them, before she moved aside with her pipe, and settled down with her back against one of the seven great roof trees.

The dancers formed a wide-spaced ring about the fire, each girl with the blade of her left-hand dirk lying across the blade of her neighbour's right, and as the first notes of the elder-pipe thrilled out, began to move slowly round the fire, with little short weaving steps. So far it all seemed very childish and pretty, Phaedrus thought, still coldly angry, though one might have expected the girls to be linked by a garland or a coloured ribbon rather than by crossed daggers, and he wondered why every man in the Hall caught a quick breath and sat more upright; why Conory just behind him, muttered, 'Gods! The Wildcats indeed!' He had not seen this particular dance before.

At first there had been no sound but the piping and the light pad of the dancers' feet on the flagstones; then, one after another, the men began to pick up the rhythm as they had done before, and the rhythm itself was changing from white to red, growing fiercer, more urgent. The dirk-blades pointed now up, now down, began to nuzzle each other, blade licking round blade as though each had a life of its own. Faster and faster, the

blades flickered and leapt, the shadows spun . . . and then the circle seemed to break off its own spinning, and instead of a ring of dancing girls, there were seven pairs of young warriors. And Phaedrus understood the sudden tensing in the Hall. He was watching a war-dance of the Women's Side.

He was watching, too, a Murna whom he had never seen before, whom he had never known existed. Murna with her face come to life, and a tense laughter in every line of her, dancing out her mimic battle with the dark girl so close to where he sat, that he could have reached her in one stride and pulled her out of the dance. He wondered for a passing moment if she would turn those leaping daggers on him if he did, then knew that far more likely she would simply change back into the Murna he knew, the cold, unreachable Royal Woman between his hands. And another kind of anger sprang up in him, a raging helplessness that he did not understand; but then he understood scarcely anything that had to do with Murna.

All round the circle the long knives whirled and darted, flashing their deadly interlacing patterns in the flame-light; the pipes shrilled higher and higher against the throbbing rhythm that the men were stamping out from the shadows, and the ring of blade on blade. And then at last, in each pair of warriors, one girl dropped to her knees and flung herself round and backward, to lie with outspread arms, radiating like the petals of some great dagger-tipped flower from the fire that was its heart, while the other made the victory leap high across her body; and the dance was over.

The vanquished sprang to their feet again, the dark girl picking a stray bracken-frond out of her hair. And Murna tossed her two dirks back to the woman who had piped for them, and left the dancing-floor without a backward glance, freeing her skirts as she did so. She was the cold Queen again; even the Moon Diadem, held secure by the thongs that knotted it into her braids, was not a hair's breadth out of place. To the Envoy she said, still breathing quickly, 'Can your women do better, across Druim Alban?'

The Envoy also was breathing quickly, and there was a

curious line of whiteness round his nostrils. 'Beyond Druim Alban it is not usual for women to dance the War-Dance, for a guest who comes in peace.'

'And on this side of Druim Alban, it is not usual for a guest to demand that the women should dance for him at all,' Murna said gently.

'There are those, among my people, who might count such a choice of dance for an insult.' The man rose to his feet, drawing his cat-skin mantle about him, and stood flicking the peace bough of green juniper as an angry cat flicks the tip of its tail.

But Phaedrus was up in the same instant. 'An insult for an insult, shall we say, and cry quits?' And before the man could answer, he reached out and caught Murna by the wrist. 'Come, my Queen. It grows deep into the night, and we must remember that our guests have had long journeying and will be taking the home-trail tomorrow. My Lord of the Green Branch, may you and your Companions have sound sleeping in the guest-huts; we meet here again in the morning.'

With the general sound of rising and breaking up, behind them, he said again, 'Come, my Queen,' though, indeed, there was little need of the order for his hold was still on her wrist; and for the first time since he had pulled the red mare's-skin mask from her face, they left the Fire Hall together, and by the curtained doorway giving on to the huddle of linked huts that made up the women's quarters.

In the empty Queen's Place, when he had roughly ordered out the Queen's bond women who waited for her there, Murna said, 'And now, will you be letting go my wrist, Midir?'

She had left the Hall with him as though his hold on her wrist had been only the lightest touch, and he had not realized until that moment that he was still gripping it, and gripping it with an angry strength.

He let go instantly, and as she drew away, he saw in the light of the seal-oil lamp, the darkening bruises that his fingers had left. Any other woman he thought, would have been cherishing her wrist, but not Murna. And most of his anger went out, leaving only the baffled helplessness behind.

'I am sorry,' he said. 'I did not mean to hurt you.'

'Did you not?' she said, without interest, and turned from the subject. 'There is something you would be saying to me?'

'Murna, why did you do that?'

'Make our dance for the Lord Envoy?'

'Yes.'

'Because he called for the Women's Side to dance. Would you have me refuse the demands of an honoured guest within the gates of Dun Monaidh?

'Maybe not. But need you dance yourself? You, who are the Queen?'

'I could not be asking the other women to dance at his call, and myself refuging behind my queenship.'

'Sa, you have an answer for everything. But why in the name of Thunder, choose the War-Dance?'

Her eyes widened gravely. 'Oh my Lord, would you have me accept his insult for the Women's Side? "An insult for an insult." You said as much yourself. . . . Ah now, it will make no difference to the terms they offer. The Caledones do not bargain. That man will have come over our borders already knowing to the last word what it is that he will say tomorrow.' Her voice was scornfully consoling. 'We have nothing to lose, my Lord of the Horse People, by spitting an insult or so back at them.'

'That I know well enough, no need that you should speak me gently like a child afraid of the dark. However long they talk tomorrow, with spring they will take the war-trail, and so shall we.' He laughed. 'Na, it was a fine war-dance, and you are as skilled with the dirk as your mother with poison. I did not know the danger I was in, when I pulled the bridal mask from your face, my Royal Woman!'

Maybe that would get through her guard to make her drop the mask again. But nothing moved behind her face, only a waft of blue peat-smoke, side-driven by the wind through the smoke-hole, fronded across between them, and she avoided his jibe with the cool skill of a swordsman. 'I was afraid that the skill would have left me, for it is long since I danced the dirk-dance with my Wildcat sisters. But it came back to me well enough. None the

less, it is in my mind that I shall go down to the practice grounds again, tomorrow.'

He looked at her, frowning, not quite sure of her meaning, and she half smiled. 'There will be many of the Women's Side brushing the rust off their spear-throw, in the next moon or so. Did you not say that when the spring came, the Caledones and the Dalriads would both be taking the war-trail?'

'The war-trail is for the Men's Side,' Phaedrus said quickly.

'When there are men enough. The Caledones are a great tribe and the overlord of other tribes; we are a small people, still. You will need the women on this war-trail.'

'None the less, we shall ride without them as long as maybe. If a warrior chooses to take his own woman with him into battle, that is his affair, and hers; I shall not call out the Wildcats, or any other of their kind.'

'Why?' she demanded. 'Why go against the custom when you have most need of it?'

'In the world I come from——' Phaedrus began, and caught back the slip. 'In the world where I have been these seven years, war is men's work, and the women bide at home.'

'You allow them to bear the sons for it, of course? That is generous of you. But otherwise—the sword for you, and the loom and the cooking-pot are all that concern the women. How glad I am that I do not belong to the world where you have lived these seven years!'

She had begun to unfasten the thongs that secured the moon head-dress, and it seemed that she had only half her attention to spare from the fastenings. Phaedrus, watching her, thought, in the way that one does think of small unlikely things in the middle of something else, tnat they must have cut the thongs on the night that she took the diadem from her mother and wore it in her stead. And the thought of that night hardened him against her. He said, 'Be very sure of this—if the time does come that I must send the Cran-Tara among the war bands of the Women's Side after all, still I shall not call for the Royal Woman—remembering that she is *Liadhan's Daughter!*'

Her eyes dilated, like Shân's when she was angry, became

enormous and full of light. 'How *dare* you speak so to me!' she whispered. 'To me, the Queen!'

'Do not be forgetting it was I that made you the Queen.'

'Was it? To me it seemed rather that by marrying me, the Royal Woman, you gained the kingship that you could not have held without me!'

Phaedrus's hands shot out to catch and shake her. 'You cursed vixen——'

But he never began the shaking. She stood quite still, the cool, brilliant stare meeting his. 'Yes, that is much better, much more the man I should have expected to flower from the Midir *I* knew!'

And Phaedrus dropped his hands to his sides, turned with a curse, and strode out of the Queen's Place.

Next morning, in the Fire Hall, the demands of the Caledonian Envoy were clear and simple. Liadhan the Queen was to be set back in her rightful place, to rule as Goddess-on-Earth over all Earra-Gyl. Conory, the Chosen One, was to take his rightful place also, at her side. The tribe was to turn again to the Old Ways and the old worship.

'And myself?' Phaedrus inquired, interested. 'Liadhan the She-Wolf, and Conory the Captain of my Guard have both their places made ready for them; what place then, in all this, for me?'

'For yourself, the word of King Bruide is this; that you go free, so long as you go far from here. If you set foot again in the hunting-runs of the Dalriads, then death, for you and for those who raised you to the place where you sit now,' the Envoy said insolently.

Phaedrus wondered with a detached interest just how far he would get on his way into exile, before he met with a fatal accident or simply disappeared. He looked Forgall in the eyes, and laughed; it was a laugh that surprised himself, short in the throat, and cold. 'For myself, I am the Horse Lord! I have seen enough of wandering, these past seven years, and have no mind to turn wanderer again. For Conory my Captain, if he chooses, he is free to go back with you to this Goddess-on-Earth and be

her Seven-year King; but he shall not be Seven-year King among the Dalriads!'

Conory, standing just behind him, with Shân in her favourite position curled across his shoulder like a fur collar, bent forward with lazy grace and spat into the fire, and the cat, startled at the sudden movement, dug in all her claws, her ears laid back and her pink mouth open in a soundless snarl. '*Sa, sa,* we are generally of one mind, you and I,' Conory murmured to her, gently detaching a claw that had drawn blood.

'As for Liadhan, once the Royal Woman of the tribe, who without right calls herself Queen: death on the day she sets foot in the hunting-runs of Earra-Ghyl.' Midir's anger was rising in Phaedrus's throat, and he had lost all sense of playing a part, as he leaned forward to stare contemptuously into the dark face before him. 'That is the answer that you may carry back to Bruide your King—and to the She-Wolf who calls herself Queen of the Dalriads!'

The eyes of Forgall the Envoy were dark and opaque, as those of the Old People, whose blood ran strong in the Caledones; but little red sparks glowed far back in them, and his face was beginning to have the same pinched whiteness round the nostrils that had been there last night in the Fire Hall. 'The claim of Liadhan the Queen holds good according to the Ancient Law. It is yourself, Midir Mac Levin, no more than the son of a son of a son, who sit where you have no right to be! You have forsaken the Mother and the True Way, to follow strange Gods, and the curse of the Cailleach lies on such as you—on all Dalriads who would seek to drive her from her rightful place in the heart of men!'

'Listen,' Phaedrus said. 'Listen, little man: for the Epidii, and the Old People before them, the way was the Old Way; but it is we, the Dalriads, who rule now in Earra Ghyl, and for us the way is a different one. Before ever we came over the Western Sea, we made the Noon Prayer to Lugh Shining Spear, and called to him on the trumpet of the Sun; and our kings were the sons of kings, and not merely the mates of Royal Women. For us, that is the way. Shall we therefore come to you and say, "You shall turn away from the Mother—you shall cast out your King

Bruide who rules only because he wedded the Queen's daughter, and set in his place Conal Caenneth, who is your last king's son; and you shall follow our way because it is *ours*?" The Caledones are a free people; and so are the Dalriads, and being a free people they ask no leave to breath under the sky, from the dwellers beyond Druim Alban!'

'Bold words,' the Envoy said. 'Bold words from the small people to a great one!'

'Whoever came away whole by bowing his head to the wolf,' Phaedrus quoted roughly. 'Listen again—it would be a fine thing for the Caledones, that you set your kinswoman back in the High Place of the Dalriads and keep her there with your swords, and a fine hold it would be giving you over this tribe for so long as the Sun rises in the East and the wheat springs in the ground. You have gained other vassals so. But the Dalriads are not minded to be vassals of yours, and we are a stubborn people, little like to change our minds.'

'And that is the last word you have to say?'

Phaedrus had meant to consult with the Council and the Kindred before making an end. But he scarcely remembered even that they were there in the great Fire Hall. 'That is my last word. Yes.'

There was a long silence. Then the Envoy took one step back, and ceremoniously broke the green branch, and threw the pieces into the fire.

'Whet your spears then, Midir of the Dalriads.'

'The spears are already whetted.'

14

Chariots in the Pass

THE storm that had burst upon them in the night had cleared
the air, and high overhead the clouds drifted against a sky of
clear rain-washed blue, trailing their shadows after them across
the mountains. But here in the low-lying stretch between the
river and the alder woods, with Beinn Na Stroine heaving its
slow height out of the woods ahead of them, and Cruachan still
white-maned with snow in the high corries, filling all the world
north eastward, the air barely stirred. The heat shimmered over
the ground though spring had scarcely turned yet to summer,
and the gad-flies fidgeted weary men and still more weary horses
unbearably. Head after head was tossed impatiently, hooves

386

stamped, and tails swished all down the chariot line. Brys spoke soothingly to his team, holding them on a light rein. 'Softly! Softly, my children! It will not be long—soon there will be a wind of our going that shall blow the biters clean over Cruachan! Softly now! Softly, I say!'

Phaedrus, squatting on the warrior's seat to the left of the charioteer, longed to fling off the stifling plaid fastened on his sword-shoulder with the huge buckler-pin of gilded bronze and blue enamel that was the war-brooch of the Horse Lord. But the Lord of the Dalriads, though he might go stripped to the breeks under it, did not drive into battle uncloaked like a mere foot-fighter. At least the heavy folds were some protection against the biters. Phaedrus thought that he as well as the fidgeting team, could do well with the wind of their going; and meanwhile, sweltered on, the sweat prickling on his forehead and upper lip, and the war-paint running on his face.

His hand opened and shut, opened and shut, on the shafts of the three light throw-spears he held in the hollow of his bull's-hide buckler. It was two full moons since they had sent the Cran-Tara through Earra-Ghyl, summoning the warriors to the hosting-place, more than one since they had taken the war-trail; but in the first weeks, the fighting had been little more than a breaking surf of skirmishes and cattle-raiding among the high moors that lay between Royal Water and the Firth of Warships, and through the steep Druim Alban glens. But today's fighting would be no mere skirmish, and Phaedrus, feeling the throw-spears in his hand, had again the old familiar sense of waiting for the arena trumpets.

He had been in the south with the main War Host, turning a thrust of the Caledones who had seized on the few hours' darkness at the black of the moon to swim their horses across the narrows of the Warship Firth and coracle-float the light chariots over, when the word had come. Word brought by a wounded man on a foundering horse, that a vast chariot horde were swarming through the Drium Alban passes, heading for the glens of the Alder Woods and the Black Goddess, and the ways down to Loch Abha. The light chariot bands led by old Dergdian who

were on guard there would hold them—ah yes, to the last man—but it could not be long, if help did not reach them, before that last man went down. Aye, the man said, another rider had set off at the same time as himself for Dun Monaidh; they would have the word before this, for the old chariot road made swifter travelling than these accursed hills. . . .

Then he died.

Chariots. That would mean the Glen of the Black Goddess, steep as it was; there would be no way for chariots through the crowding alder woods. The Leaders had taken hurried Council almost while the teams were being harnessed, and Gault had remained with a strong force, including all the foot fighters, to finish with the southern thrust, and Phaedrus and Conory had taken the flower of the horsemen and chariotry and flung them northward like fighting geese, spare chariot horses harnessed as wheelers for extra speed and to fill the places of any yoke horses that foundered on the way.

The distance was less than it would be from Dun Monaidh, but as the messenger had said, the old chariot road made swifter travelling than these accursed hills. And the storm, bursting on them last night, maddening the horses and bringing down all the hill burns in sudden spate, had held them up still further. Three days they had been on that desperate ride, and at least seven horses they had killed with the merciless speed of it. But when they had come down through the pale, storm-spent dawn into the low, wet country of the Loch Abha Gap, the scouts sent on ahead had found the light chariots still holding, with the reserves that had reached them yesterday; still holding but cut to pieces, and the fight already joining again after the few hours' darkness.

No time to rest the men and horses, as he had hoped to do; no time for any counsel. Phaedrus remembered looking over at Conory, the question and the agreement passing between them unspoken, then giving the needful orders. He remembered the sharp trampling of hooves as the scout wheeled his pony and was off again with word to old Dergdian and the hard-pressed and dwindling chariots far up the Glen of the Black Goddess. 'I send

horsemen to cover your flanks; be ready to fall back when they come. We stand ready to catch you.'

And almost on the heels of the messenger, the weary horse-band had been away, riding into the early mists, each man eating his morning barley-bannock from the bag tied to his horse's pectoral strap, as he rode.

Now, with their own morning bannocks eaten and the horses tended as best they could be, there was nothing to do but wait, here in the glen mouth, with the wide woods and marshes running to Loch Abha behind, the river guarding their left flank, and ahead of them the bare rocks and plunging bracken slopes of the Glen of the Black Goddess, shimmering in the heat.

Phaedrus had no experience, before this past few weeks, of leading a War Host, but his gladiator's training and a natural trick of leadership had stood him in good stead; and now he glanced along the chariot line, taking in the placing of the rough-riding cavalry, with the eye of one who had at least a fair idea of how to place his men to the best advantage. The gaps left in the chariot ranks were there to let the hard-pressed squadron through; the little companies in the rear standing ready to swing forward and close them before the enemy could follow. Phaedrus, used to the disciplines of Rome and the ordered sham fights of the arena, had given the order for the battle-move but the tribesmen had never heard of such a way of fighting and now he knew that in trying to carry it out with an undisciplined horde of chariots, he was running the most hideous risk. What would happen if the gaps did not close in time was a prospect that sickened him to think of, but unless they were going to leave valiant old Dergdian and his squadrons to their fate, it was a risk that had to be taken.

A gad-fly stung his wrist, and he swore and cracked his hand down on the place, brushing the small, crushed body away. And went on waiting. There should be some sign of them by now. He was straining his whole attention out ahead of him up the rocky sweep of the glen, for any sign of movement—any sound. . . .

With the air full of the soft, wet rush of the river, it was hard to be sure when the first rumours of sound came at last. Suddenly,

far off from the slopes of Beinn Na Stroine, a curlew rose, crying its alarm note, thin and small with distance. And away down the chariot line a pony flung up his head, and another pawed the ground, snuffing the eddy of cool air that came down the glen from the high hills of Druim Alban. A faint, formless murmuration that seemed to drift on the little stir of wind, died with it into the fern, and then came again. Then clear on the heat-bloomed air, broke the sound of a hunting-horn. Someone still in command up there was calling back the survivors of that first heroes' stand, as a huntsman calls off his hounds.

Something—a kind of boiling and thickening of the heat-haze—was gathering far up the glen; and out of it came a blink of light, and then another, sunlight on weapon or wheel-hub or glittering horse-pectoral. Darkness was growing under the dust-cloud, and a sound muttered out of it like thunder among the hills. It grew to the rumble and drum of wheels and hooves, the clash of war-gear and the shouting of men; all the ragged turmoil of a running fight. Phaedrus, on his feet now like all the rest, could see their own chariots falling back—back. The war-horn of the Dalriads boomed hollowly from the skirts of Beinn Na Stroine; and suddenly the bracken slopes below it were alive with running figures with long spears in their hands, while the cavalry came sweeping down to join their fellows covering the flanks of the hard-pressed chariot band.

They were so near now that Phaedrus could see through the dust-cloud how in every chariot that still carried two men, the warrior rode faced about to the pursuing enemy, spear still in hand, and shield up to guard both himself and his driver's back. They were pouring in through the gaps, like the squadrons of some terrible ghost army, tattered and bloody; chariots with only one man in them, chariots with driver and warrior slumped against the wicker side, or dragged askew by one wild-eyed and wounded horse with the harness dangling where a dead team-mate had been cut free. The wild cavalry were swinging right and left towards either flank of the War Host. The weary horses in the chariot line, roused by their comrades and the tumult and the smell of blood, had forgotten their weariness and were

fighting for their heads. Conory, next in line, was looking to him, but Phaedrus, sweating with more than the heat now, set his teeth and held the whole War Host in leash that one moment longer, until the very last of the retreating chariots were safely through; while the enemy behind them, maybe in fear of a trap, reined their horses in and swerved aside for a few moments from their charge, and the waiting bands in the rear were swinging forward to close the gaps; waited one racing heartbeat of time longer, and then with the Caledones on the very lip of spilling forward again, raised the bronze ox-horn to his lips, and winded one sharp blast that flung to and fro among the hills until the high corries of Cruachan caught and flung it back, startling every shore bird in Earra-Ghyl.

But long before that last echo had died into the wild crying of curlew and sandpiper, the chariot line of the Dalriads was away at full flying gallop to meet the onrushing hosts of the Cailleach. Phaedrus heard himself raise the war-cry: 'Cruachan! Cruachan!', heard it taken up and hurled back by the long-drawn battle yell of the enemy. He flung his first spear as they came into javelin range, and one of the leading charioteers went down, his plunging team bringing confusion on those behind him, and almost in the same instant the two chariot hordes rolled full tilt together, with a great shouting of men and a screaming chaos of horses; a ringing crash that seemed as though it must shake the very roots of the mountains.

How long they struggled there in the mouth of the glen, the whole battle mass swaying now this way and now that, Phaedrus never knew. Time was not time any more, it passed with the speed of a lightning flash, and yet it seemed to him that they had been fighting here all their lives, to hold the Caledones back from Loch Abha levels, and the way into the heart of Earra-Ghyl.

The battle had long since lost all pattern and broken up into a swirl of scattered fighting. The whole glen was full of dust now, like a vast threshing floor; the chariots careered and circled, wheel locked in wheel, while the horsemen hung on the fringes of the battle, driving in a thrust of their own wherever the chances

opened, and everywhere the foot-fighters swarmed with daggers reddened to the hilt. It seemed to Phaedrus that many of these on foot were women, but he had no time to think of that just then.

Ahead of him in the smother of flying dust and flung weapons, he saw a chariot covered with black ox-hide, whose team of bright duns flashed back fire from their gilded pectorals in the dusty sunlight, and whose half-naked warrior daubed with the woad and red ochre of the Caledones' war-paint, wore about his neck the broad golden torque of a Chieftain.

His throw-spears long since spent, the broad in-fighting spear in his hand, he shouted to Brys. The boy laughed and crouched lower, and the red team sprang forward from the goad, scattering blood-stained foam from their muzzles. The splendid chariot rushed nearer on Phaedrus's sight, almost broadside on. He nerved himself for the shock, caught one searing sight of the horses' upreared heads and flying manes, and the blue-eyed, snarling face of the Caledonian Chieftain, as the darting spear just missed his shoulder; and then in the instant before the crash, the enemy team plunged away left-hand wise and Brys wrenched the reds aside, and as one chariot hurtled across the hind-flank of the other, with no more than a thumb's breadth between wheel-hub and wheel rim, for one splinter of time the enemy driver's back was exposed as he fought to get his plunging team under control. And Phaedrus drove home his spear, and dragged it out again with a satisfied grunt, and was past before he could see the man crumple forward on to the haunches of his team. *That* was a battle-move that the tribes knew well enough. He had hated the killing in the back, the first time, but he was used to it now.

A shout from Brys brought him round to see a second chariot charging down upon them. But the boy was a better driver, or maybe more fortunate, than the other had been. Almost at the last moment, he dragged the reds back on their haunches and brought them plunging round towards the onrushing team. The chariot leapt and twisted like a live thing in pain, and from somewhere under the floor came an ominous crack. They were

scraping the side of the enemy war-car, and it seemed that in the next instant the wheels must lock; and then somehow, they were clear, while the other swept by and turned to charge again.

It was the driverless dun team, whose warrior, like many of his kind, had sprung down to fight on foot, that cut across and fouled the on-sweeping enemy, bringing all into confusion; and in the instant before the sweating charioteer could get clear, the warrior, with a yell of rage, drew back his spear-arm and flung the great, broad-headed war-spear as lightly as though it were no more than a javelin. Arching high, it took Phaedrus on the temple as he flung up his shield, and sliced downward, laying his left cheek open, and tore its way out through the young red beard along his jaw-bone.

For one terrible moment, as half his sight went out in red darkness, brought to his knees and clinging to the chariot rail, he thought his left eye had gone. Then as he freed one hand and flung it up to his face, he realized that he was only blinded by blood.

He heard Brys shouting something, and he spat blood and shouted back above the tumult, '*Na*—I am well enough.' But from the feel of it, the chariot was far from well enough, some vital lashing had given under that terrific strain, and it was little fit for more fighting that day. Phaedrus had got himself to his feet again, wiping the blood out of his eyes with the back of one hand as strength came back to him. 'Only a gash. Much mess but little matter. Try to keep near me, but above all, hold the horses out of trouble.' And drawing his sword, he sprang down to meet the Chieftain in the gold torque, who came roaring in on him again.

The battle had swept them closer to the river than he had realized, and on the bank above the yeasty water they met and locked in combat, while the battle swung to and fro about them. They fought close, each with his back to his own hunting-runs. The Chieftain attacked with the courage of a wild boar, but against his tremendous strength and two good eyes, Phaedrus could set those four years of the Gladiators' School. The two things cancelled each other out and made the fight an equal one.

And the fierce joy rose in him, and with it a kind of fever-haze, so that he was scarcely aware of making his kill at last, only of a different enemy before him, a younger and lighter man who sprang in and out like a dancer as he fought, making the Horse Lord suddenly aware that his own feet were growing slow and his sword-arm heavy. He knew that deadly creeping weakness from an earlier time, and the shouting and hoof thunder and the clangour of the war-cars all about him blurred for an instant into the roar of the circus crowd. He shook his head to clear it, and saw the steep fall of the river bank almost beneath his feet; and the dark flash of his enemy's blade coming at him like death made visible—and dived in under the man's guard, driving his point up under the buckler rim.

The Caledonian's eyes widened suddenly, with a puzzled look in them, his guard flew wide, and with a choking cry he crashed backward down the bank, almost dragging Phaedrus with him by the sword still in his body. Phaedrus flung himself back on his heels, and the blade came clear with a grating of metal on bone and a gush of blood, and as the man disappeared with a splash, he stumbled round, his sword reeking to the hilt, to face whatever came next.

A knot of enemy horsemen was bearing down on him. In the shifting patterns of battle he had long since become separated from the Companions, and Brys was nowhere to be seen; and in all the dreamlike chaos, he realized with a small, cool certainty that this was the end of his fighting, and prepared to take as many of his new assailants with him as might be when he went down.

And then with a thunder of hooves and a whirling clangour of wheels, and a yelling that might have come from the dark throats of devils, three war-cars of the Dalriads were sweeping towards him. He turned and stumbled to meet them. He saw a hand with bead bracelets on its wrist like a woman's, and caught it—or was caught by it—as the foremost chariot swept by, and half scrambled, was half dragged aboard, the horses scarcely slackening their wild career.

The wind of their going cleared his head somewhat, and he

395

realized for the first time that the eternity of surging to and fro over the same ground was over, and the tide of battle had set all one way; up the Glen of the Black Goddess, away from the Loch Abha levels, and back—back— towards the hills that bordered Caledonia!

The Caledones were breaking almost everywhere, falling back and streaming away, save here and there where some knot of warriors, cut off from their fellows, turned to go down fighting. There were broken chariots among the fern and the trampled wreck of young foxgloves; dead horses, dead men, and the pursuing chariots swept over the bodies of friends and foe alike. It was Phaedrus's first experience of driving at speed over a spent battlefield; the wheels lurched and bucketed over corpses in the bracken, and came up with the iron tyres wetly red; blood splashed up at the axle tree and even forced its way between the leather straps of the floor, and he wanted to lean over the chariot rail and be sick; but he swallowed the vomit in his throat, and got to his feet, holding to the side of the chariot. He was the King, the Horse Lord, leading the victorious pursuit that spread behind him and on either side. He shook the blood out of his eyes, and looked round at them and it seemed to him that there were fewer than he expected. . . .

There was another sound in the air; the screeching, venomous war-song of a wildcat, and looking down, he saw Shân, her tufted ears laid back and tail lashing behind her, crouched along the yoke-pole, where she always rode in battle. Conory, himself, was driving, crouched low on wide-planted feet, with the reins knotted round his body, as many of the charioteers drove, so as to have a hand free for his spear.

Phaedrus demanded thickly through shut teeth, 'Where is Brys my charioteer?' But in his heart it was all those others he asked for, as well.

'Somewhere behind us, with a spear hole in his thigh,' Conory said. 'Mine is dead. You must be making do with me for your charioteer this time.' And he crouched lower yet over the haunches of the team, calling to them by name: 'Come on now, Whitefoot—Wildfire! They run now; keep them running! Drive

them as the wind drives the storm-clouds from Cruachan's crest—so shall thy mares be proud to bear thee many sons!'

It became a kind of song in Phaedrus's head, a triumph-song that rose and fell with the hideous war-song of the great cat. The fog of unreality was thickening all about him, so that he knew nothing very clearly any more, save for the smell of blood and the fiery throbbing of his wound. Certainly not how the hunt ended, or who gave the order to call the hunters off.

But suddenly there was no more tumult, no more lurching chariot floor under him; and he was sitting on the stinking yokepole, while the spent horses, with hanging heads and heaving flanks, were led away. Someone was bending over him, holding a cold wet cloth to his face, and a voice said, 'He's left his beauty behind him up the glen, I'm thinking.' And another answered, 'The bleeding has slacked off, anyway, and that will be the chief thing.' And then a third voice—he thought that both it and the hand holding the wrung-out cloth were Conory's—said, 'Gods! He's come near to losing that eye!'

And he wondered, as though he were wondering it about someone else, what would have happened if he had. Did one eye count the same as both, where the kingship was concerned?

Someone was holding a flask of mead to his mouth. The rim jolted against his teeth, and he raised his head and tried to suck the drink between them. His face was set rigid as though with a grinding cramp, and some of the fiery stuff came out again through the great torn place in his cheek. But he managed to swallow a few mouthfuls, and the fog seemed to roll back a little.

He looked about him through the sick throbbing that seemed to pound inward from the wound and fill his whole head, and saw that it was evening, the shadows lying long across the woods and marshes; Cruachan towering sloe-dark against the sunset, with gold and purple storm-clouds flying like banners from its crest. Across the level towards Loch Abha, the shadowy scrub was alive with camp fires, and between the fires the horses were tethered to their chariot rails. But again, it seemed that there

397

were surprisingly few of them, fewer of everything, chariots, horses, men—many fewer men. . . .

Phaedrus made to struggle to his feet, but someone pushed him down again by the shoulders. 'Bide still, the Healer Priest is coming.'

He shook his head, and put up an exploring hand to the ruins of his left cheek. 'It is scarcely bleeding now. Let you give me that clout to take with me, and I'll do well enough.' The words came thick and slurred between his teeth, for his throat and even his tongue were swollen.

'Wait for the Priest.'

'That can come later. I've other things to do now—and so has he.'

But the hands were on his shoulders still, and he was too weak to rise against them. Instead, he asked after a moment, 'What of Dergdian's chariot bands?'

And the voice of Dergdian himself answered him. 'Here in the camp, and wolfing stir-about—those that are left of us.'

Phaedrus heaved up his head—it was so heavy he could scarcely lift it—and saw the old warrior bending over him. 'We—came as fast—as we could.'

'Surely,' the other nodded.

'And the rest of us? There—seems so few.'

There was a small, leaden silence, and then Conory said with an odd gentleness quite different from his usual silken tone, 'It is in my mind that the Caledones have their wounds to lick, too— more and deeper than ours.'

'Ours are deep enough, seemingly! *Na*, I must—see for myself——' Phaedrus gathered whatever strength was still in him, and lurched to his feet. 'Take your hands away—I must— see——'

They let him go, and he never knew that Conory was close behind him, as he stumbled away towards the nearest fire.

Before he reached it, a voice called weakly, 'My Lord! My Lord Midir!' and he checked and looked round. Only a few paces away, his red horses were tethered to the rail of what remained of the Royal Chariot, a few armfuls of cut grass piled

before them, and close beside them lay young Brys, straining up on to one elbow, blood still seeping through the strips of someone's cloak that had been bound about his thigh.

Phaedrus turned unsteadily in his tracks and doddered towards him. 'Lie still, you'll start bleeding—like a pig again if you—writhe about like that. And—we've lost enough men as it is, seemingly.'

'My Lord, I——' The boy glanced at his bandaged thigh. 'I got this, and—when I could get up again, I had lost you—and I wasn't good for much more, save to get the horses out of harm's way.'

'You did that finely, and there was—no more you could do. Ach now, lie still, will you—I'll be wanting my charioteer another day.'

He tried to grin, but his whole face seemed set rigid as though clay had been plastered over it, and pain clawed at the wound, almost blinding him again, and he turned away quickly, so that the boy should not see.

The sudden turn set the world spinning round him. For a moment the camp fires swam into a bright sun-wheel, and a roaring cavern seemed to open in his head. And then straight in front of him, but a long way off, he saw a face. A face that was curd-white under the coloured streaks of war-paint, with the eyes in it so dark that they seemed to cast a shadow over all. And he saw without the least surprise, that it was Murna's.

He did wonder vaguely why she looked like that, not knowing what he looked like himself, blood-stained from head to foot and with that terrible torn face like a ragged crimson mask. Without knowing what he did, he started towards her, and the ground tipped under his feet and began to slide away. Somebody caught and steadied him—and in the same instant Murna was there, and above the roaring in his ears, he heard her say, 'Give him to me.' Her arms were round him, and he felt her brace herself under his weight as his knees gave under him and he slipped to the ground. She was kneeling beside him and holding him as he leaned against her with his broken and bloody face in the hollow of her shoulder.

399

The world steadied again, and he pulled his head up with a great effort, leaving dark stains on the shoulder of the boy's tunic she wore. And then a thing happened that seemed surprising afterwards, but at the time did not surprise him any more than finding her there had done. She took his ruined face between her hands and kissed him. And this time she did not feel for his dagger afterwards.

He mumbled thickly, 'Now you have blood on your face as well.'

'It will wash off with the war-paint,' she said.

'Begun Among the Spears'

PHAEDRUS lay on piled bracken in the little branch-woven
bothy, covered by his cloak with the worst of the blood washed
out of it, and watched Murna burnishing his weapons by the
light of the fire that burned before the opening. Outside, he
could hear the voices of the Companions—not Loarne's voice or
Domingart's, or Ferdia's—they had gone with so many others,
on to yesterday's death fires, in the Glen of the Black Goddess,
and their voices would not sound among the Companions again.
He could catch a glimpse of Conory leaning on his spear, and
Shân beside him playing some small, self-contained deadly game
with her own leash.

   He stirred uneasily, made restless by the fever in him, though
the salves of the Healer Priest and the life that he had driven into

the wound through his forefingers had eased some of the pain; and she checked in her burnishings and looked up, her eyes anxious and questioning. It was strange how different her face looked, now that it had come to life. The same shape as it had always been, the same colour, and yet even in the fire-light the difference was there.

He said, 'If you burnish my weapons, who will burnish yours?' It was still hard to talk, and the great wad of salve-soaked cloth that covered all the left side of his face did not make it easier. But there were so many things that he wanted to say to Murna, and he could not wait any longer.

'I lost my spear in the fighting; I've only a dirk like the foot-fighting women.'

'So you called out your Wildcats.'

'When the word came to Dun Monaidh, we knew that there would be need of everyone who could hold a weapon.'

'Even the Queen?'

'I could not be asking the other women to make the War-Dance, and I refuging behind the queenship,' she said, almost exactly as she had said it on the night the Caledonian Envoy came. And suddenly there was a rather piteous twist to her mouth. 'Not even though you forbade me because I was my mother's daughter, and not to be trusted.'

Phaedrus watched in silence as she turned his shield to come at the other half of the rim. 'Don't be holding that against me, Murna,' he said at last. 'Murna—*she is your mother!*'

'And so? Did I give you the poison at her bidding?'

'That is one thing, but to take the war-trail against her in another.'

'How if I say to you that the Caledones have always hated us, because they fear that one day we shall grow strong? That when Liadhan my mother fled to her own kin among them, they saw their chance and took it, and that I take the war-trail against *them*, because I would not have them trailing their cat-skin cloaks lordlywise through Earra-Ghyl?'

'I should say that you spoke the truth—but not all the truth.'

'I will try again, then—I am my father's daughter as well as

my mother's. Do you remember how big and warm and golden he was, before she drained him out until he was only the poor hollow husk of a man? Just such a husk as Logiore was at the end?'

'Yet it was your cloak that saved her from Conory; and you stayed behind, wearing the Moon Diadem, that she might escape.'

'She was the Goddess-on-Earth.'

'You believe that?'

'I did not have to believe it. She *was* the Goddess-on-Earth. I do not have to believe that you are the Horse Lord. I saw you crowned.'

'Then how is it different now? If she was the Goddess then——' He checked, not knowing quite how to go on.

Murna did not answer him for a long moment, then she said in a voice so low that he could scarcely catch the words, 'Maybe she lost that, when she fled—when the time came for her and she—would not make her own sacrifice.'

The words made a kind of echo in Phaedrus's mind as though somewhere, he had heard them—something like them, spoken before. But he could not remember where, or when. 'If so, it is small loss,' he said. 'She made a somewhat ungentle Goddess.'

She said, patiently, as though she was explaining something to a small child, 'What has the Great Mother to do with gentleness or ungentleness? She does not *do,* she only *is.* She is the Lady of Life and Death. When a man and a woman come together to make a child, she is in it, and when a pole-cat finds a thrush's nest and tears the young to shreds while the parents scream and beat about its head, she is in that, too.'

'And when a boy is—made away with, that another may take what is his?' Phaedrus wished that he could stop this probing, but something in himself could not stop. There were things that he must get unsnarled between himself and Murna.

She ceased her burnishing, and laid the shield aside before she answered. Then she said, 'Let you believe me. I knew nothing of that until the night you came back. I knew only what all Earra-Ghyl had told; that you were drowned in the river that runs by Dun Monaidh, and your body carried away.'

Still he could not stop. 'That I believe; but Murna, you were knowing, when you would have knifed me on the night I pulled the bride-mask from your face.'

'What does a hunted wild-thing do when the hounds bring it to bay? It turns and uses whatever weapons it has of teeth or claws or antlers.'

'As simple as that,' Phaedrus said, after a surprised pause.

'As simple as that. You hunted me and I was—very much afraid.' Suddenly and surprisingly, she laughed, but it was laughter with a little catch in it. 'No, you still do not understand, there is so much that you do not understand, Midir. Listen—my mother loved my father, and she loved Logiore, until she had sucked out all that there was in them to love. And—she loved me.'

Phaedrus, a chill shiver between his shoulders, reached out in the half dark and caught her hand without speaking, and she turned it over inside his until they came palm to palm and fitted.

'I can scarcely remember a time when I did not know that I must keep her out, and—I do not know how to be explaining this—I learned to go away small inside myself, where she could not reach me. I made walls to keep her out, and all these years that I have done and said and maybe even sometimes thought as she bade me, I have been safe from her behind my walls. Only, to be strong enough to keep her out—they had to keep me in. . . . If I had passed, that would have broken them down, you see.'

Phaedrus's hand tightened on her. 'I am trying to see. Go on, Murna.'

'And then you came back and turned the world to red fire, and when you stood leaning on your sword and looked at me, after the fighting was over, I knew that presently you would come breaking through my walls and find me, however small I had gone away behind them.'

'And was that such a bad thing?'

'It is frightening, to come to life. I do not think I should be so afraid to die, as I was when I knew that I must come to life.'

'Does it seem so bad now, Murna?'

'No, not now. I think maybe I should have been a little less afraid if I had known—how much you have changed.'

There it was again, this talk of the change in him. Phaedrus was brought up with a jolt, and found himself on the edge of dangerous ground. But he had to know. 'Murna, you said before that I had changed, you said that I did not care what I broke and did not remember afterwards. Murna, I *don't* remember, let you tell me what I did.'

There was a little pause, and then Murna said, 'In the early times, I had one chink in my wall. Just one. It was a tame otter. I found him abandoned when he was a cub—maybe his mother had been killed—and I reared him in secret, lest my mother should know. You found him and set your dogs on him one morning when you had nothing better to do. He didn't know about being hunted, so he was very easy to kill. Too easy, you said; there was no sport in it.'

Phaedrus felt sick. 'I couldn't have known! I must have thought it was a wild one,' he said after a moment. 'Murna, I *couldn't* have know he was yours!'

'Oh yes, you knew; I was there. But I was not ten, then, a girl-child of no account, and you hated and feared my mother. Maybe you did it because I was the nearest thing to her that you could hurt. But my otter was the only thing I had to love, and after, I closed up the chink, and never dared to love so much as a mouse again, for fear of what might happen to it.'

So Midir had done that, and not even remembered after-wards, or he would have told him during those lessons in the cock-loft at Onnum on the Wall. But though the story sickened Phaedrus, it did not hit him with any feeling of discovery about Midir, nor make him feel the bond between them any less close. Instead, he felt a sudden rush of pity for the boy who had been so much afraid, and he'd had good cause to be. And fully and freely he took the weight of that long-ago piece of wicked cruelty on to his own shoulders, not only because he had to, but because in some odd way it seemed as though by doing so, he could lift it from Midir's. 'Oh, Murna, I'm so sorry—so sorry! It is in my heart that I deserved the dirk!'

'No,' she said. 'No, I know that, now. It was because you—because that boy was so afraid. We were both so afraid.'

'You're not afraid any more?'

'No.'

'But you're shivering—I can feel you.'

'Only because I am tired.' Murna made a little sound that was almost like a whisper. 'I am so tired.'

Phaedrus flung back the folds of his cloak with his free hand. 'Then come and lie down, there's room for us both.' And when she was lying in the piled bracken, he pulled his coak over both of them, and sleep gathered him in like a tired hound after a hard day.

The wound-salves of the Healer Priest did their work, and before many days were passed Phaedrus was out with the war bands again, as sound as ever, save for the great half-healed scar that dragged the left side of his face askew. He had most assuredly 'left his beauty behind him up the Glen of the Black Goddess'; and he knew it and did not like it, for he had been good to look at—the arena had taught him that; a gladiator's good looks, if he had any, were part of his stock-in-trade—and now he was only good to look at if he stood with the left side of his face turned away. He caught himself actually doing that one day, and for the rest of the day the Companions wondered why he was in such a vile temper. Only Conory, whom he had been speaking to at the time, knew the answer. He never did it again.

But, indeed, he had other things than his lost beauty to think of in the months that followed.

All summer, though there were no more full battles, the fighting went on, now dying down like a fitful wind into the long grass, now flaring up in some new place, or in many places at once, as the People of the Cailleach drove in thrust after thrust, now down the Drium Alban glens, now across the fords and narrows of the Firth of War-Boats. But gradually, as summer wore on, the scattered fighting began to draw in to one point, narrowing into the country round Glen Croe that ran up north-westward from the Firth. It started with a skirmish there, no

greater as it seemed, than a score of others that had gone before, but where the Caledonian war bands had been driven off, others, many others, came spilling back. Quite suddenly it seemed that the country for half a day's trail up and down the Firth shore was swarming with them. And always there was enough going on elsewhere to make sure that Phaedrus could not concentrate his whole War Host to the one task of driving them out. The dwindling war bands of the Dalriads swept down on them again and again, but even when for the moment they were driven back, almost before the defenders of Earra-Ghyl could draw breath, they were flooding in again, more and always more, until it seemed to Phaedrus and Conory and grim, bow-legged Gault, struggling to hold the whole coastline of the Firth against them, and close the narrow lands between the Firth-head and the loch of Baal's Beacon, that they were springing out of the ground like the War Hosts magicked from puff-balls and thistle-stalks of which the ancient legends told.

The whole glen was theirs now, and the heights on either side, and they held the old forsaken strong-point of Dun Dara on the high shoulder of Beinn Na Locharn that commanded the pass through the mountains to Royal Water. Soon, when they were just a little stronger, they would come pouring over that pass, and now that they held the coast all about Glen Croe mouth, there was little to stop them bringing over every warrior they had.

The leaders looked at each other with one question in their eyes. How much more strength had the enemy still in reserve? It was as the Envoy had said: the Caledones were a great people and the Dalriads a small one; the Caledones had other tribes to call on, while the men of the Western coasts and islands had only themselves, and had come to the end of their reserves, even the boys and women. Yet surely even the Caledones must come to the end of their strength one day. ...

But for Phaedrus, that wild and bitter summer had a kind of broken-winged happiness of its own. All through the long night rides and the swift bloody fighting, while the rowan-trees blossomed and the blossom fell into the hill burns running low

407

with drought, Murna rode with him and Conory among the Companions, proving herself as hardy and as skilled with the throw-spear as any of the young warriors. And at night among the steep glens and wooded hollows of the moors, or in some hill dun long since cleared of cattle and all else that could be driven or carried away, when the warriors slept with their spears beside them and their shields for pillows, she spread her own cloak on the ground between the wheels of the chariot for Phaedrus to lie on, and lay down beside him with his cloak to cover them both. And there were times when they would laugh together at some foolish jest; and once when there was a night attack on the chariot ring, they fought together behind one shield.

But as summer drew on towards its end, and the heat-parched heather began to fade, Murna had a look about her eyes that Phaedrus did not understand—and he knew the looks of her well enough by then. He wondered if the sword-cut she had taken across the ribs a few weeks back were troubling her. But when he asked, she laughed and showed him the place, and he could see that it was cleanly healed.

He told himself that he was imagining things, and turned his whole mind towards gathering the remains of the War Host for what all men knew must be the last battle.

Through those last crackling, drought-baked days of summer, they gathered in from the scattered ends of Earra-Ghyl; war bands brought up to strength with men who were too old for fighting and boys who were too young, hastily mended chariots drawn by unmatched horses, each the survivor of some other team. They gathered in the steep glens northward of Dun Dara, and in the midst of them the Horse Lord and the men of Dun Monaidh made their great chariot-ring on the grassland slopes of Green Head.

And then one morning, with the last battle as it were already brewing, Murna disappeared when the scouting chariots were being harnessed. And Phaedrus, going in search of her, found her crouched beside the low-running, hazel-fringed burn, being very sick. He squatted down and held her head for her, just as he would have done for Conory or young Brys, and waited until the

spasm was over and she was gathering up palmfuls of the cold peat-brown water and bathing her face. Then he demanded urgently, 'What is it? Are you ill?'

She turned to look at him, with the colour creeping back into her face, smiling at him a little behind her eyes. 'No, I am not ill. But it seems that I must turn to women's work after all. I am carrying a child for you, Midir.'

It was a time of lull, one of those uneasy lulls that come on the edge of fighting, or he would have sent her away at once. As it was, there were a few hours more, and the scouts reporting no signs of movement from around Glen Croe, Phaedrus was even able to leave the War Host for a little while, to set her on her way.

And so at about the same time next day they stood together on a ridge of the high moors a mile or so westward of the main Host, to take their leave of each other, while the small escort of Companions who were to take her back to Monaidh waited at a little distance. Early as it was, the sky arched, cloudless and already heat-pearled, over hills that were shadowed with fading heather or tawny as a hound's coat; a warm, dry wind went blustering across the moors, making a sea-sound in the dark glen woods below, and Phaedrus remembered afterwards that there was a scattering of late harebells among the furze.

Murna said almost accusingly, 'Why did you come seeking me yesterday? If you had come then, you need not have been knowing. Not yet, not for a few days more. It was only a few days more I hoped for.'

And the warm wind through the furze and the impatient harness-jingle of one of the horses were the only sounds again.

A few days more . . . in two or three days now, the thing would be settled, one way or the other, and she knew it as surely as any of them, and had tried to keep her secret long enough to share the last battle with him; and part of him wished sore that she had been able to keep it; she had been a good fighting-mate.

'Let me stay, then,' she said, as though she knew what he had been thinking. 'Just three more days.'

409

'They might be three days too many.' He looked her very straight in the eyes. 'Murna, this one time, *you will obey me!*'

'*Sa*; this time I will obey you.' There was a small wry attempt at a smile on her mouth. 'I am not wanting to—but the babe is stronger than I am. And he wants to be born and live.'

'He? You are sure, then, that it will be a man-child?'

'Of course. A son to lead the Horse People after you.' She flung up her head and laughed, a laughter that seemed to ache in her throat. 'How could he be anything else? He was begun among the spears!'

Ever since he had first known about the babe Phaedrus had been taking care not to think too closely about the fact that Murna believed it was Midir's, but now, at her words, suddenly everything in him was crying out to tell her the truth. She had the right to know, and for himself, he felt that something at his heart's core would tear out by the roots if he had to part from her with the thing untold, raising a barrier between them. But he never must tell her; in all his life or hers, no matter how long or short it may be.

He put his arms round her, loosely, and carefully at first— strange that he was holding two people in the circle of his arms—then fiercely close. 'Listen now: whatever happens, whether I come back to Dun Monaidh to make the victory dance, and we grow old together and watch this son who was begun among the spears become a man, or whether we are not together any more this side of the sunset—*whatever comes*, what- ever you hear of me, remember I love you, my Murna.'

She put up her hands and took his scarred face between them, and kissed him, and stood for a few moments straining up to rest her forehead against his. 'I love you, my gladiator, that shall be helping me to remember.'

Phaedrus held her tight against him for a heartbeat longer, then he almost pushed her away. 'Go now, go quickly.'

And she obeyed without a backward glance.

He stood and watched her going away from him through the tawny, knee-high grass between the furze, striding like a boy in her breeks and tunic, towards where the Companions waited.

He saw her fling her hand to them, and mount into the waiting chariot. ... He went on standing on the ridge, watching until a distant fold of the moors took the chariot and its little escort from his sight.

Then he turned, cursing in his heart with the dark enduring curses of the Gael, so much more potent than any that he had learned in the Gladiators' School at Corstopitum, and headed back towards the camp on the skirts of Green Head.

Midway, he met Conory, strolling up through the hazel scrub with Shân's leash swinging in his hand. 'You'll not have seen my striped she-devil?' he inquired. 'She has slipped her collar.'

Phaedrus shook his head. 'Never a tail twitch of her.' But he had a feeling that it was not really to look for Shân, who was skilled at slipping her collar and was sometimes away on the hunting trail for whole days at a time, that the Captain of his Companions had come that way.

'Ah well, she will come back when she has killed,' Conory said, and turning about, fell into step beside Phaedrus.

They walked some way in silence, and then Phaedrus said, 'Murna should be safe in Dun Monaidh within three days.'

And Conory said, 'She will be finding it dull in the women's quarters, after this summer, and she almost alone in there.'

'The whole War Host will have heard by now,' Phaedrus said savagely after a moment.

'Most of them.'

'It is an accursed tangle.'

'Were you never thinking it was a thing that might happen?'

'Ach, I suppose so.'

'And were you never wanting it should happen?'

Phaedrus said, 'Murna is *my* woman—mine to me, in the way that no woman ever was before, and it is warmth in my heart, to know that we have begun the making of a child between us.'

'But.'

'It is my child—but not Midir's.'

'The few who know will keep silence.'

Phaedrus made an impatient gesture. 'That is the kind of

thing Sinnoch the Merchant might say. *Sa, sa,* I know it is true. They will keep their side of the bargain as I have kept mine. Besides, they have too much to lose if they let it through their teeth.'

'But?' Conory said again.

'Fiends and Furies! She thinks that I am Midir,' he groaned, 'and I had to let her go, still thinking it.'

Conory looked at him thoughtfully, as they walked. 'It is in my mind to wonder—just wonder—if she does—or if for her too, the balance of the blade was wrong, after all.'

And Phaedrus stopped dead in his tracks, remembering how she had said 'You' and then changed it into 'That boy' when she told him the cruel story of that long-ago otter-hunt. How she had said, 'I love you, my gladiator'; not giving him Midir's name. 'You think —that?' he said very slowly.

'I don't know. You may know one day; no one else ever will.'

'She would never foist a child that she knew was not Midir's on to the tribe to rule as Horse Lord after me.'

'She is a woman, not a man; there's a difference,' Conory pointed out kindly. 'Women will do strange things for a man, and never feel that they are breaking any faith so long as they do not break it with that one man.' And after a silence, 'There is this, also, that for the tribe your son may be better than no Royal Son at all—if it is a son. Remember it will be of the Royal Blood on its mother's side, the same blood as Midir—or as Conory the Captain of your Guard, come to that.'

They were moving forward again, threading the steep midge-infested hazel woods that skirted the lower slopes of Green Head, and again they kept silence for a while. Then Phaedrus laughed savagely. 'It is a jest for the Gods, isn't it—Liadhan seized the rule and brought back the old worship and the Old Ways; and the kings killed each other and came to kingship only by marriage with the Royal Woman; and the daughters were all and the sons nothing. Then Gault and the rest of you rose against Liadhan, to bring back the ways of the Sun People, and you set me up to be Lord of the Dalriads in her place. And what have I done? I killed the Old King and married the Royal

Woman, and my son will draw his right to rule after me from his mother.'

'I am not Tuathal the Wise,' Conory said after a moment, 'but it is in my mind that maybe all the Gods men worship blur into each other a little at the edges. It is in my mind also that there must be Earth Lady as well as Sun Lord, before the barley springs in the furrow.'

Phaedrus nodded. He supposed that was the answer. All the answer there was, anyway. Meanwhile they were going close to the camp, and there was something else he wanted to say to Conory, something that had been in his mind to say to him, ever since he knew about the babe. 'Conory, if I am killed tomorrow—if I go beyond the Sunset before the boy comes to his time for taking Valour—and you live after me, let you guard him and Murna for me.'

'You are very sure that it will be a son.'

'Murna says that it will be a son.'

'The women have ways of knowing—so they say. See then if the rule passes to a son, the old pattern is broken after all.'

'And you will guard them?'

'I will swear to it, on whatever thing you choose.'

'A plain promise will serve.'

Conory's sweet, mocking smile was in his voice. 'You forget that I also am of the Royal Blood, and may have sons of my own one day. I will swear.'

'Swear then, on the bare blade.' They were both half laughing, both in earnest under the laughter. Phaedrus whipped out his dirk, and held it out to Conory as they walked. And Conory, his hand flat along the blade, swore the oldest and most binding oath of the Gaelic People.

'If I break faith with you, may the green earth open and swallow me, may the grey seas roll in and engulf me, may the sky of stars fall and crush me out of life for ever.'

Something had happened in the camp of the War Host while they were away, maybe some news come in. It was in the very air as they came up towards the chariot lines, and glancing aside

413

at his companion, Phaedrus saw that his head was up and his nostrils widened as though to catch an unfamiliar smell. A knot of charioteers parted at their approach. Phaedrus called to one of them, young Brys who had lately returned to him, and the boy came, running lame like a bird trailing a broken wing.

'What is in the wind?' Phaedrus asked.

'My Lord Midir, it is all over the camp that the She-Wolf herself is yonder in Dun Dara!'

Phaedrus and Conory exchanged a glance. 'So,' Phaedrus said softly, 'the Goddess herself come to be in at the Kill.'

'That or'—Conory checked an instant, his odd eyes narrowed in thought—'could it be that the Caledones have brought her to put fire into the hearts of their warriors? Could it be that even *their* strength has an end, and they are throwing in their last weapon against us?'

Phaedrus said, 'We have already thrown in ours. Ah well, one way or the other, we shall soon enough be knowing.'

16

The Last Weapon

WHEN the sun went down behind Cruach Môr two evenings later, the Dalriads were once again masters of Dun Dara; and as the great hills dimmed into the dusk the old stronghold within its turf banks, and the steep slopes that dropped away from it on three sides, were red-flowered with the watch fires of the tattered War Host. But away down Glen Croe the great out-thrust shoulder of Black Crag was flowered in the like way, with Caledonian watch fires, so many watch fires, even after these past two days of fighting. And the dead of the Horse People lay mingled with the dead of the Caledones all down the glen.

Sitting before the blind doorway of what had once been the Chieftain's Hall, Phaedrus put the situation into words, as much to get it clear in his own mind as anything else, for the men gathered about the Council fire knew it all as well as he did. 'This is the way of it, then. We have not the strength left to drive

them back to their own side of the Firth; and if we pull back ourselves, leaving them Lords of Black Crag and the lower glen, they'll be over into our herding lands like a stampede of wild horses, and we'll not get them out again until Cruachan falls into Loch Abha. We can keep them penned in the glen just so long as we can hold out here in Dun Dara. But you all know how it is. This has been the driest summer that the oldest of us can remember—see how the furze flares and crackles in the flame— and they have been here before us. They have drunk the old wells dry, and the spring runs so low that it will scarcely serve to water the men, let alone the horses, and the burn is foul with the dead men they heaved into it. We can last out the few days to burn our dead and get our wounded away; no more—while they have all the Firthhead above the burn's outflow to drink dry before they feel the lack of water.'

'May it rot their bellies!' growled Oscair, his big, freckled hands clenched on his knees.

'If it would, that would be the solving of our problem,' Phaedrus said; 'but it is in my mind that we will need to be doing something about it ourselves.'

Gault, with a bloody clout round his head, looked up from the fire. 'And what thing would that be?'

'I do not know yet. Before we can be making any plan, we must come at surer knowledge of the numbers that yet remain to King Bruide and the defences of his chariot-ring. So, my brothers, I am minded for a little night hunting and a closer look at this camp of the Caledones.'

There was a quick stir of movement among the Companions, and Diamid said, 'We are with you, Midir.'

Conory, who had been playing lightly with his dirk as a girl might play with a flower, sheathed it, and made a small, soft throat-sound to Shân beside his knee, so that she ceased washing herself and with an answering cry, sprang to his shoulder. 'So, all's ready. We will have a fine hunting, eh, my fanged flower?'

'Three of us should be enough,' Phaedrus said quickly. '*Na*, not you, Finn; you're as brave as a boar, and when you move

416

you make as much noise as one. Nor you, Cathal, with that wound only half healed. Conory, and you, Baruch; you two I take; no more.'

'One more.' He had already risen heedless of protests, and begun to strip off his necklaces and arm-rings, when he heard the dry tones of Sinnoch the Merchant, who had ridden in that day with his last reserves of horses, and turned to meet the faintly amused gaze under the horse-trader's wrinkled lids. 'If this were a war-trail, I would bide quiet in the shadows, as befits a man of peaceful ways—seeing also that I am but half-born to the tribe and carry no warrior patterns on my skin. But since it is no more than a hunting trail after all—will you take me for a fourth? I can still move with less noise than a boar, and I know these hills maybe somewhat better than the rest of you.'

'The smuggling of mares has its uses,' Phaedrus said. 'Come then, and show us the way, peaceful merchant man.'

And so in a little while, the four hunters stood ready to set out, each with the dirk in his belt for his only weapon, each stripped to the waist, his face and body daubed with fire-black over the blurred war-paint, and everything that could betray them by fleck of light or jink of sound laid aside. And already, in the light of the Council fire, they seemed to have become shadows; nothing quite distinct about them save for the eyes of the cat on Conory's shoulder that caught the flame-light and shone like two green moons.

'We are ready? Then good hunting to us all,' Phaedrus said; and the other three caught it up and answered him:

'Good hunting to us all.'

Sinnoch the Merchant soon proved his value, for it seemed that he did indeed know these hills as other men know the ways of their own steading-yard. They fell in with no Caledonian picket or scouting band and not much more than a Roman hour by Phaedrus's reckoning, after setting out, they were crouched among the furze and bilberry-covers above Craeg Dhu, the Black Crag, peering down at the watch fires of the Caledones. Fifty fires at least, Phaedrus reckoned, covering all the great out-

417

thrust shoulder of the hill-side; and if one allowed for the usual count of fifty men to a fire . . .

'There's always the chance that they have spread the men more thinly, to make us believe them stronger than they are,' Conory murmured.

'It could be. There is no telling from here. I am going in for a closer look.'

'I also.'

'You also—and Baruch. You are not called the Grass-Snake for nothing, Baruch. Get across to the far side yonder, and see what chance an attack might stand by way of the eastern scarp. Sinnoch, let you bide here. It is best that one should stay, lest we need warning of danger, or a diversion making for us. At worst, someone to carry word of what has happened to us back to Gault.'

'Have a care, then—remember that they may have dogs. Remember also that there will be watchers posted beyond sling-range of the camp.'

'*Sa, sa*, all this we will remember. Do you remember to keep your eyes and ears open for any threat behind us. Give us a vixen's scream for a danger signal, if need be.'

And with the words scarcely spoken, Phaedrus was creeping forward again, Conory close behind him, and the little striped shadow that was Shân slipping ahead through the bilberry cover. Baruch had already disappeared.

The furze thickened as they dropped lower, so that soon, instead of crouching from clump to clump, they were belly-crawling by narrow winding ways among the furze roots, oozing forward, hand's length by hand's length, every sense on the stretch for danger; but no warning cry came, no sudden leap of spearmen or fanged war-dog. In the end it seemed as though it was the furze itself that would stop them; an impenetrable wall of furze, black-dark in the light of the moon that had begun to rise. Only, as they cast about for a way through, the smell of dog-fox led them to the mouth of a fox-run almost hidden among root-tangle and spiney branches, at which Shân arched her back and spat, before flowing forward into it like a liquid shadow. The two men followed her. The run seemed very long,

and the stink of it came up into Phaedrus's throat and almost
choked him; but just as he began to feel that it must go on for
ever, it curved sharply downhill and he caught a glint of firelight at the end of it, and a little later found open ground before
him, and one of the picket fires scarcely a spear-throw away.

He froze instantly, putting back a foot to warn Conory behind
him. He felt the other's touch on his ankle in answer, and a few
moments later Conory was oozing up beside him, with infinite
caution parting a spy-hole for himself among the furze stems.
Shân was crouching between them, and he felt the tense flick of
her tail tip against his neck; but she would make no move on her
own account, not when she was hunting with Conory.

Crouching shadow-still in the furze, Phaedrus scanned the
men about the picket fire for any sign of sleepiness, but they were
awake and watchful, leaning on their spears and staring into the
night. Well, he could see enough from here. . . .

Not much out of sling-range from where they lay, Bruide's

warriors had piled a breastwork of stakes and uprooted thorn-bushes across the open hill-shoulder, and drawn up their chariots just beyond, though clearly their chief defence on that side was the furze itself; while on all other sides they were protected by the steep drop to the glen woods and the river below. The Caledones had taken to themselves a magnificent defensive position, and Phaedrus cursed inwardly as he realized the hopelessness of any direct attack. The whole strong-place lay clear in the mingled white-and-ruddy light of moon and fires—and why not? he thought furiously; the People of the Cailleach had no need to hide their strength, and they would be knowing well enough that even from the edge of the furze, if any of the Dalriads should get so far, they were out of sling range. Gods! for one Company of the Syrian Archers such as he had seen often enough ride through Corstopitum!

He could see now that the number of fires had been no bluff; the broad hill-shoulder just below him was aswarm with men; men sleeping with their shields for pillows, men wakeful and leaning on their spears. He could hear one man call to another, the whinny of a tethered horse from the chariot line, the ding of hammer on field anvil where the smiths laboured to repair war-gear broken in that day's fighting; the ceaseless, restless stir and lowing of captured cattle. In the midst of all, beside the Great Fire, the Royal Fire, two furze-built bothies stood close together under the grim stag-skull battle standard of Bruide the King. As he strained his eyes towards them, a tall figure rose from beside the fire and crossed to one of the bothies, then turned an instant in the door-hole, to look up at the dark hill as though aware of eyes watching her out of the furze cover. At that distance, and muffled in the folds of a cloak, there would have been no saying if it were man or woman; not even the gleam of barley-pale hair in the fire-light told who it was, since among the Caledones as well as the Dalriads, many of the young warriors bleached their hair. But it was as though hate lent wings to Phaedrus's vision, and he knew Liadhan the She-Wolf as surely as though she stood within hands' reach of him. He had thought that he knew about hate before, but he had never known the kind of hate that

gathered somewhere in the dry hollow of his belly as he watched; sharp and piercing hate for Midir's sake, and for Murna's, as well as a broader hate that was for the sake of the tribe. It seemed to go out from him through the fire-lit camp to reach her at the heart of it, so that it was small wonder she turned as at a touch, and stood so long staring out and up into the darkness. . . . Then she turned again and went into the bothy.

Phaedrus became aware of Shân crouched against his forward-thrust arm, and felt the little wicked currents running through her, and her fur lifting as she caught the hate from him. He felt a touch on his shoulder, a light backward pressure of Conory's hand that meant 'back, now'. Well, they had seen what they came to see, and to wait on, so near to one of the pickets would only be to bide looking for needless trouble. Yet everything in him revolted at the thought of crawling back up that stinking footrun, and carrying the bitter word to the waiting War Host that to attack the Caledones' chariot-ring would only be to fling themselves on inevitable disaster; that nothing could come at the enemy up the sheer rocks of Black Crag or through that black tide of furze on a slope that was beyond even the chariot horses.

And then almost in the same instant, two things happened. Out of the dead stillness that had made the air seem thick to breathe all day, a soft breath of wind came siffling down the glen, wind that came, for the first time in many weeks, from the west. And quite suddenly, as though of its own accord, his mind said, 'Fire could.'

For a long moment he made no response to Conory's warning touch, while the long, soft breath died away, and another starting far up the glen, came hushing towards them through the furze. There was a stillness in him like the stillness of revelation. Tuathal the Wise had told him once that it felt like that when the God spoke to you. After the summer drought, the furze and parched grass and the thin scrub that wooded the glen floor would burn like touchwood, and with even a light wind behind it, the fire would spread with the speed of stampeding cattle. . . .

He yielded at last to the touch on his arm, and slid backward

from the mouth of the fox-run. Conory waited an instant to slip
the end of the leash coiled about his wrist through Shân's collar,
and then came after. It seemed hours before at last they found
space to turn round, hours more before they were heading up
through the tongues and runnels of the looser furze, towards the
place where they had left Sinnoch on watch.

Baruch the Grass-Snake had arrived a few moments before
them, but none of them spoke any word until all four were well
clear, and halted in a little hollow of Ben Dornich well on their
way back towards Dun Dara. Then Phaedrus broke the silence
at last, speaking quickly and at half-breath—even here there
was no point in making more sound than need be. 'There must
be well above two thousand of them still in fighting shape, and
from the place where Conory and I lay hid, there was no sign of
any possible way of reaching them, even supposing that we
could gather up enough men for an attack. How was it from
your side, Baruch?'

'The same, what with the hill scarp and that black tide of
furze, a few hundred could hold it easily against our number.'

'So. Then what now, my children?' Sinnoch's voice was dry
and crackling as autumn leaves.

A small silence took them, and in it something made Phaedrus
look round at Conory. His face was in black moon shadow, but
the angle of his head told Phaedrus that the Captain of his
Companions had turned to look at him also. After a few
moments, he said softly, 'Are you thinking what I am thinking?'

'I am thinking that after this dry summer, the whole countryside would burn like a torch if one of those camp fires—or even
our own, up on the short grass of Dun Dara—should chance to
get out of control.'

'Fire!' Baruch whispered.

And the little wind freshened through the long hill-side grass.

'Or if a man chanced to drop, say, a burning twig into a grass
tussock,' Sinnoch said reflectively.

Phaedrus nodded. 'Where men cannot go, fire can,' and felt
the quickening attention of the other three. 'A while ago, it was
flat calm, but now there's this small wind rising—and from the

west! A wind that's a gift from the Gods. If we fire the hill-sides, up-valley, say about where the westernmost burn comes down from Ben Dornich, it will be on them almost before they know it.'

'The captured cattle are corralled on the western side,' Baruch said. 'They'll stampede, across the camp.'

'Surely, and on down the glen, and with our own riders to help the fires along and deal with any breakaways, that should even the odds against us somewhat. At the least, it will clear them from Black Crag.'

'Forest fire is like a wild beast on a chain,' Sinnoch said, 'not to be let loose lightly.'

'So long as the wind holds from this quarter, we are safe; and the Firth will serve for a fire-break,' Conory put in.

'And if the wind changes again?'

'Baruch,' Phaedrus said, 'will the wind change again before dawn? No, before tomorrow's noon?'

The little man was silent a moment, while they all watched him, his head cocked, his delicately twitching nose seeming, as it were, to finger the breeze. Then he shook his head. 'Before noon it will have died away, but it will not go round. And I think it will not die before it has had time to do its work.'

'*Sa.* Have you ever known Baruch mistake the wind?' Phaedrus said. 'We must pray to Lugh Shining Spear that he does not begin now.'

Baruch, who could be a fiend incarnate in time of fighting, but was oddly gentle before and after, said, 'Forest fire moves with the speed of a galloping horse. There'll be wounded among them down there in the chariot-ring, some too sore hurt to get away.'

'Would the Caledones hold their hands if the thing were the other way on?' Phaedrus said ruthlessly. 'If they have wounded, then their sword brothers must do for them what we have done for our own, before now.' For in case of a forced retreat, the Dalriads had always knifed their own wounded to save them from the mercy of the enemy. Let the Caledones save their own wounded in the same way from the mercy of the fire. He looked

423

round at the other three in the moonlit hollow. 'I know what kind of wild beast fire is when one loosens it from the chain. I know it's a wicked weapon we'll be using, and a wicked hazard we'll run in the using of it, but save for making the Caledones a free gift of Earra-Ghyl, *is there any other way?*'

'No,' Conory said after a moment, 'there is no other way.'

'*Sa;* and no moment to spare. Baruch, you are the swiftest runner of us all. Back with you to Dun Dara. Tell Gault what we have seen in the Caledones' camp, and the thing we have to do, and bid him turn out every man who can still keep astride a horse and every horse that can still put one foot before another, and send three-fourths of them to meet me in the alder woods where the Westernmost burn comes down from Ben Dornich, and himself take the remaining fourth part across the river and down the north bank to the same point. And bid him also to see that five men of his band and ten of mine carry fire-pots under their cloaks.'

Baruch was already crouching up with a foot under him. 'Any other word, my Lord Midir?'

'Bid him ride as though the Wild Hunt were on his tail. These summer nights are short, and we must set the fire upon them before the chariot-ring is astir at dawn, and be ready to throw in our attack the moment they break before the fire.'

'I will tell him.'

There was the faintest whisper of sound in the long grass, lost almost instantly in the soughing of the little west wind. And only the shadow of a furze bush in the moonlight, where Baruch the Grass-Snake had been.

Phaedrus turned back to the other two. 'We've a longish wait before us. Might as well be making up towards the meeting place, ourselves; at least up there we'll be able to move freely without fear of a Caledonian scouting party on our necks, and we can be filling in some of the time gathering dry grass and branches for torches.' He grinned at Conory. 'I was wrong when I said we had already thrown in our last weapon; we're throwing it in now.'

17

The Protection of Rome

BY noon, the west wind had died into the grass, and the white
heat-haze danced again over the glen, over the silence and
desolation that had been Glen Croe. The last weapon had done
its work. The whole valley was reddened and blackened, the
acrid smitch still rising here and there among the charred snags
of furze and birch and alder, dead men and horses and cattle, and
the jagged wreck of chariots. All across the mouth of the glen
and up the Firth shore to its head, lay the same trail of dead and
broken things, for the coracles beached where the glen ran down

425

to the shore, had served to take off only the merest handful of the War Host, little more than a bodyguard for the wild and raging woman who had been Liadhan the Queen. And for the rest, there had been the desperate, broken retreat up to the head of the Firth, and the river ford. The dead and broken things lay thickest of all about the ford; some were scattered even on the farther side.

Dead of the Dalriads among the many more dead of the Caledones. Conall and Diamid lay a little way below Black Crag, shoulder touching shoulder as they had fought, and in the mouth of the glen the women, gleaning for wounded among the slain, had found Sinnoch the Merchant: Sinnoch who had never been a warrior, who had been killed, like more than one warrior with Caledonian war-paint on his face, not by enemy iron, but by the stampeding cattle. Maybe that was why his dead face had worn a look of wry amusement as though at a bad jest, when they turned him over.

Where the slain lay thickest by the river ford, the stag-skull standard with saffron tassels torn away, propped drunkenly against an alder-tree with its bronze-tipped tines entangled in the branches, marked where King Bruide had turned with his Companions—those that were left of them—to cover the retreat of his tattered War Host. Presently, Phaedrus thought, they must raise a grave mound for him and his sword-brothers, when the death fires for their own fallen were burned out. The wolf and the raven could have the rest.

Sitting his borrowed roan beside Conory on a little out-thrust nab of the hill-side, he looked down at that scene by the ford, and drove one clenched hand into the palm of the other with sudden baffled fury. 'That is the second time! Bruide was a king worth the name, and he's food for the ravens, this noon—while *she*. . . .' His voice strangled in his throat with loathing.

Conory sitting oddly crooked on his own horse, said, 'There will be a third time.' And something, a kind of tightness in his voice, made Phaedrus look round. He saw the drawn expression about the other's mouth, but connected it almost without thought, with the loss of Shân, for the wildcat had gone into

battle with her lord as usual, and that was the last that anyone had seen of her—and his own fury claimed him again.

'It looks like it, doesn't it? She'll be half across to Baal's Beacon by now, while we sit here waiting for the word of the scouts. I was wrong; we should have pushed straight on——'

'You were not wrong. To have hunted tired hounds blindly into those no-man's hunting-runs would have been moon madness. At least the halt will give us a while to rest and bait the horses and put something into our empty bellies that may make us feel less like ghosts ourselves.' Conory laughed. 'I can smell the fat smell of cooking-fires: they do say that captured bullock meat tastes ever the sweetest.'

'Then twice captured should be twice as sweet.' No good to bide there staring down at the ford and raging. He turned his horse's head back towards their own chariot-ring. 'Come, then, or we shall miss our share.'

Conory wheeled beside him, but as he did so a stone rolled under his horse's off forehoof and the tired beast stumbled heavily. He caught his breath in a little choking gasp of pain, and Phaedrus looked round again just in time to fling sideways and catch him as he sagged forward over the horse's neck.

'Steady! What now?'

Conory managed a rather ghastly smile. 'I took a spear-thrust in the hip—it must have gone—a bit deeper than I thought.'

'You fool!' Phaedrus shouted at him in another kind of fury, because he had already lost too many friends for one day. 'You fool! Why were you not telling me?' Then as the other murmured something quite unintelligible: 'Give me the reins. Can you hold on as far as the camp, if I steady you?'

Conory made a great effort against the deadly faintness that was turning him grey-white to the lips, and said quite clearly, through shut teeth, 'I've never fallen off a horse yet.'

And he did not, though he was riding blind and slumped over the horse's neck as they came up to the picket lines, and Phaedrus, riding knee to knee with him, with a steadying grip on his arm, was almost all that kept him from sliding limply to the ground.

By the nearest of the fires he reined in and called, '*Hai!* Diamid!' before he remembered that it was no use calling Diamid any more. Two or three others came running, young Brys ahead of them, to catch the bridles, as he dropped from his borrowed horse to aid Conory down.

'Nor have I ever been lifted off a horse like a screeching captive maiden,' said Conory sweetly, opening his eyes which had been half closed, and he set his hands on the horse's withers to swing his sound leg over, and crumpled quietly into Phaedrus's arms in a dead faint.

Phaedrus gathered him up, shaking his head impatiently at the hands that came out to help. '*Na*, leave be. I have him—where are the Healer Priests?'

Aluin Bear's Paw pointed, with a hand whose back was furred with thick dark hair. 'Up yonder by that hazel-tump in the loop of the burn.'

Conory was extraordinarily light to carry, even unconscious. Phaedrus thought suddenly that Murna would not be so very much lighter. But the weight of his own weariness was added to the weight of the slight figure in his arms, so that he was gasping when he reached the hazel trees where several Sun Priests with their strangely crested heads were moving among the men who sat or lay there stretched out in the shade.

For one horrible moment, as he laid his friend down, Phaedrus thought that he was dead, but when he put a hand over Conory's heart he felt it beating faintly under his fingers; and the Healer Priest who had come up behind him said, '*Na, na*, his spirit is out of his body, but it will come back.'

'You are sure?' Phaedrus demanded.

A grey smile touched the priest's face. He also was a tired man. 'There is always a risk that the spirit may lose its way. I shall know better when I have seen the wound.' He sent one of the women for water from the low-running stream and kneeling down, began to cut away the plaid cloth of Conory's breeks to come at the spear-thrust in his hip, and clicked his tongue over it like an old woman, and called to a priest for his instruments.

Phaedrus said nothing, but stood by while the wound was

428

cleansed and salved, glad that for this while at least, Conory was out of his body and need not feel the surgeon's probe that fetched out splintered bone. When the thing was finished and the wound lashed tight, he said, 'Will it mend?'

The priest looked up with a start, having quite forgotten his presence. 'He'll go lame on that leg to the end of his days; but if he does not take the wound fever, he'll be astride a horse again by winter.' His tired face gentled. 'There's no good that you can do here, my Lord Midir. Go you and eat and get what rest you can.'

Back among the cooking-fires, the lumps of half-raw bullock meat were being given out to men who ate like starving wolves, or were too weary to eat at all; and one of the scouts had just come in with word of having picked up the trail of Liadhan and the small band with her, and followed until it was sure that they were making for the Black Glen and the Waters of Baal's Beacon.

Phaedrus listened, gnawing his way through a great wedge of meat that was black on the outside and still dripped red within. Then he spoke urgently with Gault the Strong. 'Scrape me together two- or three-score men; there must be so many among the War Host who can keep on horseback a few hours longer.'

'The War Host is something smaller than it used to be,' Gault said savagely.

'That I had noticed. None the less, I must have at least two-score to push on with me now. For the others, let you rest the men and horses but gather every single one you can and hold them ready to bring on after me when I send back word.'

'That I will do,' Gault said. 'But as to the two-score—do your own dirty work, my Lord of the Horse Herd. They're asleep on their feet; but if you can wake them, they'll answer to your call better than they will to mine.' He smiled, that harsh, bitten-off smile of his. 'Did I not promise you that you should be as much the King as you showed yourself strong for?'

'You did, and behold, I am the Horse Lord, and men come at my call.'

And for an instant, eye looking into eye, both of them remembered that quiet-surfaced struggle for the soul of a little dark hunter, that had been also a trial of strength for the leadership of the tribe.

There were only seven of the Companions left now, and of those, Baruch the Grass-Snake was away with the scouting band. Brys brought the number up to seven again; and surprisingly, Vron, Sinnoch's old fore-rider, came forward to make the eighth, with his disreputable sheepskin hat still on the back of his head. Dergdian joined them, leaving the leadership of his own men to a kinsman, and Tyrnon and Nial Mac Cairbre..... They came forward in ones and twos, men with red-rimmed eyes and scorched and blackened faces, several with a bloody rag knotted somewhere about them, until in a little while Phaedrus had more than the three-score that he had first called for.

It took longer to find the horses than it had done to find the men, for the poor beasts were utterly spent, and while that was being done, each man was making ready as best he could, bundling five days' supply of bannock and meat in his rolled-up cloak. Brys, still proudly careful of his duties as the King's armour-bearer, though now he was one of the Companions, had brought Phaedrus's cloak with the great war-brooch still in it, down from Dun Dara in the before-dawn darkness, that the Horse Lord should not ride into battle without it, and dealt with making up his Lord's bundle as well as his own, and seeing to both their weapons.

For while the ready-making was going on, Phaedrus had gone upstream to the hazel-tump where the Healer Priests were still busy with the wounded.

Conory had come back into his body again, and lay with his head and shoulders propped against the leaning stem of hazel, looking down at something that crouched against his flank. He looked round at Phaedrus's step, and moved his hand quickly in a tiny gesture that was at once warning to Phaedrus and restraint and reassurance to the thing that crouched there so tensely still, and Phaedrus, checking beside him, and looking down, saw that it was Shân.

430

Her collar was gone and she was a pitiable sight, her striped fur almost all singed off; but somehow she had come out of the fighting and found her Lord again, and her spirit was quite unquenched, judging by the way she tensed and spat at his approach, before she quietened under Conory's hand; and her narrowed eyes looking up at him were as bright and wicked as ever he had seen them.

It was stupid, he thought, at a time like this, to feel the rush of relief and gladness because one small, wicked-tempered wildcat had come alive through the fighting and the fire. And yet—it would have been even harder to leave Conory here and go on without him, if she had not. . . .

'So—she is back from her hunting yet again,' he said. It was the easy and obvious thing to say, when the things that needed saying were too difficult and stuck in one's throat. 'They do say that every cat is born into the world with nine lives.'

Conory was fondling the poor singed ears, and Shân, her fierceness now quite laid aside, was butting her head into the hollow of his hand and crooning to him. 'Then counting the day I found her, that should be leaving her six yet to run,' he said, speaking as lightly as Phaedrus had done.

Phaedrus squatted down beside him and looked questioningly into his face. 'How is it with you, now?'

'None so ill. What news is in the camp? It seems so long that I have been lying up here.'

'The first scout has come back with word of Liadhan's trail towards the Black Glen. I'm away after her now with three-score or so of our warriors. That counts what are left of the Companions.'

'How many *are* left of us? Of the Companions?' Conory asked after a moment.

'Seven, fit to ride, and you here.'

'I am sore at heart, to be missing this hunting.'

'We have hunted well together, these past months,' Phaedrus said.

And looking down into the pale, bright eyes that were so like Murna's despite the odd set of them, he thought suddenly of

how they had first met his across the heads of other men in the Cave of the Hunter, less than a year ago. Gods! Less than a year! And yet he seemed to have lived a whole lifetime since the night in that private room in the 'Rose of Paestum', almost as long since that first meeting with Conory—and the Roman world had gone away from him, small and remote and unreal as a scene reflected in a polished helmet. He remembered with sudden piercing clearness, how he had seen Conory then—a wasp-waisted creature with paint on its eyelids and strung glass beads on its wrists. And he had always thought himself a good judge of men! Fool that he had been not to see the tempered blade inside the fantastic silken sheath.

'If you should be back in Dun Monaidh ahead of me, tell Murna—tell Murna to be looking out for me. Remember, if the need be, I give them into your charge.'

Pain was pulling at the corners of Conory's mouth, but a trace of his old lazy smile was there too. 'Surely, I will tell her, but I do not think that she will need the telling. Be easy in your heart for Murna and the babe.'

Phaedrus put a hand on his shoulder and gripped it an instant, wordlessly—Shân watching the while with laid-back ears in case he meant some harm after all—then he scrambled to his feet and went back downstream to where the horses stood ready, too weary to stamp and fidget in their usual way, though not much more weary than the men who were to ride them.

They had trouble with the horses at the ford, for the smell of blood was strong there, and a raven, flapping up under the very nose of Finn's mount, sent the poor beast half wild with terror. But they got across at last, and turning aside from the trail of the main retreat, that was marked here and there by dead horses in the trampled grass, here and there by dead men, headed southwest to pick up the trail of the She-Wolf. It was Old Vron, riding ahead as he had been used to do with the pack-train, who found it first, and sat waiting for them to come up, then pointed out the hours' old horse-droppings. 'They had horses waiting on the other side,' he informed them with gloomy triumph.

The shadows were lengthening and they had come three or four Roman miles, pushing themselves and the weary horses to the very limit of endurance, when a darker shadow uncoiled itself from a tump of hill juniper, and came to meet them.

'*Sa, sa*—Baruch the Grass-Snake.' Phaedrus looked down at the little man standing at his horse's shoulder. 'What word?'

'I followed the She-Wolf and her pack till they were over the ridge yonder into the Black Glen.' He turned and pointed towards a lift of the high moors maybe a mile away. 'There, there was a camp of the Caledones, and King Bruide's Queen was waiting for her Lord. I lay hid under cover—there is good bracken cover and watched while she and Liadhan spoke together awhile. Then the first fringe of their beaten War Host came over the hill, and down to the camp, and then I heard her scream. It must have been when they told her her Lord was slain. She screamed and pulled out handfuls of her own hair. There began to be a great crowd, and I could not see what happened, nor hear anything that passed between her and Liadhan, but at last Liadhan came out from the throng in the Queen's own chariot and with her few priests riding about her, and with no one else at all—*aiee!* But the horses had terror on them! And when the Caledones harnessed up and turned northward again for the Druim Alban passes, they took the old chariot-way that leads south along the loch shore to the Red Crests' fort on the Cluta.'

With the muttered exclamation of the war band in his ears, Phaedrus said, 'A Roman fort! She could not be making for that!'

'There is no other place, I am thinking, that she could be making for, down *that* trail,' put in Old Vron, who had shared his master's special knowledge of the border hills.

'But—Light of the Sun! Liadhan to throw herself on the Red Crests' mercy!'

'And what can have parted her from the Caledones?'

Aluin asked the question, and grey-muzzled Dergdian answered it. 'Bruide who was her kinsman is dead. It is in my mind that left without a strong King, the Queen, maybe even

433

her people, may well feel that there is no room for another Goddess-on-Earth in the Cailleach's hunting-runs. I'd not put it past belief that Liadhan smells danger in that, too.'

'As I smell danger in her going to the Red Crests,' Phaedrus said harshly. 'Wherever she goes, she carries with her deadly danger to the Dalriads; and among the Red Crests, who do not know her, she will be fire in stubble.... Little Grass-Snake, get back again to Gault the Strong, and tell him all that you have just told me.' Then to the horsemen behind him, 'Come—it seems we have a clear trail to follow, anyway, but we must ride quickly on it.'

Towards evening, three days later, the little war band rode out from the thick breathless shadows of Coit Caledon, the Wood of the Caledones, and checked among the tangled thickets of hazel and elder that made up the forest verge, looking out across the emptiness of cleared land that shone tawny pale in the hazed sunlight, and up the steep tumble of thin grass and black outcrop to where the old fortress of Theodosia crouched on the crest of its great out-thrust rock above the waters of the Cluta. It might have been a further outcrop itself, it seemed so deeply rooted in its rock, with the white wing-flicker of the gulls rising and falling all about it. Even at that distance it had a half-deserted look, but Roman standards hung limp and straight in the still air above the Praetorian Gate, vivid as streaks of coloured flame against the sombre masses of storm-cloud piling up behind. And as Phaedrus sat his tired horse under the broad eaves of the forest verge, and looked up towards it with eyes narrowed against the glare, the brooding stillness was torn across by the sound of Roman trumpets that he had not heard for a year.

All their efforts to ride the She-Wolf down before she could reach the shelter of the old Naval Station had been hopeless from the start, for she had fresh horses, while their own poor beasts had been far spent before ever they began that ride. They had had to rest them again and again, and more than once they had had to lie close to avoid an Auxiliary patrol, which had not

made for speed. And so—Liadhan was safe behind Roman walls. And what now?

'What now?' Dergdian asked, like an echo of his own thoughts.

'We will try first, what the mere asking will do,' Phaedrus said, his gaze still on the distant gatehouse. 'That may at least tell us whether she is still within the fort.'

And so, when they urged the weary horses on again, each man carried his spear reversed, for a token that he came in peace; and Phaedrus, riding a little in advance, had broken a green branch from a wayfaring tree and carried it in his hand.

Trumpets sounded again, high above them, as they passed through the huddle of the small, native town at the foot of the rock and headed up the zigzag track beyond. And when Phaedrus let the red mare stumble to a halt—poor beast, he had no need to rein her in—before the high timber gate, the ramparts were manned on either side, and an Auxiliary Centurion looking down from the Guardhouse roof, demanded, 'Strangers, what is your business here?'

'To speak with your Commander.'

'And who would you think you are, to demand to speak with the Commander?'

'I am Midir, Lord of the Dalriads. I come in peace.' Phaedrus raised the green branch in his hand. 'But it would be well that the Commander come out to speak with me, none the less.'

'Midir of the Dalriads, d'ye say?'

Knowing that with Liadhan behind those walls, the name must have an effect one way or the other, he had gambled on it working in the way they needed. He could only hope that it was doing so, when the Centurion stared a moment, muttered something half under his breath, and disappeared. There was a quick barking of orders from within the gates, and then nothing more for a while.

He sat the red mare in the sultry sunlight, in the ditch causeway, reining her head up with a ruthless hand, and ignoring the sallies that the sentries on the ramparts did not suppose he understood, about One-Valley kings riding broken-winded nags and mistaking themselves for Caesar.

At last the sentries grew abruptly silent, and stood back, and a new head and shoulders appeared over the timber breastwork above him. A bronze helmet shimmered in the veiled sunlight and a red horsehair crest cut its own shape out of the heat-pearled sky; and under the forehead band was a thin, dark face with a nose too big for it, that he had seen before.

'Greeting to you, Midir of the Dalriads. You wish to speak with me across the Green Branch?'

Phaedrus spoke for the benefit of the sentries, in Latin very much purer than their own. 'Greeting to *you*, Commander. Did the mare make a good hunting-pony?'

The dark eyes suddenly alerted in the soldier's face, and he leaned forward across the breastwork. 'I have seen you before?'

'More than a year ago. I have somewhat changed, maybe.' Phaedrus, meeting the questioning stare that had no recognition in it, was sharply aware of that change, the fine bronze-hilted dirk at his side, the tattooed device that was almost like a four-petalled flower on his forehead, half hidden by the blurred traces of war-paint, the great knotted scar that made havoc of one side of his face. 'I was a pack-driver of Sinnoch the Merchant's, and you were Captain of a troop of Frontier Wolves. Quick promotion, Commander.'

'So-o, I remember. And now you are King of the Dalriads? Quick promotion, my Lord Midir; but by the look of you it did not come without fighting.'

'It did not come without fighting. When we last met, I was on my road north to win back the kingship that Liadhan, my father's half-sister, robbed me of when he died. I have fought for it; and many others fought with me, to free Earra-Ghyl from the She-Wolf. And we had the victory. But *she* escaped to the Caledones, and brought war between them and us, and now that her welcome among them grows thin, she escapes again, to take refuge under the shadow of the Eagles.'

'It is a good story, but what has it to do with me?'

'It has this to do with you, that you hold the She-Wolf even now within your gates, and I come to demand her return.'

The dark gaze flickered over the little band of tattered and

grey-weary riders. 'You should bring a greater War Host with you when you come demanding to the gates of a Roman fort.'

'There will be more of us in a while and a while,' Phaedrus said with cool affrontery.

'Then demand again, when you have enough men behind you to back your demand.'

'You refuse, then?'

'I refuse to hand over, merely because some usurping adventurer bids me, a Queen who has thrown herself upon the protection of Rome.'

Rage rose scalding as vomit into Phaedrus's throat, and he swallowed it, knowing that an angry swordsman was too often one with the edge of his skill blunted. 'I am no usurper!' (He had quite forgotten that that was exactly what he was.) 'I am my father's only son. This woman seized the rule, even as I told you, when he died. She would have had me slain, but that I— escaped—and for seven years she has ruled my people unlawfully and according to ways that were hateful to them. Therefore they rose against her at last, and I—came back to lead them. Does that make me the usurper?'

'It was not so that the Queen told it,' said Titus Hilarian.

'Would she be likely to come to you for shelter with the truth—*that* truth—on her tongue?'

'Maybe not.' The Fort Commander settled his elbows on the parapet and leaned forward conversationally. 'But even supposing that every word of this tale of yours is true, why trouble to hound her farther? You have your kingship back. She does not stand between you and the Sun. And myself, I'd say vengeance was inclined to be a waste of time.'

'While she lives she is the Shadow of Death over the Dalriads.' (No use to say, 'You do not know her as you did not know Cartimandua, a hundred years ago. You do not know that if you keep her, you will listen to her, and as sure as there is thunder coming, you will find yourselves marching north one day to set her back in the Royal Seat, and believing that the peace of the Frontier depends on it.' You could only say, 'She is the Shadow of Death over the Dalriads,' and leave it at that.)

The Commander straightened from the breastwork, and stood looking down at the horsemen below him, his mouth turning straight and hard. 'All that is nothing to Rome. Let the tribes beyond the Pale fight out their own feuds. The Queen has appealed to the protection of Rome, and until the Legate bids me give her up to you, I shall not do so. Is it understood?'

There was a long silence, and in the distance a low mutter of thunder quivered along the skyline.

Then Phaedrus said, 'It is understood,' and dashed the wayfaring branch to the ground. He brought the mare round in a plunging turn, snorting from the savage jab of his heel, and the bit tearing at her mouth. 'Away!'

There was no more talking to be done.

18

The Whistler in the Dark Woods

GUIDED by Old Vron they holed up for the night in a shallow valley, where a burn that had barely enough water to cover its stones wound out through the low-lying forest to join Baal's River on its way past Theodosia to the Firth of Cluta. And at dusk Phaedrus and the old fore-rider cut southward through the woods and marshes to the coast, and worked their way in for a closer look at the seaward side of the place. Theodosia had been a great Naval Station once, in the time of Agricola when the patrol galleys had come and gone as regularly as shuttles in a loom, up and down the Firth of Cluta; and the size of the old fort crouched on its crag above the empty docks and weed-grown slipways told its own tale of past power. Now, clearly, it was no more than an outpost fort for the Northern Wall, but strong, still. Phaedrus doubted bitterly whether there would be much that they could do against it, even when Gault brought up what

was left of the War Host. And as he watched the towering rock mass turn black and menacing against the coppery sunset far across the pale waters of the Firth, where the low shore-line of Valentia lay like a bank of mist, a beacon fire sprang up from the Roman Signal Station. Theodosia might be far from the nearest fortress on the Wall, but it was in close touch across the water.

Back in the glen where the hobbled ponies had lain themselves down too tired even to graze, the war band had made a fire. The Red Crests would know well enough that they had not simply ridden out of the district, so it seemed best to make no pretences at secrecy. They ate the last of the meat, which by now was stinking. Tomorrow and the next day they could keep going on the strips of smoked deer-meat and the last of the stir-about. After that, if the thing still dragged on, they would have to turn hunter—in a countryside that looked to have been long since hunted all but bare by the Red Crests.

Now Phaedrus sprawled on one elbow by the fire, his thoughts ranging loosely, as the thoughts of a man will when he is too tired to keep them on any one thing. Faces came and went through his mind: Murna's, and Conory's, and Sinnoch's dead face with that look of wry amusement as though at a bad jest; the dark face under the horsehair crest looking down at him from the ramparts of Theodosia. ... Sinnoch had said that he would command a fort before he was thirty, unless he was dead in a bog or broken for going too much his own way. But it was odd to see him again like this—as though the strange past year were coming full circle back to its starting-place again. Some pattern being completed, each loose end carefully secured as it was finished with, as the women fastened off each colour as it was done with, at the end of a pattern on the loom. And then he thought of Murna's face again, and the way her hair smelt when it was wet. ...

Midway between sleeping and waking, he heard something— a little plaintive whistling among the trees below the camp that might almost be the call of some night bird; almost, but not quite. Still half asleep, he cocked a listening ear. And as he listened, the whistling came again. It was the five-note call that

440

he and Midir had used as a signal to each other in that shared month in the Onnum Cock-loft!

Now he was wide awake and listening with every nerve in his body. The call came again, softly insistent, and the faces of the others in the fire-light told him that they heard it too. Finn's hand was stealing to his dirk, and he was up on one knee; others were making the same move. 'Spy!' somebody whispered.

Phaedrus sprang to his feet. 'Fools! Would a spy come whistling so near our fire. That is a call—and for me.'

'Whose call?' Dergdian demanded tersely.

'A friend's—or a friend's ghost.'

'Leave it alone, Lord.' Brys's face was sharp with sudden fear for his Lord. 'It is not healthy to answer such calls!'

And Old Vron grunted in agreement. 'The boy is in the right of it—I remember when I was a young man——'

But Phaedrus was away, heading down the slippery grass slope that dropped away into the trees. Ahead of him, the call sounded again, farther off, as though whoever—whatever—it was that called had heard him coming and moved back. It was a dark night, seeming all the darker for the brief flicker of lightning from time to time far off among the hills, the old moon not yet risen, and a thin thunder-wrack covering the stars; and once among the trees, Phaedrus could scarcely see his hand before his face. These were no thin birch and hazel woods such as those of Earra-Ghyl, but the dense black fleece of forest that covered all the low country from the great hills of Valentia northward into the unknown; damp-oak forest, thicketed with yew and holly, and on the north skirts of the hills the tall, whispering pines. An ancient forest that seemed to Phaedrus to be watching with hostile eyes that could see in the dark like Shân's. Low-hanging branches whipped his face, and time and again he blundered into a tree-trunk or stumbled into a hole left by the up-torn roots of some long-fallen giant; and always, whenever he checked to listen, the call came again, as far ahead as ever. It was leading him farther and farther from the camp. But he had no doubts—whether it was by some strange and almost unbelievable chance, Midir ahead of him, or Midir's

441

ghost, this following through the dark woods was some part of the pattern that was being worked out.

The slope of the land had levelled out beneath his feet, and he could hear the small drought voice of the burn very close in the darkness; and at last he came out on to the bank just where it spread into a chain of pools and the tail of the last pool ran out into Baal's River.

It was at that moment that he suddenly knew that the whistler was no longer far ahead, but close beside him. It was no sound or movement, just the sense of somebody there in the darkness, within arm's reach of him. He whipped round, and in doing so caught his foot in an arched root, and almost pitched headlong down the bank. He recovered himself, cursing under his breath, and something that was only a denser darkness moved close by, and he heard the merest breath of a laugh.

'A blind man has the advantage in the dark.'

'*Midir!* Is it you indeed?—of your ghost?'

'Did you think it might be my ghost, then?'

'I—was not sure.'

'Yet you came.'

'I came.'

Hands came out of the darkness and fastened on his shoulders in the old familiar way; and they were warm and strong with life, as Phaedrus put his own up to cover them. 'Feel. No ghost,' Midir said.

After the first few moments, their meeting again had slipped into place so that Phaedrus felt it to be something not at all surprising, that had simply been waiting for them in the future, until the time came for it to happen. He still did not know whether he liked Midir, and he still knew that that did not matter, that far down at the root of things, they belonged together, as though perhaps they had been meant to come into the world as one person and had somehow got split up and come into it as two.

He said, 'But I do not understand. How do you come to be here?'

'You were easy enough to follow from the fort—I heard the way you went, and that gave me the start of the trail. Tired horses smell strong, and I had the smoke of your fire to guide me the last part of my way.'

'*Sa*, that I see, but I was meaning how do you come to be north of the Wall?'

'My old master died, and still needing to eat now and then, I set out to find work for myself. Also I'd a mind to gain tidings if I could, of how this matter of the Horse Lord went, after we had taken so great pains with it. I came to Theodosia. There is always a welcome for a good leather-worker, wherever the Red Crests are. They were glad to see me in these parts.' Midir's tone changed. 'And you? You are the Horse Lord sure enough—ach, I know: news travels on the wind in these parts. Beside, if the

443

thing had gone against you, you would have been unpleasantly dead long before this, instead of standing here under my hands. ... But it seems that you have not yet taken my vengeance for me, as you promised.'

'I will take it yet,' Phaedrus said.

'Maybe. Or maybe I will take it for myself, after all.' There was a cold lingering softness in his voice that made something crawl in Phaedrus's belly. But when Midir spoke again, his voice sounded as usual. 'But I am wasting time, when there is little enough to spare. Listen, Phaedrus. The Fort Commander has sent word to the Signal Station across the Firth—the boat went at dusk. He has asked for a swift rowing-galley and an escort from the Wallsend Fort. And on tomorrow's night-tide, they will send her across into Valentia.'

'How do you know?'

'Now you sound like a Red Crest. The British town that huddles under a fort generally knows more than the Fort Commander supposes.'

Phaedrus was silent a moment, then he burst out, 'Fiends and Furies! I had hoped that they would at least have held her until some word came from the Legate or the Governor!'

'It is in my mind that the Commander, Titus Hilarian, seeks to get her away quickly lest the Frontier goes up in flames with her still on his hands.'

Phaedrus was watching the pale swirl of the water. 'The thing that is clear beyond all else,' he said at last, 'is that Liadhan must never set foot on board that galley.'

'How many spears are there with you?'

'Three-score, more or less.'

'Not enough. Where is the rest of the War Host?'

Not at home eating honey-cakes!' Phaedrus was up in arms on the instant to defend his own. 'Dead, a good few of them. All summer we have been fighting; did *that* word not reach you? Three days since, we fought—*aiee!* quite a battle, and after, I could scarcely find three-score fit to bestride a horse, to ride this trail with me. Gault is bringing on all that he can raise, so soon as they and the horses can tell night from day, but flesh and

blood is flesh and blood, for all the heart that's in it. I doubt that they can be here for two days yet!'

Midir said softly, 'Yes! I was right, I was right! Assuredly you are the Horse Lord, Phaedrus, my brother.'

'At all events I sometimes catch myself believing that I am.' For an instant memory flickered up in Phaedrus, of the little Dark Chieftain and his magic. 'Do you think that I am not the Horse Lord?' he had said; and the little man had replied: 'I do not know. But when you see that feather again, you will be.' But it was gone at once, leaving no more trace than the golden plover's feather in the narrow dark hand.

For a long moment there was no sound between them save the liquid running of the burn and the small night-time stirrings of the forest.

Then Phaedrus said abruptly, 'For the thing that must be done, I am thinking that one man might stand a better chance than a whole War Host.'

'Two men, anyway,' Midir said, and from his tone, Phaedrus knew that he had been thinking along the same lines.

'Two?'

Another silence. Then Midir broke it, speaking in short quick bursts with long pauses between, as though he were thinking the thing out as he went along. 'Listen now; this could be the way of it. The galleys will not put in until well after dark and if they will wait for dark to put in, that can only mean that they intend sailing again before dawn. At dusk, you must send in——' He checked. 'Have you a good dirk-thrower with you?'

Phaedrus's mind had caught the direction now. 'One or two,' he said, and then, 'One, at least.'

'Sa; at dusk, then, send him in. In the general run of things, they do not keep guards down there; there's not much to guard, in empty galley sheds and broken-down jetties, and they'd find it none so easy if they tried, with the town spreading into the dockyard all along the northern edge of the harbour and the fisherfolk storing their nets in the ruins, and no man to say where one begins and the other ends. But it is in my mind they'll have a guard posted tomorrow night!'

'And how does our dirk-thrower get through?'

'Ach—I leave that to you—to him. Choose a man who is used to stalking game, and he'll find a way through.'

'So. And then?'

'There's only one way down the rock on the seaward side—very steep—so steep at the bottom that it ends in a wooden stair. They must bring her that way; even the Red Crests would not be fool enough to take her out by the Praetorian Gate and half-circle round through the town. There are the remains of store-sheds and the like close up to the stair foot on the north side—good enough cover, well within knife range. Let your man lie up there, and when she comes to the foot of the stair—they are bound to have a torch or two to light her down—that will be the time for him to throw—and to pray that he throws straight!'

There was a little silence; and in the midst of the silence, somewhere away in the trees, the small, sharp sound of a snapping twig.

The two froze as they stood, hearts suddenly racing. 'What was that?' Phaedrus whispered, and the other's hand tightened on his shoulder.

'Listen.'

For what seemed an hour, they stood listening, every nerve on the stretch. But there was nothing more to hear but the little night-time rustlings and sighings of the woods behind them. At last Midir let his breath go with a little sigh. 'Nothing.'

'I will be going to make sure.'

'How?' Midir said.

No, there was no way of making sure—and no need, he had heard such little, sharp, unexplained sounds often before now. 'The dry summer has made the forest noisy with dead twigs.'

They listened a moment longer, all the same, then returned urgently to the point where they had broken off.

'I'd not say it was a good plan,' Phaedrus said, 'but it's possible, and I can't think of a better. It has one sore spot in it, though—it will be death to the man with the dirk.'

'Surely, if he were alone. That is where the second man comes in—to draw off the hunt.'

'I was forgetting about the second man,' Phaedrus said. 'Well, do I send him in with the other?'

'*Na, you* do not send him in at all. I shall wander in to talk with the fishermen when they bring in the catch at evening—it won't be the first time—and find means to go to ground until the time comes.'

'You?' Phaedrus said.

'Why not? They will not see my face when I run from them. I know that ground well; with luck I shall lead them a fair way before I fall over anything—maybe farther than they will go themselves; torches are unsure light for a chase. They will not know me until they capture me, for the blind leather-worker from the town.'

'And when they do capture you?'

'I shall have a fine excuse. See now: I went down to talk with the fishermen and bargain for a fish for my supper. I was tired, and the air thunder heavy; and I crawled into a corner and fell asleep. The sudden uproar woke me, and I was frightened. A sudden uproar is a frightening thing to a blind man, my Phaedrus—and I ran.'

'It holds together,' Phaedrus said slowly.

'Surely, it holds together.'

'But it would be madness for you to try it, Midir—don't you see——'

Midir cut in. 'No, I don't see—I don't see; that's what you mean, isn't it? You are not believing that I can do the thing, because I am blind! I know what I can do, better than you can! If any man of yours does it, he will die; there is no escape round the south side of the rock. But I can do it and like enough live to tell the tale—not that that greatly interests me just now. ... Also, it is my right. My *right* to have a small share in my own vengeance, and maybe a small share in saving the tribe also.' He broke off, and added in a tone of deliberate lightness, 'It is strange that I should trouble about that. Long ago I ceased to feel that I belong to them. But I still do not want to see the Dalriads trampled into the mud.'

'Just as I have come to feel that I belong to them, and they to

447

me. I also would not see the Dalriads go down.' Phaedrus broke off, and was silent a moment. 'Come then, and take your rightful share.' And checked again. 'I am not liking it, this slaying-in-the-dark, but it must be done; it is her life or the tribe's—*it must be done!*'

'It must be done,' Midir said.

A low, long-drawn mutter of thunder trembled into the silence. The woods seemed to have grown very still, and in the stillness the voice of the burn sounded unnaturally loud. 'The storm is coming,' Midir said. 'Phuh! There is no air to breathe.'

'It is as though the woods knew it—and were waiting.'

They stood together, a short while longer, quickly going over the few remaining details, then parted without any leave-taking, Midir turning back towards the bothy-town that huddled at the foot of Theodosia Rock, Phaedrus heading up the glen once more.

Another thread of the finishing pattern had been woven into place.

It was not until he caught the first flicker of the watch fire through the trees, that he realized that Midir had asked no word of anyone, not even of Conory. He was puzzled for the moment, and then he understood that here, so near his own people, who were so completely lost to him, his only hope lay in not asking, not wanting to know. 'Long ago I ceased to feel that I belong to them,' he had said; and that was his armour.

He whistled to warn the Companions of his coming and men were afoot and faces turned to him as he came into the fire-light. Finn began a question, and then stopped; no one else spoke, but the question was in all their faces, and Phaedrus answered it. 'No, no ghost. An old friend of mine who I did not know was north of the Wall—a leather-worker in the town, who slipped out with news for me.'

'Why did he not come up to the camp?' Dergdian asked.

'Maybe he had no wish to risk getting caught up with the War Host of the Dalriads; it was only me that he had his news for.' Phaedrus squatted down on his haunches well back from the fire, but near enough for the smoke to keep the midges away;

and sitting with his arms folded across his knees, told them of what had passed between himself and Midir—or at least as much of it as they needed to know.

When he came to the end, Dergdian, the oldest and most cautious among them, said, 'It is in my mind to wonder what price the Red Crests may demand, for the slaying of a Goddess under their protection.'

Phaedrus had thought of that, too. 'Liadhan means little to the Red Crests, and her slaying will mean little, save that by it we shall have set their authority at nought, and that they will *not* like. . . . If the luck runs our way, they may never even be able to prove that the dirk came from the Dalriads. If they do, they will maybe march north to teach us more respect for our betters. Then we shall drive off the cattle and horse-herds—giving thanks to Lugh Shining Spear that we are not a corn-growing people rooted to our fields—and take to the hills and islands, and play wolf-pack on their flanks until winter turns them south again. They may burn down a hall here and there, but thatch and turf and timber are none so hard to replace; at the worst, they may burn off what they can of the pasture. But there's rain coming soon. When the storm breaks, the weather will break with it. If Liadhan lives and has her way with them, if they march north to thrust her back into the Royal Place and hold her there with their swords, as they did in the earlier days for that other She-Wolf Cartimandua, that will be another—a darker, story.'

All round the fire, men's voices answered him quick and fierce, eyes red-sparked with an old anger above the rims of their shields.

'*Sa*, it is well thought out,' Dergdian said. 'Then it seems there is only one question left to settle: who is the best dirk-thrower among us?'

The Companions glanced at each other. Niall began, 'I——'

But Phaedrus said, 'I am.' He looked round at them in the firelight. 'The throwing-knife is not really our weapon, here in the North, but one learns strange skills in the Gladiators' School.'

Niall said quickly, 'My Lord Midir, I did not learn it in the Gladiators' School, but I've a fair aim with a dirk, none the less. Let me go.'

'No.' Phaedrus said. He looked at face after protesting face. 'I am the best dirk-thrower round this fire tonight; it is as simple as that. Also—this is a matter between Liadhan and me.'

'It is between Liadhan and all of us,' Finn said.

'But since we cannot all settle it with her, it is right that the King should settle it for the rest.'

'It is not fitting work for the King.'

'It is not fitting work for any man. But one man must do it, and only the King can do it for the whole tribe.'

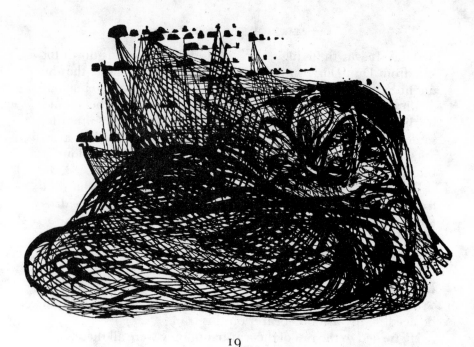

19

The Dirk-Thrower

WHEN dawn came the threatening storm had still not broken. A little wind had got up, brushing fitfully through the tree-tops, but there was no freshness in it. And the sense of coming storm made Phaedrus feel increasingly, as the day dragged by, that if anyone touched him he would give off sparks like a cat.

Thunder was grumbling again in the distance, when the time came for him to make ready, but they had heard it more than once that day, and each time it had gone away again. This time it would probably do the same. He hoped so, much as he longed for the relief of its coming, for a thunderstorm in the next few hours might complicate and confuse things hopelessly. He put on his war-tattered cloak, partly because he could pull the loose hood forward over his head if he needed to hide his face, partly with a certain feeling for the fitness of things; in a way, a play-actor's feeling for the shape of the pattern that he was

making. It was the King's cloak. Brys had brought it down for him from Dun Dara on the night they fired Glen Croe, that he might not go into battle without it. Now he was going out against Liadhan for what, he knew, one way or the other would be the last time. And he flung on the cloak as though for battle, settled the folds at the shoulder to give free play to his right arm, and thrust in the great bronze war-brooch with its splendour of blue and green enamel.

Brys, who had been standing by, came forward with his dirk freshly burnished and whetted to a razor keenness. Phaedrus took it and felt the edge with his thumb, then nodded. 'Sa, sa! With this, one could draw blood from the wind!' and slipped it silkenly into the deer-skin sheath at his belt.

'Take me with you!' Brys said, suddenly and desperately. 'My Lord Midir—let me come with you!'

Phaedrus touched the boy's shoulder kindly enough. 'I'll not be needing my armour-bearer on this trail.'

He turned to the rest of the war band; they were all there, save for the two who were watching the river fords against the time when Gault came seeking them. He had already given them their orders, that they were to bide here, no man coming with him save Old Vron as far as the forest verge, that there might be no target of moving men large enough to catch the eye of any Red Crest scouts, and whatever happened, there was to be no attack on the fort, even when Gault came with the War Host. In their present weakened state, once they lifted a spear against the fort, they were done for. He could only hope that he had got that through to them, knowing as he did, the hotness of their heads and the little skill they had in counting the cost. Dergdian understood, at all events. He could trust Dergdian to hold this lot, anyway, in leash.

They sacrified to Lugh Shining Spear together, the small, quick sacrifice of barley meal, moistened with a few drops of blood from each warrior's thumb, which the Sun Lord accepted when there was no living sacrifice to be had—for at a time like this, no God worth praying to could even wish for one of the horses.

And when that was done, there was nothing more to hold Phaedrus from his setting out.

They watched him go in silence, no one raising a protesting voice. All that had been finished with, last night. If the Sun Lord willed it, he would come back; if not, then the Mark was on his forehead. Either way, it was the King's trail and no one else's; between him and Liadhan, between him and the High Gods, and they had accepted that it was so.

It was already dusk when he came with Old Vron to the edge of the woods, close to the place where the ancient chariot road forded Baal's River. An unnaturally early dusk under a piled tumult of blue-black clouds, their underbellies stained here and there with dull copper light from the unseen westering sun. The storm had held off so far, but it was churning round them in closing circles; not long now, Phaedrus thought, before it broke.

He whispered to the shadow in the battered sheepskin hat beside him, 'Wait here and watch till I am well into the bothies; then back with you, and tell them that all goes well so far.'

The old fore-rider grunted by way of reply, a grunt which might mean anything. Phaedrus waited for no more, but slipped out from the gloom of the wood shore and down through the low-growing scrub to the Chariot road.

There was no walled or hedged cantonment at Theodosia, the steep rise of the rock left no space for more than the fort itself on the crest, and the more level ground below it was too far outside the Wall for bath-house and married quarters and granaries. Only a huddle of native bothies had sprung up along the foot of the rock on its landward side, with a wine-shop thrown in for good measure. And being in a kind of no-man's land—for within a day's trail of the Northern Wall the old tribal territories had not much meaning save in time of war—it was a place through which the rags of many tribes came and went. And so there was no encircling dyke with its gateway stopped at twilight by the night-time thorn-bush, and Phaedrus loped in by the track that turned from the chariot road, like a man at the end of a journey, without let or hindrance of any kind. Neither men nor hounds

took any especial notice of him, as they would have done of a stranger in a tribal dun, as he made his way between the crowding bothies, keeping always well clear of the fire-light that shone here and there through hut doorways or from little courtyards. If any man spoke to him or even looked at him hard, he was going to ask for the wine-shop, which he knew from Midir lay in the right direction; but no one did. It was all very easy—almost too easy....

He passed quite close to the wine-shop and saw the smoking light of oil-lamps spilling from the doorway, and heard a sudden burst of singing, that brought back with a vivid flash of memory the dark streets and crowded wine-shops of Corstopitum.

> 'Six poor soldiers, marching home from Gaul,
> Five centurions, bully-big and tall.
> Four brave Legates, who never saw a fight;
> Three grave Senators, to set the world to right.
> Two wise Consuls, going out to dine,
> But one shall be our Emperor, and pay for the wine.'

They had sung the same counting-out song to slightly different words in the Gladiators' School, and with the same clamouring of someone's name at the end—the name of whoever was to be Emperor and stand treat for the rest....

Phaedrus left the lighted doorway behind him, and walked on. There was beginning to be a different smell in the air, the smell of salt-water mingling with the stink of the little, dirty town. And he became suddenly aware of the crying of gulls made restless by the coming storm. The bothes began to thin out, and gleams of fire- or lamplight became fewer and more far between, and he knew that the time had come for going still more cautiously.

A short way farther—and he dropped to his belly in the black gloom between a store-shed wall and a ragged pile of driftwood, and lay flat, looking out across a patch of open ground, hearing the tramp—tramp—tramp of a sentry's feet, coming closer—closer—and dying away again. He could see the man, a dark

bulk in the deepening dusk, moving steadily across the open space, and before his footsteps had died away into the lap of water and the crying of the gulls, the footsteps of another sentry took up the beat, a second dark figure crossed the open space, turned, and paced back; and a few moments later the first man had reappeared. Midir had been quite right; the fringes of the old dockyard were being patrolled.

Phaedrus lay still for what seemed a long time, watching and listening, while the lightning flickered closer, showing him the pacing figures with acid clarity every now and then, trying to decide what point in that steady passing and re-passing would give him his best chance. And gradually he found that though both sentries were within sound all the while, there was one moment in each turn when one sentry had his back to him and the other's sight was blanked by the corner of what looked like a derelict sail-loft. Still he waited, getting the timing by heart, and found that it never varied; every time there was the one blind moment, just long enough, he reckoned, to get him across, but with certainly nothing to spare.

The next time it came, he got to his feet and slipped forward to the very last nail's breadth of his shelter, then froze, crouching like a runner before a race, while the second sentry came up and passed, turned and passed again, and the first returned. This time, the instant the man's back was towards him, he loosed forward like an arrow from a bow. His soft raw hide brogues made no more sound than bare feet on the sunbaked earth. The open space seemed all at once appallingly wide, the dusk still appallingly thin, and he could hear the footsteps of the second sentry—in another heartbeat he would round the corner of the derelict sail-loft.

He just made it, and as the man came into view, dropped beside a dark pile of nets against the sail-loft wall and lay still, praying that no lighting flash would betray him, praying that the sentry would not look that way and notice that the pile of nets was bigger than it had been before. The footsteps came on, close, closer—passed without checking. A few moments later Phaedrus was oozing forward again, into a narrow alleyway

between the sail-loft and the gutted shell of another building. Sand and shingle had drifted deep in the narrow space, and dry, dagger-sharp dune-thistles had seeded themselves thickly along the wall. The dry rustling of them sounded so loud in his ears every time he moved that it seemed it must bring the Red Crests down upon him every instant; but at the end of the building the sand-drift ceased and he knew with an almost sick relief that he was clear, through the patrol line. But he had no means of knowing whether there were more guards about, and his heart was still drubbing against his breastbone as he worked his way forward with agonizing caution through the wilderness of dere-lict buildings and rotting, weed-grown jetties. At last he found himself crouching in the doorway of a half-roofless store-shed of some kind, close in to the great upthrust of rock that towered over him like some vast menacing beast about to strike; and saw in the faint lightning-flicker, the wooden steps at the foot of the zigzag track from the fort above. Looking far up, as the lightning flickered again, beyond the rock ledges cushioned with the dry brown ghosts of sea-pinks, he saw the head of the track where it swerved up the last steep stretch, and the harsh outline of the fort against the sky; and at the southern end, where the rocks dropped almost sheer into the sea, he saw the out-thrust catapult platform from which in the old days, the great stone-hurler batteries must have covered the entrance to the anchorage and dockyard.

There had been no sign of the galley alongside the one serviceable jetty, or even of a stern brazier out to sea; but it was not quite full dark yet. He had a long wait ahead of him. He put his hand to his dirk, and felt that it was loose and easy in the sheath. Now that he was so near to the thing, he felt curiously empty, as though everything had been drained out of him except the knowledge of what he had to do. He did not even feel anything about that; he only knew, very clearly, inside the cold echoing emptiness of his own head, that he had come to kill Liadhan, and how, and why. Presently, he would feel again, but not now.

He whistled softly, not the old five-note call, which was too obviously man-made, but the high thin 'Pee-Wheet' of a plover,

twice repeated, which was the agreed signal. No answer came. Only the fretful gulls still wheeled crying about the face of the rock, only the lap of water and the low mutter of thunder like the first distant waking of the wolfskin war-drums.

Was Midir not there yet? Had something gone wrong? He whistled once again, and even as he did so, heard a stir of movement behind him. His hand was on his dirk but before he could whip round he felt a numbing blow on the back of his neck, and pitched forward into a darkness that buzzed and roared and was full of shooting-stars.

It seemed to him that he never quite lost consciousness, but was aware of a vast army of hands dragging and wrenching at him, and hollow booming voices at a great distance all the while. But he was trapped in a kind of half consciousness like a swimmer trapped by weed below the surface of the water. He fought against it, heart hammering and blood roaring in his ears, and broke surface at last, to find that his hands were bound behind him and he was already being manhandled up the wooden stair. He began to struggle, and somebody struck him across the mouth with a hand that had a heavy ring on it, saying with a curse, 'That's enough of that!' And he gave up struggling for the present. It was useless anyhow.

So—he was in the hands of men from the fort. He had walked into a trap—fool and double fool that he was! But who had set the trap and who had sprung it? Confusedly, through the swimming and throbbing of his head, he remembered the stick that had snapped in the summer-dry forest!

But who?—Who? That did not matter now; there was something else—someone——The sudden remembrance shot through him, bringing him back to full consciousness with a crash. If he had been betrayed, then so had Midir! Midir! What had become of Midir?

As the little knot of Frontier Wolves, with Phaedrus stumbling in their midst, started up the steep track that ended at the Water Gate of Theodosia Fort, Midir was breaking out of the small, strong lock-up behind the main guardhouse.

20

The Hostage

THE Decurion on guard had ordered a small lamp to be left
burning in a niche high on the lock-up wall, so that they could
keep an eye on their prisoner through the grill in the door, for he
seemed so crazily violent that he might be up to any lunacy. The
Decurion had known such a man bite through his own wrists
before now, and bleed to death under the noses of the guards,
and he wasn't taking any chances. The Commander had
ordered the man to be kept close till morning and brought up for
questioning again, and kept close and brought up for questioning, he was going to be.

Midir, exploring his prison by smell and delicate sense of
touch, had found the lamp within a hundred heartbeats of there
being no more heavy breathing behind the bars of the door-
squint. When he knew exactly where it was, so that he could
reach it in an instant from any part of the cell, he began
hammering on the door and yelling. Presently someone came

458

and cursed him, and he quietened for a short while, and then returned to his hammering and shouting. As time went by, the shouts became a hoarse raging, rose above the nearing storm on a growing note of hysteria, a howling that sounded more like a rabid wolf than a man—and then fell suddenly and ominously silent.

That silence fetched the Decurion at a hurried march, with one of the guards tramping behind him. When he looked through the grill, he saw the prisoner with the lamp in his hands, seemingly in the act of setting fire to his bedding straw. The Decurion shouted at him not to be a fool, cursed the Auxiliary for not having brought a torch, as he fumbled an instant with the padlock, and slammed up the door bar.

At sound of the voice and the rattle of the key in the padlock, Midir turned a wild face towards the doorway, and seemed to hesitate. Then as the door crashed open and hobnailed feet pounded towards him, he pinched out the little flame and tossed the lamp aside, and springing up, side-stepped from the line of the suddenly stumbling rush.

There was a startled shout, a curse, and then more feet. Two to one, but as he had said to Phaedrus, a blind man has the advantage in the dark. There were a few moments of chaos. Somebody pitched over his out-thrust leg, and crashing head foremost into the opposite wall, crumpled down it with a grunt. Midir's hands found a man's throat and closed on it, and his thumbs jabbed upward at the pulse under the angle of the jaw.

Next instant he was outside, the door slammed behind him. He felt for and found the bar and dropped it into place. There was a groan and the sound of somebody retching their heart up, as he turned away in search of a hiding-place—a search in which a blind man did *not* have the advantage. However, he reckoned it would be a little while before there was any serious outcry from the lock-up to lead to the discovery of his escape.

It would be too late to warn Phaedrus, but if he could escape recapture, there might be something he could do—he didn't know what but something—when they brought their second prisoner in. And even as he set off up what seemed to be an

THE MARK OF THE HORSE LORD

alleyway between high sounding buildings, a smother of voices and the clear-cut orders of an officer sounded across the fort from the direction of the gate that gave on to the old water stair. And all was swallowed up in a whiplash crack of thunder and a long hollow booming as the storm that had circled them so long burst full overhead.

He heard hurrying feet, men brushed past him, all going one way, tossing a word or a question from one to another, and he went with them, partly because he did not have much choice, partly because he guessed the meaning of the sudden stir, keeping his head well down, for somewhere not far off, he smelled the resin smoke of a pine-knot torch.

To Phaedrus, sagging between his captors, in the open space inside the sea-gate, that clap of thunder seemed part of the dizzy roaring inside his own head. Vaguely, he was aware of torches, and the jink of torchlight on bronze, and faces pressing in, all eyes and mouths, and he was confronting the Duty Centurion. 'So our friend in the fox-face hat *was* telling the truth!' the Centurion was saying. 'Bring him up to the Praetorian, the Commander wants a word with him.' Then, rounding on the crowding Auxiliaries, 'All right, you lot, get back to your barrack rows; there's nothing more to see here.'

A flash of lightning cut like a knife between earth and heaven, picking out every detail of the scene with a blue-white glare, and the thunder broke with a coughing roar, like the War Song of the wolfskin drums, as the onlookers began to melt away.

But the Centurion was wrong, for as the white whip-crack of lightning came again, suddenly the challenge of the sentry sounded from the ramparts. 'Who comes?'

And a woman's clear, scornful voice answered, 'The Queen of the Dalriads.'

And Phaedrus, wrenching round in the hands of his captors, saw in the white flicker that was now almost incessant, the tall triumphant figure of Liadhan standing at the head of the rampart stair, looking down at him. Strange to think that this was only the third time he had ever seen her. She had been so

much part of his life, this past year. ... She seemed something that belonged to the storm; the lightning made a silver wild-fire of her hair, and the lightning was in her eyes. 'I came to see this—this *thing* that would have called itself Horse Lord and King of the Dalriads in my stead; this *thing* that tonight would have slain me, who am the Goddess-on-Earth!' And she laughed until her laughter was swallowed up in the echoing crash of the thunder.

There was a moment of utter blackness, for after the lightning the flare of the torches was not so much light as a red flowering of the dark. And in the dark, Phaedrus sensed rather than saw something move in towards the foot of the rampart, and cast about oddly, like a hound seeking for a lost scent, until it came to the steps.

It was half-way up when the Decurion of the Gate Guard saw it, and started forward, shouting, 'Here! You——'

The figure flung itself forward and up, and seemed to reach the rampart-walk at a bound. And in that instant the lightning flared again, and Phaedrus saw that it was Midir.

Liadhan saw, too. Her eyes stared in her head, and her mouth opened to a cry. '*Midir!*' But the name was blurred in her throat, and in the tumult and confusion of the storm, no one save Midir himself, and Phaedrus standing rigid in the grip of his captors, knew what name she cried.

Midir spoke softly, bitterly mocking; and in the instant of prickling silence before the next thunder-peal, every word came clear to those below. 'Goddess-on-Earth, it was not wise to cry out,' and sprang towards her. She flinched back and turned to run, with death close at her heels.

The instant's stillness exploded into action. Men were running from all directions. The Commander's voice cut through the tumult. 'Spear! Bring him down!' A flung spear missed the blind man by a thumb's breadth and thudded into the rampart timbers—but it was scarcely possible to believe in those moments that he *was* blind. Men were closing in on him, racing along the ramparts, up the rampart steps; another spear actually grazed his shoulder, and falling, tripped the man behind him

and brought him sprawling down, causing an instant's confusion, and in that instant, Midir's outstretched hand found a
fold of Liadhan's mantle, and then his arms were fast round her.
In the gloom it was as though the two figures far along the
rampart fused into one. Liadhan screamed again and again, like
a trapped hare.

Then a searing flash split the night in two. For a long moment
the whole sky was one flickering blast of greenish light that
seemed to blind and dazzle and beat down at the very soul. And
for that one last moment, Midir appeared poised on the very
edge of the raised catapult platform, with Liadhan struggling in
his arms, the lightning flare playing all around them both.

Then, the woman still locked against him, he sprang outward
into blazing space. In the same instant, the darkness cracked
back again, and the pursuers blundered together in the place
where he had been. The dreadful hare-like screaming broke off
as though cut with a knife.

Phaedrus thought of the black
jagged rocks and the tide running
far below.

Then the thunder came, peal
on clanging, crashing peal that
seemed to shake the very roots of
the great rock, and boomed hollow
under the vault of the heavens,
and rolled and reverberated away
into the hills. For Phaedrus, the
night had turned unreal, and the
torchlight and the quick tramp
of feet and the shouted orders
seemed all a part of the chaos
within his own throbbing head.
The only thing he knew with any
clearness, as his guards marched
him away up one nightmare alleyway and down another, was that
the first of the longed-for rain was

falling in great spattering drops, and the smell of rain on parched earth rising all about him.

They came to a square courtyard surrounded by buildings, and then there was the soft glow of lamplight on the lime-washed walls of a small, barely furnished room, with the rain hushing down outside, and the lightning stabbing beyond the small, high window, and the thunder booming fainter and fainter among the hills.

Someone gave him a drink of the sour watered-vinegar that was the Legions' marching-wine, and that and the steady light and enclosed quietness of the room cleared his head. He looked about him and saw a big writing-table with papyrus rolls on it, a couple of chests and camp-chairs, a gay native rug hanging half over an open doorway that gave a glimpse of a sleeping cubicle beyond. The Commander's quarters. ... Somebody—sometime, had said something about orders that he was to be taken to the Commander's private quarters in the Praetorium, and held under guard until the Commander came. There must have been orders about giving him a drink, too.

He leaned against the wall, dragged down by a great weight of weariness, and stared at the little flame-tongue of the lamp, while the thunder boomed fainter and fainter into the distance and only the rain teemed down; not thinking very clearly of anything save that Midir had taken his own revenge, and for him the pattern was complete—and that Liadhan would never again carry the threat of destruction to the Dalriads....

A quick, heavy step came along the colonnade, and the men on guard over him straightened to attention as the door was flung open and the Commander came striding in, pulling his sodden cloak from his shoulders and shaking himself like a wet dog. His quick glance took in Phaedrus straightening from the wall. 'Ah, good—thanks, Optio, I shall not be needing you for the moment, but keep your men within call.'

When the three had saluted and gone, he spoke to Phaedrus, not as captor to captive, but with formal courtesy, as one leader of men to another.

'I regret that you have been held waiting for me so long.'

'You have had urgent matters to attend to,' Phaedrus said grimly.

'I have had—urgent matters to attend to, yes.'

The Commander crossed to his writing-table, but remained standing beside it, and Phaedrus understood perfectly, with a certain amused respect, that Titus Hilarian, for all his courtesy of speech, would not bid a prisoner to sit in his presence—the presence of Roman Authority, but that he would not sit down himself, while keeping the other standing.

'What do you know of the man who did this thing?' The question shot out and took Phaedrus unawares, for he had been expecting his own part in that night's events to be the first matter for questions or accusation.

'Know of him?' he said, to gain time. 'What should I know of him?'

'Something, I imagine, since he went seeking you with word that we intended sending Liadhan across by galley into Valentia tonight, though how he came by that information Mithras alone knows—and to plot out with you this plan for killing her, which would quite possibly have succeeded, if you had not been overheard.'

Phaedrus remembered the stick that had cracked in the dark woods. 'Who was it?' he demanded.

'One of the three priests she has—she had with her. He noticed a certain likeness between you two, and when the man—he was a leather-worker in the native village, blind, poor devil—slipped away and headed for the woods last night, it seemed to the priest that there might be something to be gained by following him. An unpleasant little beast in a foxskin head-dress, and stinks like the Black Pit of Ahriman, but it seems his instinct was sound, and his report was a true one.'

'Well?'

'It is hard to see why a blind leather-worker should take so much interest in the death of a Queen. This one took a very great interest. Now why?'

'Likely for the same reason as he killed her in the end.'

'A grudge of some sort? Some real or fancied wrong to be avenged? Do you know what it was?'

'The wrong was real enough—it was his wrong, and he avenged it. It has nothing to do with me.'

'So you do know something of him?'

'In the days when I was a gladiator he mended my sandal straps a few times.'

'No kin to you, then? He flew the same coloured hair, and it seemed to me also, when I questioned him earlier this evening, that he shared a certain likeness with the Lord of the Dalriads.'

'None that I know of,' Phaedrus said. 'There's a good deal of red hair among the tribes, and it's hard to judge the likeness between two men when one lacks eyes and the other has half a cheek torn away.'

The level eyes of the soldier looked at him for a long considering moment, with a little frown. Then he shrugged and changed the subject, as one who is not at all sure that he has got at the truth, but knows that if he has not, he will get no nearer to it.

'But it was not to ask you these things that I bade them hold you here against my coming.'

'*Na*, I would be thinking not.' The old faintly dangerous smile was on Phaedrus's lips. 'Say whatever it is that you have to say to your prisoner.'

'I had rather think of you as—a possible hostage,' the Commander said, and checked. 'Not even quite that—as a bargaining counter.'

'I—do not understand,' Phaedrus said slowly.

'Yet the thing is simple enough; I propose to hand you back to your own people, in exchange for one thousand of their young men, to serve with the Auxiliaries.'

There was a long, harsh silence, filled by the drenching of the rain. Phaedrus felt for a moment as though he had taken a blow between the eyes. He was remembering the desolation of Valentia, the deserted raths, the pasture-lands gone back to heath and bramble, because of the young men gone to fill the ranks of the Auxiliaries along the German lines. And for Earra-Ghyl there

would be a greater evil, for with a thousand of their remaining warriors gone, they would be left with none save the women to take up the swords when the Caledones seized their chance and came swarming in. No more children born, either; as it was, there were too many women, now, who would never go to a husband's hearth.

'That was the thing you had to say to me?'

'The thousand would have to be paid first, of course,' the Commander said.

Phaedrus was still thinking, with an odd detachment, as though he stood outside himself, looking on. Strange that now it was he and not Liadhan who was the danger to the Dalriads. 'And if they refuse to pay the price, or if I refuse to be ransomed by the lives of my best warriors?' he said at last.

'Then I shall most probably send you South to be safe held as—a guest of the Empire. In that case you might certainly be called a hostage. Of course there is an alternative. It might well be a simpler way in the end, to crucify you for an example to your kind.'

'An example? What am I supposed to have done?'

'Nothing. You were merely taken in the attempt. That is the injustice of life.'

'You are not afraid of bringing down the wrath of the North against your Wall?'

'It is only when the Caledones and the Dalriads link shields, that there is danger to the Wall.' The Roman's voice and eyes were inflexible, but Phaedrus knew that the only feeling between them was liking; which made it all rather stupid and sad. Hilarian was a good soldier, doing his duty by the peace of the Frontier, and not enjoying it.

'I—must have time to think,' he said, slowly.

'You have until sunrise.'

'And whatever I decide, after my thinking, I must have speech with my own people, that they may hear it from my mouth.'

'You shall have that also, as I had speech with you, from the rampart at the Praetorian Gate.'

They looked at each other, a long, straight, steady look. Then Phaedrus said, 'It is Liadhan, not Midir, who was the usurper, you know.'

'I think I believe you. That is your justification before your own Gods. But Rome reckons little of justification beside the fact of danger to the Frontier. When a spark falls on a grass tuft, here on the borders, we stamp it out before it can become a forest fire.'

He crossed to the door, his eyes never leaving Phaedrus's face, and opening it, called, 'Optio.'

There was a tramp of feet, and the Optio appeared with his two men behind him. 'Sir?'

'Take him away and keep him well under guard until I send for him again—under guard! He is not to be left unwatched one instant. We have had one escape already tonight.'

The Mark of the Horse Lord

SQUATTING under the lamp, the two Auxiliaries were playing a game of chance to pass the time. At first the rattle of the falling dice had maddened Phaedrus, sitting on the bench on the far end of the narrow, stone-walled chamber. But now it had ceased to matter; indeed, he heard it scarcely more than he heard the drip-drip-drip of rain under the eaves. He was listening for only one thing, for any sound of fighting in the world outside that would mean an attack by his own people, praying to all the Gods that ever he had heard of, that it would not come; that they would obey his orders; that at least they would have enough sense to wait till morning. ... It did not come. Once as

the night wore on, he heard faint sounds of activity that could only mean the arrival of the galley—it must have been delayed by the storm and he wondered how Hilarian would be meeting the Escort Commander. For the rest, elbows on knees and cloak huddled about him, for it had turned chilly after the storm and he was bone-cold with weariness, he sat withdrawn from his surroundings deep into his own thoughts, as he had been used to do in the old days, before the arena trumpets sounded.

He had overmuch thinking to do, and not overmuch time, for the trumpets had sounded for midnight watch-setting a good while since. He tried to think about the time to come, and the likely way that things would go for the tribe. But his mind went ranging back over the past year, remembering the surprised look on Vortimax's dead face, and the strange light feel of the wooden foil in his hand, and the moment of stepping forward alone into freedom that was as strange and lonely to him as death. ... Remembering again the cock-loft at Onnum, and the small, tormenting pain of the tattooing needle on his forehead; and the good feel of wrestling with Midir. He thought of Murna who had fought beside him all that summer, and the babe that had been begun among the spears. He wished that he could have seen the babe, even once. Well, Conory would keep his promise to guard them; he would trust Conory with his life—he smiled in his mind at the thought—he would trust him with Murna's life and the child's, which was more to the point.

But despite what he had said to the Commander, he had no need to think what choice he was going to make. It was as though the choice had been made long ago, and was as familiar as the folds of an old cloak. It was he who had led the tribe into this new danger, and only he could pull them out from it again. Rome had power over the Dalriads by right of holding him hostage. No hostage—no power; it was as simple as that, on the surface. But suddenly he was remembering that giant, horned figure on the back wall of the Cave of the Hunter, and Midir's voice saying of his father: 'He went out to meet his boar. There had been much fighting, and a wet Autumn. It was famine time, you see....' He hadn't understood, then. He did not really

understand now—his head only knew that when it had to be one or the other, there was not much else you could do but pay away your own life for the tribe's. But something deep within him understood that it was not only among those who followed the dark, ancient ways of Earth Mother, that the King died for the people; only among the Sun People, the King himself chose when the time was come.

'He went to meet his boar. It was famine time, you see....'

The odd thing was that he never once thought to himself that he was not, after all, the King; that the true Horse Lord had leapt to his death a few hours ago, taking the woman Liadhan with him.

It was as though, growing into the kingship through this past year, Red Phaedrus the Gladiator had grown into this other thing, too, because without it, the kingship would not be complete.

Outside, the rain-water still dripped from the eaves, but the rain had stopped. The lamp was guttering into the first grey light of dawn, and the trumpets were sounding cock-crow, and presently a tramp of feet sounded outside, and the two Auxiliaries pouched their dice and got up. Phaedrus got up too, even before the door rattled open and the Centurion's voice said, 'The Commander has sent for his prisoner.'

He was stiff and sore as a rheumaticky old man—he grinned to himself at the thought. That was something he would never have to put up with, anyway. He took his time with studied insolence, knowing well enough that the Commander would have given orders that he was not to be treated like a common captive, raked his hair as best he could with his fingers, settled the folds of his war-worn cloak across his shoulders—lightly touching the great brooch that fastened it. They had taken his dirk, of course—odd that no one ever thought of a brooch with a pin as thick as a corn stalk and longer than a man's forefinger as a weapon, even in a camp of the Eagles, where they learned, just as one did in the Gladiator's School, that two inches in the right place were enough.

'Quite ready, Centurion,' he said, when the last detail, even to

470

the dazzlingly insolent play-actor's smile, was perfectly to his satisfaction.

'I rejoice to hear it,' said the Centurion with feeling, and gestured him to go out first. Outside in the grey dawn light a small guard of the Frontier Wolves were waiting. Phaedrus laughed at sight of them.

'You're taking no chances! Do you think I am Cuchulain, to make the hero's salmon-leap over these ramparts and away?'

'Get on!' the Centurion said, his patience fraying badly. 'Guard, march!'

In the room where Phaedrus had stood before the Fort Commander last night, the lamp burned low and guttering, and Titus Hilarian, in the same drenched clothes, now somewhat dried on him, red-eyed and grey-faced so that suddenly he looked like an old man instead of a young one, rose from behind the littered table and the report he had clearly been writing.

'Well?' he said, when Phaedrus came to a halt before him.

'Well?' Phaedrus said, a little mockingly.

'Have you made up your mind?'

Phaedrus gave an exaggerated shrug, 'I've little enough choice, come to think of it, have I? A tribe doesn't thrive without its leader—and they say it's none so bad a life in the Auxiliaries. Yes, for myself, I accept your terms.'

He thought he saw a flicker of disappointment in the Roman's eyes. But he only said, 'So. A wise decision.'

'There were conditions, remember. I am to have speech with my people and tell them of these terms, myself. The final word must be for them to speak.'

'Surely.' The Commander reached for his sword, which lay on the bench beside him, and slipped the belt over his head. 'The sentries report a band of them waiting before the Praetorian Gate now: your reserves, it seems came in last night, and their leader—a dark man, broad-shouldered and short in the leg——'

'Gault the Strong.'

'So? He is well named, I should judge—Gault the Strong came in with a band of them, demanding word of you. I spoke with him in the Gate, and swore to him that you should be safe

until dawn, so long as he and his men attempted no attack on the fort, and that at sunrise you would speak to them yourself as to the terms for your release.'

Phaedrus settled the folds of his cloak again on his shoulder, and said pleasantly, 'I think I heard sounds of the galley a good while after midnight. She was delayed by the storm?'

'Yes.'

'How inconvenient for you that she was not delayed a while longer. Ah, but I am sure you will find means to carry out your plan despite any counter orders.'

Hilarian's brows flickered up. 'Fortunately the Escort Commander has not the power to give me counter orders. All he can do is to take back my report to the Commander of the Wall.'

'*Sa*. That should give you time.'

'Time to handle the thing my own way, and maybe avoid a clash along the Frontier.'

'Yes, you want the quiet of the Frontier. You told me. That is why you will exchange me for all that is left of Earra-Ghyl's fighting power.' Phaedrus looked at him straightly. 'Has a mere Fort Commander the right to do that?'

'No,' the other said crisply.

'And how if the Governor Sylvanus prefers the kudos of a captured King to the more serviceable but less dramatic gain of a heavy draft for the Auxiliaries, which after all, will go to strengthen the Eagles for another Governor in another province of the Empire? Will he be pleased with the Fort Commander who made that choice?'

'No,' the other said again, 'but it so happens that I am more interested in the peace of the Frontier than in Sylvanus Varus's chance of catching the Emperor's eye.' A small, bitter smile flicked at the corners of his mouth for an instant. 'Rome will not risk losing face before the Barbarians by repudiating my action, though undoubtedly she will repudiate *me*.'

'*Sa*. I was thinking that. You will be broken for what happened last night, in any case, Commander.' Phaedrus glanced at the half-written report on the table and felt a stirring of sympathy for this man who would have to go on living and

face in all likelihood, unjust disgrace and the ruin of his career. 'Best keep me to sweeten the Governor, and leave the peace of the Frontier to the man who takes your place. That way at least they may give you another Cohort in another part of the Empire, after they have kicked you enough.'

'Is that the faith they taught you in the arena?'

Phaedrus laughed. 'The world is a hungry place for a broken soldier, just as it is for a gladiator who has won his wooden foil. If you grow hungry enough you may come to the arena yet, as you would have had me come to the Frontier Wolves.'

'Maybe.'

'Offer a pigeon in my name, for old time's sake, the first time you sacrifice at the Altar of Vengeance.'

'I'll remember.'

Phaedrus half turned towards the doorway, beyond which the courtyard was coming back to form and colour, and the sky over the roof-ridges was already full of light. 'Shall we be going? A pity, it would be, if the Sun were before us.'

'Surely.' The Commander crossed to the door beside him and spoke to the Centurion of the Guard. 'Escort to the Praetorian Gate, Centurion.'

The escort formed up, and with the tramp of nailed sandals all round him and the Commander at his side, Phaedrus fell into the long-paced, swaggering parade march, as they went through the camp, where men were beginning to stir and horses shifting and stamping in the stable lines, towards the Praetorian Gate.

He outpaced his escort in the last few yards, and turned to face them on the lowest step of the rampart stair. 'I go to speak with my own people, and I go alone. From this place you can hear every word that I speak; there is no need that any man of the Red Crests come farther with me.' His eyes met Hilarian's, and their gaze locked and held for a long moment. Then the Fort Commander put up his hand in a gesture that might very nearly have been a friendly salute. 'Very well.'

So Phaedrus climbed the rampart stair alone. Out of the tail of his eye he was aware of a knot of soldiers standing some way

along the rampart-walk on either side, but they were a good distance off and it would take almost as long for them to reach him as it would for the men behind him to come springing up the rampart stair.

The sun was just rising, and it was going to be a glorious day after the night's storm. The morning seemed clear-washed and new as the first morning of the world, and above the hoarse never-ceasing surge of the tide below the headland, rose the thin, sweet crying of the plover and the harsh laughter of gulls. Far off north-westward, clear in the cool after-storm light, Cruachan caught the first rays of the sun. Phaedrus suddenly knew again the feeling of being light on his feet and lucky, the feeling that most of the arena-trained knew well, that it was your lucky day, the day when the God's face was towards you. . . .

He looked down. Yes, he had been right about the drop. Clearly the Red Crests thought that it was enough to hold him from escaping that way, or they would not have allowed him up here without the guards close at his sides, and they were probably right. But here on the landward side, it was not far enough to be sure of the other thing, even if one dived head foremost, especially for a man trained how to fall. Well, he had his means of making sure.

Lastly, he looked at the knot of horsemen who had been waiting a little way off, and now at sight of him were urging their horses in closer. He saw the squat, dark figure of the leader, a bloody clout round the head, and was glad that it was Gault, good, level-headed old Gault, who had had the sense not to bring the War Host out in force and so betray its strength—or rather its pitiful weakness—to the Red Crests.

They were quite close under the Gate now; the hand of the Centurion away to the right flashed up: 'Near enough!'

And they checked their horses.

They were looking up at him, tossing up their spears to bring them crashing down across shield rims in the Royal Salute, and now they sat their horses, silent, waiting for him to speak. Gault and Dergdian, Niall and hairy Aluin and Finn, young Brys with a white, sullen-set face. . . . He wondered if they were thinking in

their hearts that he had betrayed them now. It was Brys that he minded about most.

He leaned forward, his hands braced on the split-timber coping of the breastwork. They were quite close, he need scarcely raise his voice to reach them across the dry ditch.

'The Light of the Sun on you, Gault the Strong; you are well come.'

'And on you, Midir of the Dalriads. I have brought men with me—enough, maybe; you have but to say the word——'

Was that in some way for the benefit of the listening Red Crests? Or simply that the squat, dark warrior with the bitten mouth was so much a fighting-man through and through that his heart turned to battle even when he knew that battle, any attempt at rescue, had no possible place in what was happening at all, or was it a direct question from the only man among that little band who knew the truth about him. 'You are willing? You who are not the King?'

Either way, the answer was the same. 'There shall be no fighting, my brothers. No attack on this fort.' He had spoken in the common British tongue that would be understood both by the knot of horsemen across the ditch and the Red Crests in the fort behind him; but now he changed quickly to the highly inflected speech of Earra-Ghyl, which would be scarcely, if at all, intelligible to the Red Crests. 'No fighting now—or afterwards. To attack this place with the war bands we have left to us would only be to fling them on disaster. It would mean the death of the Dalriads as surely as though Liadhan stood beside you to urge you on. I keep my faith with you, now; and after, you shall keep yours with me.' Out of the tail of his eye he saw the men on either side begin to move in closer, distrusting the almost foreign tongue, and changed back to the common British speech. 'Sinnoch would have said that was a fair bargain.'

'We will keep faith with you,' Gault said simply.

And Phaedrus saw in all their upturned faces, even on Gault's, that they knew and accepted what he was going to do, because he was the King, the Horse Lord, and had the King's Right.

475

How loudly the plovers were calling, disturbed by the horses. For a moment their pied wing-flicker seemed all about him as a whole cloud of them swirled across the fort, and among the thinner calling of the rest, he thought he caught the sweeter woodwind whistle of golden plover, who sometimes flock with the lesser of their kind. They swept on and sank again like a falling cloud of storm-spray. And out of the sky where they had passed, a single feather came drifting down, twisting and circling on the quiet air. It drifted past Phaedrus's face and settled on the parapet, almost touching his hand—a dark feather, spangled with the clearest and most singing gold—clung there an instant, and then lifted off again, and went circling and side-slipping on down towards the ditch.

Phaedrus said, 'It was told to me that you have had speech already with the Chief of the Red Crests here in this fort, and that he gave you his word that I should speak with you at sunrise, and see, he has kept his word.'

The men below were silent, waiting.

'The Chief of the Red Crests offers these terms for my release; that he will sell me back to you at his own price, and his price is one thousand of the best of our young warriors, to serve as Auxiliary troops with the Eagles.'

There was a faint stir among the little band of horsemen, and a pony threw up its head in protest against a sudden jab of the bit. But nobody spoke. They were waiting. They were his people.

'But it is in my mind that I do not like to be bought and sold, I who have been a slave; and so I have thought of a better way——It is this!'

He had been playing idly with the great enamelled brooch at his shoulder as he spoke, working it free. He had it in the hollow of his hand now. His fingers closed over it so that only the tip of the deadly pin that was almost as long as a small dagger, projected between them. He had plenty of time to find the place, the two-inch place just to the left of the breastbone, that meant a quick death. A good exit. The old instinct for good exits and entrances that the arena had trained into him, was still with him now.

The freed folds of his cloak fell away from him as he got a knee across the rampart coping and next instant had sprung erect. There was a shouting and a running of feet behind him and on either side, and a strange deep cry from his own men below, but it all came to his ears like the roaring of a circus crowd. The sun, still rising far north with summer, had sprung clear of the hills and shone full into his eyes as he turned a little to face it, in a golden dazzle that touched as though in greeting the Mark of the Horse Lord on his forehead. He opened his fingers, freeing the whole deadly length of the great pin, and drove it home.

The taste of blood rushed into his mouth. He plunged forward into the sun dazzle and felt himself falling. He never felt the jagged stones in the ditch.

PLACE NAMES MENTIONED IN THIS STORY

ARE-CLUTA	Dumbarton
BAAL'S BEACON	Lomond (Loch and Ben). Connected with *lumen*, light. Lugh the Sun-God had Baal among his other names.
CLOTA	River Clyde.
COIT CALEDON	'The Wood of the Caledones'—the great Caledonian forest.
CORSTOPITUM	Corbridge.
DRUIM ALBAN	'The Ridge of Britain'. Now Drum Alban.
DUN MONAIDH	Dunadd.
EARRA-GHYL	'The Coast of the Gael'. Roughly Argyllshire.
EBURACUM	York.
FIRTH OF WAR-BOATS FIRTH OF WARSHIPS (Loch Luinge)	Loch Long.
GLEN OF THE ALDER WOODS	Glen Orchy.
GLEN OF THE BLACK GODDESS.	Glen Lochy.
INSHORE ISLAND	Kerrera, off Oban.
LOCH ABHA	Loch Awe.
LONDINIUM	London.
NORTHERN WALL	The 'Antonine Wall'. Built by Lollius Urbicus, Legate of the Roman Emperor *Antoninus Pius*, *circa* A.D. 143.

ROYAL WATER—LOCH FHIONA	Loch Fyne.
SEGEDUNUM	Wallsend.
THEODOSIA	Dumbarton Rock.
THE OLD WOMAN WHO SWALLOWS SHIPS	Corrievrechan.
VALENTIA	Roman province between the Northern and Southern walls. Broadly speaking, Lowland Scotland.

KNIGHT'S FEE

CONTENTS

THE NEW LORD OF ARUNDEL

His name was Randal, Randal the Bastard, Randal the Thief. His father was a Breton Man-at-Arms, and his mother a Saxon lady, one of several who had waited on the old Countess. She, having nothing to live for, had died when he was born; his father had been killed when he was four years old, in the constant warfare along the Welsh Marches, and neither among his father's people nor his mother's was there any place for Randal. The only person who had ever shown him any kindness, and that was of a somewhat rough and ready sort, was Lovel the Huntsman, who had taken him over from the time when the woman who sold cheap wine to the men-at-arms had thrown him out like an unwanted nestling because with his father dead there would be no more money for keeping him. Lovel had brought him up, or rather, allowed him to bring himself up in the kennels along with the hound puppies, and treated him as he treated all the rest of his charges, thrashing him mercilessly with the same long oxhide whip when he was wicked, purging him with buckthorn in the spring, and sitting up with him when he had the colic.

He was nine years old now, going on ten, and officially a dog-boy, but in actual fact just something of no account, to be kicked by anyone who felt like kicking, and plenty of people did. Sometimes, when he had been kicked particularly hard, or Lovel had used the whip more savagely than usual, or when he was especially hungry, he would crawl away into a dark corner and indulge in a welter of self-pity, wondering if his mother knew what they were doing to him, until the tears made white stripes down his dirty face to echo the red stripes that the oxhide lash had made on his scrawny brown back. But for the most part he contrived, somehow, to enjoy life.

He was enjoying it now, in this hot, blue August noon, lying on the gatehouse roof to watch for the new Lord of Arundel. He should not, of course, have been on the gatehouse roof, and at any ordinary time, since the only way of reaching it was up the guardroom stair, there would have been no chance of his getting here. But the workmen who had been doing something to the roof had left their ropes and tackle for pulling timber up in position, and where there was a rope, Randal could climb, especially with a projecting buttress to shield him from interruption. They had left some of their timber up here too, ready for use, and between the stacked beams and the parapet was a small secluded strip, well out of sight of the sentinels who paced to and fro on the roof of the great Keep.

Randal lay on his back, lapping up the sunshine until he felt that it was pouring right through him so that if he got up he would have no shadow. Nothing to see but the coping stones of the high, crenellated parapet on one side, the stacked timber on the other, and overhead the burning blue laced with the flight of swallows. He heard the bustle of preparations going on in the bailey far below him, the Master-at-Arms bellowing orders, the high voices of the women, the pad of hurrying feet on the beaten earth, all small and distinct with distance. Somewhere below the gatehouse two men were talking. Their voices carried up to him along the face of the wall.

'They should be here soon,' one of the men said. 'It must be full two hours agone that Gilbert Goaty-Beard rode out in state to meet them.'

'A fine thing 'twill be to have a Lord of Arundel here in his stronghold again,' said a deeper voice with a note of recklessness in it. 'Three years of Steward Gilbert and our saintly Lady Adeliza is more than enough for any man's belly, while the Old Lion sits in his own abbey of Shrewsbury, making his peace with God.'

The first gave a snort of laughter. "Tis to be hoped he managed it by the end. It must have taken quite a bit of doing . . . Aye well, at least we shall have better living than we've had in these past years, with the Lady so busy feeding the Poor and the

Church that there was naught but outworn plough-ox beef and watered beer for her own men-at-arms.'

'Aye, young Montgomery won't make *that* mistake.' There was a deep chuckle.

Silence followed, and then the first man spoke again, reflectively. 'Young Montgomery . . . You'd think, seeing what's come of the Conqueror leaving England to a younger son and only Normandy to the eldest, that the Old Lion would have more wisdom than to do the same thing.'

'Meaning that the two cubs will be at each other's throats? Na, na, I've known those two since they were children. They were devils then and they're devils now, but they don't turn their devilry against each other. If 'tis true as they say, that de Bellême rides in with his brother today, then I'd say more like they're planning to turn it against—someone else. 'Twouldn't be the first time. They have no more love for Red William than have most of his Barons, I reckon, and they're as fire-headed as he is himself.'

'Careful with that sort of talk,' the other man growled in sudden caution, and Randal, listening in his sunbaked corner, heard their feet scuffle, and the lowered grumble of their voices as they moved away.

He reached for one of the three dried figs that he had stolen from the kitchen—he always stole anything he got the chance to, because nothing ever came to him otherwise—flicked away a couple of flies, and bit into it. It was soft and very sweet, sticky with the heat, and added to his sense of holiday. He sat up, then scrambled to his feet and peered out through the nearest crenelle.

It was like being a kestrel, up here; a kestrel hanging in the sky, looking down on the thatched roofs of the little town beneath their faint haze of woodsmoke, on the Hault Rey looping out through the downs, brown and swift under its alders, winding away through the tawny marshes to the sea; and nothing as high as you were yourself until the oakwoods on the far side of the river valley started climbing the downs again. A little breath of wind came siffling over the shoulder of the woods, and blew a long wisp of hair that would have been barley pale if it

was not grey with dirt, into the boy's eyes, and he thought that
it brought with it the faint sound of a horn.

He thrust the hair out of his eyes with the back of his dusty
olive brown hand in which he held the rest of the fig, and pulled
himself up with a foot in the crenelle, staring out along the track
that followed the flank of the downs. Far off where it ran out
from the deep-layered shade of the oak woods, a faint cloud of
dust was rising.

A few moments later the trumpets of the Castle sang from
high on the crest of the Keep. The new Lord of Shrewsbury and
Arundel was in sight.

Truly in sight now for the dust cloud was rolling nearer, and
under it Randal could see a dark skein of men and horses. Nearer
and nearer. They were pouring up the track through the town,
between the staring townsfolk and scratching dogs who had
crowded to their doorways to see them go by. Colour and detail
began to spark out from the general mass, and the blink of light
on sword hilt or harness buckle. Some of the Arundel knights
who had ridden out with Sir Gilbert that morning wore the new
fashionable long sleeves and trailing skirts to their tunics that all
but tangled in their stirrups; but the newcomers, straight from
warfare and the Welsh Marches were shabbier and more grimly
workmanlike. Several of them wore their padded gambesons,
and here and there was even a glint of ringmail from men who
had worn harness so long that they had forgotten how to wear
the gayer garments of peace time.

Randal leaned farther and farther out, his half-eaten fig forgotten in his hand, his gaze fixed on the man who rode at their
head. It was the first time, at least to remember, that he had
seen this new Earl of Arundel, Hugh Montgomery, whom the
Welsh called Hugh Goch—Hugh the Red—from the colour of
his hair and maybe for other reasons also. He was a tall man in
an old gambeson, who rode bareheaded, flame-haired in the
dusty sunlight, managing his black Percheron stallion as though
he and the beast were one. Sir Gilbert the Steward rode beside
him, leaning confidentially toward his ear; and on his other side
rode another man, red also, but a darker red, the colour of a
polished chestnut. Randal knew him well enough, for he had

seen the Old Lion's eldest son before; Robert, not Montgomery but de Bellême, for he had taken the name of his mother's lands in Normandy. His gaze flickered from one brother to the other and back again. The man-at-arms had called them the cubs, because the old Earl their father had been called the Old Lion, from the strange golden beast on a red ground that he had on his war banner; but Randal thought suddenly that what they really were, were birds of prey—like the great, beautiful, half-mad hawks and falcons in the Castle mews.

Half a length behind de Bellême rode another man who stood out from the rest almost as much as the red-headed brothers, a long, loose-limbed man clad from throat to heel in monkish black—save that no monk ever wore garments of that outland-ish cut, and the long, fantastically wide sleeves falling back from his arms were lined with the shrill, clear yellow of broom flowers. He carried no sword, this man, but a light harp on his saddle bow, and played and sang as he rode, his voice coming up on the little wind, light, but strong and true above the swelling smother of hoof-beats; and him also Randal knew, for anyone who had seen de Bellême before must also have seen Herluin, de Bellême's minstrel. But it was on Hugh Goch that all the boy's attention was fixed, as he leaned farther and farther out from his perch while the head of the cavalcade swept nearer, the baggage train of its tail lost behind it in the white, August dust-cloud.

The trumpeters on the Keep were sounding again as the fore-most riders swept up to the bridge. The horses' hooves were trampling hollow on the bridge timbers. Hugh Goch was directly below him now, in another instant the dark tunnel of the gate arch would have swallowed him and it would be time to dart across the roof and hang over the other side to see him come riding into the bailey; and in that instant, as the new Lord reined back a little, looking up at his inheritance, the thing happened. A very small thing, but it was to change Randal's whole life. He dropped the half-eaten fig.

Before his horrified gaze the dark speck went spinning down-ward for what seemed an eternity of time. It struck the black stallion full on the nose, and instant chaos broke loose. The

great brute tossed up his head with a snort of rage and fear, plunged sideways into de Bellême's bay, and flinging round in a panic that was as much temper as anything else, went up in a rearing half-turn. There was a flurry of shouts above the savage drumming of hooves: 'Look out, for God's sake! . . . Ah, would you now?—Fiends of Hell . . .' The stallion had become a mere plunging and squealing tempest of black legs and rolling mane and flaming eyes and nostrils. He would have had a lesser rider in the ditch before a heart might pound twice, but in Hugh Goch he might have been trying to shake off part of his own body. The red-haired man clung viciously to his back, and Randal, staring down with wide, horrified eyes, saw him whip out his dagger and hammer with the pummel between the laid-back ears. In a few moments it was over, the black Percheron trembling on all four legs again, and the chaos that had spread behind him sorting itself out. Hugh Goch swung him round once more to the gate arch, and reining him back with a merci-less hand that dragged his bleeding, bit-torn mouth open against his throat, sat looking up, straight up along the face of the gatehouse wall, until his eyes met those of the boy, still lean-ing out from the crenelle and no more able to move than if he had suddenly become one of the Castle stones.

Hugh Goch's face was white and thin under the flame of his hair, long-boned and almost delicate, but his eyes were the cold, inhuman, gold-rimmed eyes of a bird of prey, and looking into them, Randal was more afraid than he had ever been in his life before. For a long moment the two looked at each other, the dog-boy and the new Lord of Arundel, and then the power of movement returned to Randal, and he darted back from the crenelle, and turned and ran.

Half-sobbing in terror, he made for the ropes and scaffolding that he had come up by, and almost flung himself over the edge. The ropes tore the skin from the palms of his hands as he dropped, but he scarcely felt it, and a moment later he was crouching in a bruised heap on the narrow rampart walk be-hind the curtain wall. He heard the hollow clatter of hooves pouring through under the gate arch, and a reckless burst of laughter caught up by a score of voices, and knew that Hugh

Goch was turning the thing into a jest. But it would be an evil jest for him, if the Lord of Arundel knew him again. With one hunted glance at the scene in the bailey, where the Lady Adeliza and her women stood waiting and all the Castle had turned out to see the new Lord ride in, he gathered himself up and bolted. He ducked under the hand of a grinning man-at-arms stretched out to catch him, hurtled down the rampart steps and dived panting into the dark alleyway behind the armourer's shop.

Over the years a veritable town had grown up round the inner side of the curtain wall, like the fungus that grows up round a tree stump; barracks and mews, stables and kennels, granaries, armouries, storehouses, baking and brewing sheds, all jumbled and crowded together in higgledy-piggledy confusion, and Randal knew the ways round and through and under the confusion better than almost anyone else in the Castle. So now he took to it as a small hunted animal taking to furze cover, making for the only sanctuary he knew, the kennels, right round on the far side of the bailey behind the vast mound of the Keep.

He reached it at last, stumbled in through the walled court where they turned the hounds out while they cleaned the kennels every day, and dived, still sobbing and shivering, into the darkness of the open doorway. Inside it was surprisingly cool under the thick thatch, and sweeter smelling than the Great Hall, for they changed the hounds' straw every few days, the Hall rushes only two or three times a year. There were no humans there, for Lovel had been sick with some kind of fever in his own quarters these three days past, and Gildon who was supposed to be in his place would be round on the far side of the Keep with everybody else. But the hunting dogs greeted him with thumping tails, great tawny shapes rousing from their noonday sleep; Beauty stood on her hind legs to lick his face, but Garm sniffed at him whimpering, as though he smelled the boy's fear. Randal stumbled straight through them, up the long, barnlike place towards the little shut-off lair at the far end, where Lovel kept his whips and leashes and medicines, and had a fire-place for warming sick puppies. Next to this lair was a corner partly screened off with hurdles, and into this he turned, and flung

himself down in the straw between the two huge, brindled shapes that already lay there.

Bran and Gerland accepted his coming, though woe betide any other hound that came trespassing round their side of the hurdles. The two great Irish wolfhounds had been the old Earl's constant companions until he left the world for his abbey three years ago, and since then, refusing their allegiance to anyone else in the Castle, they had chosen to take up their quarters here with Lovel, who had the right smell. The only person, save for the huntsman himself, who could do anything with them was Randal, who stood little higher on his two legs than they did on their four, for they were about the size of ponies.

Now they made room for him as an equal, and he crawled between them and lay shivering with his face buried in Gerland's neck, telling them over and over again in a terrified whisper, 'I didn't mean to do it—I didn't mean any harm—I didn't . . .'

For a long while he lay there, his heart hammering against his ribs as though it must fly out of his body, his breath coming and going in little jerks, his ears on the stretch for any sound that might mean the hunt on his trail. But he heard only the usual sounds of the Castle, and bit by bit his heart quietened and his panic died down a little. 'He'll forget,' he told himself. 'If I can keep out of his way for a few days, he'll forget all about it. And he *did* laugh—afterwards. Maybe he wasn't so very angry after all, maybe it was just the sun that made his eyes look like that.'

So he lay, telling himself over and over again in the same frightened whisper inside his head, that the Lord of Arundel would forget, while the long, hot summer's day crawled its length towards evening.

About sunset, Gildon came with the great baskets of raw meat, and the baying and snarling that always broke out at feeding time sounded from end to end of the long kennels. Bran and Gerland got up and shook themselves and went out, proudly pacing, to demand their share, the royal share, and Randal was left quite alone. He was hungry too, as hungry as the hounds. Usually at this time of day he went up to the Keep

and hung about the kitchen below the guardroom, waiting for the food that the Great Folk had not eaten to come down from the Hall. He had eaten with the hounds before now, but he did not really like raw meat. But this evening he was too afraid, too afraid even to creep out of his corner and fight one of the hound puppies for a lump of worn-out horse meat.

He heard Gildon grumbling and roaring away as he always did, between cracks of the lash, until at last the feeding time uproar dwindled down into contented snufflings and the sound of bones being gnawed and Gildon hung up the lash and went tramping off.

In a while Bran and Gerland came back and lay down again with contented grunts, stretching themselves out for sleep. Randal was hungrier than ever, but at least, now that they had come back, he did not feel quite so alone. Presently it was dusk in the kennels, and the sky turned water green beyond the little high window just above him, and there was one star in it, not bright as yet, because the sky had still so much left of light, but like an infinitely small white flower hovering there. Randal lay and looked at it, curled into Bran's warm, brindled flank, and the soft, sleepy sounds of the hounds stirring and settling all about him. And little by little, despite his fear and hunger, the familiar sights and sounds that he had gone to sleep with almost ever since he could remember, wrapped themselves around him.

It seemed that he had scarcely fallen into an uneasy sleep before he was awake again, to the golden gleam of a torch through the screening hurdle, casting a ring-streaked freckling of light across the piled straw and himself and the brindled hide of the hounds. The light wheeled across him, footsteps were coming along the central aisle, and Gildon's voice called, 'Randal—Randal! Rouse up now!'

The next instant the full, fierce light of the torch was flaring raggedly into the narrow corner, making him blink with the dazzle of it, as he crouched back against the wall. Gildon stood in the opening, holding the torch high. 'Come on now, up with you—you and the hounds.'

He made a sudden movement as though to catch the boy and

jerk him to his feet; Randal ducked, as he always did when anyone looked as though they were going to hit him, and Gerland
whined deep in his throat, troubled by the torch, for even a dog
that has been free to sit by the hearth all his life does not like
fire that comes at him on the end of a stick.

'Wha—what do you want? What is it then? Leave me to
sleep,' Randal began, and slid down again into the straw, playing desperately for time.

"Tisn't me that wants you,' said the man. 'It's Earl Hugh
that's finished his supper and taken a fancy to see his father's
wolfhounds again.'

Randal gave a little choking gasp, and pressed back against
the wall, his eyes darting from side to side as though in search
of some way of escape.

'Lovel,' he protested stupidly, 'it's for Lovel to take them.'

'Lovel is sick, as you know full well, *and* you know that you're
the only other living thing in Arundel Castle that those brutes
will pay any heed to!' The man stirred him roughly with a foot.
'What's amiss with you? Come on now, do you want to keep
Hugh Goch waiting all night?'

Randal stared up at him, wondering desperately if he could
tell Gildon the truth and throw himself on his mercy, but he
saw that it would be no good. Gildon was angry because he, a
grown huntsman, was having to rout out a boy of nine to do
what he could not do himself. It showed all over his broad,
piggy face in the torchlight. He would have no mercy. Well
then, if he set Bran and Gerland on to him, while he, Randal,
ran away? But that would mean noise enough to rouse the whole
Castle, and he could not escape while the gates were shut for
the night, and so he would be hunted down and most likely
dragged before Hugh Goch, which would make it all the more
sure that Hugh Goch would know him again. The thoughts in
his head ran round and round in circles like frightened mice, refusing to stay long enough for him to think them; and he found
himself obeying, because he could not think of anything else
to do, scrambling to his feet, catching up the hound leashes
that the man tossed to him. One leash with the special knot on
to Bran's wide, bronze-studded collar, the other on to Gerland's.

Somehow, fumbling because he was blind and half-crying with fright and his sense of utter helplessness, while Gildon swore at him for being all thumbs, the thing got done.

'Come then, Bran—Gerland boy—good hounds!'

A few moments later he was scurrying across the still crowded bailey in the warm summer darkness, with the huge, feather-heeled wolfhounds loping on either side of him, and Gildon with the torch following hard behind. They climbed the Keep mound by the covered way, and were passed through the inner gatehouse into the courtyard in the midst of the huge shell Keep, and, with the hounds leaping ahead on the ends of their leashes, climbed the outside stair to the Great Hall.

The skin curtains over the Hall entrance were drawn back because of the warmth of the night, and the archway was full of smoky, amber light. The flaring brightness of the torches, the colour and noise and press of life within, stopped Randal on the threshold like a blow between the eyes, but Gildon thrust him forward, and all chance of escape was cut off.

2

A GAME OF CHESS

THE rich smell of food lingered in the air from the meal that
was just over, mingling with the sour smell of the rushes on
the floor, and the smoke of the torches held by a score of squires
stationed round the walls hung in a drifting haze under the
rafters, so that the light was thick, and the whole scene swam
in it as in murky, golden water.

The new Lord of Arundel sat in his great chair, leaning an
elbow on one carved front-post and his chin in his hand, to
watch a man who was dancing on his hands before him while
another played a bagpipe; but as Randal stood just within the
arched doorway, his mouth dry and his heart hammering,
Hugh Goch looked up and saw him with the hounds in leash,
and impatiently gesturing the strolling tumblers out of the way,
crooked a finger to him in summons.

Somehow Randal found himself walking forward up the
crowded Hall, the two great wolfhounds stalking on either side
of him. He kept his shoulders hunched and his chin tucked
down, staring at the rushes as he walked, with a crazy hope that
if he did not look at Hugh Goch, Hugh Goch might not recognize him. He had reached the step of the dais now, and halted,
still staring at the rushes.

'Ohé—a sight from old times, eh, Robert?' He heard the
Lord of Arundel's voice above him. 'I scarce ever remember
our father in Hall that he had not these brutes or others of
their kind lying at his feet.' And then, 'Bring them here to me,
boy.'

Randal had just enough sense to know that the order was for
him and that he must obey. He climbed the step, and stood
again staring down—at a pair of feet shod in rose-scarlet cloth
with fantastically long toes. Ever after he remembered the
chevron pattern of gold that ran down the instep, and the
withered yellow head of ragwort among the rushes beside the

497

left one, that made him think of the salt-smelling marshes where they took the hounds for exercise when they were not hunting. Hugh Goch was snapping his fingers to the two great hounds, laughing as he failed to get any response from them. 'Hai! My Bran—my Gerland, don't you know the bad black smell of the Montgomery blood?'

'Since you so clearly remember our father with his hounds, Little Brother, have you forgotten 'twas his pride that they answered to no one else—even of the Montgomery blood?' De Bellême's voice was like Hugh Goch's, but with a note of mockery, darker in tone as the flame of his hair was darker in colour.

'It seems that they answer to the boy,' Hugh Goch said. 'Look up, boy. You should be proud that you can handle my father's hounds, not hanging your head. Look—up—I say.'

It was smoothly spoken, with almost a sheen of laughter, but the smoothness was terrible. Slowly, Randal raised his head, feeling as though his eyes were being dragged upward, over the great iron-hilted sword lying across the man's knees and the beautiful, ruthless hand that held it there, over the violet-coloured breast-folds of a cloak, until they came to Hugh Goch's face, white under the flaming hair, with the red, rough marks that his mail coif had worn at cheek and chin and forehead giving it somehow the look of a mask. He was leaning forward, his gaze waiting for Randal's face as it turned slowly up to his, waiting, as it were, to swoop. And the boy knew as he met the golden eyes that Hugh Goch had known him from the first moment he entered the Hall.

'Do they always do what you tell them, my father's hounds?'

Randal, his eyes caught and held so that he could not look away, whispered through dry lips, 'Mostly, my Lord.'

'Show me.'

'What—would my Lord have them do?'

'Bid them go back to their kennels,' said Hugh Goch, softly.

Randal, terrified as he was, suddenly found himself able to think again and think quickly. But all his thinking told him was that if he did not send the hounds away, they would fly to his aid when he needed it—as he would need it—and that then no

matter whose throat they tore out first they would be cut down, here in this dreadful place full of men with swords; and Hugh Goch knew all that, and was enjoying the situation.

'Bran,' he whispered, 'Gerland,' and as they looked round questioningly into his face, he slipped the leashes from first one collar and then the other. 'Go back! Off to kennels. Off now!'

He stood watching them as they bounded away down the Hall and disappeared through the archway into the darkness; and the panic whimpered higher into his throat as he saw them go.

'You are indeed a hound boy,' said the soft, amused, terrible voice behind him. 'They say that the Saxon blood always makes the best hound boys and huntsmen. Now turn again to me, you Saxon brat.'

Randal turned.

'So,' Hugh Goch said conversationally, 'we meet again, boy who throws rotten figs at his Lord.'

'I didn't——' Randal protested wildly, staring like a trapped hare into the white face with the gold-rimmed eyes of a bird of prey. 'I did not—it was not me—it——'

'No? In this Castle of Arundel, there are no doubt many boys with skin as dark and hair as pale as yours?'

'I didn't—I didn't——' Randal babbled. 'Oh my Lord, I meant no harm.'

'Oh no, you meant no harm.' Hugh Goch's laughter became suddenly a snarl. 'The gadfly that stings my wrist means no harm, I break it under my thumb-nail, none the less.' His hand flashed out and gripped Randal's shoulder, the long fingers biting as though they were tipped with iron, and began to drag him to and fro, shaking him with short, snapping movements like a dog with a rat, until he was sick and crowing for breath, his neck all but broken and his eyes set in his head.

When at last the Lord of Arundel flung him down, he fell all asprawl, gasping and crowing and clutching at his shoulder that felt as though it had been torn out by the roots, then somehow struggled to his knees.

'Take this *thing* away and thrash it,' Hugh Goch was saying,

499

'but stop short of killing it. It is too good a hound boy to waste, and we can always thrash it again another day.'

Randal heard the words, and with the certainty of a ruthless hand already swooping to catch the scruff of his neck, gazed wildly and imploringly among the faces on the dais. He saw de Bellême looking on as at a jest, the Lady Adeliza with her mouth buttoned and her eyes cast down; faces that laughed, or were uneasy, or simply did not care; and out of them all, one face that was not shut to his agonized appeal, looked back at him. At the last instant, with the hand of one of Hugh Goch's squires in the act of closing on the neck-band of his ragged tunic, he rolled clear, scrambled across the dais on all fours and flung himself at the long black legs of de Bellême's minstrel, clinging to them with small, desperate hands.

He felt a quick movement above him, and an arm was laid across his shoulder—but so casually that it seemed as though it had happened by chance—and a light and lazy voice said, but not to him, 'Hands off, my friend.'

Out of the startled hush in the Great Hall sounded Hugh Goch's voice.

'You have something there—an ill behaved puppy—that belongs to me. Pray you hand it over to my squire, for training.'

And the lazy voice replied, faintly drawling, 'Let the Lord of Arundel forgive me, I fear I am something too busy.'

A gasp riffled round the Hall, a laugh bitten off before it was begun; and then complete silence save for a dog scratching under one of the benches. Randal, whose face had been hidden against the minstrel's knees, looked up, and saw the two men watching each other above him. Hugh Goch's eyes were all golden, the pupils contracted to mere pin-points of black. 'Too busy? And what then is this busyness that has no outward showing?'

'I make a song,' Herluin the Minstrel said blandly, his own eyes wide and very bright under the lock of mouse-coloured hair that fell across his high, sallow forehead. 'I make songs as well as sing them, did you know? And the songs I make, folk sing and whistle afterwards—and laugh at when they are meant for laughter. This song that I make now is meant for laughter;

it is a song of how a great Lord spent as much rage as would set all Wales in flames on one small boy who dropped a half-eaten fig on his horse's nose. It will be a good song—very funny.'

By now the whole Hall, breath in cheek, was watching the two men who faced each other on the dais. Years after, when he was a man and had some knowledge of courage, Randal knew that for sheer, cold courage he had seldom seen the equal of Herluin the Minstrel, that night in the Great Hall of Arundel.

It seemed that Hugh Goch thought so too, for he said after a few moments with his lips smiling over the teeth, 'You are a very brave man, Herluin, my brother's minstrel.'

Herluin shrugged thin, expressive shoulders, his brows drifting upward under the hanging lock of hair. 'I leave the martial virtues to my Lord and his kind. My toy is the harp, not the sword.'

'A toy that you use for a weapon, and to good account for your own ends, however,' said Hugh Goch, dryly.

'Nay, I am a peaceable man, and a lazy one. But—I am such a creature of whim—I have a mind to this boy.'

'So-o?' Hugh Goch said softly. 'And do you then suggest that I give him to you?'

Herluin smiled. 'Ah, la no. There must be so many who come craving boons of my Lord, and I was never one to run with the pack; while my Lord, generous though he is, must grow weary of so much giving. No, since—I think—my Lord finds poor entertainment in the juggling turns that we have endured through supper, I would suggest that we change the order of the evening to something that may prove more amusing, and play a game of chess for the boy.'

For a long, silent moment Hugh Goch looked at his brother's minstrel, red brows knit above the fierce golden stare, while Herluin, his arm still lying across Randal's shoulders, smiled sweetly back, and the whole Hall waited. Everyone knew—even Randal, still clinging desperately to the minstrel's long black legs, knew, for in his kind of life one learned many things—that the new Lord of Arundel was a gambler to the bone. He saw little flecks of light begin to hover far back in the golden eyes.

'Truly there was never a minstrel like you, Herluin,' said

501

Hugh Goch, 'but how if we say that tonight we are all of us suddenly in the mood for minstrelsy, and cannot spare you from your harp?'

'As to that, Little Brother'—de Bellême spoke in that dark, mocking voice, with a flash of pointed teeth in the fashionable red, forked beard—'I never yet found any means to persuade this Herluin of mine to wake his harp when he was not minded to.'

Herluin cocked one eyebrow at him. 'Na, I do not think you ever have,' he said in a tone of cordial agreement; and a moment later, detaching Randal from his legs with a 'Hy my! What is all this clinging for, Small One?' lounged to his feet with the slow, somewhat fantastic grace that was very much a part of him, and made a deep bow to the Lord of Arundel that expressed without words how completely he was at my Lord's service and ready to play chess.

Hugh Goch stared at him a moment longer, then flung up his head with a snarl of laughter. 'I have done many things in my time, but never played chess for a human stake before. So be it; I am in the mood for something new.' Then, with a long, contemptuous stare at the thronging faces all turned in his direction, stamped to his feet. 'But not here, to be a raree-show in my own Hall . . . Ohé, Reynald my Squire, set out the chess board in the Great Chamber, and bring wine there, and a torch that we may have light to play by. No, since the outcome of the game concerns the brat somewhat nearly, let him come and hold the torch for us himself.'

And so, a short while later, everything seeming unreal about him, Randal was standing with a long resin torch flaring in his hands, in the Great Chamber above the Hall. The Great Chamber was by right the private quarters of the Lord and his Lady, and since the Old Lion had been away making his peace with God in Shrewsbury Abbey, it had of course been used by the Lady Adeliza and her women. But now there was a new Lord of Arundel. Sir Gilbert the Steward had ventured one trembling protest, earlier that day, when he found that Hugh Goch intended instantly to dispossess the Lady. 'It is but a short while before your Lady Mother goes to the nunnery where she has

chosen to spend her widowhood; might it not be kind to leave her the Great Chamber until she goes?' But Hugh Goch had made the situation quite clear. 'If she were indeed my Lady Mother, who knows, I might scrape up enough of filial piety to leave her in possession. She is my father's second wife and her long sheep's face raises the devil in me by the mere sight of it. Splendour of God! Cannot you find her another corner of this place to patter her prayers in? You had best try, for I warn you that I lie in the Great Chamber tonight if she lies in the brew house!' So now he sprawled in the carved chair beside the empty hearth, his sword still across his knees, while Herluin the Minstrel had settled himself, long legs outstretched, on the cushioned bench opposite; and on the table between them, at which the dispossessed Lady of Arundel had taken her supper, for she seldom supped in Hall, lay the chess board with its white and crimson morse-ivory pieces marshalled like opposing armies.

Hugh Goch had drawn red, when they tossed a silver penny for sides, and said laughing, 'It is fitting that I should command the Red Queen and her train. I warn you, I always play better with my own colour.'

And so it was for Herluin, sitting with the white ranks before him, to make the first move. He took his time, considering, then put out a long musician's hand and moved one of the pawns forward.

Randal heard the faint click, very sharp and clear, as he set it down.

Hugh Goch, leaning his elbow among the thick, harsh hairiness of the great brown bearskin flung across his chair, took up a piece that glowed in the torchlight deep ruby red, and set it down in its new position with the same clear, decisive click.

All his life, Randal was able to remember that scene in its every least detail, the torch making a ragged core of light in the heart of the crowding gloom, and in it, the intent faces of the two men, and their intent hands, and between them, on the magpie-chequer of the board, the two armies of fantastic shapes that marched and pranced and wavered to and fro, each with its finger of crowned or helmeted or horse's-headed shadow

moving beside it; the half-seen, half-lost glint of a bird with a serpent's tail gold-embroidered on the bed hangings; the king-fisher fire in the heart of the jewel that held Hugh Goch's cloak at the shoulder; the click and silence and click again of pieces picked up and set down, against the distant surf-sound of voices and bagpipe music from the Great Hall beneath their feet; the very smell of rosemary and hot resin from the torch in his sore and smarting hands. And yet, at the time, none of it seemed quite real. It was all like one of those dreams so vivid that when you wake the taste of them remains with you all day.

His shoulder ached where Hugh Goch had all but torn it from the socket, his legs ached with weariness as the time went by, and his head swam a little with hunger and the strangeness of everything. Somehow he went on standing and standing, as the time crawled along, shifting his weight from one leg to the other and back again, trying to hold the torch steady so that it did not dribble or flare; and all the while, with an aching intensity, watching the board. He had never seen chess played before; until this evening he had never even heard of it. He had no knowledge of opening gambits, of a pawn sacrificed to better a knight's position, of cunning combinations played out, and the skilled marshalling of pieces in the face of a devilish red attack and a menaced white king. He did not know what they were doing, these men with their intent faces and hovering, deliberate hands, only that they were moving about carved figures of kings and queens and little squat knights on horseback and high-mitred churchmen; and that in some way that he could not at all grasp, his whole life from that time forward as long as he lived, depended on the pattern that they made.

At first they played easily, as it were lightly, leaning sideways to the board, pausing sometimes to drink, when a squire came in to pour more wine for them into the cups that stood at their elbows; sometimes talking with the people who wandered up from the Great Hall to see how the game was going. Presently de Bellême came up, his sword chape ringing on the circular stair, to lean on his brother's shoulder and watch the play, pointing with a finger. 'Watch out for your bishop.' And a little later, 'Ye-es, I've seen almost this game played out before—

between Red William and Duke Robert.' He laughed 'Maybe our Red King should challenge his brother to play for the lordship of Normandy and England. He might get the thing settled in that way; it seems he's not likely to by tramping round the Duchy with his hired mercenaries as he's been doing all this summer.'

Hugh Goch looked up quickly, echoing the other's laugh with that soft laughter of his that was like a snarl. 'Have a care with that kind of talk, Great Brother . . . Maybe Red William feels something safer with a hired army behind him than with a dumb-sullen English rabble that trusts him as little as his Barons do, or as he trusts his Barons—and maybe with as good reason.' A long, meaning look, lit with reckless amusement passed between them, while Herluin pondered over his next move.

Randal had some idea what they were talking about, at any rate in part, for he knew (had not the whole South Country been grumbling with it for a month past?) that Red William had called out the fyrd, twenty thousand English foot to serve with him against Duke Robert, and then sent his own chaplain, Ranulf Flambard, to meet them at Hastings and take from each man the ten silver shillings coat-and-conduct money provided by his district, and send him home again, while the money went to the King to hire mercenaries.

'A trick such as last month's at Hastings does not earn trust,' de Bellême said. 'And so, with bad blood between the King and his English, comes maybe, sooner or later, the chance that *other folk* may turn to good account. Watch out for your bishop, I tell you, or my minstrel will have you checked in three moves.'

The game went on again, and gradually, as it laid a stronger hold on the players, their faces grew more absorbed, they straightened little by little from their lounging positions and sat square to the table; the wine was left untouched at their elbows, and they ceased to be aware of onlookers. Presently de Bellême shrugged and strolled off down to the Hall again, where the strolling jugglers were still amusing the company. And then at last, a long time later—but Randal had lost all count of time by then—Herluin took up one of his knights and made a move

505

with it that seemed no different from the many moves that had gone before, and set it down with a small decisive click, and said, 'Check, Montgomery.'

'Ah? What?' Hugh Goch snapped, dropping back his own hand which had been poised for a move. His gaze went quickly, questioningly, over one after another of the pieces, while Herluin suddenly relaxed in his place, watching him with a little smile hovering behind his cool, light eyes.

Hugh Goch's white face seemed for the moment to darken and narrow. Then, abruptly, he laughed, and crashed up from his great chair, oversetting several of the pieces as he did so.

'Checkmate is it? Checkmate to the Lord of Arundel? Aye well, so it is; and the brat is yours now. Take and do what you will with him.'

A few moments later he had gone striding from the room, shouting for his squires, and Herluin rose and stretched until the small muscles cracked between his shoulders, looking down at Randal where he stood gazing dazedly up at him, the torch dribbling unheeded in his numb hands. 'What a thing is life, that it can be changed by moving a few carved ivory pieces on a chequered board—or even by dropping half a fig on a horse's nose, eh, Imp?'

A squire came running to clear the chess board, and the minstrel swung round on him, saying with a flick of one long forefinger towards Randal, 'I have just won this from your Lord; will somebody take and feed it, and put it in whichever of the wall chambers has been made ready for me.'

The squire looked startled and resentful, and muttered something about the wall chambers being for the family, and sleeping in Hall like everybody else.

Herluin's brows drifted upward. 'But then I am not "everybody else", and it pleases me not at all to sleep with the common herd of squires and the like. I am de Bellême's minstrel, my good boy. If no chamber has been kept for me, then I fear, I greatly fear, that you must dispossess someone else, even as your Lord has dispossessed his saintly stepmother . . . Meanwhile I am away to snatch a mouthful of fresh air before sleeping time.'

And so in a while, without any clear idea of how it came

about, Randal found himself, his stomach full of bread and cold sucking pig, lying curled at the foot of a bed of skin rugs and piled rushes in a narrow chamber in the thickness of the wall, opening off the guardroom stair. It was pitch dark, for there was no window to see the white star through, and a curtain of some heavy stuff hung over the entrance. The darkness itself was like a curtain—a black curtain that hung close before Randal's face as he lay staring into it, and made the air thick to breathe. He heard distant sounds, a snatch of song from the guardroom below, the murmur of movement and voices from the Great Hall where those who slept there would be settling for the night, the scream of a hawk. But they were all muffled and far off. Here in the darkness there was no sound at all, no familiar stirring of hounds in the straw; nothing but his own breathing. And quite suddenly he began to be frightened again. A new fear now. So much—a whole life-time of things—had happened to him since he lay on the gatehouse roof at noon, that now, alone in the dark, dazed and bewildered by the rush of events, he was not sure whether any of it had happened at all. But if it had been a dream, was he awake now, or still tangled in it like a fly in a cobweb? And if Hugh Goch was a dream, then Herluin must be a dream too. He could not bear that Herluin should be only a dream. Panic was rising in him, and he began to whimper a little, threshing about on the piled rugs of the bed. His outflung hand found the corner of a soft, thick leather bag with something hard inside it; he reached out farther, exploring in the darkness. Herluin's harp that someone had brought in—he remembered now—and laid on the bed. He could feel the shape of it inside the thick, soft leather of the bag, and the raised scratchiness where the leather was enriched with gold and silver threads.

Comforted, he must have fallen asleep on the instant, for he heard no footsteps on the guardroom stair, but between one moment and the next the curtain over the entrance was thrust back, and light flooded into the narrow chamber, and Herluin was on the threshold holding up a rushlight that glimmered like a star.

Randal crouched up in the straw, the harp held against his

knees, blinking at the tall man as he came in and let the curtain fall again behind him.

Herluin crossed the little chamber and set the rushlight on its pricket in a niche high in the rough stone wall, then turned, stretching and yawning, to look down at the small figure on the foot of his bed. The long, wide sleeves fell back from his up-spread arms, revealing the brilliant lining like the blink of yellow on a goldfinch's wings.

'Now why did I never bethink me before, that I should keep a guard-dog?' Herluin said, his gaze taking in the harp that Randal held against his knees. 'Have you kept it safe for me all this while?'

Randal nodded.

Herluin sat down on the carved stool that, save for the make-shift bed, was the only piece of furniture, and stretched his long, loose legs all across the narrow space.

'By what name do they call you? Or do they only whistle?'

'Randal—I'm called Randal,' the boy said hoarsely; and without knowing that he did so, crept close against the bony black knees, his gaze fixed on the minstrel's face.

'Randal. Hy my! What a man's name for such a small imp,' Herluin said, his face cracking into its winged and twisted smile, and put his hand on the boy's rough head. 'Aye, well, you'll grow to it one day. Meanwhile I shall call you Imp.'

THE WATER STAIR

In the world outside the strong walls of Arundel, things were stirring that autumn; a muttering of unrest from end to end of the Kingdom, a sudden flare of revolt in Wales. And in October, the King being too deep in his war with Brother Robert to handle any other troubles himself, Henry of Coutances, his younger brother, landed in England to deal with the disturbances.

Randal heard of these happenings, as he heard the autumn wind siffling over the ramparts, and with as little thought. Indeed, he had not much thought to spare for anything, just then, from the strange experiences of belonging to somebody for the first time in his life.

Soon, before winter closed the seaways, de Bellême would be sailing to take up his heritage in Normandy, and Herluin with him, and Randal with Herluin. Any day now, Hugh Goch would ride with Henry of Coutances, back to his Welsh wars; but meanwhile, it was glorious hunting weather, and both brothers remained at Arundel while the Wealden Forest flamed gold and russet in the October sunshine.

The fine weather broke at last, some days after they heard of Henry's landing, and a gale came booming up from the southwest, salt with the taste of the sea, and the grey, driving rain blotted out the downs behind its trailing curtains of nothingness. And at dusk the storm blew to the gates of Arundel a drenched and weary man on a drenched and weary horse.

He was brought into the torch-lit Hall where half the folk and hounds of the Castle were gathered, waiting for the trumpets to sound their Lord in to supper; a tall bony man in an old leather gambeson black with the wet, who stooped a little as though from a lifetime of wearing heavy mail. And at sight of him, Herluin, who had been singing for them beside the fire—one of the songs of Roland—ceased his singing and laid down his little

bright harp between one note and the next, and came to his feet in a kind of lazy bound.

'D'Aguillon! Why, Sir Everard, by all that is most wonderful! And what do you, de Braose's man, here in the Honour of Arundel?'

The crowd had parted to make way for the newcomer, as he came through them to the fire, and Randal, looking up from where he squatted at Herluin's feet, saw the knight's very dark eyes lighten with pleasure.

'Ohé, Herluin the Minstrel! I thought it was your voice. But I need not have doubted finding you here, knowing that de Bellême as soon moves without his minstrel as without his shadow . . . I have been up to Henry's camp at Portsmouth, with words from de Braose about the Bramber levies—the old man grows too gouty for war; young Philip must lead them if they are called out. And now I am on my way home—or was, when the storm caught me.' He was putting back the coif of his gambeson as he spoke, and the thick, badger-grey hair flattened under its pressure sprang slowly erect. 'Grace of God! What a storm! Already the ford is impassable and so I come to claim shelter until the floods sink and I can get across the Hault Rey and be on my road again.'

'What word from Henry's camp?' someone asked.

'That Mowbray of Northumberland has plundered four Norwegian trading ships, and is likely to make trouble when the King calls him to account for it,' d'Aguillon said briefly.

There was a little silence, then someone said with a reckless laugh, 'Well, with matters as they are at present, that's as likely a thing as any other to set spark to stubble.'

D'Aguillon bent to hold cold, rain-wet hands to the blaze, the steam already wisping up from his sodden gambeson, while one of the squires hurried to fetch him a cup of wine. No one commented on the last speaker's words.

For two days more the storm raged. The gale beat wild wings about the Castle, and the rain fell spitting and sizzling into the fire; and they lived by torchlight with the shutters drawn across the high Hall windows slamming and rattling in the gusts, be-

cause with the windows open they would have been flooded as well as blown inside out. As it was, they would have been smothered with the smoke that billowed down the smoke-vent, if it had not been for the draught that wailed along the floor stirring the dusty rushes. Randal could have lain much more snug in his old corner of the kennels, tucked down under the shelter of the curtain wall, but now that he belonged to Herluin, and had the right to sit in the rushes and the icy draughts at the minstrel's feet, nothing would have induced him to sit elsewhere.

On the third morning they woke to broken skies and a sunrise laced with thin, watery fire, and by evening the sky was clear save for great sheep's-wool clouds trailing their shadows across the valley from one rim of the downs to the other. And Herluin said to the stranger knight, laying aside his harp in its bag of embroidered leather, and stretching as he rose, 'Come away on to the downs for a mouthful of air before supper. We have been too long mewed in the dark like moulting falcons.'

'Say rather like smoked hams hung too long in the chimney corner. Surely I will come.' Sir Everard scuffled his feet in the rushes, and got up also, hitching at his sword sheath.

Randal, squatting in the rushes, cleaning Herluin's spare pair of shoes, sprang to his feet and tugged at the minstrel's wide-falling sleeve imploringly. 'I also! My Lord, take me too, and Bran and Gerland!'

And so a while later, with Randal and the great feather-heeled hounds flying ahead, the minstrel and the old knight passed out through the castle gates, and turning northward, set their faces to the long slope of the downs.

The wind was not as strong as it had been, but up on the downs behind Arundel it still came booming up through the oak woods, and the seagulls whirled overhead like blown leaves. On the edge of the oak woods a great dyke, blurred by time until it was curved and gradual as the trough of a wave, cut across the shoulder of the downs, made—but Randal knew nothing of that —by the Bronze men, two thousand years before, to guard their turf-banked fortress where Arundel Castle stood now. And by

and by the two men fell to walking to and fro along its lip,
while Randal, scrambling down into it, found a spot that was
warm as summer, with the westering sun spilling down the
bramble-choked slope at his back, under the wind that whirled
the flocks of brown leaves overhead and laid the long grass at
the edge of the dyke over all one way; and squatting down there,
began to pick fleas out of Gerland's brindled coat, while the old
hound lay and groaned in ecstasy. Leaving Bran and Gerland
—the other hounds too, but Bran and Gerland most of all—was
the one thing that he was going to hate in leaving Arundel.
Would anyone bother to pick the fleas out of Gerland's coat
when he was gone? The thought made him extra thorough
now; but between fleas he watched the two men walking to and
fro, the one lithe and loose-knit, his mantle flying like black
wings about him, the other stiff and soldierly in his old gambeson, with his sword gathered in his arms as he walked. He wondered what they were talking about, and wished that the wind
were the other way so that he might hear. He was not at all sure
that he liked the strange knight, who had a mouth like a trap
and the kind of eyes that you could not lie to.

From the seaward end of their walk, where the land began to
drop too steeply for comfort, Herluin and Sir Everard could
look down over the marshes and the estuary, and see where the
Hault Rey came looping out through the downs, round the last
sinking shoulder of the hillside on which the town and Castle
stood. The river was still in tawny spate, but already it did not
reach so far up the half-drowned alders as it had done that
morning, and the wind-ruffled water that spread in great lakes
all across the marshy valley seemed shrinking almost while they
watched.

'Truly, it has been a most noble storm,' said Sir Everard, as
they checked as by common consent, and stood looking down.
'But from the speed that the floods are sinking, I think that it
cannot have broken far inland. If not tomorrow, then surely at
the next day's low tide, I shall be able to get Valiant across the
ford and go on my way.'

Herluin said slowly, 'Since the wind blew you into Arundel
Great Hall three nights since, I have been thinking—a little.

514

D'Aguillon, will you do something for me, for your Richard, his sake?'

'What would you have me do?'

'Take the Imp with you when you ride from here.'

The old man looked quickly at the younger one, but nothing was to be read in the cool, faintly bitter face, the pale eyes, in the windy, westering sunlight. 'Why?' he demanded, after a few moments.

'Because I have known you—somewhat—since Richard and I learned our book together at Bec Abbey, and I would liefer give him into your hands than those of any other man I know.'

'Surely you honour me,' d'Aguillon said, deep in his throat. 'That was not my meaning, however, as you know full well. Why give the boy into any man's hands, out of your own?'

'Hy my! For a number of reasons. Firstly, because the life of minstrel or jester is a chancy thing, as all men know—playing with fire was never yet a safe pastime, though amusing; and—' his light tone hardened—'if ought should happen to me, I would not have him left in the hands of the Montgomery brood.'

They had turned inland again, with the wind over their left shoulders, and Sir Everard nodded, his gaze on the wooded crest of the downs ahead. 'Aye, bad men, both of them . . . It is sometimes in my mind to wonder——'

'What?' said Herluin gently.

'No matter. I was going to say that I sometimes wonder you still hold to de Bellême yourself. But to each man the secrets of his own heart.'

Herluin shrugged, the slow expressive shrug that showed him for no Norman but French to the bone, and rolled his eyes heavenward. 'I am something of a fool as well as a minstrel . . . But we are talking of the Imp, not of me. I have given you one reason concerning him. For a second—I am fool enough to care that he should have a chance in life more suited to him than any I can give. It would be different if I saw the least likelihood of making a minstrel of him, but there is no music in the Imp. Mercy of God! There is *no* music in the Imp!' Herluin shuddered as a shrill tuneless whistling reached them down the gusts. 'If

I keep him with me, he will find no place of his own, ever; he will strike no root, and he needs to strike root, greatly. You could give him that. Will you take him?'

'What as?' Sir Everard said, twenty paces farther along the dyke.

'As a fellow for Bevis. You were saying only yesterday that the boy was growing up too solitary; that you feared you did wrong to train him up yourself, instead of sending him to one of the great houses.'

'And that is true enough.' Sir Everard gave a quickly suppressed sigh. 'But Richard was my only son, and he is Richard's, and when Richard was killed . . . I am a selfish old man; I delight in the boy's company, but he—he needs company of his own age, and not merely that of the villeins' children.'

'Give him Randal to be varlet with him, and squire with him when that time comes,' Herluin said. 'He'll make a good squire. He has lived so long with hounds that along with most of their faults he has learned the hound's chief virtue of faithfulness.'

The old man did not answer until they had turned seaward again, the wind snatching at his words. 'And in ten years or so, Bevis will be made a knight however unworthy, because he is my grandson and gently born and it is the custom. What place for your Randal then?'

'A squire's place at all events, which is none so ill a thing. Give him his chance, d'Aguillon.'

They paced on in silence a little farther, then Sir Everard said, 'You have, I think, some fondness for the child.'

'It is easy to grow fond of a stray dog,' Herluin said lightly.

'And the child has some fondness for you.'

'Because mine was the first hand that ever touched him in kindness, no more. He is a small cub; he will soon forget.'

Sir Everard looked round at the man strolling beside him, and the grim gash of his mouth that Randal liked so little had unexpectedly gentle corners. 'And you? Will you also forget so soon?'

'I?' Herluin flickered up his eyebrows and laughed, lazy, light, mocking laughter into the wind, that seemed echoed by the sea-birds' crying. 'I shall have forgotten him in three days!

I am Herluin, de Bellême's minstrel; any man will tell you that I have no heart to remember with!'

And Randal, pulling a tick from behind Bran's left ear, thought, 'It cannot be anything that matters, after all. It must be something funny, or Herluin would not laugh like that.'

The men had come to the seaward end of their walk again, and halted as before, looking down to where the Hault Rey swirled the colour of heather ale over its paved ford.

'I'll take him,' Sir Everard said abruptly. 'And this I promise you, that save for knighthood, which is beyond my hands, he shall have what Bevis has, both of the kicks and the honeycomb.'

Not that night, but the next, when it came to sleeping time, and he had propped his harp in its usual corner of the narrow wall chamber, Herluin lounged down on the roughly carved stool, and crooked a finger for Randal. 'Come here, Imp.'

Randal, who was spreading his own rug just within the doorway, where he had slept ever since Herluin had objected to his sleeping across his feet, came and stood against the minstrel's black-sheathed knees looking up at him inquiringly.

'Tomorrow, when the river ford is passable at low tide, Sir Everard goes home to his own place, across the downs,' Herluin said.

Randal was glad, and showed it as clearly as a pup wagging its tail; but his gladness lasted for only a heartbeat of time.

'And you,' said Herluin, 'you go with him.'

Randal stared at him, startled, and beginning to be afraid; and then burst into a flurry of words. 'Why? I do not understand—for how long? I must be back before we sail for Normandy.'

'You are not coming with me to Normandy, Imp.'

'But you said—you promised——' Randal was sick and breathless now, staring at Herluin with dilated eyes.

'Did I so? Then it must be that I am breaking my promise.' Herluin's voice sounded faintly bored. 'Never trust a minstrel. Hy my! Anyone will tell you that de Bellême's minstrel changes his mind as often as a swallow changes course.'

'But I don't understand!' Randal protested frantically. 'Have I made you angry? Tell me, and I'll never do it again— only don't send me away.'

There was a little silence and a queer smile rather like a shadow flickered across Herluin's face without ever touching his eyes. 'Na na, there is naught amiss. Never think it, Imp.' For the moment he had dropped something of his usual drawl. 'It is in my mind that here is a better way for you, that is all. It may even be that when you have as fine a beard as Sir Gilbert the Steward, you will think so too. Or it may be that you will not. A fine thing it would be if a man might foretell how the moves in life will turn out, as clearly as the moves in a game of chess.' Then, with a deliberate return to the cool, affected drawl that his world knew, he yawned hugely, stretching with his fantastic winged shadow stretching on the wall behind him. 'So—I change my mind; the thing is settled. Sleep now, Imp. They tell me that low tide is at some barbarically early hour in the morning.'

Randal stood back a little, still staring at him, breathing short and quick. 'Yes, I will go and sleep,' he said thickly, through the sob in his throat. 'But not here! I will sleep with the hounds as I used to do. *They* do not change their minds!' And he turned and stalked out with his nose in the air and his mouth tight shut on the grief within him.

He went down the spiral stair, past the entrance to the guardroom where the men-at-arms were settling in for the night, and down again, slowly, his hand on the great stone central core of the stairway. Half-way down, he checked altogether, not quite able to believe, even now, that Herluin would not call him back or come after him. But the moments dragged out long and thin, and no lazy voice called, no step sounded on the stair behind him, and he went on down, into the darkness. The man-at-arms on duty at the stair foot passed him through without trouble, thinking that he was on some errand for Herluin, and he came out through the archway into the courtyard in the midst of the great shell Keep. He knew that the gate to the outer bailey would be shut now, and certainly no one would open it again for the likes of Randal. That was no matter; in the

flying autumn moonlight another archway opened like a black mouth; that was the entrance to the water stair that led down to the Castle well, outside the Keep, and in normal times it was not kept guarded.

Randal oozed his way along the wall to it, taking advantage of every blot of shadow. There was no reason why he should not have walked boldly across to it, no law against his sleeping in the kennels again as he had used to do, though it might have meant answering questions that he did not want to have to answer, if he were seen. But before Herluin came, his night-time comings and goings about the Castle had mostly been furtive affairs, and now that Herluin was gone from him again, he returned without thought to his old, secret ways. He reached the dark mouth of the stairway unseen, and slipped into the pit of blackness that it made, as an otter slips into the water without a splash. The hollow feel of the tunnel was all about him, and the cold, green smell of water coming up from below.

There was another smell too, that brought him up on the third step, sniffing delicately and cautiously like a hound. A very faint scent, it wafted up on the stronger water smell, seemed to whisper in his nostrils, and then before he could lay hold of it, was gone. He stole down two more steps, and now he had it again, more strongly this time, more surely. Once, a great lady had walked close by him, and her mantle had given out a strange scent that was heavy and warm and sweet, but animal. He had asked someone what made the lady smell like that, and been told that it was musk; and now he knew the scent again, infinitely thinner and fainter, but the same. But why was the scent of musk creeping up the water stair? One of the Lady Adeliza's women meeting in secret with someone among the knights or men-at-arms? He thought he caught the murmur of voices in the darkness far down the stairway; but it seemed to him that both voices were men's, and even in the midst of his misery, a little stir of excitement shimmered through him. He crept nearer, slipping his feet silently from step to step. Near the foot of the steps was a recess where a narrow doorway led to some chamber deep in the foundations of the Keep, and

just below that, the stairway turned a corner before it ran out into the vaulted well-house. It was from below this corner that the murmur of voices came. Randal gained the recess safely, and flattened himself against the slimy stonework, listening with all his ears.

The voices were close below him now. One of them spoke in low-toned, fierce impatience, and he knew it for the voice of Hugh Goch.

His carefully held breath caught in his throat in a cold moment of terror. He knew that he was in deadly danger. Whatever it was that Hugh Goch did here, whoever he met in dead-of-night secrecy, he would not welcome eavesdroppers. He knew that if Hugh Goch caught him, he would kill him here in the dark; and he longed to turn and run, leaping upward to the silver moonlight at the head of the stair. But as before, when the Lord of Arundel had looked up at him as he leaned over the parapet of the gatehouse roof, he seemed turned to stone and built into the wall.

The other man was speaking in his turn, answering Hugh Goch's impatient words.

'It is too late in the year to start anything now, more especially with Brother Henry playing watch-dog.' It was a curiously smooth voice, a hairless voice, with a faint suggestion of a lisp. 'De Lacy sends you word to go to Shrewsbury, as many of your knights with you as maybe, and hunt your Welsh forests towards winter's end, that you may be ready in the Marches before spring. The King will summon Mowbray to appear before his Easter Court on the matter of the Northman's trading vessels; Mowbray will refuse, and then——'

'The revolt will flare up as at a signal.' Randal heard Hugh Goch's soft, snarling laugh in the darkness. 'A fine signal for our purpose, and one that can be relied on to bring in the whole of the Marches. We Marcher lords, we're all pirates and reivers to a man—but at least we do our reiving openly and not under cover of self-made laws as the King does!'

'Be ready when the time comes, and before high summer we'll have done with Red William and his self-made laws, and mount Stephen of Aumale in his place.'

'Bid de Lacy to have his own weapons sharp,' Hugh Goch said scornfully, 'and never doubt that I'll have mine!'

Randal heard the formless sound of movement, and a soft footfall on the water stair. The two voices sank to a mumble, mingling with the brush and pad of stealthily retreating footsteps, dwindling away. The sounds had quite died now, nothing left of what Randal had overheard but his own wildly drubbing heart, and the faint, lingering echo of the scent of musk. The boy drew a great gasp of air, the first full breath that he had drawn in all that while, and gathered himself together to run. But even as he did so he heard one of the men coming back. He had just time to flatten himself again into the embrasure of the door behind him, before the man, whichever it was, swept by.

The heavy folds of a cloak actually brushed Randal, but no scent of musk came from them. The dark figure swept on and up, taking the water stair two steps at a time. He saw it silhouetted for an instant in the stairhead arch; even the bleaching moonlight could not quite drain the red from Hugh Goch's hair. Then it was gone.

RIVER OF NO RETURN

RANDAL waited awhile in the darkness, his heart hammering. But he could not stop there for ever. He must go forward, or back, and he was not going back. The man with the hairless voice must be well out of the way by now. . . . He crept on down, round the corner of the stairway, the last faint traces of the womanish scent dying into the cold smell of the water strong in the enclosed spaces. He saw the well-house empty in the backwash of reflected moonlight, and the whiteness of the night hanging beyond the arched doorway, and flung himself at the steps up to it as though at this last instant hands that smelled of musk were closing on the back of his neck, and shot out into the thick moon shadows at the foot of the Keep mound.

There were still people about in the outer bailey, which always kept later and more uncertain hours than the Keep, and Lovel, long since well of his fever, his battered old lantern in his hand (it was only Gildon who took a naked torch among the hounds, and then not if Lovel was there to see him) was just snibbing the door of the kennels, after his nightly prowl round, as Randal came darting across the bailey.

Randal flung himself against the door, tearing at the latch under the huntsman's surprised hands. 'Let me in! You let me in!'

'So, so? I thought that you were Herluin's man these days,' the other grumbled, peering at him in the light of the lantern.

'Na!' Randal spat the words between his teeth. 'Tomorrow I go with the old knight he is for ever talking to—him with a mouth like a trap—but tonight I sleep with my own again!'

Lovel grunted, not interested enough to ask questions, and let him through, rattling the door to again behind him.

Randal stumbled forward into the familiar rustling and snuffling, dog-smelling darkness. He knew the place so well that it was as though his feet could see the way for themselves. But

there was light at the far end of the place; a silver sword of moonlight slanting down from the high window; and at the foot of it, Bran and Gerland lay outstretched, their brindled hides bleached to cobweb grey in the shadows, frosted silver where the moonlight fell.

They greeted Randal with softly thumping tails, and he crawled in between them as he had done on so many nights, and lay down with his back against Gerland's flank and his head on Bran's shoulder, and his face hidden under his arm from the white, fierce sword of moonlight. He was shaking from head to foot, and it seemed to him that he could smell musk everywhere, and hear the nightmare smoothness of a voice that lisped a little, in the darkness. But already he was not quite certain what he had overheard; the whole incident seemed to be dissolving as an evil dream dissolves when the dreamer wakes from it, leaving only a sickly taste of the evil behind. Gradually his heart quietened from its pounding and his breath that had been coming in little, whistling gasps grew steady again. But as his terror ebbed away, the furious misery that it had almost driven out for a time came back and engulfed him.

'Tomorrow I go away,' he told Bran and Gerland in a small, cracked whisper. 'I will never forget you—do not forget me, old Bran—old Gerland . . . I told him hounds did not change their minds. I told him—I told him . . .'

Bran licked his face sleepily.

Next morning at low tide, so early that it was not yet full daylight, and the white mist lay across the marshes, Randal left the great Castle of Arundel that had been the only home he knew in all his first ten years, mounted before Sir Everard on his tall roan stallion. Herluin strolled down with them to the paved ford, but Randal would not look at Herluin again, at which the minstrel grew mocking-merry under the alder trees.

Randal had crossed the Hault Rey often, when they took the hounds to run on the marshes, but this time, as Sir Everard gentled the horse down into the swift, brown water, and he saw it swirling and boiling mealy with foam about the great brute's legs, it seemed to him that this was more than just the Hault

Rey; this was something strange and terrifying, wild water sweeping between the unknown world that he went to, and the old familiar one that, with all its badness, was the only world he knew.

'Up, my Valiant, come up!' said Sir Everard's voice above him, and he saw the strong, dark hand on the reins, and felt the upward heave, the slipping scramble of the great horse under him, as Valiant lifted his hind quarters clear of the swirling flood. And they were across, with the old life left behind on the far side, the good and the bad of the old life, Bran and Gerland, Hugh Goch with his bird of prey face under the flaming hair, and the queer, evil, musk-scented dream—it really did seem like a dream now—that he had had last night on the water stair, and Herluin, standing among the alder trees.

But Randal did not look back.

He never afterwards remembered much about that long day's ride. Indeed, it never seemed to be part of his life at all, but just a kind of bridge between one thing and the next. Usually it would have seemed, to the boy who had never been on a horse before, both splendid and terrifying to sit so high above the world, feeling the liveness and the willing strength of the great roan surging under him, and hear the drub of the strong round hooves on open turf or miry track spooling by so far beneath. But afterwards he could scarcely remember it at all.

Late in the day there was a town of reed-thatched houses under the downs, that Sir Everard said was called Steyning, and a little later still there was suddenly a familiar thing; a grey, stone-built castle on the last low shoulder of the downs, with a river casting a bright loop through the marshy valley about its foot. 'That is Bramber,' Sir Everard said. 'De Braose holds it from the King as Hugh Goch holds Arundel—as I hold Dean from de Braose.' And almost as he spoke, the roan turned aside of his own accord through the dusty wayside tangle of bramble and seeding willow herb, heading southward, where the downs fell back to let the broadening river through. Sir Everard chuckled deep in his throat, a contented sound. 'Valiant knows the way home, you see.'

It was not yet dusk, but the 'tween-light was blurring the

outline of all things, when they came at last, two or maybe three miles down-river, to the ford of a stream brawling down from the high chalk, and saw through the smoke-soft screen of willows and alders the gleam of a firelit doorway reflected in the glossy darkness of a mill leat. 'Yonder is the Manor Mill,' Sir Everard said, as he steadied Valiant down to the ford and they splashed up on the farther side. 'And now—does the wind smell different? We are on Dean land;' and a while later still, pointing, as the woods fell back, 'See, up the valley yonder. There is Dean. That is your home, Randal.'

Looking where the finger pointed, Randal saw a straggle of deep-thatched huts and bothies strung along the track where it wound upwards towards the downs, the faint, irregular pattern of field strips striping the valley, and at the upper end of the straggle, set about with hawthorn and old fruit trees, a long low hall with its byres and barns around it. Beyond, only the steepening coomb winding upward, and the whale-backed ridge of the downs against a sunset that was like the echo of a brighter sunset somewhere else. Soft blue wafts of evening woodsmoke lay across the village, and the sunset looked as though there were trails of smoke across it, too. And as he looked, a queer thing happened; for it was as though something in Randal much deeper and older than his ten years, said softly and with certainty, 'Yes, this is home.'

A man crossing the track from the woodwright's shop with a new ox-yoke on his shoulder, turned to greet his returning Lord with a welcoming growl; a couple of women, one with a squalling baby on her hip, heard the clop of hooves and came to cottage doorways, and a scattering of children appeared from nowhere and ran grinning at Valiant's feathery heels, until their mothers called them in to supper. And all of them stared at the strange boy with the fair hair and dark skin, whom d'Aguillon carried before him. And tired as he was—it was a long ride from Arundel to Bramber, farther still from an old life to a new one—Randal felt their interest and curiosity, and stared back at them under his brows, wondering about them as only somebody whose chief experience of people is that they kick can wonder. But all the while, unwillingly, rebelling

against it because he did not want to be happy in this new life that Herluin had betrayed him into, the queer sense of home-coming was with him.

They were half-way up the village street when, with ears and tails streaming, three great hounds came bounding to meet them.

'Ohé, Luath—Luffra! Ohé, Matilda lass,' Sir Everard greeted them as they came yelping and weaving about him. 'Sa, sa! Here's a clamour! You will let them know through half Sussex that the Lord of Dean comes home!'

They did not jump up, having been trained like all good hounds not to leap upon a mounted man and startle the horse; but Luath, who was the tallest of them all, reached up and nosed Sir Everard's foot in the long Norman stirrup, while Valiant dropped his head to touch muzzles with the bitch Matilda, and Luffra, who was little more than a puppy, skirmished about them with tail and ears flying.

A big, half-wild pear tree, gnarled and twisted with age, hung over the gateless gap that led from the village street into the Hall garth, the little brown pears showing among the rusted leaves, and as they drew near, something that was not the wind made a sudden frowing and flurrying in the branches, and Randal, looking up, saw a long, thin leg in loose, russet-coloured hose appear from among the leaves. It was followed by another, and next instant a tall boy dropped lightly into their path almost under Valiant's nose, making the horse snort and sidle, and came to Sir Everard's stirrup as the knight reined in to a trampling halt.

'Bevis! That was a fool trick!' Sir Everard growled, patting Valiant's neck. 'Softly, softly my Valiant. Have you never seen the boy before? Have you no more sense, Bevis, than to come dropping out of nowhere under a horse's nose to startle him half out of his wits?'

'He's not really startled, only a bit surprised,' the boy said, with a breathless laugh in his voice. 'And I didn't drop out of nowhere. I was up in the pear tree, watching for you.'

'So? And how did you know that I should come home this evening?'

'Ancret said you would. She said she heard Valiant's hoof-beats this morning in the wind, and you would be home by dark.'

He was a tall boy, maybe a year or so older than Randal, with a thin, eager face that looked white in the twilight, under a feathery tangle of dark hair; and as he spoke, his gaze flicked from his grandfather to the boy riding before him, lingered, frowning a little, and flicked back again.

'Who is that?'

'A boy called Randal. Herluin, de Bellême's minstrel, who was your father's friend, sends him to you for a fellow varlet. For the rest—doubtless he will tell you himself, whatever he wants to tell you, by and by.'

Bevis turned his gaze again to meet Randal's, which had been fixed upon him since the moment that he dropped out of the pear tree. And they looked at each other, both frowning, a little wary, like two young dogs who walk round each other on stiff legs, uncertain whether they are going to be friends or fly at each other's throats.

'How long is he to be here?' Bevis said at last.

'That is as God wills. He will be varlet with you, and squire with you when the time comes.' Sir Everard sounded a little stern.

'I don't mind that'—Bevis spoke with a faint challenge, after a moment's silence—'so long as he remembers that it is *I* who have the right to be your body squire when *that* time comes, grandfather.'

Sir Everard laughed, deep in his throat, his sternness forgotten, and set Valiant in motion again. 'Since you have already been my varlet for two years, and so he must be two years behind you all the way, you may surely sleep secure on that score, unless of course I decide that your manners are too ill to fit you to be any decent knight's body squire—in which case I shall send you up to de Braose to herd the Bramber swine.'

The boy Bevis gave a crow of laughter, apparently completely reassured by this dire threat, and padded along at his grandfather's stirrup, with the hounds flowing all about him,

as they headed for the long, low Hall that was already shedding dim, saffron firelight through high windows and open doorway to greet them.

A sharper note of light, ragged and jaunty like a dandelion, came round the end of the Hall, and a little man, knotted like a tree root, came with a stable lantern swinging in his hand, to take Valiant as they clattered to a halt.

'Not washed away by the floods, you see, old Wulf,' said Sir Everard, and dropped stiffly from the saddle, lifting Randal down after him.

Randal was so tired and stiff from the long journey that his legs buckled under him, and he stumbled and all but fell before he got his balance. The lantern light swam round him for a moment, or he round it, like the autumn moth that had come fluttering out of the dusk to circle about and about the candle flame, beating soft, spread wings against the horn panes. Ever after, when he thought of that first coming to Dean, he remembered old Wulf's brown, toothless face lit from below by the lantern, and the powdery white moth turned to silver in its airy circling.

'Take him with you to help Wulf stable Valiant.' Vaguely he heard Sir Everard's voice above him. 'If he is to be varlet with you, he cannot begin too soon.'

And then, a little behind the boy Bevis, he was stumbling after the swinging lantern and Valiant's feathery heels, into the new life that was waiting for him to learn its ways.

RED AMBER

THE Hall was the heart and centre of the Manor, a long, low
timber-framed building deep-thatched with reed that was
bee-brown save where the new reed of a mended place shone
pale as honey, with its fire burning on a long hearth down the
centre of the floor, and the smoke-blackened beams showing
still where firelight or torchlight touched them, the red and
blue and saffron paint that had made them gay for a Saxon
master before the Normans came. D'Aguillon had made little
change in the place, save that for comfort he had built on a
small solar at the far end, raised up a few steps over an undercroft where they stored farm implements and spare bee skeps at
one end and the Manor's quota of war bows and leather jacks
in great iron-bound kists at the other.

The byres and barns huddled about the Hall, all within the
tangled hedge of hawthorn and the little half-wild fruit trees.
Below the Hall garth, the reed and turf and bracken-thatched
bothies of the villeins straggled downhill, each with its kale and
herb plot, its tethered cock among his clucking hens, its woodpile beside the door, its bee skep at the back; and beyond the
village stretched the three great arable fields, each divided into
long narrow strips, lord's land and villeins' land all mixed up
together, with the long, communal pasture lying between it and
the high, wind-haunted stride of the downs above, where
Lewin Longshanks kept the Manor sheep. It was all Dean land,
from the river in the east where the trading ships passed up to
Bramber or down to the open sea, away up to the whale-backed
ridge of Long Down, a mile and more to the westward; from
the ford by the mill where the Manor corn was ground, down-
river until the Bramble Hill thrust half across the valley, and,
so they said, the King of a forgotten people slept with his golden
treasure about him, in the heart of the green grave-mound
against the sky.

This was the share that Sir Everard's sword had earned him
thirty years ago, when he was young and followed de Braose
who followed Duke William from Normandy. A knight's share
of English land, held for the usual knight's fee, five mounted or
ten foot soldiers to follow his Baron in time of war, and in war
or peace alike, for the Lord of the Manor himself, a month in
every year spent on Castle guard duty at Bramber.

A small, self-contained world that, as the years went by, had
woven itself very closely into the fibres of d'Aguillon's being.
And it was the new world to which Randal woke, on his first
morning, lying in the deep fern beside the fire, with Bevis and
the hounds and the rest of the household; stiff and sore, bewildered, bruised and aching in heart as well as body, and yet
still with that unwilling feeling on him of having come to the
place where he belonged.

But in the next few days he lost something of that feeling.
The new life that he had to lead now was so very strange to him.
and it irked him like a too-tight garment. In the mornings, until
ten o'clock dinner, he must go across to the small, thatched
church just outside the garth, and sit with Bevis at the feet of
Adam the Clerk who looked after the souls of Dean and kept
the Manor Rolls, sniffing the smell of mice that always clung
to the little man's rusty gown, and struggling to make sense of
the marks that he scored on wax tablets and then smoothed out
and scored again. He must learn to handle light weapons, and
to tend old Valiant and Hector, Sir Everard's second horse,
and to handle hawk and hound; and all that part he liked. (He
knew already, of course, more about hounds than Bevis was ever
like to do.) But at meal times in the smoky Hall he must bring
water for Sir Everard to wash his greasy hands, and help to
serve him as Bevis did, for Bevis might speak with his grandfather as man to man, but that let him off none of his duties,
and he served the old knight on bended knee as the varlets and
squires served Hugh Goch in his Great Hall at Arundel. He was
quick to learn all these new things—his old life had at least
taught him to be quick-witted—but they still irked him because
he could see so little sense in them. And these were only the
surface things, for underneath there were others even more be-

wildering. Different ways of living inside oneself and treating other people from any that he had known before, things that he could only guess at, feeling in a confused and half-painful way that they might be good to know about, but not even beginning to understand.

Bevis might have helped, but Bevis and he were still watching each other from a long way off. They did their work together but when they were free, each went his separate way, and Randal was left to his bewilderments.

It was more than a sennight after his first coming to Dean, that the change came about. It was the day they started cider-making—perry-making would follow after when the later-ripening little brown pears had had time to go part rotten—and half the folk of the Manor were gathered at the top end of the Hall garth, where the cider press stood among d'Aguillon's apple trees. The cider press, like the mill and the dovecot, belonged to the Lord of the Manor, and everybody brought his own pears and apples to it for crushing. Randal and Bevis had been pressed into service with everybody else, fetching up the willow baskets of apples that the two villeins in charge tipped into the press, and though this also was new to Randal it was something that he liked wholeheartedly. The whole cheerful, crowded scene under the apple trees, centred about the great stone press with the plough-ox treading his patient circle harnessed to the pole, the sweet, heady scent of the half-fermented apples, the clear, amber stream of juice trickling down the narrow trough into vat after vat, had all the feeling of holiday that he loved.

So much so that presently he had forgotten that he was supposed to be working at all, and was standing on the outskirts of the throng with a basket of apples dumped at his feet, watching a flock of small birds busy among the seeding thistles in the corner of the garth. He had seen their like before, on the downs above Arundel when he was helping to run the hounds, but had never wondered about them. They were very beautiful little birds, and as they flittered from thistle head to thistle head, he saw the golden bars on their wings, and the patch of chestnut crimson on their foreheads. And then a gleam of sunlight woke

533

under the apple trees—it was a grey, drifting day of broken lights and shadows—and suddenly they were feathered jewels.

Delight sprang up in Randal, and he said to Bevis, who happened by at that moment with an empty basket, 'What are they? Oh, they look as though they had rubies in their foreheads!'

'Goldfinches,' Bevis said checking in his tracks. That was all; they didn't even look at each other, they were both watching the gold-touched and jewelled finches among the pale, silky thistle heads. But for the moment their delight leapt between them, making a bridge from one to the other.

Next instant, as though at some signal, the goldfinches burst upward in a puff, a flurry of little birds. They swept right overhead, the brief sunlight striking through their pulsing and quivering wings to touch them with fire, before they wheeled in a cloud and flittered out over the hawthorn hedge. Randal took a quick step back to follow their flight, caught his heel in something and sat full in a vat of apple juice that had been set aside under the hedge.

Amber juice sluiced over the edge of the vat, deluging Bevis who stood nearest, as with a breaking wave. And Randal, kicking and spluttering, saw the other boy's usually grave face above him, splintering into helpless laughter even as he grabbed his hands to pull him out. A splurge of voices had broken out all round them, half grumbling, half richly satisfied, according as grief for the loss of so much good cider or joy at seeing someone sit heavily and unexpectedly in a vat of apple juice was uppermost in this man or that. And in the midst of it all, Randal and Bevis stood dripping with sticky, golden juice, snatching at their breath and crowing with laughter and trying not to, because with Reynfrey the Steward, who had been one of d'Aguillon's men-at-arms, bearing down on them, they had a feeling that it might be no laughing matter.

'You young devils!' said Reynfrey, towering on them, his thumbs in the belt that held up his big stomach. 'I'll teach you to go playing the fool with the year's cider, that better folk than you have had the work of pressing!'

'But we weren't—we didn't—I stepped back into Randal

534

without seeing he was there, and Randal stepped back into the cider vat,' Bevis spluttered helplessly. 'Oh Randal, look out for that bee, you'll have it down your throat. It thinks you're a foxglove full of nectar or something!'

Reynfrey caught them each by an ear and banged their heads together, just to sober them a little, then turned them round in the direction of the Hall.

'Pull up your roots, and march, my fine young foxgloves, and don't let me see either of you again today.'

By the time they reached the Hall they were more or less in their right minds again, and Bevis said, 'If we can slip in quietly without Sybilla catching us, we can snatch a clean tunic each, and go and wash off in the stream, and no fuss.'

But Sybilla caught them just as they were letting themselves into the storeroom under the solar, where, among all the other things, the clothes kists lived, threw up her fat hands in horror and also decreed clean tunics and washing, but not in the stream and not without fuss.

Sybilla oversaw the household and the cooking, and Bevis and his clothes so far as he allowed anybody to do that. Now she shooed the boys into the storeroom as though they were chickens, and dared them to disappear again while she fetched the water that she had been heating for kale broth over the Hall fire. And they stood in the middle of the beaten earth floor, not daring to move for fear of where their drips might go, exchanging rather hesitant grins and rubbing one foot over the other, until she came back, lumbering from leg to leg and panting as she always did, for she was very fat.

'Ah, now, I did think at least you'd have had the sense to take off those sopping rags while I was away!' she scolded, setting down the great crock. 'Dear o' me! However am I to get these stains out? And me with my hands full enough already and naught but those lazy sluts to help me——'

It was when they were stripped that Bevis, standing a little behind the other boy, said suddenly, in a tone sharply drained of all laughter, 'Randal—let's look at your back.'

It was the first time that he had seen Randal stripped, for they slept in their shirts, and it was too late in the year for

river bathing except when one was really uncomfortably
dirty.

'Why—what is amiss with it?' Randal asked in a small,
guarded voice.

'It's all stripy. Did they—beat you a lot at Arundel?'

'Lovel beat me sometimes, like the other hounds.' Randal
screwed his head over his shoulder in an attempt to see his own
back. He had not been beaten since Herluin won him from
Hugh Goch, and that was more than two months ago now.
'Does it still show, then?'

'Didn't I say? It's all stripy.' Bevis sounded almost angry.
And then in quite a different tone, thoughtful and a little won-
dering, 'I never saw anybody with their backs all stripy before
. . . Yes I know, Sybilla, I'm *coming*.'

Sybilla clucked and scolded all through scrubbing them, and
seeing them into fresh shirts and clean woollen tunics smelling
of the herbs they were stored with to keep out the moth, then
threw the dirty water out of the door, where it deluged a flurry
of indignant hens; and finally surged away, leaving them to
follow or not as they chose. There was no question of locking up,
too many people had things in the storeroom that they might
need to get at, and the door was not secured in any way save
by a stout pin to keep out the hounds; things such as the war
bows that had to be kept close were locked in the great armoury
kists against the wall.

Randal was hitching at his tunic, pulling it up through his
belt in the Saxon way; it was Bevis's and too big for him, but he
had not a second tunic of his own until Sybilla or one of the
other women found time to make him one.

'Bide a moment,' Bevis said, rooting in the little carved kist
that held his clothes and belongings. 'Something to show you.'
He straightened and turned round, holding whatever it was in
his hand, gently and carefully, as though it were alive. 'Look,
now.'

It was an irregular lump of something roughly the size and
shape of two walnuts joined together, and of a dark, dusty,
greyish-reddish colour that looked as though there was some
other colour underneath.

'Take it in your hand,' Bevis said.

Randal took the thing, puzzled; he had expected it to weigh like a stone, but it weighed like a feather. 'What is it?'

'Red amber—a piece of very old red amber. A man called Laef Thorkelson who goes long voyages to the other end of the world gave it to me. It's a sort of magic; when you warm it, a sweet smell comes out, and when you rub it very hard in your hands something wakes up in it that pulls things towards it—threads and flakes of chaff and things. There isn't anything in here, but I'll show you another time. Laef Thorkelson called it the Gold of the Sea.'

'Gold?' Randal said, still staring at the dark lump.

'Hold it up and look at the light of the doorway through it.'

Randal, with a puzzled, half-frowning glance at the other boy, did as he was bid, and instantly caught his breath in wonder and delight, the same delight that he had felt in the goldfinches, but somehow sharper because the thing was more strange. For as the light struck through the dark lump in his hand it was transmuted. It became a thing of flame, like a flower when the sun strikes through it, shadowed and dimmed at its edges, burning with all the fires of life at its heart. Herluin had said that Randal had no music in him, and nor had he, not so much as would serve to set two notes together in their right order; but something in him answered to the smoky flame in the heart of the amber as the music-maker and word-weaver in Herluin might answer to a new song of Roland that no one had ever heard before.

'It is beautiful!' he whispered. 'It's so beautiful it's as though it would burn your hands! It's—it's Sea Fire, not Sea Gold.'

'Sea Fire,' Bevis said consideringly. 'Yes, that's what it is! Oh, I knew you'd like it, Randal.'

They looked at it together a few moments in a shared silence of delight. Then Randal gave it back into the other boy's hand.

It was a mere lump of dusty darkness again, the fires quenched, as Bevis stowed it away once more in the bottom of the kist. 'I keep it hidden under my shirts and don't show it to everybody, but you can see it whenever you like. Now come on,

let's take the hounds and run them up to Long Down and talk to Lewin and old White-Eye before supper.'

From that time forward, with nothing spoken on either side, Bevis and Randal began to hunt in couples, and Randal's feeling of having come to the place where he belonged returned to him.

And then a few days later he was lying up in the barn where the barley was stored to wait for threshing, and the big oxcart stood with its shafts pointing toward the rafters. Bevis had been captured by Reynfrey, who took the boys for sword and buckler practice, and set to hacking at a stake in the ground as though it was one of Duke Robert's men. Reynfrey, standing by, would call out the different kind of strokes that were to be used, and it was good practice, but not exciting. More fun, Randal thought, stretching all out like a hound, to lie hidden among the gold of the stacked barley and the sharper yellow of the drying beans that filled the barn even on this grey and blustering autumn day with something of sunshine, listening to the wind soughing across the thatch, when you should be doing something else.

A speckled hen appeared in the barn doorway, looked round her with a bright purposeful eye, and strutting across to the loose pile of bean stalks in a dark corner, settled herself to lay an egg. She had three there already, but Randal, who had a fellow feeling for her, and might himself one day need not to be betrayed, had not betrayed her. Presently Cerdic the Ox-herd came in and began to work tallow into the axles of the oxcart, which needed greasing, whistling as he worked, and all unaware of the boy peering down from the shadows between the unthreshed barley and the roof, and the little speckled hen watching him with an alert, gold-rimmed eye. It was all very pleasant and peaceful.

But Sybilla with a big rush basket on her hip surged into the doorway just as the hen arose with a triumphant cackling from the fourth egg. Sybilla pounced, with a speed surprising in anyone so fat, sent her streaking for the barn door with an outraged squawk, and gathered up the eggs, adding them to those already in the basket.

'As if I hadn't enough work already, without the hens laying in every corner of the garth!'

Cerdic laughed, rubbing the back of a tallowy hand across his nose. 'Reckon you'd expect them to come and lay their eggs in rows on the Hall doorsill, then?'

Randal, unseen in the barley straw, grinned with delight. Sybilla snorted. 'Get on with your greasing, and don't try to be more of a fool nor you are already!'

'Sour as a crab-apple,' said Cerdic, reflectively.

She hitched the egg basket higher on her hip. 'Well, 'tis enough to make anybody sour. The nicest little sucking-pig all dressed for d'Aguillon's supper, I turn my back on it for so long as it takes to go pull a few leaves from the bay tree, and now where is it? Gone!'

'Gone?' echoed Cerdic.

'Stolen! And if you were to ask me who stole it, I should say that scrawny little ferret d'Aguillon brought home with him from Arundel! The boy hadn't a-been here three days when I caught him stealing honeycomb!'

Randal, who, honeycomb or no, had seen Luffra behind the woodpile with the remains of a sucking-pig, on his own hurried flight from Reynfrey, was not grinning now.

Cerdic, who was big and patient like the oxen he worked with, had returned to his axle greasing, and said quietly over his shoulder, 'Be there all that harm, in a child stealing honeycomb?'

'Maybe not, so long as it *is* but honeycomb. But what d'Aguillon should want to bring him here for . . . Oh I'm sorry enough for the child. God be thanked there's no child in this Manor has marks on its back the like of those there are on his—though I make no doubt he earned them with his thieving ways. But if I'm never to leave my kitchen for a breath of time with an easy heart . . .'

'I'd not think too hardly of the boy. He and the young Master seem good enough friends.'

'Aye—since young Master saw his back.' She shrugged with a kind of fond exasperation, and her voice grew faintly doting. 'Soon as he saw Randal's back, a' course Bevis would do ought

in the world to make it up to him. Dear o' me, the soft little heart he has—I mind me how when he was scarce four year old, he would ha' given the little Sunday shoes off his own little feet to old Horn down at the mill because he'd cut his foot on a bramble root.'

Cerdic grunted, his head between the wheel and the side of the oxcart, and Sybilla hitched up her basket again, saying, 'Ah well, I can't stand here chittering to *you* all day with the pottage only half made,' and surged out.

Cerdic returned to his whistling, finished his greasing, and went out too, leaving the barn alone to the boy who lay with his head on his arms, hidden in the stacked barley.

Randal lay quite still for a long time. Once he thought he heard Bevis calling him, but he did not answer. He hated Bevis, he hated the whole world, but Bevis most of all. There was a feeling of black betrayal on him, worse even than when Herluin had changed his mind. He lay there while the long hours passed and at last the light began to thicken and grow mysterious in the great barn, as it does before twilight, telling himself that he didn't care. Presently he knew that it must be near supper time, and he was hungry; and because he didn't care, of course he didn't care, he slithered down out of his hiding place, shook himself like a dog, and stalked out and across the Garth where the evening mist was just beginning to rise among the old crooked apple trees, towards the Hall.

If the storeroom door had been shut, he might not have done it, even then; but some careless soul had left the storeroom door ajar. It gaped, a little cramped oblong of darkness, in the angle made by the solar's outside stair, as Randal came by. And he checked, half moved on, and checked again, staring in. The low undercroft was full of crowding shadows, but he could just make out, among the great armoury kists and new axe heads and spare bee skeps, the corner of Bevis's little carved kist: the corner in which the lump of red amber lay, with its fires quenched in the dark, waiting for the light to waken it again.

He glanced round quickly. No one was in sight, though he could hear the voices of Sybilla and the other women at their cooking in the Great Hall. Then he slunk down the four steps

into the narrow doorway. He was crying a little, though he did not know it, crying with a desperate sense of loss, as he eased up the lid of the kist, and thrust his hand inside. His fingers explored down through layer after layer of Bevis's clothes and belongings, and at last, at the very bottom, met the lump of amber. He pulled it out with a gasp, and without waiting to look at it—there was not enough daylight left to wake the fire, anyway—stowed it inside his tunic and shirt where it lay, not cold like a stone but light and oddly living against his skin. Then he shut the lid of the kist again, and stole out, as secretly as he had come.

Just outside the postern door to the Hall, which opened from the foot of the solar stairs, Bevis all but ran into him.

'Randal! I've been looking for you half the day! Where away have you been?'

'Out,' Randal said, and followed the other boy back into the Hall with his shoulders hunched and his head down.

That evening he was very clumsy in serving d'Aguillon at table. He spilled the salt, fell over Matilda, upset a cup of wine, and finally had his ears boxed by Reynfrey to teach him to attend to what he did; and when Bevis whispered to him, 'I tipped a whole wheatear pie on the floor the first time *I* served at table,' he turned his back on him. All evening he would not look at Bevis; had he done so, he might have been surprised at the puzzled and hurt look in the other boy's face.

For the past three nights they had spread their sleeping rugs and straw-filled pillows close together beside the fire, but tonight, when the time came for sleep, Randal waited until Bevis had spread his bed, and then took his own rug and pillow round to the far side of the hearth. Bevis had given up trying to talk to him by that time and so said nothing about this new arrangement. And Randal lay down and rolled over with his back to everybody.

As he did so, he felt the lump of amber against him. Tomorrow, before Bevis went to his kist and found it missing, he must find a safe hiding place for it. A very safe place where Bevis would never find it; Bevis, who had everything, who, from his secure world could give the shoes from off his lordly

541

feet to someone below him in the mud because they had cut their foot, who had shown him the red amber with fire in its heart, as the Lady Adeliza scattered largesse to a beggar, just because he was sorry about the stripes on his back.

But Bevis would not have the red amber any more; everything else, but not the red amber. Randal would have that; all the fire and beauty of the red amber for himself, because he could never have any of the other things.

THE WISE WOMAN

WHEN he woke in the morning he had thought of the perfect hiding place in his sleep.

All he needed was the chance to slip off on his own for a while, but at first it seemed that he was never going to get it. For after the early morning spent as usual over the writing tablets and trying to read Latin from a book with Adam Clerk, and after dinner in the Great Hall, Sir Everard summoned both boys to walk out with him to see how the autumn ploughing was going on in the South Field. Alfwine was ploughing with the big wheeled ox-plough that the whole Manor shared, his boy far ahead leading the patient, wide-horned oxen, and the cloud of gulls wheeling and crying in his wake. At the head of each furrow, where the field ran up towards the downs, the earth that turned up from the shear was mealy pale, but as the furrow went valleyward, the soil grew richer, until just above the edge of the River Woods it was deep, leaf-mould brown, with a glint of almost harebell colour where the light touched it.

That lovely and unexpected sheen of colour waking on the slabby darkness of newly turned earth made Randal think again of the flame springing up in the red amber where there was no flame before. He pressed his hand secretly against his stomach above the belt, and felt the light hardness of the amber lying there. He must find a chance to take it down to the hiding place before Bevis found that it was gone . . .

Both the chance and the need were upon him sooner than he expected, for when they came into the Hall garth again Reynfrey was waiting for a word with d'Aguillon about the choice of beasts for the autumn slaughtering, and Sybilla called to Bevis from the Hall doorway. 'Master Bevis, Master Bevis! *Where* is your shirt with the blue chevron bands?'

'In my kist,' Bevis called back.

''Tis not, then, for I've looked all through.'

'It must be!' Bevis said—they had closed in from shouting distance now.

'Go you and find it, then.'

'I will,' said Bevis, and he disappeared in the direction of the storeroom.

D'Aguillon was deep in discussion with his steward, and with a little sick lurch of the heart, Randal caught his chance, and disappeared in the opposite direction.

There was no time to be lost. Any moment now, Bevis would find that his treasure was gone. He wriggled through the weak place in the garth hedge that Bevis had shown him, and ran. He was making for the woods that licked in a long tongue up the steeply-winding coomb following the course of the chalky stream. They were mostly of stunted oak, hazel and hawthorn and elder, but in one place an ancient pollarded ash leaned out across the stream, and it was for this ash tree that Randal was making. A faint honey scent and a humming sound like the song of bees round the hive on a summer evening reached him even before he pushed his way through the tangle of dry hemlock stalks and seeding willow herb, to emerge on the bank where the ash leaned out over the water. It was the same scent, the same sound that had first drawn him to the place, days ago; for the stunted shape of the old tree was mantled in ivy and the ivy was in flower, though the oaks and alders were brown with autumn and growing bare, and the bees and wasps and drone flies had gathered to this last harvest of the year.

Randal reached up, and pushed aside a hanging swathe of ivy, pollen-powdery and sticky with the nectar of the green-gold flower balls, disturbing a painted butterfly as he did so, and felt underneath. Yes, there it was, a little hole in the ash trunk, just large enough to take four fingers. It was dry and tindery inside so that one could easily scratch it bigger with a bit of sharp stone. He had meant to show it to Bevis. . . . In frantic haste he searched about, found a bit of flint of the sort he wanted in the stream bank, and set to work. The hole had to be big enough to take his hand holding the amber, so that he could get the treasure out again as well as pushing it in. Fungus-speckled flakes of rotten wood crumbled away and fell, light almost as

dust, to the foot of the tree, and he got a splinter under his thumbnail and had to stop to suck it; and then at last the hole was big enough. He fished the lump of amber up through his neck-band, and thrust it into the crumbling, rough-edged hole, and settled it inside. Presently he would plaster up the opening with earth and moss, and it would be quite in the dark again. He had not looked to see the fire wake in it since he stole it out of Bevis's kist. Stole, stole, stole! He chanted the word inside himself. He was Randal the Thief; very well then . . .

There was a sudden swift brushing through the undergrowth behind him, and he let the ivy swing back over the hole and spun round just as Bevis came thrusting through the tangle of willow herb. Bevis's face had a queer pearly whiteness and his mouth looked exactly like d'Aguillon's as he halted and stood looking at Randal.

Randal gave a kind of whimpering yelp, like a puppy that is very frightened, and then stayed quite still. And so they stood, staring at each other.

'I thought something was amiss, ever since last night,' Bevis said at last. 'Where is my red amber?'

'I didn't—I don't—I don't know what you mean,' Randal stammered. 'I—oh *no*!'

For Bevis had taken a quick step towards him with fist upraised. '*Don't* you?' he said. '*Don't* you?' and there were queer little lights flickering in his eyes. And then the movement of the ivy that had not quite ceased swinging caught his eye and he looked beyond Randal, and saw the powdery trail of rotten wood and fungus powder down the bark of the old ash tree and lying at its foot. He looked at Randal once more, then reached out and thrust the ivy aside and saw the little hole with its freshly enlarged edges. He put in his hand and took out the piece of red amber. He stared at it, and then at Randal, his eyes wide and bright and his nostrils flaring above the clamped mouth. Then, still without taking his gaze from the other boy's face, he thrust the thing down the front of his own tunic. And all the while there was no sound but the sucking of the stream under the bank and the deep song of the bees in the ivy bloom.

Then Bevis cried out at him in a strange voice full of furious

grief, 'Oh, Randal, why did you do it?' and flung himself upon him like a wild beast.

In any ordinary fight, Randal would have held his own against Bevis, though the other boy was nearly two years older than he was, simply because Bevis had learned to fight fair, and he had not. But this was not an ordinary fight. Bevis seemed possessed of a devil. It was as though he did not even feel the blows which Randal, sobbing as he fought, drove into his white, furious face. He knocked Randal down and when the younger boy scrambled to his feet knocked him down again. Randal's nose was bleeding and his right eye was full of jagged stars; he was dazed and dizzied by the blows that seemed to come at him from all directions at once, and when he kicked or struck out his blows no longer found Bevis at all. He was down on the ground now, with Bevis on top of him panting in his face; they were rolling over and over together in a vicious flurry of arms and legs; his head was being banged on the hard, exposed ash roots, and everything was going dim and blurred and far off . . .

And then suddenly it seemed that it was over, and the devil was out of Bevis. Randal waited for more blows, but they did not come. Slowly he humped himself on to his knees and crouched there, one shoulder leaned against the ash trunk, his head hanging, and the blood from his nose dripping *splat—splat—splat*, like the ripe mulberries that he had once seen dropping from a tree at Arundel and making crimson stains on the flagstones. Bevis stood over him, drawing his breath in a queer, whistling way.

'Why did you do it?' Bevis said again at last; but whereas the first time it had been simply a cry, this time it was a question that demanded an answer.

Still crouching against the ash trunk, Randal looked up at him slowly, and saw with fierce satisfaction that there was a broken bruise on the other boy's cheek bone. 'Because I hate you!' he said hoarsely. 'I hate you, Bevis d'Aguillon, you and your old bit of red stone that you go round showing to people like—like a king giving something to a beggar! I never asked you to tell Reynfrey you pushed me into the cider vat when I fell in all by myself! I never asked you to be sorry for me and—

and *kind* to me because of my back! I don't mind my back—I don't *mind* being beaten.' His furious torrent of words fell over itself and his voice cracked into a wail. 'And all the while I thought—I thought——'

Slowly, the white rage in Bevis's face gave way to bewilderment. 'Randal, stop talking gibberish—I don't understand. I don't know what you're talking about.'

'Oh, yes, you do, because it's true—it's all true, isn't it?' Randal flung at him, sniffling through his bleeding nose.

'No it's not, then!' Bevis shouted. 'You're a horrible boy to think such things.'

'I'm not so horrible as you are!' They were both shouting now, shouting and glaring and ridiculous; but to them it was not ridiculous. 'You're the most horrible boy in all Sussex, for all that Sybilla thinks you're so wonderful!'

There was a little silence, and then Bevis squatted down on his haunches, close to the other boy. 'Did Sybilla fill you up with all this?'

Randal nodded. 'At least—she was talking to Cerdic; it was after Luffra stole the sucking-pig, and she thought I'd done it, and I heard——' He choked. 'I heard all she said.'

'Sybilla is a fool,' said Bevis as his grandfather might have said it. 'She's a *fat* fool—and you're a worse one for paying any heed to her.'

Randal did not answer. They squatted staring at each other among the tangle of the past summer's willow herb. Far off across Muther-Wutt Field they heard someone whistle to a dog, the low of a plough ox, the ring of hammer on anvil from the smithy, and above them the bees were busy in the ivy bloom. At last Bevis said, 'Well, of course I was sorry about your back; wouldn't you have been sorry about mine? It—it made me feel I wanted to hit somebody. But it wasn't anything to do with that, my showing you my bit of amber.'

Randal scowled at him out of the one eye he could still use. 'Why did you, then?'

'Because of the goldfinches, I suppose. And then you fell in the cider vat and we all started laughing; and after that everything was friendly, until—until——'

His voice trailed away, and the bee-haunted silence settled on them again. Strange things were happening in Randal. Something swelling up big and painful in his chest. So Bevis had wanted to be friends after all, and he had spoiled everything by stealing the red amber, spoiled it before it was well begun.

'Bevis,' he said in a small cracked whisper, 'oh, Bevis,' and could say no more, because there did not seem anything more to say, and because his throat was full of tears as well as the taste of blood.

And then the wonderful thing happened; for Bevis suddenly reached out and laid an arm across his shoulders and began to shake him, the small, easy, companionable shake that means friendliness as well as exasperation. The queer, pearly look had quite gone from his face.

'Don't you ever go listening to people like Sybilla again!' he said. 'Do you hear me? Don't you ever——' He stopped shaking. 'I've made a wicked mess of your face! Come on, let's wash off the worst of the blood, and then we'll go down to Ancret and ask her to salve it. Sybilla's hands are heavy, and besides she asks too many questions.'

They dropped down by the twisted alder roots on to the tiny spit of shingle, and set to work to clean up, in the swift, icy, downland water that smelled of watercress.

When they had got rid of as much of the blood as they could, both from themselves and the front of Randal's tunic, they set off to visit Ancret—the same Ancret who had heard Valiant's hoof-beats in the wind, on the morning of the day that d'Aguillon came home. Randal had heard stories about Ancret, queer stories, and he knew that she was herb wise, and doctored all the ills of the Manor. He knew that she had been Bevis's foster-mother after his own mother died, and that Bevis loved her, and he had seen her in the distance, about the village and the Manor lands, but he had not gone to see her in her own place before.

The shadows were lengthening as they crossed the familiar driftway that led up from the ford to the village, and headed southward, for Ancret lived withdrawn from the rest of the Manor folk, away beyond the cultivated land, within the fringe

of the woods below the Bramble Hill. A thrush flew out of a
hazel bush as they stepped out from the trees into the little
clearing that was Ancret's herb plot; nothing else moved, not
even the air. In that first moment Randal would not have
thought that there was a cottage there at all, save for the dark
oblong of a doorway in the side of a little green mound in the
midst of the clearing, and the whisper of woodsmoke, curling
out through a hole in the top to mingle its blue tang with the
wet wood and fallen leaf and coming frost smells of the autumn
evening. Certainly he did not see anyone besides himself and
Bevis in the clearing, until there was a movement by the door,
under the elder tree that grew there, and he saw, in the way that
a sudden movement will show a herd of fallow deer where there
was only dappled sunlight the moment before, that there was a
woman standing there. A woman in a faded, grey-green kirtle
exactly the colour of the bothy's turf roof behind her, who
looked as though she had known that they were coming, and
was waiting for them.

She was a small woman, slight and narrow-boned, but standing there under the elder tree she looked tall. Randal was to
find later that she always looked tall, that if she wore her rough,
homespun cloak with the great earth-coloured patch where she
had torn the hem, it fell about her like a queen's mantle. All
he saw now was that she had dark eyes—dark and full and
bloomed with light like a deer's, in a narrow, work-worn,
weather-browned face; and that her hair, hanging in thick
braids over her shoulders, had cloudy lights in the darkness of
it, the colour of the ripe elderberries, and was much younger
than the rest of her, like a girl's hair.

'Good fortune be to you, fosterling,' she said.

'Good fortune come with me, Ancret my foster-mother,'
Bevis returned, as they halted before her.

'You have come, then.' Again it was as though she were expecting them. She looked from Bevis to Randal and back
again. 'So, there has been the fine blood-letting. How did that
come about?'

'I hit him,' Bevis said, and shut his mouth exactly like his
grandfather.

Ancret looked at the bruise on his cheek, and the laughter shimmered at the back of her dark eyes. 'It is in my mind that he hit you also.'

'Well, of course he did.' Bevis rubbed the place and then hurriedly stopped as he found how sore it was. 'But mine's only a bruise and 'twill mend quickly enough on its own. I've brought him to you to put his face to rights, Ancret.'

She stooped, and took up a pitcher that stood beside the door. 'Then go you and draw me some water from the well,' and as he took the pitcher from her and went to do her bidding, she turned full to the younger boy for the first time. 'And you, come your ways in with me, Randal.'

She must have heard his name long before this, from the other Manor folk, but it made him feel a little queer all the same, to hear her call him by it, with her strange dark eyes upon him, and for a moment he was not sure that he wanted to go into the bothy that was like a little green mound; he had always heard that the fairy kind lived in mounds. But he remembered that she was Bevis's foster mother, and the laughter was shimmering again behind her eyes. So he nodded, and followed her down the three earthen steps through the low, dark doorway.

Inside it was not so dark after all, for the bothy faced west: the evening light came in down the steps and the smoke hole was so big that he could see a patch of milky sky and the shadow-flash of a bird's flight across it. The fire burned on a raised hearth in the centre of the round house-place, and little barley cakes were baking on the hot hearthstone, adding their own friendly, new-bread smell to the heavy smell of earth and the blue reek of woodsmoke and the aromatic tang of nameless herbs.

Ancret made him sit down on a stool at the foot of the steps where the light from the doorway fell strongest, and taking the pitcher from Bevis, when he brought it dripping from the well, she poured a little into a bowl and set it to heat in the hot fringes of the fire. Then she fetched a bundle of leaves from somewhere in the farther shadows, where it seemed to Randal that there were many strange things hanging that he could not

552

quite see, and took seven leaves from the bundle and set them
to seethe in the water. And all the time she spoke no word.
Randal had hoped that Bevis would come in too, when he had
brought the water, but Bevis had gone out again, and he could
hear him hammering something, a sound like a woodpecker but
sharper, *tap-tap-tap*, all the while they waited, he on his stool
and Ancret standing withdrawn into herself beside the hearth,
for the water to boil. *Tap-tap-tap, tap-tap-tap.*

When the steam rose and the surface of the water crept and
dimpled, Ancret took the bowl from the fire with a piece of
cloth wrapped round her hand, and broke other herbs into it,
and shook cold water into it from her fingers until it was cool
enough to use. Then she stripped back Randal's tunic, and with
the leaves themselves bathed the bruises on his arms and body
and face. She bathed his black eye, which was the sorest of his
hurts, last of all, and then laid her hand over it, and said in a
tone of authority, as though to someone or something that he
could not see,

> 'Out fire and in snow,
> In weal and out woe.
> Sorrow of flesh bid you go.
> In the name of St Luke of the Ox's Horns.'

She kept her hand there a long time, and it seemed to Randal
that a lovely coolness flowed out of her fingers, soothing away
the fiery throbbing that had been there before. And when at
last, with a long sigh as though something had gone out from
her, she took her hand away, he saw, squinting out of his usable
eye, that the palm and finger tips were reddened as though she
had scorched them.

It seemed that the thing was finished, and he got off the stool,
and stood looking up at her with a vague idea—he was too
battered by all that had happened both within him and without, to think of anything very clearly—that he should thank
her. But before he could find the words she took his damaged
face between her hands and bent to look into his eyes, holding
them with her own, so that he could not look away. 'You're no
Norman, like Bevis my fosterling and no Saxon either, despite

your hair. What are you, that Sir Everard brought home with him?'

'My mother was a Saxon lady, and my father was a Breton man-at-arms,' Randal said.

'Breton? So—the old blood comes back,' Ancret said musingly. 'Breton–Briton, Briton–Breton . . .' Then as Randal looked at her, frowning in bewilderment, she smiled. 'The Saxons drove out your kind, many and many of your kind that fled across the narrow seas and took refuge in the place they called Brittany; but when the Saxons' time was done, the old blood came flowing back, at the heels of Count Alain of Brittany, to Hastings over the chalk yonder, on the day that Harold died.' It was almost as though she were singing now, crooning to herself rather than to him. 'But we, who are an older people still, who were an old people when they raised the grave mound on Bramble Hill in the days when the world was young, we see the conquerors come and go and come again, and marry and mingle, but we know that all things pass, like a little wind through the bramble bushes. There are few of us, of the pure blood, left now, but something of our blood runs dark, dark like the veining in an iris petal, through all the people that come after. Even through you, under your thatch of Saxon hair.' How dark her eyes were, so dark that you felt as though you might lose yourself in them as in the stillness of deep water. 'Aye, the old blood runs strong, and comes into its own again; you should know that, you that Sir Everard brought home on his saddle bow.' In another moment, he felt, the dark, still water would close over his head and he would know something— something that he did not want to know. Then, in the very instant before it happened, she let him go, turned him to the little doorway that was mostly in the roof, and said, 'Out, after the other one.'

When he climbed up into the last of the sunset, Bevis was sitting on the sloping turf edge of the roof, with his knife in one hand and a heavy flint in the other. He stuck the knife back in his belt and sent the flint skittering away into the bushes, and drew his legs up with his arms round his knees. Randal scrambled up beside him—the roof came down so low that he only

had to put his hands on the edge and give a little hop—and settled himself with his legs swinging. He was not quite sure what they were waiting for, but he was content, with a content like the quietness after a storm, to be with Bevis and do whatever Bevis wanted. And in a few moments Ancret came out after them with two of the barley cakes hot from the bakestone and dripping with some dark, sweet, pippy mess which Randal had never met before.

'There,' she said, giving one to each of them, 'never say that Ancret sent you away hungry—though indeed it must be near your supper time, up to the Hall.'

Bevis looked at her contentedly, already licking the dribble of dark sweetness round the edge of his cake. 'I wish you still lived up at the Hall, Ancret.'

She stood with one hand on the branch of the elder tree that arched above them all, smiling a little secret smile. 'I lived for years up to the Hall, herded among other folk, for your sake, little fosterling, because I love you. Now I live my own life again in my own way, and when you want me, it is you who must come to find me. I shall always be here for your finding—while you need me.' The smile that had been secret flashed open in her dark, narrow face, 'I—and my bramble syrup.'

So that was what it was, this dark, sweet, pippy stuff. Randal took a bite of barley cake and chewed, then licked a blob of the syrup from his thumb, his tongue enjoying the sweetness even while the deeper part of his mind was still full of the things that had happened between himself and the boy beside him. Through the berry-laden branches of the elder tree he could see the Bramble Hill against the sky, and the turf hummock on its crest that Ancret said 'they' had raised when the world was young, and the other hummock of brushwood and furze roots that the Manor folk had been raising for days now, ready to be lit on All Souls' Eve, Reynfrey said, as the fires had been lit up there every All Souls' Eve and every May Day Eve since before the memory of man. All bloomed with shadows now, shadows crowding among the bushes and the bramble domes, quiet under a windy sky that was suddenly flying with the manes and tails of wild horses.

He licked up another blob of the stuff, crushing the pips between his teeth. 'It is good!'

'In all the Manor—in all this reach of the downs,' Ancret said, 'there is no bigger and sweeter fruit than you may find on the Hill of Gathering.'

'The Hill of Gathering?' Bevis said, questioningly.

'Did I say the Hill of Gathering? It is an old name; folk do not use it any more.'

Bevis swallowed the last of his barley cake and sucked his fingers. 'Maybe they called it the Hill of Gathering because of the great gathering that there must have been when they raised the barrow on the top—or maybe it's because of the gatherings when they make the fires and the Sun Dance on All Souls' Eve.' They were all three looking up towards the hill, through the elder branches, seeing it withdrawn into its own shadows, its own secrets, dark against the sunset.

'I wonder if it's true,' Bevis spoke again in a little while. 'I wonder if there *is* a king buried up there with all his treasure about him; gold cups and crowns and arm rings under the bramble bushes.'

Randal said without knowing why, 'It might be just a champion, with his sword.'

'Whatever there is,' Ancret said, sweeping round on them almost, for the moment, as though she were angry, 'you let him sleep. There's never aught but sorrow come yet to mortal man from the gold of the Hollow Hills. Now let you be off, for it's time and more than time that you were home to your supper.'

It was twilight as they came up towards the Hall, not by the driftway but over the fields, and just outside the weak place in the hedge, Bevis halted, holding out something that he had just fished from inside the front of his tunic.

'Here,' he said, shamefaced all at once. 'Take it, Randal.'

All Randal could see in the 'tween light was a dark lump about the size of a walnut, but the moment he touched it, his fingers knew it by the light, live feel. So that was what Bevis had been doing with his knife and the pebble outside Ancret's bothy: splitting his treasured piece of amber in two.

He stood with the thing in his hand, looking from it to Bevis

and Bevis and back again. Then he shook his head. 'You don't —have to do that, Bevis.'

'No,' Bevis said. 'That's why I'm doing it. Not because I have to—because I want to.' Suddenly he was in desperate earnest. 'Then we shall both have a piece of red amber—don't you see? Please, Randal.'

There was a long pause before Randal said gruffly, 'All right,' and then the moment after, in a small, hoarse rush, 'I shall carry it with me always.' And he thrust it into the front of his own stained and filthy tunic. Sybilla was not going to be at all pleased when she saw that tunic.

Sir Everard looked at their faces with interest when he saw them at supper, but made no comment. And that night Bevis and Randal spread their sleeping rugs and hard, straw-stuffed pillows alongside each other again.

THE CUSTOM OF THE MANOR

ALL Wales went up in flames that winter and they heard that Hugh Goch had called out almost every knight in the Honour of Arundel to follow him on a new, bloody campaign into the mountains. So the Lord of Arundel would have a better excuse than hunting in his Welsh forests, to account for being in the Marches when spring came. But de Braose was not a Marcher Lord, and so in the Honour of Bramber all was quiet as that winter went by.

The river woods that had been softly dark as smoke all winter broke out into the mealy gold of hazel, and the curlews were crying over the downs. D'Aguillon rode away to render his thirty days' knight's service at Bramber, leaving the boys in Reynfrey's charge; and by the time he returned, the spring ploughing was upon them. The swallows came back to the great Manor barn, and soon after the swallows, a wandering friar, who said, 'Have you heard the news? The news about Mowbray who sacked the Norwegian trading ships last year? Since the King summoned him to face his trial at the Easter Court, he has come out into open revolt! Arundel and de Lacy and William of Eu have all joined him, and most of the Marcher Lords. May the sweet Mother of God have mercy on us, for we are all sinful men!'

Randal went away by himself after that, and thought about the voices on the water stair that he had shut his mind to and managed not to think about for months, and would not tell even Bevis what was the matter.

Haymaking came, and then barley harvest. And a wandering minstrel came to sing for them at the boon feast afterwards, when the whole Manor supped with d'Aguillon in the Great Hall.

'You'll have heard that the King has marched north?' said the minstrel, tuning his harp. 'Oh yes, almost three months ago. Fé! Don't you ever hear *anything* in this corner of Sussex? He's got Mowbray, they say—captured him by a trick outside his own walls, and made his Lady yield up the castle to save her Lord's eyes. Very fine eyes, so I've heard, but they'll not be much use to him now, save to show him his prison walls or maybe the shadow of the noose dancing.'

Autumn came, and the nights were full of droning dorbeetles, and they brewed the year's perry. Winter came and went, and Sir Everard rode for Bramber again, to return thirty days later with the news that the King had brought Mowbray and his rebellious Barons before his Christmas Court at Gloucester. 'Aye,' he said, kicking his spurs beside the fire, and shaking the rain from his heavy war mittens, 'it seems that the loyal Barons dealt out hanging and mutilation with generous hands —the more so, maybe, because for the most part they would have been on the rebel side themselves, had they been more sure of success.' He generally spoke to his varlets as though they were grown men. 'Arundel? Arundel got off with a fine, being maybe too powerful even for the King.'

So it was finished, Randal thought, finished and done with as though he had never heard those voices on the water stair; and he felt as though he had escaped from something. He was wrong, quite wrong, but it was to be years before he knew it, and meanwhile, life was good.

He and Bevis were up on Long Down one wild evening not long after Easter; the second Easter of his life at Dean. They had been hoping to take out Bevis's new sparrow-hawk and fly her at starlings—Randal had no hawk of his own yet, but Bevis was going to help him catch and train one next spring, when Sir Everard judged that he would be old enough—but the wind had got up since morning, a wild wind with flurries of rain and bursts of sunshine on its wings, that set the cotters' geese scurrying and stripped the early fruit blossom and roared like a furnace in the river woods. Hopeless weather for hawking, but not the kind of weather when one could bear to remain indoors; and so they had come up to Lewin the Shepherd, their particular

friend, on Long Down where he had just brought the sheep up to their summer pasture, now that the lambing season was over.

They were huddled one each side of him in the shepherd's cave that he had made for himself in the heart of a thorn clump. He had two or three caves in different parts of the Dean sheep runs, but this one up on Long Down was the best. From outside there was nothing to be seen at all but the blackthorn tump, greyish white now with its fleece of blossom, but crawl under the low branches and you were in a sort of lair, part hollowed out of the ground, part out of the blackthorn tangle overhead. lined with straw and old skins, snug from the wind and the rain that drove across the shoulder of the down, yet with the whole countryside open before you.

And what a countryside, from up here on Long Down! Craning forward, Randal could look southward to the sea, northward to the Weald, Andred's Weald far below him, rolling away into the distance—the vast oak forests that cut this high down country of Sussex off from the rest of England far more surely than the sea cut it off from Normandy. Ahead of him the world fell away into the sweeping whorls and hollows of the river valley, then rose again like the waves of a slow sea gathering themselves to the crest of Thunder Barrow full four miles away, with nothing between him and it, but the emptiness of wind and rain and flying sunshine, and the wings of a sailing gull. Far below, and a mile or more away, he could make out the huddled roofs of Dean with its three great fields running to the river woods and the marshes seaward. And on the long curved slopes of the coomb-head below them, sheltered somewhat from the wind, Dean's sheep grazed in a quiet, grey crescent, watched over by Lewin and his dogs.

There were three dogs in the shepherd's cave, for beside Lewin's two, Bevis had brought up his new hound puppy, Joyeuse, one of Matilda's last litter. With three dogs and three humans in it, the little cave was somewhat close quarters; but to Randal it seemed to have a deeper feeling of shelter than a proper house could ever have, shelter as a wild thing in its lair might feel it. And when the sunshine that for the moment had been all about them fled on, and suddenly the next shower was

hushing overhead, with never a drop coming through—three days of steady rain, Lewin had once told him, before it came through the roof of a properly built cave—he shivered luxuriously and pressed his shoulder closer against Lewin's in its oily-smelling sheepskin cloak.

'It is good up here! Better than sitting round the fire in Hall, cracking last year's nuts!'

'Why so late in the day to come up, then?' Lewin Longshanks said in his deep, gentle, grumbling voice, never taking his gaze from the sheep below him in the coomb-head. ''Tis a'most time to be going home again, before you've well come, I'm thinking.'

'We couldn't get off earlier,' Bevis said, sitting with the puppy's leash twisted round his wrist. 'It's the day for the Manor Court, and grandfather likes us both to be there in Hall while he gives his judgements—he says it's part of our training. And such a lot seems to have piled up while he was at Bramber. Alfwine and Gyrth squabbling about their boundaries again, and Cerdic wanting leave to graze two more geese on the common grazing, now that he has another son, and Gudram claiming the Custom of the Manor that he should be forgiven six boon-days' work because the gale before Easter blew down his best apple tree. Quite a lot of them were things that Reynfrey could have dealt with just as well but——' his voice was suddenly thoughtful. 'They won't go to Reynfrey if they can help it, they save it all up for grandfather.'

Lewin turned on him a pair of very blue eyes that were wrinkled at the corners as the eyes of seamen and shepherds often are, though he was still quite young. 'Reynfrey is a Norman,' he said simply.

There was a little sharp, surprised silence, and then Bevis said, 'So is grandfather.'

'D'Aguillon is d'Aguillon, and Reynfrey is his paid man.'

'Reynfrey is kind enough, and just,' Bevis said hotly. 'Grandfather wouldn't have him for his steward if he was not.'

'But d'Aguillon is d'Aguillon of Dean,' said Lewin, and somehow the argument was unanswerable.

Nobody spoke for a while, and then Lewin broke the silence again. 'I mind my grandfather claiming the Custom of the

Manor from Wulfthere, our Thegn, when his apple tree blew down, the year before Hastings's fight.'

Hastings again. The Senlac that Reynfrey talked about sometimes, if you could get him into the right mood, stripping up his sleeve to show the long, white, puckered scar on his forearm. Senlac to the Normans, Randal thought, Hastings to the Saxon kind. 'Lewin, were you at Hastings fight?'

'I?—I was six years old on the day that Harold died. I remember Wulfthere riding off with his sons and house-carls, their weapons keen for war . . . I remember the women weeping. And then later came d'Aguillon your grandfather, and Reynfrey with a bloody clout round his sword arm, but never the old Thegn and his sons again.'

'I'm glad grandfather forgave Gudram his six boon days,' Bevis said, after a while.

The rain had swept on now, and the sun was out, dazzling the wet blackthorn blossom. 'The shadows are growing long,' Lewin said. 'Time you were away home, and the flock gathered in.' He drew his long legs under him and ducked out from the cave, the boys and dogs behind him, and cupping his hands about his mouth, sent the long-drawn folding call echoing down the valley.

'Coo-oo-oo-o-up! Coo-om along! Coo-oo-o-up!'

They knew that he would have no more time for them today, and took their dismissal in good part, for they were used to being sent packing by Lewin whenever he had had enough of them. Besides, it must be drawing on towards supper time. So they took their leave, doubtful if he even heard them, and set off for the distant huddle of roofs that was home. They walked quietly until they were through the flock, keeping Joyeuse on the leash, but once clear of the sheep, Bevis slipped her free and they ran, boys and hound puppy, laughing and shouting with the wind behind them, racing the long cloud shadows that swept along the shoulder of the downs.

When they burst into the firelit warmth of the Hall, with sticks and dead leaves and wet, torn-off petals of pear blossom and the first spatterings of the next rain squall clinging about them, they found the household already gathering for supper,

and a stranger there with Sir Everard. At least he was a stranger
to Randal; a fat man with pale blue eyes in a round, weather-
beaten face, who wore his sandy hair in braids like a woman
over the shoulders of his stained and greasy leather tunic, and
had beads of red coral round his neck and copper rings on his
bare arms. But Bevis greeted him as Laef Thorkelson, and asked
if his ship was at Bramber.

Laef Thorkelson! Randal's ears pricked at the name. So this
was the man who went long voyages to the other end of the
world, and had given Bevis the piece of magical red amber.
Almost without being aware of it, his hand went up to feel the
little bag hung round his neck under his tunic, in which he
always carried the half of the red amber that Bevis had given
him. And the huge, sandy stranger standing in the firelight
seemed just a little larger than life, as he gazed up at him.

Laef Thorkelson stood with his feet planted wide apart as
though they gripped the leaping deck of a ship, and grinned
down at Bevis. 'Aye, safe and fast in the lea of the downs, under
the Castle. And maybe tomorrow I shall sell de Braose a pipe of
wine or a damascened blade; but meanwhile here come I to
warm myself at the Dean hearth fire again—and find you a
good span taller than when I saw you last.' His small, bright
eyes, wrinkled at the corners as Lewin's were, turned from one
boy to the other, and he said to Sir Everard standing beside
him, 'It seems that your household has increased; I mind me
there was but one whelp when last I came this way.'

It was Bevis who answered, before his grandfather could do
so, flinging an arm across Randal's shoulder. 'He came to us
from Arundel, more than a year back, and his name is Randal
and he is my friend and will be squire with me by and by.'

After supper in the Great Hall, which Laef Thorkelson with
his great laughter made to seem as full as it did when the whole
Manor supped with d'Aguillon at Christmas or Easter or the
boon feasts between, the Lord of Dean and his guest settled
before the fire in the solar. Bevis and Randal had been allowed
to come too, and now they squatted in the firelight, Randal
busy oiling and burnishing Sir Everard's sword, while Bevis,
with Joyeuse asleep against his knees, did the same for the nut-

shaped helmet. For some time now it had been their task to keep d'Aguillon's war harness in good order, and it was a task that they loved, for it made them feel as though they were squires already.

Randal was glad that he had got the sword this time. It was a huge and beautiful sword, forged by the armourers of Saragossa, who were the best armourers in Christendom or beyond it; the firelight played on the blade like running water, and d'Aguillon's seal was cut into the fine reddish stone of the pommel. D'Aguillon sat on the foot of the low sleeping bench, with Matilda between his knees, the bitch crooning with half-shut eyes as he gentled her ears; and Laef Thorkelson, merchant and sea captain, sat in d'Aguillon's carved chair, with his great feet stretched to the fire. And so, sitting with the flicker of the burning logs on their faces, the two men talked companionably, the talk of old friends. They were very old friends, and it seemed that Sir Everard had even made one voyage to the far north with Laef Thorkelson in their early days. 'That was in the beginning of time,' he had said, speaking of it at supper, 'when I was young and not bound by wife or bairns or holding of English acres.' But just now they were discussing the news of the outside world, which was disappointing to Randal who had hoped for adventures and marvels and sea dragons, from the man who had given Bevis the red amber with fire at its heart.

He turned Sir Everard's great sword over to come at the other side, laying the wave-rippled blade across his knee, and set to work again with the oily rag, huddling closer to the fire as a fresh gust boomed against the house. The shutters rattled and the smoke drove down the chimney in a billowing cloud that made them all cough. Then the smoke cleared, and Bevis leaned forward over the helmet in his lap and flung another log on the fire, and the flames leapt up, reaching even to the corner where Tyri, Sir Everard's Norway goshawk, sat on her bow perch with her black and white mutes striping the wall behind her.

And at that moment, out of the quiet rumble of voices that he had long ago ceased to listen to, the name that even now could make Randal's heart lurch unpleasantly, caught his ear.

Hugh Goch!

'The King would have done well to remember that de Lacy and Hugh Goch are Marcher Lords.' It was Sir Everard who spoke. 'And that the Marches are ever the quickest part of his Kingdom to spark into revolt.'

Laef Thorkelson chuckled. 'Lucky for Hugh Goch to get out of that affair with no more than a fine, when William of Eu paid for his part in it with his ears and most of his fellows found their way to the Tower or the scaffold.'

'Aye, our Red King was lavish enough with the noose and the branding iron,' d'Aguillon said, drawing Matilda's soft ears out like wings on either side of her head. 'A stronger hand for dealing with his own Barons than he has for Normandy, seemingly.'

Laef grinned in his sandy beard. 'Maybe he'll not need to take Normandy with the strong hand, after all. There are more ways than one, so I've heard, of killing a cat.'

'So-o?' D'Aguillon's hands checked on Matilda's twitching ears. 'And what might you mean by that?'

Laef Thorkelson looked round at him, his elbows on his knees. 'Last November, Pope Urban, being taken with a vision, preached a Crusade at Clermont.'

'And?' said Sir Everard.

'Long before Christmas, Duke Robert was chafing to take the Cross. The thing is veritably cut to his measure, fighting, adventure and the hope of plunder besides—and all in God's sweet name. But to take the Cross, he must first come to some sort of settlement with Brother William. Also, he must have money. So—it is beautifully simple—they meet and come to terms. Robert has pledged his Duchy to William for ten thousand marks. So William has Normandy while Robert is away smiting Saracen's heads from their shoulders; and if Robert comes not back, he has Normandy still, and if Robert comes back—why then, William is within the gates, and it is Robert, even if he can raise the ten thousand marks again, who must drive him out.'

In the silence that followed, a burned log fell with a rustle into a red hollow on the hearth. Joyeuse whimpered in her sleep, chasing dream hares, her paws and muzzle fluttering, and

Bevis stroked her tawny flank, then went on burnishing the heavy, nut-shaped helmet.

'And all this is sure?' Sir Everard said at last.

'Have I ever brought you news that was faulty?'

'Not so far as I remember.' The corners of the knight's grim mouth quirked a little ruefully. 'It is news that concerns all England and much of Christendom somewhat closely; but the thing that I am chiefly wondering at this moment is—how are the ten thousand marks to be raised?'

'Not out of Red William's pouch. By you and de Braose and le Savage of Broadwater . . . All England is to pay another Dane Geld, so they say. Glad am I, and give thanks to Thor and the White Kristin, that *my* plough cuts its furrow in the salt sea, and no King may tax my acres.'

Sir Everard sat a moment staring into the fire, while Matilda whimpered and nosed at his hand, wanting to have her ears pulled again. Then he said, 'Ranulf Flambard must be taking great pleasure in life. I hope Red William is sufficiently grateful to his Chancellor who squeezes England for him like a ripe fig. Aye well, if 'tis more than three shillings the hide, we must do without the new yoke of plough oxen for a while.'

'Pass it on to your villeins and make them pay for their own field strips,' suggested the sea captain.

Sir Everard looked up from the fire, with the odd gentleness at the corners of his wolftrap mouth that came there sometimes, but not often. 'Who have had the same poor lambing season as my own . . . I've held Dean for half a lifetime, friend, but not in *that* way.'

And in a while they returned to an earlier part of their talk, and the knight was asking, 'What of young Henry? Does he take the Cross with Robert, or join William to help him reive away Robert's Duchy?'

'So far as I have heard, neither, but bides him quiet in his own Castle of Domfront, which is about all that the other two have left him.' Laef Thorkelson let out a harsh bark of laughter like the bark of a dog-seal on a foggy night. 'Na na, you cannot blame the young one for the times that he has joined whichever brother offers the best chance for his sword, against the third,

since whenever they make common cause it is to turn against *him*. Munin and Hugin! What a brood of wolves, these sons of the old Conqueror! Brother ready to tear brother's throat at a word!' And then, with a sudden change of mood, he leaned across and brought down a hand like a hammer on d'Aguillon's bent shoulder. 'Not such brothers were we, in the days of our hot youth, eh, old lad?'

And now at last they were away into the sort of talk that Randal had hoped for. Wonderful talk of steep green northern seas, and icebound lands where the sun never set all the summer long nor rose in the winter days; of hunting great white bears for their skins, and the strange flickering lights that played across the northern sky like a vast diadem of flame in the winter nights, and made a sound like the rushing of mighty wings overhead. Strange, heady talk that flashed and flickered like the northern lights in the small, firelit room where the rushing of wings was the spring gale roaring in from the sea over steep miles of English downland.

Randal's head was still singing with it, like the echo of harp song, when at last it was time for bed, and he went with Bevis to bring up the little dried apples and late night cups of wine for Sir Everard and his guest. But under the singing, the thing that he was really thinking about, was the old Norman knight in his Hall saying, 'I've held Dean for half a lifetime, but not in *that* way'; and Saxon Lewin, in his shepherd's cave on Long Down, saying, 'd'Aguillon is d'Aguillon of Dean'; and the six days' boon work that Gudram had been forgiven because it was the Custom of the Manor. He thought about those things, which were really one thing, a good deal.

ALL SOULS' EVE

THEY had been down in the river woods, helping Lewin Long-shanks to make hurdles for the lambing pens, and now they were on their way home. The woods were very still, with the still-ness of an autumn day drawing on towards evening, frost-scented, leaf-mould-scented, woodsmoke-scented where they had been burning scrub, and the boys, with Joyeuse running ahead like a tawny shadow, loped along through the stillness without dis-turbing it save by the occasional contented cracking of a hazel nut. The blackberries were over, but there were still nuts in their green-frilled cups to be found on the hazel bushes, and Bevis and Randal gathered them as they went along and cracked them in their teeth, picking the milky, brown-skinned kernels from among the broken shell shards, and crunching happily.

Two and a half years had gone by since Gudram claimed the Custom of the Manor when his apple tree blew down. Good years, and very full ones. And this one the best yet, Randal was thinking, remembering bitter cold night-time visits to Lewin at the lambing pens, hot summer evenings spent lazy by the river with nothing stirring in all the valley save the plop of a water rat under the bank, the joy of the first time his hawk came back to the lure after making its kill . . . Bevis had been made a squire at summer's end, on the very same day that they had heard of Hugh Goch's death in Wales, shot through the eye in a skirmish with Norse raiders.

'The Old Lion led the Norman centre at Hastings,' Lewin said softly into his golden beard, when that news came. 'Now the cub dies of an arrow through the eye, as Harold Godwinson died.' And he gave one of his own ewe lambs to Steyning Priory as a thank offering.

So Hugh Goch was dead, and de Bellême was Lord of Arun-del after him, and Randal wondered whether perhaps now he would see Herluin again. But de Bellême had been campaigning

with the King all this while, helping secure the Marches of Normandy, and had not yet come to take possession of his English lands. Maybe later he would come—there was a rumour that the King was returning in the spring—and Herluin with him. It was not so very far from Bramber to Arundel . . . It would be good to see Herluin again. He had known that for quite a while now. Little by little through the four years since it happened, he had come to understand that it had not, after all, been betrayal, when de Bellême's minstrel changed his mind.

They had reached the place where the woods opened, and slowed to a halt, turning as by common consent to look up at the Bramble Hill that Ancret had once called the Hill of Gathering. There was a little wind stirring on the Bramble Hill, though down here on the edge of the river woods the air was still. Randal could see the shivering and frowing of the bushes and bramble domes that crowded thick about the long green barrow up there against the sky, and on the level space before the barrow, the dark, beehive shape of furze branches and piled brushwood, for once again it was All Souls' Eve. Tonight, as soon as dusk fell, the fire would be lit, and almost every soul on the Manor, and as many as could get away from the Manors round, would be up there dancing with home-made torches kindled at the blaze, making of themselves a great spinning wheel of light in the autumn darkness.

'I wish d'Aguillon would let us join in the Sun Dance,' he said suddenly, using the name for it that he had heard Ancret use, and Bevis after her.

Bevis nodded, still staring upward with eyes narrowed into the westering light. 'So do I, in a way, but they wouldn't really want us up there. It's—a thing you have to be part of, not just join in from the outside.' He laughed. 'And poor old Adam Clerk would nigh on throw a seizure, I'm thinking. He is upset enough every year, as 'tis, because grandfather will not stop the fires altogether.'

'Yes, but I don't see why,' Randal said seriously.

'I suppose because he's a Christian priest and thinks it is his duty to stamp out all that has to do with the Old Faith. But the

trouble is that there is such a lot of the Old Faith, and he's such a very gentle stamper!'

Joyeuse, who had been foraging to and fro in the undergrowth, came trotting up with a piece of rotten wood in her mouth, rippling with proud delight from her moist, mushroom-pink muzzle to the tip of her sweeping, golden tail. They had taught her to retrieve for them when they went hawking or shooting, and retrieving for Bevis—it was always Bevis she brought the fallen birds to, even when it was Randal's arrow or hawk that had made the kill—had come to be so much a part of her that when there were no dead birds, she brought him sticks and flints and anything else that she could find. Bevis took the bit of wood from her, laughing; it was part of a rotten birch branch, with fungus that looked like a scatter of red-hot sparks clinging to it, and stooped and caught her muzzle in his hands and shook it, while she danced about him with lashing tail, and a few moments later they were on their way again, the matter of the Sun Dance quite forgotten.

Presently they came over the shallow neck of the woods that ran up between North and South Fields, and saw in the distance their own Mill, and the ford of the Dean stream above it. The few elm trees by the Mill stood up tall and stately golden, the hazels and alders by the ford kindled to a more russet fire by the setting sun: the whole wide, wooded valley wound its way up to Bramber touched with apple colours, bonfire colours, as though the woods too made their Sun Dance, and the faint mist of the frosty evening was already rising blue as bonfire smoke under the trees. Among the hazel scrub that half hid the track from the ford, there was a flicker of movement, and a glint of sharp emerald colour that was alien to the tawny hues of All Souls' Eve.

'Look, Bevis,' Randal said, 'there's someone coming up from the ford.'

Bevis looked in the same direction. 'Stranger, by the look of him. I wonder whether he's for us, or only heading down the river for Durrington or Broadwater—come on, let's go and see.'

They whistled Joyeuse to heel, and went swinging down

through the hazel scrub at top speed, for in their world strangers were always an event.

The man whom they met on the river track rode a fine bay palfrey, and his tunic, with its long, trailing sleeves turned back with fur, showed lizard green under the darkness of his cloak. A man with a plump, smooth face and brilliant, colourless eyes on either side of a surprisingly thin, high-bridged nose. But his voice, though smooth like his face, and with the barest trace of a lisp in it, was pleasant enough when he spoke, reining in his horse as the boys and hound reached him.

'God's greeting to you. I am a stranger in these parts. Can you tell me if I am on the right road for Shoreham?'

Bevis shook his head. 'You are on the wrong side of the river for Shoreham, sir. You should have crossed over at Bramber.'

'I had a feeling that was the way of it. I was misdirected by some fool of a villein. Would I had the flogging of him.' The man showed his teeth for a moment, then turned the furious grimace into a smile, and shrugged. 'Assuredly this is not my fortunate day—which comes, maybe, of journeying on All Souls' Eve. If I turn back now I shall not be in Shoreham, if 'tis as far as they say, until long after dark, and to crown all else, Grisart here is working loose a shoe. Who's Manor am I on now?'

'This is Dean, sir,' Bevis said. 'My grandfather, Sir Everard d'Aguillon, holds it from de Braose. In his name I bid you most welcome to all that the Manor can yield, both for yourself and your horse.'

'Ah, a cup of wine, maybe, while your Manor smith sees to Grisart . . .'

Bevis smiled, with the quick back-toss of the head which was so much a part of him. 'I am very sure that my grandfather will not be content to lose your company before morning, if your business in Shoreham will wait until then.' He set his hand on Grisart's bridle. 'Come, this track to the right leads up to the Hall.'

Randal had said nothing all the while, looking up at the stranger knight under his brows. There was something he had known before about the man, and yet he was sure that he had

never seen the plump, smooth face until this moment. The half-memory made him uneasy, because mingled with it was a queer feeling of evil, a feeling of a shadow falling across him, across all Dean.

The man had wheeled his horse into the track that led up towards the village, Bevis walking at his stirrup and Joyeuse running ahead, and Randal fell in behind them, still frowning. He never took that track, even now after four years, without remembering the first time, and feeling again something of that lovely, unexpected sense of home-coming. He felt it now, so sharply that it hurt him.

Ancret, who had come up to tend old Wulf for the ague, was crossing the Hall garth with a crock in her hand as they came in through the gate gap under the ancient pear tree. She turned to look up at the stranger, herself aloof as a shadow, drawing back her skirts a little as the horse went by. It was a strange, deep look, and when they were past, the man made the sign of the Cross, saying half-angrily, 'That's a darkling look to meet at the day's end! I wonder you care to keep such a bird of ill-omen about the place.'

'That is Ancret, my foster-mother,' Bevis said quickly and a little hotly. 'She is herb wise and heals all our ills hereabouts. I don't think she would waste her magic putting the Evil Eye on anyone.' But he too made the sign of the Cross, not for any fear of Ancret, but because it was not good to talk of the Evil Eye, especially towards dusk on the eve of All Souls.

The sound of horses' hooves clattering to a halt before the Hall door brought Sir Everard from the storeroom, where he had been checking over the Manor's stock of war-bows with Reynfrey. He greeted the stranger with the grave and somewhat stiff courtesy that he had for all guests, as Bevis held the stirrup for him to dismount. And a little later, while the older boy went indoors to help the stranger wash off his dust and see to the laying of an extra place at table, Randal was leading Grisart down through the village again in the direction of the smithy.

He waited, sitting on the horse-block outside, while Cissa, the little black-browed Manor smith, dealt with the loosened shoe; then he brought the big bay palfrey up to the Hall again.

By now it was the time of the evening that Lewin called owl-hoot, and in the long, thatched stable where all the Dean horses had their stalls it was already deep dusk, filled with the good scent of the horses and the evening hay in the mangers, and the lazy sound of champing. Randal called for Elli the stable boy, and bade him light and bring the stable lantern and hang it in the spare stall, then fetch water and fill the empty manger, and while the bay, having drunk as much as he judged good for him, grew busy with the hay and beans, he fell to rubbing him down. Bevis came in before he was half-way through and set to work beside him. In public they were careful to keep up their relative position of squire and varlet, but in private they did all things together, as they had always done. Elli had gone off again to his supper, and they were alone with the horses.

'What is amiss, Randal?' Bevis asked suddenly.

'Nothing,' Randal said, shaking out the big horse rug. 'Have you heard what his name is yet?'

'Sir Thiebaut de Coucy. Why? Do you know something about him?'

'I? No I——' Randal stumbled; 'I don't think so. Bevis—I don't like him.'

'I don't like him either,' Bevis said after a moment. 'But he'll be gone in the morning.'

They finished rugging Grisart, then turned towards the door, Randal carrying the lantern. At the next stall he checked, and went in for a good-night word with Swallow, his own horse. Swallow was grey; not the hard, iron colour of most grey horses, but a soft, smoky grey, deepening almost to black at ears and muzzle. Randal had loved him even before he was old enough to manage anything bigger than a pony, when the tall grey was just one of the Dean horses. It still seemed to him a wonder that Swallow was his, and just as the old sense of home-coming had hurt him earlier that evening, so now his joy in possessing Swallow was suddenly so piercing sharp that it hurt him too. He put his arm over the arch of the grey neck, as the horse whinnied softly and swung his head to greet him, and pressed his face a moment against the horse's cheek, holding to him as though for

comfort against this queer feeling of a shadow having fallen across them all, that he could not shake off.

Bevis had strolled on, pausing for a word with his own Durandal, and with the old war-horse Valiant in the end stall. Now he checked again in the doorway to call, 'Come on, Randal. We shall be late for supper.'

And Randal gave Swallow a parting pat, and went after him.

The household was already gathered when they entered the Hall; d'Aguillon and their guest sitting at the high table, and the rest of the household, Ancret among them this evening, at the lower tables set up on trestles in the body of the Hall. It was a fast day, but with thick fish soup flavoured with saffron, and eel pies and kale and good, dark barley bread, and baked pears stuck over with sorrel and rosemary for the high table, nobody felt the lack of meat. And when the meal was over, and Bevis and Randal with the house churls to help them had cleared the tables and stacked the trestle boards away, they drew the benches to the central hearth, and settled with the Lord of the Manor and his guest and the hounds about the fire.

It had been autumn out in the woods, but it seemed full winter now, and they put up the shutters and huddled close about the hearth, stretching out their feet among the dogs who lay blinking at the flames. Often after supper Sir Everard played chess with the boys, as part of their education, or sometimes Adam read to them from his treasured *Lives of the Saints*. But tonight they had a guest, and instead of chess or reading, they turned to him for news of the outside world.

And so, sitting with his back propped against the blackened kingpost of the Hall, his face with its pale, brilliant eyes now lit, now lost, in the flare and fall of the firelight, Sir Thiebaut talked. He talked well and interestingly, telling them the latest news of the Crusade that was now sweeping to the very gates of Jerusalem, speaking the great names, of Duke Robert himself, of Raymond of Toulouse and the bold Tancred, talking of the sieges of Nicaea and Antioch, the battle of Dorylaeum (the names sang themselves like a charm, like the runes on a Norseman's sword). And all the while Randal, heel-squatting against Luath's warm, rough flank, watched his face in the red light of

the fire; that queer half-memory still teasing and tugging at him with the certainty that somewhere he had known Sir Thiebaut de Coucy before.

He talked of London too, of the splendours that were to be found there, a little condescending in his manner, while the Sussex draughts set the rushes eddying on the floor and blew the acrid smoke into one's eyes.

'If Saxon Harold could rise from his grave now, my Faith! His one eye would start clean from his head to see the change that Norman power and skill has wrought in London.'

Randal, still watching the man's face, felt the Saxon half of him stiffen, the hair rise a little on his neck like a hound's when it is angry. One did not speak so of Harold Godwinson here in this corner of Sussex where so many of the Manors had been his own. And Sir Everard seemed to feel the same, for as though to cover the other man's slip of courtesy that had set the house churls bristling, he said quickly, 'Doubtless London is a fine city, these days. To us, with all Andred's Weald between, it seems like a city of another world. But even here in our remoteness, we hear things from time to time. Is it true that they have built a stone bridge across the Thames?'

'Aye. That is Ranulf Flambard's handiwork. These two years past he has been raising for our Red William such a city as no King in Christendom can better.' He laughed at the back of his high-bridged nose. 'Indeed, 'tis so that I am in these parts—on Flambard's behalf, to beat up your Sussex Barons into providing me more drafts of craftsmen to work your Sussex oak for the roof of the great new Hall at Westminster . . . Say now, have you any skilled woodwrights or trained dressers of stone on the Manor?'

Sir Everard's stern gash of a mouth quirked a little at the corners. 'Edda who can build and patch a flint wall, and Wilfram who can make a wagon wheel with any man in Sussex, but not such, I think, as would serve to work the roof of the King's Hall. Why do you need more workmen suddenly at this stage of the work?'

'To hurry it to its finish. You will have heard the rumour that the King comes again in the spring? Red William has as good as

finished his campaigning in the Norman Marches; and what is there, once Normandy is safe, but to return to England? Aye, and once returned, there are those who prophesy that he is to be crowned again—and where but in his own new Hall? That would mean a bishopric for Ranulf Flambard, and Ranulf Flambard knows it.'

'But why crowned again?' Sir Everard said. 'Once knighted, one does not kneel a second time for the accolade.'

The stranger shrugged. 'He has been crowned before, yes; with the crown of England alone; but see you, now he has made all again as it was in his father's day, he is King of England and Count of Maine and Duke of Normandy.'

'Only Duke of Normandy until Robert rides home from his Crusade.'

'Why as to that, there may be two thoughts concerning the matter: Brother Robert's and Brother William's.'

The two men looked at each other in silence, and then, as though to change the subject, Sir Thiebaut glanced about him at the faces in the firelight, and said in a tone of faint amusement, 'You have a strangely shrinking household, Sir Everard. Surely there are fewer of us round the fire than rose from supper a while since.'

For a moment nobody answered. Randal thought of the brushwood pile that he and Bevis had seen on the Bramble Hill. For some while past he had been aware of one after another of the household folk rising and melting away after Ancret into the darkness, and he was sure that Sir Thiebaut had been aware of it too.

Adam Clerk broke the silence, twisting his thin hands together in deep distress. 'I do try—I do most humbly and truly try to bring them with a whole heart to Christ, but they come to Mass on Sundays and Saints' Days, and turn at all other times to their Horned God, no matter how hard I strive to make them see that he is the Devil. And Ancret is the worst of them, for all that she gives the wax from her bees to make candles for our little church. It is my fault—I am sure that it is my fault—but really I do not see what more I——' His eye fell on Bevis raking in the hot ash with his dagger, and he shook his head. 'Even the

boys burn nuts in the fire to read their futures when they should be thinking, on this night of all the year, of their immortal souls!'

'So?' The amusement deepened in Sir Thiebaut's silken voice. 'I had thought it might be that. Do you dance round a sacred thorn tree? Or is it a Fire Festival, hereabouts?'

Sir Everard rose, touched the little clerk's drooping shoulder kindly in passing, and turned to the lower end of the Hall. 'Come to the door and see what we do hereabouts.'

Bevis and Randal had risen too, the hounds all about them, and slipped ahead to raise the heavy doorpin and have the door open for the Lord of Dean and his guest; and a few moments later they were all outside in the darkness of the foreporch. It was very cold, with the tang of frost sharp in the air, and a little mean wind that had risen with the coming of dusk; and below in the darkness of the river woods the owls were crying. Southward, upward of two miles away, the Bramble Hill rose blackly against the crackling brightness of the stars; blackly, but wearing a feathered crest of fire. And even as they watched, flecks of light brilliantly and deeply coloured as the heart of the red amber seemed to break off from the main brightness and go circling and swooping about the dark shoulders of the Hill.

The Sun Dance had begun.

Randal was standing very close to Sir Thiebaut, and as the man moved, huddling his cloak around him, it seemed to the boy that a faint, sweet, animal scent stole out from under the dark folds. It was very faint, the merest ghost of a perfume put on days ago. The warmth of the hearth fire must have woken it, but in the Hall it had been masked by the stinging tang of woodsmoke that blunted one's nose. There was no woodsmoke out here, and instantly Randal knew it for what it was, the animal sweetness of musk.

Even as he realized it, Sir Thiebaut spoke again. 'So—a Fire Festival indeed! Doubtless the sun will be greatly encouraged to return in the spring, thereby.'

And now that it had no face to it, now that Randal was standing in the dark with the scent of musk in his nostrils, the voice did the rest; a smooth voice with a trace of a lisp, so smooth that

there was about it an odd suggestion of hairlessness. The voice that he had heard on the water stair at Arundel, four years ago!

His heart began to race, and the scent of musk suddenly made him want to retch. He pressed back against the doorpost behind him, telling himself that it didn't matter now, it couldn't matter. The plot to kill the King and set his cousin in his place was three years dead, and though, seemingly, this man had been one of the lucky few to slip through the net afterwards, his being here could not matter now, could not possibly bring any harm to Dean. His sense was telling him all that, desperately, over and over again, but far down below the level of sense, he was struggling like a fly in a spider's web, caught in horrible dark, sticky strands that reached out to him from the old life behind him, struggling but unable to get free. It only lasted a moment; then he took a deep breath and told himself not to be a fool, and straightened from the doorpost.

Sir Thiebaut must have asked some question while he was not listening, maybe something about the Hill itself, for Sir Everard was saying, 'It has been in some sort a sacred hill, and the Manor has made its fires there since before the memory of the oldest man in the valley and his grandfather before him. There's a legend of a king buried in the green howe up there, with all his treasure about him, and whether that was aught to do with the thing, I would not be knowing, I who am mere Norman. I doubt if they know themselves.'

De Coucy made a small, abrupt movement, and the smoothness of his voice sharpened a little, as he took up the one word that really interested him. 'Treasure! It would be gold, think you?'

'Gold, I imagine, and fine weapons which have ever been the treasure of the fighting man—if indeed it be not merely the gold of legend.'

'But do you tell me that you have never taken measures to find out?'

'I have never felt the smallest desire to find out,' Sir Everard said simply.

'Ah, you are wasted on this greedy world. You should be in Steyning Priory,' said the smooth, faintly-amused voice. 'Faith!

If it were on my land I'd have every villein on the place to work, and the whole barrow laid open to the sky.'

'It would have gone hard with our fields the while. Besides, if men that we have forgotten laid a king's treasure there with their dead King, it was not done that men of a later year might dig it out and put it to their own uses. If it is only the gold of legend, then 'twould be a pity to rob it of its shining.'

'Such niceties are beyond me,' Sir Thiebaut said impatiently, then deliberately lightened his tone, and shrugged, half laughing, and shivered. 'But to each man his own affairs . . . It is cold out here, my friend. In Heaven's name let us go back to the most pleasant warmth of your fire.'

Randal took his chance as the others turned back to the firelight, and slipped out into the night, and round the end of the Hall towards the stables. His heart was still beating uncomfortably fast, and the palms of his hands were sticky despite the cold, and he knew that he was running away from something; but he always ran away from things.

Bevis found him squatting in the dark, safe shadows of Swallow's stall a while later, and demanded with worried exasperation, 'Randal, what *is* amiss with you tonight?'

Randal shook his head. He had never kept anything from Bevis except this one thing. But if he told him about Sir Thiebaut he might feel that he must tell Sir Everard, and Sir Everard might feel it his duty to tell de Braose, and who knew where the thing might end. He was afraid, desperately afraid of what might happen if the old evil were woken up and dragged into the daylight.

'I felt sick,' he said. 'I ate too much eel pie for supper, and I felt sick.'

And that was a kind of running away, too.

THE HAWKING PARTY

Sir Thiebaut rode off next morning, leaving behind him a feeling like an evil taste lingering in the mouth. But little by little the day to day life of the Manor closed over the whole incident, and at last even Randal almost forgot about him.

The King returned in the spring, and at Whitsun he was crowned a second time. Crowned in his great new Hall at Westminster, under the roof of Sussex oak. And Ranulf Flambard duly received the Bishopric of Durham. 'King of England, Duke of Normandy and Count of Maine' ran the Red King's titles. But with the first autumn gales came the news that Brother Robert was on his way home from Jerusalem.

Christmas came, and then it was New Year; a new year and a new century.

'An old world has passed and a new world stepped into its place in the last hundred years,' Sir Everard said to Bevis and Randal as they walked back from Midnight Mass in the tiny, flint-walled church, ice crackling in the ruts underfoot, and checked to watch the winter fires of Orion swing low above the Bramble Hill. 'And what this new, untouched century holds for men, God, He knows. But I think that before it is half spent, there will be no more talk of Saxon and Norman, but only of English. I shall not see that, my children, but you may—you may.'

'You—don't think the world is going to end this year, as they say?' Bevis said, as though the words stuck a little in his throat. So many people believed that, but somehow it had not seemed so near until the New Year was actually upon them.

'No,' Sir Everard said simply. 'I do not. It seems to me that so many things are beginning now, and I cannot believe that God would let them spring, only to cut them down before they come to flower.'

At the end of January Sir Everard received the usual yearly

summons to Bramber. In the earlier years, before Bevis was a squire, he had gone unattended on his month's knight's service, and then last year he had taken Bevis. And now Randal, miserably grooming Valiant until the old war-horse's flanks shone like copper, was facing the prospect of being left behind alone once more.

'Next year you will be a squire, and then you'll be coming too,' Bevis said wretchedly. He was more wretched about it even than Randal. And Randal nodded, and went on grooming Valiant's tail, and said, 'I shall have a fine time while you are away. I shall help Lewin with the lambing.'

But they both knew that next year would not be quite the same. For one thing, old de Braose's son was being married this February, and though the wedding would of course be at the bride's home, he would be bringing her back to Bramber, and there would be feasting and revelry, harpers and jugglers and merchants from foreign parts, hunting and hawking, and Randal would have loved the clash and colour and swarming life of it all. For another, at the back of everyone's mind there was the thought, whether one believed it or not, that the world might indeed be coming to an end this year. That there might never be another February to be a squire and ride to Bramber behind Sir Everard.

Bevis said suddenly, as though he was thinking the same things, 'I could not bear it to happen before grandfather makes you a squire.'

The two boys looked at each other across Valiant's hind quarters. Randal didn't think he could bear it either. 'I don't believe the world is coming to an end, not really,' he said. 'I'm sure Lewin doesn't, or he would not have planted that new elder sapling in the sheep fold for sheep-medicine. No, I'll get to be a squire, sure enough, and then—you'll be a knight.'

There was a little silence while they both thought about that. And then, propping his shoulder against the side of the stall, Bevis said, 'Randal—if you were to get your chance of knighthood too—say that one day we were to fight Duke Robert, and before the battle de Braose thought to make some more knights, and he sent for you and said, "Randal of Dean, I would that

you receive knighthood of me this morning," what would you do?'

'Refuse,' Randal said simply. 'I have no land. I couldn't furnish my helm.'

'Not every knight holds land.'

Randal did not answer at once. He had turned his head, the harsh liveness of Valiant's tail still under his hand, and was looking out through the stable door, across the garth where the hens were scratching after dropped corn, to the familiar tawny lift of the downs beyond the still bare branches of the pear tree by the gate, and suddenly he was wondering what it would be like to hold Dean. He had never, after the first baffled and rebellious days when he stole the red amber, envied Bevis his foster brother for the things he had, only for the things he was; he envied him for being the sort of person who did not run away from things, but not because his grandfather was d'Aguillon of Dean. He did not envy him that, now, only he wondered for the moment what it would be like.

'A landless knight is no better than a man-at-arms,' he said at last. 'I should not mind being an ordinary man-at-arms like my father, but I should hate to be a man-at-arms wearing a knight's sword, having to sell it to whoever would feed me, maybe even my helmet my Lord's property and not my own; sitting in my Lord's Hall, looking for insults from the very dogs, and seeing them everywhere.'

It was Bevis's turn to be slow in answering, while Randal finished his task and put away the brushes and currycomb, and all the while outside they heard a green woodpecker laughing his first derisive laughter of the year. Then he said, standing away from the side of the stall, 'I'm rising two years older than you, but sometimes you make me feel like a babe in swaddling bands, Randal.'

'You haven't run with the hounds in Arundel bailey with your eyes and ears open,' Randal said. And then as though in some way their positions were reversed, and he was trying to comfort the other boy, 'I don't at all mind that I shall never be more than a squire, you know—so long as I'm your squire, that is.' Something swole up in his throat and made him sound gruff,

although his voice had only just finished breaking. 'I shall like being your squire—and I'll be the truest squire to you that ever knight had to carry his shield for him.'

And then that evening when they were both at work in the solar, burnishing Sir Everard's ring-mail hauberk—it was always bright as a salmon skin, but they could not risk a speck of rust now—the old knight's tall shadow fell upon them from the doorway.

'Let me look,' he said, bending down to watch them with the silver sand. 'Sa, sa, the work is well done. But it is work for a squire. Why do you make Randal do half your work for you, Bevis?'

'I wanted to,' Randal said quickly, and looked up in reproach. 'I have done squire's work for you for as long as I have been your varlet, d'Aguillon.'

D'Aguillon nodded, his dark eyes narrowing into a shadow of a smile, and sat himself down in his carved chair, leaning on one elbow to watch the boys still. When he spoke again, it was to Bevis, but clearly his words were for Randal as well.

'I have been thinking, these past few days: Bevis, do you remember how when first he came among us, you bade him understand that you and not he were to be my body squire when the time came, and we decided that since he must always be two years behind you in his training, there could be small risk of his forgetting that?'

Bevis flushed like a girl. 'I was a jealous puppy!'

But Sir Everard took no notice of the interruption. 'His full time is not up until the autumn, but how say you, shall we forgive him the last few months, this Randal of ours, and give him his squirehood tonight?'

And so, when Sir Everard rode for Bramber next morning, not one squire but two rode behind him.

The south wind was booming in the elm tops, and the cloud shadows were sweeping up the valley and over the downs like a charge of cavalry, and as they brushed by the hazel bushes at the ford, the yellow pollen-dust clouded the sunlight for yards around them. It seemed to Randal that winter had flowered

into spring overnight, and he did not care if the world ended tomorrow, he was a squire with Bevis, riding behind his knight today.

The life of the great Castle was both strange and familiar to Randal. He knew as he knew the feel of his own skin, the talk of the men-at-arms in the crowded bailey, the baying of hounds from the kennels and the scream of hawks in the mews, the sour smell of the Great Hall and the richly greasy one of the kitchens: all the teaming, furtive, sweating, laughing, brawling life of the place. It was the life that had bred him and been part of him until he was ten years old. But now he was seeing it all from a different level, and so came the strangeness. It was odd and disturbing, like being two people at once. It was not only that the dog-boy had become a squire; but that the Randal who had slept with the Montgomery's Irish wolfhounds had become a different Randal altogether. The change had come on him so gradually through the years at Dean that he had not noticed it until now, and it made him feel a little strange inside his own skin.

It was eight days before the return of young de Braose and his bride, when Sir Everard and his squires rode in to Bramber, but already there were many more people in the Castle than usual, guests invited and uninvited, for the door stood open to all comers at such a time. Priests and jugglers, merchants to spread their wares in the courtyard, knights and squires, a Saxon harper, a wild-eyed Welshman with sure tidings of the end of the world, a horse dealer, a goldsmith, a seller of charms against colic and the Evil Eye. More and more they came, and all the while, among the in-swarming of new faces, Randal was looking out for Herluin, de Bellême's minstrel. He knew that de Bellême was campaigning in Wales, but he might send his minstrel to the wedding festivities, just as a man might lend his cook to a neighbour for a special occasion. But the days went by and Herluin did not come.

Instead, on the very day before young de Braose was expected, Randal came out of the stables where he had been overseeing the Dean horses at their evening fodder, just in time to see Sir Thiebaut de Coucy clattering into the bailey on his bay

palfrey. He drew back instinctively at sight of the man, fancying even at six spear-length's distance that he could catch the scent of musk, and the queer dark smell of evil that de Coucy seemed always to carry with him. Then he told himself not to be a fool, and turned off about his own affairs. And in the days that followed there was so much happening, so much to do, that he managed for a while to thrust Sir Thiebaut out of his mind.

Next day Sir Philip de Braose rode in with his bride. The King had made the marriage, as he made all the marriages among his nobles, for his own advantage, mating this great house with that, as old Lovel had mated his hounds. But in spite of that, Sir Philip and the Lady Aanor, riding with his young knights and her ladies behind them, looked as though they might do well enough together. Randal, pressing forward with the rest of the crowd about them, saw a tall girl with a grave face that had laughter and eagerness somewhere at the back of it, who rode her fine white mare with the ease and freedom of a boy, despite the graceful, hampering folds of crimson silk that hung down on either side of her almost to cover her feet in the silver stirrups. But he looked with a quicker and deeper interest at the young man beside her, who would be Lord of Bramber one day. A thick-set young man with brown hair and a square, steady face, who might have passed easily enough for one of his own men-at-arms but for something of mastery in the level, iron-grey eyes. Sir Philip de Braose would not be an easy lord to serve, but Randal thought that he would be very well worth the serving.

After Sir Philip's coming, life at Bramber seemed even more crowded than it had done before, and it was three evenings later before suddenly Randal had bitter cause to think of Sir Thiebaut again.

That evening there had been much harping and merry-making in the Great Hall, and when the company split up and the fires were smoored for the night, Randal's head was still full of the bright harp music and the jewelled, bird-like flash of the juggler's cups and balls, as he huddled himself in an old cloak to lie down with the squires and hounds and lesser folk about the hearth. Bevis had gone after Sir Everard to the closet above

the guardroom where the old knight was housed, to help him disarm and take charge of his harness; but it seemed that he had scarcely left the Great Hall before he was back beside Randal, saying quietly and quickly as he bent over him, 'Grandfather wants you.'

Randal looked up in quick anxiety from the warm nest he had been making for himself in the rushes. 'What is amiss? He is not ill?'

'No. I don't know what it is. He told me to fetch you, that's all.'

Randal nodded, and turned with him and they slipped out together, down the steep spiral stair to the guardroom, then up again and along a narrow passage in the thickness of the wall, groping their way in almost total darkness, until a bar of light shone to meet them down three steps from the chink in a leather curtain over a doorway.

Sir Everard was standing beside the narrow shot-window, making—or rather pretending to make—some adjustment to the buckle of his sword belt. He had lately come from guard duty, and still wore his hauberk, though he had slacked off the lacing of the coif and let it slip down so that it lay about his neck like a monk's cowl of glimmering mail. And as he turned from the window at their coming in, Randal thought that his face in the light of the candle on its ledge was grimmer and more sternly set than he had ever seen it before, his mouth an even straighter gash.

He gestured them to come and stand before him, but did not speak for a long moment.

'Bevis, Randal,' he said at last, 'I have something that it is in my mind I should tell you both—you, Bevis, as my grandson, and you, Randal, because I know that in any case Bevis has no secrets from you, and because I think that to you, also, Dean is very dear.'

Randal's heart gave a small, sick lurch. His eyes on d'Aguillon's face, he waited for what was coming next.

'I have been with de Braose this evening since coming off duty. He sent for me to give me warning that Sir Thiebaut de Coucy has cast hungry eyes on the Manor.'

There was a long, stunned silence, and then Bevis said, 'You mean that Sir Thiebaut de Coucy has cast hungry eyes on the gold that he thinks to be buried on the Manor land.'

'Undoubtedly. But that makes little difference so far as we are concerned.'

Randal said in a thick, hot rush, 'But Dean is yours! Sir—sir it can make no odds what de Coucy thinks; Dean is *yours*!'

D'Aguillon smiled, a smile that made two hard lines run from his nose to the corners of his mouth. 'That was your Saxon mother speaking, Randal. By our Norman custom, all land is the King's. The Barons hold from the King, and we lesser folk from the Barons. Have you forgotten that? I pay knight's fee for Dean, as all men pay for their manors, though, like most other men, I have come to look on the Manor, both land and folk, as mine—have come to love it very dearly.' He looked up into the darkness of the shot-window, and fretted with his sword belt. 'Bone of my bone, it has become, flesh of my flesh . . . But Sir Thiebaut has the ear of the new Bishop of Durham, who owes him something in the matter of the roof of the new Hall at Westminster, and the Bishop of Durham has the ear of our Red William. And Red William is ever joyful at any excuse to change about the holders of his fiefs, lest with passing from father to son the bond between lord and land should become too strong, and something of the King's power be lost thereby.'

Bevis shook the dark hair back from his forehead in that swift, defiant way of his. 'What are we going to do?'

'So far as I can see—and I have given some little thought to the matter already—there is nothing under heaven that we can do.' Sir Everard sounded unutterably weary. 'There is no appeal save force of arms against the King's decision in such a matter, and we can scarce expect de Braose to raise his banner and bring out the Honour of Bramber in revolt against the King and the rest of the Kingdom, in the cause of one knight's fee.'

In the silence which followed, Randal carefully traced out with his eyes the shape of a greenish damp-stain that made the likeness of a grotesque face on the wall behind d'Aguillon. Then Bevis said very gently, 'If we lose the Manor, what will you do, sir?'

'De Braose will yield me another fief, out from among his own manors. If I were a young man, I think that I should not take it, but turn my back on Sussex and my face towards Constantinople and the Emperor's Varangian Guard. But I am old, my children . . .'

Bevis said quite quietly, and quite seriously, 'Would it help if I killed him?'

And Sir Everard swung round from the window, and looked at him with a queer mingling of expressions on his stern face. 'No, Bevis. When there is killing to be done, I kill for myself, and do not delegate the task to a squire scarce seventeen summers old. How shall it avail us that you are hanged or made Wolf's head? And even though by some miracle the deed were not brought home to you'—he leaned forward a little, his dark eyes holding the boy's gaze—'I will not hold Dean by right of murder in cold blood, *and nor shall you!*'

And all the while Randal said nothing, and all the while he was thinking—thinking that there was one weapon that might save Dean, and he held it in his hand; if only he had the strength and skill, and the courage, to use it properly.

Sir Everard slipped free the buckle of his sword belt, and crossed to the sleeping bench and laid it down. The tiny golden roses that diapered the worn and scuffed red leather of the scabbard caught the candlelight, and made a pattern in Randal's mind that he did not see at the time, but that powdered the darkness for him all night, afterwards.

'No use that we talk more of the thing tonight,' Sir Everard said, and raised his arms slowly above his head. 'Come and aid me out of this lizard skin of mine, Bevis, for tonight it weighs as heavy as the whole world on my shoulders.'

When Randal got back to the great Hall, somebody else was of course asleep in the warm corner he had marked out for himself, but he had a heavy heart and too much to think about to trouble with turning him out. He crawled in among the hounds for warmth, and lay down with his head on the flank of an old wolfhound. But there was no sleep for him that night. Instead he lay going over and over in his mind the words that he had overheard on the water stair at Arundel. He had almost

593

forgotten for so many years, but now every word, every inflexion of the smooth voice, the snarling softness of Hugh Goch's laugh, were clear in his inner ear again, as though he had heard them not an hour ago. 'Be ready when the time comes, and before high summer we'll have done with Red William and his self-made laws, and mount Stephen of Aumale in his place . . .'

If he went to Sir Everard or straight to de Braose with his accusation against de Coucy it would be only his word, the word of someone who had been a child at the time, against that of the knight; and having tried and failed, there would be nothing more he could do. But perhaps the threat might serve where the actual deed would not . . .

He was coldly afraid. He had always been afraid of things and people. Men had put that fear into him with many kicks when he was so small that it had become a part of him. But when he tumbled up with the rest before it was daylight, shaking himself like a hound and rubbing the dusty feel of the long night's wakefulness out of his eyes, he knew exactly what he was going to do, and the only uncertainty in his mind was how he was going to get word with de Coucy alone.

But that was to be made easy for him, for on his way down to feed and groom Valiant, he was overtaken by a fellow squire in a kind of cheerful ill-humour, who demanded of him, 'Does your knight ride with the hawking party this morning?'

Randal shook his head. 'No.'

'Neither does mine, but I'm lent to de Coucy to tend his horse and saddle the brute for him. If a man comes travelling without a squire, he should saddle his own horse or leave it to be done by the stable churls, say I,' and he darted on.

Randal followed more slowly. So there was a hawking party planned for this morning, and de Coucy was riding with it. Well, that might be his chance. He turned into the long, thatch-roofed stables that were already alive with grooms and squires hard at work, and went to Valiant's stall. He brought down hay from the loft and filled the manger, then set to work to groom him. While he was still at it the horses for the hawking party were already being led out, and he heard the falconers gathering, men's laughter, and the baying of a hound in the still frosty

air; and the trampling of hooves dying away as he turned from Sir Everard's horse to his own. Swallow greeted him with a whinny of pleasure, thrusting a soft muzzle with delicately working lips against his shoulder, but Randal had no time to give the grey more than a hurried pat, and a couple of handfuls of fodder in his manger while he saddled up. He was not worried about the hawking party being away ahead of him; they would ride slowly and he could easily overtake them. But at any moment Bevis might be here to groom his own Durandal and there would be the need for explanations. And any explanations that there had to be would be much better left until later.

He was done now and ready to be off. He led Swallow out into the bailey, where the fowls were beginning to scratch around the garbage pile and the breath of hurrying men hung in little puffs of cloud on the grey air that was turning silvery as the sun rose; he swung into the saddle and headed for the gate-house, settling his feet in the long Norman stirrups as he went. He had a story all ready for the gate guard in case of need, about having been sent after one of the hawking party with a message; but the men-at-arms lounging in the guardroom doorway seemed to assume, despite the lack of any hawk on his fist, that he was one of the party who had overslept, and made no attempt to check him.

'Up river, or down?' he asked of one man-at-arms leaning against the wall and idly picking his teeth with an old goose quill.

'Up,' said the man, pointing with the feather and returning to his pastime as Randal, with a word of thanks, clattered out over the bridge.

Swallow was fresh and eager to be away and broke forward into a canter, shaking his head and scattering foam over his breast as they headed down the steep track that curled about the Castle mound. Once past the thatched huddle of St Nicholas' Church and College among the willows at its foot, Randal turned him up-river, into the marshy country that ran in a long, watery tongue far into the Weald, and settled down to overtake the hawking party.

Presently he saw them, through a screen of still bare alders

595

and crack-willow. The hounds had been slipped from leash and were working the rushes and dank tangle of last year's hemlock and willow herb on the river bank, while the horsemen, falcon on fist, gentled their horses to and fro on the fringes of the tangle, watchful for the heron to break cover. Randal drew rein among the alders, looking for de Coucy among the rest, and found him without much trouble, some way farther down the bank. The party was a large one, and well scattered. No one was likely particularly to notice his coming.

After a few moments he urged Swallow out of the thicket, and rode forward at an amble. The hounds, who had been working in silence, gave tongue at that instant, and amid a flurry of baying and shouting, a heron broke from cover of the rushes and leapt upward in swift, spiral flight. Three of the knights loosed their falcons at her, and the chase was on. The heron climbed desperately the blue circles of the upper air, striving to gain height to use her own weapon, her dagger bill; and behind her the falcons mounted steadily, dark-winged death on her track. Randal could hear the hawk bells ringing, a shining thread of sound as thin as lark song, as they climbed, and narrowed his eyes to follow the deadly chase. Up and up and up into the sun-lit blue and silver of the February sky, until at last the foremost falcon, soaring like an arrow from a bow, overtopped her and stooped, avoiding the despairing dagger thrust of her beak, and made his kill.

Randal brought his dazzled gaze down out of the sky as the falcons dropped, and while the hounds were searching the river-bank cover for the fallen heron, and everyone seemed riding here and there, brought his horse up beside that of de Coucy.

'God's greeting to you, Sir Thiebaut.' His mouth felt uncomfortably dry.

Sir Thiebaut looked round, his plump face startled for an instant, then covered as with a mask. 'D'Aguillon's varlet, is it not?' he said after a pause, and there was something guarded in his voice as well as his face.

'D'Aguillon's squire.'

'So—— Have you some message for me?'

'No message. I came to speak with you on my own account,' Randal said. 'When the rest move off, fall behind a little, that we may talk the more easily.'

Sir Thiebaut sat his bay palfrey and looked at him, his brows rising a little over those brilliant, colourless eyes. How assured he seemed, in his dark gown turned back with fox fur, the peregrine on his fist unhooded and made ready for flight: how coldly formidable. Randal was aware to the depth of his being that he was a boy of fifteen, and had been less than two weeks a squire; he felt very small and naked to be challenging such as de Coucy.

'Surely your new squirehood has gone to your head like too much cider,' de Coucy said contemptuously. 'But I am not used to that tone from an equal, let alone from a mere squire. Thank your patron saint that I am a patient man, and go away, my good lad, and cool that hot head of yours in the river.'

'I will go when I have said what I came to say,' Randal told him. 'If you like I will speak it before these others.' He glanced about him. 'There's more than one within shouting distance. But I think that maybe what I have to say, you would as lief not hear cried aloud to the world.'

He watched something flicker far back in the man's eyes, and wondered whether he was remembering the water stair at Arundel, or whether there were other matters.

Then the knight shrugged, still with a show of contemptuous good humour. 'What man that is flesh and blood and no cold saint has not something that he does not particularly wish his world to know? Nay then, I'll hear you, since you seem so set on it,' and he wheeled his horse as he spoke, and began, Randal beside him close as a shadow, to separate from the rest of the hawking party. The falcons had returned to their lords' fists by now, the heron had been recovered and the hounds leashed again, and the whole company were drifting off up-river towards the next patch of cover.

Randal and Sir Thiebaut dropped farther and farther behind, until the hawking scene grew small and bright with distance as it had been when Randal first saw it through the screening alders. Finally, in the lee of a tump of still bare blackthorn, they reined in and turned to look at each other.

'Well?' Sir Thiebaut said. 'Now, before I lose all patience, what is the thing that you would say to me?'

Randal's heart was suddenly banging against his ribs.

'Firstly, Sir Thiebaut, by way of sweetening what comes after, to pass on to you some words I once heard from that Ancret who dared to look at you in a way you did not like, when you came to Dean a year and a half since. "There's never aught but sorrow come yet to mortal man from the gold of the Hollow Hills." Remember that, if you think, by gaining Dean, to gain also a king's fortune from the crest of the Bramble Hill.'

'So you have heard tales,' de Coucy said after a moment, dropping pretence.

'Yes, I have heard tales. Maybe you can tell me that they are not true?'

Sir Thiebaut smiled. 'Come to think of it, why should I?'

He was hatefully sure of himself. Randal longed to smash his fist into the plump face and take some of the sureness out of it. He steadied his voice with an effort, terrified that even now it might betray him with an unbroken squeak.

'You have some influence with His Grace of Durham——'

How pompous that sounded! He felt that his enemy was mocking him for it.

'A little, I hope. And His Grace of Durham has—have you heard it?—some influence with the King.'

'Then, if you have not already spoken of this matter of Dean, let you leave it unspoken. If you *have* spoken, then let you use this influence that you have with His Grace, that he give the words back to you as though they had never been.'

'And why?' said de Coucy again, pleasantly.

'Because five years ago last October, I, who was then a dog-boy at Arundel, overheard what passed between you and the Lord of Arundel on the water stair of his castle.'

Sir Thiebaut made no sign, save that his eyes narrowed a little, but the peregrine on his fist suddenly bated wildly, filling the silence between them with her scream and furiously clapping wings. When the bird was quietened, the knight said gently, 'Yes, and how do you know me again?'

Something clicked in Randal's brain, and he saw the danger.

Many men might wear musk, and a voice was such a small thing to swear to—to those who had not heard it as he had done.

'It was dark in the stair-way,' he said, taking a risk, 'but once outside, the moon was very bright.'

The knight inclined his head as though giving him best on that point, but smiling, because he could afford to. 'You were then, perhaps, ten years old? Whatever you heard, whatever you dreamed you heard, who, think you, is going to take your word against mine? The word of a boy scarce yet a squire, and at the time only a child, and it appears a mere dog-boy at that, against the word of a knight?'

'In these days even a knight cannot afford to have suspicion fall upon him,' Randal said, thinking out his words as he went along. 'The King is half mad with suspicion—all men know it—and loves not those who are even whispered to have plotted against him. And'—his voice did shake a little then, but he steadied it instantly—'I am ready to take my story before the Bishop of Chichester and offer myself for trial by ordeal to prove that I speak the truth!' (What would they do? Make him plunge his hand—his sword hand—into boiling water? That was the most usual ordeal. He must cling to the faith that, whatever it was, the God that Adam Clerk had taught him about would strengthen him and bring him through unscathed to prove that his accusation was a true one.)

'So, a fighting cock indeed!' Sir Thiebaut said softly, and then, 'Have you not thought that it might be no very hard matter to have such a troublesome boy—cleared from the path?'

Randal had thought of that, but not the answer. His quick wit furnished him with that now, in the moment of his need. 'Yes; and therefore I have set a written and sealed report in the hands of—someone, to be opened and acted on, if any harm comes to me.'

He watched the odd little flicker behind de Coucy's eyes again. He did not think the man believed him, but saw that he could not be sure; and he knew that while he could not be sure, de Coucy would not dare to risk it.

Something from the long-ago night when Herluin had won him with a game of chess came into his mind.

'Checkmate, Sir Thiebaut,' he said.

Sir Thiebaut seemed to be watching the distant hawking party, but after a moment he looked round once more at the young squire. And Randal, meeting the narrowed gaze of the pale, bright eyes, found himself looking into sheer hate. A personal hate that went far deeper than the question of Dean.

'No, only stalemate,' he said, very, very gently. 'And I think that one day you shall weep blood for this day's work, my kennel-bred squire.'

THE FLOWERING FLINT

RANDAL rode back to Bramber, stabled Swallow, and went in search of Sir Everard. At the head of the Keep steps he met Bevis, looking very white and taking his position as senior squire heavily—the more so, perhaps, because of last night—who caught him by the shoulder, demanding, 'Randal! What in Satan's name do you mean by skulking off without leave like this? Where have you been?'

'I went after the hawking party,' Randal said. 'Where is Sir Everard?'

'Well, next time you think to run off to play——' Bevis began furiously; and then something that he saw in the other boy's face halted him. 'Randal, what is amiss now?'

'Nothing,' Randal said. 'No, I think—everything is going to be well enough. But I must speak to Sir Everard.'

Bevis dropped his hand. 'Go along and make your peace with him then. He is in the armoury with de Braose, and I warn you, he's angry.'

The armoury was on the ground floor of the Keep, with the dungeons and storerooms, beneath the guardroom; a kind of undercroft with its low, barrel-vaulted ceiling supported on short, immensely strong piers, so that the place was like a church that had gradually sunk down squat and bow-legged under the immense weight of the great Keep above it. There among the pike stands and stacked shields and iron-bound armour-kists, with a couple of torch-bearing squires to light them—for though the armoury was above ground it had no windows nor outer door—Sir Everard and the old Lord of Bramber were looking at several sword blades laid on a kist top between them.

Sir Everard glanced up as Randal came clattering down the steep, curling, guardroom stair, and looked at him a moment, deliberately, his black brows drawn together.

'Ah, Randal, wait there,' he said, as though there had been

603

no question of his squire being absent without leave, and turned his attention back to the sword that de Braose was holding to the light. His mouth was at its grimmest, and the frown lingered between his eyes, but clearly he did not intend to take his squire to task before onlookers.

Randal waited, standing stiffly in the archway at the stair foot, while the two knights bent their heads over this weapon and that. They were old friends, old comrades in arms; but it was hard, Randal thought, seeing the Lord of Bramber, fat and gout-ridden, with his pouchy, used-up face in which only the eyes still seemed really alive, to think of him, young and strong and maybe much as Sir Philip was now, leading his squadrons to the charge, at Senlac, over the downs: he was so long past his fighting days, though he could be no older than d'Aguillon. But, past the use of them though he might be, he had kept the same passion for fine weapons that another man might feel for horses and a third for jewels. Now, smiling a little, he passed to his old companion a damascened blade on whose dark surface the torchlight played changeably as on a stormy sea.

'Feel. Is not the balance sweet? I had to have a new hilt made for it: the Saracens have narrower hands than ours, seemingly, and the grip was too small.'

'From Laef Thorkelson?' Sir Everard said, making the blade sing as it cut the air.

'Ah, I forgot that you were a friend of Laef Thorkelson's. He has brought me more than one of my best weapons; fine Arab blades that have no equal in the North.'

'It is a lovely weapon'—Sir Everard felt the balance again and squinted one-eyed along the blade—'though a little light, to my mind, maybe because I have carried a heavy sword all my life . . .' He gave it back, and took up another from the kist top. 'This has more the weight of my own sword that I carried at Senlac, and that Bevis will carry after me.'

Clearly, since it seemed that there was nothing to be done about Dean, they had set the matter behind them for the time being, in cleanly and civilized fashion, to take pleasure in their old companionship and the keenness of damascene sword iron.

And still, at the stair-foot, Randal waited.

At last the time drew near to noon—dinner had been set back two hours to suit the hawking party—and de Braose bade his squires to wrap the blades again in their oiled linen swathings and lay them away in the open sword kists, before they all climbed back into the dim daylight of the guardroom above. When the Lord of Bramber had ambled away leaning on the shoulder of one of his squires, Sir Everard gestured Randal to follow him up on to the rampart that cut the inner from the outer bailey.

Randal followed the tall old man as he descended the Keep stair, crossed the inner bailey and went tramping up the rampart steps with the chape of his sword ringing on the stones beside him. The rampart walks, not greatly used except in time of war, for the look-out was kept from the roof of the Keep itself, were good places to be safe from interruption or unwanted listeners.

'Randal,' Sir Everard said, strolling a little ahead, his shoulders hunched in his old, rust-stained leather gambeson, 'you know the duties of a squire. If you have any excuse to give me for going off this morning without first asking my leave, give it to me now.'

'I went after the hawking party,' Randal said to his stooping, leather-clad shoulder. 'De Coucy rode with them, and I had to get word with him alone.'

Sir Everard stopped in his tracks so abruptly that Randal all but bumped into him; then he turned round quite slowly, and stood looking at his squire.

'If I had come to you for leave first, you might have asked me why I wanted word with him,' Randal urged, to the stern uncompromising face.

'Randal,' said Sir Everard in a voice that grated a little. 'What have you been doing?'

Randal leaned against the side of a crenelle, surprised to find that he was shaking. But he had been shaking without knowing it, ever since he left de Coucy and the hawking party.

'Sir—I knew something about de Coucy that I thought I could maybe use as a weapon against him.' He checked, stumbling for the right words. He could not tell d'Aguillon the whole

story. For himself, his only loyalty was to Dean, but d'Aguillon's loyalties were wider and he might feel it needful to go to de Braose . . . But something he must tell him. 'When I was in Arundel, I overheard de Coucy once, in a place where he had no right to be, with a man he should not have been with, and they made a plot that—would not have pleased the King. I think that he will leave Dean alone.'

There was a long silence. The little February wind hummed through the crenelles of the rampart, and below in the courtyard the hawking party was returning, and folk beginning to make their way towards the Great Hall for dinner. Sir Everard brought up both hands and set them on Randal's shoulders, and looked at him very straight out of those dark eyes that would be so hard to lie to. 'Tell me the truth, Randal; this plot you speak of, is it finished, a thing altogether of the past, or does anything of it reach out to the future?'

'It is altogether of the past,' Randal said, 'but the King loves not those who plot against him, even in past years.'

'True,' Sir Everard said slowly. 'So be it, then, I will ask no other question. A bargain is a bargain, even with such as de Coucy.' And then, as Randal heaved a sigh of relief. 'No. One more question. How did you contrive to make such a bargain— your word against his, and you were a child at the time?'

'I—reminded him of how half-mad with suspicion the Red King is; I said I would take the thing before the Bishop of Chichester and submit to being proved by ordeal. I—oh, I know it was a weak enough weapon, but it was all I had, and— and it worked!' Suddenly there was a great swelling in his throat and he could say no more. He was aware of the warm trickle of tears on his face, and he stuck out his tongue like a puppy to lick them up.

D'Aguillon was shaking him very gently, very kindly. 'You young fool! You very valiant young fool! Fifteen is too young to be making yourself a deadly enemy!'

Next day Sir Thiebaut de Coucy was gone, seemingly forgetful that he had ever looked in the direction of Dean. A week later, Sir Philip de Braose took his wife away to his own Manor

at the northern end of the Honour; and the great Castle guarding the pass through the Downs settled to its usual way of life again. The month of Sir Everard's guard service drew to a close once more, and on a day of soft rain sweeping in from the sea, the old knight and his squires rode home.

The alders were dropping their little dark catkins in the water of the ford, and the elm trees below the Mill wore their brief purple mist of blossom, and as they drew towards home the babble of the young lambs came down to them from the lambing pens. Bevis let the reins drop on Durandal's neck, and stretched his arms wide above his head.

'Oh, it is good to be back. We have been away too long!'

Randal, with his head up into the soft rain that tasted a little of the sea on his lips, heard the babble of the lambing pens, and the deep content welled up in him because Dean and the Dean sheep would not suffer a change of master this year.

'There'll be a-many lambs come already by the sound of it,' he said, and he and Bevis looked at each other as they rode, sharing the contentment. He had told Bevis the whole story. That was a different matter from telling Sir Everard, though he would have been hard put to it to find words for the difference.

Sir Everard glanced back over his shoulder. 'You have run in strict leash all these past thirty days, and it is time that you were slipped. Bide for supper, then away with you up to Lewin and his lambing pens. It is in my mind that you would liefer spend the night there than lying decently by the Hall fire, at this time of year.'

And so, when Sybilla had done fussing over them, and supper was finished, they left Sir Everard to talk over the Manor affairs with Reynfrey and Adam Clerk, and took Joyeuse who had been bringing Bevis all that the house had to offer, including the best kitchen ladle and a hen's egg warm from the nest, and set out for the lambing pens on the sheltered skirts of the downs. It was still raining, the fine, soft rain that seems at any moment ready to turn into mist. The branches of the old pear tree dripped and splattered on them as they went out through the gate gap and turned uphill for the open downs, and away to their right they could hear the voice of the little winter bourn

that began to run when the springs broke in November and would dry up again by May. It was not very dark for there was a moon behind the clouds, and in a little they saw the dark mass of the lambing pens on the sheltered southern slope of the little coomb, silent now, save for the occasional bleat of a lamb waking to find itself separated from its mother. A dim flicker of firelight shone from the opening of the bothy through the mizzle rain, and as they drew nearer, there sprang up a gleam of paler and stronger yellow that spoke of a lantern, and a great baying broke out, at which Joyeuse pricked her ears and whined, pulling against the leash.

Then Lewin's voice sounded, quieting the dogs. He was standing, big and peaceful, beside the opening of the bothy, his old battered lantern half shielded under his sheepskin mantle, when they came up.

'The thirty days are finished, and 'twas in my mind to wonder whether you would be up tonight,' he greeted them.

'It seems more than thirty days,' Bevis said. 'Oh, *Lewin*, it is so good to be back! How goes the lambing?'

'Well enough. Aye, well enough this year. I was just going to take my look round the pens now. Coming with me?' It was a question that he had asked often before, and he knew the answer so well that he did not even wait for it. 'Tie up the bitch then, and come.'

Bevis made her fast by her leash to the elderwood doorpost, and the great hound sat down quite unprotesting, for she was used to being tied up there. She was friends with Ship and White-Eye, and friends with the sheep, but no dogs save their own were allowed among the ewes at lambing time. She licked the hands of both boys, and lay down nose on paws with no more than a liquid whimper of protest as they turned away after the shepherd.

Lewin heaved back the hurdle at the entrance to the big lambing fold, and they followed him in, Randal fixing the hurdle in place again behind them. He had spent many hours up at the lambing pens every year since he first came to Dean, and the scene was as deeply familiar to him as any other part of the Manor's life; yet tonight, all at once, he was seeing it dif-

ferently, with a new awareness that was almost painful, as though he had one skin less than usual: the deep bracken litter underfoot catching running gleams of light, coppery gold, from the lantern under Lewin's rough cloak, the man-high hurdle walls laced thick with furze branches to keep out the wind, the huddled, woolly shapes of the waiting ewes through which they waded knee deep, feeling the faint, live warmth rise from them like the mist of their breath. Ship and White-Eye moved ahead, running quietly among the ewes, looking, just as surely as Lewin, to see that all was well; and the rest followed. Every now and then Lewin halted and stooped to feel a woolly body, or to let a meagre beam of light shine on to one of the ewes from the lantern that he kept so carefully shielded. 'There's some fools that goes swinging a lantern round among the ewes and then wonder that the lambs get trampled on,' he said in that soft, caressing growl of his. 'And there's some, not much wiser, that reckons 'tis the light that terrifies them.'

'And it isn't?' Randal said, bending with him over one of his charges.

'Na, 'tis the shadows that the light casts . . . 'Tisn't often, save in the hardest winters, that we get wolves on the hill nowa-days, but a light carried heedless sets the shadows leaping and prancing and running—ah, just as the wolves must have come leaping round the folds in the winter nights way back; and the sheep remember.'

The next ewe was standing head down to nuzzle at some-thing on the ground, and as he let a careful gleam fall on her from the lantern, two little damp, sprawling shapes flashed out of the shadow into sharp-edged reality on the trampled, russet bracken. 'Sa, sa, here's one for the side-pens. Bravely done, my girl!' Lewin gave the lantern to Randal, and scooping up the two limp creatures, turned towards the small hurdled-off pens round the sides of the fold, where the ewes were housed with their new-born lambs for the first day. The mother followed, bleating distressfully and sniffing at her nearest lamb, and Randal brought up the rear with the lantern carefully shielded under his own cloak.

When they reached the pen, he uncovered the lantern at a

word from Lewin, while the shepherd made sure that all was well with the ewe and persuaded the lambs to suck; and the fine rain that drifted across the top of the hurdles caught the gleam of it and became a spitting, golden smoke. Ship came thrusting into the pen, and his shadow, running sideways from him before the lantern, was suddenly the shadow of a wolf. Hurriedly Randal spread his cloak to shield the light, and the shadows came crowding in, jagged, leaping shadows of wolves that prowled beyond the corner of the eye; and Lewin's crook lying beside him might have been a spear.

Lewin glanced up from the ewe, and his eyes met Randal's. 'You see?' he said.

Perhaps it was remembering, as Lewin meant it when he spoke of the sheep remembering. It was gone now. Come and gone in the time that it took for the shadow of the boy's cloak to swing across the little hurdled pen. And the shepherd got up, and held out his hand for the lantern, stowing it again beneath his thick sheepskin mantle. 'She'll do well enough,' he said, and turned back to the main fold where Bevis was waiting with White-Eye.

They finished the round of the lambing fold, found another lamb newly born, but nowhere any sign of trouble. 'Looks like an easy night,' said Lewin in rumbling content. They went into the big enclosure beside the other, where the ewes that had given birth within the last few days were folded at night with their lambs. Here, too, all was quiet. And in a while they went back to the bothy, where Joyeuse greeted them with softly thumping tail, before them the prospect of warmth and shelter, until presently Lewin would take down the lantern that he had just hung from the roof, and start the same round all over again. There was little rest for the shepherd folk at lambing time.

Now he shook the rain from his shoulder, and drew the old sheepskin rug across the opening of the bothy that was built of hurdles like the folds, and thatched with furze; and blew up the fire of crackling thorn branches in the hearth, made of a few stones, in the corner, and propped a pot of water to heat over it. Often there would be a motherless or ailing lamb before the

fire, but not tonight. They huddled close, for the wind seeped through the hurdles for all the lacing of furze branches, Ship and White-Eye and Joyeuse lying nose on paws among their feet. Randal sat with his hunched shoulder leaning against Bevis who leaned companionably back, and stared a little sleepily into the fire, where a red hollow like the gaping mouth of a dragon had opened under the crackling thorn branches, and listened to the soft rush of the wind across the thatch.

'And all the time, the wind blows over,' he thought. 'Ancret's people, and the Saxons, and Harold dead at Hastings over yonder, and now the Normans: and all the while the wind blowing over the downs, just the same.' Half asleep as he was, he was suddenly aware of the new life in the lambing pens, the constant watchful coming and going of the shepherd and dogs and lantern, as something not just happening now, but reaching back and back, and forward and forward, into the very roots of things that were beyond time.

Something of the same mood must have been upon Lewin also, for when he had brought out the meal bag and tipped barley meal into the birchwood bowl, thrusting away the dogs' soft, expectant muzzles, he rose—but he could not stand upright in the little bothy—rooted in the willow basket hanging from the roof, in which he kept his few personal belongings, and brought out something wrapped in a rag of yellow cloth.

'I'll show you a thing,' he said to Randal. 'Sitting here at nights I've had it in my heart to show you, a good while past. Showed it to the young master when he stood no higher than my belt,' and as Randal looked up expectantly from the fire, and Bevis watched with the interest alight in his thin, eager face, he unfolded the yellow rag, and put into the boy's hand a thing somewhat like a double axe-head made from flint, mealy grey and tawny with the outer weathering that flint gathers through the years—an axehead, but with no hole to take the haft, nor any flanges for binding it on.

Without quite knowing why he did so, for he was not left-handed, Randal put out his left hand for it, and felt his fingers close over it as something infinitely familiar. But he had never seen such an object before.

'What is it?' he demanded.

'What it is called I do not know, but with such things it is in my mind that men fought the wolf-kind, and maybe each other, very long ago. I have seen others turned up on the downs, but never one to equal that one. I found it up on Long Down, years ago, and kept it because it was made for a left-handed man, even as I.'

Randal shifted it to his right hand, and found that it was true. One could use it perfectly well with the right hand, but it did not lie there happily, as in the left.

'Left-handed, or one-handed.' He did not know what made him say that. He leaned forward, looking at it in the light of the fire. And then, maybe because of the strange mood he was in, maybe because he was half asleep, maybe because of that dark thread of the old blood that Ancret had recognized, running in his veins, an odd thing happened. Once, in the outer bailey at Arundel, he had watched spell-bound while a wonder-worker who made live pigeons come out of an empty basket, had made a striped pebble picked up from the dirt where the fowls were scratching, grow in his hand without any visible change, into a yellow iris flower. He could see now the shimmering, silken fall of the petals, the dark, hair-fine intricacy of the veining that sprang from the slender throat, the sheer, singing strength of the colour. And as the pebble had become a flower, so the thing he held was suddenly warm as though fresh from the knapper's hand, and the outer crust of the centuries all gone like a little dust, leaving the beautiful, dark blue flint in all its newness. It was as though the thing flowered between his hands. He had an extraordinary sense of kinship with the unknown man who had first closed his fingers over that strange weapon, who had perhaps seen the wolves leaping about the lambing folds as he, Randal, had almost seen them for an instant tonight; an extraordinary feeling of oneness with Dean, of some living bond running back through the blue, living flint, making him part of other men and sheep and wolves, and they a part of him.

This was the true seisin. He had the oddest feeling that because he had earned some right that he had not had before, because, coward that he was, he had set out with the only weapon

he had against Sir Thiebaut de Coucy, Dean itself was letting him in . . .

The water in the pot began to bubble, and Lewin took it off and poured it into the bowl of barley meal, stirring with a stick as he did so, until he had a good steaming, porridgey mess, and added a lump of honeycomb—Ancret gave him a honeycomb from time to time—saying, 'That is in honour of the day that you come back from Bramber. 'Tis not every night that White-Eye and Ship and I have our stirrabout sweet.'

And Randal shifted, rubbing the firelight and the dust of sleep out of his eyes with his free hand, and grinned at Bevis who grinned back, and returned the strange flint weapon into the hand that Lewin held out for it. The warmth in it was only from the fire after all, and the flint was covered with the grey and tawny weathering of the years.

But the feeling of being given seisin, of being let in, remained with him.

WITCH HUNT!

LIFE at Dean went on in its usual way. The swallows came back to the great barn. Bevis and Randal dammed the stream and dipped the sheep, taking their turn to stand waist deep in the cold water, heaving the terrified and struggling beasts off the hurdle jetty. Hay harvest came and went, and the barley in Muther-Wutt Field was almost ripe to the sickle.

But under the surface of things, there was an uneasiness like thunder in the air, gathering ever more thickly as that spring and summer went by. People whispered together that maybe the end of the world was indeed coming. Strange things happened; omens and marvels. Last winter there had been strange lights in the northern sky; now a calf with two heads was born up at Durrington. People had queer, unchancy dreams and talked about them at half-breath afterwards; and as always when people were afraid, they turned back to the old gods. The Prior of Steyning complained of difficulty in getting the tithes in, or any work out of the Priory villeins, and on Lammas Eve, Adam Clerk came to Sir Everard in deep distress, having found the trunk of a certain ancient thorn tree on the Manor smeared with blood.

The next day Sir Everard had some business with de Savage, over at Broadwater, and riding home with the two boys behind him as usual, just where the Bramble Hill dropped into the woods, they came upon Ancret gathering simples. They would not have seen her, but that she heard the soft thud of the hoof-beats on the track, and straightened and came down to meet them, trailing her dusty-coloured kirtle like a queen's mantle through the dusty-coloured flowers of late summer, the wild marjoram and the swaying yarrow among the dusty hazel bushes. Randal thought, looking at her, that he had never seen anything human that took on the colour of her surrounds as

perfectly as Ancret did. Only those deer's eyes of hers, darker even than Sir Everard's, were bright.

Sir Everard reined up and greeted her courteously as he always did. And she returned the greeting, 'God's joy to you, Sir Everard,' and stood waiting, her eyes on his face, as though she knew he had something to say to her.

'Ancret,' said Sir Everard after a moment, fidgeting with his sword belt, 'if I had not met with you this evening, I should have come to your cottage. Adam came to see me yesterday with a tale of having found the big thorn tree below Long Down smeared with blood.'

Randal, watching her, had a feeling of a curtain being drawn behind her eyes, though they remained as bright as ever.

'Did he so, my Lord?'

'Don't pretend to me that you did not know about it,' Sir Everard said sternly.

'What would d'Aguillon have me do?'

'Put a stop to it; it is dangerous.'

Ancret came a step nearer, and laid her hand on Valiant's neck, looking up into the knight's face with those dark, curtained eyes. 'This year is not like other years. This year the people are afraid. And when they are afraid, men turn back to the gods that they knew before ever they knew Christ. Be glad that it is no more than a cock's blood smeared on a thorn tree.'

There was a pause, Valiant standing stone still under Ancret's hand, though Randal's and Bevis's horses fidgeted behind him, swishing their tails against the flies. Then, leaning down a little from his high saddle, Sir Everard asked quietly, 'What is it, Ancret? Is it the End of the World, as the priests say?'

'I do not think so. But this is a strange year, and strange things moving in it.' She hesitated, as though making up her mind whether or no to say something more. Then she said, 'In the time that it takes for the news to come through Andred's Weald, we shall hear that the King is dead.'

Sir Everard straightened in the saddle with a jerk. 'That kind of talk is folly. How can you know, before the messenger arrives?'

'I dreamed last night that I saw a red-haired man lying under an oak tree, with an arrow in his heart,' Ancret said simply,

'and his blood soaked down into the roots of the tree, and the tree strengthened and put out new leaves, so that he and the tree were one.'

A few days later they heard that the Red King was dead, shot while hunting in the great New Forest that he had made for his pleasure.

Some people said that his friend Sir Walter Tyrrell, who had been with him that day, and was not to be found afterwards, had shot him, either by accident or sick, like most of England, of his harsh rule. Some believed that Brother Henry, who had lately joined him in England, had loosed the arrow. Certainly he had been quick and purposeful in action after his brother's death, securing the fealty of as many of the leading Barons as he could gather in two days, and crowned at Westminster on the third, before the Archbishop of York could get to him, so that the thing must be done by the Bishop of London. But still, deep under these surface reasons for the King's death, ran a dark whisper that no man spoke aloud. Red William had belonged to the Old Faith, scarcely paying even lip service to the faith of Christ, all men knew that; and he had red hair, even as the man under the oak tree of Ancret's dream. Red, the colour of fire, of blood, of sacrifice. Was it not always a red-haired man who died for the life of the people?

The new King issued promises of just government to his Kingdom; he flung the hated Ranulf Flambard (no longer Bishop of Durham) into the Tower gaol; he brought back the gentle old Archbishop of Canterbury, whom William had hounded into exile. Late that autumn he took for his Queen Eadgyth, the orphan daughter of Malcolm of Scotland, who was descended through her mother from the great King Alfred whose White Horse of Wessex still had power to set men's hearts aflame. Most of his Norman subjects mocked at the marriage, but when the news reached Dean, Sir Everard, standing at the head of the South Field to see the great ox-plough turn at the autumn ploughing, said to Bevis and Randal beside him, 'Our Henry may be his brother's murderer, but he is a wise man as well as a strong one. Did I not once say to you that the time will

come when there will be no more Norman or Saxon, but only English? This marriage, for all that the fools among us laugh at it, will help to make one England.' He paused, watching the wheeling cloud of gulls behind the plough. 'Already we begin, a little, a very little, to be one people. And I think that before so very long, maybe even before another harvest time comes round, we shall need all the unity we have if we are not to fall under the Norman's heel again.'

'How odd,' Randal thought, watching him. 'He has forgotten that he is Norman himself.' But both boys knew what he meant. William was dead, and Robert home from his crusade and sitting in his Duchy again without even having to pay back the ten thousand marks for which he had pawned it. But assuredly he would not be content to sit there long, while for the second time a younger brother wore the crown of England.

'It is between the two brothers, now that William is gone to his account,' Sir Everard said after a while, 'and neither will rest until one is the death or the master of the other.'

But all that seemed very far away from the ordinary men in the fields, more concerned with the winter wheat than the affairs of their lords. The year that had seemed so strangely fated was passing; they felt that the shadow which had lain so dark across the land was slipping away behind them. They were no longer afraid, and so they left the old gods, and went to church again; and because the clergy preached hell fire and their consciences were tender, they grew afraid as they had not been before, of those among them who still danced for the Horned One in the woods or smeared honey on an oak tree. So there were a few witch hunts, and folk looked askance at any old woman they passed gathering simples in the lanes, and made the Horns with their fingers to avert evil. Even Ancret, going into Steyning to sell her spare honey, found that the folk were careful not to meet her gaze or step in her shadow, though on the Manor they had too many memories of warts charmed away and fevers cooled by her for any such folly.

Summer came again, a still summer evening with sheep shearing over and the hay making almost done. And the time of which

618

Sir Everard had spoken, when Saxon and Norman English must stand together or fall again under the spurred heel of Normandy was almost come.

Through the spring, news had come on every south wind of supporters flocking to Duke Robert's standard. As early as February, Ranulf Flambard had escaped from the Tower and fled to him (though there was a whisper that his escape had been arranged, and he was gone overseas as a spy for King Henry). Now, in these last weeks, the news was of a war fleet gathering on the Normandy coast. The English fleet was at sea already, the feudal levies and the Fyrd had not yet been called out, but the more alert of the knights up and down the coast were making ready their men and stores against the call-out that they knew must come.

That day Sir Everard had been going through the Manor's war gear, with the two boys to help him and gain experience; making sure that the leather jacks were well oiled and stout, and that no dagger had a sprung rivet, testing the war-bows and seeing to the supplies of arrows and spare bowstrings. (Every man kept a hunting bow hidden in the thatch of his hut, though it was against the law; but the stout, four foot war-bows that could send a shaft through ringmail were kept locked away and only issued for practice or the real thing.) Now, after supper, he had strolled out to sit on the edge of the cider press at the high end of the garth, with the two boys and the hounds sprawled at his feet.

The sun was westering behind Long Down, the shadows creeping towards them across the turf, but the tops of the apple trees were still touched with sunlight that seemed all the more golden because there had been rain earlier. The rain had brought out the good smells of the summer earth, and Randal, sitting on his heels and playing with a half-grown puppy of Joyeuse's, caught, through the tang of woodsmoke and stable droppings, the scent of the hay in the long pasture, and a whisper of something else that might be honeysuckle but was more likely elder. The thrush who had had his nest in the pear-tree by the gate was singing as he sang at this hour every evening; and there would be a new moon presently.

Reynfrey had gone into Steyning to take their tithe of strawberries to the Priory. The Dean strawberry bed, begun by Bevis's mother with wild strawberry plants gathered from all over the Manor, as well as plants that Sir Everard had had specially brought for her from Normandy, and later tended by Sybilla and Ancret for her sake, was the only one in that part of Sussex, and every year the Prior of Steyning made a great point of receiving his tithe of the little sweet, scarlet fruit. What an odd world it was, Randal thought, in which you saw to the rivets of your helmet and sent your tithe of strawberries to the Priory on the same day. The Prior would have kept Reynfrey for supper, but he should be back soon.

'Everything looks so peaceful,' Bevis said suddenly, glancing about him. 'It seems almost too strange to believe, that in a few days we shall be facing Duke Robert's army.' His eyes were wide and bright, and he sat with his new sword across his knees, fondling it. As d'Aguillon's body squire, he would be going with him as a right; but Randal was going too. He did not think he could have borne to be left behind, and the stronger the hay smelled and the sweeter the thrush sang, the more he thought he could not have borne it. Well, there had been no question of that; he was sixteen, and Sir Everard had said to him days ago, 'When the call-out comes we shall need every man we can raise. There's an old leather gambeson in the armoury kist, Randal. Go and see if it fits you.' It did not fit him very well, being somewhat large, but it had horn scales on the breast and shoulders. Only Reynfrey was to be left behind, and Randal did not see how the old man-at-arms could bear that. Maybe one did not care so much when one grew old?

Matilda, sitting against d'Aguillon's knee, raised her head to listen. She was very old now and quite blind, so that her eyes in the evening light were milky, but she could still hear as keenly as any of the other hounds. Luffra pricked his ears and sat up, and Joyeuse swung her tawny head towards the gate. A few moments later they all heard it; the beat of horse's hooves drumming up the track from the ford.

'That will be Reynfrey now,' Randal said.

...ng with a little frown. 'If it is, he's
...unt were behind him!'

...gh.'

...nearer, nearer, came to a trampling
...rgent voices sounded, and a few moments
... on their feet by now—Reynfrey appeared
... the Hall and came half-running up the garth
...

...od, man, what's amiss?' Sir Everard said, for the old
... was panting so much when he reached them that for the
...ent he did not seem able to speak.

'All Hell broken loose in Steyning, that's what's amiss!'
Reynfrey rubbed the back of a hand across his sweating forehead. 'There's some wandering friar been stirring them up
for days, Brother Thomas at the Priory told me—and there's
the market crowd, o'course, today, and they'd been drinking—
and then the shout went up——' He drew a deep breath
and seemed as though he were trying to straighten out the
urgent tumble of words. 'There's a witch hunt started and
they're heading this way over the downs. They'll be here by
dusk!'

'This way? Why this way?' Sir Everard snapped.

The two men looked at each other for one sharply silent
moment, and then Reynfrey said, 'Ancret.'

Randal felt everything go still and unreal about him. 'Witch
hunt! Witch hunt!' The words, hideous as leprosy, seemed
mouthing, gibbering, screaming themselves over and over in his
head. If there had been wind and storm and the tree tops bending double he could have taken it in more easily; it might even
have seemed less horrible; but on this still, hay-scented summer
evening . . .

Sir Everard had swung round to his grandson. 'Bevis, go and
fetch Ancret up to the Hall.'

'I'll go too,' Randal said, as his fellow squire swung on his
heel to obey, but Sir Everard stopped him.

'She will come for Bevis alone, if she will come for anyone;
and I have other work for you. We must get in all the men near

at hand, and for safety's sake the women and children a
best come up to the Hall.'

Afterwards, Randal's memory of what came next was a
blurred, as though he were remembering it through runn
water or drifting smoke. He was pelting down the village stre
scattering dogs and cats, pigs and chickens, thrusting into on
after another of the villeins' hovels, shouting his warning of the
witch hunt, shouting to the men, 'D'Aguillon wants you!' To the
women, 'Best get the bairns up to the Hall out of harm's way.'
Pelting on again with the women squarking behind him as
loudly as the scattered poultry. Bevis joined him before the end
with a couple of the house churls with him and the news that
Ancret was safely up at the Hall; and they finished the round-up
between them. When they got back to the Hall at last, Randal
was carrying a sick child for its mother, and Bevis and another
man were dragging a wildly bleating goat between them, because the miller's wife, whose darling it was, refused to come
without it.

In the Hall, Sir Everard stood by the hearth, with Reynfrey
and the men of the Manor gathered about him, and the women
huddled in the farther shadows against the gable wall.

'Na, na, there is naught to huddle like sheep for,' he was saying with a touch of exasperation. ''Tis not Duke Robert coming
down on us, but a mere market crowd from Steyning with too
much cider in their bellies.'

But the fore-shadow of the witch hunt was on them, and
Randal could not help seeing how even some of their own
Manor women had drawn aside from Ancret, looking at her a
little askance, as though in some way the fact that the witch
hunt was for her made her something to fear, a kind of danger
point like an oak to draw the lightning.

She stood, tall-seeming as always, and looked round at them,
then turned her dark gaze to Sir Everard. 'You should have left
me to take to the woods.'

'I'll have no one of my Manor hunted across country like a
deer,' Sir Everard said briefly.

She walked out from among the women, her dusty-coloured
kirtle drawn contemptuously close about her, and came to the

re. None of the men drew away from her, but Alfwine the ploughman made the sign of the Horns, carefully hidden behind his back. But not carefully enough. Ancret flicked him with her eyes. 'At the least I should have had the deer's kinship with the woods, and the woods would not have been afraid of me.' Suddenly she turned from them all, to the young squire loosening his new sword in its sheath, the only one of them all who mattered to her. And her narrow face broke up a little. 'Young Master, are you afraid of me, too?'

Bevis left his sword to itself, and put his arms round her as though he was comforting a child. 'You are all the mother I ever knew. How should I be afraid of you, Ancret, dear?'

It was growing dusk by now, though outside the thrush was still singing. The sick child whimpered, and was hushed by its mother. All colour and substance was draining out of the Hall, save where, close about the hearth, the light of the low fire woke the warm, earthy colours of the villeins' homespun, and showed the look on their waiting faces.

There was not much longer to wait. Suddenly head after head turned, eyes widening; one man licked his lower lip, another half-pulled the knife from his clumsy leather sheath, as the first distant sounds of shouting splurged up into the evening quiet beyond the thrush's song.

'Here they come, then,' Cerdic the oxherd said.

Nobody answered him.

The sounds were drawing nearer; a ragged surf of shouting, with something of the same note of menace that sounds from a disturbed nest of wild bees; the ugly, inhuman voice of a mob. Randal, waiting with his hand on the dagger in his belt, his eyes on d'Aguillon's face like a hound that waits for orders, realized that they were coming straight over the shoulder of the downs towards the Hall, and even in that moment it struck him as odd that they should not seek Ancret in her own cottage; for there must be some among this Steyning crowd who knew where she lived.

Sir Everard, his sword still in its sheath, strode towards the door, Bevis and Randal at his shoulders. They could see the witch hunt coming now, over the shoulder of the turf below

Long Down; a ragged, loping skein of figures strung out like
hounds on the scent. Some of them had torches, and the flames
streamed out behind them in rags of smoky brightness on the
dusk. They swarmed down into the village kale plots, their mass
growing denser as the stragglers in the rear caught up with those
in front; they were pouring through the gateway under the pear
tree from which the thrush had flown in terror, breaking down
the hedge on either side, bursting and jostling their way through
into the garth. The sparks from their ill-made torches whirled
up into the quiet branches where the fruit was setting, and their
faces in the tattered flare of flamelight were both afraid and
vicious. Randal saw the brightness of their eyes, the dark gape of
their yelling mouths, and the torch-glare on cudgels and quar-
terstaffs and the sharper weapons, the scythe blades or but-
chers' knives that some among them carried; saw also the friar,
face hidden in the forward-drawn folds of his cowl, who strode
in their midst.

'Why doesn't d'Aguillon draw his sword?' he thought, as the
mob, catching sight of them in the doorway, set up a fiercer
yowling and closed in at the run. 'Why doesn't d'Aguillon
draw his sword? The sight of it might stop them. *Why
doesn't*——'

D'Aguillon had flung up his arm, shouting above the tumult.
'What is this garboil that you raise on my Manor? What do
you here on Dean land?'

They were right before the door now, milling round it, but
something in the three purposeful figures standing there and the
glimpse of others beyond, something in the tall old knight confronting them on his own threshold, for a moment pulled them up.

'Send out the witch that you have in your house!' someone
shouted.

'What wicked folly is this?' d'Aguillon's deep voice cut
through the ugly surf of sound. 'You have drunk too much perry
in the Market Place, and dreamed dreams.'

'Do not listen to him!' It was the friar now, crying out in a
high, cracked voice. 'He has the woman in his house and the
woman is a witch! Remember the cow of yours that fell sick the
day after she looked at you, Rafe One-Eye! The Wrath of God

is on this house for the witch's sake. Go you in and fetch her for the burning!'

The surge forward began again, weapons were brandished aloft, torches up-tossed above distorted, howling faces. Sir Everard had left his sword in its sheath as long as might be. Now he seemed to make scarcely any movement, but suddenly it was naked in his hand, a streak of glittering steel barring the doorway. In the same instant Bevis's sword was out, and Randal whipped his dagger from his belt.

'Get back!' Sir Everard cried. 'Get back, you fools! Go home and cool your hot heads and be wiser in the morning! There is no witch here, and I give up to you no woman of my Manor, though you choose to name her ten times a witch!'

They drew back a little, snarling as an animal snarls that is baulked of its prey, but the friar, with arm outstretched in accusation, was screaming them on, lashing up their fear and frenzy.

'Will you give ear to this shielder of Satan's women? Woe, woe to those who suffer a witch to live among them! She will put the murrain on your cattle and the mildew on your fields! She will cast her spells about you to suck out your souls while you sleep, and God will not save you because you have turned your face from Him to leave the witch alive!'

Suddenly there was a rush, and the thing had gone beyond shouting and became fighting: fighting that reeled to and fro in the doorway where Sir Everard still struggled to use the flat of his blade and not the edge. Someone had tried to fire the thatch, yelling that they would smoke the witch out that way if they could get her no other; but the thatch was damp after the rain, and the flames guttered out in a black reek of charring that Randal smelled thick and acrid at the back of his nose as he tramped to and fro with the press of struggling men in the door-way.

Then a man with a broad face made stupid by fear, and a butcher's knife in his upflung fist, leapt in at Sir Everard. Randal caught the flash of the descending blade, heard a sharp cry that seemed torn off before it was well begun, and saw out of the tail of his eye the old knight stagger and go down.

625

A howl went up from the mob, and they seemed to waver, some to half-surge back in horror at what they had done, while others yet thrust forward. Bevis had sprung across his grandfather's body, the house churls behind him; there could be no more fighting with the flat of the blade. And all the while in the midst of the turmoil the friar was still urging them on, mouthing and shrieking curses and wild accusations.

'Na na, never mind the old one! Kill the young one—the yellow-haired one—I see the witch-light shining round his head! Kill! Kill! *Kill!*'

His hand was outstretched, pointing at Randal, his whole figure seemed contorted by a wild spasm of malevolence, and in the same instant, in the milling press about him, the black folds of the cowl slipped back from his face, and Randal saw it in the leaping red glare of the nearest torch, distorted with hate and rage, but unmistakable.

He gathered himself together and sprang as a wild animal springs; but quick as he was, Sir Thiebaut de Coucy had flashed a dagger from the loose sleeve of his habit to meet him, and the two blades rang together. Some instinct, something in the way the man moved, told Randal that de Coucy wore mail of some kind under his black habit, and a body blow would be well nigh useless; and something in him knew, though there was no time for thought, that failing a kill, the thing was to mark him—a mark that could be recognized afterwards . . . For a few heartbeats of time they reeled to and fro together, unaware of what went on about them, aware only of each other. Randal broke his blade free and struck again, and again felt the blow parried with a shock, as steel met steel, that jarred all up his arm. De Coucy's dagger leapt once more, and Randal felt a fiery flick of pain in his left forearm, and sprang back an instant out of touch, then in again, striving to close with the man—the great black cat, he seemed in that habit, whose claws were one bright dagger-point of death—and beat down his defence. Then de Coucy's weapon darted past his shoulder as he side slipped, with such force in the blow that for one split instant of time the man was off balance; and in that split instant Randal had him by the dagger-wrist and closed with him. He saw the rage and hate in

de Coucy's eyes, the man's whole face, close to his own, a blazing mask of hate, and slashed it across the cheek once, twice, the second gash crossing the first.

Sir Thiebaut dropped his dagger and staggered back with a strange, high cry like a woman's, clutching at his face. Randal sprang after him and caught him by the breast of his habit, twisting his hands in the black folds, dagger raised for another blow; but the thick stuff tore in his grasp, dragging away at the shoulder, and the torchlight fell full on the quilted gambeson he wore beneath it. And next instant the man had whirled about with the swiftness of desperation and kicked Randal in the groin.

The boy doubled up, as his world darkened and swam in agony, and when it cleared again, de Coucy was gone. He was on his knees, winded and retching. He glared up at the aghast faces that wavered round him in the torchlight, and used the first shuddering breath that he could draw to rave at them. 'You fools! You duped fools! Don't—you know the difference between a friar and one of Ranulf Flambard's gore-crows?'

Vaguely, as he staggered to his feet, he heard Reynfrey's bull voice calling to the Manor men as a huntsman calls to his hounds. The witch hunt was over and the rabble was in full retreat, blundering away and breaking down the garth hedges as they went. It was partly the stunned realization that they had wounded, perhaps killed, a knight whom all men knew was dear to the old Lord of Bramber who held all their lives in the hollow of his gouty hands, partly the sight of a knight's gambeson under a friar's habit, and the hated name of Ranulf Flambard flung into their midst, that had acted on them like a bucket of water flung over fighting dogs. They wanted nothing now but to get away, to reach their own homes and leave the harm that they had done behind them in the hope that in the morning it would all be a dream.

Reynfrey and half the men of the Manor were away in pursuit of de Coucy, but Randal had just sense enough to know that he could not at the moment join in any chase. If he could be any use anywhere, it would be back in the Hall. He dragged himself back to the doorway, his dagger still naked and red in his hand, heaving aside with his foot the body of a respectable Steyning wool merchant that blocked his way. Then he turned on the threshold, without knowing why, and looking up, saw the pale sliver of the new moon that he had known would be here later, caught like a white feather in the branches of the tallest cider tree at the head of the garth.

12

DE BRAOSE'S BANNER

D'AGUILLON lay just within the doorway, with the hounds crouching about his feet, his head on Bevis's knee, and Ancret kneeling beside him, busy by the light of a brand pulled from the fire that one of the remaining men was holding for her. And Randal, pushing through the throng to his Lord's side, felt a shock of sudden hope. He had thought that d'Aguillon was surely dead, but if he were dead, they would not be cutting away the sodden cloth over the wound and hurrying to staunch the blood like that. Still sweating and sick, he dropped to one knee at the old knight's other side, thrusting away Matilda's anxious white muzzle, and fixed his eyes on Ancret.

She had uncovered the wound now, a stab wound just under the collar bone, not wide, but deep, with the bright heart-blood welling up from it. A hoarse, inarticulate murmur that was like a groan ran through the Manor folk pressing about them, and Ancret looked up.

'Back! Get back now and give him air to breathe.'

Bevis, with very straight lips, said, 'Is it mortal?'

She shook her head. 'How can I tell? Even I? Sometimes the pictures come, the pictures of what will be, but never for any looking of mine. If anyone can save him, then I can, and if I can, then I will . . . Bring me clean linen for the wound, and rugs to carry him up to his own chamber.'

Two or three of the men hurried to bring her the rugs she wanted; and Sylbilla came lumbering with the linen and knelt down beside her, her face all puddled with tears. The fear that had stirred between them and the Wise Woman so short a time ago seemed quite forgotten now, as though maybe Sir Everard's blood had washed it away.

So in a little, Sir Everard was carried up to the chamber over the storeroom, his hounds padding alongside him all the way, and laid on the low sleeping bench. Randal remained beside

him, partly to help Ancret, partly for the simple sake of being
with his Lord, as the hounds were with him. Bevis, who had the
better right, was needed elsewhere, with the search for de
Coucy to be sped, and the safety and welfare of the Manor folk
to be seen to.

Randal never forgot that scene; Sir Everard lying so still on
the bed, his face set and quiet as the face of a knight carved in
stone, his great nose pointing to the raftered ceiling, and his
shield with its painted device hanging in its usual place on the
wall above his head, like the harness of a dead knight above his
tomb; the dark woman kneeling beside him, her hands laid
with a curious, light purposefulness over the newly dressed
wound, rising and falling a little—a very little—with his
shallow breathing, as though she sought to drive some life or
strength through them into his spent body (and watching
her, Randal thought suddenly of the way she had held her
hands over his bruises on the day he stole the red amber); the
hounds crouching whimpering by the fire that had been made
on the hearth; the big Norway goshawk hooded on her perch,
with her hooded shadow on the wall behind her.

Presently Bevis came back. He came silently up the outer
stair and through the doorway which had been left open to the
summer night, and stood with his eyes on the still figure on the
bed.

Ancret looked up, never moving her hands. 'I think he will
wake soon,' she said.

Bevis let go a little breath like a sigh, and came to the hearth,
thrusting back the wild, dark hair wearily from his eyes.
'We're keeping some of the outlying folk and the ones who got
hurt in the Hall for tonight. Not that there'll be any more
trouble now. De Coucy will be away for the sea coast, if he can
see his way for blood. I suppose he was making for his Master
overseas, anyway—and the rest are damp timber without him.'

'They have not caught him, then?' Randal said, stupidly,
still kneeling beside Sir Everard.

Bevis raised his eyes slowly from the unconscious man, to
look at him. 'Oh no. They're still searching the woods, but I
haven't much hope now.' There was a puzzled frown between

his brows. 'I suppose because Ancret was here when he came before, and I told him she was my foster-mother, he thought she lived under this roof.'

'Ancret was only the excuse.'

'Oh, I know . . . How he must hate you, Randal!'

'Almost as much,' Randal said softly, through shut teeth, 'as I hate him.'

He had risen to his feet as he spoke, and they stood looking at each other in the firelight. Then he took a step towards the door.

'Where are you away to?' Bevis said.

'To Bramber, to de Braose.''

There was a little silence, and then Bevis demanded, 'And what will you tell him?'

'The whole truth,' Randal said. The bargain was dead now, and surely de Braose, with all the resources of Bramber at his sword hand, might succeed with the hunt where they, it seemed, had failed.

The older boy nodded. 'I wish you joy of getting de Braose out of bed at this hour of the night, but any chance of getting de Coucy will be gone by morning. Off with you, Randal.'

Some while after midnight, when the faint light shining from the window of St Nicholas' Church showed where the Canons were at Matins, Randal was hammering with his dagger hilt on the great gate of Bramber Castle, crying out in answer to the gruff inquiry from within, 'Sir Everard d'Aguillon's squire, with an urgent message for the Lord of Bramber!'

Probably if he had been another man's squire they would not have let him in at that hour of the night, but though d'Aguillon was only the holder of one knight's fee, and there-fore not of much importance, the whole castle knew him for a friend of the old Lord's. There were grumbles and protests, but the gate swung open, squealing in the still summer night, and Randal on Swallow clattered through. There were more pro-tests, more grumblings, but somehow his blazing urgency got things done. Someone took Swallow, and he was following a man-at-arms across the courtyard and up the Keep stair. The smokiness of the guardroom gave place to the smokiness of the Great Hall and the sleepy stirring of human and hound shadows on the rush-deep floor. In the Hall they bade him wait (who 'they' were he did not know, he was too dazed by the things that had happened since sunset). He heard a mutter of voices somewhere, and de Braose's squire came down the snail-curled stair, rubbing the sleep out of his eyes and yawning, as though he were mere mortal instead of body squire to the Lord of Bramber.

'What is it?' he demanded. 'Oh, it's you; you're d'Aguillon's squire, aren't you? What do you want at this hour of the night?'

'Word with de Braose,' Randal said hoarsely.

'De Braose is in his bed.'

'Beg him to see me, all the same. Tell him d'Aguillon lies wounded, maybe to the death, and there is that which he must know——'

'Wait here,' the squire said, and turned again to the stair.

Randal waited for what seemed a long, long time, fretting with his feet among the rushes, the centre of curious stares from all directions. And then the squire came back and bade him follow.

A few moments later he stood on the threshold of the Great Chamber, above the Hall. The huge box bed with its hangings of embroidered stuffs showed tumbled and empty in the light of the newly kindled and smoky torch, and de Braose himself, who had never yet received a messenger in his bed, and clearly did not mean to begin now, half sat, half lay in his great chair before the empty hearth, a cloak of some dark, glimmering eastern stuff powdered with silver flowers flung round him over his nakedness, and his great sword laid across his knees. Two great boarhounds crouched at his feet, and he had been fondling the savage, rough head of one of them; but his eyes, like the eyes of a sick hound themselves, were already fixed on the doorway when Randal appeared in it.

'What is this that you have come to tell me?' he demanded harshly.

Randal crossed to him, limping still from de Coucy's kick,

and dropped on one knee between the hounds. 'It is true, sir—a witch hunt——'

'Ah!' de Braose leaned forward. 'I heard there was a garboil in the Market yesterday, and half Steyning out after a witch. There are many witches and I took no heed. Was it a Dean woman, then?'

'Yes. Bevis's foster-mother, Ancret—At least, it was meant to look like that, but in truth it was stirred up by Sir Thiebaut de Coucy, in revenge for being worsted over Dean.' Randal covered his face with his hands, and groaned. 'It's all my doing.'

'Never mind whose doing it is, beyond de Coucy's.' The old Lord's voice cut like a north wind. 'So it was de Coucy, was it? I wondered why he forgot his designs on the Manor so suddenly. Stop talking in rags and ravellings, boy, and get up and tell me the whole of this thing, from the beginning, whatever that may be.'

Randal drew a deep breath, uncovered his face and straightened his shoulders and got drearily to his feet. And standing before the empty hearth, he told to the fat, sick old man slumped in his chair, the whole story from the beginning, from the soft voice and the scent of musk in the darkness of the Arundel water stair, as he had told it to no one save Bevis.

De Braose's gout-swollen hands tightened on his sword as he listened, but he spoke no word until the whole ugly story was told.

'We've beaten the woods for him,' Randal finished desperately. 'They were still searching when I rode away—but it is in my mind that he has slipped through our hands.'

'And so you come to me to raise the countryside against him. But can you swear that this friar-leader of the witch hunt *was* de Coucy? In torchlight it is easy to be mistaken.'

'Even though he wore a gambeson under his habit?' Randal said quickly. 'At least the leader of the witch hunt did not go unmarked. Bid your men to look for a man with two fresh dagger cuts in the face, crossing each other—here,' he touched his own left cheek, 'and see if it be not indeed de Coucy.'

'Your dagger, I take it,' de Braose said.

'My dagger, de Braose.'

The Lord of Bramber seemed to ponder for a moment. Then with a suddenness that made the hounds leap up in bewilderment, he burst into action, hammering on the hearth stone with the chape of his sword and bellowing for his squires in a voice to rouse the whole of Bramber Castle. His body squire, from his place just outside the door, was there on the instant; others came running. He shouted orders at them, sent them hurrying for this man and that, for his chief huntsman and the captain of his men-at-arms. And through it all, Randal stood by the empty hearth, dazed by this sudden, wild explosion of activity in the midst of the sleeping castle, the hardly roused and half-dressed men hurrying in and out, while their sick old Lord sat in his great chair and issued his orders as crisply and clearly as ever he could have done at Senlac.

Presently Randal found that the Great Chamber was quiet again, and empty save for the squire who had returned to his place across the doorway. He could hear a voice somewhere below in the bailey, and the dogs lay down again with protesting grunts. And he saw that the old Lord was looking at him out of the little sick eyes sunk in his pouchy face.

'So? That is all; there is no more that we can do. The hunt is up, and within a few hours there will be a search of every ship or fishing smack that sails from this part of the coast; but—like you, I've a feeling we shall not net him. He must have decided to slip overseas and cast in his lot with Duke Robert, or I think he would not have risked it. He's a coward in some things, and he's no gambler; he'll have had his plans laid.' De Braose's voice deepened suddenly to a rumbling growl that seemed to come from somewhere in his chest. 'But if we do not get the ring-leader, we can still hang half Steyning for this night's work.'

Randal said quickly, though it was quite against his will, for he would have liked to do the hanging himself, 'The man who stabbed Sir Everard is dead, and one or two others. They were all no more than tools of de Coucy's; and I—do not think Sir Everard would want any hanging.'

De Braose was silent a moment, one hand still clenched on

his sword, the other plucking at the silver threads of a flower on his cloak.

'Maybe you're right,' he said at last, broodingly. 'A gentle soul, d'Aguillon, overly gentle, maybe, but it has brought him the love of his stubborn Saxons . . . And if he dies, though I hang all Steyning high as the Keep of Bramber, it will not bring him back to fight old battles with me again.' He seemed to be talking to himself rather than to Randal, and suddenly he noticed it, and glared at the boy as though daring him to notice it too. 'Get back to your Lord, boy; there's nought to keep you longer here, and the Lord of Bramber is away back to his bed.'

It was the first silky greyness of the summer dawn when Randal rode into the Manor garth of Dean again, abandoned Swallow to old Wulf who came hobbling with the spent lantern pale as primroses in the growing daylight; and without waiting to ask news of Sir Everard—he could not ask, the words stuck in his throat, and he must see for himself—stumbled up the outside stair.

The door at the head of it stood open as he had left it, and the solar was awash with torchlight and dawn light that mingled without mixing; the fire had sunk to frilled grey ash on the hearth, the hounds still crouching before it, the Norway goshawk on her perch, with her hooded shadow that had been so black grown thin and tenuous on the wall behind her. Ancret still knelt beside the bed, and Bevis stood beyond it; it was as though nothing, no one, had moved since he left the room. But there was a sound of harsh, quick breathing in the solar that had not been there before, and as he halted in the doorway, suddenly d'Aguillon's voice, hoarse and rattling, said, 'Is that you, Randal?'

Randal was across the room in two limping strides, and dropped on his knees beside the narrow bed. 'Yes, sir, I am here.'

Sir Everard's eyes, seeming darker than ever and sunk into his drained face, looked up at him, frowning a little. 'Bevis has told me—the whole story. And—you have told de Braose?'

Randal nodded. 'I wish—God knows how I wish I had told it before,' he groaned.

'Nay, you judged—that the threat might serve—better than the deed; and you were right, for—has not the threat served—all this while?'

'But afterwards—I should have told you.'

'Na na, a bargain is a bargain, even with—such as de Coucy. Did I not—say that to you before? Never be—sorry for faith kept, Randal.'

They did not find de Coucy; and two days later the message came down-river from Bramber that Sir Philip de Braose was carrying his father's banner to join the King's army at Pevensey, and Bevis in his grandfather's stead was summoned to bring in the Dean men to follow him.

The summons came in the evening to march next day, and before the messenger was a bowshot on his way to the next Manor, Dean was leaping into activity very different from the slow, circling rhythm of the farm that had held it before. The ten men were called in from the last of the haymaking, and Randal, coming into the Great Hall with his own leather gambeson, found the women making ready food for the march, and Reynfrey issuing arrows and spare bowstrings. He said to Bevis, who was there also, 'It must be hard for Reynfrey.'

Bevis looked at him quickly, with some trouble in his face, then gave a tiny backward jerk of the head into the shadows behind him; and when they had drawn aside from the rest, turned to look at him again. Bevis, very tall, very dark, very grave, suddenly not a boy any more, but a man. 'Randal, I—don't know how to ask this of you.'

'What is it?' Randal asked, but even as he asked there was a shock of misery in him, and he knew.

'Randal, it isn't only Reynfrey it will be hard for. You too.'

'You mean—I'm not to go with you to join the King's army?'

Bevis shook his head. 'It is for me to go. While grandfather is sick of his wound, I am d'Aguillon, and it is for me to take his levies into battle. But it is for you, who are also his squire, to stay with him.'

Randal said, mutinous for the moment, 'What would you do if you were all the squire he had? You would have been if

638

Herluin hadn't won me in a game of chess and given me to
d'Aguillon as though I were a hound puppy.' That was unjust
to everybody, and he knew it, but he was too miserable to care.

'Then le Savage would have taken the Dean levies with his
own, and I should have stayed here. That is the way it must be
when a knight has only one squire, this is the way it must be
when he has two.' He flung an arm across Randal's shoulder.
'Don't you think I'm heart-sore enough about it?—Oh, curse
you, Randal, we've done everything together so many years, I
never thought one of us would have to go into his first battle
without the other!'

Randal was silent a long moment. He had set so much store
by this marching out to join the King's army; he had had
impossible dreams of doing great things, the kind of dreams,
connected with honour and other shining matters, that you
do not talk about even to a stranger, let alone to your nearest
friend.

'Very well,' he said at last, hoarsely. 'I'll stay with Sir
Everard.'

'Good old Randal,' Bevis said. '*Good* old Randal,' and gave
his shoulder the little shake that he used sometimes instead of
words. 'Try to send me news at Pevensey, if—when there's any
news to send.'

And Randal nodded, and turned away to carry the old
leather gambeson with the scales on the shoulders back into
the storeroom again.

Next morning Sir Robert le Savage came by, leading his
Broadwater levies, and would have gone tramping up to see Sir
Everard, who was in a high fever and quite unfit to see anybody, while his men waited below, but that Ancret refused to
allow him up the solar stair. He fussed and fumed a little, his
big nose reddening as it always did in times of stress, but had to
accept her ruling; and Bevis, himself white with worry, soothed
him with a cup of the Manor's best cider, before they went on
together. Randal, standing in the Hall doorway, watched them
ride away, Bevis beside their stout neighbour, his hand on his
long new sword, and Dean men and Broadwater men loping

behind them, their bow-staves across their backs. Cerdic looked round once, at the turn of the track, as though wondering if he would ever see the village under the downs again. Then they disappeared, heading for the ford.

Randal turned to the steward who stood beside him, thumbs in belt, staring after them too, and said, 'Does it get to matter less, when you're old?'

Reynfrey laughed and cursed on the same breath, and clipped him on the shoulder and bade him get back to d'Aguillon; but he didn't answer the question.

Randal had little time for brooding in the weeks that followed. There was work and to spare for everybody, with the Manor running ten men short and barley harvest drawing on; and when he was not helping Ancret to tend the Lord of Dean, he was working like a villein in the fields. Joyeuse followed him wherever he went, seeming to think that where he was, Bevis could not be far off; and even, as the weeks went by, brought him a flint or a piece of firewood once or twice, though always in a bothered way as though her mind was not quite on what she did. News trickled over the downs from time to time; de Bellême had come out for Duke Robert, bought by the promise of more lands in Normandy, and on the other side of them, de Warrenne, Lord of the Honour of Lewis, was out too. They heard of the King's army mustered at Pevensey, waiting for the invasion, and then that the King's fleet had gone over to the enemy; and they slept at nights half listening for the hoof drum of Norman cavalry sweeping across the downs. They heard that Duke Robert had landed, not at Pevensey as his father had done, as any right-minded conqueror would do, but at Portsmouth; and the King's army was hurrying westward to give him battle. On the day that d'Aguillon, looking like his own grey ghost, first came out leaning on Randal's shoulder to sit in the sun before the Hall doorway and listen to the voices of the reapers in Muther-Wutt Field, they heard that there was to be no fighting after all. The two armies had come together at Alton, and the two royal brothers had met between their armies and come to terms. Henry was to keep England but pay Robert two thousand pounds a year. Robert was to keep all

640

Normandy save for Henry's own Castle of Domfront, and each
was to be heir to the other if he died without a son.

The English army was disbanded again, and soon after the
last sheaves were carted, Bevis and the Dean men came marching home, Bevis bright-eyed and mocking, saying to Randal,
'Well, you didn't miss much, save for seeing the King's camp
like a city of tents. All we did was to sit on our rumps and
scowl at each other, while Brother Henry and Brother Robert
haggled.'

Somehow it all seemed a little flat.

For a while, Sir Everard continued to mend. The wound
under his collar-bone was healed, thanks to Ancret's salves and
the spells she crooned over them. They had a golden autumn
running late into the winter, and towards the end of it, when
the perry making and winter slaughtering were over and the
pigs had been driven down into the Weald to fatten on acorns,
he was out and about the Manor again. But then the winter
came, with its whistling winds through the Great Hall, its cold
and dark and shortage. Sir Everard developed a dry cough, and
when at last spring came again and the fires of May Eve flared
on the Bramble Hill, it seemed to Randal that his Lord was
thinner and grew tired more easily than he had done last
autumn.

That summer Dean was left in peace to harvest its barley
with its full tally of men, for the King did not call out de Braose,
though he himself spent the campaigning season driving de
Bellême from one to another of his castles; from Arundel to
Bridgenorth, from Bridgenorth to Shrewsbury, and at last back
to Normandy where he would inevitably make common cause
with Duke Robert. Randal thought of Herluin when that news
came, thought of him with a small aching sense of loss. Whenever he heard that de Bellême was at Arundel, he had always
had the feeling that at any hour, at any moment, he might look
down the track to the ford, and see the long, fantastic figure in
monkish black with the golden sleeves come riding up it. And
they would wave to each other in the distance, and when they
came together, Herluin would sit his horse looking down at him,
with that twisted smile of his, and say, 'Well, Imp, was I

right?' and he would say, 'Herluin, you were right.' But now, that would never happen.

There was another sense of loss on Randal, too, that autumn, or rather, the shadow of a loss that was yet to come.

Sir Everard's cough had seemed to improve through the summer, but with the autumn it returned. And on a wild evening of early December, just as he was making ready to go down into the Hall for supper, he suffered a bout of coughing deeper and more racking than any that had gone before. He pressed his hand to his mouth, half leaning over the back of his big chair for support, and when at last the attack spent itself and he took his hand away, it was stained with bright spots of blood.

The eyes of his two squires met for one shocked and sickening moment; and then Bevis, his arm round his grandfather's shoulders, said, 'Go and get Ancret.'

Ancret had lived up at the Hall since Sir Everard was wounded, just as she had done when Bevis was a baby. Randal found her without trouble, and she dropped her work in the strawberry plot and came hurrying, but not, it seemed to him, surprised, rather as though it were a summons that she had been waiting for. When they reached the solar, Sir Everard, looking much as usual, though somewhat spent and grey, was lying back in his great chair beside the hearth, his head turned to watch through the narrow window, the windy sunset beyond the downs that was echoing the colour of the burning apple logs. Bevis stood beside him, and old blind Matilda, who spent all her life now dreaming in the sun when there was any, or by the fire when there was not, lay at his feet. There was a great deal of silence in the room; more silence, Randal thought, than he had heard in a room before.

Ancret went to the old knight, and stooped to look into his eyes. She seemed no more shocked or upset by what had happened than he did himself, and something passed between them that was almost a smile, as though they shared some secret that nobody else knew. Then she brought water with certain herbs broken into it, and bathed his face and hands.

Bevis, watching her, said more harshly than he had ever

spoken to her in his life before, 'Can you not do more than that? More than just wipe off the stains? Something to stop it happening again?'

Ancret looked up. 'Nay,' she said, 'neither man nor woman of this world can do that. The blade pierced my Lord's lung. It is finished.'

And Randal knew what the secret was; the secret that she and d'Aguillon had shared between them this year and more.

Sir Everard looked at his two squires, and his straight mouth curled up at the corners. 'Na na, never wear such down-daunted faces for me. I am an old man, children; I have had a good life, and now the time draws near to lay it down; there is nothing for beating the breast in that.'

His gaze, the dark, straight gaze that Randal had disliked so much in the early days, had gone back to the flaming colours of the sunset that seemed spreading into the room itself. 'I should like to see the spring come running into this valley of ours, once more . . .'

Bevis, with his hand on his grandfather's shoulder, stood also staring into the sunset. His face was suddenly thin and taut, and nothing about him moved except the muscles in his throat as he swallowed.

Randal broke down and cried like a child, with his head on d'Aguillon's knees, the great hounds whimpering against him.

D'Aguillon looked down at his tangle of pale hair with a kind of half-amused wonder, and said, 'Randal—do you love me, then?'

'If you take a half-starved dung-hill whelp and bring it up to be your hunting dog and hearth companion, you're likely to find in the end that the silly brute loves you!' Randal wept, almost defiantly.

D'Aguillon was to see the one more spring that he longed for. Christmas passed, and Candlemas, and the valley was full of the babble of lambs again, and the plovers at their mating up on Long Down; and before the night frosts were over, they made him a little wattle hut like a hunting bower among the apple trees behind the Hall, for he found it easier to breathe there than between walls.

Once or twice that winter, messages had passed to and fro between Dean and Bramber where the old Lord too was dying. The last came on an evening early in April, clerk-written on a scrap of parchment as the others had been.

I am away; see that you follow my banner as close as you did at Senlac.

Adam Clerk read it to Sir Everard, and the old knight smiled at the grim jest, and bade them send back word that he rode in the very shadow of de Braose's banner. But de Braose never got that message. A few hours after, they heard that he was dead.

Two days later, Sir Everard, always a quiet man, died on the quietest of spring evenings, with the first white pear blossom unfurling on the old tree by the garth gate, and the first nightingale of the year singing in the river woods.

Matilda, who had lain beside him all that long while, died the same night. Privately, Randal thought that was Ancret's doing. The old hound could not have been left to grieve, and it saved Bevis, who would have had to give her the mercy-stroke, just so much more of sorrow.

So the dark Norman knight who had held his English Manor for more than half a lifetime, was laid beside his wife in the little flint church in the land that had become home to him; and his Saxon villeins grieved for him as deeply as they could have done for a Saxon Thegn. Bevis took his great sword with the damascened blade and the seal cut in the pommel, and swathed it in oiled linen and laid it away in the armour kist.

'When I am a knight, I shall take it out again,' he said, 'if ever I come to my knighthood now . . .'

If. That was always the question for a squire whose knight died, for he must find another knight with whom to finish out his squirehood; and since a knight was seldom made before his twenty-first birthday, Bevis had still two years to go. No good worrying about that at the moment, though. The thing that mattered now was to see that the spring ploughing got finished and the bank of the stream properly made up again where the winter rains had torn it down.

They had been helping with the torn bank, and were returning, thigh-wet, a few days later, when the hounds pricked up their ears, and Bevis said, 'Hallo, someone's coming.'

Looking down-stream through the hazels by the ford, Randal caught a glimpse of russet and blue cloth and the black arch of a horse's neck, followed by a flicker of chestnut colour where a second rider came after the first, up the steep slope of the bank. A knight, and maybe his squire behind him.

'I believe it's Sir Philip himself,' Bevis said. 'Come on.'

It was Sir Philip de Braose. A few moments later he reined in his big Percheron and stood looking down at the two muddy figures that had broken out of the hazel thicket to meet him. He held his left arm at the stiff falconer's angle, a hooded goshawk on his fist, and Randal saw the little wind ruffle her breast feathers that were barred and splashed brown on creamy amber, like that of an enormous missel thrush. Young de Braose looked at Bevis with the cold, grey eyes that were so exactly the colour of a sword blade. 'Ah, we are well met, Bevis d'Aguillon. I was coming up to the Hall in search of you, but now I need not ride so far.'

'Will you not come up to the Hall in any case, de Braose, and drink a cup of wine?' Bevis said, dripping chalky mud where he stood, but mindful of his duties.

De Braose shook his head. 'When you are a knight, then I shall come and claim a stirrup cup at the door of Dean . . . It was on the matter of your knighthood that I came to speak with you. You have—what—two years of your squirehood left to serve?'

'Yes, if I can find some knight to take me.'

De Braose quieted his fidgeting horse. 'I'll take you. Aylwin here'—with a beck of chin over shoulder towards the young man on the chestnut behind him—'will be made a knight at Whitsun, and after that I shall be in need of another squire. Come up to the Castle tomorrow.'

There was a silence, broken only by the tiny silver ringing of the goshawk's bell as she raised one foot. Then Bevis said, 'You are most kind, my Lord——'

'Nay, you will find that I do not do things for kindness. I

645

remember the friendship that was between my father and your grandfather, that is all.'

'—but there are two of us. Unless you can do with two new squires . . .'

De Braose turned his gaze from Bevis to Randal, and raked him with a long, cool stare. 'Both or neither, eh?'

'Don't be a fool!' Randal babbled under his breath, his eyes on de Braose's face, but his urgent muttering for his foster brother beside him. 'Bevis, don't be a fool—I'll do well enough. I can fend for myself. Maybe I'll do a voyage with Laef Thorkelson. I'll come back to you when you're a knight.'

But Bevis simply was not listening. 'Both or neither,' he said to de Braose with a curious gentleness.

De Braose looked from one to the other, frowning. Then abruptly the frown vanished and he flung up his head and laughed. 'God forbid that I should part Roland and Oliver! Come up to the Castle tomorrow, both of you.'

13

THE RED-HAIRED GIRL

SUNSHINE through the hinder door of the kennels splashed on the brindled and tawny coats of the hounds newly in from exercise. A fly with a dark blue, iridescent body danced and hovered above their heads, just out of reach of their snapping jaws, then zoomed out through the door into the kennel court where more of the great Talbots and Alaunts lay sprawled on the little plot of summer-dry grass. Randal watched it go, his hand still fondling the great rough head against his knee. He had come down from the Keep with word for Guthlac the chief huntsman that de Braose wished to see him about the choice of young hounds for the hart hunting. And when the huntsman had stridden off to answer the summons, he had lingered behind to make much of old Rollo, who was a favourite of his. The afternoon was his to do as he liked with, but he never knew quite what to do with off-duty time when Bevis was not off duty also. Thuna oozed towards him, jealous of the attention he was spending on Rollo, and nosed at his hand, gazing up at him with eyes of liquid amber and bee-brown. Her soft coat in the sunlight was tawny gold, like Joyeuse's at home at Dean.

Dean. His thoughts, lazy in the afternoon heat, went off to the Manor under the downs. It would be good out at Dean now. Probably they would just have finished getting in the hay. It was more than a year since he and Bevis had come to Bramber as de Braose's squires, and the Manor had passed into de Braose's keeping until Bevis reached his knighthood. But Reynfrey was still the steward, and when they got the chance of a few hours at home, everything was just as it always had been, save that Sir Everard was not there. Not that the chance came very often. As far as work went, life was easier as well as gayer than it had been at Dean; there were plenty of amusements, hunting and hawking, minstrelsy in the Great Hall at nights; but the squires were always with their Lord, or at least on call, and it was seldom enough that they could count themselves free for a day or a half-day, to have out Swallow and Durandal and ride home. Maybe it was because these visits were so few and so brief, that they seemed always to shine a little in the remembering, as though they were woven of something richer than the fabric of every day.

Rollo had fallen asleep. He was wise and strong with the garnered wisdom and strength of his many years' hunting; but he was old. Probably this would be his last season. He was hunting now in his sleep, paws and muzzle fluttering, and tiny, oddly pathetic whimpers breaking from his throat as he picked up the scent of the dream hart and belled and bayed the proud and eager message to the dream pack behind him.

'Ho moy, ho moy, hole, hole, hole!' Randal encouraged him softly, his hand on Thuna's head. 'Oyez, a'Rollo, hark to Rollo! Hark to Rollo the valiant.'

Suddenly he became aware of other voices in the kennels, voices away up at the far end, from the direction of the stall where Linnet, de Braose's favourite bitch, lay with her new litter of puppies. The stubborn growl of a boy's voice, and a girl's clear tones raised and angry.

'Let me pass! Let me pass this instant!'

Better go and see what was happening. Randal gave a parting pull to Thuna's left ear, and got up. He went through the next bay of the kennels into the far one—the long range of the building was divided into three so that they could shift the hounds about to clean and air the compartments—and found himself in the midst of a fine battle scene.

In the entrance to the stall where Linnet and her puppies were, Perrin the dog-boy was confronting a tall girl with hair as red as Hugh Goch's, as red as winter bracken with the sun shining on it, that seemed just now to be all but flying out of its two thick braids with fury.

The youngest of the Lady Aanor's maidens had only been at Bramber for a few weeks and Randal had scarcely spoken to her, but he knew vaguely that her name was Gisella, that she was fourteen, and that she came from a manor away northward into the Weald where there were too many daughters even though two of them had been given to a nunnery. Fine, warlike nuns, if they were anything like Gisella, he thought, checking just inside the doorway, and wondering what, if anything, he was to do.

'My Lord gave orders her wasn't to be disturbed by strangers,' Perrin was saying doggedly, with the air of one repeating what he has said before.

'Disturb her? Who talks of disturbing her? Do you think this is the first time I have ever been near a bitch with young puppies?'

'I don't know aught about that, young Mistress. De Braose gave orders——'

'I will explain to de Braose afterwards,' said the red-haired girl with her nose in the air.

'It will be me that'll have to do the explaining afterwards, if I let you in,' Perrin said simply. And then, as she showed no sign of giving way, his voice rising into something that was almost a howl of injury and exasperation. 'Oh *why* don't you go back to your stitch-craft and leave what doesn't concern you to them as it *does* concern?'

The girl's eyes widened. 'Why, you—you impertinent oaf!' she spat, her face bright with fury. 'How *dare* you speak to me like that!' Her hand shot out, and she dealt him a sharp blow, not open-palmed as Randal would have expected a girl to hit, but with her clenched fist on the side of his face.

The sound of the blow fell, duller than a slap, into the close, dog-smelling quiet of the kennels, and for a long moment afterwards nothing and nobody moved. The boy had clenched his own fist, but gave no other sign, and stood staring straight before him with sullen blue eyes, while the mark of the blow flushed slowly crimson on his cheek and jaw.

All the careless blows and casual cruelties of his own early days surged up in Randal in that one moment as he watched, and he longed to catch hold of the girl and shake her until her teeth rattled in her cruel, stupid head. But the feeling was mingled with an exasperated helplessness, because he knew the ways of men and hounds but not girls, and certainly, save for giving her the shaking, which he supposed regretfully was out of the question, he had not the faintest idea how to deal with a girl as angry as this one seemed to be.

'Gervase is trying out a new horse in the river field,' he heard his own voice saying with careful courtesy, as he stepped forward. 'Maybe you would like to come and watch him, Mistress Gisella.'

She swung round and stood looking at him as he reached her side, her eyes flickering with scorn. 'You sound just as though I was four years old and you were trying to coax me out of here with a sweetmeat.'

That, Randal realized with fresh exasperation, was perfectly true.

'If you'd not be treated as though you were four years old, maybe you'd best not behave as though you were,' he snapped. 'Now you come out of here and leave Perrin in peace.'

For a long moment they stared at each other, the girl's eyes stormy and challenging, Randal's grimly determined. Then, with a small, furious shrug, she turned to the outer door. Randal followed behind her as she stalked out with her nose disdainfully in the air.

Outside in the bailey where the heat danced a little on the cobbles, she rounded on him in a fine, singing passion. 'And you a squire—going to be a knight some day, I suppose—and you take that wretched dog-boy's part against *me*, after you heard how he spoke to me!'

'He was in the right,' Randal said levelly. 'He had de Braose's orders. And de Braose was right, too. Bitches are easily upset in the first few days.'

'Do you suppose I don't know that? Always I went among my father's hounds whenever I would; I helped tend the bitches and their puppies. I've been with them when they whelped before now.'

'They knew you; Linnet doesn't,' Randal told her flatly. Then, as he saw her mouth open for a furious retort, he added, 'And maybe you did not hit whoever was in charge of them. It was a coward's trick to hit Perrin.'

She flushed, but said defiantly, 'Why?'

'For the obvious reason that he couldn't hit you back.'

652

Gisella swallowed, and said in a slightly smaller voice, 'Because I'm a girl, you mean?'

'Oh no. If you had been one of the kitchen wenches I don't doubt he'd have clouted you back as you deserve. Because you are one of the Ladies from the Great Chamber.'

There was a little silence, while they stood in the midst of the crowded bailey and glared at each other, and he saw that she was in some sort driven into a corner. Then she gathered herself together again and lashed out, jibingly. 'It seems you have a vast deal of fellow-feeling for a dog-boy—almost as much as though you had been one yourself.'

Randal's temper went with a twang like a snapped bowstring. 'I was a dog-boy at Arundel, until de Bellême's minstrel won me from Hugh Goch with a game of chess, and gave me to Bevis d'Aguillon's grandfather to be bred up with Bevis,' he told her through clenched teeth. 'I've had a good many cuffs and kicks in my time, more than Perrin, maybe, but none from such a stupid, cruel, heartless little creature as you are!'

'Not until now!' Gisella said, also through clenched teeth, and flashed up her hand and dealt him a stinging, open-palmed slap—a girl's blow this time—on the cheek. 'There! I'm not a bit sorry I hit Perrin, and I'm *glad* I've hit you! That's what I think of dog-boys!' And she whirled about and ran from him back towards the Keep.

Randal stood for a moment watching her, the marks of her fingers burning on his cheek. Then he carefully unclenched his own fists, shook his shoulders as though to shake off the whole stupid incident, and strode off by himself to watch Gervase and the new horse.

Bevis was to be made a knight at Easter time. There would be many new knights made that Easter, five of them from Bramber, for the King was gathering his forces to invade Normandy, and a good supply of new knights was always made on the eve of a campaign.

Duke Robert's popularity when he returned from the Crusade had been shortlived; now his Duchy was in a state of chaos, and his harrassed lesser folk begging Henry to come and

take them. It was the younger brother's chance, and Henry
seized it as he had seized his chance before. The days of the
Lenten Fast were full of the steadily mounting din from stable
and store and armourer's shop. Harness was being readied up,
war gear forged and mended, great bundles of arrows brought
from the fletchers, horseshoes, spare mail and weapons sealed
in barrels against the salt of the sea crossing, sheaves of spears,
bales of bandage-linen and wound salves that the Lady Aanor
and her women had provided, wine and salt meat and coarse
barley meal in sewn skins, all made ready for taking down to
the merchant ships that lay waiting at the wharf below the
Castle mound. And all day and all night the great Castle rang
with the clash of the armourer's hammers, the voices of men,
the neighing of horses and the tramping of feet.

Now Easter was one day past, and the ring and throb of last-
minute preparations that had been silent since Good Friday, had
sprung up again more urgent than ever. Tomorrow the can-
didates for knighthood would keep their vigil in the Castle
chapel, kneeling with the new swords that they were so soon to
use laid before them on the altar steps; Randal, hurrying up
with Bevis and Gervase de Machault to the Keep at supper
time, thought that the ring of hammer on anvil, where the
Master Armourer was renewing a link in a hauberk, sounded
like the note of a struck bell; a fiercely insistent note that seemed
to get inside your head and go on beating there, bright as the
sparks that flew up from the anvil in the hurrying grey and
silver of the windy day.

De Braose's senior squire, a strong and very ugly young man
with a disarming grin and a trick of making friends, flung an
arm across Bevis's shoulder as they hurried. 'I wish you were
going to keep your vigil with the rest of us tomorrow. What do
you want to go skulking off to that Manor of yours on your own
for?'

'Not on my own. Randal is going with me,' Bevis said
quickly. And then, 'Being knighted is one of the things that can
only happen once—like being born or dying. I want it to happen to me in my own place, with my own folk around me.'

'De Braose wasn't best pleased, was he?'

'No.' The seriousness that had touched Bevis's voice the moment before, splintered into laughter. 'He said I was a pest, and the Lord of Bramber had other things to do just now than ride half over to Shoreham for the very doubtful pleasure of dubbing me knight.'

'What did you say to that?'

'I told him I was very sure that le Savage would ride over from Broadwater to give me the accolade, for my grandfather's sake.'

Gervase whistled dolefully. 'And you would really take your knighthood from that old cider barrel instead of de Braose, just for the sake of being at home?'

'He was my grandfather's friend,' Bevis said, carefully avoiding the question, as they swung into the alleyway behind the long row of workshops.

But it had not come to that, thought Randal who had been present at the interview. De Braose was not the man to have it said that one of his own squires had had to turn elsewhere for his knighthood. He remembered the Lord of Bramber saying with a bark of laughter, 'Have it as you wish, then; go free of your squirehood a day early, and take Randal with you. I ride down to Shoreham after the ceremony here is over, on some business of horse transports; and I'll turn aside to give you the accolade if you will give me the stirrup cup you once promised me.' He had even given Bevis in advance the tall Spanish stallion he would have given him afterwards, for it was his custom, as it had been the old Baron's, whenever he made a knight, to give him his first war-horse.

So tomorrow they would ride home to Dean, the Bramber years behind them, and ahead, only a handful of days away, the time when Sir Bevis d'Aguillon and Randal his squire would be sailing with the King's host for Normandy.

At that moment two things happened in quick succession. Firstly Randal saw that somebody had left the garden door open. Usually the door of the narrow Castle garden where the Lady Aanor and her women brought their sewing in the fine weather was shut to keep out stray dogs, pigs wandering from the butcher's yard, scullions and other such creatures. But now it stood wide, letting out the luminous, grey-green turmoil of wind-tossed, budding branches into the garbage-strewn and rain-puddled alleyway below the Keep. Secondly there broke out behind them a great baying and snarling, followed by a rush of flying paws; and two of de Braose's great wolfhounds came streaking past, the foremost carrying a red bone from the butcher's yard, the other in furious pursuit. Math and Mathonwy were brothers, even as Bran and Gerland of the Arundel days had been, but all the Castle knew how little brotherly love there was between them when either had a bone.

'One day these brutes will kill each other,' Randal said, as they circled a pile of stacked timber and sprang yelling into view again; and even as he spoke, Mathonwy, seeing the open door and the sheen of grass and leaves beyond, swerved in his tracks and shot through, followed by Math with every hair along his spine bristling like a wolf's.

Randal heard the rush and scatter of their paws, and the sudden sing-song snarling as Mathonwy, finding that there was no other way out, turned to rend his brother; heard also one small human cry, cut short and not repeated.

'Someone is frightened in there,' Bevis said. 'Come on.'

'No, I'll go. We're late already and you two are on duty for supper,' Randal said over his shoulder, already doubling in his own tracks towards the garden door.

Inside the narrow garden, a tall girl with red hair stood pressed back against the wall in the far corner where the two great hounds had penned her, half engulfed in their struggle as they rolled over and over, each striving for a throathold. Randal saw the strained stillness in her face above the whirling slavering turmoil of their bodies, and dived into the fight himself, no longer Randal the squire but Randal the dog-boy. How many yelling dog fights he had broken up, and how many scars of old bites he had to show for them! He twisted one hand in Math's throat, hammering between Mathonwy's eyes with a clenched fist, snarling at them, not as a man giving orders, but in something very like their own tongue. This was something they were not used to, and it seemed to puzzle them and come between them and their deadly purpose. Mathonwy snapped at the boy's wrist, but did not hang on. Sullenly, panting and snarling, they allowed themselves to be flung apart. Randal caught up the bone from where it lay at Gisella's feet, and turned back to the door, holding it above his head, the two great brutes with every hackle raised along their spines leaping and slavering about him as they tried to reach it. He kicked them out into the alleyway, and flung the bone over the nearest wall, where he thought it might take them some time to find it, then rattled the little deepset door to, and turned again to Gisella.

She had come out from her corner, and stood beside the turf seat under the still bare quince tree. The blue of her torn and muddied kirtle made a patch of strong colour in the hazy greens and greys of the awakening garden, but not so strong as the angry, sparkling red of her hair.

'All's over,' Randal said. 'They can't get in through the closed door even if they wanted to, and they'll take their quarrel elsewhere now.'

'Good,' said Gisella breathlessly, with the colour coming back in two little crimson patches on her cheek-bones. 'So now you can go away and—and not have to stop here and play the hero any more!'

Randal felt slightly jolted in the stomach. He had not expected to be thanked, but he had not expected quite such a rebuff, either. He stood and glared at her, while she glared back. They had taken great care to ignore each other ever since their first encounter, but if she still wanted an open fight, then she could have one.

'If you feel like that, I am sorry I came at all,' he said at last. 'I don't suppose Math and Mathonwy would actually have killed you, they were too busy trying to kill each other. But I thought you sounded frightened—despite being so used to your father's hounds.'

'I wasn't frightened, I was startled,' she said crossly. 'I wasn't expecting anything, and I've never actually had two brutes the size of war-horses fighting on top of me before.'

Something in her crossness struck Randal as funny, and despite himself, he grinned. 'Well, if you want no more rescuing,

657

I'm away. You had best come too, or you will be late for supper.'

'Go and get your supper. I've still to find the Lady Aanor's scissors. She thinks she dropped them here——' And then, glancing down as though she thought he might be hiding them somewhere about himself, she saw his wrist, where the close-fitting linen of his shirt sleeve was torn and stained with crimson, and her face and voice changed on the instant, as though she turned before his eyes into another and very much gentler person. 'Oh! You're bitten! Show me.'

Randal had been bitten so often before he was seven years old that it no longer seemed to him a thing to make a fuss about. 'Not much,' he said. 'Mathonwy was not really giving his mind to it.' He pulled up the tight sleeve and sucked his wrist and spat blood into the roots of a rosemary bush.

'Show me,' she persisted, and when, with a shrug, he held his arm out to her because it was less trouble than refusing, she touched the torn skin with one finger. 'Oh, it *is* a bite! It must hurt—and I didn't even thank you.' She swallowed, and looked up. 'But I do thank you. It was splendid, the way you parted those two!'

'It is a thing I've done often enough,' Randal said. 'I'm a dog-boy—remember?' Odd, how that rankled.

There was a long silence in which he heard the insistent bell note of the armourer's hammer ringing to war, but small and shut out beyond the high wall; and the soft hushing of the wind through the budding twig-tangle of the Lady Aanor's beloved briar roses. Then Gisella said in a small, steady voice, 'I am sorry about that. And I'm sorry I hit you, and I'm sorry I hit Perrin.'

Randal was so surprised that he simply stood and stared at her. And after a few moments she said in the same small, steady voice, 'Now it is for you to say you are sorry that you called me a stupid, cruel, heartless little creature.'

At first he was not sure whether she was laughing at him; then he realized that she was completely in earnest. But he still hesitated. He was not going to say he was sorry for the things he had said if it was not true; oddly, he felt he owed the

658

red-haired girl that, not an empty apology for courtesy's sake, but the truth. But even as he hesitated, he knew that if she was sorry, so was he.

'I am sorry I called you a stupid, cruel, heartless little creature,' he said at last, without a shadow of a smile.

Her eyes were fixed on his face, very wide and grave. Grey-green eyes with a feathering of tawny gold. 'I'm not really,' she said. 'Not stupid and heartless, I mean. But I was so miserable and—and homesick, and I *did* have a lot to do with my father's hounds, and when they said Linnet had got puppies, I thought —I thought I would go and see them, and it would be just a little bit like being at home. And then Perrin wouldn't let me in, and I got angry because I was so m-miserable, and then you came, and I was ashamed as well as miserable.'

'And that was why you smacked my face and flung "dog-boy" at me—because you were ashamed?'

'Yes,' said Gisella simply.

They were sitting, turned to face each other, on the turf seat now, without any recollection of having sat down there, without at all noticing that there was anything odd in their doing so, when they had been enemies so short a time ago.

'Are you still homesick?' Randal said after a little while.

'Often. But I'm more used to it now.'

Another silence, and then she added hesitantly, 'I suppose that is a thing that cannot happen to you, anyway—feeling homesick?'

Randal was gazing into the wind-ruffled grey-green depth of the rosemary bush, as if he were looking through it, and seeing a track leading from a ford, and a thin old knight on a great war-horse riding up it, with a small boy with a whip-scarred back and strange feelings waking in his small, sore heart, mounted on his saddle bow. 'You don't know Dean,' he said, 'or you'd not say that.'

'Dean?'

'Bevis's home—and mine since I was ten years old—over the downs that way, towards the sea.' He turned again to her, with a deep contentment. 'And I'm going back there tomorrow.'

'You? Are you going tomorrow?' she said quickly. 'I knew

Bevis was going, because he wants to be knighted among his own folk. But you're de Braose's squire—you're not going to be knighted yet.'

'I'm only de Braose's squire until Bevis is knighted. When we sail for Normandy, I shall be d'Aguillon's squire, not de Braose's.' Randal hesitated a moment, and then added, 'I shan't ever be knighted, you know.'

She sat and looked at him out of a sudden stillness, frowning a little. 'Why not, Randal?' It was the first time she had used his name.

'It is no good being a knight, when you have not the where-withal to furnish your helm. And it's none so bad a life, being a squire.'

'But that's not fair! You'd make a better knight than some that hold a dozen manors!' Gisella said in swift championship. 'Look at the way you got rid of those hounds—and after I had been so horrible to you!' She looked down at her hands folded in her blue lap, with the shadows of the bare quince branches dancing over them; then up again. 'I am glad it was you that came, Randal.'

'I am glad it was I that came, too, Gisella.'

A gust of wind stronger than any that had gone before swooped into the narrow garden, booming like a breaking sea in the branches of the quince tree, and setting the briars streaming like green spray. The rosemary bush flung up its arms in a silvery turmoil, and as it did so, something bright among the twisted roots flicked at the corner of Randal's eye. He stooped quickly, and picked the thing from its hiding place. 'Here are the Lady Aanor's scissors that you were looking for.'

With the finding of the scissors, remembrance of the time and the rest of the world rushed back to them. Gisella snatched them from him and sprang up. 'Oh we're so late—so dreadfully late for supper. We must go!'

Randal also had come to his feet, and they stood for one moment looking at each other with a queer, unexpected wretchedness for something that they were losing before it could even be said to have begun. Then Gisella swooped down, and with the Lady Aanor's scissors clipped a sprig from the heart of the rosemary bush—the only sprig that was yet come into flower—and held it out to him.

'There, take it,' she said incoherently. 'You'll be going into battle—it's good to have something that somebody gave you, to take into battle with you.'

Randal took it from her, and stood looking at it, seeing as clearly as though he had never seen a sprig of rosemary before, the shape and the faint, washed-out blue of the fragile petals, and the silvery green of the narrow leaves; catching the dry, aromatic scent that came up to him from between his fingers.

When he looked up, Gisella was already gone, running as she had run that other time.

Randal fished inside the embroidered neck of his tunic and brought out the little washleather bag in which he carried his precious lump of raw red amber, opened it, and slipped the sprig of rosemary inside. He drew up the string of the little bag again, and returned it to the breast of his tunic. Then he too ran, but remembering to close the door in the wall behind him.

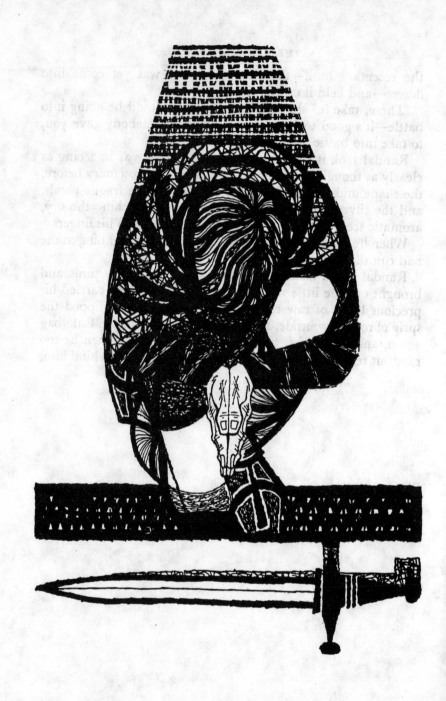

14

SIR BEVIS D'AGUILLON

ABOUT an hour before noon next day, Randal and Bevis rode into the Hall garth at Dean, Bevis on the tall bay stallion that de Braose had given him, and Randal leading Durandal beside his own Swallow; the hounds as usual leapt all about them, and the squire years at Bramber were left behind. They were expected, and Reynfrey, who had been watching the track from the ford all morning in the intervals of the other things he had to do, came striding to hold Bevis's stirrup as he dismounted.

'Home again, then, d'Aguillon.'

It was the first time he had ever called Bevis by that name, and Bevis flushed a little as he heard it. 'Aye, home again to be made knight among my own folk, before the ships sail, Reynfrey.' He turned to greet Adam who had come scurrying up from his little cell behind the church when he heard the horses' hooves. 'Come to keep my vigil in our own church, where you made Randal and me keep so many vigils with our Latin when we wanted to go fishing.' And he took the little man's thin, brown hands and stood smiling down at him, then turned to the silently waiting Ancret, and hugged her without a word. Others of the household and Manor had come running at the sound of hooves, and Bevis in the midst of the growing knot of them was greeting and being greeted. But the smell of mutton pottage that had been stealing out to them from the big pot over the cooking fire in the Hall turned suddenly to the smell of burning, and Sybilla fled with a squawk, followed by their laughter.

Presently they ate in the Great Hall, Bevis sitting in d'Aguillon's place at the High Table, with Joyeuse crouched against his knee, and when dinner was over, Adam brought the Manor roll that must be checked and gone through. Reynfrey came with matters of his stewardship to be gone into in readiness for de Braose's coming, and Bevis must go over the equipment and stores of the ten men that he would be leading in a few days to join the King's army. For Dean in its small way was humming the same deep war-song of preparations that they had left behind them in Bramber; all just as it had been nearly four years ago, when the witch hunt came. The witch hunt! There had been no more word of de Coucy from that day; he must have got safely out of the country to join the Duke. Randal, helping Bevis and Reynfrey to check bowstrings, wondered if perhaps he might meet de Coucy in Normandy this summer, and cherished the thought as though it were a smoothly rounded pebble in his hand, everything in him reaching forward to the coming campaign, and Gisella already forgotten altogether.

But towards the day's end, when all things were seen to and set in order, Bevis and Randal went up the valley to find Lewin the Shepherd, and lay on their stomachs as they had done when they were boys, watching the shadows lengthen across the downs.

'If I were going to be made a knight tomorrow,' thought Randal, his nose in the sheep-nibbled grass, 'this is just how I should choose to spend the last few hours: up here with Lewin and the sheep. Nothing moving but the cloud shadows, and all Dean spread out below me from the Bramble Hill to the ford.'

When they got back to the Hall, le Savage had just ridden in from Broadwater. He had sent word that he would come, and here he was, clattering into the garth, his great round face shining in the April sunlight that dappled through the branches of the old pear tree.

Bevis ran to hold his stirrup as he dismounted, exclaiming, 'God's greeting to you, Sir Robert. This is kind of you, when you must have so little time to spare just now from Broadwater's affairs!'

Le Savage clapped a hand like a mottled ham on Bevis's shoulder, his big nose red with emotion. 'All things are in train at Broadwater and I've left Hugo in charge. Couldn't leave you without a made knight beside you at a time like this. Na na!'

Again they ate in the Great Hall; le Savage a good deal—especially of the wheatear pie—and Randal and Bevis rather less than usual. Randal was suffering from an odd breathlessness, a feeling of unbearable solemnity in his stomach that left little room for food. He jibed at himself for a fool; it was not he who was to spend all the long hours of this night's darkness alone in the little church beyond the garth, kneeling before his naked sword laid on the high altar, not he who would kneel down here in the Hall still a squire, and rise up a knight, sheathing his new sword—d'Aguillon's great sword with the seal cut in the hilt . . .

Supper was over and the daylight fading, and Bevis had left the table and turned in the doorway at the foot of the solar steps, looking back for him. They left the Hall and climbed the outside stair together, Joyeuse at their heels. Le Savage looked after them as though wondering whether he should come too, then shook his head and settled down with his cup of home-brewed perry, beckoning with his head for Reynfrey to come and talk to him by the fire, while the churls cleared up the Hall.

Randal set the torch he had brought in the socket beside the empty hearth, and the smoky yellow flare of it sent the grey daylight scurrying into corners where it hung like cobwebs under the rafters. The room felt extraordinarily empty; there had been no life in it for two years. But the sleeping-bench against the wall was made up, with hard, straw-filled pillows and the best sheepskin rug ready for the new Lord of Dean.

Bevis went to the carved kist where d'Aguillon's war gear had always lain, and flung back the lid. The smell of oiled linen and long-stored leather came up to them as he lifted out the great sword in its linen wrappings. Randal took it from him and laid it on the bed; the worn crimson belt with its powdering of tiny golden roses swung free as he did so, a bright slash of colour across the greyish fleece of the rug.

'I'll give it a rub up before you belt it on,' he said.

Bevis was already arm-deep in the chest again. 'I'm no knight that you should be my squire yet, Randal.'

'I shall be your squire tomorrow,' Randal said. 'It is but a few hours. Let me clean your sword for you, Bevis.'

They brought out the nut-shaped helmet in its oiled wrappings,

665

the stained and weather-worn gambeson that Sir Everard had worn so often, the studded leather legstraps; finally, together, they lifted out the great ring-mail hauberk that chimed and rang faintly even inside its linen cloth as they moved it. Sir Everard's shield, the bright bird-snake on it freshly painted and the straps renewed (Reynfrey had seen to all that) hung where it had always hung, on the wall over the bed.

Everything was in perfect readiness, evidently Reynfrey had been busy; and Randal knew that it was really only for a whim that he was rubbing up d'Aguillon's great sword, even as he un-sheathed the long streak of wavering, sheeny brightness that was the blade, and began his burnishing, while Bevis, his outer tunic pulled off over his head, stood watching him.

After a few moments he sheathed the blade again, and rose to help Bevis with his arming, and as he did so, their eyes met in the flaring torchlight, with a brightness shared between them. They had shared so many things in their time, but this was something greater even than their red amber had been. Then Randal took up the old gambeson and held it for Bevis to push his arms into the short sleeves, and when that was laced on, set to work on the legstraps. Bevis, being something of a dandy, wore close-fitting hose in the new fashion, instead of the old loose breeks, and the heavy, studded cross-gartering struck Randal suddenly as looking quite ludicrous over them. The laughter rose in his throat, as it will do sometimes when one is not in the least in the mood for it. He gave a kind of whimper-ing snort, and Bevis, still fiddling with the lacing of his gambe-son, looked down to see the jest, saw his own legs, and caught the quick, strained laughter from him so that they rocked to-gether like the veriest pair of urchins. And le Savage, in the Great Hall by the fire, heard them and grumbled to Reynfrey, 'Ah, we did not laugh so, on the eve of knighthood, when I was a boy. But it is different in these days; nothing is sacred to the wild lads now.'

In the cold solar, by the light of the flaring torch, Bevis and Randal had sobered from their laughter, and Randal was help-ing Bevis on with his hauberk. The thing weighed more than half as much as a man, and hung heavy with the dead, cold

666

heaviness of its interlinking iron mesh as he heaved it up and Bevis, stooping, plunged his head and arms into it. Randal slipped round behind him and heaved it further on over his shoulders. The mail jarred and chimed as Bevis threshed with his arms, heaving also; then he stood upright, his usually pale face scarlet, and the hauberk slid down over his body, a darkly glimmering gown of mail to the knee, the torchlight jinking on his shoulders in flecks and fish-scales of light.

'Phew! Somebody ought to invent a better way of getting into a hauberk!'

Randal brought him the great sword and belted it on; lastly the war-mittens. The helmet would be left standing ready on the armour kist until tomorrow, since he must go bareheaded to his vigil; and the mail coif hung loose on Bevis's neck. He hitched at his sword belt, making sure that all was secure, then crossed the solar to take down the gaudy shield, moving less swiftly than usual. He was well used to wearing mail, as was Randal, for it was part of the training of a squire, but however well one was used to it, there was always that slowing up, that faint ponderousness in the movements of a man in full war harness.

He slipped the guige of the shield over his head, and stood a moment as though getting the feel of the harness, with Joyeuse snuffing in bewilderment at his feet and legs. 'It's a good thing grandfather and I were much of a size.' He looked about him. 'Is that everything?'

'Everything save the helmet. You're a credit to your squire.' Randal cast a quick look at the window, where the spring dusk hung blue and opaque beyond the torchlight. 'Time we were away. It is almost dark.'

Bevis glanced once more about the room, as though wondering what strange things would have happened inside himself before he came back to it in the morning with his vigil behind him. Then he whistled to Joyeuse, and turned to the head of the short stair.

Randal lingered just long enough to take the torch down and quench it on the hearth, then he followed.

In the Great Hall the men round the hearth heard the

weighted footsteps on the stair, and looked up, and as Bevis came into sight and checked in the stair-foot doorway, Randal, following close behind, saw their eyes widen in the firelight.

'Splendour of God!' le Savage growled. 'It is d'Aguillon.'

Reynfrey chuckled exultantly. 'Aye, 'tis d'Aguillon. Did you never see before that the boy was somewhat like his grandsire?'

'It is uncanny!' le Savage said. 'He even frets with his sword belt as Everard used to do. I mind him doing it while we waited by the horses on the morning of Senlac Fight.' He tramped to meet Bevis, and clapped him on the mailed shoulder. 'Well, boy, are you ready?'

'Quite ready, Sir Robert.' Bevis looked about him at the familiar faces. 'Where is Adam?'

'Gone to light the candles,' Reynfrey said.

Ancret came through the rest, like a dark shadow cast by the firelight, and set her hands on his shoulders. 'Ah, you have grown into such a tall man that I cannot reach you. Stoop down, little nursling,' and kissed him as his mother might have done.

They were all at the foreporch door now, spilling out into the deepening dusk, Bevis in front with le Savage, Randal following close behind, and the rest coming after him. Candle-light shone dimly gold from the high window of the church as they made their way across the garth; but it was not full dark yet, and Randal could see the familiar outline of the downs high above them, and the pale blur of blossom on the branches of the old pear tree that arched against the humpbacked darkness of the thatch.

Adam was waiting for them in the lime-washed church, still fiddling with the wicks of the two altar candles, and the scent of the bees' summer gathering stole out from the warm, golden wax. He came down to them by the door; a thin old man in a rusty brown habit, suddenly near to tears.

'Ah, Bevis, Bevis, my old heart is very full. It is a brave day for Dean that d'Aguillon comes home to keep his vigil in our own little church and be made knight among his own people.'

'For d'Aguillon also,' Bevis said, very quietly.

They stood in a little huddle in the doorway, watching him as

668

he walked forward alone. He was standing at the east end now, dark and narrow against the candles. He drew the great sword from its sheath, and laid it on the Lord's Table, and knelt down, his head bent over his joined hands. The candlelight made a rim of brightness round his dark head; above him in the shadowy saffron of the gable wall the small east window was deeply and luminously blue, and behind him his shadow lay pooled across the long flagstone that marked Sir Everard's grave.

When Randal turned away, he found that the others had gone already. He followed them on feet that dragged a little, like the feet of someone very weary, or very sad; and there was a feeling on him of having just parted from something, a feeling that nothing would ever be quite the same again.

Back in the Hall, they gathered round the fire against the chill of the spring night, and flung on more logs so that the sparks flew upward. Randal, sitting with Joyeuse hunched disconsolately against his knee, heard the others talking, but not what they said; saw their faces in the firelight with a piercing clearness: old, brown Adam growing to look more and more like an autumn leaf these days; Reynfrey who looked, as always, to have been made of harness leather; le Savage with his big red face and bald yellow head—he was the only person Randal had ever seen who had face and head of two completely different colours, and the peculiarity had always fascinated him. But all the while he wasn't thinking of what he was seeing, at all; he was thinking of the little church just outside the garth, and Bevis kneeling with his drawn sword before him at the altar where the tall candles smelled of Ancret's bees.

When the time came, Randal helped as usual to make the Hall ready for sleeping. He brought rugs and straw-filled pillows and made le Savage's bed on one of the broad benches in the warmest and most secluded corner, serving him as Hugo his own squire might have done if he had not been left at Broadwater. But he did not lie down himself in his old place among the hounds by the hearth. Instead, he slipped out through the door at the stair foot, and made his way down to the foreporch end of the Hall, from which he could see the light shining—

more brightly now in the full darkness—from that small, high window under the pear branches.

He could not sleep tonight, warm among his fellow men, while Bevis . . .

A cold muzzle was thrust into the palm of his hand, and as he looked down, a furry shadow pressed itself against his leg, whimpering. Joyeuse too. He stooped and patted her.

'Come too, then, Joyeuse; faithful old Joyeuse—come, girl.'

He crossed the garth, the hound padding beside him, and slipping out through the gate gap, turned aside into the narrow green, tangled alleyway between the church and the hawthorn hedge. It was very quiet as he knelt down—something rustled among the grass and brambles, and then was still again; so quiet that he could make out the faint voice of the winter bourn, that he had always thought you could only hear from the Hall when it was in spate. He wondered if Bevis was hearing it too, inside the church. Joyeuse settled herself against him with a sigh, her great rough head under his hand, and their own quietness became part of the quietness of the night. Bevis need never know that his squire and his hound had kept his vigil with him.

At first light, when the green plover were crying over the downs, Randal got to his feet, cramped, cold and weary; and with Joyeuse still at heel, crept back to the Great Hall. The rest of the household were beginning to stir and must have noticed his absence, but they asked no questions. And now it was almost time to go and fetch Bevis from his vigil.

Randal and le Savage went together, the squire walking a little behind the knight.

The candles had guttered down to their prickets, and Bevis was kneeling exactly as they had last seen him. He did not move when they entered the church, indeed Randal did not think he even heard them. When le Savage stooped and touched his shoulder, he started, and looked up, blinking; then got slowly to his feet and stared about him, as though for the moment he was too dazed to be sure where he was. Then he saw Randal, and smiled ruefully and stooped and rubbed his knees.

They brought him up to the solar, with the first sunlight of a fine spring morning splashing through the tiny eastward-facing window, and stripped him naked, naked as the day he was born; they laid him on the sleeping bench, and piled the sheep-skin rugs over him, carrying out the long, complicated ritual that went to the making of a knight; and all with scarcely a word between them, for it seemed one of those times when there is no use for words. A knight in the making was supposed to sleep before the next stage. Randal wondered if anyone ever managed it, unless from sheer exhaustion. Bevis lay still with his eyes closed, his breath just stirring the curly hairs of the fleece drawn to his chin. But Randal knew that he was only making the pretence of sleeping that custom demanded. Well, he would rest for a while, anyhow, after those long, cramped hours. Le Savage went down to the Great Hall where the morning meal of bread and perry would soon be on the tables; but Randal had no more wish for food than he had had last night. He set Bevis's clothes and harness all in order to be put on again, then went and sat in the sunshine across the threshold of the open doorway, his back against the doorpost, his arms round his updrawn knees.

He heard a blackbird singing in the pear tree, and the deep, full-throated murmur of bees already busy in the fruit blossom, and little by little his head went down until his forehead was resting on his knees.

The next thing he knew was le Savage shaking his shoulder in kindly exasperation, and trumpeting into his ear. 'Splendour of God! Is this the time to be sleeping and snoozing? How if de Braose comes, and our young knight not ready for him?'

Randal glanced at the sun and shook his head. 'He'll not be here yet. But it is time we started, all the same.' He got up and crossed to the bed. Bevis's eyes were open, looking up at him with a little smile. He flung off the heavy sheepskin and stretched his arms wide above his head in the way that he used to do on fine summer mornings when the two of them had slept out on the downs. His arms above the elbows were very white; all his body where the clothes covered it from sun and wind was white as the flesh of a just-ripe hazelnut. He brought his hands down on Randal's shoulders, laughing, and sprang up.

671

It took a good deal longer to arm him this time than it had done before, because of le Savage's determined efforts to play his part, blundering about them like a good-natured bumble bee, mingling advice on the aims and behaviour proper to a knight, with hearty tugs on the wrong straps and laces at the wrong moment. They bore with him patiently, as though he were a well-meaning, very small child, but it was not easy. Presently Randal looked up from the sword belt. 'Look, I've only slipped it through the buckle and under the loop, and not put the tang through. One pull, and it's off.'

Le Savage snorted in approval. 'Aye, aye, can't spend half the day wrestling to get your sword belt off while the priest waits with his hands out, as I had to, I remember.'

While Bevis was being armed, they had heard the continual tramping of footsteps and the growing splurge of broad Sussex voices from below.

'The whole Manor must be packed into the Hall by the sound of it,' Randal said, standing up from his task. 'And 'tisn't only for free drink. I wonder if any of the old men among them are remembering that Sir Everard was an enemy overlord when they were young.'

Bevis looked at him as though it was a new idea. 'I expect so,' he said slowly, after a moment. 'But maybe it's only with their minds, not with their hearts. I hope it's like that.' He had begun to pace to and fro with that firm, slightly cumbered tread. He could not go down until de Braose came. He went and stared out of the window, leaning his mailed elbows on the sill. 'If blossom is anything to go by, we should have a good crop of pears this year, and enough perry to make the whole Manor drunk at Christmas. I wish de Braose would come; my belly is full of foam.'

De Braose came at last, with a nearing tramp of hooves that swung into the garth and clattered to a halt before the door. They heard the trampling and snorting of horses, the ring of a sword chape on stone. Reynfrey's voice sounded in greeting, and then de Braose's level, rather harsh tones and the jingling tramp of mailed feet. In the solar the old knight and the young, unmade knight and the squire looked at each other. Time to go down.

The Hall was as full of Manor folk as it was at Christmas, when they entered it a few moments later, the ten men of the levy standing together in a knot as though they felt themselves already a little apart from the rest. Even Lewin Longshanks stood just within the doorway, leaning on his crook, huge and quiet as always, and seeming to dwarf the whole place. The Lord of Bramber stood on the slightly raised dais, three other grey-mailed Bramber knights with him, and Adam beside them in the old brown habit that even *looked* as though it smelled of mice.

There was a stir as they crossed the threshold and every face from de Braose's to the boy who scared the crows turned towards them. Le Savage gave Bevis a small friendly push, and he walked forward alone as he had walked last night towards the Lord's Table and the glimmering candles. It came to Randal, watching, that the business of being made a knight was one of the lonely things of life, like being born, or dying.

Bevis mounted the low steps of the dais; Randal saw him give a quick tug to his sword belt, and drew a breath of relief as it fell open in his hand. Bevis laid d'Aguillon's great sword in little brown Adam's hands, and knelt down to take his vows. Adam fumbled with the sword, blessing it, then set his free hand on Bevis's bowed, dark head and bent over him a little. Bevis took his vows very quietly, so quietly that Randal could scarcely catch the words; it seemed as though he were making them to something deep within himself, and there was no need for anyone else to hear.

His vows taken, he rose, and knelt again, this time to de Braose, and set his joined hands between those of the Lord of Bramber. And this time the whole Hall heard him clearly enough, as he took the vassal's oath to his feudal Lord.

'Here, my Lord, I become liege man of yours for life and limb and earthly regard, and I will keep faith and loyalty to you for life and death; God helping me.'

He remained a moment kneeling at his Lord's feet, then rose and turned to take his sword again from Adam. Le Savage stepped forward to belt it on him, and Randal, standing in the doorway, suffered a stab of jealousy. The old fool was fumbling and bumbling with the buckle. He felt Bevis's exasperation as though it were his own and it was all he could do not to start forward and take the strap from the man's fat fingers. But the thing must be done by a knight, and not a mere squire. It was done at last, and Bevis turned to kneel once again, with bowed head, before the Lord of Bramber; and while the whole Hall held its breath, de Braose leaned forward and gave him a blow with his mailed hand, between neck and shoulder.

'Rise, Sir Bevis d'Aguillon.'

Bevis blundered to his feet a little blindly.

There was a long silence, while it seemed to Randal that the almost painful solemnity drained out of the air; and they heard, as he realized they must have been hearing it all along, the horses being walked up and down outside.

Bevis was looking round him as though in search of something or somebody. His eyes lit on Randal by the door, and clearly he had found what he was looking for, and for the moment nobody else in the Great Hall, including de Braose, mattered in the least to either of them.

The Manor folk, his own folk, were thronging round d'Aguillon now, even up on to the dais with de Braose still standing there fiddling with his riding gloves. And as Randal with a sudden joyful sense of having found again something that he thought was lost thrust his way through at last to Bevis's side, the Lord of Bramber brought his hand down once more on the shoulder of his newest knight, laughing. 'Now what about the stirrup cup that you promised me two years since, Sir Bevis? One cup of wine to drink damnation to Robert of Normandy, and I must be away. The ships are ready and we sail on the fourth morning from now if the wind holds. Get your fellows down to Shoreham by the morn's morning.'

15

THE WEALDEN BLACKBIRD

IT was strange, but in after years that summer of his first campaign which should have been vivid in his mind with the sharp-edged vividness that belongs to all First Times, never stood out much in Randal's memory. It was as though all the time something within him knew that next summer, not this, was to be the one that mattered.

The day after Bevis was made knight, they marched out with their ten archers down the marshy river valley through the downs to Shoreham, where the horse transports were waiting. They embarked with the rest of de Braose's following, and sailed on an oyster-pale morning tide. They joined a great and ever-growing fleet at sea, and glimpsed among them a vessel flying a pennant like a licking gold flame, which someone said was the King's. Most of them, Randal included, and all the horses, were miserably seasick. And then there was Normandy, dusty already in a dry spring. Henry landed at Barfleur in the Cotentin; his old Lordship called in his vassals and the allies—Flanders, Main, Anjou and Brittany—that he had been making for a year and more past, and marched on Bayeux. So Bevis and Randal went into their first battle together, after all. And through that early summer, with the last apple blossom falling and the fruit setting in the Normandy orchards, at Bayeux and Caen and on the rough march to Falaise, Randal gained the experience of a shield-squire, riding into action behind his knight; always a line of squires behind the knights, each to second his own lord in every way, help him if he were thrown, carry his spare lance, receive his prisoners, and in between whiles, maybe strike a blow or two on his own account. Randal came to know the sights and sounds and smells of battle, the dust kicked up by the horses, the rank smell of sweat and the sharp smell of blood, the flying thunder of hooves and the tempest-roar of shouting and the weapon-ring; the vicious sound that an arrow makes, passing within a hand's span of your ear.

When the English army returned home soon after harvest, he had seen his full share of fighting, and had the fading scar of a sword-cut on his forearm to compare with Reynfrey's; but still, none of it seemed very important. They came home with nine of the ten men they had marched out with, leaving Alfwine the ploughman dead before Caen, and the wailing of Alfwine's widow remained ever after the thing that Randal remembered most sharply about that summer's campaigning.

The whole campaign had left nothing settled either way. And next summer it would be all to do again. Henry would not leave matters as they stood; he could not. It must be a fight to the finish between Brother Henry and Brother Robert, now. And according to whichever of them went down, so would Normandy be master of England, or England master of Normandy.

The Manor grumbled when the preparations for war began again, as every Manor in the Kingdom was grumbling, and always had grumbled at such times. 'Ten men short, we were, last harvest and seemingly we'll be getting this one in ten short again—na, eleven, counting Alfwine . . . If our Norman overlords want fighting, let 'em have it to themselves, wi'out troubling the poor folk . . .'

Bevis, hearing two of them in this strain, told them with a flash of angry impatience, 'If you had not all talked like that when your Harold, that you sing so much about, called you to arms forty years ago, maybe you'd not have had us Normans with our wars to trouble you now!'

The villeins withdrew into silence. More than anything else, they were shaken by Bevis having spoken of 'us Normans' when it had been 'us English' with him all his life, as with their old Lord, and on one Manor at least, the grumbling ended.

The swallows were late that year, but they came at last to nest again in the great barn. The May Fire blazed on the crest of the Bramble Hill, and in the midst of making ready for war, it was time for sheep shearing. And then there came a day in early June that was the last day before they marched again to join the King's army. Bevis and Randal were both of them far more sharply aware of tomorrow's march than they had been the year before, maybe because then there had been Bevis's knighthood to think about as well. But they did not speak of it much to each other until darkness came, and they went out together as they always did, escorted by Joyeuse who had long since made it clear to the other hounds that it was her place and her's alone to go with her Lord on his evening round, for a last look at the horses before they slept. It had been raining off and on all day, a soft growing-rain that whispered through the river woods and dripped from the Hall thatch, but it had passed now, and the deep, still darkness was breathing with the scents of wet, refreshed earth; and as they came out from the stables, Bevis checked a moment, sniffing, his head up like a hound's, and said, as he had done so often when they were boys, 'Come away, Randal; there'll be a moon later, and we can't waste tonight snoring in the rushes.'

They did not. Part of that night they spent with Lewin Longshanks up at the summer sheep fold. Later, moving on again, they made a wide cast over the downs that brought them at last valleyward again by the bluff, out-thrust shoulder of the Bramble Hill. The smell of the summer dawn was already in the air, but the moon that had risen now swung high over the downs in a glimmering harebell sky, and the world was bathed in a light that seemed tangible as silver water, so that Randal felt suddenly that if he held out his cupped hands he would feel it trickling between his fingers. Joyeuse, loping ahead of the two young men, and looking round from time to time to see that they were following, was silver too, with no hint of her daytime gold; a silver hound running through a silver night, like some great feather-heeled hunting dog of the Fairy People.

As they came down to the Bramble Hill, the valley began to open to them, and they checked, looking out and down over marsh and woodland and strip-patterned field, to where the Hall trailed its straggle of village down the side coomb, all lying asleep in the remoteness of the moonlight. No, not all asleep, for as they looked, from somewhere at the foot of the village, a flicker of warm yellow light blinked out, telling of a kindled lantern.

'Someone is early astir,' Bevis said.

'Looks like Gudram's cottage; he'll be making ready to do you credit on the march—never one for a last moment flurry, our Gudram.'

'They're good lads to lead, even if they do grumble,' Bevis said, his pride in them lit with laughter.

'We English always grumble,' Randal said, still looking down through the elder scrub towards the tiny blink of gorse-yellow light. 'We always have grumbled and we always will.'

They moved on again, the old companionable silence falling between them once more. But after a while Bevis said, as though he had been following a train of thought, 'We English ... Randal, do you remember grandfather saying that one day there would be no more Norman or Saxon, but only English? If this summer brings us victory in Normandy—one great victory gained by Norman and Saxon English fighting side by side—I think it will do more than all else could do to hammer us into one folk.' Another long silence, and then, thoughtfully. 'That would be an odd kind of revenge for Senlac!'

The scar of the May Day Fire still showed black on the turf, and at their right hand the great barrow rose, still under the rustling of the night wind through its elder bushes, with the strange potent quality of stillness that it always had—as though it shared in the stillness of the name-forgotten king who slept in the dark heart of it with his wrought gold and his weapons about him.

As Bevis and Randal, touched by its stillness as though it were a great wing that brushed over them, walked slower, and stopped, out of the darkness of the river woods below them rose one clear, perfect note of birdsong, long drawn and insistent, repeated again and again, then breaking into a shining spray of notes, a cascade of runs and phrases that seemed to shimmer on the ear. It was a song that the two young men standing up there among the bramble domes had heard often enough before; but surely it had never sounded quite like this, so that it was one with the white flood of moonlight and the smell of the elder flowers.

'Oh, listen!' Randal whispered, stupidly, for the whole night was already holding its breath to listen. 'Listen, Bevis, it's the nightingale.'

Bevis stood as though he were rooted, like the brambles and the elder scrub, into the hill beneath his feet. His head was up, his gaze not turned down to the dark woods below from which came the song but going out up the curving length of the dearly familiar valley to the long, low huddle of the Hall that he had been born in, under the steep stride of Long Down, and the Manor Mill by the ford. His thin face was remote and far off, as Randal glanced aside at him, as though he were hearing something else, something that was beyond the singing. In a little, he shook his head. 'It's a song spun from the moonlight. But if it were me up here in the hollow hill, and I were to wake tonight, it would not be the nightingale but the speckle-breasted thrush or our Wealden blackbird I'd be listening for, to tell me I was home again.'

Joyeuse, who had been rooting under an elder bush, came padding back to lay a rolled-up hedgehog at his feet. She was the only dog Randal had ever known who would carry a hedgehog without tearing her soft mouth to shreds. And Bevis stooped to fondle her head as she thrust against him. 'Nay, now, leave poor Tiggy be; what harm has he ever done you? But thanks for the parting gift, all the same.' He straightened up with a little shake of his shoulders and looked about him. 'It's been a good night, this one; the kind of night that is good to remember. But we must be getting back now, or we'll be all unready when the time comes for the march.'

The first blue mist of the September evening was beginning to rise, though the swallows still swooped and darted in the last of the sunlight about the battlements of Tenchebrai and over the heads of the two opposing armies encamped below. Randal, on his way back from seeing to Durandal, who like most of the spare horses was picketed at an outlying village, paused where the woods fell back a little, to glance out over the wide valley of the Orne. He could see the great castle still flushed fiercely tawny by the westering sunlight, though the huddled roofs of the little town at its foot were already dimming into blue and violet shadows, and the faint blue twilight and the autumn mists were creeping out from the oakwoods to mingle with the smoke of countless cooking fires that made a drifting haze of their own all across the great camp. Knowing where to look for them among all the other tents, the awnings and flying banners, the crowded fires and horse-lines, he could just make out the big, checkered tents of the Counts of Maine and Brittany, each pitched among their own men, and closer at hand, on a knoll of rising ground in the midst of the English camp, that had been an orchard before they cut most of the trees down to make room for it, the great weather-worn, crimson pavilion of Henry himself.

It was more than a fortnight since the English army with its Cenommanian and Breton allies had come out of the oakwoods by the wild road north from Domfront, and settled down to besiege this great Castle of William de Mortain—de Mortain, Lord of Pevensey in his day, until, like de Bellême, he had forfeited his English lands for rebellion against the King, and, also like de Bellême, had made common cause with Duke Robert in revenge. More than a fortnight—the smell must be getting somewhat thick in Tenchebrai by now, Randal reckoned. Well, one way or the other, it looked as though the siege could not last much longer, not now that Duke Robert had brought up his own forces to relieve his henchman's stronghold. Couldn't see the Norman camp from here, it was hidden by the oakwoods, but awareness of it seemed to quiver like thunder in the air over the whole valley; and every soul in the English camp knew that somewhere—not in the great crimson pavilion, but out between their two armies, maybe in the lea of a beanstack or under a poplar tree by the track side—Brother Robert and Brother Henry were met this evening as they had met between their armies before, to talk of terms.

Would anything come of it this time? Randal wondered. Fiercely he hoped not, as most of the camp were hoping not. Nothing save fighting could settle the thing in the long run, but one great battle now might do it, the one great victory that Bevis had spoken of, that would bind Norman and Saxon together in the common bond of Englishry. Was that what was coming tomorrow?

The chatter of a magpie from the woods behind him called him back from tomorrow, and he remembered that it was no part of a squire's duties to be standing thinking his own thoughts on the fringe of the war-camp. He strode on again, whistling tunelessly as he went, casting wide through the edge of the woods so as to come down from above on the derelict tanning shed where Bevis and a handful of other young knights had taken up their quarters; it was quicker so, than trying to make one's way through the teeming thickness of the camp.

But without knowing it, he must have made a cast wider than usual, and so he came on a place in the woods that he had not found before, a small clearing among the denseness of the moss-floored oakwoods, and in it a hovel of wattle and daub under a ragged thatch that gave somehow the effect of a filthy old straw hat pulled over its eyes, squatting amid seven gnarled and ancient apple trees, two bee skeps and a tethered goat. On one of the trees, and only one, the apples were already ripe; small, greyish apples with a scent of fennel about them that reached his quick nose even as he checked and stood looking up into the lichened branches. It was one of the tasks of a squire to forage for his lord, but in any case the idea of apples, the crisp juiciness of apples, at the end of that dusty day—Normandy seemed to him dustier than England—would have pulled Randal up in his tracks. While he stood there, a woman came out through the smoky darkness that hung like a curtain at the doorway of the hovel, with a wooden milking pail in her hand.

She was a very old woman, scrawny and twisted as one of her own ancient apple trees, with her head tied up in a folded cloth and little bright black eyes in a face all fallen together and made up of earth-coloured wrinkles. She checked at sight of Randal, and fixed him with a bright, beady stare, blowing her crumpled and toothless mouth in and out, but she did not seem surprised at his appearance; probably he was not the first of his kind to pass that way, and he rather wondered that she had managed so long to keep the goat.

683

'Well then, Englishman or Breton or whatever you be, and what is it that you're wanting?'

'Apples,' Randal said. 'A handful of apples for my knight.'

She let out a squawk of laughter and set down the pail. 'Sa, sa, it is only a boy after all! How old is your knight?'

'Two years older than I am,' Randal told her with dignity.

She flung up her hands. 'Does Henry of Coutances fight his wars with children, then?'

Randal would have protested hotly at this, but he had a feeling that to leave well alone, though bad for the dignity, was the way to get the apples he wanted. So he grinned cheerfully at the little old woman, standing with his feet planted wide apart, and towering over her, with his helmet, which he had unbuckled and pulled off, swinging in his hand.

'Maybe—but give me the apples, old mother.'

She looked up at him slantwise like a bird. 'Aye then, take as many as you can carry in that iron cap of yours, and give me a kiss for them. 'Tis a long and a weary long while since a fine young man kissed me.'

It seemed fair enough. Randal stooped, and put his free arm round her for good measure, the helmet still in his other hand. She smelled sour, but it was not the kind of sourness that a hound would have objected to, and nor did Randal. He kissed her, laughingly and kindly and clumsily, and stood back, grinning still.

The old woman cackled like a hen. 'None so bad, my bold young squire! None so bad for the first time.'

Meeting the snapping, cackling amusement in her little black eyes, Randal felt himself flushing. 'How do you know it was the first time?'

'Easily enough!—Any woman could tell you as much,' she said scornfully. Then, voice and manner abruptly changing, 'Aye, but there's another thing I'll tell you that's none so easy, about yourself,' and before he knew what she was about, she had put up her old, clawed hands and taken his face between them, and drawn it down to look into his eyes. 'When to-morrow's sun goes down, you'll be no man's squire, but your own knight.'

Randal felt a little prickling chill in the back of his neck; but he laughed, and shook his head between her hands. 'I shall never be my own knight. I'm the kind that stays a squire always. It costs money and acres to be a knight, and I have not anything of my own, save my sword and helmet.'

'None the less,' said the old woman very softly, 'knight you will be, before another sun goes down, and as to the acres——' Her voice trailed away; her hands were still on either side of his face, and he felt that he could not break from their hold on him, or maybe from the hold of her eyes. They were small, hard, bright eyes, their darkness very different from the shadowy darkness of Ancret's eyes, and he saw the reflection of himself in them, and the leafy reflection of the apple branches behind his head. Yet suddenly he had again the feeling he had had once when Ancret held him so, of sinking down into their darkness as into dark water, only this time it was a darkness of rustling leaves. In another moment they would part and let him through and close again behind him, and he would see—he would know—something that he could not bear to know. Already he could see it dimly, moving to meet him through the leaves . . . And then a bird flashed across from branch to branch of the apple tree above him, so close that the beat of its wings was in his ears; the sudden movement broke the spell, or else, as Ancret had done, at the last instant she let him go. 'Ah, but leave that for now—leave that until the hour brings it,' and she dropped her hands and stooped for the milking pail.

Randal stepped back, oddly shaken, and not sure why. For the memory of the uncanny moment was passing almost as soon as the moment itself.

'If you can foretell the future, tell me if we shall join battle tomorrow,' he said, jeeringly.

'Oh, aye, there'll be fighting tomorrow,' she told him, almost without interest. And something in her tone made him think again of Ancret, and Ancret's people, watching the later folk come and go, conqueror following conqueror, like a little wind through the bramble bushes. But if tomorrow did not matter to her, it mattered to him . . .

'Shall we win? Old mother, shall we win?' The question stuck in his throat.

She shot her lips in and out at him. 'Maybe you will, and maybe you will not. Have I not told you enough? Whoever has victory, I must milk the goat.' The last words were tossed to him over his shoulder as she hobbled towards the tethered animal. 'Away with you now. Fill your helmet and go.'

Randal stood for a moment looking after her, frowning a little as he tried to remember—something that he felt he had only just forgotten. Then he turned his attention to the apple tree, and picked his helmet full of little grey, fennel-scented apples. He hesitated when he had done, looking again towards the old woman, but as she still kept her back to him and had seemingly no more thought for him nor for anything save her milking, he finally shrugged, called out to her, 'God keep you, old mother. Thank you for the apples,' and set off once more on his interrupted way back to the tan shed.

He walked with the apple-filled helmet in the hollow of his arm, not whistling any more; thinking. Had she spoken truth? Was he really to win his knighthood tomorrow? Oh, but how could he ever be a knight? He shook his shoulders and determined to think no more about it, and of course went on thinking, dreaming a little, as one does dream of the shining and impossible things happening . . .

When he got back to the tan shed the day had faded almost to dusk, and the fire of brushwood and heathersnarls that burned in the wide, nettle-choked entrance had begun to cast a fluttering, tawny light over the faces of the men gathered about it and up into the lower branches of the giant old hornbeam that grew before the door. Martin, Gervase de Machault's squire, was roasting a rabbit over the fire on the point of his sword, and Gervase was there, and several of the young knights who had been squires with Randal and Bevis at Bramber. But of Bevis himself there was no sign at all.

'He's gone off to settle some trouble between his fellows and de Salynges',' Gervase told him, without much interest. Quarrels were common between the different Manors.

Randal hesitated, wondering whether he should go after him,

and if so what he should do with the apples, and in that moment a square and freckled youth said, 'Hé! I smell apples!' and reached out to grab. Others followed the action, and Randal stepped back, laughing but determined. 'Hands off, sirs! I forage for my own knight, not for you!'

'How many have you eaten yourself?' the freckled one demanded cheerfully. Wilfred was a Saxon. There were beginning to be a few Saxons and half Saxons among the young knights, these days; and, surrounded by Normans, he and Randal had always bickered together in friendly fashion when they were both squires. But it was not quite the same now that one of them was a knight.

'Does my helmet look half-empty?' Randal demanded, suddenly a little stiff.

One of the others sat forward, grinning in the firelight, his arms round his updrawn knees. 'Squire Virtue! Don't you like apples, then?'

And a third joined in the good-natured baiting. 'Splendour of God, you shock me, Roger! Do you suggest that Randal would pleasure himself on apples meant for Bevis's belly? Don't you know that Randal would give Bevis his head if Bevis had a use for it?—Randal, wouldn't you give Bevis your head if he asked you?'

Randal laughed, but felt himself flushing, and before he could answer the sally, Gervase struck in, saying as Randal had done a few moments before, 'Hands off, sirs!' Then with a grin towards his own squire, carefully turning the rabbit on his sword point, 'I'd like to think Martin would do as much for me.'

It was full dusk by now, and growing misty. Below them the cooking fires of the main camp were a little blurred, and shadows of bowmen and men-at-arms came and went between them and the brightness. A shadow loomed up through the twilight, and took substance, and Bevis emerged into the firelight that jinked on his ringed hauberk and the nasal of his nut-shaped helmet. The others greeted him with a cheerful clamour.

'Ohé Bevis! You've been a long time! Have your fellows slit the de Salynges throats to a man?'

687

'Not quite,' Bevis said, folding up beside the fire, and tipping his head for Randal to unlace his helmet, 'though there were knives out when I got there.'

'Were there so?' Gervase said. 'And what did you do about that?'

'Called them every name I could lay my tongue to in Saxon *or* Norman, and banged a couple of their silly heads together. All's well now . . . That rabbit smells good.'

'Never mind that rabbit,' Wilfred sniffed. "Twill do no more among this lot of us than to flavour the black bread. Here's Randal come by a whole helmet full of apples and will not let us so much as smell one until you have eaten your lordly fill.'

But the one they called Roger, sobering all at once, said, 'Never mind the rabbit *or* the apples. Is there any news?'

'Yes.' Bevis ducked his head out from under the helmet as Randal lifted it off, and pulled back the mail coif from his flattened dark hair. 'Henry's back in camp. No terms.'

'So——'

'So we fight tomorrow.' He cocked up his head as he spoke, his eyes full of little dancing lights from the fire. 'Listen—you can hear it running through the camp, now.'

They listened, all of them sober for the moment. Randal, leaning back on his knees to lay Bevis's helmet beside his shield against the fire-dappled bole of the hornbeam, heard the voice of the little stream that had once fed the tan pits, and beyond it the evening voice of the great camp that seemed, even as he listened, to rise and quicken and take on a new urgency. So the old woman had been right in that at least . . . Oh, but it was an easy guess, anybody's guess. When he had asked her who would have the victory, which was a harder thing, she had turned sour and gone to milk the goat. And as for the other things she had said—there was a sudden flutter of wings among the branches of the hornbeam, as of a bird disturbed in its roosting by the firelight and the voices, and he half remembered something—something that had to do with the old woman . . . then lost it again as Gervase said quietly, 'It's Michaelmas Eve tomorrow. I'd forgotten; but one of our old men-at-arms was saying that it was forty years ago on Michael-mas Eve that the Conqueror landed at Pevensey.'

'Forty years to turn the tables,' someone else said, and all round the fire the young men looked at each other.

Then Bevis stretched his arms above his head, his thin face splintering into laughter. 'That's for tomorrow. Meanwhile—apples! Where are those apples of yours, Randal?'

The moment passed, and a little puff of laughter caught from Bevis blew in behind it, for it seemed to them good to take life none too seriously on the eve of battle. And in a little they were all munching the small, grey, fennel-scented apples from Randal's helmet that stood propped beside the fire, while they waited for the rabbit to finish scorching.

16

MICHAELMAS EVE

It seemed odd to be waiting on foot to meet the shock of the Norman charge. Always, until now, the time of waiting for battle had meant to Randal the smell of horses, the uptossed mane and ceaseless, restless trampling; Swallow fidgeting under him, the nervously flicking tail of Bevis's war-horse just ahead. But the Saxon in him found it familiar, all the same. 'This is the way my mother's folk waited for war. This is the way we waited at Hastings, forty years ago.' And he was glad of it because it meant going into battle with one's own men, instead of being cut off from them in another part of the battle line, as had to happen if one's own men were foot soldiers. He was as proudly and harshly aware of the Dean men somewhere among the archers of the ranks behind him, as he was of Bevis standing spear in hand just in front.

Henry had dismounted his whole vanguard, indeed most of his army save for the Breton and Cenommanian cavalry on the left, and formed them into a solid phalanx to confront the Norman cavalry. It was only partly the old Saxon battle formation, for the men who had waited dismounted with Harold at Hastings had formed a single line of wedges; and this solid phalanx, built up of three such lines close behind each other, was of the Byzantine school. The combination was a new thing that had not confronted Duke Robert's cavalry before, and whether it was a good thing or a bad only that day's fighting would show.

Away ahead of him through the spears, through the blue and green, russet and crimson of lesser banners, Randal caught the golden gleam of the King's banner, lifting and spreading sideways on the dry, gusty wind, and only a little behind it the blue and gold of the lion battle badge that de Braose had taken after his father. It was a day of changing lights and eddying, dust-laden wind, this Michaelmas Eve; a day of pale, dry colours, the weather-worn stones of the great Castle itself that frowned

out over the two armies, the sombre, gold-flecked darkness of
the oakwoods, the fading tangle of wild marjoram along the
river banks, and the stubble of the spent corn-land, all a little
paler than usual. And even among the two great armies, no
depth of colour nor spark of light on hauberk ring or shield
boss; only the constant dry, dusty movement of banners and
pennoncels in that little fretting wind, and the darting to and
fro of swallows overhead.

Duke Robert, Randal knew, was in command of the Norman
centre, William de Mortain of the vanguard and de Bellême of
the rear. De Bellême . . . Looking out over the empty strip of
corn and beanfields between, to the dun-dark masses of the
Norman cavalry with the farther woods behind them, he remembered with sudden, startling vividness the white face under
the flame of red hair that was just a little darker than Hugh
Goch's, the voice with its hint of mockery that was just a little
darker, too. And where de Bellême was, there would de
Bellême's minstrel be also. Odd to think of Herluin somewhere
among those waiting enemy ranks—or maybe, since he was a
singer of songs and no fighting man, with the camp servants and
the baggage train. But Taillefer, the Conqueror's minstrel, had
ridden with him at Hastings—had led the charge, singing one
of the songs of Roland, tossing up his sword and catching it
again as he rode. He could imagine Herluin doing that, Herluin with his casual, loose-limbed grace and drawling courage.
He could imagine how the sword would flash in the sunlight,
bright as the images of the Song of Roland . . .

But there was no sun, nothing bright and flashing save the
notes of a Norman trumpet blowing thin on the fitful wind, for
the end of the waiting time and the onset of battle.

Randal felt his heart tighten under his breast bone as the
trumpet echoed away into silence between the oakwoods, and
in its place came the sudden, swelling thunder of horses' hooves
rolling towards them. The English ranks braced themselves for
the shock, the dismounted knights and squires of the foremost
ranks settling each his spear butt under the hollow of his instep
as though to take the shock of a charging boar. Randal, crouching to his own spear with the rest, saw with painful acuteness

how the pattern of the hauberk rings across Bevis's slim, braced
shoulders slid with the tensing of the muscles underneath. Then
the whole Norman van led by de Mortain was upon them. The
English ranks shuddered as a dyke shudders under the blow of a
breaking sea, but stood firm, and a roar burst up from both
sides as defiance and counter-defiance and the blood-rousing
battle-shout was flung to and fro above their heads.

How long that phase of the battle lasted Randal never knew;
it was a thing without form and without time; a blind, slow
reeling back and forth of two great armies locked together like
two wild beasts that have found a hold but cannot shift it to a
death grip. It might have been a few heart-beats of time or a
whole day before he became dimly aware of a fresh outburst
of cries and shouting, a fresh sweep of drumming hooves away
to the right, and supposed that the Bretons and Cenommanians
were charging in on the flank. But he saw nothing of all that,
and after the one moment, thought nothing of it either. For him,
Tenchebrai Fight was the trampling struggle of the mere handful of men and horses nearest about him, and the sudden fierce
exultation as he realized that they were no longer reeling to and
fro over the same ground, but the English were moving forward, slowly but remorselessly forward, after the golden flame
that was the King's banner.

It was no longer the time for spears, but out swords and drive
home the slow, deadly charge that was gathering momentum
as a wave; drive forward, plough forward into the Norman foot,
following the King's banner, and the gold and azure of de
Braose's lion; and above them, no swallows now, but the dark
deadly flights of arrows lacing the pale September sky.

'Bramber!' They were shouting all about him.

'Bramber!' Randal roared at the full pitch of his lungs, his chin
driven down behind his shield, and his sword busy in his hand.

And then, seemingly out of nowhere, a flying squadron of
Norman cavalry crashed down upon them, and the world exploded into a tangled and swirling welter of pounding hooves
and slashing sword-iron and savage, up-flung horses' heads
with wild eyes and flaring, blood-filled nostrils. Randal saw a
horseman stoop from the saddle at Bevis, and as Bevis sprang to

693

meet him, he heard, even above the vicious uproar of battle, the crash and grind of blade on blade. And in the same instant another Norman swung his horse down on them and assailed the young knight on his unprotected side. As in some horrible dream, Randal, locked in desperate combat on his own account, saw the man lean from the saddle with upswung blade, and the crashing blow that tore away Bevis's shield and bit deep into his shoulder. He saw Bevis stagger and go down, beaten to his knees. And even as, breaking through the guard of his own enemy, he sprang forward to cover him, the second Norman spurred forward his snorting and wild-eyed steed, trampling the crumpled figure under the great, round hooves.

It was all over almost before it was begun, but for one jagged instant of time that had the intensity of a lightning flash, Randal saw the face of the second Norman. In the heat of battle, and part covered as they were by the mail coif and the helmet with its broad nasal, he might not have known the snarling features again, but there could be no mistaking the livid criss-cross scar on the left cheek, that his own dagger had set there.

He gathered himself like an animal to the kill, flung back his hampering shield, and sprang.

De Coucy had just time to recognize his assailant, just time to see death coming at him in the white, blazing face of the young squire, and no more. Randal sprang sideways under his guard and flung himself across the horse's withers, making the great brute plunge and rear. He had hurled the man back half out of the saddle by the impact of his own body against him, his left arm was round him as de Coucy's sword arm flew wide, and for one instant they glared face to face, even as the Norman toppled sideways from the saddle with Randal still clinging to him: down and down among the plunging hooves of battle. They were broken apart by the fall, but Randal, falling uppermost, was on his knees almost before he hit the ground. He flashed up his own sword and brought it hissing down on de Coucy as he struggled to rise. The blade hacked through the rings of the Norman's hauberk, through flesh and bone, and he slumped back, his head all but smitten from his shoulders, while his great horse plunged away riderless into the mêlée.

Randal, struggling up through the trampling press, knew no hot joy of vengeance, the vengeance he had waited for so long, no thought for anything save Bevis. But the fight had closed over between him and the place where Bevis had fallen, and he was being picked up and borne along like a bit of flotsam on the slow, resistless flood of the English advance. There could be no beating back against that flood; nothing to do but go on. He went on. The smell of blood was in the back of his nose and a crimson mist of it swimming before his eyes, and only one thought in his bursting heart—if Bevis were dead, to avenge him on the whole Norman army. The red, uncaring, berserker fury of his forefathers woke in him and roared up like flame, and he forgot that he was anything but a high wind and an avenging sword. He thrust forward into Bevis's place, into the ranks of the knights storming at the tasselled heels of de Braose's golden lion, into the mass of the Norman infantry that had already begun to crumble and break apart.

English Henry's new formation had proved its worth. They said that de Bellême and the rear squadron had been swept clear off the field, that Duke Robert had been captured by Waldric, Henry's Chancellor, and de Mortain by the Bretons. They said that four hundred knights had been killed or captured besides countless men-at-arms and foot soldiers. But none of it had any meaning for Randal. The sun that had begun to make a brightness in the breaking sky was still high above the low wooded hills, for at the last it had not taken many hours of this Michaelmas Eve to reverse the work of that other Michaelmas Eve, forty years ago; and he was squatting beside Bevis, who had been carried back to the derelict tanning shed where they had made their headquarters last night.

The shed was crowded with wounded; but Bevis had demanded to remain outside, telling the men who carried him that he had liefer do his dying in the open air. So he lay under the great hornbeam, by the scar of last night's fire, with his head and shoulders propped on his high, crimson saddle. He was still in his hauberk; they had unhelmed him and twisted a mass of rags round his shoulder to staunch the bleeding, and that was all. Gervase, nursing a gashed arm of his own, knelt at his other side, and a little knot of Dean men had already gathered, and stood leaning on their bow-staves in silence close by; but Randal was not aware of them at all, only of Bevis.

'But you'll mend,' he was saying, desperately, stupidly, as though by repeating it he could force it to be true. 'You'll do well enough by and by. You'll be all right, Bevis——'

But he knew, all the time, that Bevis would not be all right.

'De Coucy's horse—trampled on me. I'm—about broken in half as well as—bled white. Shan't last till evening, old lad.'

Randal's fists were clenched and driven together in his sense of utter helplessness as he looked down into the grey, sweat-streaked face of his foster-brother.

Bevis turned his head slowly on the high, red saddle, to return the look, frowning with the effort that even that small movement cost him. 'Randal, I—something I want to tell you.'

Randal nodded, his gaze never leaving the other's face.

'You remember once when we—were lads, I asked you what —you would do if ever your chance of knighthood came, and— you said you'd refuse because you—couldn't furnish your helm?'

Randal nodded again, wordlessly. How odd that that had once seemed to matter.

'You'll be—able to furnish your helm—after all. I have spoken with de Braose—oh, long ago, and he—it is in my mind that he will give you Dean to hold in my stead.'

There was a long, long aching silence. They heard the distant sounds of the camp and the spent battlefield, the voice of the little stream, and the soft stirring of wind in the mazy branches of the hornbeam; but all from far off, beyond the borders of their own stillness. Then Randal said dully, 'But I am not a knight.'

'That is a thing that—can be amended.' There was a shadow of laughter in Bevis's face, an echo of it in the painful, breathless whisper that his voice had become. 'You're too—humble-minded, that's—your trouble. You've proved yourself—well enough, all these two summers in Normandy. And today— they've been telling me how you—fought today. Like three

696

men! Go you to de Braose and—ask for knighthood at his hands. He'll—give it to you.'

There was another silence, and then Randal said unsteadily, 'I had sooner ask for it at yours.'

'At mine? Nay now, that's—foolishness fit for a woman. Stand you in better stead in—after years—to have it from the Lord of Bramber.'

Randal shook his head, stubbornly, blindly. 'I'm not very interested in after years, not now. If I am—if you judge me worthy of knighthood, let you give it to me, Bevis. I—don't want it from anyone else.'

Bevis lay looking up at him, his face very still under the shifting shadows of the leaves. Then he said, 'Have it your own wilful way. Gervase, you'll be his sponsor? Raise me up . . .'

Gervase raised him against his shoulder. Randal came slowly to his knees, his head bent, lower, lower. He knew, through all his own body, the effort that it cost Bevis to raise his arm. He felt it fall in a light, fumbling blow between his neck and shoulder. So little ceremony needed, in the end, to make a knight; no ceremonial arming, no vigil—oh, but he had kept his vigil, a year and a half ago—nothing but Bevis's spent hand falling on his shoulder in the accolade. 'Sir Randal of Dean.'

So Randal, who had never thought to be a knight, had his knighthood after all; and would have given all the world to be only Bevis's squire again.

Bevis looked about him at the Dean men, as Gervase laid him down, seeming to notice them for the first time.

'Well, I've done my best for you both,' he said. 'Lord and villeins. Na na, don't all of you look—as though it was end of—the world that we didn't have—six years ago.' And a little later 'Will—somebody bring me some water?'

One of the men—it was Gudram of the apple tree—took up the nut-shaped helmet and turned away to the stream, and came trudging back with it half full of water. This time it was Randal who raised Bevis against his shoulder, and taking the helmet from Gudram's hand, held it to his foster-brother's dry, white lips. Bevis drank a little, but he could not keep it down. It came up again, beaded with dark grains of blood. Randal wiped the stain away, and did not lay him back but continued to hold him.

Gervase had withdrawn a little, and sat nursing his arm, with his back to the hornbeam bole. No one moved among the Dean men, and amid the swarming life of the English camp, and the tramp of men bringing in more wounded, it seemed that Randal and Bevis were alone with each other as they had so often been alone on the high downs at home with only the green plover calling.

'My sword——' Bevis said after a while, his lips scarcely moving. 'Grandfather's sword—yours now, Randal.'

Randal was still holding him when, an hour later, he opened his eyes once more and looked up into his face, with the quiet contented look of so many summer morning wakings.

'Randal,' he said again. Then his gaze drifted past the other's face, into the brightening sky beyond the rustling branches of the hornbeam. 'Look, the clouds are flying like banners above Long Down. We shall have wild weather tomorrow.' He stretched himself all out with a long sigh, and turned his head in the hollow of Randal's shoulder as though to sleep again.

A soft gust of wind swooped at them under the hornbeam branches, setting the shadows flurrying, and when it died into the grass, Randal laid Bevis's body down, with a stunned emptiness inside him as though something of himself had gone too. As he did so, the tramp of spurred feet checked behind him, and a shadow long in the westering light, fell across the grass. He looked up slowly, and saw de Braose standing beside him.

'They told me d'Aguillon was wounded,' he said. 'I came as soon as might be.'

'You're just too late,' Randal said. 'Just—too—late, de Braose.'

De Braose looked down at the body of his youngest knight. 'So I see,' he said in his harsh, clipped voice. The iron-grey gaze shifted deliberately to Randal. 'Come up to me in my tent, in an hour's time.' And with a brusque nod, there being no more that he could do here, and many things that he must do elsewhere, he turned on his spurred heel and tramped jingling away.

When he was gone, Randal turned his attention with a dull, conscious effort to the Dean men, where they stood looking to him now to make the decision and tell them what to do.

'Ulf, go you and find out where they are taking the slain. The rest of you go down to the cooking fires and get something in your bellies, you'll be needing it. Come back after; we shall have to carry him somewhere—wherever it is.' And as they trailed heavily away, and only Gervase was left, sitting against the grey bole of the hornbeam, he bent again over Bevis's body. There was something that he must do before he took the great sword, something that to him mattered even more. He slipped his hand into the breast of the loosened hauberk, and pulled out the little washleather bag which Bevis wore round his neck, and from the bag, bloodstained now, Bevis's nut of red amber. It lay dark in his hand, keeping its secret, until a gleam of the westering light striking through it woke a spark of the old fire even as he watched. He dragged up the little bag that hung round his own neck, opened it with fumbling fingers, and took out his own piece that was twin to the other: precious, half magic Gold of the Sea that Laef Thorkelson had brought from half the world away. As he did so, something else spilled out with it; a sprig of rosemary, dried and crushed, its flowers shrivelled to brown wisps that crumbled at a touch. He picked it up, and the aromatic ghost of a fragrance came up to him from between his fingers, bringing for an instant other ghosts with it; the narrow, waking garden at Bramber, a girl with red hair . . . With a sudden confused feeling that the thing was in some way precious, he dropped it with his own half of the red amber into the bag round Bevis's neck and slipped it back inside the loosened hauberk, over Bevis's quiet heart.

Bevis's half of the red amber he stowed in his own breast. Then he set to unbuckling the great sword with the d'Aguillon seal cut in the hilt.

17

KNIGHT'S FEE

It was sunset, and the clouds which Bevis had seen as flying like banners from Long Down, were banners indeed: vast, tattered, gold and purple, fire-fringed banners of victory streaming all across the sky, as Randal made his way through the camp towards de Braose's tent. The wind had begun to rise, and smoke from the cooking fires billowed all across the camp, and he heard snatches of talk around him that had the same ragged, shining, torn-off quality. An old knight, leaning on his sword, cocked an eye upward and said to another beside him. 'Splendour of God! Will you look at that sky! Just such a sky we had on the evening after Senlac fight, as though Harold's golden banners had been caught up in the sunset.' And an archer, squatting with his bow-stave across his knees beside one of the great cooking fires, spat contentedly into the flames, and announced to the world at large, 'Eh, lads, if ever Norman cries Senlac after us in the roadway, I reckon we just turn and cry 'Tenchebrai' in his teeth, from now on.'

Randal heard them as he strode by, but as though they came from a long way off, outside some black barrier that walled him in. He had left Bevis lying with the dead in the Abbey Church below the Castle, and the stunned emptiness that had been all he felt at first was beginning to wake into intolerable pain. He wanted to crawl away into the woods, away from all men, like an animal that has its death hurt. But de Braose had bidden him come in an hour, and the habit of obedience had been drilled into him.

De Braose's pavilion was pitched not far from the greater one of the King, which stood dark and empty now, for Henry supped in Tenchebrai tonight. The entrance flaps were looped back, and the flames of the dead apple branches burning on a field hearth just inside seemed in the shadows to echo the streaming banners of that fiery and victorious sky. The aromatic scent of the woodsmoke reached Randal before ever he came to the threshold, stealing out to swirl and eddy with the autumn wind through what were left of the apple trees. Squires were setting out the trestle table for de Braose's own supper, while two or three camp curs who had wandered in in the hope of bones and gristle later, were sniffing expectantly among the rushes. Several knights were gathered there already; among them Randal saw vaguely the round, red face and kindly, rueful eyes of le Savage of Broadwater. And de Braose himself, his helmet off and his coif hanging loose about his neck, stood by the fire, face to face with a tall man in black, sombre as a monk, save that no monk would wear garments of that outlandish sort—a slender, loose-limbed creature with pale, mocking eyes, and a lock of mouse-coloured hair hanging limply across a high, sallow forehead: nothing changed in twelve years, save that the bitter, laughing, twisted lines of his long, mobile face were bitten a little deeper than when Randal saw them last, and he carried no little gilded harp, but wore a sword belt and an empty sheath of fine, embossed leather, the sword that had evidently been in it standing propped against the bench behind de Braose.

And so, checking in the opening of the tent, after twelve years Randal saw Herluin the Minstrel again.

'We must see that you are well bestowed. Robert de Bellême's own minstrel should fetch a good ransom,' de Braose was saying bluntly.

Herluin shook his head a little. 'I doubt it, do you know. They tell me that de Bellême has come in to make his submission, and will of a surety be stripped even of his Norman possessions, now that Henry is Lord of Normandy. Not, I fear me, the moment to be indulging in luxuries such as the ransom of a mere minstrel.'

'A pity,' de Braose said, meaningly.

'Yes, is it not? It seems that you will have to trade me cheap —hy my! Almost for nothing!—or have me on your hands for life.'

'Not on *my* hands,' de Braose returned with a glimmer of a smile, stripping his great war-mittens between his fingers. 'I dare say Henry may well find it amusing to possess a minstrel captured from one of his brother's barons—especially since Rahere shows signs of exchanging his motley for a monk's habit and his harp for a rosary.'

'It was once said of me by de Bellême, my Lord,' Herluin said in a tone of gentle reverie, 'that so far as he knew there was no way of—persuading me to wake the harp against my will.'

'I wonder. Henry has ways of—persuasion . . .' de Braose's hard eyes flicked towards the tent opening, and he saw Randal standing there with the fires of the windy sunset behind him. But Randal was not looking at him, he was still gazing at Herluin; and in the same moment, as though feeling the intensity of the gaze upon him, the minstrel turned and saw the haggard young man in the opening.

'Herluin!' Randal said, as their eyes met.

Herluin looked in silence for a moment, and the wicked, winged lines of his eyebrows drifted upward. 'Well, Imp! Not maybe the happiest of ways to meet again.'

'Ah, of course.' De Braose's hard voice came between them. 'I had forgotten that you two were of old acquaintance.' He gestured with his war-mittens to Herluin to stand aside, and turned his full attention to Randal. 'Come here!'

Randal came, walking heavily like an old man, and stood before his overlord.

'You know why I sent for you?' How intently the man was looking at him, the hard, grey eyes raking into him as though seeking to uncover what lay behind his outward-seeming and form some judgement.

'Yes,' Randal said. 'Bevis told me—before he died,' and was aware of a sudden movement from Herluin, who never made sudden movements.

'I will give you Dean to hold for a year,' de Braose said abruptly. 'At the end of that time—we shall see. Meanwhile, the end of a campaign, when the shield squires have proved their mettle, is as good a time to be making new knights as the beginning of a campaign, when one makes them for the sake of fresh fighting blood. Kneel down.'

Randal remained standing. No longer like an old man, but

very young, very straight, very proud for all the haggard misery in his face.

'I have my knighthood already, de Braose.'

He saw de Braose's brows snap together, and added, his hand on the engraved pommel of the great sword at his side, 'At Bevis's hand. Sir Gervase de Machault stood sponsor for me.'

De Braose's iron-grey gaze flickered a little in the silence that followed. 'So-o. It seems that I am too late for all things today— Sir Randal.'

Sir Randal. How strange it sounded. Sir Dog-boy, Randal thought, with the harsh mockery of it tearing at his chest. All that way he had come, and he would have been so proud to be a fellow knight of Bevis's—and it was only by Bevis's death that he could furnish his helm. Life was very bitter, very cruel, and he wished rather desperately in that moment that he too was dead. He was saved from his moment of black despair by the sudden ripple of reflected firelight as a log fell, on the blade of Herluin's captured sword where it leaned against the bench behind de Braose. Herluin's sword—Herluin a captive, and in need of help . . . Herluin had said once that Randal had lived with hounds so long that, together with most of their faults, he had learned their chief virtue of faithfulness. Randal could not know that, but it was true.

'De Braose, it is the custom, I know, to make some gift to the Church or to the poor, for the first act of one's knighthood. May I, instead, pay the ransom for a friend?'

'Meaning de Bellême's minstrel,' de Braose snapped.

'Yes, sir.' Randal caught at the tail of his eye another movement from Herluin, startled and quickly suppressed. His eyes were on his overlord's square, uncompromising face, begging him to understand and show mercy. He knew that he was taking on a crushing burden for Dean. 'Oh, I know that I could only pay it off a little at a time; Dean is not a rich Manor, but if you will set Herluin free now, I will clear the debt though it takes me twenty years.'

'And I have promised you Dean for only one,' de Braose said. 'If at the end of that time I do not choose to renew the fief—what then?'

Randal was silent. He simply did not know what then. He felt how ridiculous his offer had been; there must be something he could do—some other way—but he could not think of it.

'I am not a man given to easy kindness, as you will know by now,' said the Lord of Bramber. 'I give nothing for nothing. For your good service these two summers past, and for the old friendship between d'Aguillon and de Braose, I have given you Dean to hold by knight's fee. I take that back now, and make another offer. I will give you the minstrel to do with as you choose, *or I will give you Dean*. The choice is yours.'

There was a long, dragging silence. Randal's fists clenched slowly at his sides, and he no longer looked into de Braose's face, but into the red heart of the fire brightening as the windy daylight faded. Le Savage, on the edge of the firelight, protested explosively down his nose. 'That's too cruel a choice to set the boy! You can't do it, de Braose!'

'I can, and I will,' de Braose said, simply; and something of the cold iron that showed in his eyes sounded also in his voice.

Every face in the dim, fire-reddened pavilion was turned to the two standing beside the field-hearth. Herluin's expression, as he looked on, was a strange one under the circumstances; a look of interest that seemed to be quite detached from himself, and something that was almost amusement in his pale, bright eyes. A dog began to scratch in the silence, and scratched on, and on . . . Randal was still staring into the fire, while slowly but without any kind of wavering, his mind made itself up. A few moments ago, he had thought that he had nothing more to lose; now he knew that he had, and he must give it. He knew that it had been Bevis's last wish that he should hold Dean, but Bevis would understand. There were certain things that a man could not do, certain debts that he could not leave unpaid. In an odd way that he could not have put into words, he felt that Bevis, whose body would sleep in Normandy, was part of Dean, part of the marshes and the downs and the river woods in springtime, woven into them by his love. Nothing could ever take Dean from Bevis now; the Wealden blackbird would always sing for him . . . For himself, it meant that he must go all his life in exile, but there was no other way. He raised his head

705

slowly, and looked at de Braose through the faint waft of wood-smoke fronding across his face, and ran the tip of his tongue over his lower lip because it was uncomfortably dry.

'I beg you give the Manor to someone like Gervase, who will be good to it—to the land and the villeins,' he said.

There was a soft rustle of movement among the watching knights. Herluin made a small gesture of applause that was only half fantastic. The dog finished scratching and wandered out. De Braose stood for a long moment more, looking at the young knight, and still stripping his great war-mittens between his hands. Then he turned and tossed them on to the bench behind him with an air of *finish*, and swung back to Randal.

'So.' He nodded. 'The colt is worthy of his breakers. I was none so sure, before, though you should have had the Manor at least for the year to prove your worth; but it is in my mind that he who keeps faith in one thing, even to the breaking of his heart, is like to keep it in all. You're a fool, Randal, but such a fool as I would have among my fief knights. Take Dean, and this minstrel of yours also. Pay me for the one with a stirrup cup each year over and above your knight's fee, and for the other— do with him as you will.'

In the first instant Randal was not quite sure that he had really heard it. Then, very slowly, the words sank in and became part of himself. His eyes were on de Braose's face all the while. If the Lord of Bramber knew that in that instant he had gained for life a liege man who would follow him into Hell fire to bring him a cup of water if he were damned and thirsting, he showed no sign of doing so; but every other man there saw it plainly enough.

Randal did not attempt to thank him; he had no words— no words of his own, only the words of the vassal's oath, that Bevis had spoken at his own knighting in the Great Hall of Dean, a year and a half ago.

In the smoke-filled and fire-flushed pavilion, with a few battle-weary knights and a captive minstrel looking on, while outside the triumphal cloud banners faded over the battlefield of Tenchebrai, he knelt in a passion of gratitude, and set his hands between de Braose's.

'Here, my Lord, I become liege man of yours for life and limb and earthly regard, and I will keep faith and loyalty to you for life and death, God helping me.'

Two dawns later, Randal took his leave of Herluin the Minstrel, in the lea of an apple orchard on the edge of the English camp. The camp was smaller than it had been, for the King and his Bishops and certain of his English Barons had by now made their quarters within the walls of Tenchebrai. De Bellême had been dismissed, humiliated and raging, with his freedom but little else, to almost the last of his Norman estates left to him. The dead were buried, and the swallows, gathering for their flight south, swooped and darted once more about the Castle walls.

It was raining, soft swathes of rain that were scarcely more than mist, and the moisture spattered cold from the branches of the apple trees. Somewhere in the rain a trumpet sounded thinly for watch-setting, and a horse whinnied, and someone went by whistling a snatch of a Breton tune. The blue waft of woodsmoke from the cooking fires drifted to them, mingling with the chill, grey freshness of the dawn. Beside one of those fires they had sat together late into the night before, silent for the most part, talking by fits and starts, of all that had happened in twelve years; of Dean and Arundel, of Sir Everard and de Coucy—of Bevis . . . But it seemed to Randal now that he had left unsaid so many of the things that really mattered. At the last moment, he said one of them.

'Herluin, come with me back to Dean.'

Herluin's brows drifted upward under the lank forelock, and his winged mouth curved in mockery. 'Hy my! Are you, then, one of the Barons of the land, to keep a minstrel in your Hall?'

'I did not mean as a minstrel,' Randal said. 'I just meant—come.'

'Nay then, what should I do, save grow moss, on a downland Manor?'

Randal was silent a moment, rebelling against the implication, yet knowing the truth of it. Herluin and Dean were of two different worlds.

'You'll go to de Bellême, then?'

'At least life will never be dull, where de Bellême is.'

'And you think it would be, with me?'

Herluin's face cracked into its slow, twisted smile. 'I think it more than likely.'

And then he set both hands on Randal's scale-clad shoulders, and stood looking at him, almost as searchingly as de Braose had done, two evenings ago. 'You are not yet bearded to compare with Sir Steward Gilbert at Arundel; but tell me now, was it a good thing that I did, when I gave you to Sir Everard, twelve long years ago?' He was not asking in a spirit of 'did I not tell you so?' He was asking the question because he wanted, wanted badly, to know the answer.

Randal gave him back his look, levelly—even in that moment it seemed to him odd that Herluin's eyes were on a level with his own instead of glinting and glancing down at him from somewhere tree-tall above him.

'Two days since, when I was yet Bevis's squire, I would have told you yes, a thousand times,' he said at last. 'Now, I am a knight, and Lord of my own Manor, and Bevis is dead; and I should maybe have a less sore heart if you had never even played the game of chess that won me from Hugh Goch.' His voice, which had been hoarse and steady, cracked desperately in the middle. 'I don't know, Herluin, I don't know.'

But even as he said it, he knew that it *had* been good; for the sake of all that Dean had given him and made of him, for the sake of the friendship he had shared with Bevis, that could not be lost, even though Bevis was dead. He brought up his own hands and set them over the minstrel's and bowed his head for an instant on to the other's neck.

'It was a good thing, Herluin,' he said, 'a good thing that you did, all those years ago,' and dropped his hands and stood back.

Herluin kept his hands on the young knight's shoulders a moment longer. 'So; and truly I think that for Dean also, for the folk and the fields of the Manor, which must otherwise have passed to a stranger's hand, the matter will prove to be none so ill. God keep you, Imp.'

He slipped his long musician's hands from Randal's shoulders so lightly that Randal never felt them go, and turned away, leaving the boy standing there under the apple trees in the rain, with the waking sounds of the English camp behind him.

18

THE LORD OF DEAN COMES HOME

Towards evening of a wild day in late October, Randal dropped from Swallow's saddle in the courtyard of Bramber Castle. He was quite alone; the Dean men and Bevis's horses which were his now, left behind him in Normandy with le Savage, for the King and the main part of his army were not yet coming home. Henry had held a Council at Lisieux and soon there would be another at Falaise, for the reforming and future handling of the Duchy that was once again one with England. But there was so much to do, and already the year grew late for embarking an army; so it could not be before spring, now, that the King would be home. Meanwhile de Braose had sent Randal back with letters for his Seneschal at Bramber, and for the Lady Aanor, before the winter storms shut the seaways.

The rain that had come with him all the two days' ride from Pevensey had fled away for the moment, and the streaming cobbles washed clear of their accustomed filth shone silver-gilt, the puddles reflecting the ragged lake of clear sky over the battlements, and in the old days Randal's heart would have lifted to the sudden blue and silver flashing out of the grey like a sword from its sheath; but not now: all that seemed dead in him now, and left behind him with Bevis at Tenchebrai.

An ancient stable-hand had come hobbling out to take Swallow from him, and a small, impudent varlet not much older than he had been when Herluin won him from Hugh Goch came darting down the Keep stair, grinning as he recognized the mired and weary knight who had just ridden into the courtyard, and shrilling like a curlew to know whether de Braose and the rest were near at hand. Already a little crowd was gathering,

711

of women and boys and old men. There were few of fighting age in Bramber now.

'Na na. De Braose and the rest will not be home before spring,' Randal told him, standing with his hand on Swallow's wet and drooping neck. 'I am come back with letters from my Lord to the Lady Aanor. Where may I find her?'

'In the Great Chamber. Have you seen much fighting?'

'Enough . . . Run then, and tell her that I come, and that all is well with the Lord of Bramber.'

The boy darted off again, and behind him, slowly, wet and saddle-stiff and desperately weary, Randal was climbing the familiar Keep stair. He was passing from the wind and the scudding silver-gilt light that was beginning to fade, into the smoky dimness of the guardroom; climbing still, from the guardroom to the Great Hall and then to the Great Chamber above it: the Great Chamber that he had come to know so well since he spoke there with the old Lord of Bramber on the night of the witch hunt. Now a fire leapt on the hearth, and the fluttering light of it warmed the grey stone walls and the hangings of the huge box bed against the chill and the changing lights and glooms of the wild autumn day. The Lady Aanor sat in the carved chair by the hearth, where the old Lord had sat that long-past summer night with his sword across his knees, her year-old son sprawling with the wolfhounds among the strewn rushes at her feet, while scattered about the room two or three of her women were busy at their spinning.

She had been busy, too, on the embroidery of a wall-hanging to keep out the draughts, but she had let the work fall in a drift of soft, dark storm-colours across her lap, and sat looking towards the stairhead arch as Randal appeared in it.

'Why, Randal, God's greeting to you. Garin says that you bring me a letter from my Lord.'

Randal shook the beading rain from the horn-scaled shoulders of his hauberk, and crossed the floor to kneel among the hounds and sprawling baby, holding out the packet that he had brought from his wallet.

'De Braose greets you, and sends you this, my Lady.'

She leaned quickly forward and took the packet from him,

her plump face alight with eagerness—for the marriage, made by Red William for his own ends, had grown to be a happy one, and the Lady Aanor, who had first come to Bramber riding her big white mare as lightly as a boy, was running to soft, sweet fat, like a full-blown rose in the sunshine.

'You are welcome twice over, then, once for yourself, and once for what you bring!' she said, and made a little gesture to him to rise, before she took her scissors to break the yellowish wax with its impress of de Braose's seal, and opened the crackling sheet of parchment.

Randal got to his feet again, and stood looking down at the embroidered stuff that flowed from her lap to the floor. He saw an oak tree with three acorns and seven leaves, a hare and a fallow doe beneath it, a bird in its branches, all worked in those sombre greys and russets and dim violet colours, and one unexpected note of brilliant blue in the bird's wing that was like the sudden flashing out of blue and silver from the grey tumble of storm-clouds that had greeted him for a brief moment in the courtyard.

But the brightness had fled onward, and the Great Chamber was already darkening with the next storm of rain. The shutters of the weather windows were closed against the wind and wet, and the rain rattled on them and drove hissing down the slanting smoke vent into the fire, making the ash logs spit and steam; but under the steam and the smoke that billowed into the room, the hollow heart of the fire seemed to glow all the brighter, red gold, the colour of Randal's red amber—Bevis's red amber—with the sun behind it.

There was another note of fire colour in the Great Chamber, flaming out of the greyness by one of the open windows. It teased at the corner of Randal's eye until he raised his head and glanced towards it, and saw Gisella sitting in the deep embrasure, watching him, with the grey storm-rain driving behind her head, and the back-wash of the wind fretting the wisps of bracken-red hair about her face.

He had not seen her since the evening in the Castle garden, a year and a half ago. Bevis and he had not come up to Bramber at all last winter, there had been so much to do at Dean. And

713

when they had come up to the Castle in the spring, with preparations in full spate for Henry's second invasion of Normandy,
she had not been there. He remembered vaguely having heard
that she had gone home on a long visit to help with an elder
sister's wedding; he remembered still more vaguely that at the
time he had been sorry. But with so much else happening, he
had scarcely thought of her since. He remembered that evening
in the Castle garden now, sharply and painfully, even to the
way the shadows of the budding quince tree had danced, and
the dry aromatic scent of the sprig of rosemary that she had given
him. And because Bevis was dead, the memory hurt him unbearably, as the sudden dazzle of blue and silver in the courtyard had hurt him, so that he swerved away from it in his mind
and would not remember at all, and stared back at Gisella with
almost hostile eyes.

Gisella in the window met his look, puzzled. She seemed to
be waiting for something, and then he saw her give up waiting.
She cocked up her chin with a sudden resolve, and laying aside
her spindle and distaff with its load of saffron wool, got to her
feet and came to stand before him.

'I will take your helmet for you,' she said, and put up her
hands to the strap that held it to his mail coif.

But Randal's own hands were before her, and he stepped
back a pace until his head struck against the raised stone of the
hearth. 'Na, I can do well enough for myself.' He freed the
buckles with a savage tug, and pulled off the heavy, nut-shaped
headpiece.

Two bright patches flamed up on Gisella's cheek-bones, and
he saw the war-light that he remembered of old flickering in
her eyes. 'Are you afraid that I shall dint your precious helmet?
You are not the first knight that I have unharnessed, Sir
Randal!'

Randal looked at her again, quickly, startled by her words.
'How did you know that?'

'Well, of course I know who I have unharnessed and who
not! Does it seem that I am quite a fool?' she retorted, wilfully
misunderstanding him.

'No, I meant—about my being a knight.'

714

'You are, are you not, in spite of telling me that you never would be?'

'Yes.'

Gisella hesitated, her eyes moving over him with a kind of ruthless, detached interest, and returning to his face. 'I do not know. You don't look like a squire any more—and that sword; it's no squire's blade.'

'It was Bevis's sword,' he told her after a moment.

Her face changed in the swift way it had, all the sparkle of temper draining out of it. 'Oh no!' she said quickly and softly. 'Bevis—is Bevis——?'

He looked at her with dull eyes. She was outside the dark barrier of his misery, and he could not reach her, even if he had wanted to.

'Bevis is dead,' he said, and turned his shoulder on her. He saw the Lady Aanor look up from her letter, and forestalled her kindness as he might have shielded a raw wound from someone's too searching touch, saying roughly, 'My Lady, I have letters also for Sir Herbrand the Seneschal. Give me leave now to go and find him.'

The storm blew and drenched itself out in the night, and the world had turned gentle when Randal set out next morning for Dean. The tall elms by the Mill stood up, half bare already, but lamp gold against the tawny paleness of the downs beyond, and the dog-rose tangle among the hazel bushes was set with the scarlet flame-points of rose hips as though to light him on his way through the quiet, grey morning as he rode up from the ford. But Randal saw nothing of that. To him it was dusk, under a sunset sky that was like the echo of a brighter sunset somewhere else; and he rode with ghosts, hounds long dead that came running to meet him, and old Sir Everard's voice calling to them, 'You will let them know through half Sussex that the Lord of Dean comes home!' A long-legged boy in russet hose dropping out of the pear tree by the gate . . .

'The Lord of Dean comes home.'

It was the thrusting and barking of real hounds about him now, as he swung down from the saddle in the Hall garth, and he realized that he must have come right through the village without seeing it at all—or rather, seeing it across twelve years. The hounds fawned about him, Joyeuse carrying an old shoe of Bevis's in her mouth. The household was gathering in the wake of the hounds. Randal stood with his arm curved over the warm grey arch of Swallow's neck, and looked back into their eager, questioning faces, and knew that this was the worst moment of all. He heard their voices without knowing what they said. He did not know if he answered them; but if not, they must have read his news in his face, for he felt his own grief reaching out to engulf them too. He saw them standing back from him a little, staring at him, without noisy sorrow, in a silent and almost sullen grieving, after the manner of the Saxon kind. He saw Adam Clerk's face among the rest, white and stricken and suddenly very old. Reynfrey's big hand was on his shoulder, and he felt it shaking; Sybilla, making less outcry than for many smaller griefs, though the tears trickled down her fat cheeks, was bidding him come in, promising him something to eat. Odd how one still had to eat . . .

But the worst thing of all was Joyeuse pattering round him, looking for something—someone—who was not there. She nudged the old red shoe against his legs, whimpering, but would not give it to him when he stooped for it. It was not for him she had brought it. He fondled her head, seeing the greyness of her muzzle, and realized for the first time that Joyeuse was old. They had called her Joyeuse, though it was a sword's name and not a hound's, because she had been such a joyous puppy; but now she was old and grey-muzzled and not joyous any more.

'He is not coming,' Randal told her, choking; and she looked up into his face with a piercing whine, trying to understand. 'No good looking; he will not come again—poor old lass, not any more.'

Suddenly he had had all that he could bear. 'I—am not hungry,' he told Sybilla. 'Give me some supper when I come back—someone look after Swallow . . .' and he turned and strode blindly out from the garth, round the end of the little flint-walled church, and up towards the downs.

Joyeuse followed a little way at his heels, then turned with a distressed whimpering and padded back towards the Hall, and Randal went on alone.

There were goldfinches on the seeding thistles and wild marjoram beyond the garth, jewelling the grey day with their forehead-rubies and the blink of gold on their quivering wings, but Randal did not see them, he did not see the familiar upward sweep of the downs that was tawny as a hound's coat, silvering as long, cool swathes of air went by. He climbed on, blindly, leaving the tilled land and the woods behind him, into the emptiness. He did not know, he did not even question in his own mind whether it was the downs or Lewin Longshanks that he was going to; in a way they were the same thing in his mind. Strength and unchangingness; and he needed them now . . .

He saw Lewin from a long way off, sitting on the crest of Long Down against the drifting sky, with the Dean sheep grazing in a quiet grey crescent in the steep coombhead below him, and in the same instant the shepherd stirred, put up one arm in a slow, wide gesture of greeting, and got to his feet. He did not come loping down over the rolling fall of turf to meet him, but remained quietly leaning on his crook, with the dogs crouched on either side, to wait for his coming. And Randal, returning the greeting gesture, climbed slowly on and up. He climbed straight through the flock, the sheep raising their heads as he passed to stare at the armed man in their midst, then returning peacefully to their grazing.

The two men came together on the broad downland ridge with nothing higher than themselves save a kestrel hanging in the sky above them. The big, fair shepherd in his sheepskin mantle, with the quiet of the high and lonely places about him; the young knight still in hauberk and helm with his shield strap creaking across his shoulders, still mired with yesterday's long, hard riding, haggard and red-eyed. They stood looking at each other for a few moments, without any further greeting. Then Lewin asked in his gentle growl, 'Where's d'Aguillon, then?'

'Dead,' Randal said. It sounded such a little word, in the immensity of the downs.

In the silence that followed, he heard suddenly the faint

shish-shish-sh of those long, cool swathes of air moving through the tawny grass, and the thin, shining song of a lark lost somewhere high overhead.

'Aye, I thought it might be that,' Lewin said at last, his quiet gaze still on the younger man's face.

How they came, soon after that, to be sitting side by side on the sloping turf, Randal never knew, save that when one was not going anywhere or doing anything, it always seemed more natural to sit than stand on the slow, quiet swells of the downs. There they sat, with the prick-eared dogs, Lewin with his crook lying beside him, Randal dandling his great sword across his knees. Lewin glanced aside at it, after they had kept silent for a good while. 'D'Aguillon's sword.'

'He gave it to me,' Randal said.

'When was he killed then? Was it at Tence—Tenchebrai? We heard there was a great battle at a place called Tenchebrai.'

'Aye, at Tenchebrai. It was a great fight—broke the power of Normandy.' In a dead, level voice he began to tell the other how it had been. 'Henry dismounted most of his army to take the shock of the Norman charge—so that in a way we fought as Harold's men fought at Hastings. It was queer, that. We held the charge and we pressed on against the Norman foot, and the battle began to break up; but a squadron of their horse came against de Braose's men—de Coucy was one of them.' He turned a little to look at the gravely listening man beside him. 'Always de Coucy, as though even in the chances of war his fate was woven with Dean's. I was close behind Bevis and saw it all happen. Another Norman took him first, and while his sword was busy to the full, de Coucy took him cross-wise and cut him down before I could reach him to cover him with my shield, and the horse——' he bowed his head for a moment on to his sword arm that lay across his updrawn knees. 'The horses trampled on over him. He died before evening.'

Lewin said, 'You killed de Coucy?'

'Oh yes,' Randal said very gently. 'I killed de Coucy.'

A long time passed before either of them spoke again. Presently one of the sheep wandered too far from the rest of her kind. Lewin pointed her out to the dogs beside him, and they streaked away, running silently, belly to ground, to head the straggler back into the flock, and then, their task accomplished, returned to fling themselves down again, panting, beside their master. Then Lewin said, 'Who is the new Lord of Dean?'

The skies had begun to break up, and faint blurs of brightness to drift across the downs. Far below them and a mile away, a ragged wing of sunshine brushed across the thatched roofs of the Manor Hall and its byres and barns, waking the colour of the three great fields, fresh from the autumn ploughing, and the gleam of the tall straw-stacks in the garth.

'I'm afraid I am,' Randal said.

It was so long before Lewin answered that he looked round. The shepherd was watching him with those far-sighted, very blue eyes of his, that met his own haggard gaze and held it in a long, considering scrutiny. At last he nodded. 'That's as it should be. 'Tis a thankless time any stranger would have had of it, I'm thinking, but the Manor will accept you. Aye, and for more than that barley-coloured thatch of yours.'

Yes, Randal thought, the Manor would accept him. In an odd way it had already done so on the night that Lewin showed him the nameless flint weapon, the night that he had seemed, for one instant that was outside time, to see the shadows of the wolves leaping about the lambing fold . . . His thoughts turned, as always when he remembered that night, to Ancret, who belonged to the world that he had glimpsed then. Ancret with her ancient wisdom and her ancient magic, who had been Bevis's foster-mother. And he drew his legs under him to get up. 'I must go to Ancret. I should have gone to her first, before someone else told her about Bevis.'

'No hurry for that, then. You'll not find Ancret on the Manor, no more.'

Randal checked his movement to get up, and looked at the older man with startled eyes. 'Not find her? Not—dead too?'

'Na, na.' Lewin shook his head. 'Cerdic saw her walking up over the shoulder of the Bramble Hill, way back a moon and more gone by—'bout the time of Tenchebrai Fight, I reckon. Her didn't come back, and her won't now.'

Randal said, 'But she's part of Dean!'

'Aye, her's part of Dean; a villein, tied to the land like the rest of us,' Lewin agreed, watching his new Lord. 'Send after her and fetch her back, if you can find her.'

'Don't be a fool,' Randal said wearily, his arm across his up-drawn knees, and his forehead on his wrist. He was remembering, against the darkness of his closed eyes, Ancret's face as he had seen it that first time of all, shadowy against the berry-laden branches of the elder tree, hearing her voice as she told Bevis that she would always be there for his finding, so long as he needed her. So long as he needed her. She must have known when she walked up over Bramble Hill and away, that her foster-son's need of her was finished, and he would not come seeking her again. She must have known how it would be, that first time of all. He remembered her hands on either side of his face and her eyes holding his own, so that he seemed to be sinking down into the darkness of them, down and down . . . 'The old blood runs strong, and comes again into its own again; you should know that, you that Sir Everard brought home on his saddle bow.'

Why had she not hated him? Knowing what she knew even then, why had she not hated him? The answer came to him in Ancret's voice, remembered across twelve years, but clear as though the words were murmuring that moment in his ear, sounding in the faint soughing of the air through the long grasses. 'We, who are an older people still, who were an old people when they raised the grave mound on Bramble Hill in the days when the world was young, we see the conquerors come and go again, and marry and mingle, but we know that all things pass, like a little wind through the bramble bushes.'

Only the downs went on, the downs, and life itself, whatever happened to the people who lived it. The wolves leaping about the lambing folds, and the men with their spears; Harold dead at Hastings, and Bevis at Tenchebrai, and all the while, the little wind blowing over the downs, and harvest following seed-sowing, and the new life coming at lambing time. In a few days,

he thought suddenly—and the thought woke in him as unexpectedly as the blue of the bird's wing flashing out from
among the dun and grey and violet colours of the Lady Aanor's
embroidery—he would take time off from the autumn work of
the Manor, and go up to Bramber and get word with Gisella
again. He did not get as far as thinking that now he was a
knight, standing well with de Braose and holding his own
Manor, her father would likely enough give her to him if he
asked. It was much too soon for that. He simply thought that he
would go and get word with Gisella again, and tell her that he
had carried her sprig of rosemary through those two long,
blood-stained summers in Normandy. But not how he had
parted with it; that was between himself and Bevis, for all
time.

'It's a good Manor,' he said. 'Looks as though we're ready
for the autumn sowing.'

Historical Note

THE Mowbray revolt of 1095 really did happen, and Hugh Goch
was caught up in it, just as I have told in *Knight's Fee*. All the other
campaigns and uprisings in the background of the story are histori-
cal. In 1094 there was a great rising of the Welsh, and in the next
year William Rufus marched into North Wales, but the expedition
had little effect; in 1096, having lent his brother, Duke Robert of
Normandy, the money he needed to go on the First Crusade, he
crossed the Channel to hold the Duchy while the Duke was away. In
the spring of 1097 more Welsh troubles called him back, and again
he marched into Wales, but when the revolt died down in the
autumn, he returned to Normandy and set himself to secure and
make strong the Norman borders. That done, he returned triumphantly to be crowned a second time in his new Westminster Hall.
But less than a year later, on 2 August 1100, he was shot while hunting in the New Forest; and it was for his younger brother Henry to
hold England.

Henry did not have an easy time, for Robert was back from his
Crusade now, and wanted England as well as Normandy. He bought
the allegiance of several of Henry's greatest Barons with promises of
lands in Normandy; and on 20 July 1101 landed at Portsmouth. On
this occasion the two brothers came to terms without a battle. Henry
was to keep England but pay Robert £2000 a year, and Robert
was to keep all Normandy save for Henry's own castle of Domfront.
Afterwards, Henry dealt with the Barons who had turned against
him; and by spring 1102 it was Robert de Bellême's turn, and the
King drove him out of one after another of his English castles, and
finally overseas.

Meanwhile, the people of Normandy who had been so glad to see
Duke Robert back from his Crusade, were becoming sickened by his
weakness and his cruelty; and they appealed to Henry to come and
take the Duchy. In April 1105 Henry invaded in force, and though
he had to draw off in August, in June of 1106 he invaded again, and
in September the great battle of Tenchebrai was fought, which ended
all Norman resistance to the English for a long while to come.

So much for the events. For the people—most of them are real too, the greater folk anyway; de Braose and de Bellême and Hugh Goch; but not Herluin the Minstrel nor de Coucy nor Bevis nor Randal. D'Aguillon is not a real person but he comes of a real family; several d'Aguillons followed Duke William from Normandy, and by the time the Domesday Survey was made they were settled here and there throughout Sussex.

You may wonder how the Saxons and Normans in the story talk to each other so easily; but I believe that very soon after the Conquest, certainly as soon as the first Norman children born in England had begun to talk at all, they would have used one tongue as easily as the other, speaking Norman French to their fathers and their fathers' friends, and Saxon with their nurse and the grooms and dogboys, and sometimes—for there were many mixed marriages—with their mothers too.

The Old Faith was the faith of all Europe, long before Christ. It lasted on, side by side with Christianity, right through the Middle Ages, though by then most people had forgotten what it was, and called it witchcraft. The people who held to it believed that a God-King had to die every so often, and be born again in a new God-King, just as the year dies in the winter and is born again in the spring, and that only so could life go on. William Rufus belonged to the Old Faith, and many people still believe that he was chosen to be the 'Dying God' for that particular time. If so, he may have been on the whole a bad man, but he was certainly a very brave one.

Glossary

ACCOLADE   The blow on the neck that makes a knight.

ALAUNT   A kind of hound.

CHAPE (OF SWORD)   The metal guard on the end of the sheath.

COIF   A close-fitting hood.

FEALTY   Allegiance.

FIEF   A knight's holding of land.

FURNISH ONE'S HELM   A colloquialism: to provide one's own horse and armour and keep up the way of life fitting to a knight.

FYRD   Militia.

GAMBESON   The padded tunic worn under the hauberk.

GARBOIL   Unseemly noise and turmoil.

GUIGE   The strap of a shield that goes round one's neck.

HAUBERK   A chain-mail or scale-mail shirt.

HONOUR   A Baron's holding.

JACK   A leather tunic

KIRTLE   A shirt or tunic.

KIST   A chest.

NASAL   The nose-guard of a helmet.

PRICKET   A kind of candlestick with a little spike on which to stick the candle.

SEISIN   A piece of turf or a small object given in token of ownership of land etc.

SENESCHAL   Steward and manager.

TALBOT   A hound.

TITHE   The tenth part of the harvest etc. paid as tax to the Church.

WOLF'S HEAD   Outlaw.